First Edition
signed by author
1987

Paul Butterworth

Their Pride and Joy

also by Paul Buttenwieser

FREE ASSOCIATION

Their Pride and Joy

by

Paul Buttenwieser

DELACORTE PRESS/NEW YORK

Published by
Delacorte Press
1 Dag Hammarskjold Plaza
New York, N.Y. 10017

Copyright © 1987 by Buttenwieser Literary, Inc.

All rights reserved. No part of this book may be reproduced or transmitted in any form or by any means, electronic or mechanical, including photocopying, recording or by any information storage and retrieval system, without the written permission of the Publisher, except where permitted by law.

Manufactured in the United States of America

First printing

Library of Congress Cataloging in Publication Data
Buttenwieser, Paul, 1938–
Their pride and joy.
I. Title.
PS3552.U855T44   1987   813'.54
ISBN 0-385-29567-7
Library of Congress Catalog Card Number: 86-23958

To my parents with love and gratitude.
And to the memory of my sister, Carol, and Linda Miller.

Their Pride and Joy

Prologue

The Gutheim family spent its happiest times at Rosefield, during the summers of World War II. Peggy Gutheim always liked to say that her mother ran the best hotel in Westchester. Relatives, refugees, servicemen on leave, strays of all sorts, anyone stranded in the city could come out for a night or a weekend or a few days in the country. The procession was unending. Mrs. Altman's hospitality was legendary, and no one was ever turned away, however tenuous the connection with the family, however crowded the house might be on a given night. During the day everyone spilled out onto the lawns and the gardens, spreading out over the meadows and into the woods, where they would find children brought out from the city for a day in the fresh air, Boy Scouts on bivouac, local kids over for a swim. The air was one of holiday, but no one forgot for a minute that a war was being fought. How could they, with so many boys and men seeing action, among them Alan Gutheim himself? Newspapers, visitors, letters brought the latest information; the phone was in constant use; and every evening life stopped for the news broadcast. Even the idyllic landscape of Rosefield was now and then bloodied by a telegram or a call bringing news of death: a distant cousin, a friend's son, an acquaintance, lost in action. Amid all that beauty tears were shed in private, and no one spoke of the terrible anxiety hidden away just under the surface.

Still, it was an exhilarating time, and Rosefield was a wonderful place to be, especially for the children. The war summers were a long house party for them. With Alan stationed overseas and Gerald Altman traveling back and forth to Washington, it made sense for everyone else to group together for the summer at Rosefield. It was a noisy and complicated arrangement. The Gerald Altman household included two French children taken in for the duration of the war, as well as the four Altman children themselves, Randy having arrived just as the bombs were landing on Pearl Harbor. Peggy Gutheim had not only her own Phil and Joan to look after, but also assorted German relatives, recent widows, temporary orphans in and out of her home throughout the war years, and in the last summer of the war in Europe her first DP's arrived: twins, a girl and a boy of ten, who had been smuggled out somehow in 1942 but had been stranded in Uruguay since then. They had almost no English, and German was not appreciated in those days, so they struggled to make themselves understood in a Spanish that was dimly comprehensible only to the French children. Phil, two years their junior, ordered them around in imperious, German-accented English when no adults were around, but Joan took pity on them, and tried to make them feel at home in the huge, chaotic household.

The only absentee among the children was Carl Gutheim, not yet born. It was his fate to miss out on life's greatest experiences, as the others so often reminded him. They never tired of recounting, detail by loving detail, the wartime days at Rosefield until he incorporated them into his own memory. Those days became as vivid and personal to him as if he had lived them, except that they were flavored with the special poignancy of a dream that leaves the dreamer famished with longing. The legend of a golden age he would never know cast a shadow over his life; but the same legend went on to darken the lives of the others in time. No one put it into words, but after Joan's death everyone knew that the family's best years were irretrievably in the past.

At the time, though, Rosefield was heaven for the children. With the head gardener's three children and the daughter of Holberg, the chauffeur, they formed a permanent cadre that was supplemented by houseguests, friends, and children of the neighborhood, if nearby estates could be considered a neighborhood. This horde spent the hot summer days roving back and forth between the house and the grounds, loosely tended to by any number of nurses, nannies, governesses, maids, and an occasional mother or aunt. They biked and triked along the back roads to the duck pond, the chicken coop, the vegetable garden, the brook in the woods. They played baseball and football and running bases and keepaway. They had picnics in the meadow and parties in the formal garden. They all had their own victory gardens to tend to and one summer Dickie Altman had everybody working on a treehouse that never got finished.

Usually, though, when the weather was good, activities centered around the swimming pool. If a grown-up was in the water, gliding along in a placid breaststroke, there couldn't be any games. But as soon as the last adult was out, the pool churned with races, water fights, or a wild aquatic version of cops and robbers. All the cousins were ferocious swimmers, and the competition frequently got out of hand. Once in a while all the children were made to get out of the pool, and a game of hide-and-go-seek would ensue. The trellised arbor was always home base, and common hiding places included the bushes surrounding the pool lawn, the large trees in the near meadow, and the far side of the playhouse. But the favorite place to hide was in the pool itself, under the murky surface. It was tricky: You had to slip in silently while whoever was "it" counted, and duck below the surface to avoid being seen. The youngest children were not supposed to hide there, but it made poor Mrs. Altman nervous to see even one of the older kids disappear for long stretches underwater. If she was there, you could tell that someone was hiding in the water just by looking at her face, which was a study in horror. The leaves and shadows provided camouflage, though, and the seeker couldn't spend too long searching there or everyone else would come in home free. Still, if one hid there he had to be prepared for a pretty long immersion, and it really was a miracle that no one ever drowned.

On rainy afternoons Mrs. Altman almost always had a bridge game. If there were enough guests, she would have two tables. The children were allowed to watch, but not to speak, which made the ground floor a pretty dull place to be. Helga had a fit if anyone came into her kitchen in the afternoon, and the back part of the house was generally off-limits while the servants were resting. The head gardener's children for some reason didn't have quite the easy access to the house that they did to the rest of the estate, although the chauffeur's girl did. Because of the gasoline rationing, friends couldn't be driven over on a moment's notice. On Saturdays there might be a trip to a movie: White Plains had four theaters in those days, and in a pinch one might venture as far as Bedford Village to the north or Scarsdale to the south. But as often as not, nothing was playing that was considered suitable for the children, and life could get dull, even at Rosefield. Until Carl came along with his odd ways, no child in the family ever dreamed of reading a book for pleasure and of course there was no television in those days. It was not a resourceful group for indoor activities. The house was, needless to say, well equipped: games, blocks, clay, paints, and costumes abounded. There was a small puppet theater, several toy cars that one could drive down the hallways, and a library of jigsaw puzzles. There was a Ping-Pong table in the screened porch on the second floor. Even so, boredom loomed large. The governess of the moment would make suggestion after suggestion. Whining would break out, a silly argument would escalate, the summoning of a parent would be threatened. It was at times such as those that Phil would really come into his own.

Peggy always said that Phil was a born manager, but he surely owed something of his later success to those rainy afternoons at Rosefield. There he was king of the castle. In those small but telling matters among children, he always prevailed. He had no obvious authority over the others—Dickie Altman was older, and blustered even back then—but Phil always prevailed. Except for an occasional visitor, no one even challenged him. The two Parisian children who clung to the Altman family for dear life throughout the war were bigger and no doubt stronger, but they wouldn't have dared to assert themselves while France was still occupied. The hangers-on in the Gutheim family were mostly nonentities, and the German twins were treated by the children as prisoners of war. The only person who might have given Phil a run for his money would have been an older Randy Altman, but Randy was only three by V-J day, and his career as a troublemaker was still some years in the future.

Some might say that the question of who would run the show among a group of small children was too trivial to care about. It is certainly true that nothing earthshaking was at stake. The choice of which game to play or what record to put on the Victrola couldn't conceivably have mattered much even to Dickie Altman. But it must have galled him to have his younger cousin call the shots, even as it gratified Phil to call them. It's amazing how early one child can learn, for example, how to be impotent, while another finds out how to stay where he is and let people come to him.

Phil's undeclared quest for superiority was helped by the fact that Marian and Barbara Altman, who agreed on nothing else, both cordially loathed their brother Dickie. Phil could always count on their support in any dispute. Randy was too young to have a say in anything, Carl wasn't born yet, and the visiting children had no franchise. Joan, of course, was on his side before she knew what was at issue. She, too, disliked Dickie—who didn't?—but that had little to do with it. Her loyalty to Phil was absolute, at times too fierce for the petty squabbles of those rainy afternoons. Her admiration for him was almost excessive. It certainly contrasted with her feelings toward an inconvenient younger brother when he came along. But everyone knew that Joan adored Phil from the day she was born to the day she died.

To the grown-ups at Rosefield these resentments, these rivalries, these seeds of future bitterness, didn't exist. Peggy, of course, knew of them, as she knew of everything, one way or another, and no doubt Eleanor had a pretty good idea of what was going on. But the others— Gerald on his weekends off, Alan home on leave, the guests, the household help, the gardeners—saw only a happy band of youngsters merrily playing their way through the tense war summers without a care in the world. Even Miss Georgina, that incomparably horrid governess the Altmans had for years and years, mistook the united opposition to her attempts at discipline for solidarity.

Miss Georgina may actually have been on to something; for if anything could override the jealousies and grudges and bring the children together it was the hope of getting rid of her. No opportunity of tormenting that poor woman was passed up. During the last summer of the war nothing, short of the surrender of Japan, was more fervently hoped for than that she would break down, or quit, or, best of all, both. She did neither, as it turned out, but not for lack of provocation. The various skirmishes were later recounted along with other war stories, and in the Altman history of the war the Battle of Iwo Jima, for instance, became blurred with the Capture of Miss Georgina's Wig.

Miss Georgina wore a wig—it was no secret from anyone who ever laid eyes on her—that was a true object of wonder. Probably no artifice could have salvaged much for her appearance, but the wig only exacerbated matters. From a distance it slightly resembled the severe, sharply outlined coiffure of the woman in Mrs. Altman's Ingres portrait, but when you got close the resemblance faded. The hair itself had the consistency of straw, with some loose, spiky strands sticking up. Miss Georgina had chosen, for reasons probably connected with her personality, a jet-black color that did little for her pasty complexion and was mocked by the reddish-blond hairs of her light mustache. If it ever fit, by the time she came to the Altmans it had shrunk to the point that it could cover only a portion of her skull, and was applied to a different location every day.

Naturally the children were wild to get their hands on it. Some last thin line of decency, or more likely fear, prevented them from snatching it directly off her head, although if she had ever dared to go in the pool with them she might have undergone that ultimate indignity. But Miss Georgina didn't swim, and she didn't join in on games, so the chance of a direct steal was slim. It was generally thought, though never proved, that she took it off when she went to sleep; but the idea of going into her room to get it was too horrible to contemplate. Even the DP's, who had been hidden in the closet when the Gestapo came, shrank from that assignment.

The only plan that held any promise revolved around Miss Georgina's bath. Because her duties included nighttime surveillance, Miss Georgina didn't stay in the servants' wing but had a bedroom next to Marian and Barbara's, and shared a bathroom with them. The bathroom was off a little corridor, itself divided off from the long second-floor hallway by its own entrance. Miss Georgina was strict about her privacy. She would never allow the girls to see her in the corridor in anything less than a robe, and she invariably locked the bathroom door even if she was only washing her hands. But she did, on occasion, go back into her room to get something after her bath before completing her rituals. She always called out to make sure the coast was clear, which gave rise to a theory that she made the brief trip wrapped in a towel, and without the wig, which was presumably left in the bathroom, begging to be swiped.

Even if it was true, the enterprise was fraught with difficulties. To start with, Miss Georgina did not take her bath at a time when it was likely children would be milling around her door. She usually waited until late at night. Once in a great while, if the children were out of the house and she was off duty, she might allow herself the luxury of a midday soak. If the children were to take advantage of such an occasion, it obviously called for the utmost in planning, secrecy, and precision of execution; none of which was in strong supply in that gang.

But the idea was discussed over such a long period of time that it became first attractive, then irresistible. Phil, in particular, was obsessed with it, and if Phil wanted to do something, it was only a matter of time before it was at least attempted. He made his calculations, and bided his chances. One weekend, shortly after D day, he decided the time had come.

It had been a hot week, and by Saturday everyone was virtually living in the pool. Gerald Altman was home from Washington for the weekend, and there were several houseguests as usual. On Saturday, a collector of Mrs. Altman's acquaintance came over to discuss paintings, and the children, who ordinarily had lunch with the grown-ups, were fed earlier. When they were finished, because it was so hot, they appealed to Peggy and Eleanor to skip their naps and go back outside. They were allowed to on condition they not go swimming until an hour after lunch, and the younger children were to have a nap later.

The conditions were perfect. With the children presumably safely out of the house, poor Miss Georgina had every reason to think she could count on a half hour's peace and quiet to refresh herself. She ran a tepid bath and moved herself in with her salts and soaps and lotions. It must have been a great relief to lower herself into the tub and find respite from heat and the trying children all at once. It's possible that in the drowsiness of a July afternoon she allowed herself to doze off. At any rate, she didn't hear the muffled sounds of the children who had reentered the house via a cellar door and had come up the back stairs to the second floor, where they scurried around barely suppressing excited giggles.

Phil was, of course, in charge. The plan was not too complicated. His main problems were the high spirits of the younger children, and Marian's threatened defection. Marian, who in later years was to participate in far more atrocious acts of protest, was developing cold feet. She alone of the children had a bond of sorts with Miss Georgina, and she suffered the only pangs of conscience in the group. Phil had counted on her to do some crucial reconnaissance, but had to be satisfied with her promise not to betray them. Her place was taken by Charlotte, one of the French children, who crept in with Barbara to eavesdrop from her room while Miss Georgina hummed contentedly in the bath. At the first sound of Miss Georgina arising dripping from the tub and letting the water out, Charlotte slipped out the back door of the bedroom to give the signal. Barbara remained at her post to give warning in case something went wrong, and Joan was moved up to the hallway door. Hearing the bathroom door open and Miss Georgina's door close, she dashed in and grabbed the wig, which was, sure enough, standing in stiffened

majesty on the bathroom stool. It was too good to be true. She raced
back out with her prize, followed by Barbara, whose job it was to close
the door noiselessly behind her. That was the end of the silent part of
the raid.

Unable to contain themselves a moment longer, the younger children broke out into shrieks of laughter. The older ones joined in, and
even Phil had to raise his voice in hopes of maintaining some semblance
of discipline. But it was too late; and besides, no one had any idea what
happened next. All the planning had gone into filching the wig, and no
one had thought what to do with it once they got it. Miss Georgina,
alerted by the commotion, must have discovered the theft, although obviously there would be some delay before she could do anything about
it. Some of the children wanted to wait and see her come out—how?
Bald? Stark naked? Driven to murderous insanity?—but most couldn't
bear the prospect. The wig, on closer inspection, turned out to be even
more hideous than anyone had suspected. Its texture was creepily un-
natural, its underside a thicket of netting and pins and snarls. After
everyone had had a look at it, it turned into a hot potato. They all threw
it at one another, and there was a rush for the stairs. Dickie, who had it
last, put it onto Marian's head, and she, with a cry of disgust, jammed it
onto Randy's. It covered his eyes as he was stumbling down the steps,
and in his confusion and terror he burst out with a piercing shriek.

The grown-ups, at their peaceful lunch, had already heard the
ruckus from upstairs, and now the children invaded the dining porch
where they were eating. It was hard for them to make much sense of the
combination of laughter, wails, and breathless incoherence that poured
forth. At first no one recognized the wig, thinking perhaps that a bird's
nest had been brought into the house and was being disputed. Only
when Barbara took the wig from her distraught brother and put it on
herself did they realize what had happened. Amid the general amusement, Eleanor took the wig back up to Miss Georgina, where, judging
from the length of her absence, it must have taken all of her considerable
tact to persuade the poor woman from resigning on the spot. The children were given a mild scolding, contradicted with hugs and more
laughter, and sent back out to play. Joan and Randy were sent for their
naps.

What fun they all had that day! What summers those were! By the
time Carl came along, the war was over, Alan had come home, the refu-

gees were reunited with their relatives, and the families spent their summers in separate houses. Everyone visited Rosefield often, and there
were more good days there, but it was never the same. Those had been
the great years, the happiest times.

Carl had been hearing those stories for years and years before he
ever put it together that the day Miss Georgina's wig was stolen was the
same day his mother miscarried. Which was strange, when he thought
about it, because the one event followed immediately after the other. In
a different era, it might have been suggested that the excitement over the
wig had in some way precipitated the miscarriage, but Peggy would
have been the last person to credit such an outlandish theory.

It had all happened without any warning. Peggy and Eleanor had
gone upstairs to settle Joan and Randy down for their postponed naps—
Miss Georgina could hardly have been asked to perform that duty just
then—while the other children went outside, and lunch was resumed.
Peggy had just bent down to kiss Joan when she was seized with a
cramp. The pain must have been quite severe, because she suddenly fell
to the floor. She always maintained she never passed out, but Joan
thought she had had a heart attack and died. With what was always
referred to as great presence of mind, but was more likely sheer terror,
Joan didn't yell or become hysterical. All she did for the minute or so
her mother lay immobile in front of her was to kneel down and look into
her face and say softly: "What am I supposed to do?" But there was no
need for her to do anything, as it turned out.

Peggy remained perfectly calm. When she regained her voice, she
reassured Joan that she was perfectly fine, and told her not to worry.
Those were the days of air-raid drills, and people were prepared for
emergencies. Everyone responded beautifully. The doctor was called,
the hospital notified, the chauffeur was sent for. The children, except for
Joan and Randy, were off in the woods and never knew a thing until it
was all over. Neither did Randy, for that matter, since he was already
asleep, or as good as. There was only Joan to be tended to. Peggy, not
one to be thrown by cramps and blood and the prospect of losing a baby
with her husband thousands of miles away, managed to convince Joan
that she was not going to the hospital in order to die. She refused to
budge until Joan recovered to the extent of a tearful smile and a doubtful agreement that everything was fine. Only then did Peggy let them
help her down the stairs and out into the waiting car.

From there on in it all went about as smoothly as could have been expected, except for one further hitch, and that one minor. Miss Georgina, whose humiliation had gotten lost in the shuffle, reappeared and quite generously asked if there was anything she could do to help. Although the answer to that question was no, under the circumstances she could hardly be rebuffed. Peggy, as she hobbled through the hallway, asked her to take Joan back upstairs for her nap, thinking the distraction would help both the child and the governess. Unfortunately, no sooner was she out the door than Joan dissolved again. Miss Georgina was understandably not as sympathetic as she might have been, and she tried to insist on Joan's marching straight up to bed. Even at the age of five, Joan wasn't one to be pushed. She had been through a lot for a young child and she was too confused and worried about her mother to go off docilely. For Miss Georgina, who'd put up with more than her share that day as well, it was the last straw. She went flying out the front door to complain to Peggy, who had just been gotten into the car. Meanwhile, Joan went to pieces in the hallway.

Poor Miss Georgina! It wasn't her day. At that point no one could take her seriously. Peggy was in the car with her mother and sister-in-law, and at the sight of the hapless governess, her wig looking more frightful than ever, the three women burst into helpless laughter. Luckily, one of the houseguests up from Washington with Gerald happened to be an English diplomat. He saw that his professional skills were in demand, and was able somehow to mollify Miss Georgina. He then took charge of Joan, who was in any case so exhausted by the emotion of the ordeal that she let this handsome stranger carry her up to her nap without further protest. The car drove off to the hospital, where Peggy finished up her miscarriage. They wanted to keep her overnight, but they didn't realize they were dealing with Peggy Gutheim. She raised such a fuss that they let her go home when the bleeding stopped. She was back at Rosefield in time to read Joan her bedtime story.

Peggy Gutheim was not one to dwell on the unpleasant. For example, she didn't write Alan about the miscarriage. It came so early that she hadn't even had a chance to tell him about the pregnancy itself, so she saw no reason whatsoever to upset him needlessly by letter. His next leave came just before the Battle of the Bulge, and she presumably told him then. But if she could have been sure he wouldn't find out inadvertently, she might not have ever bothered him with it. Why dredge up something dreary from the past? What earthly good does it do? Better by far to forge ahead, and if one feels obliged to look back, why not remember the best times? Memory is only finite, after all—and Peggy Gutheim's memory was more finite than some—why fill it up with sadness, especially when there is so much to be grateful for?

And so Rosefield during the war came to be bathed in the shimmer and haze of a lovely summer day. Events that took place became blurred, sharp edges softened, unpleasant details forgotten. The story of Miss Georgina's wig was recounted often, with the embellishments and exaggerations suitable to a beloved family tale. Peggy's miscarriage was hardly mentioned at all, and never in connection with the earlier event. The fact that he had an abortive predecessor was no secret to Carl or anyone else—there were no secrets in the Gutheim family. Peggy didn't believe in them. Nevertheless, it wasn't generally spoken of.

"I'm only too happy to discuss it with you," Peggy told Carl once, when he asked her about it. "Only there isn't much to say. There was a war going on at the time, there were lots greater tragedies taking place every day, I can assure you. Besides, you came along not so terribly long afterward. No, I never really wasted much energy thinking about it. What good would it have done?"

And that was about it. Peggy's utilitarian view of thinking was pretty much shared by the rest of the family, and no one seemed to have wasted much energy thinking about it—except for Carl, who brooded somewhat melodramatically on his close brush with early extinction. He was goaded to it, admittedly, by Phil, who liked to remind him. "That could've been you, Carlie," with the implication the world would have been better off if it had been. But everyone else forgot about it.

What about Joan, who had got caught up in the middle of it? Did she forget the sight of her mother, crumpled up in front of her, to all intents and purposes dead? Did she really believe her mother a few minutes later when she said everything was perfectly all right? What was she to make of it all?

"What am I supposed to do?" she had moaned in desperation when she thought her mother had died. But Peggy wasn't dead after all, and needed no help.

"I'm fine," she reassured the poor child. "Everything's perfectly all right." She picked herself up off the floor and went off to the hospital, laughing, and came back in time to read Joan her bedtime story. There was nothing left for Joan to do but to forget the whole thing. Or if she remembered anything, to remember that her mother needed no help from anyone; certainly not from her.

Over the years, the story of Miss Georgina's wig was told and retold with so many variations that eventually no one remembered what had really happened. But in every version Joan was the heroine. What fun they all had! What summers those were!

One

Peggy picked up the receiver, but there was no dial tone. It was annoying. She was late, having dashed home from her last meeting, and she didn't have a lot of time to waste if she was going to return at least some of her calls, get a bath, and be ready to go out by six forty-five. Carl was practicing, and she wanted to be able to go sit and listen to him for at least a few minutes before having to rush out again. She had called her mother, and was now frowning at the list of messages, trying to decide which ones could be put off. To when, though? She'd get home too late to call anyone, and tomorrow would be just as frantic as today had been. With an inward sigh, she picked up the receiver and had almost started to dial before she noticed she didn't have a dial tone.

"Hello?" she said.

"Hello?" a voice replied.

Obviously some wires had gotten crossed. Peggy pushed down firmly on the bar in order to clear the line, and released it.

"Hello?" The same voice was still there.

"You must have crossed some wires," Peggy said, as patiently as she could. She was always annoyed by people who blindly continue whatever they're doing despite clear evidence it's not working. "You'd better hang up or neither of us will be able to get a line."

"Is this Mrs. Gutheim?" the voice persisted.

"Who's this?" Peggy asked sharply, alarmed that a stranger whose wire had crossed hers should somehow know who she was. It took a moment for her to realize that a call must have come in just as she was lifting the receiver.

"I'm trying to reach Mr. or Mrs. Alan Gutheim," the voice said, betraying some irritation of its own.

"This is Mrs. Gutheim."

"Mrs. Gutheim?"

The woman must be a little dense, Peggy decided. "You *have* Mrs. Gutheim," she declared.

"Oh! Mrs. Gutheim! The phone didn't ring, and I thought I had cut in on someone else's call by accident. This is Eileen Cattell, at Bennington College? I'm the dean of Student Life. I'm calling about Joan. There's nothing to worry about."

Peggy thought, how stupid can one woman be? A dean calling a parent at six in the evening, and then saying there was nothing to worry about. Fortunately, Peggy was not one to panic. "What can I do for you?" she asked as calmly as could be imagined.

"Well, we're a bit concerned about Joan, and we thought we'd better be in touch with you about it. She's a lovely girl, we're all terribly fond of her, as I expect you know."

Really, the woman was an idiot. It didn't speak well for Bennington that she was the dean of Student Whatever-it-was. "Yes, I do know that," Peggy said, just as evenly as before, but somewhat more coldly.

"It's just that Joan was found on the pathway to the library. She had fainted."

What on earth was this all about? Peggy waited to hear the rest, but nothing more was forthcoming. That was evidently all there was. "You called me to tell me Joan fainted?" she asked incredulously. "Don't you think she could have told me that herself?" Then she felt an instant of alarm that perhaps Joan wasn't able to tell her anything, she was lying in a hospital bed unable to speak or move; but the image was so unlike Joan that it quickly dissolved of its own accord.

"Well, of course, we would have *preferred* that, Mrs. Gutheim," the woman said in her unctuous dean's tone. "I asked Joan to call you, and I must confess I assumed she had. When I saw her again today, to find out how she was, I found out she hadn't. I urged her to do so once more, but she was really quite adamant about it. I thought it important that you know, and I did inform her that I would have to call you myself. She raised no objection, I must say, but she simply refused to be the one to do it. So I've had to be the bearer of bad news."

Peggy didn't reply immediately. Even she needed a moment or two to take it in. "I gather from what you say that this didn't happen today?"

"No, it happened two days ago. I wouldn't have waited, but as I say I just assumed Joan would have called herself."

There was no point in going into that, and for a moment Peggy felt there was no point in going into any of it. Something about this didn't make sense. Maybe it was the delay in hearing about it, as if some distant star had exploded, and had already disappeared before the phenomenon was observed. Or else it was the saccharine voice of the dean, having to say something distasteful to a potential donor. Fainted! People don't faint anymore. Not in this day and age. No, something didn't fit.

For Peggy Gutheim, it was important that things fit, that they run well. The smooth functioning of her life was important, not so much as an end in itself, but because it released her to her main occupation in the world, which was to be of help. Peggy had no job, no career as such, but she made it her business to help wherever she could. She spent her days running herself ragged, rushing around town taking care of half the city. She put herself at the service of an astonishing number of people and organizations in countless ways, large and small. She didn't look for recognition, and in fact didn't particularly like to be thanked. She got her satisfaction from simply being involved with the lives of the people she helped. The good life for her was the useful life, and all she asked for herself was an orderly world so she could do her best; a world where things fit and each element had its proper place.

Right now, Joan's fainting on a path at Bennington had no place whatsoever in Peggy's world. Peggy had never been happy about Joan's choice of college. Bennington was all perfectly well and good for a certain type of girl, but Joan was simply not that type. She had gone there, Peggy always thought, because her friend Ellen Frankel had gone, and at that point in her life if Ellen Frankel had jumped off the Empire State Building, Joan would have jumped too. Peggy had said nothing, of course: her children led their own lives. She hadn't thought Joan would last at Bennington, and if this had happened two or three years ago, Peggy wouldn't have been the least surprised. She would have known what it meant, and they would have found some graceful way for Joan to come home without actually having to admit that it hadn't worked out. Peggy had absolutely no interest in proving to someone they were wrong. What earthly good did that do? It would have been enough for Joan herself to know it, and do what she needed to do. If that meant fainting on the path, well, there were worse ways for a girl to get herself out of college.

(Peggy had the fleeting thought, quickly dismissed, that Joan was pregnant. Joan, she realized, had too much common sense for that.)

But this wasn't three years ago, this was now. Joan was a senior, she didn't have that much time left. There was no reason whatsoever for her to leave now. Of course, people have been known to faint for medical reasons, but that seemed hardly likely. Joan was perfectly well. Always exhausted, but then that was the Gutheim style. Otherwise she was the picture of health. No, it didn't make sense. It didn't fit.

There was no point dwelling on that, however. Joan had fainted, and no matter how little sense it made, there it was. It had to be dealt with. Peggy was a realist above all, and she would handle whatever needed to be handled. Her immediate problem was what to do with this woman who continued babbling on, to very little purpose. Then she would decide what to do about Joan. The dean seemed to have the idea that Joan should go into a hospital, of all things, and even suggested "a good place right here in Vermont." Vermont might be the last word in maple syrup, but Peggy had never heard of anyone going there for medical care. "If it comes to that," Peggy said, "I think we might be able to find something in the city." Even without her mentioning that Alan was on the board of Mt. Sinai, it provided the only light moment in an otherwise pretty humorless conversation. In any event, it wasn't going to come to that. Knowing nothing more than the little she had been told, Peggy knew perfectly well Joan wasn't going into any hospital.

She needed to talk to Joan, and before that she needed to think. Her first task was to get the dean off the phone. It wasn't as easy as one might think. When she had finally gotten rid of her, Peggy sat for a minute, deliberating. She had lost her bearings and needed a few minutes to recover from the impression of dreaming that always accompanies unexpected news.

She was sitting on her bed in her gray suit. The heavy beige curtains had been drawn for the evening, but the beds hadn't been turned down yet. Peggy's bedroom was her haven. The rest of the apartment paid homage to their at times uncompromising paintings, but she wanted to be caressed in her own room. It was large enough for four armchairs and the two beds, but it was cozy there all the same. In the two alcoves the bureaus were built-in, both of the same rich mahogany as the bookshelves over the beds. The lamps, outfitted with cream silk shades, cast a soft light on the whimsical Klees and Mirós that decorated the walls. Over on the dressing table, her three children looked uncharacteristically serious in their formal photographs. On a hook inside the open closet door, the maid had hung her midnight-blue taffeta dress for the dinner party. Her mail was on the small shelf in the recess by her bed, next to the telephone, letters and bills on top, *The New Yorker* and *Life* underneath.

Her sense of order restored, she looked again at the messages, which now seemed even more insignificant than they had before. Still, they weren't going to go away. Her sister-in-law Eleanor had called. It was probably the least important, and Eleanor Altman was the last person on earth Peggy would ever ask advice of, but Peggy was tempted to call her. It would take forever, though, and besides, Peggy didn't want either to tell Eleanor about Joan, or not tell her, just yet. Eleanor's own children were forever causing no end of trouble, and Peggy invariably held her hand through whatever crisis was on at the moment. But it was not in Peggy's nature to turn to anyone for help, not even Eleanor; or perhaps, especially not Eleanor. People relied on Peggy Gutheim, not the other way around. It would take more than her daughter fainting before Peggy Gutheim would say, in any way, shape, or form, "I need you."

Before she had decided what to do, the phone rang. It was Alan's sister Marjorie, of all people. There was almost no one Peggy would less rather talk to at any time. Right now she barely had the patience to force herself into the sugary sweet tone she used with Alan's family, not that Marjorie was taken in by that. Marjorie might be one of the more unpleasant people on the face of the earth, but she was no fool. Anyway, it was Alan she wanted, she had no particular interest in talking to Peggy. She much preferred to bitch to Alan behind Peggy's back. She'd called to find out if Peggy and Alan were going to the benefit performance of the new musical, for the Jewish Guild for the Blind. "What new musical is that?" Peggy asked. Marjorie, of course, couldn't remember the name, but it was supposed to be darling, and they could all have dinner before. "If you think of the name of the musical, and it turns out we're going that night, we'd be only too happy to go with you," Peggy said, making a mental note to give away the tickets as soon as possible. The call was mercifully brief, and before anyone else had a chance to waylay her again, Peggy placed a call to Joan's dormitory.

The girl at the phone desk didn't think Joan was in her room, and she asked Peggy to wait while she tried to locate her. Peggy started to open her mail, but she realized she wasn't taking in what she was reading. She heard Alan's voice in the hallway, saying good evening to the maid. When he didn't come down the hallway, she guessed he had gone in to the living room to listen to Carl practicing. She was still waiting for Joan when he appeared in the doorway with his briefcase. He chirped several kisses at her and raised his eyebrows in inquiry.

"*Nu?*" he asked.

Peggy wrinkled her nose. It was not one of her favorite expressions. "I'm waiting for Joan," she told him.

His face clouded. "Everything okay?" he asked.

Peggy hesitated. "Everything's fine," she said. "Go get ready."

Alan looked at his watch. "I'll talk to her when you're done?" he asked.

"You'll be in the shower," Peggy informed him.

A flicker of disappointment passed over his face, and then he brightened again. "Give her my love," he said, and went on down to his dressing room.

And then Joan came on the phone.

The minute she finished talking to her mother, Joan got her suitcase out of the storage room and started to pack. She was going home. That much was decided. Everything else was up in the air. She didn't know how long she would stay in the city. She had no idea what they were going to do to her when she got there. She didn't really understand why she had to go in the first place, except that it was better than the alternatives. The nurse had wanted to keep her in the infirmary. The dean would settle for nothing less than a hospital. She had staved those two off, but now her mother had threatened to come up to Bennington. Nothing she could say would convince them all that she was fine, everything was perfectly all right, the world wasn't going to come to an end. Other people faint, she had pointed out, and go on about their business without everyone becoming hysterical. "You're not other people," Peggy had said. "I'll be up tomorrow." Joan had no choice. It took all she had to be allowed to take the train down. Peggy wanted to send Mrs. Altman's chauffeur up to fetch her. She supposed she was lucky to escape being carted off in an ambulance. She could see herself, battened down on a stretcher, speeding along the Merritt Parkway with sirens wailing, lights flashing, doctors poised to give her artificial respiration in case she stopped breathing. She wondered if they'd meet her at Grand Central with a wheelchair. It wasn't beyond the realm of possibility.

It's your own damn fault, she told herself, for collapsing in the middle of campus. That had not been smart. Definitely dumb. She had been coming from the dining hall with a bunch of girls, just after lunch, when she felt suddenly giddy. "That's what you get for not eating anything," Ellen had said, and the next thing she knew she was flat on the ground. People were putting books under her head and throwing coats over her. They wouldn't let her get up. It was absurd. She wasn't even sure she had lost consciousness. She kept saying, "I'm fine," but of course no one paid the slightest attention to her. They took her over to the infirmary, where the perpetually frantic nurse, Miss Denehy, had all but administered the last rites. It was actually funny, in a way, and she had come close to giggling in front of Miss Denehy, only she had a splitting headache. Also, it would not have been tactful at that particular juncture.

What struck her as ridiculous was that they were making this *monumental* fuss—and it wasn't even the first time. She'd passed out twice before, only no one knew about it. She'd had the sense to do it on those occasions in seclusion: the first time she'd been in her room, and the next time she had been coming back from the library, at night, alone. She knew the signs by then and had felt it coming on. Somehow she'd got herself over to a clump of bushes where she did her nosedive, but at least no one had seen her. When she came to, she'd heard some girls on the path near her, and she'd had to lie there for several minutes to avoid being discovered. She was afraid when she did come out someone would spot her and wonder what she'd been doing behind the bushes; but she was alone, on a deserted quadrangle. It was a little creepy, really. She'd wondered then if she oughtn't to tell someone, or see the doctor, but she was glad she hadn't. If one lousy swoon provoked this much uproar, imagine what three would have done! They would have been convinced she was pregnant, at the very least.

Even she had considered the possibility. Two months before, she had lost her virginity in the tritest possible fashion, after a Williams frat party, to a boy she hardly knew and cared for less. She would have liked to believe she'd been too drunk to know what she was doing, but in fact she was cold sober. She should have been drunk. That way she would either have enjoyed it or forgotten it. She had her sobriety to thank for a clear memory of some awkward and unpleasurable thrashing, followed by embarrassment and faint disgust. He had evidently been as unprepared as she was, and she hadn't had a period since. The only reason she wasn't frantic with worry was that it had been almost six months since she had menstruated. She seriously doubted she could get pregnant right now, even if she wanted to.

But what had gotten into her? she had to wonder. When she had broken up with Johnny Krieger the summer before, she had felt so tremendously free, it was like being able to breathe again after having nearly smothered to death for—what? two, almost three, years. She had told herself she didn't want the confinement of having a boyfriend again for a long time. She had looked forward to being at college, for once, without feeling that in her every action she was beholden to someone else. Not that Johnny had been difficult or jealous or demanding. Not Johnny! The most selfless man in the world. But just the idea of being on her own excited her. She would study seriously, date now and then, decide on the spur of the moment what she would do with her time. She would discover, she told herself, just what kind of a person she was. God knows, it was time she found out.

It hadn't turned out that way. Far from feeling liberated, she had found herself apathetic, listless, dispirited. She had no appetite, and at times the very thought of food nauseated her. Academically, she was at loose ends, drifting aimlessly through her classes. She was still in the center of everything going on, but she herself only went through the motions. She had no plans past graduation, and could think of nothing she wanted to do. Although she couldn't put her finger on it, there were times when a feeling of dread would run through her. She would not have called herself lonely—there were far too many people around for that—but she felt herself alone, terribly alone.

Of course the inevitable had happened. She became preoccupied, in spite of her resolve, with men. She paid too much attention to the few males on campus, dated indiscriminately on weekends, allowed herself to respond to the advances of the most notorious, if also most attractive, professor at the college. Unable to handle that, she had fled smack into the arms and ultimately the bed of this perfectly harmless boy, ten of whom wouldn't have been worth one Johnny Krieger, who had paid her the most ardent court for years without once touching her below the waist. Although in retrospect that may have been part of the problem.

She looked in her mirror, turning from side to side to see if there was some telltale sign. She had to tip the mirror downward and stand back to get a view of her midsection. It wasn't very satisfactory. The tan slacks she was wearing hung too loosely on her to tell anyway. She thought she could see a hint of protuberance. Most likely it was her flannel shirt, stuffed carelessly in the waist. She tipped the mirror back up and caught a quick impression of her face. It always surprised her, she looked so different from her image of herself. She had never set any store by her appearance. She'd been called lovely often enough, but people say that, she thought. She didn't see it herself. Her mouth was much too large. Her gray eyes lacked intensity. She'd escaped the Altman nose, thank God. Recently her cheekbones were taking on that dramatic prominence she saw in the Botticelli goddesses they'd been studying, with their hollow cheeks and abstracted gazes; although she lacked their calm indifference. She was too reactive. People did tell her she had such an expressive face, so full of life. She was supposed to have a wonderful smile. She tried to produce one, but could manage only a joyless grimace. Letting go of it, she was taken aback by the defeated expression left in its place. What's the tragedy? her mother would say. She recoiled from the accusation of self-pity, and gave up her inspection. Which was just as well, since a moment later Ellen burst in the door.

Although Ellen Frankel was fiercely devoted to Joan, their friendship had started off on a rocky footing. When the two girls had first met fifteen years before, swimming at the Silverlake Country Club, one of them had splashed the other—in the many tellings of the story the original aggression was hotly disputed—and they had cordially hated one another for the first summer of their acquaintance. They didn't see each other until the next winter, when the first snowfall brought them both into Central Park. Pilgrim Hill proved a more congenial environment than the Silverlake pool, and they sledded together all afternoon till the gathering twilight interrupted their sport. From that day on they had been nearly inseparable. When Ellen announced she was going to Bennington, there was no question where Joan would go. At college, despite their large circle of friends, they were known as the Siamese twins. Even three years of rooming together hadn't parted them.

Physically, no one would have taken them for sisters. In contrast to Joan's unconventional beauty, Ellen was short and dumpy—the kind of good kid that friends desperately advertise to boys as having a great personality. She had developed a self-deprecating banter to defend herself from chronic disappointment, and when she was with Joan she invariably played the sidekick role. For what it was worth, she was a painter of considerable talent. In New York her painting had been regarded as a mere hobby by everyone except Joan, who was more loyal than convinced; and her mother, who doted on her. When she came to Bennington, she was shocked that people took her work seriously. She was considered one of the more promising talents in her class. A gallery in New York had shown interest in her work, and for her final winter project at Bennington she was going to San Francisco, to study at the Art Institute. Joan dreaded her coming absence. She had considered going to the Coast at the same time, until she realized she had nothing to do out there. She was facing the prospect of a winter without her friend. She wasn't sure what that was going to be like.

Ellen came in and stopped dead in mock surprise. "What's this?" she asked, indicating the suitcase, open but still empty on Joan's bed. "Eloping?"

Joan continued the joke: "Hugh's picking me up at midnight," she said, naming the professor who had been running after her earlier in the fall. Ellen put her hand to her forehead and mugged a faint. "Actually, I'm going home," Joan said, as if that was as fanciful as running off with Hugh McIntosh.

"On a Tuesday night?"

"I'm going tomorrow."

"Oh, that makes a lot more sense." Ellen still didn't believe her. "Seriously, why the suitcase? You're not moving out, are you?" Her laugh was a bit forced. It had been a strange fall in many ways.

"I am serious. I just got off the phone with my mother. She's heard. Cattell called her. She had a cow, as you can imagine. She said I had to come down to New York. I've never been so shocked in my life. I asked her why on earth, but of course she just talked in circles. It didn't matter. You know Mother. When she wants something to happen, it happens. I'm going home, and that's that."

"Oh, my god," Ellen said in sympathy.

"Of course, I have no idea what to pack." She started transferring piles of clothing indiscriminately from her bureau to the suitcase. "I've got about a million papers to write, I'll have to take all my books."

"Don't you think the papers can wait?" Ellen asked, aghast at the amount Joan was packing. "Jesus, how long are you gonna be gone?"

Joan shrugged. "Who knows? They want me to see a doctor. There was no use arguing about that, it's a lost cause. I did point out that there are doctors in Vermont, this isn't exactly the Belgian Congo, but of course that didn't cut any ice. Then I asked how long I had to stay, and she said 'As long as it takes to find out what's the matter with you, dear,' in that oh-so-reasonable tone of hers, as if it's completely out of her hands. How long do you suppose 'as long as it takes to find out what's the matter with you, dear' is?"

"I wouldn't think more than a couple of days."

Joan gave her a wry look. "We're talking about Mother, remember?"

"Your mother *hates* doctors," Ellen reminded her.

"It's just an excuse. Once she has me down in New York, she'll find a thousand reasons why I shouldn't come back. You know how she feels about Bennington."

"I know how she feels about me," Ellen said.

"She likes you!" Joan protested. "Mother's always liked you."

"Oh, I know she *likes* me." Ellen laughed. "She just thinks I'm a bad influence on you, with my strange ideas and bohemian ways. I should live so long. What your mother doesn't realize is that you don't listen to anyone. I'd like to meet the person who has an influence on you."

Joan wasn't paying attention. She had gone over to the closet and was rummaging around in it. "Do you think I can get away with wearing blue jeans in the city?"

"Oh, sure. Especially to your grandmother's. I'm sure she'd be delighted to have you come to lunch in blue jeans."

"I guess not," Joan said, coming from the closet with several plaid skirts over her arm. "You don't by any chance know where my cashmere sweater has wandered to, do you?" she asked in a light tone.

"You realize what a hardship this is causing me," Ellen replied. "I'll freeze." As she went to find it in her own bureau, she saw Joan taking a framed photograph off the table next to her bed. "You're not taking The Picture!" she wailed.

Joan smiled. It was always hard to tell when Ellen was being serious. The picture was a blown-up snapshot of Phil and Johnny Krieger the summer before, just after the final round of the Silverlake men's doubles tournament. They had lost the championship, but the two of them were grinning as broadly as if they had won. All the girls in the dorm were constantly mooning over the picture. Phil wore his characteristic smirk, as if he had just done something he shouldn't have, while Johnny, shy as always, looked every inch the young god, two months out of Dartmouth, handsome as all get-out. The photograph had special irony: It was later that night, after the club fair and dance, that Joan had broken up with Johnny. No one—not even Ellen—knew what had gotten into her. They were everybody's dream couple. Everyone assumed they'd get married. Johnny had walked around for the rest of the summer looking dazed, and in retrospect it seemed as though Joan had started her decline then. Not that anyone spoke of a decline; not out loud, at least.

"I'll leave the picture," Joan said, putting it back on the table. "I wouldn't want to deprive you."

"You'll have Phil right there, after all," Ellen pointed out. "And it wouldn't come as a complete shock to hear that you had laid eyes on Johnny."

"I'm not going to see Johnny," Joan said, with such finality that Ellen didn't venture anything further on that score. The gang had discussed the subject of Joan and Johnny endlessly for the remainder of the summer, and also in phone calls to Ellen, when Joan wasn't around. Everyone agreed they ought to get back together. Johnny's face was the first thing Joan saw every morning, the last every night, and his name was virtually taboo in her presence. No one could figure it out.

"Anyway, you'll be back before you miss it," Ellen maintained.

Joan was kneeling, looking through the bottom drawer of her bureau. "I don't know when I'll ever get back," she said. When she stood up, Ellen saw that she was tearful.

"Oh, Joanie!" she cried, rushing to give her friend a hug. "Don't say that! This is really for the best. They'll find out what's wrong with you, and have you back here in no time at all. You'll see!"

"I don't want them finding out what's wrong with me!" Joan said, barely keeping from sobbing. "There's nothing wrong with me! Why does everyone think there's something wrong with me all the time?"

She broke away from the embrace. Ellen looked at her roommate, pale, gaunt, exhausted. It seemed as though she might keel over again any moment. She looked terribly sad and precarious, a piece of porcelain about to shatter of its own fragility. All fall Ellen had watched her friend grow thinner and had said nothing. Where once Joan had confided everything in her, now she grew secretive and evasive. Ellen, of course, knew perfectly well what was going on. She knew about the Williams boy, the fatigue, the missed periods. She kept track of what Joan ate, which wasn't enough to keep a small bird alive. She could see her friend disintegrating in front of her eyes, and she couldn't say anything. Not a thing. "I'll get that sweater," she said, and started to look through her own bureau for it. "It isn't here," she said, trying to slam the drawer shut, but it stuck as usual. "Ginny must have borrowed it," she said, and ran out of the room.

As soon as she was alone again, Joan stopped packing. She sat on her bed amid the disorder of underwear and blouses, unable to make any more decisions. She was too tired. Let them come, she thought, she would offer no resistance. They could take her wherever they pleased. In truth she wasn't altogether sorry to be leaving. She loved her friends, she leaned on Ellen, but she had to get away. Bennington was giving her claustrophobia. There was no privacy there. You were constantly in the spotlight. Your every movement was watched. Left to herself, she wouldn't have chosen to return to New York, but where else was she to go? It was a big city, after all. Surely she could find a corner of it where she wasn't known, where she could escape her mother's watchful eye. She was ready for new possibilities, the unknown, adventure. She wanted to live another life, be a different person. She would be just like the immigrants, leaving everything behind, starting over again, unhampered by the constraints of the past. New York would surely take her in.

New York!

Peggy and Alan had their usual disagreement after leaving the Kaplans'. The night was clear and mild, and Alan proposed that a stroll home might be pleasant. "Have a lovely walk, dear," Peggy wished him. "I'm taking a cab." With some regret, he meekly followed her into the taxi that the doorman hailed for them.

Once they were under way, though, he settled back happily and said, "Well, I found that a terribly interesting evening."

"I'm glad you enjoyed it, dear," Peggy said. "Personally, I was bored to tears."

"Really?" Alan was astonished.

"What else could you expect? Sidney is the dullest person on the face of the earth, and I doubt that Ruth knows the time of day."

"Sidney's no ball of fire, I know, but I thought that Secretary or whatever he was from the Liberian delegation was worth meeting."

"He had on a colorful costume," Peggy conceded. "I couldn't get a word out of him during the entire meal. Every time I asked him anything, he said he couldn't comment on it."

"I imagine he has to be quite discreet. I thought he was very knowl-edgeable, considering. He seemed terribly interested in the election. He was quite up on what's going on there."

"He knew who Nixon and Kennedy were, I'll grant you that. Be-yond that I didn't see any great evidence of his being up on anything."

"Oh," Alan said, deflated. He tried to come up with an example of the diplomat's grasp of the issues, but he couldn't think of one.

They rode on without talking. Alan wanted to salvage something of the dinner party, but he knew his wife's intransigence better than to persist. He thought she was being a bit harsh on the Kaplans, and won-dered if she wasn't off her feed, a bit. It didn't occur to him that she was preoccupied, and had been all evening, with thoughts of Joan. He him-self was relatively untroubled. Peggy had given him too little informa-tion to arouse any real anxiety. All she had told him was that the dean had called, there was some vague question about Joan's health, the up-shot of which was that she was coming down. The fainting episode had been downgraded to a dizzy spell, and Peggy gave her opinion that it was probably nothing more than sheer exhaustion. Alan was concerned, of course, but he was also pleased Joan was coming home. He missed her terribly, and although he realized she did have to go to college, he was always happier when all the children were home. The dinner party had distracted him from worrying about her, and only now, in the silence of the taxicab, did his thoughts return to her arrival the next day.

"Wouldn't it make more sense for me to meet Joan?" he asked. "I'm two steps from the station, and it would save you the trouble." Alan's firm had, over his strenuous objections, moved its office from Wall Street to midtown the year before.

"You do just as you like, dear. I wouldn't dream of not being there." Peggy had no intention of allowing anyone to usurp her place at her daughter's side. She'd be just as happy if Alan wouldn't come, but there were other ways of getting him to stay away. She would of course be there when Joan stepped off the train. If she'd followed her instinct, she would have skipped the dinner party—no great loss there—and been up at Bennington by then. She was burning to know what was afoot. Joan had been puzzlingly cryptic and evasive over the phone. On the one hand, she insisted nothing was the matter. On the other, she all but begged to be allowed to come down. She didn't put it in those words, but Peggy knew that was what she wanted when she refused to accept any other alternative. If she wanted to get away from Bennington, that was fine with Peggy, but she didn't have to go through all this rigama-role to do it. When Carl had started school, he had worked himself into such a dither that he was constantly having mysterious stomachaches, until finally Peggy had had the sense to tell him he didn't have to be sick in order to skip school. That was the end of the stomachaches. Was that what was up with Joan? Did she think she had to be sick in order to come home?

"Are you going to have her see Gelbert?" Alan interrupted her reverie.

"Darling, Gelbert is a pediatrician. I can hardly have him see her."

"I suppose not. What do you think, Plotkin?" Plotkin was the chief internist at Mt. Sinai, an oily little man whom Peggy utterly loathed. She and Alan really had no family physician. Alan got his checkups at Mt. Sinai, and Peggy avoided doctors like the plague. She decided what was wrong with her, and if she needed a prescription, she called her obstetrician.

"I think we could do better than Plotkin," she said.

"He's said to be one of the top three in New York," Alan countered. He was a devotee of rank lists, although it was not always clear on what authority he compiled them.

"Not by me he isn't," Peggy said firmly. "I don't mind if some younger member of the staff sees her. As long as they don't go over-board. I find when they don't know what's going on, they simply order more tests. That I can do without."

"I'll get someone to see her—what do you think, Thursday? She won't want to see someone tomorrow."

"Thursday will do, I suppose," Peggy said, resigning herself to the necessity of at least a pro forma medical examination. She was going to add something about Joan not being in any hurry to get back to college, but stopped herself. Alan wouldn't understand, and she'd have to ex-plain it to him, and he still wouldn't understand. "I don't think there's any mad rush about it" was all she said.

After a while she asked him, "When do they decide about this Bar thing?" Alan had told her earlier that evening that he was being seri-ously considered as the next president of the Bar Association of the City of New York.

"That's very hush-hush, you know," he whispered, glancing ner-vously at the driver.

"Darling," Peggy protested.

"I think I should have a pretty good idea how it's going in a month or so," he said. "They'll decide by the end of the year. It's still quite iffy."

"Not in my book, it isn't," Peggy said, patting his leg. "If anyone deserves it, you do. No one's worked harder."

"I appreciate the vote of confidence," Alan said. "I hope some of the others see it your way."

When they got home, Carl was in bed, or at least his door was closed, and Phil was not yet home. He generally spent the evening at the apartment of his girlfriend, Betsy Schine, ostensibly coming back to sleep in his own bed, although Alan, who stayed up late, had his doubts. He didn't mind, and in fact was glad to believe that Phil was doing what any normal, healthy young man would, but if he were Harold Schine he'd think twice about letting his daughter have an apartment by herself.

They both got into their nightclothes and sat in their respective beds to clear up the unfinished business of the day. Alan read the evening paper, while Peggy went through the mail, putting on the recessed night table between their beds the letters Alan needed to look at. From time to time he would comment on an item in the paper, or she would ask him what he wanted to do about the solicitations that had come in that day. Alan had a system to determine their response to various charities. It was based entirely on who was doing the asking. Appeals from relatives and close friends and big givers to Federation or Mt. Sinai were automatically honored. Others would get a donation carefully calculated according to what Alan hoped they might do in the future for his or Peggy's projects. Those who had failed to come up to previous expectations got little or nothing, while the irredeemably bloodless stones got what Alan was pleased to call the finger, and suffered the indignity of having their letters crumpled savagely by him before being thrown into the wastebasket.

There were several requests that needed decisions, including a couple of benefits, and when they had finished with them, Alan had worked up an appetite. He went off to the kitchen to see what he could snack on, and left the paper for Peggy. She looked through the first pages without paying much attention. Her mind was elsewhere. She turned out the lamp set over her bed, and closed her eyes, but sleep did not come easily.

It disturbed her, about Joan. If she had thought Joan was really ill, that would have been upsetting, but there were accepted ways of dealing with that. Peggy was sure that the trouble with Joan lay elsewhere. She had almost no reason for her supposition, but then Peggy needed very little in the way of evidence in order to leap to very firm conclusions. No, she was going to have a difficult time on her hands. She didn't fool herself for a minute it would be any picnic, having Joan home. Lovely as it would be to see her again.

The trick was to find something for her to do. The Gutheims had a tradition of working themselves to exhaustion, and it would be awful for Joan to be sitting around brooding while everyone else was running around like mad. New York was far too exciting a city to sit around in, doing nothing. This could be a wonderful opportunity for Joan, if properly used. Peggy herself had never finished college, and had never regretted it for one day. Joan would do fine if only she had a purpose, a goal, something to draw her outside herself. She would absolutely blossom, Peggy thought, if she could do something for others, if she could really be of use. What would be the most stimulating, most rewarding work for an energetic, intelligent girl who wants to contribute? What would Peggy herself do, if she were twenty-one again, with her life before her and that kind of opportunity, waiting to be seized?

The idea of Meyer House struck her as so right, so obvious, that she felt like an idiot not to have thought of it sooner. Working in a settlement house would be ideal. Not only were they desperately in need of all the help they could get, but it would be the very thing for Joan: a chance to be useful, see an aspect of life that was new to her, serve those who really needed her, all under the aegis of one of the most exciting men in the city. The plan rapidly took shape in Peggy's mind as she worked out the details, and she felt the tremendous relief of someone who has had a heavy burden lifted from her shoulders. She lifted herself up on an elbow, and with her free hand wrote a note on the pad by the telephone. She tore the page off and propped it up over the dial so the first thing she would see in the morning would be the reminder: *Joan— Martin Perry.*

Two

Peggy always found the lobby of Meyer House one of the most fascinating places in the city. It reminded her of the concourse in Grand Central Station, without the huge Kodak ad but with that same madhouse atmosphere of people rushing through: staff, clients, visitors, total strangers, as colorful a crowd as one could find anywhere in New York.

She was watching from the side, seated in one of the deep maroon armchairs that dated, she was sure, from the earliest days of the settlement house. Her fellow onlookers were elderly men and women, mostly women, reading magazines, chatting, crocheting, dozing, or making no pretense of doing anything other than gaping. She was conscious of the gulf between herself and them, but they smiled pleasantly when she said hello, which pleased her. Joan was keeping her waiting, but she couldn't have minded less. "I never think it's a waste of time to look at people," she always said. "Everyone has a story to tell, if you could only guess it."

In the midst of all the bustle, a little girl limped slowly across from the elevator to the front door. Such an adorable little girl, surely no more than eight or nine years of age, with braids someone had tied with more love than skill, and a thin little brown coat over her plaid gingham dress. Right out of a picture book she was, and to eat. The girl clumped by Peggy in her brace, her eyes fixed ahead, her face set in that petrified smile of the handicapped. What next? she seemed to ask. Peggy ached just looking at her. She could barely resist reaching out and scooping the child up and giving her the most tremendous hug before letting her go on to wherever she was going. What a struggle life was for her! If only one could do something. God knows, Peggy tried; but it was so little. She would have given anything to be allowed to tie the girl's shoe, wipe the smudge off her face, button up her coat. As if that coat had the slightest chance of keeping out the harsh cold of a gray November day; or Peggy the slightest chance of smoothing out, even a little, the rocky path the girl would have to clump along for the rest of her life.

Meyer House in its last incarnation had been a clothing factory; that is to say, a sweatshop. In the previous century, large numbers of immigrant women had worked there under the most appalling conditions. After the ghastly Triangle fire, when rudimentary safety measures were finally enacted, the owner had decided that compliance would cut his profit margin too sharply, and he had shut the place down. Many such factories closed around that time for similar reasons, and were abandoned, or burned, or turned into squalid tenements at no great gain to the health or welfare of the former workers. Guided by vision, compassion, and disciplined outrage, the local rabbi, Josep Silivitz, had somehow gotten himself into the uptown mansion of one Ephraim Meyer, a retired drygoods merchant not previously noted for philanthropy. Meyer was, however, a widower without known heirs, and for some reason agreed to accompany the rabbi down to Rivington Street for a first-hand look at conditions there. After looking around the neighborhood and touring the empty factory, he had a glass of tea at the tenement flat of Ida Pilanski, a blind former seamstress. Meyer found to his astonishment that he was speaking Yiddish for the first time in over thirty years. The next morning his lawyer called on the owner of the former factory and bought it, cash on the barrelhead. Within the month, Esther Meyer House opened its doors, and had been in continuous operation ever since. By the time Peggy had come on the board, Meyer, Rabbi Silivitz, and Ida Pilanski had all died; but the older clients of the house still remembered the factory, where some of them had actually worked. Looking around the lobby, Peggy wondered if any of the old ladies sitting there could remember it, and the early days of the settlement house. Their reminiscences must be fascinating; someone ought to set them down. She made a mental note to speak to Martin Perry about it.

The thought of Martin made Peggy decide that it would be rude after all not to let him know she was there. She didn't want to disturb

him, but it would be awful if he found out she had been and gone
without his knowing; and of course he would find out. Nothing happened at Meyer House he didn't know about, even something as unimportant as a trustee dropping in. So she just poked her head inside the
door marked DIRECTOR and asked the secretary to let Mr. Perry know she
was there, she had come to pick up her daughter, and under no circumstances was he to interrupt what he was doing on her account. She was
very firm about that. But no sooner had she settled herself again than
she was startled by the sudden appearance before her of Martin Perry.

"If I'd had the slightest idea you would stop your important work
just to come out and see me, I would never have told your secretary I
was here," she protested.

"And I would never have forgiven myself to have had you here and
missed the opportunity to say hello, Mrs. Gutheim," Martin replied.
Peggy thought he was a remarkable person. She had never had a moment's regret about insisting that he be hired, over the objections of the
fuddy-duddies on the board.

Martin was telling her about a new program he wanted to start,
working with some of the young people who seemed to be getting involved with drugs, when Peggy noticed a slight young woman appear at
the far side of the lobby. It took a moment before she registered that it
was Joan, so lost and forlorn did her daughter look. She could have been
one of the waifs off the streets the settlement house was there to serve,
all but lost in her tan loden coat. They'd have to get her something more
suitable for New York. For the first time since this had all started, Peggy
entertained the thought that Joan might really be ill. She had always
dismissed it, but just at that moment Joan looked so deathly pale that
Peggy felt a chill in the pit of her stomach.

But Joan spotted them and underwent a complete transformation.
Her eyes lit up. Joan had the eyes of someone completely caught up in
life. "They're the most expressive eyes of any child I've ever known,"
Peggy always said. Joan couldn't conceal anything, not if her life depended on it. Whatever she felt, she showed in her eyes. She would
drink in everything that was going on, and then she would respond
vividly, generously. She loved nothing better than to laugh. She herself
was not a great wit, but she brought out the humor in others and made
people feel happy. She had that special knack of bringing out what others had to offer. In any crowd she would be at the center, her large
mouth wide with surprise, just on the verge, at any moment, of pouring

forth cascades of the most infectious laughter, accompanied by streams of helpless tears. Everyone around would be filled with pleasure and warmth; people loved to be with her.

The minute Peggy saw her eyes, she knew that the day had been a complete and utter success. Joan hurried over, full of apologies for keeping her mother waiting. "Nonsense, dear, when is it ever a waste of my time when I can talk with Martin. Did you get something to eat?" she asked, nervous over Joan's pallor. The doctors had wanted to put Joan in the hospital immediately. Peggy had put out that fire, but she had promised Joan would start slowly. "I hope you aren't taking on too much all at once. We had thought something part-time," she added to Martin, who looked surprised. She wondered if she should have told him the reason Joan had come down from college; but since she wasn't sure herself, it seemed best to say nothing.

"Mother!" Joan exclaimed. "I couldn't come just part-time. There's much too much to be done. You should see those kids!"

Peggy's only response was a tolerant smile. Martin Perry pointed out, "I think your mother has seen the kids."

"I should have known this would happen if I left her here with you," she told Martin, laughing. "I just don't want her exhausting herself before she even starts. That's my only concern."

"Everyone exhausts themselves at the beginning," Martin said ruefully, but with pride. "After that they're just plain bone tired. Kevin! Good luck tonight!" he called to a young man who had waved at him. Turning back, he said, "You would be amazed to know how far that particular boy has come. When he first turned up here, he was barely keeping himself from serious trouble with the law. Now he practically runs our teen sports program. He has a boxing match himself tonight. He's a fabulous athlete. Fabulous."

"Handsome-looking boy," Peggy said, glancing at Joan to see her reaction; but Joan evidently hadn't seen him.

A short, fat woman with a pleasant face had come over and was standing a little to one side, waiting patiently. "Yes! Etta! What can I do for you?" Martin cried.

"Just a word with you, Mr. Perry, when you've got a minute. Don't let me interrupt."

"You're not interrupting," Martin replied genially. "Mrs. Gutheim, you know Etta, of course."

"I don't believe I've had the pleasure," Peggy said graciously.

"You haven't? How can that be? Etta is one of our Rocks of Gibraltar. Runs our nursery practically single-handed. Etta Sevitsky, Mrs. Gutheim."

"Oh, I'm so pleased to meet you, Mrs. Gutheim," Etta said, flushed with embarrassment and pleasure. "I've known of you ever since I came to Meyer House."

"And this is her daughter, Joan," Martin continued. "She's joining us next week. She's going to help Leona with the crippled children."

"Oh how nice," Etta said. "Following in your mother's footsteps."

Joan was horrified. "I'm not going to be on the board! I want to *do* something for the kids!" The three grown-ups smiled indulgently.

"Well it's nice you're going to be here. I'll get you over to meet our tiny ones. Mr. Perry can tell you, I'm the Pied Piper of Meyer House. Anyone who isn't nailed down, I come and steal them." She laughed her pleasant laugh, and Martin Perry nodded in vigorous agreement.

"Why don't we be off," Peggy suggested. "Martin has his hands full, and I've got to get you to a store this afternoon. You know, she's just come back to town," she confided in Etta, woman to woman, "and we have to get her something to wear."

"Don't I know!" Etta cried, thrilled to be included by Peggy, although she had no children of her own and thought that Joan was very nicely dressed. Most of the ladies at Meyer House, including Etta, wore some sort of smock, and to her Joan looked charming in her plaid skirt and sweater underneath the loden coat. "You must be so pleased to have her back."

"We're ecstatic," Peggy replied. "Shall we leave it that we'll talk next week about the arrangements, Martin?"

"We've already made the arrangements," Joan said, with an edge in her voice.

Martin, picking up the tension, added quickly, "If that's all right with you, Mrs. Gutheim."

"Oh, there's no question of its being all right with me," Peggy said. "Joan runs her own life. I'm just here to make sure she doesn't take on more than is realistic right now. Oh, no, she makes her own decisions. The day I had anything to say about it is long since gone."

"Then it's settled," Joan said testily.

"Wonderful!" Peggy said. "When do I get this young lady back to you, then, Martin?"

"Did we say something about Monday morning?" Martin asked gingerly, as if testing a very uncertain rung on a ladder.

"Monday morning," Joan said firmly.

Peggy frowned. It was all very well, but there was the specialist Joan was supposed to see Monday morning. "We can certainly discuss it on the way home," she temporized. "No need to keep Martin waiting while we settle it."

"I thought it was settled," Joan said sarcastically. Peggy smiled at Martin and Etta, who looked understanding. Everyone said good-bye. As Peggy and Joan walked toward the front door of the settlement house, Martin Perry was leaning over, listening to Etta with a serious expression, completely absorbed in what she was telling him. Peggy nodded pleasantly at the people she passed. They could talk about the schedule later, when Joan had recovered her humor. The girl was obviously exhausted. It made no sense for her to be going out that evening with Phil. Peggy wondered if she was even up to shopping. Hopefully the taxi ride would revive her.

They saw no taxis on Rivington Street, so Peggy suggested they walk over to Allen Street. "I gather you found Martin terribly exciting," she said. "I can't tell you how rare it is, this gift he has of getting people caught up in whatever it is he's doing." She was disappointed not to see more of a reaction in Joan, but she didn't flog it. "I would have given my eyetooth to have had a chance to do this when I was your age. But of course in my day it wasn't 'done.' This was before I discovered you could actually do things that weren't 'done.'"

"I thought you worked at that old people's place, or whatever it was."

"Well, yes, but in those days, you see, when a young woman 'worked' at that sort of thing, what she did was to go over there once a week and pour tea. You were never allowed to do anything useful. You weren't supposed to dirty your hands. I was, of course, a terrible nuisance. I asked if there wasn't something I could really do. Oh! You should have seen the shocked looks! You would have thought I was proposing something immoral. In a way I suppose they thought it was." They had come to Allen Street. "No, I started shocking people early on."

She stepped off the curb and waved at some taxis coming up the street, but they were all full. "And then, a young woman could hardly hold a job in those days, because you were expected to pay calls all the time. I had to visit every single one of my aunts at least once a week. It was a deadly bore, but you couldn't get out of it. The afternoons I spent in your great-aunt Ethel's drawing room, yelling as loudly as I could because she was as deaf as a doorpost, and the most disagreeable old woman imaginable. That's why I put my foot down when it came to you kids doing that sort of thing. Of course, your father's sisters have never forgiven me for that. Among many other things, I may say." She laughed. "Many, many other things."

Joan relented, and smiled at the thought of her mother outraging her dreadful aunts. You had to hand her that. Peggy persuaded a taxi to stop, and they got in. Joan's good humor was coming back, but when Peggy said, "Bergdorf's, if you please," she sighed wearily. "I think you'll find Bergdorf's less stuffy than you remember it," Peggy assured her. "They've really smartened it up."

"It can't possibly be more stuffy than I remember it," Joan replied. "Is this really necessary? They'll send my stuff down from college in a few days."

"I know that, dear, but what did for Bennington doesn't necessarily do for New York." Peggy didn't mean to sound quite so snooty, but the fact was that none of Joan's clothes seemed to fit right. They made her look like a little girl, dressed up.

Joan leaned back against the seat and closed her eyes in tacit protest. Peggy looked at her anxiously. Her color was poor. Probably had nothing to do with the . . . She was just exhausted after too full a day. All the same, it was worrisome. She wondered what this specialist would say. Lamartine. The doctors at Mt. Sinai were none too happy about his being brought in, but that was just too bad. They had, as she suspected they would, wanted to put Joan straight to bed and run every test in the book. "Over my dead body," she'd told them. She'd used those very words, and it had all but come to that. She had had a terrible scene with them, and a none too pleasant one with Alan, whom they had scared to death. Joan, of course, knew nothing about that. All she knew was that she wouldn't be going back to college for a while, but she could stay at home and work at Meyer House until everything was cleared up. Peggy had been tempted to bring her in on all the discussions, all the arguments, and let her see who was going to bat for her; but it was too delicate a situation. The less said, the better. She could live without Joan's gratitude.

That old people's place . . . Peggy smiled to herself to hear the

Reisenberg Home referred to that way. That was what it was, though. As good an agency as any to start in, although it had been a terrible disappointment at the time. She had wanted desperately to go out to Chicago and work under her idol, Jane Addams. Her father had of course refused to hear of such a thing; and it would never have occurred to her mother, who was secretly on her side, to oppose her husband in the slightest way. That was how marriages worked in those days, and even Peggy hadn't questioned it. She had argued herself blue in the face, but to no avail. Peggy had always adored her father, but he was, really, the stubbornest man she had ever known. Her brother came in second, but even Gerald couldn't hold a candle to Nathan Altman in his prime. So Chicago was out, Hull House was out, and by the time she woke up to the fact that she could do what she pleased with or without his permission, Jane Addams was dead. Peggy had never admired anyone so fiercely, and never again wanted anything so badly. Nothing she did subsequently, not all the charity work and board work and taking care of everyone who crossed her path, could ever make up for having missed out on the great opportunity of her life. Her only consolation was the knowledge that her own children could do anything they wanted, that they would never be deprived of fulfilling their deepest ambitions. It pleased her no end that Joan was about to embark on this adventure, and start living her own life to the fullest. In the privacy of her thoughts, she congratulated herself. If it had been left up to the others, Joan would fast be turning into an invalid, and they would all be sitting around bemoaning her fate.

Peggy had no patience with that sort of thing. Life is too short, she always said, to waste time wringing one's hands.

Without opening her eyes, Joan said, "I wish you wouldn't tell people how 'ecstatic' you are to have me home."

"Why on earth not?" Peggy asked. "We are ecstatic."

"Well I'm not."

"I don't expect that you should be. But that doesn't mean we can't be. It's lovely to have you home. I'm sorry for the reason, but your father and I are happy to have you back."

"The whole thing is lousy. You make me come home for no reason at all, like I'm going to die or something, then you go around telling everyone things are simply divine." When she opened her eyes, the tears were there.

"Darling, no one is saying things are divine. Of course we all wish none of this had ever happened, but since it has, it made a good deal of sense for you to come home. I think I can be pleased to have you back without necessarily being glad that there are . . . difficulties."

"Blackouts, Mother. It's called a blackout. It's not a 'difficulty.' Jesus, can't you ever call something what it is?" She started to say something more, but stopped, and closed her eyes again.

Peggy decided to talk to Phil. Joan shouldn't go out that evening. Nothing could be clearer.

Meanwhile, she needed to get Joan's mind off this upsetting business. She cast about for some neutral topic. "Percy Weinstein died," she said.

"That's too bad," Joan said without emotion.

"Well, it is and it isn't. He had been desperately ill for months, in terrible pain. It was really a blessing. The funeral's Sunday, by the way."

"The funeral!" Joan exclaimed. "I hardly knew the man. He wouldn't know me—wouldn't have known me if he passed me in the street. Why do I have to go to his funeral, of all things?"

"Nobody said anything about your having to do anything. I just thought you'd like to know, in case you want to go. Your father and I will go, of course, and I suspect Phil will. But you suit yourself."

"I would never in a million years have thought of going to Percy Weinstein's funeral!"

"Darling, it's entirely up to you. It couldn't matter less to me." Peggy looked out the window with studied nonchalance. They had gone west, and were driving up the Bowery. Not the route she would have chosen. She started to tell the driver to take another avenue, then decided not to. She couldn't run everything. "Personally, I think funerals are for the birds, but it's very important to your father. Also he was very close to Uncle Gerry and Aunt Eleanor." Percy Weinstein had been a partner at Altman & Sons, Gerald's firm.

Joan didn't respond. The two women looked out at the gray, littered sidewalks and crumbling buildings. The streets were virtually deserted. Occasionally a derelict stumbled out of an alley or a doorway, and if you looked closely you could see that what at first appeared to be a sack lying up against a wall was really a person. None of the buildings looked occupied. The stores had been out of business for years, it seemed. Those which still had signs were hollow shells, the windows smashed or boarded up. Rows of tenements, fire-gutted, were permanently filthy with the soot and refuse of the years.

"This part of town used to be such fun," Peggy said wistfully. "You know, in my day you used to come here all the time. There used to be markets and restaurants and stores where you could always find the most marvelous things. You couldn't get them anywhere else in the city. The sidewalks were jammed with people. You could walk down any street without the slightest worry in the world. In fact, you could go anywhere in the city in those days: Brooklyn; Harlem. We used to go to nightclubs in Harlem. It was quite the thing to do. They had the most wonderful jazz music. But the Bowery was great fun. You know that song?" Joan nodded. Her father was forever singing it, in his tuneless croak. "Now look at it," Peggy said bleakly.

They had stopped for a light. A shabbily dressed man walked unsteadily across the street. When he got directly in front of the taxi, he staggered and reached out to steady himself against the hood. He stopped, as if surprised to notice what he had bumped into, and peered through the window. The light changed. He remained where he was, supporting himself with one hand and using the other to shield his eyes as he looked into the cab. His unfocused gaze stopped on Joan. He seemed fascinated by her, as if he were visiting a zoo and had spotted an animal concealed in the corner of a dark cage. Joan felt exposed and trapped. There was no place to hide from his insolent, threatening stare.

The driver honked. The drunk didn't take his eyes from Joan, but moved slowly on. Pushing himself away from the taxi, he took an uncertain step, like a patient rising from a sickbed, twisting his head to keep Joan in his gaze. He swayed as he tried to stand upright. The cabdriver, infuriated by the insulting delay, cut his wheels to the right and the taxi jerked forward. The man staggered, startled by the sudden movement of his support, or perhaps by the screeching tires. He either fell against the rear fender or was actually hit by the taxi swerving too close to him as it went back into the lane. There was a dull thud. "Fuck him!" muttered the driver, not quite under his breath. Peggy looked straight ahead, as if she hadn't heard a thing, but Joan twisted sharply around and saw the man collapse onto the street. "We've hit him!" she cried.

"He bang on de fender wid hees feest," the driver told her. "Heet's an old treeck."

The light had changed again, and they had to stop, just a block uptown. The drunk remained motionless on the street. "I think he's hurt," Joan said urgently.

A black Pontiac turned into the avenue two blocks back and pulled up next to where the drunk lay. The driver of the Pontiac stuck his head out the window and looked down at the crumpled heap. Then he pulled his head back in and rolled up the window."We have to go back," Joan insisted. The taxi driver looked straight ahead. "Have him go back." Her voice was thinning and shaking. The light changed again and the driver gunned the cab. A car ran the side street against the light and they only missed a collision by a sudden jamming of the brakes and another swerve to the right. As soon as he was clear again, the cabdriver floored the pedal.

"Be careful!" Peggy ordered sharply.

"Have him go back!" Joan begged.

"I think we'd better leave him to drive the taxi as best he can," Peggy said in a tense undertone. She checked the name on the ID card. Julio Nunez. The mild, slightly startled face in the photograph bore little resemblance to the swarthy, agitated man in the driver's seat. Maybe the taxi had been stolen by a maniac.

"It's hit-and-run, Mother!" Joan insisted. "We have to go back."

The driver veered the cab over to the side of the street and screeched to yet another stop. He turned fully around in his seat and shouted at Joan: "He knock heeself agains' my cab. I get out, see wha' de matter. He pool de knife on me. Take my money, eef I'm lucky he no slash my face. Maybe he got a friend in de doorway, come in an' rape you and you' moth'. Wha' you gonna do den? Huh? Wha' dey care about heet-an'-ron?"

Joan didn't answer. Peggy, trying to maintain a semblance of reason in the taxi, said, "Just drive on to Bergdorf's, if you would."

Joan was trembling with anger and fright. The basic laws of civilization had been abandoned in favor of paranoia. But she had no reply to the driver. Seeing his accuser silenced, Nunez turned around again and threw the gearshift back into drive with a smack of his hand. The taxi roared uptown again, and for the third time got only to the end of the block before the light changed again. "Friend of mine, he get slash' last week. Up in Harlem." Nunez chopped his hand through the air to describe the knife's deadly descent. "Another one, he peeck up a fare, da man pool a gun on heem, make heem drive to Brooklyn. Crown Point. Den he make heem get out of de cab and he shoot heem in de foot. He drive off in de cab and leave heem wid a bullet in de foot. He limping aroun' Crown Point in de middle on de night wid no money and a bullet in de foot, how he gonna get back anywhere? He lucky he no get mugged again before he find a cop."

The light turned while he was talking, and he threw the cab back into the uptown race. As the traffic grew thicker around them, he wove in and out to get around cars that were turning, dragging with other taxis, all the while continuing his accounts of friends who had been assaulted, incidents he'd read about, stories he'd heard, rumors, apocryphal tales, the lore of the city.

When they reached the ramp going up past Grand Central Station, the driver paused. It was as if a boil had burst, and with the release of copious amounts of purulent material he felt some measure of relief. Emerging on the other side of the station, the city looked ordered and peaceful. Park Avenue lay ahead of them, divided by its regular islands of grass and trees as far as one could see. The Waldorf reigned on their right, flags flying, festive and solid. St. Bartholemew's romanesque calm sent forth a benediction as they passed it in the next block. Farther uptown the new glass buildings rose cleanly to reassure them that the drunks, criminals, decay, filth, and violence were somewhere else—behind them now—not in this part of the city at any rate. The driver drove them serenely to 57th and Fifth, past Tiffany's, to the entrance of Bergdorf's. He took the fare and accepted the tip with the surprise of an old friend who had by chance given them a lift.

After the squalor of the Bowery and the unnerving brush with violence, the crowded store was familiar and safe. Joan followed her mother through the aisles, past the counters of luxurious nonnecessities behind which pale, bored salesgirls stared blankly outward. She was swept into the elevator, which deposited them on the sixth floor. Misses' and Juniors' apparel. Unhesitatingly, Peggy struck out toward the Misses' department, making straight for a rack of dresses that she proceeded immediately to inspect. She rapidly pushed the dresses past, pulling out one every so often and making a brief comment. Joan nodded wordlessly, giving no indication of her preferences. A saleslady, fortyish, appeared at their side and asked, in a sour baritone, "Can I help you?"

"This young lady has just come back to town, and she needs mainly something to wear to work, although I imagine if you have some dressier things she might be interested, am I right, darling?"

"I have some lovely things," the saleslady said with rote enthusiasm. "You're in the wrong section, though." She moved Peggy and Joan to the left-most part of the rack. "If we don't find just what we want here, we can always try the Juniors'," she said, noting Joan's indifference.

"I'd just as soon not have her look like Alice in Wonderland," Peggy cautioned.

"Oh, we carry some very sophisticated clothing in the Juniors', you'd be surprised," the saleslady promised. Cocking an appraising eye at Joan, she added, "In her size, she'd have more selection there." She drew out one or two dresses and as quickly let them fall back, as if searching for some particular outfit she had in mind.

"Let's have a look at that one," Peggy said. The saleslady took out a green dress with gathered sleeves. "No, the blue one," she corrected her.

"Oh, that's a nice one," the saleslady said in her monotone, taking out a simple dark blue wool dress and holding it up against Joan. "You could wear that to work and go straight on to a cocktail party. What kind of work do you do?"

"She's just started at Meyer House," Peggy said.

"Oh, how nice," said the saleslady, who had never heard of Meyer House and had no idea what it was. "Well, you would look very chic in this."

"I have no interest in looking chic," Joan said.

"Why don't you just try it on," Peggy suggested.

"The dressing rooms are over there," the saleslady pointed out. Joan raised her eyes to the ceiling as she went over with the dress. "Meanwhile, I'll show Mother some other things."

But Peggy declined to look until Joan came back. "There's no point in doing anything without her. She's the one who's going to wear them," she explained.

"Oh, that looks lovely on you," the saleslady exclaimed when Joan came out.

"It doesn't feel right," Joan said.

"Why don't you have a look at yourself in the mirror before you decide," Peggy suggested. Joan looked quickly at herself in a mirror, and shook her head.

The saleslady searched through the rack to find a basic black dress in the right size, but Joan had no interest in a basic black dress. Peggy backed her up on that one. "I think they're for the birds, frankly," she said.

"Let's look at the Juniors'," the saleslady said, seeing what was up. The three women walked across the aisle to a rack opposite. Joan looked at the dresses without touching them, and finally pulled out a dress with a quilted skirt and flowered bodice, somewhat on the peasanty side for Peggy's taste. "Oh, that's darling," the saleslady said.

Peggy kept her mouth shut.

The dress swam on Joan, but she decided to take it anyway. She also settled on a simple plaid dress and one or two skirts. Peggy wanted her to get a few more things, but she saw nothing else she liked at all. She wandered over to look at sweaters while Peggy was giving the charge account information to the saleslady. "Why don't you send that first blue dress on over with the rest of the things," Peggy said.

"Certainly," the saleslady replied without looking up from her sales pad. "Sometimes we don't always realize at first what we're going to really like."

After finishing with the sixth floor, Peggy shepherded Joan through one department after another. Gradually, Joan let herself unbend a little, and she allowed her mother to indulge her freely. They went through accessories, sportswear, costume jewelry, luggage, shoes, purses, virtually the entire store. To Peggy's great relief, they found an attractive brown coat Joan liked. Peggy would have liked to have left the dreadful loden coat right there, and have Joan wear the new one home; but it had to be shortened. The only thing they couldn't settle on was an evening gown, which Joan protested she didn't need. "You can't tell, something is sure to come up, and when it does you'll need it in a hurry. These things can't be gotten overnight." She took Joan over to Bonwit's, but they had similar difficulties there. Peggy thought several gowns were lovely, but Joan dug her heels in, and refused one after another. Finally she found one that might do, a chiffon of pale blue, and tried it on. She was on the verge of taking it, but while it was being fitted she caught sight of the price tag and was horrified. While the fitter was pinning up the hemline and dictating notes to the saleslady, Joan protested that she didn't need an extravagant dress she would wear conceivably twice a year, if that. Out of courtesy to the tailor, she allowed the fitting to proceed, but when she brought the dress back after changing, she virtually flung it on the counter, saying sarcastically, "I don't want it, but that's of course irrelevant."

The startled saleslady looked to Peggy for guidance, which Peggy provided by telling her to charge it and giving her the name and address with exaggerated enunciation, spelling out *Joan* as well as *Gutheim*.

On the way out of the store, Joan gave herself a silent scolding. She had been awful to her mother. She knew how little Peggy liked to shop, and here she had taken a whole afternoon to traipse around Bergdorf's and Bonwit's. She was generosity itself. Joan stammered out her awkward thanks, which seemed to suffice. "You couldn't be more welcome, dear," Peggy told her. "It was a lovely afternoon." As was so often the case, Joan had no idea what on earth her mother really felt. How do you apologize to someone whose feelings can't be hurt?

The two women reeled from the store and found themselves in the dark swirl of rush hour on Fifth Avenue. The air was sharply laced with the late autumn cold, carrying a hint of the holidays coming up, and in the faint distance the threat of a harsh winter. People surged along the sidewalks. The lights had come on in all the store windows. A long urban midway stretched down the avenue as far as they could see. It felt as though the first snow of the year might fall any moment, covering the carnival scene with a shower of white confetti. "Isn't it exciting?" Peggy exclaimed happily. "I don't know anyplace in the world as exciting as New York. I've been lucky enough to have seen some wonderful things, but nothing is as thrilling as this city. No, after all these years, I still haven't gotten over it."

Except for the lumbering buses, the street was filled entirely with taxis. None of them was free, though. A number of people were already in the street, putting their hands out to signal cabs that didn't stop anyway. Peggy stepped boldly into the street, but after a minute she came back and said to Joan, "They're not exactly desperate for fares. Do you feel up to walking?"

"Of course I do," Joan replied, trying to echo Peggy's gaity despite her mounting fatigue.

They strolled uptown for a block or two, looking in the windows. At F.A.O. Schwarz the electric trains had stopped running for the day. One of the caravans was parked in a miniature Alpine village, the other one spending the night in a mountain pass. On the next block they paused to see what books were on display at Chaucer Head. "Have you read *To Kill a Mockingbird?*" Peggy asked. Joan shook her head. "You'll like it. It's terribly well written. I've loaned our copy. I'll be damned if I can remember who to. I'll get another one for you."

"Don't bother, really," Joan said. Peggy made a mental note to pick up another copy, just in case Joan changed her mind.

North of 59th Street there were no more stores. The Savoy Plaza faced the statue on the Grand Army Plaza, across from the Plaza Hotel itself, and then came the park. A couple of heavily harnessed horses waited impassively in front of their buggies. The evening was not one to tempt people to a ride in the park. "I always like to look at people's faces," Peggy told Joan in her schoolteacher's tone as they walked along. "You can always find something interesting in a person's face. Everyone has at least one story to tell, if you could only guess it."

Joan didn't reply. She had heard the maxim often. An elderly woman dressed in a thin cloth coat came toward them. She walked heavily, laboriously, as though something was wrong with her legs. She carried two large shopping bags: one, from Ohrbach's, held scraps of materials, while the other, from S. Klein, appeared to contain papers: letters, pamphlets, leaflets, and clippings were all visible in disarray near the top. The woman herself looked ill. She breathed stertorously, and was either groaning or mumbling to herself. Joan tried to look at her, in compliance with her mother's suggestion, but something about the woman's face—the pain, the fear, the red, watery eyes—made her feel as though she was intruding, and she looked away in embarrassment. "I have no patience with people who say they're bored," Peggy went on. "I don't have the time to be bored myself. Life's too short."

On the next block they didn't pass anyone. A wind blew over from the park, a harsh, biting wind that stung their faces. "Does Phil have something particular planned for tonight?" Peggy asked as casually as she was able. She so much wanted Joan to stay home, but tried to be nonchalant. "Wouldn't it make more sense for you all to have dinner at home?"

"I don't know. I suppose we could. It's up to Phil."

Peggy spotted a chink. "I take it you'd be just as happy to stay put."

"I don't care, really," Joan said wearily.

"I told Gerta to have enough in case you decided to stay in. I just need to be able to tell them how many to set the table for. We're having leg of lamb."

"I'll ask Phil when we get home."

"He probably won't be there. He plays squash at the Meridian on Fridays." Joan didn't reply. "You could call him there," Peggy hinted; but Joan still said nothing.

By the time they had gotten to the next corner they were struggling against the wind, and had to stop once or twice to turn their backs to it. "There's a phone booth," Peggy said. "Why don't you call? That way you won't have it on your mind." She opened her purse and found a dime. Joan placed the call. It seemed the easiest thing to do. It seemed the only thing to do. The locker room attendant said Phil was on the court and asked if he should interrupt the game. Joan said not to.

"You could have left word for him to call you at home," Peggy pointed out.

"I thought you didn't need to know."

"It couldn't matter less to me," Peggy said airily. "I just like to give Gerta some idea how many we're going to be. As far as I'm concerned, I don't need to know until we sit down to the table." They started walking again. "Also, your father has Dean Stoddard coming tonight, he's dying to have Phil there. I think he has an idea the dean could be helpful to Phil over this clerkship. I tell him again and again to quit meddling, Phil can get the clerkship just fine on his own. I love your father dearly, but he never knows when to leave well enough alone."

Joan took refuge from her mother's chatter by trying to look at the faces of the passersby. But people were walking too fast, and bending their heads against the wind. She herself had to put her head down to protect her face. Peggy looked anxiously at her. "Why don't we take a taxi, dear, if you're cold."

"It seems silly, really. It's not that much farther."

"There's no sense in being miserable. We only did this for our pleasure, and if it's not a pleasure, what's the point?" She stepped off the curb, but there were few cabs, and the empty ones were picked off by doormen blowing whistles. She would have stuck it out until through sheer force of will she got one to stop, but Joan said, "We might as well walk," and they set off again in grim silence. They turned east and were crossing Madison when Joan staggered and seemed as though she was about to faint. She tried to brush it off, but Peggy made her go stand in the barred doorway of Delmore's China, closed for the night, and would have gotten a cab for the last three blocks, only there were simply none to be had.

When they got home at last, Peggy let them in the apartment with her key and went automatically over to look at the messages on the foyer table while Joan sank gratefully onto the tan leather couch. It was such a relief to walk into the slightly overheated apartment after being out in the bitter cold. Peggy had put the couch and a companion chair there on the theory that people needed a place to sit and take off their galoshes or skates or what-have-you in the wintertime. A large mirror on the left and the curved wall leading to the corridor on the right had startled guests with their modernity when the Gutheims had moved in before the war, but to Joan the large hall, with its leathery smell, was always comforting to return to on a bad day.

"I should have had you stay put at Bonwit's, inside, until I got a taxi," Peggy said, shuffling through the pieces of paper. She looked up and caught sight of her daughter, half dazed on a chair where she had sunk. "Let me have a look at you, sweetie." Joan stayed where she was and allowed her mother to come over to her and gaze anxiously into her face. Peggy gasped in shocked sympathy. The child was pale as a sheet. The wind had lashed her face into a mask of resignation without raising any color, except for some splotches on her cheeks that looked like unhealthy discolorations. "Poor lambie!" Peggy cried. "Really, I could kill myself, letting you walk home in that cold." She was beside herself with remorse.

"I'm fine, Mother, really," Joan said, too weakly to be convincing.

"What can Noreen get you to drink?" Peggy asked, the maid having come out to bid them good evening.

"They said not to have any alcohol until they finish the tests," Joan told her. The familiar surroundings were beginning to revive her a bit. She longed to get to her room, and be alone, but for the moment she was too weak to move. "You go ahead, though," she urged.

Peggy was abashed. "They said that? None?" Joan nodded. "I would think it would help relax you."

"I wouldn't know about that, but they said none."

"Remind me to speak to Lamartine about it. They probably tell that to everyone. I doubt that there's any earthly reason why it should apply to you."

"Mother, I wish you wouldn't always act as if I were some sort of exception that none of the rules apply to," Joan said irritably.

"As far as I'm concerned, dear, there are no rules. Not in my book. And if there were, you'd be an exception to a lot of them. It runs in the family."

"I don't like it," Joan insisted. She had recovered enough to get up and start walking toward her room. "Some day I'd like to be ordinary, and be treated just like everyone else," she cried.

"I doubt you'd like it as much as you think you would," Peggy called after her.

It wasn't clear whether Joan heard her. Peggy would have followed her down the hall if Noreen hadn't just then asked, "How many will there be for dinner, Mrs. Gutheim?"

"I don't know yet," Peggy snapped, to Noreen's dismay. Peggy was rarely short with the help. She leafed through the messages: Mr. Gutheim. Donatello's Florist, to see if she wanted the flowers to be sent to Mrs. Weinstein's or the funeral home. As if Peggy would ever send flowers to a funeral home! Mrs. Altman. "Which Mrs. Altman is this?" she asked, exasperated that a maid who had been with them for five years hadn't yet registered that her mother and sister-in-law had the same name.

"Mrs. Nathan, ma'am. She said not to bother calling her back, she was just going to rest."

"Would you please be sure to put the *full name* of the person calling," Peggy lectured her. "Otherwise I have no way of knowing who it is." Noreen nodded and stood meekly awaiting further orders.

But Peggy's mind was on other matters. She was so terribly worried about Joan. How in the world could she have been such an idiot as to let her daughter get that cold and exhausted? It had all been so avoidable, and now what should have been a lovely afternoon was spoiled. Peggy had wanted so much for it to be nice for Joan, and instead see what she had gone and done. Joan had not enjoyed herself. She had lashed out at Peggy several times in uncharacteristic fashion. Well—that was nothing, really, an aberration, the result, no doubt of . . . whatever this thing was. Peggy paid no attention whatsoever to that sort of thing. What mattered was that Joan should be excited to be in New York, and forget about Bennington altogether. That wasn't happening. The afternoon had not been auspicious.

Peggy felt wretched. She herself was tired, and chilled to the bone. She wanted to go in and see Joan and assure herself the child was all right, not angry, and so forth; but she thought Joan might prefer to be alone. Peggy was a great believer in privacy. She'd have to wait. The maid was still standing by patiently. "I will have a drink myself, please, Noreen," she said more gently, adding, "We'll just have to wait until Phil comes in to know how many for dinner."

Joan just made it to her room. Her legs barely supported her, and after her cold ordeal the overheated apartment made her light-headed. Thank God her mother was so wrapped up with the damn question of how many to set the table for, and didn't see her staggering down the hall. Her hands were shaking so badly that she had to put both of them on the doorknob to wrench it open. She stumbled to the bed like that horrid drunk they had nearly run over, and collapsed. She didn't know, maybe she fainted again. It was hard to know what state she was in these days.

What if her mother followed her into the room and found her collapsed on the bed? The expression on her face! Joan started to giggle. Take this seriously, she scolded herself. This is not one of Phil's awful jokes. If he could see her now, he'd have a field day, describing to all the world how unladylike she was being. She'd never be able to show her face in public again.

The afternoon had been truly unbearable, beyond her worst fears. She had told herself a few hours couldn't be so bad, but she had forgotten what it was to spend that length of time with her mother. No one was more generous, more tireless, more eager to please, and the net result was like being buried alive. If she'd had to try on one more dress, she swore she would have fallen to pieces right there in the middle of Bonwit Teller's, for all of New York to see. And then the walk home! The cold and wind were bad enough, but it would have been at least tolerable if not for her mother's incessant attempt to persuade her how pleasant it was. She felt brainwashed. Next to that, freezing to death would have been a blessed release. If only she would be allowed to think her own thoughts and die in peace. Joan didn't know by what miracle she had avoided going stark, raving mad.

How would she ever endure it? How was she literally going to survive? She had told herself that coming down to the city wouldn't be such a bad idea. It had this much to recommend it: It wasn't Bennington. She'd had to get away from there, that much had been clear. She couldn't bear any longer having Ellen watching her morning, noon, and night, seeing everything she did, noting everything she didn't do. Joan couldn't bear to have those eyes, those disappointed eyes, watch her any longer.

And now she was out of the frying pan, heading fast toward the fire. She'd been fooling herself to think she would be left to herself in New York. It wasn't the doctors she worried about. She could handle them. Let them put her in the hospital if they wanted, let them observe her to their heart's content. She had no fear on that score. But her mother was a much more formidable clinician. Joan had counted on her being so busy, what with her charities and committees and board work and God only knew what else she ran around town in a frenzy doing, that she wouldn't have the time or the inclination to monitor her daughter. Joan now saw she had miscalculated badly. Despite the constant barrage of words, Peggy took in everything: where she went, who she saw, what she did. She could come and go as she pleased, it went without saying; but those comings and goings would be noted. What she put in her mouth, and what she didn't put in her mouth, all would be duly registered. Few questions would be asked. Peggy Gutheim had many other ways of gathering information. She had eyes, she always used to say, in the back of her head.

Meyer House! Her one place of refuge. It had been a thrill, those few hours there, to be away from the family, out of the searchlight, on her own. No one knew her there. No one had any expectations. She could disappear into Meyer House every morning, and become the person she wanted to be: her true self, without hypocrisy or sham. No one who knew her before would recognize her.

As she lay there, thinking of her new life at Meyer House, a sense of anticipation stole over her. Who knew what lay ahead for her? New possibilities, new experiences, new people. Those kids! She was ready to devote herself to those kids. They needed so much, there was no limit to what she could give to them. She was eager to begin.

What was that boy's name, Martin Perry had called to? She hadn't gotten much of a look, because Peggy was watching her like a hawk, but it was enough to excite her curiosity.

Kevin, that was his name. "So long, Kevin," Martin had called out.

"Handsome-looking boy," Peggy had said.

One more reason to look forward to Monday.

Someone was knocking on her door. Her mother, of course, to ask if she wanted something; or if she was feeling all right; or if anyone could do anything for her. Also—not that it mattered in the slightest!—was she staying home for dinner? How many should they set the table for? Had she called Phil since coming home? Peggy would be only too happy to dial the number for her, save her the trouble.

But it wasn't her mother, it was Phil. Joan's relief was enormous.

He was dressed spiffily in brown slacks and a pale yellow shirt, with his beige sport coat draped over his shoulder. He had dark wavy hair and mocking brown eyes, and Joan had a bigger crush on him than she ever had on any of the boys she went out with, Johnny Krieger included.

"Why aren't you ready?" he demanded with mock severity.

"You never said what time! Also, Mother is putting heavy pressure on us to stay home for dinner."

"I know all about that. She started telling me before I was in the door. You're exhausted. Nothing could be easier. We're having leg of lamb."

"What did you tell her?"

"I told her it was no concern of mine if you were exhausted. They're paying all these world-renowned doctors enormous fees to look after your health. I see no reason whatsoever why I should do it for free. Get yourself dressed. You look like a mess."

"Don't you want to stay home? Dean Something-or-other is coming for dinner, and if you kiss his ass he'll nominate you to the Supreme Court, or something."

"I couldn't think of putting my career before your happiness," Phil replied.

Joan smiled. "Where are we going?"

"Laurent," he told her.

Joan wasn't used to elegant French restaurants. "Jesus, what do I wear for Laurent?"

"If you just bought out Bergdorf's and Bonwit's combined, I should think you'd have something."

"It's all being sent, dummy. I have nothing but my disreputable Bennington clothes. Can I come in them?"

"I could care less, as long as you've got the manure scraped off."

"What's Betsy wearing?" Joan asked.

"I haven't the vaguest," Phil told her. "You have fifteen minutes." He opened the door and stood in the threshold.

"Phil! I have to take a bath!"

"Fifteen minutes. Be ready, or I'm leaving without you." He slammed the door behind him.

"Phil!"

Three

Through the door of City Hall emerged Alan Gutheim: alert, expectant, exuberant. A trim, bantam man, he wore no overcoat, summer or winter, counting on his energy and enthusiasm to ward off the chill of a November day. His face was shrewd, but saved from sharpness by an open, eager expression and a perpetual curiosity. Alan found the world on the whole hospitable, and always fascinating. Coming out onto the steps, he paused and prepared himself, like a swimmer about to plunge into a turbulent and exciting sea.

The city lay spread before him. Although the sky had clouded over while he had been in his meeting, he decided he would walk anyway. Alan never rode when he could walk. Walking through New York was his recreation, his delight, his gazette. "I learn more in a brisk walk of a mile or two through any part of this *burg* than I do from a week's worth of the *Times,*" he always said, although not within earshot of his good friends the Sulzbergers, who published the paper. "If you keep your eyes and ears open, there's no telling what you can find out." Alan had sharp eyes, and there was nothing much wrong with his hearing either. If pressed, he would admit to being well informed, up-to-date.

He rubbed his hands against the cold and prepared himself for the next item on his agenda. He felt ready to take on all comers. He loved this kind of day, rushing from one thing to another, committees, boards, conferences, advisory sessions. He had just come out of a meeting of the mayor's Select Commission on the Problems of Youth in New York City, on which he was honored to serve. Now he had just enough time, he noted with satisfaction, to walk to Altman & Sons, where he was to meet with his brother-in-law Gerald Altman. Then he would have to hurry like mad up to a special meeting of the board of Mt. Sinai Hospital that was sure to take the rest of the afternoon. He'd be lucky if he got back to his office at all. Guests for dinner, a concert—he'd be up late with work, make no mistake. A big day. He loved it.

He wondered what Gerald wanted. Alan was counsel to Altman's, and there might be some business matter. Or else one of Gerald's children was in some sort of scrape or other, and Alan would have to fix it. An open agenda with his brother-in-law always made him a little uneasy. Gerald had a way of springing little assignments on him that seemed innocuous enough on first blush, but later proved vexatious.

If he had a chance, he would put in a word against Gerald's latest madness, this Morty Pines affair. It seemed that an old and moribund real estate firm in the city, Abbott & Strawbridge, was about to die a natural death when out of the clear blue a brash young adventurer named Mortimer Pines came along and offered to buy it out. Now, Morty Pines might have fancied himself the next John Jacob Astor, but no one else took him seriously, and his bid was predictably given the back of Abbott & Strawbridge's feeble hand. Whereupon this little upstart decided to mount a hostile takeover, of all things; not only that, but he had come to Gerald for financing. To Alan's utter dismay, Gerald was actually considering the request. Jacob Altman & Sons, in the middle of a proxy fight, of all things! Old Will Strawbridge might be practically senile, but not so senile as to let his family business pass without a struggle into alien hands, and Jewish ones at that. He was digging in for a long, hard fight. After years of inertia, Abbott & Strawbridge was building a huge office complex on Third Avenue. Gotham Tower, they were calling it. No one had the foggiest idea how it was being financed. No reputable bank would touch it. The construction company they'd gotten had appeared from nowhere, overnight. Bertino Bros., it was called, hardly a name to inspire any great confidence. You'd have to be out of your mind to want to get mixed up in this, but Morty Pines was chomping at the bit. What was more, Gerald seemed to have taken complete leave of his senses, and was prepared to bankroll Pines to the hilt. No, Alan was going to have his hands full with this particular piece of craziness.

Gerald wasn't his only headache, either. Mt. Sinai was about to start a new medical school, and Alan could see the handwriting on that wall. Although no one had said anything yet, he was sure they would ask him to chair the fund drive. It couldn't be coming at a worse time: he was drowned in work, and he had a few other commitments, if he did say so himself. He had just finished raising the money for a new pavilion, and had cashed in a number of his chips for that. It was someone else's turn this time. "No one else can do it, Alan," he could already hear them plead. And how could he refuse? How do you say no to the training of physicians, one of whom might, who knows, save his life, or the life of a loved one? Or who might, God willing, find the cure for cancer —that scourge whose latest victim, Percy Weinstein, had died during the night, in the very pavilion Alan had gotten built, God rest his soul.

He wondered if he should call on Harriet Weinstein on his way home. Maybe a phone call would do. He was so pressed for time. Also, he hated to go into those death-scented rooms. He remembered the numb, uncomprehending look on his mother's face, accepting the condolences for his father. Did she somehow know she would be following him so soon? Her death had been far sadder for him, but the ceremonies had been like a dream, going through them a second time in a year. Thrift, thrift, Horatio. The funeral baked meats furnished cold. The pain had come later.

Enough of death! When he got home, Joan would be there! His beloved Joan. He thought of Jephthah returning from the wars, greeted by his daughter who ran out to welcome him in joy. Alan was not a great reader of the Bible, except for the Psalms, which he found beautiful and consoling, and some passages in Ecclesiastes, majestic if a bit pessimistic. "There is a time for sowing, and a time for reaping," and so on. Marvelous stuff. His religious education hadn't been neglected: when he was a child a young rabbinical student had come every Wednesday evening to his home to read Bible stories and recite the sad history of the Israelites; and, of course, he had been coached within an inch of his life to chant for his Bar Mitzvah. He probably could reel them off today, if called upon: "*Vayomer Kach-na et bincha et yechidchaasher ahavta et Yitzchak . . .*" He might need an occasional prompt, but it was all still there. He had wanted his children to have lessons, too, but Peggy had nipped that one in the bud. The story of Jephthah was therefore not thrice familiar to Alan. Nonetheless—it was great to have Joan home again. Her health wasn't all it could be, but the doctors would have that cleared up in no time at all. Thank God for them.

He decided he'd take the chairmanship of the fund drive.

There was more to look forward to: they had taken tickets for the Legal Aid Society benefit concert, to be given by none other than the great Rubinstein, and had invited the dean of Columbia Law School and Mrs. Stoddard, who were coming to dinner beforehand. Peggy had, of course, accused him of all sorts of ulterior motives, but she couldn't have been more wrong. He and the dean had become great pals through the Bar Association, and Pam Stoddard was a great music lover. It had been the farthest thing from his mind that the dean might be helpful to Phil. Phil was being seriously considered for a clerkship with Justice Klingor of the U.S. Supreme Court, and if it should happen to come up in the conversation, it would be the most natural thing on earth for the dean to take an interest in it, perhaps even offer to put in a word on Phil's behalf; but it hadn't been Alan's intention in inviting him, so help him God.

At any rate, nothing could be more heavenly than to end the day hearing the music of his beloved Chopin, rendered by its foremost interpreter alive. If Rubinstein would play just one nocturne that evening, Alan was certain he could die contented. "If it were now to die, 'twere now to be most happy," as Romeo put it.

Or was it Juliet?

A busy day, one filled with the opportunity to serve his fellow man; the advancement of science; the welfare of future generations; and his beloved city. New York! The greatest city, he could say without the slightest fear of contradiction, in the entire world.

As he stood there on the steps of City Hall, a feeling of intense pleasure suffused him. He thought back to the meeting he had just come from. First of all, they had received a report written by none other than Philip Gutheim, the newest member of the commission staff—Alan had had nothing to do with that, no matter what Peggy said, Phil had gotten the job completely on his own hook—and it was a hell of a report. Even Dave Hurwitz, the very capable executive director of the commission, had said it was a damn fine job.

But then, toward the end of the meeting, who should drop in completely unannounced but the mayor himself. He'd stayed only a minute or two, just to say a few words of encouragement, boost the commission's morale. He'd given a little pep talk, and finished by saying,

"There's nothing more important to this city than our kids. They're our future. You gentlemen are doing a splendid job. Keep it up." They'd all applauded, and as he was leaving he added, sotto voce, which could be heard clearly throughout the room:

"Keep 'em honest, Alan."

You could have heard a pin drop. The others were dumbfounded, none more than poor Dick Utley, the chairman, who was practically drooling for the word of recognition that never came his way. Alan had, of course, dealt with mayors before this and he had more than a nodding acquaintance with political figures who made Michael Flaherty look like a pygmy in comparison. No, he took it in stride. Still—the man was the mayor of the city of New York. He might not be the most progressive man ever to hold the office, nor the most scrupulously honest, for that matter, but he was the people's choice. And he did have that broad Irish grin. It hadn't hurt the morale of the commission one bit to have him take a personal interest in its work. Or that he was on a first-name basis with one of its members.

Peggy would be pleased.

Basking in the memory, Alan looked out over lower Manhattan. To his left the Brooklyn Bridge soared out over the East River. With its filigree of cables and wires hung between the brick stanchions, it had always struck him as an emblem of New York, celebrating its enterprise, its energy, its complexity. All those poor souls who had flung themselves from it over the years, hurling themselves into the swirling river below, their hearts, it was said, broken by the immense city itself. New York was incomprehensible to the outsider. You couldn't hope to grasp it until you had lived here for years and years. Better by far to have been born here. Alan's proudest boast was that he was a New Yorker, born and bred.

Coming down the steps, he waved at a policeman who was leaning up against an illegally parked limousine, chatting through the open window with the chauffeur. The policeman straightened up. "Top o' the mornin' to you, Officer," Alan called cheerily, intending the Irish greeting to convey also his magnanimity toward a mild winking at the law.

"The same to you, sir," the policeman replied, touching his hat in salute. Alan was pleased, although in principle he thought an officer of the law, even a cop on the beat, shouldn't have to show deference to anyone, prominent citizen or otherwise. Warmed in any case by the fraternal exchange, he was about to cross the street when a voice behind him called out, "A chilly day to be going about without an overcoat, isn't it, Alan?"

He turned around and saw a man in clerical dress making his slow way down the steps with the aid of a cane. "Never use such a thing, summer or winter, Monsignor," Alan replied, delighted to have the policeman see him hailed by a man of the cloth. Alan didn't number all that many clerics among his friends, and would never have met Monsignor Nugent except for the commission. As he got to know the priest, Alan had found him to be surprisingly broad-minded, and possessing a great sense of humor in the bargain.

"Can we share a subway uptown?" he asked. "I'm just on my way back to the Chancery." The Archdiocese of New York was run out of a handsome building in back of St. Patrick's Cathedral, on Madison Avenue at 51st, not far from Alan's office.

"I'd like nothing better," Alan answered with unfeigned regret. "Unfortunately I have a luncheon meeting down here. At Altman's."

"Oh, well, you'll be well fed, from all accounts. I'm trying to get the Cardinal's permission to float a school bond issue, and I mentioned your brother-in-law, thinking, I must admit, more of the superb food than the interest rates. Of course, His Eminence wants it financed by a good Catholic bank, not that I'm aware any such entity exists," he added with a roguish smile.

"There are none that I know of that are predominantly Catholic," Alan said, furrowing his brow and rapidly reviewing the partnership lists of the major non-Jewish investment banks. "Although I think you'll find some of your more distinguished communicants carry quite a bit of clout over at First Continental, and also at Chemical Fiduciary. And of course there's Jim O'Malley, who's president of the Broad Street Bank. He'd be able to offer you favorable terms, I daresay."

The priest laughed. "Alan, you never fail to amaze me. Is there anyone doing business down here about whom you don't know everything there is to know?"

"I try to keep track of these things," Alan replied modestly.

"By the way, Alan," the Monsignor said, taking Alan's arm with his free hand as they walked slowly toward the BMT station; even with the cane, the poor man limped badly. Alan admired him for going about on the subway. Surely the chancellor of the archdiocesan schools rated a car and chauffeur if he wanted them. "Did you hear the one about the woman who brought her baby to be baptized? Have you heard that one, by any chance?"

"No, I haven't," Alan said, chuckling in anticipation.

"Well . . ." Monsignor Nugent began expansively. "It seems this woman brought her baby in to St. Timothy's to be baptized, you understand. She asks to see Father McDonough, and when he comes out, she says to him, 'Father,' she says, 'I'm wonderin' if you'd be so kind as to baptize the baby.'" The priest had a wonderful way with the dialect. "Now, Father McDonough doesn't recognize the woman as one of his regular parishioners, but he figures, what the hell, a soul is a soul. You understand these things, Alan, don't you? So he says to her, he says, 'Sure'n I'd be only too delighted to perform the blessed sacrament.' He looks at the baby, who's sleeping peacefully in the mother's arms, and of course the first thing he notices is this great shock of flaming red hair. 'Sure'n that's a grand head of hair the lad has on him,' he says. 'Does his father also have red hair?' The woman being a brunette, you understand; a pretty slip of a girl, but of course the priest doesn't notice that. We celibates! You know how it is, don't you, Alan? But he can see plainly she has hair as black as any raven, while the baby's is a fiery red. 'Does his father also have red hair?' asks Father McDonough. 'Oh, Father!' comes the reply, 'I wouldn't know. He didn't take off his hat!'"

And at the foot of City Hall, in full view of a doubtless devout policeman and several astonished passersby, the Right Reverend Monsignor Joseph Nugent flung his head back and exploded in a decidedly nonecclesiastical laugh. Alan joined in, amazed and delighted.

The next moment, as if to atone for his ribaldry, Monsignor Nugent stopped walking and looked Alan directly in the face. "To be serious for a moment, though, Alan, that was a fine report your son wrote. The one on the recreational facilities. A very fine job. Clear, thorough, realistic without being cynical, and containing some valuable suggestions. You must be very proud of him. Very proud indeed."

Alan glowed. "The boy's got a head on his shoulders," he conceded.

As he turned to descend into the subway, Monsignor Nugent asked, "Family well, I trust?"

"Fine, just fine," Alan said. He hesitated, then added, "Although my daughter is having a spell of poor health just now, actually."

The priest's kindly face fell. "Nothing serious, Alan, I hope," he said, subdued.

"They don't have a diagnosis as yet, but I'm sure it's nothing serious. We have the best doctors at Mt. Sinai on the case, plus Peggy's got some hotshot in from Presbyterian in the unlikely event they miss anything. They'll have it cleared up in no time at all, I haven't the slightest doubt. In the meantime, though, it's given her mother and me some worry, as you can imagine."

"Of course I can, Alan. Of course I can," Monsignor Nugent said gravely. "Would you mind if I offered a prayer for the girl?"

Alan flushed. He was terribly moved. He wasn't altogether sure whether such an action, on behalf of a non-Christian, might not constitute sacrilege; but certainly the priest was the better judge of that. "It would be wonderful, Monsignor. I'd be terribly grateful." He wondered if he ought to offer some kind of donation.

"I'll say it at Vespers. I'll ask for a speedy recovery. Till the next time, then, Alan. Take care."

"The same to you, Monsignor. Thanks." Alan watched nervously as the priest hobbled down the steep steps into the subway. A wonderful man, that; truly holy, underneath the worldly facade. And to be able to do something for one's fellow man as tangible, as comforting as offering a prayer! Whether or not one believed in any of it, it was good to have a priest on one's side.

Feeling wonderfully ecumenical, Alan crossed the street and entered the park. His shortest route would take him down Broadway, but that was a noisy, unpeopled thoroughfare over which furious buses, taxis, and enormous trucks raced along in grim earnestness. On Nassau, he would be able to see what was in the shops, to look down the little side streets, and generally to find out what was going on. He liked to know which stores were doing well, which were going out of business, what new ones were opening up.

But first he would walk through the park. Alan walked through parks on principal, on the grounds that they had been put there at some expense and trouble to provide respite and refreshment, a bit of sylvan relief from the bricks and concrete. City Hall Park, unfortunately, was a shabby affair, open on all sides to noise and traffic, lacking either charm or repose. When there was a ceremony, it barely served as a village green; but today it was almost deserted, and quite desolate. Alan thought they should put a statue in it, at the very least. Peter Stuyvesant, or Peter Minuit. Or a great writer: Poe, for example, whose birthplace was not far from the spot; although he was perhaps too morbid. O. Henry might be better, the great chronicler of the city. Whitman had greater stature, but he was more national than civic, and also he was from Brooklyn. Still, those immortal lines:

> *"When lilacs last in the dooryard bloom'd,*
> *And the great star early droop'd in the western sky in the night,*
> *I mourn'd, and yet shall mourn . . ."*

So moving. He must look it up again that evening.

Taking the diagonal path, Alan passed a man sprawled on a bench, halfway to oblivion but still clutching a paper bag that certainly contained a bottle of some rotgut. The stubble of a beard shadowed the man's face, his clothes were redolent of many garbage heaps. Such sordidness shouldn't be allowed in City Hall Park, Alan thought. Foreign visitors, dignitaries—schoolchildren, for God's sake, regularly visited City Hall. They shouldn't be exposed to that sort of sight. The generosity of a great city could be abused as readily as that of a great philanthropist, which in some respects New York resembled. Anywhere else, such a person would be locked up or run out of town. Only New York felt this responsibility, this obligation to embrace every derelict, feed every vagrant, shelter everyone who was down-and-out. "Give me your tired, your poor, your huddled masses yearning to breathe free . . ." Alan couldn't remember exactly how it went after that. He would look it up along with the Whitman. Emma Lazarus. So moving.

Quickening his pace, Alan took the next path out of the park, crossed Park Row, and took Beekman over to Nassau. Running between the massive municipal buildings to the north and the great houses of finance at the lower end of the island, Nassau Street ignored both. It was Main Street, U.S.A., plunked down in lower Manhattan. Drugstores, stationary stores, candy shops, florists, coffeeshops, thrift shops, delicatessens, clothing emporia, appliance outlets, jewelers, book dealers, shoe repair shops—the stores that got people through life, day by day, lined the street. The pace was less frantic. Pedestrians looked you in the eye, smiled as they passed. Shopkeepers recognized you when you came in. A friendly street.

At Wormrath's he stopped to see what books were on display. *To Kill a Mockingbird.* Stirring, he'd heard. Anger toward Southern bigots welled up in him. New York had its problems, he'd be the first to admit, but the preponderance of its citizens—its leaders, its clergy, its ordinary people, the guy on the street—all were on the side of tolerance and brotherhood. Yes, they could do better, and he himself was doing his best to move them even further along. He'd tried his damnedest, for example, to get more Negroes on the boards he sat on. Mt. Sinai, for example, ought to have an eminent resident of Harlem, which was literally on the hospital's doorstep. He wondered if they could get Ralph Bunche. Alan would have been proud to sit on a Board with Ralph Bunche. Also the Bar Association: surely there must be a distinguished Negro attorney somewhere in this town. Another Thurgood Marshall, if one existed. He saw himself nominating Thurgood Marshall to the Bar Association board. There'd be some stiff opposition, make no mistake. He was ready for that: "While any man is a slave, I cannot be free . . ." Alan would have loved to see someone try to oppose the immortal words of Abraham Lincoln. *(When lilacs last in the dooryard bloom'd . . .)*

Next he stopped at Klein's Haberdashery. FAMOUS BRAND NAMES— PRICES SLASHED the sign declared. Arrow shirts, Three G's, Hathaway, Hart Schaffner & Marx. Alan was disturbed. When premium items were discounted, it meant that inventories were too high. People weren't buying. Another sign, in case one was needed, that the economy was in trouble. He worried about the little guy: the man with mortgage payments to meet, the bright kid from the slums who wants to go to college and pull himself up by his bootstraps, the factory worker who gets laid off and has a bunch of hungry mouths to feed at home. The country was sound, he didn't question that. But the ingredients for disaster were always lurking just underneath the surface: irresponsibility; mismanagement; stupidity; yes, laziness; and above all, greed. Greed had caused the last depression and would cause the next. They said it can't happen again, but of course it can always happen again, most likely when least expected. Life is like that: catastrophe could strike any time.

He moved on. They'd opened a new restaurant. The Regency. A bit hoity-toity for essentially a luncheonette. Its predecessor had been strictly a quick-and-dirty, just looking in the window could give you ptomaine. Alan peered at the menu, pricing the hot turkey sandwich, the tuna surprise, the chef's salad. Pretty steep. Rents must be going up. He made a note to give the Regency a wide berth.

"Feel like a nice blueberry knish?" a high-pitched voice behind him asked. "With sour cream? And a cup coffee?" Turning around, he found Irv Friedman with his mouth half open, waiting for him to collapse with laughter. Why a man who had come from nowhere and made a fortune in the hotel business should want to remind everyone he started out as a bellhop in the Catskills always mystified Alan. Still, Irv had never put on airs, and he gave very generously. "Had lunch?"

"I couldn't be sorrier, Irv," Alan said, truly regretting passing up Irv, if not the Regency. "I'm on my way to Gerry's."

"Oh, well—knishes you won't get, but you'll eat well. The day they serve knishes at Altman's . . . !" He suddenly extinguished his idiot grin and lowered his voice: "Sad news about Percy."

"Yes, it is. Although, you know, he'd been suffering terribly, in a way it was a blessing."

"I suppose. Still, it's tough to see him go. A hell of a nice guy, Percy. Tell Gerry I'm sorry to hear it, will you?"

"I will, Irv. Thanks." The two men stood with their heads bowed for a moment. While they were showing respect to the memory of Percy Weinstein, Alan realized that Irv was just the person to ask about Abbott & Strawbridge's new building. After a decent interval he broke the silence: "Irv, you keep track of these things, let me ask you: You know this new building that's going up on Third Avenue and 48th? Going to be an office building, I don't know how many hundred thousand square feet? You know the one?"

"Gotham Tower?" Irv spoke the name derisively. "Now I can pretty well guess why you're interested in that building. I'll tell you this, Alan—that property was offered to me. Everyone knows I've wanted to put up a hotel near Grand Central, and I won't deny I was tempted. It would've been a good location. You know something? I took one look at that deal, and I wouldn't touch it with a ten-foot pole. You know what I mean?"

"I know what you mean, Irv. That's why I asked."

"You know something about real estate in this town, Alan, to put it mildly. Some of those buildings they pulled down for this still have thirty, forty good years in them, and they went for a song. You figure that. Third Avenue real estate, now that the El is down should be worth a fortune, it went for peanuts, from what I hear. And then there's that bar."

"O'Donnell's?"

"That's the one. I'm sure you know it well, Alan, one of your regular hangouts, I've no doubt. Well, O'Donnell's—I looked into this very carefully—O'Donnell's turns out to be two of the toughest Irish broads you ever want to meet. Sisters, they are, both in their seventies, sharp as two tacks, not to mention hard as nails. They were asking a cool fortune for that bar. It does a terrific business, not all of it pertaining to the sale of alcoholic beverages, if you follow me. But they let it go for peanuts. I doubt that they did it out of any great love for Will Strawbridge."

"I've wondered about that," Alan said. "I didn't think Abbott & Strawbridge had that kind of dough."

"Alan, dough is the least of what they don't have."

"What about this Bertino outfit they've brought in? Do they know what they're doing? I've never heard of them before."

"There's a reason for that, Alan. I think if you looked into it, you'd be hard pressed to find out any project they've done in this city. Ask your friend Hurwitz, at your commission. If he can find one building they've put up, I'll eat my hat. Don't quote me. And all of a sudden they're building a skyscraper on a hundred and fifty feet of Third Avenue. You figure it out."

Alan looked worried. "You think there's shady money involved here?"

"Ah, Alan!" Irv cried gleefully. "You always go to the heart of the matter! That's what I love about you. One of the many things."

"I don't think this is something Altman's ought to be getting involved with," Alan said, as if just coming to that conclusion. "I really think Gerry ought to get out while the getting's good."

"It might not be a bad idea," Irv advised. "Especially if he has any interest in enjoying his old age."

Alan was shocked. "You think it's that bad?" he asked.

"There's a lot of money in New York these days that no one's exactly sure where it came from, Alan. If Gerry takes over Abbott & Strawbridge, he might find himself doing business, if that's the word, with some people he's not used to associating with. They don't all belong to the Bankers' Club, either. To say nothing of putting his money on Morty Pines, who'd be hard-pressed to put up an outhouse in a vacant lot. I don't know what Gerry can be thinking!"

"I better warn him off," Alan said, shaking his head. He looked at his watch, and added, "I'm really grateful to you, Irv. Sorry I can't join you for lunch. Let's get together soon."

"Love to Peggy," Irv called with a wave, and turned back to look hungrily in the window of the Regency.

Alan continued down Nassau Street, but the shop windows no longer captured his attention. He was worried and upset. He knew perfectly well that the city had its seamy corners, its prostitution, numbers running, heroin traffic, that organized crime had penetrated certain parts of the construction industry. Everyone knew the mob controlled the waterfront. But basically New York was a sound city, its leaders— not the politicians, but the real leaders—were honest and civic-minded. What Irv had told him amounted to a diagnosis of cancer: early, to be sure, but in danger of spreading if something wasn't done quickly.

As a first step, Gerald would have to be warned off.

He had reached the corner of Maiden Lane. He stopped and looked down the improbable winding course of the Lane, so incongruent with the straight lines and right angles of the city, as though an ambling cow had laid out this one particular street. On the other side there were no more stores, only grimly serious buildings. People walked faster, more determinedly, their faces set. He was nearing the Stock Exchange.

Striding toward him was Roger Montgomery. He didn't see Alan, and Montgomery not being one of his favorite characters, Alan was tempted to let him pass by. Still, he was influential at the Bar Association, and it went against Alan's grain to let an acquaintance cross his path without a greeting. Also, he could broach his idea of getting a Negro on the Bar Association board, where Montgomery carried no end of clout. He called out.

" 'Lo, Alan," Montgomery responded dully. "What brings you down here?" He could never quite keep a flicker of disdain from his patrician face, or maybe he never tried. He was a Montgomery, after all, his mother had been a Howard, and his wife was an Islington. He still didn't give a plugged nickel to anything, so far as Alan could tell.

"I'm just coming from City Hall," Alan answered.

"Oh, yes, the commission," Montgomery said, not bothering to hide his contempt. "How's it going? Have you solved the problems of our city's youth yet? It would appear you still have a way to go." There had been a story in the paper that morning of several particularly gruesome caped Puerto Rican thugs who had taken to terrorizing the elderly.

"It takes time, Roger," Alan said apologetically. "You know that no commission is going to solve anything overnight. But we do our part."

"Yes, yes," Montgomery said, unconvinced.

Alan saw that he was about to move on, and thought he'd better seize the moment. "On a completely other subject, while I have you, Roger, I've been thinking that it's high time we did something about Negroes in the Bar Association. I think we ought to have one on the executive committee."

Montgomery's brow creased with annoyance. "Whom do you have in mind?"

"No one in particular," Alan replied, embarrassed not to have even one name to offer. "It's mainly the principle. I imagine there must be several distinguished attorneys of color in this Bar."

"I don't know." Montgomery bent his head and shook it like a horse trying to rid itself of a pesky fly. "I don't think you do these people any real service by lowering the standards, just for appearance's sake. It doesn't do them any good in the long run, and it sure as hell doesn't do the Bar Association any good."

Alan was indignant. "Who said anything about lowering the standards?" he exclaimed. "Look at Jackie Robinson. They didn't lower the standards for him. Look at Marian Anderson. Ralph Bunche. Thurgood Marshall."

"Thurgood Marshall is a moron," Montgomery pronounced. Alan was outraged. It might be that Marshall wasn't the most brilliant lawyer in the city, but he had cleared the path, for God's sake. He had argued the school desegregation decision, whoever wrote the brief. Jack Greenberg, no doubt. Still, Marshall had done a great deal more for his fellow man than Roger Montgomery could ever hope to do, if he had any inclination in that direction, which he didn't. "Find me a Jackie Robinson and I'll second the nomination," he went on smugly. "Until then I think we're on sounder ground to continue our policy of strict merit. Look, Alan"—he saw that Alan was girding himself to debate the point —"I'd love nothing better than to chat with you some more, but I really must fly." He tipped his hat in cold formality and left Alan, fuming, on the sidewalk.

Well, he had been a fool, Alan told himself despite his anger. Roger Montgomery was the last person he should have raised the subject with. Like all bigots he had no end of plausible arguments to support his prejudices. It hadn't been smart. Not only had he done nothing for the plight of the Negro, but he hadn't done Alan Gutheim any big favor either. If he wanted to be president of the Bar Association, he couldn't go around antagonizing influential members of the board.

No one could fairly call Alan Gutheim an ambitious man. He was sensible of all that life had bestowed on him—a lovely wife, three wonderful children, good health, a comfortable way of life that stopped short of indulgence—he had everything a man could reasonably want. He feared God enough to be grateful for what he had, and not to covet

what he didn't. If he had any wishes whatsoever, they had solely to do
with the welfare of others. If, say, the presidency of the Bar Association
of the City of New York allowed him to serve his community and the
people in it, then that was something he wanted, yes; but not for himself. If it was bestowed on him, so be it. If not, well his cup ranneth over
as it was.

Or perhaps it would fall to Phil to finish what he began; to be
Joshua to his Moses. If he wasn't to be the first Jewish president, let the
honor fall to his son. The clerkship would be the first step on a glorious
career. The one danger was that he might somehow be trapped in Washington, and never get back. It was inconceivable that Phil would ever
choose to live elsewhere than New York City; but circumstances might
overtake him. Alan worried about that.

One block beyond the Federal Building, on William Street, stood
Jacob Altman & Sons. One of the few firms still to have its own separate
building, Altman's occupied the handsome quarters bought just after
World War I by Peggy's father, Nathan Altman. Alan entered the imposing door and passed between the oil portraits of his late father-in-law
and of the old man, Jacob Altman himself. The artist had painted Jacob
Altman's eyes in such a way that they seemed to follow you as you
passed, adding to the uneasiness Alan always felt on coming into his
brother-in-law's domain. His firm had been counsel to Altman's since
long before he and Peggy were married, and he had never heard even
the whisper of a suggestion that he had made an opportune marriage.
Nonetheless, he always felt like a lackey when he came to see Gerald, a
feeling Gerald did nothing to discourage if he knew about it, which he
most likely did.

Scorning to take the elevator, Alan bounded up the staircase to the
second floor. The partners' dining room was a clubby, paneled room
with leather wing chairs drawn up to large square tables, big enough for
papers to be spread out alongside the plates without danger of gravy
splattering a confidential memorandum. On special occasions the tables
were pulled together into a banquet setting for a visiting VIP, but today
they were separate.

The maître d' hurried over to tell Alan that Gerald would be late,
and took him to a table where a waiter brought him a Manhattan without his having to ask for one. Several partners and guests said hello to
him as he walked across the room, and Gerald bustled in a minute or
two later. "Sorry to keep you waiting, Alan," he said. "I was on the

phone with Harriet." Gerald always had an unimpeachable reason for keeping Alan waiting; but he always kept him waiting.

"How is she?"

"As good as could be expected, all things considered. They drag these things on far too long, if you ask me. When my time comes, I want to be put out of my misery. I count on you to see that it's done, if I'm non compos, which would seem likely at this point." The waiter brought him a large glass of orange juice.

"We don't have euthanasia at this point," Alan advised Gerald.

"We damn well should."

"I don't know. Tricky business. The entering wedge. A convenient way to dispatch disagreeable relatives who are spending capital. Aunt Tilly complains about her rheumatism, next thing you know someone's pulled the plug. It'd be very hard to control . . ."

"Oh . . . well . . ." Gerald said morosely. "How's Peggy anyway? Family?"

"Peggy's fine. Joan could be better. She's down from college, so we can look into these . . . episodes . . ."

"Oh, yes, I heard something about that," Gerald commented vaguely. "She all right now?"

"It's hard to say. They're looking her over pretty thoroughly. They've brought in this fellow Lamartine from P and S. He's evidently the hottest rock going for this sort of thing. Meanwhile, Peggy's arranging for her to do something down at Meyer House, for Martin Perry. I gather it's terribly important to give her the feeling she is still useful. Keep her cheered up."

"Of course," Gerald said. He hadn't any idea what Alan was talking about. Having shown what he considered a proper concern for a distasteful matter, he moved quickly on. "And Phil? Job going well at the commission?" Phil was his special favorite, having had both the sense and the brains to follow Gerald's path to Yale. Randy was struggling to stay in Brown, while Dickie's college career had consisted of enrolling in and subsequently dropping several courses at CCNY and The New School for Social Research.

"Everyone's raving about him. He just wrote a report that's, if you ask me, a hell of a job. Hell of a job. In fact"—he was struck with a thought—"I wonder if Klingor oughtn't to see it."

Gerald held up his hand while he took a long drink of his juice. Putting the glass down, he pronounced: "I think not. My sense is now is the time to soft-pedal this thing. Too much pushing at this point might well put the kibosh on the whole thing."

Alan was deflated. "Whatever you think," he said, but he wasn't happy about it. The situation was ticklish. Gerald knew Klingor from the International Committee for Jewish Relief, and had used his relationship with the Justice on Phil's behalf. Without that, it was doubtful that Phil would even have a foot in the door. Klingor had made it his invariable practice to get his clerks from Harvard Law School, and although he had on occasion interviewed some whiz kid from Yale, he had never reached down all the way to Columbia. Over Peggy's objections, Gerald had been asked to recommend his nephew, and Phil had been called to Washington for an interview. Now Gerald wanted to run the show, much to the mounting frustration of Alan, who hated to leave any stone unturned. "If you change your mind, I can get a copy sent to him in no time at all."

Gerald gazed off at nothing, which was his way of ignoring any unwanted suggestion. Alan was angry, but said nothing. He might just have to send the report on and not say anything to Gerald. Why should Gerald call all the shots where his own son's future was concerned? The day was beginning to turn sour. It wasn't like him to misjudge two situations in a row: first Roger Montgomery, now his brother-in-law. Alan prided himself on few things, but he did think of himself as a persuasive man. Two setbacks in a row! He'd have to regroup.

He asked after Eleanor. "She's fine," Gerald allowed. "She'd be a damn sight better, though, and so would I, if Barbara would see her way clear to dumping this latest of hers." Since her divorce, Barbara had had a succession of affairs with men of unsavory character and no visible means of support. "We're not supposed to know he exists, of course. Right now I'm just waiting for more information before having it out with her."

Alan looked pained. "She's your daughter, Gerry. Personally, I don't like the idea of using private detectives. Nasty business."

"Nasty!" Gerald exploded. "Who do you think this piece of garbage is? Sir Galahad?"

Alan shook his head in sympathy. "There's not much you can do no matter what you find out. She's over twenty-one. If worse comes to worst, we can try to persuade her to let me draw up a prenuptial agreement this time." Barbara's trusts had fallen in at about the same time her marriage had crumbled, and Alan had had his hands full stemming the threatened hemorrhage of Altman capital.

"Oh, God!" Gerald groaned, and turned his attention to lunch, which had just arrived at the table.

After the pause while the waiter served the food, Alan thought the time was right for bringing up the Abbott & Strawbridge matter. The subject of Gerald's children had sobered him, and he might be more inclined toward caution. "Incidentally, I wanted to talk to you about that building Strawbridge is putting up on Third Avenue," he said.

Gerald put down his fork and pointed his knife accusingly at Alan. "If they think for one minute that the stockholders are going to be fooled by that kind of grandstand play!" he said angrily. "They sit on their fannies for the past twenty-five years, all of a sudden when someone tries to buy them out and get things going, they put up their first building anyone alive can remember. People aren't that dumb. They won't fall for that."

Alan shook his head. Gerald as usual wasn't following his line of reasoning at all, but was going off in his typical bullheaded fashion. "It isn't that I was talking about. I'm not at all happy about the financing of it. No one seems to know this Bertino outfit. The contractors. It looks like a completely fly-by-night outfit. I heard on good authority they haven't put up a single building of any consequence in this city."

"Who told you that?" Gerald demanded.

Alan looked around nervously. The tables were spaced far apart, and none of the waiters were hanging around. Still . . . "This can't leave this table," he said, and after Gerald's nearly imperceptible nod of agreement, whispered, "Irv Friedman."

Gerald turned out his palm in concession to the hotelier's information, but said, "What's it to me how they're financing? If the terms are as bad as I imagine they are, Morty can refinance it when we take over the company, or else we can simply default, and let whoever's holding the paper have their pile of rubble."

"You don't know the terms. What if they used other assets as collateral? What if there's an accident, and their liability isn't properly covered? You could gain control of the company and find out you've just taken title to a huge debt."

"Alan, if there's anything, no matter how improbable, to conceivably worry about, you'll find it," Gerald scoffed.

"That happens to be my job," Alan said testily. "What if you went ahead with this, and this improbability came to pass, and I hadn't warned you? Would you prefer that?"

Gerald laughed. "I'm terribly grateful to you for always imagining the worst," he said. "Consider me warned."

Alan reddened at his brother-in-law's condescension. "You're not still thinking of going ahead with this, are you?" he asked in disbelief.

"I'm not thinking of it, I'm doing it," Gerald told him. Alan pressed his lips together in silent dissent. "You don't approve, I take it?"

"I think it's sheer madness, if you want to know my candid opinion," Alan told him.

"I guess I do," Gerald said doubtfully. After a moment's hesitation, he leaned forward and said: "Alan, I'm getting someone else in on this."

Alan felt a stab of betrayal and alarm. Whatever other considerations there might be, he couldn't afford to lose Altman's as a client. It was his firm's biggest account, the mainstay of his practice. Money wasn't the only issue, either, although the loss would be considerable and the firm would have to scramble to make it up elsewhere. More important, though, his reputation as a lawyer and an advisor would be impugned. His whole standing in his profession and in the community was at stake. How much chance would he have of becoming president of the Bar Association on the heels of being fired by his own brother-in-law?

When he could speak, Alan said only "I think I'm capable of handling this." His voice was trembling, but there wasn't much he could do about that.

"It isn't your capability that's in question, Alan. I don't need a wet blanket just now."

"If you want a yes-man, you're right to get someone else," Alan said, flaring up.

"Oh, for Christ's sake," Gerald said in exasperation. "You know what I'm talking about, and it isn't that."

Alan didn't say anything for a moment. Finally he asked, "Who have you gotten?"

"Jack Bernstein."

The name was no surprise. Bernstein was a young whippersnapper, one of the new breed of aggressive lawyers who, in Alan's opinion, were running the profession into the ground. Bernstein had already made himself known as the man to handle buy-outs, proxy fights, hostile take-overs, deals where there was a lot of money to be made and no one worried overly much about the niceties. "Mazeltov," he said bitterly. "I hope you two will be very happy together."

"You're still my lawyer, Alan," Gerald said. "He'll just be handling this one matter. You have to be up on the latest for these things."

"Sure."

"I don't see why you should go off into a huff about this," Gerald said crossly. "You didn't want to do this in the first place. You can't blame me for wanting someone who I can count on to support me."

"I think you've always been able to count on me," Alan said, his quiet voice concealing his anger.

"Yes, but you know whenever there's any unpleasantness, you don't like it. If there's even the whiff of a fight, you get cold feet."

"I don't think that's fair, Gerry," Alan nearly whispered. He was stung, as much by the truth of what Gerald was saying as its unpardonable distortion.

Gerald shrugged. "You can't go through life trying to please everyone, Alan. Some times you have to offend people to get what you want."

"I couldn't agree with you less!" Alan retorted. "I think it's perfectly possible to do quite nicely without antagonizing everyone, and still make a decent profit. What's the great attraction of a fight? Even if you win, you show yourself to be grasping, greedy, pushy—"

"That is to say, Jewish," Gerald shot back.

Alan flushed. "In a word, yes." He hated to put it in such terms, but there was no avoiding it now.

"Why do you have to hide it?" Gerald challenged him.

"No one could possibly accuse me of hiding anything, God knows," Alan said hotly. "But I don't see what we gain by playing up our worst side. It just confirms the accusations of our enemies, and embarrasses our friends."

"Our so-called friends."

"Why put everyone to the test? A friend is a friend."

"Your trouble is that you're willing to let people walk right over you rather than have them think you're obnoxious. God! It's the old story: Don't make trouble. How many Jews have gone off to the gas chamber reciting that line?"

"No one's sending you to the gas chamber," Alan said irritably. "You can't justify everything, no matter how outrageous, on the ground that they killed four million or whatever number it is Jews. That's exactly the sort of thing that irks me about Israel, frankly. They always have a chip on their shoulder, and they always know they're right."

"I'm not ashamed of Israel, and I don't see any need to apologize for it," Gerald said; it was his turn to be indignant.

"I'm not ashamed of Israel per se. I just don't like all that arrogance."

"And I don't like timidity. Where has it gotten us?"

"Where has it gotten us?" Alan exclaimed. "Look where we're sitting right now!" He took in with a sweep of his arm a roomful of prosperous Jews. "Within our own lifetimes things have changed drastically. There isn't an opportunity in America closed to us. There isn't a school worth going to our children can't attend. I don't say there aren't a couple of clubs no one in his right mind would want to join that might not welcome us with open arms, a few dances our kids don't get invited to, but in everything that really means something that sort of discrimination is a thing of the past."

Gerald shook his head slowly. "You're living in a dreamworld, Alan," he said. "It's dog-eat-dog out there." Involuntarily, Alan's eyes were drawn out the window, down onto the street. All he could see was a number of men much like himself, except that they were all wearing overcoats. And to hear himself called timid! Living in a dreamworld! It was not to be borne!

The clouds had thickened by the time he left Altman's, and it looked as though the snow might start any time now. His own day had fallen apart as well. Lunch had been a complete disaster. He had allowed himself to be bullied, humiliated, all but fired by his brother-in-law, virtually in public. Old-fashioned, he had heard himself called; overcautious; weak. Did others see him that way? Did Roger Montgomery, for example? Alan knew he ought to disdain the opinion of a bigot and a snob, but in truth the man carried great weight at the Bar Association.

With a gloomy foreboding he saw himself cast aside, passed over for someone more forceful, decisive, strong. The Roger Montgomerys of the world would be only too happy to let him continue running from one end of town to the other, raising money, solving problems, mediating disputes. They would never put him in at the top. He was destined to be at someone else's right hand, whispering advice in unheeding ears, letting others take the credit. He had always told himself he didn't care about the limelight; but he had his pride, after all. He wanted what he deserved.

It was late. He hurried toward the subway station and cantered down the steps. As he approached the turnstiles he heard the train coming into the station. It was going to be close. Luckily he had change. He pushed through the turnstile and made a dash for the train. Exiting passengers drew aside to make way for his sprint. The doors were in motion, but he slipped in neatly. He'd made it!

He turned around to receive the congratulations of his fellow passengers. Most of them hadn't noticed. They were absorbed in their paperbacks or the afternoon paper or their own thoughts. One kid, a shabbily dressed but clean Negro boy, still in his teens, was looking at him with what he hoped was admiration, mixed with apparent surprise that a successful-looking man should be running for the subway. It suddenly struck Alan that this boy was the personification of the youth of New York City. Here, in person, was the reason for the commission's existence, the representative of those it would benefit. Right now this boy was no doubt poised on the razor's edge: tipped one way, and he could slide into a life of crime; a slight push in the other direction, and who knows? Another Jackie Robinson, Ralph Bunche, A. Philip Randolph. A timely word might conceivably make a difference. "It'll be ten minutes till the next train," he explained to the boy. "I always believe in trying my best. No one ever got rich wasting time."

The boy looked around to see who Alan was talking to. When he realized it was himself, he ducked his head down toward the floor. He kept his eyes averted all the way to Grand Central, where he got off, casting an apprehensive parting look at Alan as he left. Alan didn't mind. He would never know the result of his advice, but at least he'd done his bit. That was what counted. If every citizen would put his shoulder to the wheel, they could really move this city ahead.

An elderly woman across the aisle looked up and their eyes met. She hesitated, and then her frightened face relaxed into a tentative smile. A moment of joy. His day was back on course.

Four

The mayor's Select Commission on the Problems of Youth in New York City, Richard Utley, chairman, David Hurwitz, executive director, held its meetings at City Hall. The commission staff did its work, however, tucked away in two shabby rooms on the seventh floor of the Municipal Office Building. The rest of the floor was occupied by the sections of the Building Authority that dealt with zoning, permits, and inspection. One might think it an unlikely location for a commission dealing with youth unless one knew that Dave Hurwitz and his counterparts in the other offices were among the mayor's closest advisors. The seventh-floor mob, as it was called, was Flaherty's kitchen cabinet. Whenever the door to Hurwitz's office was closed, it was a sure sign that a meeting was taking place that had little to do with the problems of youth.

When Phil arrived at the commission, at about the same time that Peggy was calling for Joan at Meyer House, the door was closed. Hurwitz's office was nothing more than a corner chunk of the larger room, partitioned off in a previous administration, and soundproofed when the commission had taken up residence. It wasn't hard to guess the topic of conversation, muffled but audible behind the door. Michael Flaherty was proud of his close ties to the senator from Massachusetts, and the size of the Democratic turnout in the city next week was ultimately the responsibility of the four men in that room. Phil stopped momentarily and stared at the roughly painted plywood wall, trying to ascertain the political weather from the rise and fall of voices coming from the inner office.

"Better put your ear to the keyhole. You won't hear anything from that distance," the sardonic voice of Lou Mazerowski broke in. Phil masked his surprise. He had thought he was alone. Friday afternoons the office was usually deserted. He turned to see Mazerowski's weasel face grinning at him. "Go ahead. Be my guest. My lips are sealed."

A slip. He had let himself be caught unguarded, and by the last person he wanted to catch him. Phil had no real friends at the commission, which was understandable; but Mazerowski was gunning for him. On Phil's first day he had introduced himself: "Lou Mazerowski. CCNY, 1954. Fordham Law, night school. Glad ta meetcha." There was very little Phil could do after that. He went out of his way to be friendly, helpful, deferential even, but all Mazerowski could see in him was privilege and pull. He needled Phil constantly, and when Hurwitz wasn't around it could get pretty nasty. Phil had tried to go about his business quietly and unobtrusively, but the guy wouldn't let him alone.

"How are you, Lou?" Phil said, instantly regretting the inopportune rhyme, which made him sound supercilious. "Burning the midnight oil?" he pushed on.

"Oh, someone has to stick around to take your messages. Your whole family's been trying to reach you all day," Mazerowski replied. He swiveled his chair around and looked through the litter on his desk. "Dreadfully sorry I didn't have a chance to copy these over," he said in a mock English accent as he held a scrap of paper up over his shoulder.

"Thanks," Phil said to the back of Mazerowski's head as he came over to take the paper. He glanced quickly at the barely legible scrawl. The first message read: *Your father. Don't call back, can't be reached. Send copy of report to Gerald Altman immediately.* The second read simply, *Call R. Altman, urgent.* The two *Altmans* were circled, and arrows drawn to them from the question *Are these two by any chance related?* written at the side. On the bottom, as an afterthought, *They aren't by any chance related to you?* It was already a stale joke.

Phil put the paper in his pocket, and went over to one of the desks. These battered wooden government-issue items were not placed in any particular pattern but had been added one by one as needed, with those already there shoved aside to make room for new ones as they arrived. There were no longer enough for everyone to have his own desk, and every inch of surface space was cluttered with typewriters, files, folders, documents, handwritten drafts on yellow lined paper. Phil, the latest staffer at the commission, simply camped out at whichever desk happened to be free at any given time, and kept his papers in one of the file cabinets that lined the walls. Since he had just finished a report, he had no work in progress and nothing to do that afternoon. He had come in to see Hurwitz so he could discuss his new assignment. He was hoping to get something to work on this time more exciting than playgrounds and gyms. Maybe even something that would call on his legal training. He had come all the way down, on a Friday afternoon, counting on finding Hurwitz alone. It would be hard to maneuver in front of Mazerowski.

"Who's 'R. Altman, urgent?' " Mazerowski asked, his back still to Phil.

"He's a cousin of mine. Works at Altman's," Phil said. At first he had tried to be as forthcoming to Mazerowski as possible, but the man's curiosity was insatiable. Phil's policy now was to say as little as possible, volunteer nothing, and, as the family's familiar maxim went, "When you have to lie, use the available truth." So far he'd learned nothing more useful at law school.

"Don't let me keep you from returning your urgent calls," Mazerowski said. "If you need more privacy, just say the word. I'll go out in the hallway and wait till you give the sign."

Phil didn't answer, nor did he pick up the telephone. Dickie could wait. It was inconceivable that the matter was urgent. Nothing in Dickie's life rose to the level of urgency. It was true that he had an office at Altman's, and the use of a secretary, but to say he worked there was already stretching it. After a few pathetic attempts at holding jobs elsewhere, Dickie had finally allowed himself to be taken in at Altman's. He was given no real duties, but he could presumably be watched and kept relatively out of mischief. He periodically concocted wild schemes for making money that tended to be hopelessly naive, slightly shady, or both. When he came to the realization that his father didn't even listen to them, he tried to get Phil interested. For a variety of reasons, Phil hadn't yet given him the brush-off. If Dickie was cut off completely from the family, there was no knowing where he might turn. Without needing to be told, Phil understood that he was expected to keep an eye on his cousin. These things were not spelled out in the family. They didn't need to be.

"Lotta action at the commission meeting this morning," Mazerowski said when he saw he wasn't getting anywhere with the subject of Dickie Altman.

"Oh?" Phil replied, showing interest, but not too much interest. He knew his report had been on the agenda, and he didn't want Mazerowski catching him with his tongue hanging out again.

"Hizzoner made an appearance. Your report was discussed." Mazerowski paused teasingly. When Phil didn't rise to the bait, he continued: "Unfortunately, those two events were separated by about half an hour." Phil could see that one coming a mile away. He wasn't even disappointed. Coming to Flaherty's attention wasn't high on his list. Not yet. The timing wasn't right. "Your report was unanimously adopted," Mazerowski conceded. "Several favorable comments. I had the feeling Commissioner Gutheim thought highly of it. Say—he isn't by any chance related to you, is he?"

Phil ignored the gibe. "What did the mayor have to say?" he asked, wanting to show proper disinterest.

"Oh, the usual profundities." Mazerowski softened a little. He swiveled his chair back around, and addressed Phil directly. "This commission will decide the entire future of New York City. Our youth, blah, blah, blah. Most precious resource, blah, blah, blah. Education, employment, rights, blah, blah, blah. Simultaneous translation: Find a way to get rid of all the niggers and spics in this town. Now *that's* leadership. Utley was so pleased he came in, he practically wrote him out another campaign check on the spot. That is, until the mayor called your father 'Alan.' That stopped him in his tracks. 'Keep 'em honest, Alan,' he says on his way out. I thought Utley was going to fall off his chair. I thought your father was going to fall off *his* chair. God, it never ceases to amaze me, the cosmic importance of infinitesimal trivialities. I guess that's politics."

"My father eats that sort of thing up. He could live on it happily for the next week," Phil said, reciprocating the glimmer of warmth coming from Mazerowski. Feeling more at ease, he asked, nodding toward Hurwitz's office, "What's up in there?"

"I heard somewhere there's an election coming up next week. I believe those gentlemen have some slight interest in the outcome."

Phil asked, "Do you know what we're all supposed to actually be doing on Tuesday?"

"Vote early and often. You know the politician's prayer, don't you? 'Lord, give me strength and health. We'll steal the rest.' "

Phil smiled. Mazerowski was such a cynical son of a bitch. Minus the chip on his shoulder, he had a lot of qualities Phil admired: He was tough and smart, and knew what he was after. He was going to get it, too. Already he was Hurwitz's fair-haired boy. Long after the commission report was written and forgotten, he'd still be around, Phil was sure.

Just then the door to the office opened, and Hurwitz stuck his head out. "Lou!" he barked out. "Get your ass in here." Hurwitz had been a reporter on the *Post* before coming to work for Flaherty, and still liked to fancy himself a city editor. He saw Phil and asked gruffly, "What brings you in?"

"Do you have a minute?" Phil asked.

Mazerowski strode by into the smaller room. "Great timing," he mumbled out the side of his mouth as he passed Phil.

"Not till after Tuesday," Hurwitz said. "Stick around," he added, closing the door.

Left alone in the office with nothing particular to do while he waited for Hurwitz, Phil thought he might as well call Dickie. He didn't want to be caught on the telephone when the others came out, but he figured he could always hang up on his cousin. He dialed the number, and went through the farce of giving his name to the operator and then to a secretary, who told him Dickie was on another line and put him on hold. It was barely possible Dickie was talking to someone; more likely he was hanging around the back offices, where he spent most of his time gossiping with the runners if he wasn't making a pass at a stenographer.

"Phil, how's the kid!" Dickie cried out with forced heartiness when he finally came on the line. "Long time no see! Whatcha been doing with yourself?" Even with his cousin, Dickie couldn't control his nervous laugh.

"What can I do for you, Dickie?" Phil asked, curbing his distaste but otherwise all business.

"We-hell!" Dickie giggled, taken aback by his cousin's curtness. "Now listen, Phil, I know you, don't say no on this until you've heard me out."

"That could take some time," Phil observed. Already it didn't sound good.

"I know how *busy* you are." Dickie's obsequiousness could become bitter with surprising suddenness. "Listen, I have a deal that is really exciting. I'd like to tell you about it, you could make a pile on it. But don't do me any favors. If you're interested, fine. If not, we'll end it right there."

"I don't really think I am, Dickie," Phil said firmly. He didn't like to be openly rude, but sometimes there was no other way of dealing with Dickie.

There was a short silence on the other end of the line. Dickie evidently hadn't seriously considered the possibility Phil wouldn't be interested. "Don't you think that's a little hasty? You haven't heard one thing about this yet. I know your time is precious, but I should think even you might like to know what you're turning down. You could be kicking yourself in a couple of months."

"That's a risk I'm prepared to take, I guess."

"Phil . . ." Dickie began to plead, but he had nothing further to say. He hadn't counted on such a swift and final refusal. Phil, on his part, knew he ought to hear Dickie out and then dissuade him from whatever he wanted to do. That particular afternoon, however, his usual patience failed him. The real world went on, he reflected, while Dickie spun out his schemes of acquiring wealth and power with a snap of his fingers. Just this once, let him get burned, Phil thought. It's the only way he'll ever learn. Dickie didn't have access to enough money to do himself or the family any real damage. None of the Altman children had much control over their own estates. Even with three of them over twenty-one, and several trusts having fallen in, Gerald had somehow contrived to keep them all on a fairly short leash. Phil didn't know how he did it. Gerald Altman undoubtedly knew a few things they didn't teach at Columbia Law School, and Phil was eager to learn some of them.

He got rid of Dickie before the others came out. Finding himself alone in the office with nothing to do meanwhile, the idea of the keyhole had its appeal. He stayed put, however, until the meeting broke up. Voices rose in conclusion, he heard chairs scraping, and the men filed out: Hurwitz first, carrying his overcoat, followed by three grim-faced colleagues, and lastly Mazerowski, looking pleased with himself. The other men went through the door to the hallway without acknowledging Phil's existence. Hurwitz looked at him accusingly and said, "This thing could go either way."

It was always a challenge to guess what Hurwitz was talking about, since with his subordinates, at least, he never bothered with referents.

Phil assumed he was nervous about the election, although it was possible he was worried about the New York vote, or maybe some numerical goal that was turning out to be overly optimistic. "All we need is a few more attacks like this and we'll have gang warfare on our hands."

Phil needed all his mental agility to understand that Hurwitz's outrage was directed toward the mugging reported in the papers that morning, and not some last-minute campaign smear.

"The mayor wants this given top priority. Full court press. Lou's going to be working on this full-time. He'll need a lot of help on this, so I'm giving him you. Is that okay?" The question wasn't a request. Phil shot a look at Mazerowski but could read nothing on his face. Probably he didn't mind having Phil under his thumb, but he betrayed no sign of satisfaction. "I can't talk to you now, we're on our way over to City Hall, there's a meeting about these scum up in East Harlem. Lou's going to leave you his file on it, plus a bunch of other stuff he's got. See what you make of it. As soon as the election's over you can get going on it." Despite his being in a hurry, he was obviously warming to his subject. "We're not interested in sociology here. We're not trying to understand the root conditions. We know the root conditions. The mayor's interested in getting the streets safe. Find 'em, catch 'em, lock 'em up. That sort of thing. We'll let the next commission worry about rehabilitation. Of course, that's not exactly the way it'll be phrased in the final report. That's where you come in."

"How's that?" Phil asked uneasily. Hurwitz had now put on his coat and was standing with one hand on the doorknob.

"Lou will, of course, be in charge on this one," Hurwitz replied. "He's been working on it all along, and he has a pretty good grasp of what we're looking for. He's—I don't mind saying this in front of him, his head is already about as swelled as it can get—he's the ideal person for this project: he's savvy, he knows a little law, and of course he's had plenty of experience with juvenile delinquents." Mazerowski, standing next to Hurwitz, his coat already on, looked satisfied with the characterization. "He has maybe one drawback, which is that he hasn't got a damn bit of tact. Not a shred. He calls a spade a spade, which has a lot to recommend it, but not in the final report, if you know what I mean. That's your job. I want you to make sure it all comes out smelling like a rose. Lou knows what to say, and you know how to say it. Between the two of you, I figure we can turn out a hell of a report and still go to bed with the ACLU. We'll talk about it some more next week. After Tuesday." Without further ceremony he went out of the office. Mazerowski followed him out, leaving Phil with an enigmatic little wave, as if to say, "You're going to be seeing a lot more of me."

Phil was once again alone in the empty office. It was just as well. He needed some time to himself to assess what had happened. He liked to analyze his position formally, treating himself as objectively as if he were a case. This assignment, for example: What did it mean in the long run? What could he get out of it? He would be working under Mazerowski. That could be an opportunity, or it could be a trap. Should he consider this a promotion? In whose eyes? There was Hurwitz to consider, of course, and Mazerowski, but what of the other staff members? They already eyed him with considerable suspicion. Would they think he had maneuvered his way into this? It might be smart not to seem too pleased about this, let them think he was accepting an onerous assignment without complaint.

He didn't know, maybe it was an onerous assignment. Carrying Mazerowski's briefcase. Putting up with endless cracks about the Ivy League. Taking orders. Doing the work, seeing someone else get the credit. As long as Hurwitz knew, he could live with it. Hurwitz was his constituency, after all, not any of the rest of them. It was Hurwitz's opinion that mattered.

And what was that opinion? That he had tact, he could make things sound good. Should he feel complimented or insulted? Was he being praised for his maturity and common sense, or was this in some sense a reproof. Mazerowski might be a street fighter, but at least he has principles; while Phil was smooth, but unscrupulous? Was that how Hurwitz saw it?

He smacked his palms on the desk and stood up. Enough thinking. It was time for action. He had to get a copy of his report to his uncle. He could easily guess what that was about: the clerkship. His father must be staying awake nights thinking about it. Phil worried that he was overdoing it. As often as Phil had asked him to play it low-key, he was off on some new tack. The latest was the dean of the law school, for God's sake. Before Phil had even made up his mind he wanted the job, half of New York was being enlisted in his cause. He hated that kind of exposure. Better always to look as though you didn't care, than to have people see your ambitions, raw and ugly, like an angry open wound. Then, too, suppose he should be denied what everybody knew he was after? It was

the worst fate Phil could imagine: a setback in full view, a public humiliation.

He went into Hurwitz's office and looked in the cabinet where several copies of his report were filed. Strictly speaking, he should have
asked Hurwitz's permission before removing any material from the
commission, but it was very unlikely to be discovered, and if it was, he
could offer any number of explanations. As he was opening the file
drawer the phone rang. The sudden ring sounded like a burglar alarm,
and he snatched his hand away as though he had received a shock.
Quickly recovering, he answered the phone. "Utley Commission," he
announced in his most official tone. He almost gave his name, but
stopped himself.

"Is Mr. Walsh there?" a gruff voice asked.

There was nobody named Walsh on the commission staff, but the
name rang a faint bell. "Who's calling please?" he asked. It seemed irrelevant, but you never knew.

"Vinnie Bertino."

"Just a moment, Mr. Bertino."

Phil pressed the hold button, and rummaged around on Hurwitz's
desk until he found a directory for the Municipal Building. He looked
up Walsh. There were three Walshes: Frank Walsh, John Walsh, and
Patricia Walsh. He pressed the button again and asked, "Which Mr.
Walsh do you want, Mr. Bertino?"

Mr. Bertino didn't answer right away. "Who's this?" he asked.

"This is the Commission on the Problems of Youth in New York
City."

There was another brief pause, and then Vinnie Bertino hung up.

Phil stared at the buzzing receiver for a few seconds, then replaced
it. An intriguing call. He looked back at the directory. Frank Walsh
worked in the sanitation department, John Walsh in the Building Authority. Room 713, two doors down. That was why the name was familiar. Phil had never met the man but had seen his name on the door.
Could he be the one this Bertino was calling? Who was Vinnie Bertino,
anyway? And why had he hung up? Filing it away as one of the little
mysteries of life, probably never to be solved, Phil went back to the file
drawer and found what he was looking for.

He took it out, and looked at it with bemusement. "A Survey of
Recreational Facilities in the Five Boroughs, with Proposals for Increased Use." This was going to get him the clerkship? Shaking his head,

he put it in a manila envelope. He had thought to use a messenger, but that was always a little chancy. He looked at his watch. He just had time to take the report over to Altman's himself, and still make it to the Meridian for his squash game, if all went well. He put on his coat and went downstairs. It all depended on how long it took to get a taxi.

On his way to the elevator he passed Room 713. He stopped and read: HOUSING AUTHORITY—INSPECTION SECTION. He looked down the list of names and saw *John Walsh*. For a moment, he considered going in and telling John Walsh that Vinnie Bertino had phoned for him. But then he thought better of it. Something about the voice, and the abrupt hanging-up. He tried to remember if he had given his own name. He hoped not.

When he got outside the building, it was growing dark. The wind had picked up and it seemed as though snow might fall any time now. It was much too early for that. If it snowed before election day, there was no telling what kind of winter they were in for. He hoped he could get a cab quickly. He was cutting it very close.

But it didn't snow that afternoon, and within a minute Phil got a taxi. He climbed in and gave the address of Altman's. "I'll want you to wait," he told the driver. "Then I'm going uptown." He settled himself comfortably into the warm cab and took stock.

The day, he had to admit, was not going too badly. There was nothing like getting a taxi when you needed one.

Five

In the split second before the door to Betsy's apartment opened, Joan knew something was wrong. She should have been suspicious when Phil had her come up to see Betsy's new apartment. If they had really had dinner reservations, he would have had Betsy waiting for them in the lobby, and had her see the apartment some other time. But then everything had an air of unreality these days. She hardly knew from moment to moment where she might find herself, who she might see. Her days were strange and disjointed, like dreams: people appeared where they didn't belong, events took place without causes, nothing was quite as it should have been. Her sense of time was peculiar. The ordinary seemed unusual, and the unexpected inevitable.

Even so, it gave her a jolt to see all those people standing there beyond the doorway, grinning at her. Although they were her closest friends in the world, at that moment they were total strangers. She was overcome by a wave of inexplicable shame, as though they had caught her in the midst of some unspeakably degrading act. Hot blood rushed into her face. She couldn't catch her breath. Dizziness and nausea swept over her and for a terrible moment she thought she would pass out. Suddenly the tableau of frozen faces broke and everyone yelled "Welcome home!" With the noise came a hot sting of tears. She couldn't believe what was happening to her.

"Betsy Schine!" she cried. "Is this all your doing?"

"It's everyone's doing!" Betsy tossed her head, causing her thick dark hair to describe a great arc taking in everyone standing behind her. Then she stretched out both arms and came forward to kiss Joan. The others broke up the semicircle and crowded around, taking turns kissing and hugging.

"Jerry!" Joan wailed. "Oh, my God! Tinker!" The guys were engulfing her in great clinches, and Tinker was making one of his grotesque clown expressions. Everyone pressed near. "I've got to sit down before I collapse of shock!" She staggered, laughing, into the living room, Tinker on one arm, Freddie Anspach on the other. They half escorted, half carried her to the couch, where she crumpled with another little moan.

It was still hard to believe this was all really happening. "I'll never forgive you!" she called out to Betsy, who smirked back at her from across the room. "I love your apartment, by the way," she added sarcastically, thinking of her own gullibility. "No, really!" she shrieked, catching the faux pas. "I love it! The rug is gorgeous." Betsy's mother had gotten her a French provincial carpet, pale blue, with pink and violet flowers—beautiful, but a bit on the elegant side for a first apartment. Her decorator had insisted that all the furniture had to be off-white, giving the place the look of a Hollywood boudoir.

"I'll tell Mummy you like it," Betsy said, laughing.

"Do you realize how close I came to having a heart attack?" Joan told the boys, who were towering above her. "I could have actually died on that spot. Do you have any idea what it's like to have the door open and there's this entire . . . *circus*, everyone standing there and staring at you. I thought I was in a cage at the zoo! Oh, my God!" she screamed. They had brought out the enormous panda Johnny had won for her at the Silverlake fair by knocking down about a hundred bottles with tennis balls. Joan had left it with Betsy for safekeeping when she had gone back to college that fall. They thrust it into Johnny's arms and pushed him over to the couch. He made a great show of reluctance while Tinker and Freddie shoved him all the harder, making football noises as they pushed.

Johnny, the eternal boy hero. When Riverdale came to play basketball games, all the Fieldston girls turned out just to see him. He was said to be the cutest thing imaginable, which was how nice high school girls described sexy boys in those days. He was twenty-two now, and had fleshed out his six-foot-four frame a little more, but otherwise he still looked exactly the same. Lanky and earnest, with a shock of unruly black hair falling down over his eyes, he still wore the modest expression of the star who has just scored a basket and is embarrassed by the cheers. He plunked the panda down on Joan, who gave it a great squeeze. "Hey! How about me!" he complained. He bent over to collect his own panda-hug from Joan, and to show everyone they were still on hugging terms. Everyone in the room knew that he hadn't gotten over her, and there was a momentary freeze while they all watched Joan's reaction to seeing him again. It had all happened so fast that she didn't have a chance to plan her response, which in any case was constrained by her being seated and his bending over; only two giraffes would have been able to manage much of an embrace.

"You're just going to have to give me a few minutes to come to," Joan said. "God, everyone's here, aren't they? How on earth did you ever arrange it?"

"I couldn't fend them off," Betsy said. "The minute we heard you were coming down, everyone was on the phone at once, and we all agreed on tonight. So here we are. Tinker and Debbie had tickets to Mike Nichols and Elaine May, and my mother was expecting me for a dinner party so she's furious with me, but other than that it was no trouble whatsoever."

"Oh, you didn't! Mike Nichols and Elaine May! But I hear they're a riot!"

"He's taking me next week, don't worry," Debbie reassured her.

"So everybody's here," Joan exclaimed, looking around to see who was missing."

"Except Ellen, of course," Betsy reported. "And the Danzigers."

"Oh, well, really—all the way from Boston," Joan allowed.

"If you'd had leukemia, they'd have come from Boston," Phil said. "But you're only sick enough to pull them in from New Rochelle."

"Phil!" Betsy scolded; but Joan wheezed with laughter.

All the others still formed an audience, laughing a little too hard at every quip. The effort took its toll, and now a gap of uncomfortable silence fell over the group. Wendy took it on herself to fill it in. "You look *so great*, Joanie," she said, but it was too hoked up to be convincing. At one time she had nursed an ambition to go on the stage, and had done summer stock, acting classes, auditions, the whole works. Although she was over that phase, she still occasionally projected her lines as though the curtain had just gone up.

"What did you expect?" Joan replied. "I never felt better in my life. If it wasn't for my parents becoming hysterical, I'd still be up in Bennington."

"Yes," Phil explained, "our parents were so unreasonable to think that a person might require some medical attention after being found feet-up in a snowdrift."

"I wasn't in any snowdrift!"

"I was being polite. We all know what kind of drifts they have up in Vermont."

"You are the end!" Joan shrieked. "Don't listen to a word he says."

"I never have," Betsy said. "It makes life that much easier." The others, giggling nervously, started drifting off. "You ought to be spanked," Betsy scolded Phil, but he continued his grin. Nothing could shame him. Joan thought he was hilarious. Nothing he said ever offended her. He had absolute privilege. Betsy called out, "Everybody should start eating right away. I have about a ton of food, and if you guys don't get it eaten, I'll be having leftovers for the next month."

"Is Clara here?" Joan asked. Mrs. Schine often sent her cook over when Betsy had company in for dinner. Left to herself, Betsy had trouble boiling water.

"No, Mother's got this dinner party tonight, so she got Claude for me instead." Claude was the rather sinister former butler of Betsy's grandparents who had gone into the catering business after their deaths.

"Oh, no!" Joan cried. The girls, when they were little, used to scare one another with the stories they concocted about Claude's secret and horrific practices.

"Oh, he's not here, don't worry. You don't actually have to have him in person. All you do is call him up and tell him how many you're having. That's all there is to it. He tells you what you're going to have and sends it over in his own serving whatchamacallums. About three times as much as you need, naturally. Tomorrow he sends over one of his little flunkies to clean up and collect everything. You don't so much as wash a dish. Listen, let me get people eating. I have to get things out of the oven. I'll be right back. Do you want a drink? Johnny, get Joanie a drink." She went off to the kitchen, and Johnny said, "Do you want a drink?"

Joan shook her head. The others had moved away, leaving her alone with him. She patted the sofa next to her, indicating that he should sit down. He picked up the panda on her other side and sat there, putting the stuffed animal on his lap. "I'll just sit here with my old friend." The panda's head came just up to his chin, which he rested on one furry ear. "I was wondering how long it would be before you got your shoes off," he said, nodding at the black high heels already discarded at the foot of the couch. Joan had curled her legs underneath her. "That must have set an all-time record for your keeping them on."

"My mother dragged me through about a hundred stores this afternoon. She decided I had nothing to wear. She thinks a social worker in New York should look like somebody out of *Vogue*. Not that my mother ever in her life looked like anything out of *Vogue*. But she wants me to, and of course once she and I get going, we buy the whole place out. Neither of us have an ounce of self-control. We went on a binge."

"So you're doing social work?" Johnny said admiringly.

"You could call it that. You know me. The first day home I slept late, which is hardly news, except that everyone was convinced I had died. When I finally staggered out of bed, you would have thought I had risen from the grave. After that, I got so bored I could have screamed. They wanted me to stay in one place and not move for about a month. Daddy wanted to have me committed to Mt. Sinai, where they could have round-the-clock nurses taking my pulse and so on and so forth. Fortunately, Mother wouldn't hear of that. But she wanted to do it at home. The only way I could keep from going stark, raving mad was to get something to do right away, so I'm down at Meyer House, and I'm starting Monday working with the cutest kids you could possibly imagine, but what I really want to know is, how are *you*? My God, it's been ages and ages. How is B-school? I'm dying to hear all about it. Not one word, may I remind you, not one word all fall, but who's complaining?"

Johnny smiled. "I'd apologize except that, as you may possibly know, I haven't had one word, not one word, from you either, so if the shoe fits . . ."

"You know perfectly well I never write anyone unless they die, or send me a present, or I go to their houses for the weekend. You can't scold me for some deep-seated flaw I can't help, for God's sake!"

"Who's scolding?" Johnny said, laughing and putting up his hands in defense. They had actually never written each other, even when they were going together. They used to run up quite a phone bill between Bennington and Dartmouth.

"But how is school? Really?"

"In a word: tough. Very tough. You wouldn't believe how much work they throw at us. I'm booking it pretty much night and day."

"Poor Johnny! No more double features?"

"No more double features. Not a hell of a lot of single features, when you come right down to it."

"God, you must be going into withdrawal. How do you stand it?"

"There's still the Late Late Show. You can't forget the Late Late Show."

"How could I ever forget the Late Late Show?" Joan said, laughing. "You haven't given that up, at least?"

"Some things are sacred," Johnny said solemnly.

"But you do like it? Even without the movies? I mean, it must be interesting, isn't it?"

"It's okay. I guess what they say is true: Life after college is downhill all the way. I give it about a C-minus."

"Oh, dear! But then nobody ever loved college more than you did."

"More than we both did," he said, suddenly sentimental. Joan looked away from his adoring eyes. It was painful to remember the times they had had together, the long walks through the bright leaves or the sparkling snow, fraternity parties, dances, football games, lazy Sunday mornings in the dorm, Winter Carnival. Joan's memories of college were bound up with memories of Johnny, at least until that fall, which now seemed more and more like a bad dream. He took her hand. "Joanie, I'm really glad you're back. I'm sorry about what's happened, but I have to be honest: I'm glad because it means you're here."

The others were all talking, so fortunately no one heard his ardent and embarrassing declaration. "Johnny . . ." Joan began. She didn't know what to say. "It's wonderful to see you. It's wonderful to see everyone . . ." She couldn't go on. As casually as she could, she drew back her hand. He didn't resist, but his face registered everything. Joan felt awful. She'd hurt him badly enough last summer, she didn't want to start in all over. Johnny was the sweetest boy in the world; but she had nearly suffocated to death before finally breaking it off. They had been living out everyone else's fantasies. They were the perfect couple. The gang had all but seated the wedding. She couldn't stand it. She couldn't breathe.

"Well, it's great to have you back," he said quickly, to avert any further rejection. "Everyone feels the same, you know. Who else could have gotten the gang together on such short notice?"

"Oh, I know. I'm everybody's pet project now, aren't I?"

Johnny was chagrined. "No, you're not!" But he was too transparent. He never could hide a thing.

Wendy came back in from the dining room with a plate of food. She flounced down on the couch next to Joan, on the other side from Johnny and the panda. "What's that you're eating?" Joan asked. "It looks wonderful."

"It's chicken fricassee, and it's heavenly. Want a bite?" She offered Joan a forkful.

"Mmm," Joan murmured. She still loved the taste of food, and liked especially to have a bite off of someone else's plate; it seemed less as though she were actually eating it. "So—what's up? I feel as though I've been away for about ten years, and I haven't had a good gab since getting back. Any dirt?"

Wendy considered the question. "Well, this may not qualify as actual dirt, but Felicia's engaged. In fact, it's being announced tomorrow, that's why she's not here, they're having dinner with both sets of parents, if you can imagine."

"Jesus! Engaged! Phil, of course, never told me a thing! I wondered where she was, but I didn't want to act like I expected her necessarily to be here. Do I know him?"

"I doubt it," Wendy said. "His name's Henry Garber. I haven't even met him yet. I don't think anyone has, it's all been so sudden. Although they're not getting married until next spring, so don't worry, it's not a shotgun affair. He's an odd-lot broker, but for all I know he may be perfectly nice. Felicia's certainly happy. They're going to drop in later, so we'll all get to meet him. God, the poor guy! Can you imagine what it must be like for an outsider to be brought here and get the third degree from Tinker? And your brother?"

"Who's this who's going to get the third degree?" Phil wanted to know. He had been standing halfway across the room, eating and talking to Freddie but he could always listen to more than one conversation at a time. It was one of his many talents. He came over to the couch, with Fred trailing.

"Felicia's fiancé," Wendy said. "And I hope you'll be nice to him when he gets here."

"I'm nice to everyone," Phil said. Wendy snorted. "Move over," he commanded. He squeezed in between her and the arm of the couch, nearly sliding his creamed chicken onto her lap. "I'm sure I'll find him fascinating. Odd-lot brokers lead such exciting lives."

"You are such a fantastic snob!" Joan cried. Phil looked pleased with the accusation. "Really, he is impossible. The highlight of his whole entire life came when they put him on the Silverlake membership committee. He can hardly wait to blackball someone. I shudder to think what happens if this poor guy wants to join. God help him."

"Is it true they blackball you if you give less than ten thou to Federation?" Wendy wanted to know.

"They don't blackball you," Phil said with a straight face. "They just send your application over to Hartsdale." Hartsdale Country Club, which aspired to rival Silverlake, drew heavily for its membership on disappointed applicants to the older club.

"Oh, God!" Joan groaned. "I hope he boycotts the Silverlake Country Club, that'd show you. Maybe he's not Jewish," she added hopefully.

The others smiled at Joan's naiveté.

"I suspect he is," Freddie put in.

"Why do you 'suspect he is?'" Joan challenged him.

"I happen to have met him on the Exchange." Fred's father was senior partner in one of the largest brokerage firms in the city, and Fred had gone to work there immediately after college.

"What, was he wearing a yellow armband or something?" Everyone started laughing. "No, really, how do you know?" Joan insisted.

Fred crooned the familiar tune in his cracked voice:

> "*They . . . asked me how I knew . . .*
> *Ginsburg was a Jew . . .*"

The others joined in:

> "*I of course replied . . .*
> *Noses never lie . . .*"

Everyone in the room finished the verse in unison:

> "*They get in your eyes.*"

and broke into cheers, while Joan blushed with embarrassment. Her inability to tell if someone was Jewish was notorious.

"I'm getting seconds," Phil said when the whistles had died out.

"Why don't you get your poor sister firsts?" Betsy wanted to know. She and the others in the dining room had come in to see what the commotion was about. "She's starving. Not to mention she is, after all, the guestess of honor."

"I don't want to set a bad precedent," Phil said. "If I start waiting on her hand and foot, there's no telling where it'll end. Besides, Krieger is dying to do something useful. I vouldn't vant to deny him the pleasure," he ended in his mock accent.

"He sounds exactly like your father when he talks that way," Betsy observed to Joan.

Johnny jumped up to fetch Joan her dinner, but Joan said, "I'll get my own. I know these guys. They'll get in there and start talking football," she added to Wendy. The two women went into the dining room. Johnny put the panda back on the couch and told it "Stay there," while he followed the others in.

Joan knew what was going on. They were all in a conspiracy to get her and Johnny back together, as if they were high school kids at a prom, too shy to dance, but meant for each other. No one would be satisfied unless they were a couple once more. It was unthinkable that they wouldn't be. She must need him more than ever; and everyone knew that Johnny would never rest until he got her back.

But no one had asked her, and she was not about to be railroaded. She could be elusive when she wanted to. Once in the dining room, she didn't get her supper at all but started making the rounds. Johnny stood near her in constant attendance. She neither ignored him nor paid him any special attention. She drew out everybody. Playing her familiar part, she got the boys to show off. She would egg them on to their most outrageous, and reward them with the peals of laughter everyone had missed all the time she had been away. Without contriving to, she catalyzed a chain reaction and the party became increasingly noisy and hilarious. Even when Betsy handed her a plate and ordered her to eat, she never flagged. She was too caught up in the whirl to do more than pick at her food, as people pretended not to notice.

When eventually Betsy couldn't cajole her guests into eating anything more, she and Wendy began clearing away the dishes into the kitchen. Phil came in not so much to help as to talk and to see what else he could nibble at. The girls were discussing Joan.

"I think she looks great. Just great," Wendy said with more hope than conviction.

"I think she looks awful," Betsy said. She was upset. "I feel terrible about even having this tonight. I never would have if I'd had the slightest idea how exhausted she was. But of course getting any kind of reasonable report about her from Phillip is like expecting a blind man to describe a sunset."

"I don't know what more you wanted," Phil bantered. "I told you she had slept all day after she got down, and you said she always sleeps all day after she gets down. Since then you've been on the phone continuously and no one else has gotten a word in edgewise. So mea non culpa."

"What's that supposed to mean?" Wendy asked.

"It means I'm not guilty."

"He's never guilty," Betsy said sarcastically. "I asked you specifically how she looked, and you gave me one of your typical smart-aleck answers."

"I told you she looked like death warmed over," Phil said, looking pleased with himself. "Which I think is a pretty accurate description."

Betsy held out her hands to Wendy in a gesture of helpless exasperation.

"Well, I think she looks just great, considering," Wendy repeated loyally. "Of course she's been tired, who could blame her? What she's been through! Do they still have to do a lot of tests and everything on her?"

"I'm sure my father won't rest easy until every piece of equipment in the Mt. Sinai laboratory has been put through its paces. And you can be sure that any result my mother doesn't agree with will be thrown out and the test will be repeated until a satisfactory one is obtained. She's already fired all the doctors at Mt. Sinai and is sending to P and S for someone she finds more congenial."

"I can't believe she's going to work right away," Wendy said. "And at Meyer House, of all places. Isn't that terribly depressing? Why would she want to go to a place like that?" Wendy gave a little shiver of distaste.

"She wants to work with crippled children," Betsy explained. "She doesn't want to sit around doing nothing. You know her. Isn't it crippled children?" she asked Phil.

"Anything in a wheelchair," he answered. "Preferably drooling. She's very big on kids who drool."

"He really is terrible," Betsy complained, smiling in spite of herself.

"I would think she would find that horribly depressing," Wendy insisted. "I would think the last thing she would want was to be around sick people. Why doesn't she do something at the museum, if she feels she absolutely *has* to do something? Personally, if it was me, I'd climb straight into bed with a big box of Flora Mir caramels and about a hundred magazines and let them bring me everything on a tray. Mummy could buy me some of those heavenly bed jackets they sell at Léron for about a fortune apiece and you could all come and see me. After a while, if I was feeling up to it, I might go to a movie in a taxi, or maybe the Philharmonic with Aunt Clara on Friday afternoon and skip the modern piece. None of this running down to Meyer House to save the world, I can assure you."

"Joan wouldn't be caught dead in bed," Betsy said.

"She may not have a choice about that," Phil wisecracked; but not even Wendy laughed at that.

He went over to the refrigerator and looked in it. Finding some grapes, he took them out and brought them back to the table where he had been sitting. Wendy said, "I just wish we could all *do* something. I mean, it makes you feel so helpless. They really don't know what's wrong yet?"

Betsy shook her head. Wendy looked inquiringly at Phil, but he was preoccupied with eating the grapes and removing the seeds from them. Betsy had finished putting away the leftover food and she walked toward the dining room. "I don't think he's terribly interested in doing anything," she told Wendy with disgust. "Coming?" The two young women walked through the swinging door, leaving Phil with his grape seeds, which he carried, cupped in his hand, over to the garbage pail. He lifted the lid by pressing the pedal with his foot, and brushed off the seeds with swift movements of his free hand. He rinsed his hands off in the sink and looked around to see if there was anything more to eat. Seeing nothing, he shrugged and said aloud, "What's there to do?" Then he followed the others out and left the kitchen empty.

Everyone was sitting around the living room, listening to a Miles Davis record, catching their breath. Even Joan had subsided back onto the couch, and was talking quietly with Debbie and Tinker, while Johnny gazed on in silent adoration. But she was beginning to look restless already, and when she saw Betsy coming over with a maternal frown on her face, she flew into action. In a moment a Lester Lanin record had replaced Miles, and the carpet was rolled up. The gang loved to dance. At all the big parties they monopolized the floor and showed off shamelessly. They had a whole group routine they did whenever a tango was played, and Wendy always requested the Bunny Hop. She always managed to lead the snakeline, and could be seen pulling along her obedient followers, a look of intense satisfaction on her face. The record they had on now stuck to fox-trots, but the beat was unmistakably Lester's, and turned Betsy's apartment into the St. Regis Roof.

In the midst of the dancing Felicia arrived with her fiancé, who turned out to be either tongue-tied or dreadfully anxious, and amply confirmed everybody's worst prejudices. Phil and Tinker took him off to the kitchen, ostensibly for a drink, where, true to Wendy's fears, they treated him with unimpeachable courtesy thinly covering utter condescension. Joan was talking to Felicia at the time, trying to show a decent enthusiasm for her friend's engagement. Felicia kept glancing anxiously at the wall behind which her fiancé was being held. Joan, seeing her distraction, went off on a rescue mission and pulled the poor man back out and onto the dance floor. Lester Lanin had been replaced by the Dukes of Dixieland, and Henry Garber took his first steps toward acceptance by the gang—if not the Silverlake Country Club—by demonstrating a pretty mean Charleston.

Joan was delighted with the results of her Good Samaritanism. She herself had a stylish rendition of the step, and she reveled in the novelty of a new partner. Kicking out the beat and shaking her upstretched hands, she made a fetching flapper, except that in her excitement she couldn't affect the proper insouciance. Her glee was unsuppressible and infectious, and she pulled everyone along with her into the convulsive dance. Her eyes glittered and a hectic flush colored her pale cheeks as "Sweet Georgia Brown" followed "South Rampart Street Parade." Only Betsy was nervous that Joan was pushing herself dangerously, but Phil refused to intervene. By the time the Saints marched in, the party had turned into a full-fledged uproar, with no signs of letting up.

There was no stopping her. As the others dropped, couple by couple, onto the couches and chairs, Joan kept on. She ceded a flustered Henry Garber to Felicia, and pulled Johnny, who'd been sitting out like a prim chaperone, onto the floor. He exchanged nervous glances with Betsy. Joan's manic gaity was nothing new, but now it seemed forced, brittle. When the record ended, she called for the other side amid a chorus of protests. They tried to put on something else, but only Harry Belafonte would placate her. When "Matilda" came on, she wasn't content to sing along with the choruses, as they always did, but wanted the boys to limbo. She was like a drunk, although she hadn't touched a drop of liquor all evening. Everyone knew she had to stop. The party was over.

A few people got up to go home, but no one in fact left. Joan wasn't taken in. "I'm not going to be the first to go and then find out tomorrow that I missed out on something fantastic," she insisted. She wanted to go to Basin Street, or to the Metropole. She thought Ella Fitzgerald was in town, and they had to get Betsy's *Cue* out to prove to her that it wasn't so. She turned to the movie section and started reading out the double features down on 42nd Street. That reminded her of the penny arcades, and she tried to organize a visit to Hubert's Flea Circus. The others sat by too dazed to offer any objections, but too beat to accommodate any of her whims.

Finally, Johnny broke the impasse by announcing that he was taking her home. "You'll do no such thing!" she protested, but when Jeff produced her coat she let them put it on her. The coat seemed to have a calming effect on her, and she became quite docile. Everyone was relieved. People started to say good night in earnest. Debbie and Tinker actually left, and the exodus was on. As it turned out, Joan and Johnny were among the last to go. When they finally did leave, only Wendy and Jeff still remained, and, of course, Phil and Betsy. Phil never stayed the night—there were many reasons for that policy—but he never discouraged people from assuming he slept with Betsy regularly, and he called a host's good night from the door.

And so Joan and Johnny were by themselves at last, on the street. It was cold, but the sky had cleared. The threat of a storm, with its unseasonable snow, had passed at least for now. As they walked down 84th Street they could see a few stars overhead, or peeping out between the buildings on either side. More stars were there, only invisible; in New York, only the brightest stars can penetrate the perpetual aureole of light cast up into the night by the city's incandescence. The clear air was a relief after the closeness of Betsy's apartment. Wendy and Jerry were the only smokers, but between them they had managed to cloud the apartment with a dense blue haze by the evening's end. On the street, Joan realized how oppressive it had been, and what a relief it was to breathe the sharp, cold air.

They walked in the old way, with Johnny's arm wrapped protectively around Joan's shoulders. Joan would have preferred to remain free, but she made no protest. "That was terrific of Betsy," she said. "It must have been a horrible lot of trouble. I can't even stand to think about it."

"She was glad to do it. We'd all have been glad to, but she wouldn't let anyone else do a thing except come."

"Well, everyone was wonderful to come. And on such short notice!"

Johnny looked tenderly at her. "No one would have missed it, Joanie," he said, hoarse with emotion.

It was so sad. At one time, just to have him talk to her, with his earnestness and intensity, would have thrilled her. Now she found him cloying, nearly unbearable. She made a tremendous effort not to pull away from him, but she couldn't keep herself from shuddering. She tried to turn it into a shrug, as if shifting the weight of a heavy cloak that was uncomfortably draped over her. Johnny took it for a shiver, and tightened his embrace. "Don't say that," she begged him. "It makes me feel so . . . *sick*. I'm not dying, you know."

Johnny didn't reply, but his crushed look spoke for him. Joan knew the expression well. She felt its reproof. "Well, I'm not," she went on. "Why does everyone have to act as though I have only a few months to live. I'm beginning to wonder if my next breath will be my last. It's bad enough that they made me leave college and have everybody think I'm pregnant, or else having a nervous breakdown. My father talks as though only the greatest miracle of modern medicine can possibly save me, and Mother, of course, takes the position that no daughter of hers is allowed to have anything *ordinary*, or *vulgar*. She has it all figured out that I have some weird exotic condition that's stumped all the doctors, and she's the only one who knows what's wrong with me. She always knows. No matter what they find, it'll turn out she knew all along. All the doctors are running around trying to please both of them, and everyone else is trying to grant me my last wish. The only person who treats me as though I have the slightest chance of pulling through this is Phil, and I know perfectly well that's because he loves anything macabre. He can't wait for me to fall down in the middle of Fifth Avenue or somehow make a spectacle of myself so he can make one of his stories out of it."

Johnny looked miserable. "Joanie, please . . ."

"Don't! Don't say anything! Don't tell me how much everyone loves me, and don't tell me everything's going to be just fine, and don't tell me I'm really so wonderful. *Please* don't tell me how wonderful I am. I really can't stand hearing it. You don't have any idea how horrible it is

for me to hear you say that, over and over. I'm not wonderful, and I
never have been. And having this . . . whatever it is, doesn't make me
any more wonderful, I can assure you. It isn't beautiful, you know, it
doesn't make me some kind of saint to keel over like that. It makes me
feel repulsive. When you tell me I'm not, you're not talking to *me;* you're
talking to someone else. Someone you've got in your mind. I'm not that
person, and I never have been."

Forbidden to speak, Johnny said nothing. He walked on, staring
straight ahead, stoical as always. To Joan he looked noble and extremely
handsome and insufferable. She knew there and then that she had been
right to break up with him, and even righter to resist all summer his
silent, unreproaching, unanswerable plea to take him back. Even now,
seeing how wounded he was by her outburst, which he had done nothing to provoke, she knew she could do nothing but hurt him. She
wouldn't smooth it over, wouldn't apologize or temper her words with a
little kindness. He would only draw some fantastical wild hope from
what was nothing more than a little decency. He always forced her to be
bitchy with him, and then he twisted it all inside out so that she wasn't
really a bitch, she was actually an angel. Well, she was no angel. He had
reason to know it as well as anyone, but he couldn't see her clearly. He
had his own conception of her, and it had been too much for her to live
up to in the end. It had drained her and exhausted her and eventually it
had done in what they had had together.

She steeled herself for his protest, or his soothing words that would
make everything come out sweetness and light; for his somehow manag-
ing to blame himself. But for once he surprised her, and only said, "You
know, Joanie, I don't pretend to understand you. I never have, and I
doubt that I ever will."

Although it was the last thing he ever intended, his words stung
her. If there was one thing Joan didn't like in herself, it was her devious-
ness. Johnny of course never suspected any such thing in her, hadn't
meant that at all. But she took it to heart, and replied meekly, "Am I so
complicated?" There was even a note of apology in her voice.

He nodded. "You are to me," he said; meaning he was too thick to
comprehend someone as elusive and ultimately mysterious as Joan. He
looked down at her wonderingly. "No one could convince me in a million years you were sick, Joanie," he said. "You're the most alive person
I know."

The ambush was too sudden. Her tears sprang forth reflexively, welling up from some hidden place where they had accumulated for weeks without her knowing they were there. As they streamed down her face, a sob of misery escaped, and for a moment she feared she might break down entirely.

They had come out from the side street onto Lexington Avenue. Joan turned downtown and would have continued walking, but Johnny stopped her and pulled her more tightly to him. She felt she was making a fool of herself in front of him, in front of anyone else who cared to look. Her face was buried in his chest, and she couldn't see if anyone was watching. A couple was in fact passing, but they were involved in their own drama, and noticed nothing. Had Joan been able to see, she would have found that the other woman was also crying. It was a night for tears. Scattered around Manhattan a score of couples were sharing their own private sorrow. A man walking his dog did see Joan, but he barely glanced at her. He turned to the window of the Barton's candy store with greater interest. In New York, people look at everything, and take in only a fraction of what they see. If she had in fact fallen down on Fifth Avenue, foaming at the mouth, she would have attracted only fleeting attention.

In any case, she didn't break down. She stopped crying after a minute and pulled away from Johnny. She sighed, not so much over her sad plight as over the fact that it had pushed her back onto him. She felt hopelessly compromised, as if she were penniless or pregnant and forced to turn to some unscrupulous protector. Johnny, of course, was a paragon of scruples. Still, what could he possibly think now, except that she wanted his love and devotion. No one was more prepared to shower it on her. He would see her through her ordeal and ask nothing in return. Johnny was a romantic, and he was also dogged. Joan knew that after this she would never be able to extricate herself. She could say what she liked, but now he would never give up. She might as well have broken down, so completely routed was she now. There was no defense from his solicitude.

She took her compact from her purse and redid her face. Joan was not a vain person and she couldn't have cared less what she looked like at eleven-thirty at night in the middle of Lexington Avenue. But she needed time to collect herself, to gather up what little remained of her resources, before delivering herself up to Johnny again. When she had finished, he put his arm around her shoulders again. It felt even heavier than before.

They walked back to 68th Street. She would have had to say something to put him off, to keep him from coming up with her. She was too tired, and he came up by default. The elevator man greeted him familiarly, placing his benediction, too, on their reconciliation. Everyone loved Johnny.

Inside the apartment, the front hall light was on, but the rest of the place was dark. Her parents must have gotten back from their concert, Joan was sure. Peggy would be asleep in bed, Alan reading in their bedroom. When, after a moment or two, he didn't come padding out in his pajamas to kiss her good evening, she guessed that her mother, through the first veil of sleep and several thick walls, had sensed Johnny's presence and had ordered her father to stay put. "I just want to see if she wants anything," he would have protested. "Shush!" was undoubtedly her mother's reply.

Joan took her coat off and gave it to Johnny, who hung it up in the front hall closet. "Do you want something to eat?" she asked. He shook his head. "A drink?"

"Maybe a Coke. I'll get it." He ducked inside the pantry door, opened the refrigerator, and took out a bottle. Bringing it into the darkened library, the room next to the living room, he opened the liquor cabinet and took a bottle opener from the little drawer underneath the glasses. After he had opened the cap, he dropped it into the wastebasket and reclosed the cabinet.

Joan had come into the library and sat down on the couch. Johnny went over to the light switch at the door, but she said, "Why don't you leave it off." He hesitated, took a long drink from the Coke bottle, and came over to sit down next to her. In the old days he would have put on the television set and clicked over the channels until he found a movie, any movie. Tonight he left it off.

"So," he said, settling in cozily, "what's on for the weekend, Joanie?" She didn't answer him. By the dim light coming in from the hallway, he could see that she had leaned her head back against the couch and closed her eyes. She looked asleep, but he couldn't tell if she was. He finished off his Coke in a couple more swigs and looked around for a place to put the bottle where it wouldn't leave a ring on the polished wooden table. He found a silver ashtray, which he recognized as the one given to Alan in appreciation of his chairmanship of some fund drive or other.

Joan wasn't asleep, nor was she quite awake. She drifted in and out of a somnolent stupor like a swimmer bobbing up and down on the water's surface. Hypnagogic visions passed before her—faces, disconnected bodies, intertwined couples. They glided by, slowly at first, then faster and more wildly until they seemed to be swept up in a torrent. Joan tried to steady herself by clinging to Johnny, as a boat might be lashed to its mooring to keep from being swept out to sea, or dashed against the rocks.

Feeling dizzy, she opened her eyes and lifted her head. It felt heavy and wobbly, and it throbbed slightly. She was too weak to hold it up, but she didn't want to lie back against the couch and succumb to sleep. Instead she turned so that she was half lying against Johnny. Her head lay on his chest, her arm was flung over the edge of the couch. He stroked her hair. The strong beating of his heart stayed absolutely regular, with no quickening. Passion was out of character for Johnny. When he had first asked her out, she had suffered a fever of dreadful excitement. Till then he had been one of Phil's friends, older and inaccessible, and she couldn't believe he had decided to bestow himself on her. She had done her tedious apprenticeship with the boys she had gone to school with, and she was ready for ecstasy.

She hadn't reckoned with his rules. His rigid chivalry, compounded by his worship of what he imagined to be her purity, dictated a chaste two years. If he had ever guessed the lewdness of her wishes! Her cousin Barbara Altman, who was at that time being whisked off to Puerto Rico for an abortion, was considered the last word in nymphomania in the family; Joan thought herself to be worse: a secret whore. By the time she began to suspect she was not completely depraved, she also understood that Johnny's reticence had a life of its own.

That was another age; another world. In the midst of her vertigo and fatigue, Joan wasn't thinking clearly. Lying with her cheek pressed against Johnny's crewneck Shetland sweater, his warm, familiar presence surrounding her, she felt aroused; not the languorous, muted stirrings she expected, but something sharp and urgent. She felt a skittish nervousness, her body was taut, she was increasingly agitated. She wanted sensation, stimulation, something astringent; she wanted a struggle, an attack. She took Johnny's head in both her hands and pulled it down toward her face. The resulting impact fell between a kiss and a collision. Startled, Johnny embraced her as if she were made of fragile porcelain. Goaded by an unbearable tension, Joan opened her lips and pulled his head even more fiercely down on her mouth. At the same time she moved her hand down to his thigh and stroked it. She could feel him contract with alarm. She craved for him to touch her breast, be rough with her, do something dirty and forbidden. But he remained passive. It was like coaxing a statue into arousal. She wanted to rip off his clothes and be wild, terrible, scandalous. She would have had a hard time imagining what that might be, even if she didn't know that he would flee in horror. He tried—poor Johnny!—to respond to what must have seemed to him to be a manifestation of her pathological condition. Maybe it was. In any case, it was no use. He had neither the experience nor the desire to do anything more than stay at his post.

They weren't getting anywhere, so she let him go. He gamely kissed her again, more in the spirit of a tough challenge than from any remotely sexual impulse. Knowing the effort it was costing him, Joan pulled away. He faced her with the expression of a fighter who has absorbed a terrific punch without being knocked out and is bracing himself for the next one. Joan didn't assault him again. Now she only wanted him to go. She lay back on the couch again. "So what're you up to over the weekend?" he asked again. Except for the huskiness of his voice, he betrayed nothing of the intervening ordeal.

Joan didn't answer his question. She had run out of energy. "Good night," she said dully, wishing he would be gone, not wanting to go through the ritual of seeing him out the door. Johnny was so confused that he didn't know whether to feel wounded or triumphant. Cautious as he was, and familiar with Joan's capriciousness, he reserved judgment. He did understand that she wanted him to leave. He always had his good manners to fall back on. He might have felt awkward about whether or not to give her a normal good-night kiss at the door, but that at least had been rendered irrelevant. He tried to say something in parting, but she was swaying on her feet and clearly wanted him to leave quickly. He patted her arm and said, "I'll call you." She nodded, her eyes closed as she stood.

Virtually the instant the door had shut behind him, even before the elevator had come, Joan heard her father coming down the hall. He shuffled in his slippers, in contrast to the brisk gait he used when walking down a street in the city. "Mom's asleep," he said. Joan figured as much, since otherwise he would not have been allowed out of the bedroom. "How was your evening?"

"Fine," Joan said. She didn't want to tell him there had been a party. He would want to know who was there, what did they eat, all the details. "It was fine."

"How was Laurent?" he asked.

"It was good," she said. The lie came easily in her half-asleep state. "A nice place. Phil likes it."

"A bit on the chichi side for me," Father said. He thought that any restaurant more elegant than the Automat was chichi. Why pay an arm and a leg, he always said, to eat less well than you can right here at home? "Did you go somewhere afterward?"

"We went to Betsy's," she said, following Peggy's maxim "When you have to lie, use the available truth."

"Did Phil come home with you?" he asked, frowning. He knew perfectly well Phil hadn't. Alan still thought unmarried people shouldn't sleep together, but he wouldn't have said a word directly to Phil, not in a million years.

"Phil stayed there for a while. Johnny brought me home."

"Johnny! That's nice." He feigned surprise. "Nice boy, Johnny. Always did like him. Glad to see him back in the . . . well . . . swim of things. . . ." He knew he had overshot his mark. "Would you like something to eat?" he asked quickly.

"I'm not hungry." Out of the frying pan and into the fire.

His brow creased with worry. "How are you . . . feeling."

"I'm *fine*, Daddy," she said, more petulantly than she intended. "If you want something to eat, I'll sit with you," she offered by way of apology.

He brightened like a little boy who has been offered a lollipop. They went into the kitchen together. Joan sat at the table while Alan catalogued the contents of the refrigerator. Nothing tempted her, though. He hadn't said a thing since she had returned home about how thin she had become. Peggy had forbidden it, and also the doctors were supposedly attending to it, although he was dubious about that. He couldn't resist the opportunity: "Some fried chicken?" he offered. "There's some leg of lamb left over from tonight. Oooh, here's a cheese-cake that isn't to be sniffed at, I can vouch for that *poissonally*. There's also some pretty high-class gully-gully here. Some sort of mousse, I don't know, it seemed terribly rich to me, but the dean ate it like it was his first square meal in weeks. Not a bad *schmecker*, the dean. Would you like some?"

She didn't want anything. At his urging she accepted an apple.

"They're Golden Delicious," she observed, to make up for choosing something so plain.

He fixed himself a bowl of cereal, shredded wheat, with skim milk. "I never use any sugar," he said with quiet pride. "You don't eat the peel?" he asked, dismayed that she was paring away large chunks of the apple. "I think that's the best part of all. All the vitamins . . . Here, let me." He took the fruit from her and peeled the rest expertly, the skin coming off in one continuous strip, almost translucent in its thinness. "There's an apple for you!"

"How was the concert?" Joan asked.

He beamed at the memory. "Beautiful. No. Make that heavenly. There's no one in the world today who can touch Rubinstein. Some say Horowitz, but you can have Horowitz. Much too loud. No, for my money it's Rubinstein, any day of the week. Playing Chopin." Suddenly he was struck with chagrin. "Would you have liked to come? I don't know why we didn't think of it!"

Joan smiled. "Daddy, it would have been wasted on me. You know I can't tell Rubinstein from Horowitz."

Alan winced. "Just let me know," he said, still only partly reassured he hadn't deprived her of a magnificent concert, and himself of her company. "Any time you want to go, just say the word."

They sat and ate together for a moment; or rather, Alan ate his cereal while Joan nibbled at a slice of the apple like a mouse exploring a rather dubious piece of cheese.

"Mom tells me Meyer House was a great success," he said. Joan smiled wanly. "You don't think you're taking on too much there?" She shook her head. The issue was closed. Peggy had settled that. "If you get a chance, it wouldn't be a bad idea if you were to telephone your aunts. They're anxious to know how you are."

"Daddy, they find out exactly how I am from you!"

"Well—only if you want to. I know they'd love to hear from you. If you have a chance," he added warily. Peggy had settled that too.

Joan didn't reply. She had put down the apple slice and sat, not so much watching him as staring off into space. She looked to him frighteningly pale, thin, exhausted. He groped for something positive to say.

"That Johnny Krieger certainly is a nice boy," he hit on. "I've always liked him."

"I know, Daddy."

"Nice-looking too."

Joan started to be annoyed, then stopped herself. "Now don't start pushing us back together, or I won't see him again, period."

Dad looked embarrassed. "I wasn't . . . it hadn't occurred . . . not that it wouldn't be terribly nice, but I assure you it was the far-thest—"

"I know perfectly well you're just trying to marry me off," she teased him.

"Oh, sugarpie, I'm not! It's much too early for you to—" He stopped, saw she was only joking, and looked terribly relieved. "It's just that I would think it would be nice for you, if you have to be out of college for a while, to have a little fun right here. I dare say there are a few fraternities in Williamstown where your absence from Bennington has been noted."

"I can assure you, there are no fraternities anywhere where anyone gives a good goddamn."

"Oh!" Alan said, as shocked by the language as by the idea, "I can't believe that! But you do find college great fun, don't you?"

Joan sighed. Her father had a hopelessly jazz-age view of college. "I like it a lot. I would certainly like to get back as soon as possible," she said, suppressing her impatience.

"Of course you would," Alan said, seeing he was on thin ice. "We'd all like you to. Although, I must say it's terribly nice having you with us for a while. It's been a long time since we've had all you kids home. I'm sure the doctors will have you back on your feet in no time."

"Dad, I'm on my feet," Joan said irritably.

"Of course you are," he agreed hastily. He knew he was blundering, but it was so hard to find the right thing to say. She was so touchy. Part of the . . . whatever it was, he supposed. "Mom's, you know, more worried than she admits . . . just a few more tests, and I'm sure—"

"I really don't want to talk about it," she said curtly, and got up. "I think I'll go to bed, if you don't mind. I'm really beat."

Alan was alarmed. "By all means. Of course. Don't let me keep you up."

But he was disappointed. The midnight snack had not turned into the intimate chat he had hoped for. He knew he should have kept his mouth shut.

Joan saw his crushed look. "I'll see you in the morning," she said more tenderly.

"You'll be here?" he asked in confusion. He wasn't used to having her home yet. "I mean, you don't have any plans?"

"Not a one," she said, smiling once more. "We can talk some more then. I just have to get my head on a pillow now."

"Of course you do, sweetheart. You go to bed. I'll see you in the morning." He looked once more like a happy little boy, dressed neatly in his bathrobe.

Joan came over and bent down, and he gave her a soft kiss on her forehead. "Good night, Daddy," she said.

"Good night, sweetheart. Sleep well. Pleasant dreams."

He ate his cereal after she had gone, feeling a mixture of contentment and vague worry. When he had finished, he noticed the apple, barely touched on the plate. He wasn't hungry any more, but it seemed a shame to waste a perfectly good Golden Delicious apple, and it was already peeled. He ate it, quarter by quarter. He emptied the core and peels into the wastebasket, washed all the dishes so the maids wouldn't come in to a dirty kitchen the next morning, checked around before turning off the lights, and shuffled off back to his room. He had a fair amount of reading to do before he could go to sleep.

Six

The Altman family adored music. Of all the arts, it was the one that affected them the most emotionally, that gave them the deepest pleasure. Frieda Altman was an ardent concertgoer. She had a box at the Philharmonic for odd Thursday evenings and took two seats for the alternate Friday afternoon concerts. She subscribed to the lush Philadelphia and to the venerable Boston, although she missed both Stokowski and Koussevitsky. She had kept the same Monday evening seats at the Met her parents had sat in. She also attended numerous recitals and chamber music concerts, not only at Carnegie Hall but also at Town Hall, and once in a great while would patronize the Grace Rainey Rogers Auditorium of the Metropolitan Museum. Although it would have been convenience itself, she didn't go to the Sunday afternoon concerts at the Frick Collection, only a block away from her home; it probably had something to do with her great antipathy to Frick and all he stood for, and perhaps a slight touch of a collector's jealousy. She had never once been to a concert at the 92nd Street Y; an institution not in general frequented by the family, despite the fact that the hall there was named after Mrs. Altman's uncle Henry Totenberg. He and her father had not been on the friendliest of terms.

The rest of the family trooped off to concerts with varying degrees of enthusiasm. Peggy and Alan enjoyed going to the Philharmonic with Mrs. Altman whenever they could make it. Peggy also went with her to a number of other concerts when she needed company, although never to the opera, which was an art form totally alien to Peggy's straight-to-the-point philosophy of life. Also, that much raw emotion was not really to her taste. Alan especially loved piano recitals, none more than those of his idol, Artur Rubinstein. The rest of the family attended sporadically. Eleanor Altman enjoyed concerts immensely since she had not had many opportunities to go as a child. No one could remember seeing Gerald's eyes stay open much beyond the opening chords of any given piece.

As for actual musical talent, there was virtually none. Almost everyone in the family was tone-deaf. Listening to Alan butcher a melodic line in his cracked delivery was a frequent ordeal. Barbara Altman had a pleasant voice and went to a teacher for a time. But she remained steadfast in her musical illiteracy, and never progressed further than quite nice offerings of Rodgers and Hammerstein or Jerome Kern at parties. Joan was made to take piano lessons for a while, but that was a short-lived and stormy experiment.

Clearly any member of the family who could carry a tune would be considered a phenomenon. When Carl was discovered, at the age of four, picking out a melody at the keyboard, it was instantly decided that he was gifted. In the family, one didn't have mere aptitude. You were outstanding, or you were nothing. Just how outstanding he was, and how far he would go, remained a plaguing question for him throughout his childhood, but no one else shared his doubts. A governess was hired who, in addition to the usual duties, was charged with teaching him to read music. He started formal lessons in first grade. Peggy assumed he would quickly outstrip the limited capabilities of poor Miss Faber, who did her best despite the dire warning that she was nurturing a colossal talent.

He had been with her only a couple of years before he was taken to play for the great Rudolf Serkin. According to the legend, Serkin was so dazzled with his promise that he commanded the Gutheims to move to Philadelphia so that Carl could study with him at Curtis. Although that was clearly out of the question, evidently serious thought was given to sending him down. Some family friends, the Hirschheimers, were sounded out before the project was abandoned. For years afterward, whenever Carl saw them, they would tell him how crushed they were not to have had him, and all that glorious music, in their home. Alan was all in favor of it, but Peggy thought he was too young to go into orders, no matter how urgently Serkin supposedly argued the case. She was also—this was secondary—unwilling to have him raised by the Hirschheimers, who were kindly but hopelessly insipid fuddy-duddies.

As a consolation for being deprived of Serkin, a search was launched for the best teacher in New York. There was little doubt as to who that was in those days: Madame Ida Tamarovna, the high priestess of Juilliard. She auditioned him, and was perhaps a shade less thunderstruck than Serkin had been. But the upshot was that Miss Faber was immediately replaced by one of Madame Tamarovna's assistants, a bitter, disappointed man named Seymour Bloom; and when Carl was twelve he began lessons with Madame Tamarovna herself.

Carl himself had never been able to ferret out what minuscule portion of this fantastic story had any basis in reality. He remembered playing for Serkin, and there was no doubt that he wound up studying with Madame Tamarovna, whose other pupils were all either Juilliard students or professionals already launched on their careers. But he always assumed that he was among their number not because of any breathtaking talent but because his parents made it worth her while, or Juilliard's, or both. Certainly his ears never heard any evidence that he had a great future as a pianist. He loved music, to be sure, and he played with a certain precocious sensitivity, and occasionally beauty. A genius he wasn't. He hated practicing, and consequently never developed a solid technique. Through a judicious selection of repertoire, he could pass himself off to a sympathetic audience as a prodigy. But as he neared the threshold of his career, the ice he was skating on became thinner and thinner. He, if no one else, began to see cracks forming. At no time did he feel in greater peril of plunging into the freezing waters below than when he had to perform at one of Madame Tamarovna's master classes.

Madame held her classes once a month, always on Saturday afternoons at her apartment on Riverside Drive. The students would arrive at three o'clock—she disliked anyone to be either early or late—and were admitted by Sonya, a Russian émigrée almost as old as Madame herself. Madame always referred to Sonya as her companion, but she was in fact the maid. To be sure, it might have been that in prerevolutionary days Sonya had greater status, and she certainly passed herself off as a fallen aristocrat. She did attend concerts with Madame, and so in that respect fulfilled a companion's role, but on Monday afternoons she answered the door and brought in the tea and was ordered about by Madame in an imperious fashion. Then again, Madame spoke to everyone in an imperious fashion, so that wasn't a fair test. Sonya, it's true, never showed the slightest deference to any of the pupils, but that was always attributed to White Russian arrogance, found also in the salesladies in Fifth Avenue stores who had yet to get over the social outrage that overshadowed even their exile forty years earlier.

The students would leave their coats with Sonya and move nervously into the salon, as the living room was called. Madame greeted them each formally and they took their places. There was no chitchat before the music, and the interval between one's arrival and the beginning of the class was shrouded in the kind of silence usually reserved for church; except that their tension had an almost tangible quality. The lids of the two Steinways were always raised, gaping jaws of twin black monsters. On the rack of one piano were the scores of the pieces that were to be performed that afternoon. The other piano, which was used by the students, had been stripped of its rack, an ominous reminder that there was no recourse for a failing memory. Madame herself sat in the deepest armchair, elaborately dressed in one of her fantastic black gowns. She must surely have brought those gowns with her when she fled from Odessa; they could not possibly be American. She would be discovered in a deep reverie, to which she would revert between her mournful greetings to the pupils.

Years later, Carl could remember the details of that room with unwelcome clarity. He would always try to look appropriately enrapt, but his meditation was always contaminated by dread. The room was large, with high ceilings and windows that gave a view of the Hudson, or would have if the heavy curtains had not been perpetually drawn, as if in mourning. Against the wall opposite the pianos was the longest sofa he had ever seen anywhere. Six people could sit comfortably on it, and during the classes seven or eight of them were squeezed together without undue crush. Madame's armchair was upholstered in a red brocade that hinted only slightly of the brothel. Two other armchairs were supplemented for the class by folding chairs that contributed their bit to the torture if one was late enough to have to sit on one. There was a long coffee table of imitation marble and many occasional tables, draped in crocheted cloths, each of them crammed with photographs. These varied in age, the oldest being so yellow that Carl assumed they dated to Czarist days. Prominently displayed were dramatic studies of the great dead pianists—Rachmaninoff, Hofmann, Cortot, de Pachmann, Gabrilowitsch—effusively inscribed to Madame. After many years of looking at them, Carl realized that there was no picture of Josef Lhevinne, an interesting omission. Lhevinne's widow, Rosina, still taught at Juilliard, and was Madame's only rival there. Carl assumed that jealousy had either prevented Lhevinne from presenting Madame with his portrait, or she from putting it out.

On the coffee table, among the pictures, were cigarette boxes, bibelots, and other relics from Russia. Isolated in splendor was a glorious jeweled egg that when opened, revealed a delicately spun miniature piano of glittering silver. Only many years later did Carl learn, from another former pupil, that it was not by Fabergé. The pupil went so far as to suggest a provenance no more exotic than lower Fifth Avenue, but Carl was not prepared to believe him, even though Madame was by that time many years deceased.

At the time Carl attended master classes, the egg was still a magical and fascinating object. He used to exploit it as a mesmeric talisman, and he would concentrate on it in a desperate effort to hypnotize himself on those occasions when he had to perform. During the classes, Madame could draw on a full and considerable range of histrionics. There was little comfort in the knowledge that she directed her attacks, sooner or later, at everyone in the class, with no one suffering worse than the supposed "professionals"—she would roll out the word in her thick accent rich with irony—who had studied with someone else. He never knew how the others managed to weather these storms. For him, they were nearly insupportable. They confirmed his suspicion that he was an imposter without a shred of talent, kept on in sole consideration of an enormous fee. After playing in a master class, he invariably came home and begged Peggy to allow him to relapse to the pedestrian tutelage of Miss Faber; or better, to give up the piano altogether. Peggy would listen to him very calmly, as she always listened to anyone on the verge of hysterics, and would remind him that no one was forcing him to study the piano. He could, of course, do as he pleased. It would be a pity, she always added, to throw away an opportunity to contribute, to give people so much *real pleasure*; but he should do as he pleased. Which always shut him up, and quelled his sad little rebellion.

He remembered these classes by what he had to play. His first performance was a miserable rendition of a Mozart sonata, a leftover from his Seymour Bloom period. Madame commented unfavorably on the style, the technique, the tempo, and even his hand position. His only consolation was the knowledge that the real object of her scorn was her own lackey, Bloom, but he wasn't there and Carl bore the burden. She did say that his phrasing was natural, but he didn't know at the time that this was high praise.

He had a grace period of almost a year before having to play again. This time the piece was a Bach French suite. He got through the opening allemande and half the following courante, and then the roof fell in. He had thought that since he had studied the piece entirely under Madame, she might approve of one or two aspects of the interpretation. He couldn't have been more wrong. He didn't know yet that each new student was given, in his second or third performance, a thorough verbal beating. It was part of Madame's theory of becoming a professional. "If I don't say it now, the critics will later," she would say when she sensed that the student was on the verge of breaking down. Carl didn't break down, although he had no idea why he didn't. He wouldn't have been the first boy to do so, not by a long shot. The girls did regularly. It was a rare class that one or more girls didn't burst into tears. The crying was never commented on. It was considered a sign of temperament: extramusical, but not entirely discouraged if kept under decent control.

After the Bach, he had no more debacles, although every performance had its problems. He played a Schubert impromptu, a Scarlatti sonata, one of the Debussy Arabesques, and a Brahms intermezzo, which was much too difficult for him. Despite all the tricks he then knew, it still sounded like a bear growling. Madame must have been tired, or preoccupied that afternoon, because she let him off with only minor cuts and bruises.

For the class that took place the day after Joan's surprise party, he was to perform the third Chopin Ballade, the A-flat. As every pianist knows, it is the easiest by far of the Ballades. It had been chosen because, of all the major Chopin works, it has the fewest technical demands. Nevertheless, it is a major Chopin, and was a tremendous challenge for him. Actually, it was beyond him. He did his best with the notes, and by the time of the class he could just about get through it without falling on his face. The interpretation was, to be kind, still rudimentary. He had all he could do just to negotiate the passagework. Anything beyond that was a bonus. He should never have been playing it at all; but when Madame assigned a piece, there was no further discussion.

He was the first to arrive that day. Sonya was frostier than usual, but Madame, in the absence of other pupils, allowed a few moments of private informality. She asked after Joan. He was always surprised when she showed any interest in things nonmusical, but in fact she took an intense interest in the lives of her students. She was especially fascinated by their love lives, or what she fancied to be their love lives. Nothing threw her into greater ecstasy than two of her pupils having an affair. It was a rare occurrence, fraught with danger, since if it didn't culminate in marriage, it meant that Madame would have two estranged lovers on her hands. She couldn't tolerate that. Although her musical taste was impeccable and dry-eyed, in other respects she was a hopeless romantic who liked her plots simple, preferably mushy. Since she considered him far too young for sex—he never knew whether that was a carryover of some nineteenth-century Russian attitude, or a shrewd intuition about him—she kept tabs on his family instead. She may have been attracted by their wealth, although that possibility never occurred to him at the time. He was naive enough in those days to assume that no one had any knowledge of or interest in his family's status, financial or social. For himself, he disdained such matters, except when they were a source of embarrassment to him. He thought that, as the youngest of her pupils, he might have aroused whatever faint maternal instincts still stirred within her; and he was foolish enough to hope that she would go easy on him on that account. On this last, he miscalculated badly.

With the arrival of the other students, all intimacy ended. Carl's momentary calm gave way to performance nerves. It suddenly struck him that he didn't have the piece securely memorized. He tried to play it through in his mind, but the first phrase repeated itself over and over idiotically. Recognizing the first signs of panic, he stared at the supposed Fabergé egg, but it refused to come to his aid. The class assembled with disheartening speed, and he was summoned to perform.

He hadn't forgotten the notes, or at least his fingers had not. He got through the piece about as well as he could have expected. The fast passage in the left hand went surprisingly well, and as for the treacherous C-sharp minor broken chords toward the end, he just put down the pedal and plowed through with as much conviction as if he could actually play them. He knew it fooled no one in the room, but it wasn't a bad paraphrase of what Chopin actually wrote. He finished the piece with a brave flourish, and his fellow students applauded with a mixture of appreciation and disbelief. Whatever their true feelings, they were always generous to one another in public. He nodded his thanks and slumped down in the chair, exhausted physically and emotionally. Waiting for Madame's response, he imagined she might be gratified by his unforeseen . . . well, *triumph* was too strong a word; but something along those lines.

There came instead only the uninflected words "May we have the first phrase, if you please."

He didn't have any idea what to make of that. In some other setting, he could have heard it as a joke. The first phrase of the ballade consisted of the briefest melodic theme and its answer. It was simplicity itself. There was nothing to it. She must be giving me a respite, he thought, before going on to the hard parts. He played what she asked.

"I said the first phrase, not the first two phrases," she said as tonelessly as before. "Let's get one thing right before we move on to the next."

He repeated the opening phrase. With a huge effort, she emanated from her chair and went to the other piano. She played the same phrase, which was tantamount to her saying, "Words cannot convey my contempt." She glared at him, and he repeated the notes, trying to copy her exactly.

"It is impossible to produce anything other than ugliness with the wrist in that position," she said.

She then made him repeat the opening note—a single E-flat—again and again until his wrist, his hand, his finger, were held to her satisfaction. She had, of course, been teaching him herself for three years. It has also been scientifically established that the tone of one note can be produced as beautifully by an umbrella stick as by Gieseking. She nevertheless kept him at that damn E-flat for an eternity, before letting him attempt the next seven chords. After she had dissected, anatomized, analyzed, and reinterpreted those notes, she had him go on to the answering phrase, which was subjected to the same torturous process. When she then called for the entire passage, it turned out that the first phrase had slipped back and had to be relearned.

Finally he played the entire thing to her satisfaction. It had taken the better part of an hour. She lumbered back to her armchair and muttered, "We will reserve comment on the rest until you can manage the notes. Amelia?" she indicated the next performer.

He sat, stunned and shaken. Amelia appeared next to him, waiting patiently for him to cede the bench to her. Dazed, he returned to his place, which was unfortunately right next to Madame, owing to his early arrival. "A little practice presumably would not seriously damage your remarkable version of the C-sharp minor section," she added dryly, lest he might think she hadn't seen through his ruse with the pedal. "The Schumann?" she said to Amelia. She was through with him.

The rest of the class was a blur. He heard nothing of the Schumann, which was a pity, because Amelia was Amelia Ostrovski, who went on to a major career. Her performance that day must have been creditable, because he did remember Madame saying, "Not too bad," when she finished. "Not too bad" was her highest accolade. When they were drinking tea after the class, Amelia took him aside and whispered, "It happens to everyone. One time she made me do the first four measures of the 'Pathetique' for the entire class. She never even got to the next piece. To this day I can't hear that damn sonata without wanting to throw up. Don't let it get to you."

Nevertheless, her soothing words that day didn't entirely cure his despair. If, after all these years, he couldn't even play a simple phrase, what future was there for him? What hope was there if he couldn't even hold his wrist properly? He was angry at Madame for assigning him a piece he couldn't play, and angry at himself for thinking he could get away with it, and angriest at fate for its cruel joke of making people think he had talent where he was bankrupt. This would be his last master class, he resolved. He wouldn't be so weak as to let his mother manipulate him into coming back.

As they were all leaving, Madame called over to him from her armchair, "If you would be so good as to stay for a few minutes, Carl, I would like a word or two with you." The others looked pityingly at him over their shoulders as they left. If Madame had something to say that couldn't be said in front of the class—considering what she *did* say in front of them—it must be pretty dire. He was sure she was going to kick him out. He shouldn't have minded, since he had himself decided to quit, but the shame of it would be hard to bear. It would be harder to explain to his family than flunking out of school, and just as improbable in their eyes. It was not beyond the realm of possibility that they would urge Madame to take him back, perhaps adding still further inducement. There seemed to be no end to the possibilities for humiliation.

When the others were gone, she had him come and sit next to her. "I was a little hard on you today, no?" she asked. Sonya was still in the room, clearing up the teacups. She pretended not to be listening, but he could tell from the grim smile that played on her sour, wizened face that she was enjoying his discomfort. "It is not pleasant, I know, to be told that your playing is not wonderful. Especially since your family all makes a great fuss over you. I'm sure that your father would have fainted with pleasure over that performance." She spoke now without sarcasm, although Sonya broadened her hideous grin. "You and I know better, though," she continued, patting him on the knee. "And I must call a spade a spade. One day the critics will be doing it, so better at least you should hear it first from me, so you do not say afterward, Madame did not tell me the truth."

None of this was exactly balm to his wounds; still, it was evident that she was not dismissing him. She spoke with the assumption that one day he would be playing for the critics. His own thoughts of quitting were fast fading.

"Actually," she went on, "some of it was not too bad. Toward the end, after the C-minor mess was over, I heard one or two interesting ideas. Rough, still, but they may come along. If you put your mind to it, and also practice a little, I think you could play it at the next student recital." She gave him a sly glance to see how he was taking the astonishing news that he was to perform at Juilliard. It was unthinkable. After an arduous and trying afternoon, he hardly believed what she was telling him.

"You can do it," she assured him. "All it takes is practice, practice, and more practice." She patted his knee again, to indicate her confidence and also that it was time for him to go. As always, there was to be no discussion.

He did ask when the recital would be. "I don't know," she replied with her usual airiness about practical matters. "Somewhere around Christmas." Sonya was waiting with his coat.

Somewhere around Christmas, he repeated to himself as he walked out of the building onto Riverside Drive. He inhaled deeply, surprised by the cold, urbanized brine of the Hudson that came in on the west wind. Christmas was six weeks away. There was no possibility he could play that piece at Juilliard in six weeks' time. It would be a debacle. He could see a lifetime of recitals stretching out before him, each more terrible than the last, a never-ending succession of classes, recitals, examinations, competitions that would stop only when he was finally finished off. The city was filled with the carcasses of musicians who hadn't made it. He himself wouldn't starve, barring the revolution, but he could easily share the rest of their lot. He could become another Seymour Bloom with no trouble at all.

If he had any hope of avoiding that fate, he would have to make his bid for freedom. Just the idea of it scared him. He couldn't imagine telling his mother—Madame—the world—that he was giving up his nonexistent career. He doubted he could carry it off. He didn't have a whole lot of time left, either. Soon the door would clang shut, and his escape routes would be cut off.

Seven

As the rabbi intoned mournfully, "The Lord is my shepherd; I shall not want," a rustling noise, like dry leaves being stirred by a wind, came from the expectant congregation. The organ whirred into a soft accompaniment of the rabbi's recitation, while the bier, blanketed with white carnations, rumbled down the aisle on its final journey. At the words "Yea, though I walk through the valley of the shadow of death," the congregation rose to its feet with a great whooshing sound. As the Psalm ended, the organ swelled into a sonorous, lugubrious dirge.

Peggy, standing at the aisle, had an unobstructed view of the coffin as it passed. The pallbearers were all obviously employees of Frank E. Campbell. They were substantial, solid-looking men in their forties and fifties, serious, respectful, stolid. Off-duty cops, Peggy thought, retired army sergeants, reformed minor thugs. Directly following the coffin came the family. Harriet Weinstein was in black, with a veil. Peggy tried to catch her eye, so she could convey her sympathy and incidentally show she was there. The family of the deceased always closeted themselves in that cramped, unpleasant little room behind the altar before the ceremony, and then they were whisked into the front limousine, just behind the hearse. "It makes no sense," Peggy told Alan after Harriet had passed without the slightest sign that she had seen them, or anyone else, for that matter; she appeared quite preoccupied. "You come to these things for only one reason: to show consideration for the family; and then they haven't any idea who's here. You might just as well stay home, for all the good it does."

"I thought it was a very moving service," Alan said. He was always saddened when he heard the Twenty-third Psalm at a funeral, and the lines from Tennyson had particularly touched him. He made a note to look them up that night. He hadn't recognized them. *In Memoriam*, no doubt.

"I thought it was for the birds," Peggy announced. Alan didn't argue with her. Everyone's attention was absorbed in the business of getting into the aisle, so they could get out of the place, with its scent of mortality.

Ellie Bamberg squeezed in next to Peggy as the family passed her row. "Wasn't that a magnificent service?" she asked with a satisfied sigh of sorrow. "I think he does the *most wonderful* job, this new one. It must have been a great comfort to Harriet."

"I think he's for the birds," Peggy said again. She could endure just so much after being subjected to that rabbinical whine for an hour and Ellie Bamberg's sentimentality was more than she could put up with.

"I thought he spoke beautifully," Ellie insisted. Her natural horror of contradicting anyone, let alone Peggy Gutheim, was overcome by her shock at hearing a rabbi criticized. At a funeral, no less. "The old one always spoke in a monotone."

"Dear, I hate to tell you, but the 'old' one, as you call him, has been dead for about fifteen years, now."

"Thirteen years," Alan corrected her.

"Is it that long, really?" Ellie asked.

"Time moves on, dear," Peggy informed her. They inched down the rest of the aisle in silence until they came to a complete stop. Peggy tried to see around those ahead of her to find out what was holding things up. Her view was blocked by Ellie, who thereby became all the more irritating, if possible. Peggy twisted the other way around and said to Phil, "At this rate I'm afraid we may not get you home in time for your football game."

"It doesn't start until two," Phil said. "I'm all right unless someone keels over now and they have to do another service as an emergency."

Alan turned around. "I've seen molasses flow faster than this in January," he said.

Near the back of the temple, separated from the rest of the congregation, stood a small group of older people, dressed simply. They stood respectfully as the others passed. One old woman among them was weeping openly. "The servants," Peggy whispered to Alan. "Isn't that the girl who waits on table there? Or used to, we haven't been there in such a long time. Yes, I'm sure that's her." She caught the woman's eye and smiled warmly at her to make it clear that she, at least, knew servants had feelings. Probably they were more upset than most of the people who had sat up front. It angered Peggy that they were segregated from the rest, treated as second-class. "I wish I could figure out a way to see to it that the help weren't always shunted aside," she said to Alan. "I've never understood why people think that just because someone is a maid they don't feel these things as strongly as anyone else."

"I think," Alan replied with his lawyer's caution, "that, given their choice, they would elect to sit back there. They probably feel more comfortable among themselves."

"That's only because we make them feel uncomfortable if they're not. Besides which, it's not their choice."

"I doubt that they even think about it," Alan suggested.

"Well, I do," Peggy retorted, frowning. "I don't believe in making other people's decisions on their behalf. How are you doing, sweetie pie?" she asked Joan, who had come after all. Peggy thought she looked very becoming in her new coat, which they had had Bergdorf's rush over the day before when Joan had decided, completely on her own, to come to the funeral. Although she did look so terribly pale. Peggy was adjusting herself to Joan's thinness; but her pallor was really alarming, especially when she was as exhausted as she had been ever since coming down from college. The doctors would say little; they had scheduled more tests for the next day. Peggy dreaded them. She said nothing, of course, but she dreaded them.

"I'm *fine*, Mother," Joan said. She hated being fussed over, especially at a funeral when people should be thinking of Mr. Weinstein, not her.

"I see your Aunt Cissy. If she's still there when we get out of here, if we ever do, you'd better say hello. She's making your poor father's life miserable because you haven't called her since coming home. Which is of course pure stuff and nonsense, but there it is."

"Oh, God, where is she?" Joan asked, trying to see.

"She's just gone out the door. See, there's Uncle Edgar." Edgar Hirsch was more or less holding the door for presumably the rest of the congregation, since several people were going past him as if he were an usher. Cissy wasn't at all close to the Weinsteins, but she was an inveterate funeralgoer. On reading obituaries, her friendship with the deceased would begin to intensify steadily until the day of the service, when she would arrive practically prostrate with grief.

Eventually the family did reach the door. They passed through to the outer vestibule of the temple, which was just as jammed as the aisle had been. Few people were ready to go home, or to get into the cars that were waiting to speed them to the cemetery. Some of the Frank E. Campbell functionaries were trying their officious best to expedite the process so they could be on their way, but it was raw and threatening outside, and no one wanted to leave the sanctuary of the temple.

"Oh, for goodness' sake," Peggy exclaimed, looking around as soon as they emerged. "There's Albert Solomon. How long has it been since we've seen him?"

"Probably not since the last funeral," Alan guessed.

"He can't still be active in the firm, is he?" Albert Solomon had been a partner of Altman & Sons in Nathan Altman's day.

"I think he still goes down to the office once or twice a month, and they tell me he still attends all the partners' meetings."

"He must be, what, in his late seventies, wouldn't you think?"

"Easily that. He could well have seen the last of eighty by now. Hello, Edna," he called to a woman just coming out of the doorway.

"Hello, Alan. Peggy, dear. How are you? Terribly sad, isn't it?"

"Yes, it certainly is," Peggy agreed. "Still, he led a very useful life."

"He most certainly did. A wonderful person. It's always very sad, though."

"You know my two young people, don't you? This is Phillip, and this is Joan. You know Mrs. Margolis, of course." Everyone smiled and shook hands. "Joan's just down from college. We're thrilled to have her back with us again. She's going to be, you'll be interested to know, working at Meyer House, with Martin."

"Oh, how wonderful! Following in your mother's footsteps, I see. Meyer House is a wonderful agency."

"Mrs. Margolis knows what she's talking about," Peggy informed Joan. "She's been on the board of the Co-operating Settlement Houses for—how long is it, Edna?"

"Longer than I care to think. Actually, I'm no longer on the board, you know, Peggy. I got off just this fall."

"Oh?" Peggy was dismayed. "I'm sorry to hear that."

"I decided to retire before they got around to asking me to. There are so many capable young people today, it seems a shame to clutter up these boards with us ancient relics."

Peggy and Alan both protested vigorously, and then Peggy asked after Mrs. Margolis's daughter Anne, whom she had grown up with. She had never much liked her, but the woman lived in St. Louis now, which was a safe enough distance that Peggy could afford to show interest. They all said good-bye, and as Mrs. Margolis walked away, the others could see that her right hip was stiff, and she rose a little on that leg as she searched for someone else who might bridge the journey between the funeral service and the bleak day outside, with a long afternoon alone to look forward to.

"Let's stand over here, shall we?" Peggy suggested. "That way we won't be smack in the way of people trying to get out of the door." She moved everyone a few steps to the left. "Now *that*," she continued, "is a woman who has really contributed. Before she came into the picture, every settlement house was going off in different directions, no one paying the slightest attention to what anyone else was doing. I said she was on the board, but she was the one who really got Co-operating Settlement going. No, she's a really useful person. You might find her quite interesting to talk to," she told Joan. "She used to, incidentally, be quite a good friend of your great-aunt Lucy."

"I'll tell you who she is," Alan said. "She was Edna Mengleberg. Her father was Irving Mengleberg, who started Northern Gas."

"Darling, they haven't the slightest idea who Irving Mengleberg was."

"Who, Irv Mengleberg?" Alan asked in astonishment. "He was a very distinguished man, I'll tell you that. And he had a marvelous sense of humor in the bargain. That's his daughter," he said, completing the gestalt. Peggy winked at Joan. "Hello, Howie," he greeted a doleful-looking man who was passing.

"Hello, Alan," Howie answered. "Hello, Peggy." He kissed Peggy. "How are you, Phil? They keeping you busy up there at law school?"

Peggy saw that he couldn't remember Joan's name. "You know our Joan, don't you?"

"Of course I do. How are you? Down for the funeral? Still at Smith?"

"Bennington," Joan said, leaving the rest unexplained.

"Of course, Bennington. I can't keep them straight. In my day it was easier. If a girl was in the city, she was at Barnard, and if she wasn't, she was at Vassar, and that was that. Except for your mother, who never did anything the way you were supposed to, even then. Ellen is at Oberlin, which didn't even exist in those days, as far as I or anyone else knew." He was referring to his niece. Ellen Eisman was a pathetically shy girl who had shown up dutifully at all the dances and had never, to anyone's knowledge, been known to smile. "I don't know why she couldn't go to a place one can get to. Or even find on a map."

"It's a very popular college these days," Joan assured him. "And very hard to get into." Ellen had been considered a brain at Nightingale-Bamford, for whatever that was worth.

"How is Dorothy?" Alan asked, modulating his voice into the hushed tone one uses when talking about the terminally ill.

"She's the same, I'm afraid," Mr. Eisman said gravely. "No worse, but unfortunately no better. But—we don't give up. They say they're doing some new work on this in Rochester, and one of their top people there is coming down for a consultation. So—there's always hope."

"You mean the Mayo?" Alan asked.

"No, Rochester, New York. I gather it's very up-and-coming. They have a lot of Eastman money there, you know."

"Oh, don't I know! We try to get some of it once in a while for Mt. Sinai, but it all goes to the medical center there. A very fine place, I'm told. I hope something will turn up, no matter where. Give her our best, will you?"

"I certainly will. She'll be delighted to hear. She still takes just as much interest as always in everything that's going on. She'll want to hear all the details as soon as I get home. Nice to see you all."

"So long, Howie," Alan said. When Mr. Eisman had moved out of earshot, he added, "Poor soul. Must be a terrible strain on him to have to come to a funeral."

"Why does he come, then?" Peggy wondered.

"Probably wants to bone up," Phil suggested.

"Phil!" Joan gasped, scandalized but laughing.

"He and Percy were very close," Alan explained. "Bad enough to have your wife on the one-yard line, but then to have one of your best friends go, from the exact same thing."

"Is she really?" Peggy asked skeptically. "It seems to me she's been on the brink for years and years."

"Oh, this time it's for keeps, from what I hear. A matter of weeks. I think whoever they have coming down from Rochester must be to reassure her that everything possible is being done. I doubt if Saint Luke himself could save her at this point." They were all sobered for a moment, even Phil, thinking of Dorothy Eisman, wasting away in pain.

It was getting on. Phil was planning to go home to watch the football game on television, and Joan would of course go with him. "Don't wait for us to have your lunch, dear," Peggy told her daughter. "There's no telling when we'll get back. I've told them to put Phil's on a tray, and you can have them do the same for you if you want."

"I thought actually I'd come out to the cemetery," Joan said.

"Why on earth?" Peggy exclaimed. "No one expects you to."

"I'm not coming because anyone expects me to," Joan replied. "I'd like to, that's all. If it's all right."

"Of course it's all right, dear. You do just as you want." Peggy was thoroughly mystified. She couldn't imagine why anyone in their right mind would want to drive out to Valhalla on a dreary day to see a coffin lowered into the ground, but she kept her mouth shut. Joan led her own life. "It'll be nice to have your company."

Barbara Altman, looking uncharacteristically sorrowful in a black hat and coat, came over. She and Joan hadn't seen each other since Joan came down from college, and they hugged. "You look very becoming, dear," Peggy told Barbara, accepting a kiss from her niece. "Would you like to come out to the cemetery with us? Joan's coming after all, and that way you two could have a visit."

"Oh, I'd love to, Aunt Peggy," Barbara said, "but Mummy's got it all arranged. I'm sure she wouldn't want to change the seating now." Peggy smiled her understanding of her sister-in-law's inflexibility. "Why don't you ride with us?" she suggested to Joan. "Mummy wouldn't mind that. They're going with Mrs. Weinstein, so it wouldn't be too awful. You'd have to put up with Marian, but she'll sulk, and we can gab."

Joan smiled. "I'd love to come with you, but I think I'll stay with the folks," she said. "I'm dying to see you, Bobbie. I'll call you." The two cousins repeated their hugs, and Barbara went back to the Altman group.

"Wouldn't you rather go with Barbara?" Peggy asked. She was horrified that Joan might be doing this out of some sense of obligation, to hold her hand, or some such nonsense. It couldn't be sweeter, but as far as she was concerned, no one need ever worry about Peggy Gutheim.

"I'd really rather come with you and Dad," Joan said.

"It's very nice of you," Peggy told her. "Your father will be pleased."

People were starting to say good-bye to one another. Those who were going home readied themselves for a harsh journey, while the mourners who were to attend the burial allowed themselves to be led toward the waiting cars. The sociable atmosphere in the vestibule began to chill into a kind of apprehension: of going outside, of the journey to come, of what lay at its end. Peggy said they ought to go. They took their leave of Phil on Fifth Avenue, and found the limousine waiting for them. They were among the last to come, and shortly after they were handed into their car, the procession started off. As it moved slowly up Fifth Avenue, people stopped to pay their respects. Several men took off their hats, remaining motionless and somber as the cortege passed by.

Their car was one of the last to arrive at the cemetery. When they reached the grave site, most of the mourners were already there. It was cold and depressing, but Joan was glad she had come. Her father looked quite shaken now. Seeing a coffin, hearing the final prayers, thinking about the last days of Percy Weinstein, he was undoubtedly reminded also of his own parents, buried in the same cemetery. It would be a comfort to him to have his daughter next to him. When she took her place at his side, he looked terribly grateful. Peggy looked at her fondly, too, and whispered, "I like that coat. I think we did very well."

The rabbi, weighing his obligation to the last stragglers against the sharp chill of the wind, began:

"O Lord our God, King of the Universe, we lay to rest here all that remains mortal of our beloved friend, Percy Weinstein . . ."

The somber, dreadful cadences sounded somehow more fitting out in the open, with the cold air whipping people's faces and the dark clouds threatening snow again. The coffin seemed more real with the grave gaping beside it. One could believe that there was in fact a body inside; that the end had finally come for Percy Weinstein.

"As it must for all . . ."

Joan had never really known him. She had been introduced in the course of things several times, perhaps often, but she could barely visualize a face. Someday it would be her father. She wondered if he thought about it. His own father had died early. A stroke. The same age he was now. The next funeral might be his. If not her own: she had a premonition that she would go before them all. A terrible thought. She couldn't believe it, not seriously. Maybe she ought to, though. Everyone was so worried about her. They couldn't figure out what was the matter with her. She wondered if she might really be sick after all. She was no longer certain whether she was bringing all this on herself or not. Maybe something inside her was causing it, something beyond her control. Something controlling her. She imagined them coming to tell her they had found a brain tumor, she had only a month to live. She had a fleeting vision of herself stretched out on a bier, white with death. Grieving relatives, the servants weeping softly. She didn't believe any of it. She didn't believe this was all happening to her in the first place. It could be a dream, she would wake up and be back at Bennington . . .

> *Did you ever think, when the hearse went by,*
> *That you might be the next to die?*

A blessing, her mother had said. Cancer, pain, terrible suffering. The only other funeral she had been to was Aunt Lucy's. A dear old woman, but hardly a tragedy at eighty-three years of age. When Jeanette Traber's mother had died, she had wanted to go, for Jeanette's sake, but it was too awkward, at that age. She hadn't known what to say. Suicide is such an embarrassment. When Jeanette had come back to school, no one had said a word to her about it. The unmeaning cruelty of children. She must have felt completely deserted, alone.

There was that girl at college, freshman year. Joan couldn't even remember her name. She had been strange from the very beginning. No one had known her well enough to feel bereaved. What had horrified them all was that she had hanged herself. If it had been pills, would they have felt better? She would have been just as dead. Why was the idea of hanging so horrible? The consciousness of it, probably. One minute you were alive, and then in one deliberate act you were dead. It could hardly be conceived. What would you feel in that instant? What if, when you died, the last thing you felt was what you felt for eternity? Remorse; terror; unspeakable pain . . . Was it different if you died in your sleep? Did God forgive you if you didn't intend it?

She wondered where she got such strange, Catholic-like notions. She didn't even know what Jews believed about the afterlife. It didn't matter, she supposed, what you believed. What mattered was what happened, and it would happen whether you believed it or not. No one knew. All the centuries of people trying to find out, thinking about it, praying, fighting wars over it, torturing one another, burning people at the stake. Still no one knew. How could they?

Or did someone know, after all?

"Then shall the dust return to the earth as it was: and the spirit shall return to God who gave it."

A surprising number of people had come out to the cemetery, especially on such a cold day. The huge temple had been filled. Who would come to her funeral? Her parents' friends, she supposed, people she barely knew. Just the family would fill half the place to start with. The gang would sit together. It was sort of like planning your wedding, except that you couldn't enjoy it yourself. No one enjoys their wedding either, when it comes to that. If she had Betsy as her maid of honor, Ellen would be hurt. Phil would play some terrible prank or other. Would Carl have to be an usher? She scolded herself for thinking about her wedding while Percy Weinstein was being eulogized.

She wouldn't have any eulogies at her wedding. Except they weren't called eulogies at a wedding, were they? What was the word? How could she be getting weddings confused with funerals?

Toasts. The word was *toasts*.

They were saying the prayer for the dead now. Her father joined in. She was surprised to hear him recite the words as fluently as if he were a Hassidic with a beard and black high hat. Where had he learned that? He never spoke a word of Hebrew at home. The family had a seder now and then, but that was strictly in English, albeit not without a certain amount of thoroughly inauthentic davening. Joan looked at him speaking the words as though they were his daily prayers. He looked utterly devout. Some other men were chanting too. None of the women. A bit weird, Joan thought, for people whose lives are otherwise untouched by religion. But it was—impressive. Moving, she had to admit. Unaccountable tears welled up in her own eyes. Who were they for? Surely not for Percy Weinstein. For whom, then? She didn't know.

Yisgaddal v'yiskaddash shmey rabboh
B'olmoh dee v'roh chir-vsey

At the end of the prayers Mrs. Weinstein walked forward, moving heavily, stumbling a bit on the uneven ground. Her last moment, and then unremitting widowhood. She leaned on her son's arm. Tom Weinstein had turned out nice-looking, Joan noted. The other man must be the daughter's husband. The children must have stayed back in Cleveland, or Cincinnati, or wherever they lived. They were probably too young to have much feeling about the death of their grandfather, maybe too young to understand at all. Now everyone was being handed a flower, to put on the coffin.

It was her turn to go up. She suddenly froze, not knowing what to do. She didn't want to look at the coffin. Her parents were moving toward it. They had given her a white carnation, stained with drops of scarlet. It seemed a shame to put it into the ground.

Why should she give her bounty to the dead?

At the coffin she held her breath, and relinquished the flower.

They all walked away sadly. Mrs. Weinstein tripped on the way back to the car and would have fallen but for Tom's catching her arm. People were looking for their cars, struggling against the wind. Alan said to Peggy, "I just want to go over. . . . I won't be a minute." He looked imploringly at Joan and said, "You certainly don't need to come." He looked quite forlorn.

"I'd like to," she said. They walked away from the rest of the mourners. Peggy stayed behind, talking to Eleanor. It wasn't in her to go and stand at someone's grave, certainly not her parents-in-law's. Joan didn't want to either, but she felt she owed it to Alan. They walked across a road. He hesitated. "It's this way," he said, and struck out along a path toward a small lake.

Gutheim. It was a mausoleum. Something Egyptian about it, like having your own pyramid. Alan stood at the entrance. He said nothing aloud, but his lips moved. Joan hoped he wouldn't actually cry. He stood for a moment, then walked back.

She knew he was glad she had come with him, but she was relieved he didn't say anything about it. She hadn't known either of those grandparents, although her grandmother Gutheim hadn't died until after she was born. Just a few months later. They trudged back to join the others.

Peggy was surprised to see them again so quickly. "Did you get a chance . . . ?" she asked Alan anxiously.

"Yes. I just wanted a look. They keep it up nicely. Joan had never seen it. I wanted her to see it."

"Really? I would have thought she had. Still, I suppose there wouldn't have been any reason for her to. Why don't you get right in the car, dear, you must be freezing, poor lamb."

"I'm fine, Mother. Please don't worry about me."

The journey back was very quiet. One doesn't witness the final

departure of a friend without some trepidation. The day had turned
darker and drearier, and no one had much to say. Mostly they looked out
the windows. They passed several other cemeteries. Valhalla must
surely be the cemetery capital of the world. They drove along some
lovely back roads before coming out onto the parkway, but the day was
too depressing to allow enjoyment of the landscape. The trees appeared
desolate, stripped as they were of leaves, waiting anxiously for winter.
The lower part of Westchester merged imperceptibly into the Bronx. A
few flakes of snow fell, but before they could constitute any kind of real
snowfall they turned into drizzle. The driver turned on the windshield
wipers, which moaned rhythmically on the glass.

"The South Bronx is dying," Peggy said, looking out over the
burned-out buildings and trash-littered sidewalks they were passing.
"None of the politicians has the slightest stake in doing anything about
it. The people who live here have no power. No voice. They've given
up." She sounded uncharacteristically pessimistic.

Joan said, "I think I should have come up here to work. There's so
much more to be done."

"You wouldn't have found it very pleasant," Peggy told her.

They passed a group of young Negro men huddled against the wall
of a building. They were accompanied by a mangy dog that was defecat-
ing on the sidewalk. As the car passed the men stared coldly at it. The
procession had not re-formed for the drive back, and the limousine carrying Joan and her parents was the only car moving along the street.

"It's not the greatest place I could imagine to get a flat," Alan observed.

They crossed the Harlem River and drove through the slums of
upper Manhattan. The buildings looked more lived in, but there was
just as much filth in the streets. They passed a project, a cluster of huge,
ugly red-brick buildings set at a peculiar angle in a concrete island. The
driver took a cross street over to Park and drove them under the elevated
tracks of the New York Central line. A few colored people trudged
along, but most of the streets were deserted. They went over to Madison
and continued downtown, passing in back of Mt. Sinai Hospital, where,
until two days before, Percy Weinstein had lain, enduring his final agony. He was freed from that now, at least.

Riding through the gray city, Joan fell into a kind of trance. She
stared out the window, seeing nothing. She was much more tired than
she had realized. When they reached 68th, she had difficulty arousing

herself to get out of the car. They found Phil watching the football game. Carl was nowhere to be seen. The maid brought lunch in on trays. Peggy urged Joan to eat something, but she didn't have the energy for it. She went straight to her room and slept most of the afternoon. When dusk fell, she awoke, still exhausted. Johnny had phoned. She didn't return the call. She knew he would try again, and eventually she would have to talk to him, but just then she couldn't make the effort. She wondered when she would feel well again.

The next morning she was to start at Meyer House.

Eight

Martin Perry's first act when he came to Meyer House was to unlock the front door. For the first time in a hundred years anyone could walk into the building right off the street. Until then, the massive wooden door had been locked, night and day. In the factory years the door had been guarded by a shipping clerk, whose duties included reporting late-arriving workers to management. In the early days of the settlement house, the doorkeeper job was assumed by a relay of clients, and later a full-fledged receptionist presided over the lobby. She greeted everyone who entered the place, rerouted the odd bum who stumbled in looking for a handout, and generally had a pretty comprehensive knowledge of what was going on in the building at any given time. During World War II, with the personnel shortage, the receptionist was recruited for other work and never replaced. People could still get in during the daytime. There were always elderly clients in the lobby, although few of them could actually get the door open. Especially in the summertime, when the door swelled and stuck, one of the younger staff had to be gotten. In the evening, though, the lobby was empty. The bell would ring plaintively until someone, usually a perspiring basketball player who had run down three flights of stairs, swearing furiously, would answer the door, only to find that the caller had given up and disappeared into the night.

Martin Perry would have none of that. He insisted that the door remain unlocked at all times. Of course, he met with stiff opposition.

Aside from every other consideration, the fact that it was his first action as director guaranteed that the old guard would rally in opposition. They didn't like the change for many reasons, but the main one was expectable: "It's never been done that way."

Needless to say, Peggy supported her new director and his position to the hilt; all the more vigorously because "it had never been done that way." Several board meetings tortured the question. Peggy loved the absurdity of it all. "Leaving the door unlocked is a virtual invitation to undesirable elements to wander in," people said in horror. To which she replied, "What business is it of ours to keep anyone out?" She pointed out that the House's mission was to take in everyone who wanted to come, in the spirit of New York itself, great settlement house to the world. But surely not everyone, they gasped. "And just who do you propose to exclude?" she challenged them. Well!—these criminals. These derelicts. These degenerates. "And who are we supposed to help?" she shot back. Her antagonists threw up their hands in frustration and outrage. No one could do a thing with that impossible woman.

Peggy smiled, and the door remained unlocked.

Martin Perry striking off the locks of Meyer House was one of Peggy's favorite stories. Without ever actually saying so, she made it clear that he could never have done it without her. Joan had heard the saga often. Nonetheless, it came as something of a shock to her when she arrived for her first day of work to find that the front door was in fact unlocked. It really was. Even Joan found it oddly welcoming. The thought of herself as needing asylum was silly—what was she running away from, after all? What was she escaping? She herself couldn't have said; but she did feel a sense of sanctuary, coming into the settlement house.

Entering the building, she found that the lobby, teeming when she had last been in it, was completely empty. Without anyone there, the chairs and sofas revealed their shabbiness, and the whole room looked seedier than she had noticed the last time. She wondered if she was the first person there. The excitement of being alone in the building mingled with the fear that some dangerous person had preceded her and was lurking somewhere. One of those drug addicts Peggy had been so eager to invite in.

Joan was to work on the third floor, where a large room housed the crippled children. When she had visited, Martin had taken her up in a huge, antiquated elevator that now stood gaping at the far end of the lobby. It had been used in the factory to bring bolts of cloth and other materials up to the workers, and then to take down entire racks of finished clothing that were wheeled out directly to the merchants in nearby streets. Joan hadn't liked the looks of the elevator in the first place, and she was terrified to use it if she was the only person in the building. She was sure it would stall between floors and strand her; or, more likely, the ancient cable would snap and plunge her to a horrible and unwitnessed death. She headed for the stairs.

Meyer House had only one staircase. The lack of any adequate escape route from the building in case of fire had been a major reason for the factory's being closed in the nineteenth century. It was still a firetrap. The same code that had been enacted to protect the women working in the sweatshops had been winked at once the place was a charitable organization. Since the building was only four stories high, it was possible that a person could jump from the top floor, as a last resort, and still survive. That might be; what was much more unlikely was that anyone could actually get out through the windows. Most of them didn't open, and all were protected by external iron gratings. As Joan climbed the stairway, she could imagine shrieking children running down in panic. She eyed the banister nervously. It was a flimsy wooden railing, not likely to stand up against any real crush. Whoever didn't die from the flames or the smoke would surely be killed falling into the central well.

Turning the corner at the second landing, Joan almost bumped into a swarthy Puerto Rican man with a jagged, livid scar on his face. It was so unexpected that she let out a little gasp, as much from shock as fear. Although he carried a mop, it took a moment for her to realize that he was cleaning the stairs and not waiting to rape the first unwary worker to come into the building. "Hees sleepery," he apologized to Joan, grinning to show his collection of rotting teeth. "Better to take elevator." Joan thought she could get up one more flight without slipping to her death, but she couldn't quite shake the notion of danger. She didn't want to trap herself above this man, with no route of escape, so she went back down the stairs.

Reentering the lobby, she was relieved to see that two women had come in. They were sitting in armchairs, drinking coffee out of cardboard cups and eating pastries. Their presence was reassuring. As she came nearer she saw that one of them was Etta Sevitsky. When Etta saw her, she called out excitedly, "Oh, Miss Gutheim! You've come!"

Joan went over to say hello. Etta introduced her to the lady with
her: "Miss Gutheim, I'd like you to meet Estelle Klein."

"Pleased to meet you, I'm sure," Estelle said, half rising to shake
hands with Joan.

"Miss Gutheim's going to help Leona," Etta explained, nodding her
satisfaction in having inside information. "A volunteer. Following in
her mother's footsteps. We met last week. Mr. Perry introduced us. I
also had the pleasure of meeting her mother. You'll have some Danish, I
hope, Miss Gutheim?" She took her napkin and pulled a cheese-filled
pastry out of the paper bag on her lap and handed it to Joan, who was
too surprised to refuse it. "I feel so badly not to have any coffee for you.
I'll bring some in tomorrow."

"Oh, please—" Joan put in, but Etta ignored her protest.

"How do you take your coffee? I love that coat. Did you get it with
Mother last week? Miss Gutheim is just down from college," she explained to Estelle, "and her mother was rushing her off to the stores to
get her something to wear. Is that from Saks Fifth Avenue, I imagine?
It's lovely." She fingered Joan's four-year-old coat admiringly.

Joan saw that nothing she said could interrupt the steady barrage of
solicitude and praise streaming forth from Etta. It reminded her of
when she was a little girl and used to go to Furrer, Gutheim, where the
secretaries would squeal with delight over her at her every word. These
two ladies, professionals with years of experience, were clearly awe-
struck to have her among them. She nibbled microscopic bites of the
Danish while they fussed over her. Seeing there was no possible escape,
she sat on the arm of the couch and turned herself over to them. She felt
like a fraud, to be the object of all this adulation, but it was clearly the
making of their day, to have her all to themselves. She had hoped for a
certain anonymity at Meyer House, and instead she was turning out to
be a celebrity. There was nothing she could do about it.

While they were talking, a young Negro woman came into the
building. The newcomer looked over at Joan and the others, paused,
then went over to the elevator. The door was open and the car was at the
landing, but she didn't get on. Instead she waited, looking over at Joan.
When she caught Joan's eye, she made a gesture to ask if Joan was
coming up. Joan didn't know her at all, but as the young woman seemed
to be waiting for her, she saw her chance and extricated herself from the
ladies.

"I'm Jenna," the young woman said to her as they got on the elevator together. She looked a few years older than Joan, but it was hard to be sure. She dressed like a high school girl, with a tight red sweater and a surprisingly short skirt under her outer jacket, and if it hadn't been for her air of assurance, Joan would have thought she was a school dropout coming in to see her counselor. Her hospitality seemed to extend only to holding the elevator, since she didn't smile at Joan and didn't offer her hand.

"I'm Joan Gutheim," she told Jenna.

"Oh, I know who you are, Miss Gutheim." Was there a touch of resentment in her tone? "You're working with the crippled kids, right?"

"Yes, at least at first," Joan answered, nervous that she might have inadvertently grabbed a plum job. For all she knew, working with the crippled kids was much sought after at Meyer House, and she had snatched it away from someone who had been hoping to get it. There was an uncomfortable silence as the elevator inched upward with an ominous rumble. It hadn't seemed this slow last week. "Which program do you work with?" Joan asked. She didn't know how to address Jenna. It didn't seem right to call her by her first name in the face of "Miss Gutheim," but she didn't know Jenna's last name. If she asked Jenna to call her Joan, it would sound patronizing, no matter how she phrased it.

"Oh, I'm not with any *program,*" Jenna said, laughing at the pretentiousness of the term. "I'm just a secretary, that's all. I do the typing, run errands, that sort of stuff. I find things. Anything you want found, just yell for me. Everyone else does."

The elevator stopped. When Joan didn't move, Jenna opened the gate, put her foot in front of it to keep it from springing closed again, and heaved open the heavy door. "Isn't this where you're going?" she asked, holding the door for Joan, as if she were the operator.

"Oh—yes—you're not getting out here?" Joan asked. She was embarrassed to have Jenna think she expected to be waited on this way. Despite her best intentions, everyone was treating her as if she were royalty.

"I'm going up to the gym," Jenna told her. "I have to straighten it out. You can't believe what a disgusting mess it is after a weekend."

"Is that part of your job too?" Joan asked.

"Part of my unofficial job," Jenna replied with a grin. "Kevin's supposed to make sure it gets cleaned up, but he's such a slob, if you leave it up to him it never gets done. Also, he thinks it's beneath him. He says that's nigger work." She laughed, seeing Joan's shocked expression.

"He's not what you're used to, I can see that. Well, I'll see you later. Lunch?"

"Oh, yes," Joan accepted quickly. She was supposed to leave at lunchtime, in fact, but she didn't want to turn down the invitation. She could have a cup of coffee, at least, before rushing off, and still not have to eat.

The elevator took Jenna upstairs, leaving Joan nonplussed. She was no stranger to Negroes—she had several good friends at Fieldston who were colored, and she had made a point of being friendly to the few Negro girls at Bennington—but she didn't know what to make of Jenna. She had been brought up to think that skin color was trivial, that it made no difference. The idea was not to notice it. You certainly didn't refer to it, or if you were forced to, you treated it as beside the point— "She happens to be Negro"—and moved on quickly. To use the word *nigger!* Only Southern rednecks and certified bigots would use the term. Even coming from Jenna, who Joan supposed had a right to use it if she wanted, it sounded brutal and obscene. Joan would as soon say "kike." Her friend Wendy lived in an apartment house on Park Avenue that had so many Jews, Phil always referred to it as Kike's Peak, but Joan could never use the word. Phil would know how to talk to Jenna. Joan, for her part, didn't know what to make of her.

Grudgingly, she recognized a certain thrill when she heard Kevin's name spoken. Even without Jenna's suggestive grin to tip her off, it was clear he stirred everyone up. He was good-looking enough, she guessed —she'd only had a quick, furtive look the other day—but there was something more. He was—not quite safe. That was it: He was a little dangerous. Joan wondered if he was sleeping with Jenna. Maybe he slept with all the girls, made it a point of honor to get them all in bed, sooner or later. Would she be out of bounds? Or would he see her as a special challenge: the rich bitch. Certainly he wouldn't find her sexy. He would be disappointed in her breasts, find her too skinny. But her being who she was might provoke him.

Nice thoughts! she scolded herself. What's a nice Jewish girl like you doing . . . ?

Get to work, she ordered herself. That was what she was there for, after all, not to jump into bed with the first guy who came along. She was in bad enough shape as it was, without overstimulating herself with lewd thoughts. She ought instead to purify herself. She ought to concentrate her thoughts on the children, the crippled little children, she ought to concern herself with their blighted lives, their wheelchairs, crutches, braces, casts, all the instruments of their misery and hardship. She ought to dedicate herself to them, body and soul, and keep herself so frantically busy that there was no opportunity for selfishness and immorality. It was a pity Jews didn't become nuns or missionaries: Joan was ready to take the veil and go off to darkest Africa if someone would have asked her.

Having gotten only to the lower East Side, for the moment there was no work to plunge into. No one had come in yet. Leona wasn't there. For all that Meyer House was devoted to the welfare of the poor, it kept bankers' hours. Most of the morning was devoted to getting going. A few elderly clients appeared pretty early in the day, and a few children who for one reason or another weren't in school straggled in. But the pace didn't pick up until sometime in the afternoon, and the house didn't go into full swing until after dark. During the evening there were lectures, meetings, sports, rehabilitation and therapy programs, dances of one sort or another, concerts, discussion groups, and a perpetual Bingo game. These all took place simultaneously, in every nook and cranny of the building. But in the morning—especially Monday morning—the place was as sleepy as a closed-up nightclub. They had told Joan not to come in until the afternoon, but she came in early anyway, hoping to prove her seriousness and dedication.

Also today, despite it being her first on the job, she had to leave in the middle of the day. They were still trying to figure out what was wrong with her, and were poring over her inch by inch in their search. That afternoon she was to see a new doctor, this Lamartine her mother had found. Joan had made her protest, arguing that she couldn't abandon her post right off the bat, but this time not even Peggy had backed her up. There was no getting out of it. She would have to see Lamartine. Mrs. Altman had kindly offered to send the car for her, so she could stay until the last minute. The idea of stepping out of Meyer House and into a Cadillac didn't thrill Joan, but the sensibleness of the idea won out, and she had accepted the offer. If she only had half a day, she would just throw herself all the harder into whatever she could do—she was prepared to scrub floors if need be—and then just slip out unobtrusively. She would be back the next day, before anyone missed her.

The crippled children were assigned to a large room that took up half of the third floor. The outside wall ran the length of the building, and high windows that were opened with a long pole were set deep into

the wall. The grating outside the windows added to the prison-like atmosphere in the room. The wall on the hallway side was covered floor to
ceiling with pictures painted over the years by the children. They varied
widely as to size and quality: some were crude efforts, little more than
drips and splotches, while others showed astonishing talent. They were
unified only in their common medium, powder-in-water paint applied
with thick brushes onto brown wrapping-type paper. Some of them
were strikingly vivid, especially the street scenes, hallucinatory evoca-
tions of the lower East Side and of Chinatown. Joan was struck with
how many of the pictures showed children in motion: running, leaping,
dancing.

A mural covered the entire wall on the end nearest the elevator. It
had probably been painted by a client who either was an artist or aspired to be one. It was unsigned and undated, but its style identified it
clearly as Depression realism. A large group of strong, idealized figures,
men for the most part, and a few women who looked as though they
could tame a riveter, stood in a factory that itself was set in the midst of
a farm. They held the typical symbols of honest labor—shovels,
pitchforks, axes, sledgehammers, and the like—familiar from WPA art
projects. On their faces was a mixture of defiance and resignation, meant
certainly to convey socialist solidarity but unintentionally showing
something between bewilderment and fear. Joan couldn't think what
the picture had to do with children, handicapped or otherwise, but it
certainly cast a moral pall over the room.

While she was studying the artwork, Leona came in. She was all in
a flutter to find that Joan had gotten there before her. She had been
floored when Martin Perry told her Joan would be working under her,
and the prospect of actually having to give directions to the daughter of
a board member had obviously weighed on her over the weekend. And
now Joan had come in before she had. Her sense of fitness was further
violated by the idea of a Gutheim pitching in and working. Leona was a
pleasant, motherly woman in her fifties, cut from the same cloth as Etta
Sevitsky and Estelle Klein. She wore no wedding ring. Joan sensed that
even if she had a family, Meyer House stood in the emotional center of
her life. She reminded Joan of those matrons who used to work at the
movie theaters on Saturday afternoons, hapless women who had the
impossible task of supervising hundreds of uncontrollable children who
ran up and down the aisles, spilling popcorn and root beer and drown-
ing out the dialogue with their yelling. When she had visited the week

before, the crippled children's room had reminded Joan a little of RKO Keith's or Loew's Orpheum; now, with no children there yet, it seemed unsettlingly quiet.

The children were brought in sporadically over the course of the morning. Since any child who could get around at all was in school until the afternoon, the morning group consisted of only the most handicapped of the children. They were all in wheelchairs except for one poor girl who was deposited at the settlement house by ambulance, on a litter. She was recovering from a gruesome operation in which every bone in her back had been broken in hopes of straightening her twisted spine. Imprisoned for the winter in a full-body cast, she remained immobile while the rest of the kids wheeled themselves around with varying degrees of facility. One young boy, named Mark, was particularly adept at careening around the room at great speeds. One of Joan's first tasks was to try and entertain Mark, which was the only way he could be kept still.

When Joan had seen these children the week before, they had been lost in the larger crowd. Now, arriving one by one, they claimed her individual attention. They all knew who she was from her visit, but to her they were strangers. She hoped to get to know them all before the morning was over, but something about them defied any quick intimacy. They allowed themselves to be introduced to her, but then they quickly went off to their familiar activities, leaving Joan feeling superfluous. When they wanted anything, they called Leona. If she was busy, they waited. For her part, Leona couldn't bring herself to ask Joan to perform some menial task not fit for a Gutheim. She unwittingly collaborated in excluding Joan. The ostracism would have been complete had it not been for the arrival, midway through the morning, of Pearl.

Joan had been drawn to Pearl when she had first met her the week before. In fact, it was seeing the two of them together that convinced Martin Perry that Joan should work with the crippled children. Pearl was by far the most handicapped child at Meyer House. Nine years before, her mother had fallen down a flight of stairs and gone into premature labor. After twenty-four hours of excruciating agony, a misshapen, flaccid, blue fetus was pulled from the womb. The delivery was a double one: as Pearl gave her first faint cry the mother gave her last, and expired. Looking at the floppy, cyanotic infant, one of the nurses asked aloud if the child would have been better off going to heaven with her mother. She had a point. Whether because of the fall, or the protracted labor, or the agonal parturition, not enough blood reached Pearl's brain during that awful day. She came out of it with a left side that was too weak to do her any good, but still subject to painful spasms. Her neck never became equal to the task of supporting her head reliably, and when her speech finally developed it was all but unintelligible. Everybody took it for granted that she was retarded: how could a body that damaged contain a normal mind?

It took a long time to discover that it did. The deceased mother's sister, to her everlasting credit, took the baby into her home and kept her out of the institution where she would have rotted away the rest of her life. The aunt loved her and kept her decently clean, but there wasn't much else she could do, for all her goodwill. Pearl spent her days tied into a chair so she wouldn't fall over and crack her head, watching TV as best she could, what with her head bobbing and weaving like a punch-drunk fighter's. She also drooled an amazing amount. At the end of the day she would have soaked the bib she always wore, and usually through her shirt as well. She never complained—she could hardly have gotten the words out if she had had a mind to—but she accepted her lot with an idiotic cheerfulness that confirmed everyone's conviction that she was a dummy.

This existence was interrupted when Pearl was nine years old by one of those rectifying accidents in which chance masquerades as purpose. The Department of Welfare, which paid for Pearl's care, sent workers into the aunt's home from time to time to see how her health was holding up, and also to make sure that its money wasn't being diverted to support someone's drug habit. A new worker named Miss Gavrilov was assigned to the case. Unbeknown to the department, Miss Gavrilov was a secret zealot. She took it on herself, against policy, to play with Pearl whenever she visited the aunt's home, and she even went so far as to bring Pearl some puzzles, which violated not only policy but several explicit rules. Now, no one had ever dreamed of asking Pearl to work a puzzle. There weren't that many puzzles in the apartment, and it was doubtful if any of the cousins had much skill in this area. To everyone's astonishment, Pearl proved a demon with puzzles. Even taking into account that she could barely manipulate the pieces, she could do them faster than anyone in the family. Miss Gavrilov, excited by her discovery, spent more and more time with Pearl, until she finally reached the conclusion that beneath the spasticity and saliva lay a pretty high IQ.

Exhilarated, she informed the aunt of her opinion. The aunt smiled and shrugged her shoulders. It was neither here nor there to her. Whether she was a moron or a genius, Pearl still had to be tied to a chair, and fed, and all that spit still had to be cleaned up. Undaunted, Miss Gavrilov reported her findings to her supervisors. They promptly reprimanded her for exceeding her authority. She persisted until they were goaded into dismissing her claim on the grounds of impossibility. They even called up Pearl's old record from some warehouse in Long Island, and dredged up a doctor's report that proved she was technically an imbecile. Miss Gavrilov was, of course, completely untrained in psychological assessment. More important, she was becoming a pain in the ass. Eyebrows were raised. Adverse efficiency reports were filed.

Nevertheless, she continued to make a nuisance of herself. She pestered everyone interminably until finally, just to shut her up, they had Pearl retested. To the dismay of everyone except Miss Gavrilov, the results showed that Pearl was a bright child. Despite her deficits, there was no telling how far she might go. All she needed was a chance.

The question remained, how to educate this still severely handicapped girl. There was talk of a special school. The aunt, it was said, had done nothing for the child. The term *neglect* was tossed about loosely. Miss Gavrilov wouldn't hear of it. The aunt, she insisted, would keep her; and for her education she should go to Meyer House. Her weary supervisors didn't bother to argue. They knew perfectly well that no agency in its right mind would ever agree to such an impossible assignment. They naturally hadn't counted on Martin Perry. No sooner had he heard Pearl's story than he went personally to the aunt to offer the services of the settlement house for Pearl. It didn't bother him in the least that Meyer House had no program for a child as incapacitated as Pearl; or that none of his workers was trained to rehabilitate children with cerebral palsy; or that he in fact had no accredited school program at all. He simply said, "I'll take her," and then sweet-talked Leona into agreeing to have Pearl in her classroom. "What will I do with her, Mr. Perry?" Leona had asked timidly when the writhing, titubating child was wheeled, grinning and spouting saliva, into her room.

"We'll think of something," Martin Perry had replied.

But no one had actually thought of anything, until Joan arrived at Meyer House. Pearl was still more or less in storage in the crippled children's room. When Joan was introduced to the cheerful, inarticulate girl tied into the wheelchair, Martin watched her face carefully. He hadn't planned it, but it was part of his genius as a director to know that Joan could be the "something" he had promised Leona they would think of. Furthermore, he suspected that Pearl might well be the "something" for this young woman whose mother had sent her to Meyer House disguised as a charity worker. Martin Perry wasn't fooled for a minute. In his eyes, both Pearl and Joan, despite their many outward differences, were knocking at his door.

When Pearl arrived, Joan was reading to Claire, the scoliotic prisoner of the body cast. She interrupted the story to be reintroduced to Pearl. Claire had learned to be satisfied with small doses of attention, so when Joan finished she didn't ask her to read another. Instead she thanked Joan profusely, and asked to have the book left so she could look at it again, by herself. Which she did, turning the pages and looking at the pictures while replaying in her head the well-remembered sound of the last voice she had heard. She was already an expert on stretching her rations.

Pearl was much hungrier. She seemed to think that Joan had come to Meyer House especially for her. Although most of her life had been spent in some form of isolation, she accepted Joan's attention without surprise. She gave Joan a soaking kiss, and wanted to be taken onto Joan's lap. If Joan left her for a moment, she didn't complain—she hadn't in any case yet learned how to complain—but when Joan came back to her she broke out into her peculiar, lopsided grin, which she could execute only on the right side of her face. She looked as though Santa Claus himself had come to pay her a special visit. Joan put her chair close to the wheelchair, and Pearl was able to reach over with her good hand, clutch Joan's wrist, and pull it onto her lap. She transferred this new possession to her spastic left hand, which then clamped down on Joan's forearm. Owing to the irregular firing of her reflexes, her spasmodic grip would suddenly become flaccid, then tighten again, like a tourniquet. The effect was startling at first, but Joan understood what it meant. Before long she was attempting to interpret the messages Pearl was sending.

The morning passed quickly. Since Leona couldn't instruct Joan what to do with Pearl, and no one else came around, she was forced to improvise. The first priority was to be able to communicate. Pearl could make few sounds come out as they should, and to put them together in any intelligible fashion required enormous effort from her, as well as tremendous patience and an imaginative leap from whoever was trying to understand her. Joan's task was complicated, and not by any means made pleasanter by the constant extrusion of saliva, which sprayed around indiscriminately whenever Pearl attempted a labial. At first she couldn't help flinching, but the shock soon wore off. After each unintelligible sentence Pearl uttered, Joan would try to guess what she meant. At each try Pearl would shake her head and grin crazily. When Joan finally hit on the right answer, Pearl would go into a frenzy of affirmation, and Joan would hug her for a reward. It was wet, but worth it.

As the time slipped by a sense of excitement began to fill Joan. Sitting with this crippled girl, helping her, working with her, accepting with perfect patience her limitations—no activity could be more satisfying. This is real, she thought; this is worth doing. Here was an opportunity to be grasped, a mission to be accepted. There was no need to question the value of what she was doing. It was absolute. She knew she was in the right place, performing the right actions. It seemed as though a tremendous weight that had been crushing her had been removed, and in reaction she felt as though she could float upward. She felt light and giddy, almost intoxicated with her new freedom. She felt, for the first time, guiltless, as though she had been released from oppressive, painful shackles.

At noon they brought trays in for the children. Leona always stayed to help feed them, and another worker came in to spell her after they were through. Unless they were very shorthanded, she generally took her own lunch downstairs in the basement cafeteria, since eating with the crippled kids was a fairly unappetizing experience. Today, Joan volunteered to feed Pearl and watch the others so Leona could have her break earlier. Leona fretted, wondering whether she could manage. What really worried her was the thought that Joan Gutheim might have to clean up a mess, or, worse, get some of it on her clothes. Despite Joan's best intentions, even the simplest Bonwit outfit, nothing more than a plain gray woolen dress, looked to Leona too fashionable to be soiled by juice or applesauce or the glop that came out of Pearl's mouth. Joan had to all but push her out of the room, and she left still unconvinced that Joan could cope.

Lunch did prove a formidable experience. Pearl needed painstaking care if she was to get any nourishment at all. She could hold a spoon, and liked to feed herself, but it was a losing proposition. Only a tiny fraction of what she started out with wound up in her mouth. Even Joan found it a challenge to get the spoon into the moving target. Pearl's chewing and swallowing mechanisms were impaired, and she couldn't get through a meal without a certain amount of choking and gagging and regurgitation. Through it all she maintained her even good humor, never giving way to frustration or discouragement. Given her persistence, Joan could hardly do less. Still, it was a disgusting exercise, and before it was over, Joan had lost any semblance of appetite she might have had.

Before Leona got back, Jenna poked her head in the door to see if Joan was coming downstairs. Joan didn't know what to say. After a long and heated family argument about how long it would take to get from Rivington Street to upper Park Avenue, the final decision was that she would have to leave by one at the latest. It was past twelve-thirty already, but she couldn't possibly leave the children. Jenna said she'd stay, and took a turn shoving food at Pearl's peripatetic mouth. From the way she performed the task, Joan guessed it wasn't the first time she had done it.

Leona came back, and Jenna took Joan off down to the basement with her. The large room with travel posters on the walls that doubled as meeting hall and cafeteria was crowded and noisy and thick with smoke. Many—most—of the elderly clients got their one hot meal of the day at Meyer House, and they filled most of the tables. A few of the staff intermingled with them, but the workers generally ate among themselves at the back of the room, farthest away from the kitchen. One table was crammed with the middle-aged ladies—Joan was immediately spotted by Etta Sevitsky, who yoo-hoo'd her and nudged Estelle Klein, who beamed. The table across from them was occupied by younger people. Jenna went there, and Joan followed. Jenna introduced everyone rapidly by first names, leaving Joan as much the stranger as before. She had met Martin Perry's secretary, and recognized the boy who had brought graham crackers and juice to the kids in the middle of the morning. Everyone else was new to her. She noticed with regret that Kevin wasn't there, and scolded herself silently for wanting him to be. What was it to her whether she saw him or not? She had already settled it that he was irrelevant. She wasn't at Meyer House for that.

Still, she was disappointed.

These younger staff members paid almost no attention to her. She was glad, really; more relaxed, less under scrutiny than with the older ladies. These people weren't dazzled by her. She was just another volunteer. She wasn't one of them yet. They talked to each other with the kind of sarcastic banter that covers over affection at that age. They discussed the movies they had seen, the songs they were listening to, the vacations they wished they could take. They were unpretentious. Joan found them refreshing. She felt a surge of unexpected excitement as she realized that they were going to be her new friends. It was like going to a foreign country on an exchange program. She forgot about Kevin. These were the people she wanted to be with, this was the group she wanted to be accepted by. They were different from the crowd she ran around with. They didn't watch each other so carefully, nor were they so quick to form judgments. They took you as you were. If they knew who her family was, they disregarded it. It was nothing to them. That was fine with Joan. She found it easier to breathe.

Suddenly the talk had stopped. They were all looking at someone standing behind Joan. She turned around, expecting, from the looks on their faces, to find Martin Perry hovering over her. Instead, she was dismayed to find her grandmother's chauffeur, Holberg. He must have crept up behind her and waited, with his repulsive Scandinavian servility, for her to notice him. If she hadn't turned around, he might have stood there all day. He responded to her horrified look by saying, "Chust to let you know de car iss vaiting venever you might be ready, Miss Choan."

It was a supremely humiliating moment. Who would have ever dreamed that he would pursue her into the cafeteria? In all her days, she had never known him to abandon his post: she had always seen him standing stiffly by the car, at the entrance to Carnegie Hall, or outside an art gallery or theater. It had never occurred to her that he would actually invade the building. She felt her face redden as she managed to tell him, "Thank you, Holberg. I'll be right out." Turning back again, she faced a wall of inscrutable faces. If they had accepted her on probation before, she was now on the other side of an unbridgeable gulf. This spectre, in his black double-breasted uniform, holding his cap respectfully under his arm, might as well have been the figure of Death, appearing at the table to claim her. They looked that appalled. When was the last time someone's chauffeur had come to call for them in the cafeteria at Meyer House, she wondered.

Mumbling ineffective explanations of no interest to anyone, Joan got up to go. Instead of having the decency to vanish, Holberg stayed right where he was, as though he was her bodyguard. The only way to get rid of him was to leave, right away. She was sure she would never salvage the fragile friendship she had begun with Jenna; as for the others, her position was now entirely untenable. Everything she had wanted to repudiate—privilege, luxury, shelter from the hardships and realities of life—had been harshly reaffirmed by the chauffeur's appearing in the cafeteria. She could never undo that, and the knowledge left her miserable with disappointment.

She hadn't told a soul where she was going. No one knew about her illness, and she had the thought that if she offered an explanation now, it would sound as though she was making it up, trying to win sympathy for herself. The only thing to do was to get out of there as fast as she could, and hope she could start all over the next day. "I'll see you tomorrow," she said to Jenna, and hurried out of the room. Etta Sevitsky saw her leaving, and called out good-bye to her. She, for one, seemed delighted that Joan was being called for by a chauffeur. To her way of thinking, undoubtedly, nothing could have been more fitting.

Joan ran up the stairs all the way to the third floor to get her coat and purse. Her breathlessness covered over her agitation as she said good-bye to the children. Some new ones had arrived while she had been downstairs, but there was no time to meet them now. "I'll be back tomorrow," she told the children, but they looked at her skeptically. Pearl smiled her crooked smile and called out a gurgling "So long," but she didn't look as though she expected to see Joan again. Claire was at her post by the door. Joan grabbed her coat and purse and fled.

Having sprinted up the stairs, she walked down more slowly, trying to collect herself and see what could be salvaged. It wouldn't come out right. She felt hopelessly compromised. The thought occurred to her not to come back to Meyer House, but to start over again somewhere else. She had wanted to get away from the family, but she'd been thwarted. It was inevitable. If her grandmother's chauffeur hadn't shown up, something else would have happened, sooner or later. She couldn't go anywhere in New York and escape the family tentacles. She thought she ought to get out of the city. She should never have let herself be dragged back in the first place.

As she was walking down the stairs the door on the top floor opened, and a couple of teenage boys stormed past her, yelling obscenities. She shrank to the wall to avoid being pushed down the stairs by their onslaught. The first boy, a Negro, sped past her, but she was kicked by the knee of the pursuer, who looked Puerto Rican, Joan couldn't be sure. He jumped the last steps of the next flight, catching the colored boy before he turned the corner and throwing him violently against the wall. Having stunned the smaller boy, he set upon him, beating him viciously on the face. Joan was too terrified to intervene, although it seemed as though the colored boy was getting seriously hurt. The door above opened again, and an older boy, or a young man, galloped down. When he caught up to the two combatants, he grabbed the assailant around the neck and yanked him off. The boy swung at him, but he blocked the punch and answered with a short, powerful blow that ended the fighting suddenly. Grasping the front of the Puerto Rican boy's jacket in both hands, he pulled him up roughly. "If I ever see your ass in here again, you're dead!" he yelled, and shoved him hard down the stairs. The boy stumbled, recovered himself, and ran down the rest of the stairs, yelling as he went, "You motherfucker! I'll get you for this, you cocksucker!"

The Negro boy, bloody and crying, was treated hardly better by his rescuer. "You, get the fuck up to the gym, and if I have any more trouble out of you again, you're goin' out that door after him." He more or less pushed the sobbing boy in front of him as the two of them returned up the stairs. "You're all right," he assured the boy in a kinder tone. "You just gotta learn how to fight, that's all. What kind of nigger are you, anyway, letting a white boy beat you up?"

They had reached the place in the staircase where Joan was still cringing against the wall. Whether or not he had seen her on his race down, the young man seemed surprised to see her there now. He broke out into an embarrassed grin and said, "Sorry," gruffly as he passed her with his charge.

It was Kevin. He was wearing white sweatpants and a white sweatshirt, which made him look heroic. Joan ruefully noted that when he smiled at her she felt a disquieting thrill. She scolded herself, but she couldn't take her eyes off him until he turned at the next landing. Then she ran down the rest of the stairs so he wouldn't see her gaping at him.

She decided to return to Meyer House the next day after all. She'd been foolish, being so mortified by such a trivial thing as Holberg's calling for her. Of course she would come back. It wasn't merely a matter of her preference. Pearl was counting on her, and so were the rest of them. She couldn't let them down. She had others to think of now.

Alan, wrapped in a towel, took the telephone call in the lounge of the Meridian Club locker room. "Yes, Gerry," he said. "What can I do for you?"

"They didn't interrupt your squash game, did they?" Gerald asked. "I told them they were not to interrupt you if you were on the court."

"No, I wasn't on the court."

"I wondered, because it took some time to get you." Gerald didn't like to be the one left hanging on the phone. If it wasn't considerably past five o'clock, Alan would have found Gerald's secretary on the line.

"I was just coming out of the shower," Alan said.

"Good. Are you alone?"

Alan glanced around. George Flussman, also wrapped in a towel, was napping on a chaise, his large, hairy belly rising and falling rhythmically. Probably George Flussman, fully awake, would not pick up that much. "I can talk," Alan said.

"I think it's time to pull out all the stops," Gerald said without introduction.

He didn't have to explain what he was referring to. Since the tender offer for Abbott & Strawbridge had been announced, Gerald had lived for nothing else. The race was on. Each side was scrambling for every outstanding share in the company it could lay its hands on. Peggy had predicted that Gerald would call Alan in the minute a particularly sticky problem came up, Jack Bernstein or no Jack Bernstein. It was disheartening that she should be proven correct, and so soon.

"I would have thought you'd pretty much done what you could already," Alan commented.

"We have, of course. But occasionally new things turn up," Gerald said. "It turns out that the Abbott family's holdings may not be quite the closed door we thought."

"How is that?" Alan asked. Although the last Abbott in the company had died off some time back, the family still held a large bloc of stock that they would of course vote to oppose the takeover.

"Well, it turns out old man Abbott didn't leave his affairs in absolutely apple pie order when he kicked off. Not too surprising, when you consider the mess he left the company in. It seems that some of their position—we don't know how much, but probably a significant chunk—is actually being held as collateral for a loan. And there is every reason to believe that they might not find it convenient to come up with the cash if the loan was to be called in."

This was interesting. "Who's holding the note?" Alan asked.

Gerald announced wryly: "Anspach & Wellman." Alan whistled softly. "A mixed blessing, I suppose you would call it."

It was that. Anspach & Wellman was a brokerage firm that had at one time had the closest possible ties to the Altman family. They had banked with Altman's, and Alan had been their lawyer and Gerald and Fred Wellman played golf together every Saturday at Silverlake. Several years back, however, Gerald and Fred Wellman had had a falling out— one of those things that starts over a trivial matter, part business, part personality, and escalates until the situation is irreconcilable. Since then they had virtually stopped speaking to each other. They were civil to one another in public, still worked together on boards, and the young Wellman boy was great friends with the young Gutheims, but the two families virtually stopped doing business with each other. Alan's firm continued to represent the brokerage house, but Alan had asked his partner, Murray Furrer, to handle its affairs.

"Obviously, Fred could be very helpful to us on this," Gerald continued. "And just as obviously, he might not."

Alan could see what was coming: Gerald wanted him to do the dirty work. Trying to forestall the inevitable, he suggested, "Fred wouldn't go against you on something like this, would he?"

"Who knows? Oh, I don't say that if I were bleeding to death on the sidewalk he would necessarily walk by without stopping, but this is different. On this one he might cross the street." He paused. "Needless to say, I'm in no position to ask him."

Alan said nothing.

"Actually . . ." Gerald said, as if a thought had just struck him out of the clear blue, "I wonder if you mightn't be able to help us out with this."

Gerald was at least predictable. Wearily, Alan replied, "I don't see how I could, Gerry. For one thing, it would be a conflict of interest if I were to advise him on a matter in which I'm involved."

"But you're not involved in this!" Gerald insisted. "You can say that you're not handling the case. It's the God's honest truth."

Rather than respond to that absurdity, Alan forged ahead: "In any case, I don't handle Wellman & Anspach for the firm. I turned it over to Murray when there was that business, and since then I've stayed strictly at arm's length."

There was a pregnant silence before Gerald asked, "Could Murray speak to Fred for us?"

It was hardly a surprise, given Gerald's elastic sense of propriety. Of course, Alan was in an untenable position. Gerald was in the process of being very helpful to Phil. Now he was asking Alan to do him a favor; a particularly unsavory one, to be sure, but that was how Gerald played the game. Alan sighed. Peggy had warned him about that too. She had begged him not to put himself in a position of obligation to her brother. He couldn't look to her for sympathy on this one. "I don't think it would be proper," he said stiffly.

"Is it illegal?" Gerald asked.

"No, it's not illegal," Alan answered testily. "But it may well be unethical. How can Murray purport to give them advice, and at the same time solicit them on your behalf? Who is he representing there? This is just the sort of thing we're doing our damnedest to avoid."

"I'm not asking him to solicit on our behalf. All I'm asking is for him to put our case."

"It amounts to exactly the same thing," Alan said, exasperated. Gerald could pretend to astonishing obtuseness when it suited him.

Gerald pressed on: "Would you at least ask Murray, and let him decide? I don't ask you to put any pressure on him. Just ask him."

"You know perfectly well that my asking is tantamount to putting pressure on him. I'll tell you this, Gerry: If I were in his shoes, I wouldn't do it."

In response to Alan's raised voice, George Flussman gave a grunt and stirred slightly.

Gerald replied, "If you were in Murray's shoes, it would behoove you to do it." There was really no limit to his arrogance, when the chips were down.

Alan was torn. It was hard to stand up to his brother-in-law under any circumstances. But with his son's whole future at stake, to say nothing of his being seminude while he talked, he felt at a distinct disadvantage. "I'll speak to Murray," he said.

Gerald softened immediately. "I'd appreciate that, Alan," he said expansively. "Please tell Murray I'm very grateful, will you?"

"I won't tell Murray any such thing!" Alan snapped, his anger flaring too sharply, and too late. "I'm not going to suggest to him that he's doing something he oughtn't to as a favor to you."

"Whatever you think best." Gerald could be affability itself, as long as he got his way. "At any rate, I am grateful."

They said good-bye. Alan hung up the phone and looked at George Flussman, who had lapsed back into a deeper sleep. The steward, who had probably been hovering just outside the door, listening to every word, now appeared and asked Alan if he wanted a drink. Alan declined the offer and went back into the locker room. Manny Straus was telling an off-color joke, and it took some effort for Alan to join in on the laughter.

Fiona stole quietly into the anteroom off Eleanor and Gerald Altman's bedroom. Seeing Eleanor sitting in her armchair and not lying on the bed, she asked, "Mrs. Altman, will you speak with Mrs. Gutheim on the phone? She said not to disturb you if you were resting, that it would wait."

"No, I'll speak to her." The maid started out when Eleanor picked up the phone next to her chair. Before she spoke into it, she held the receiver out as a pointer and said, "Oh, Fiona, that blue dress has a spot on it. I want to wear it tonight if they can possibly get it out, but if it has to be sent out, simply let me know, and I'll wear something else. Hello, dear," she said, putting the receiver to her head as Fiona curtsied.

"Hello, dear," Peggy said. "I hope they didn't disturb you. It isn't anything that couldn't wait, especially since we're seeing each other shortly."

"No, darling, I was just sitting here reading John Gunther, so I can assure you I was delighted to have the excuse to put it down. It is a deadly bore."

"Why on earth do you read it, if it's a deadly bore?"

"Well, darling, one has to go through certain things, deadly or not, and John Gunther seems to be one of them. I find that conversations at dinner parties go better if I have something to toss in now and then, and John Gunther is a great help to me in that regard. But leaving that aside: you called to say?"

"Only that I wanted to let you know, because I thought you would like to hear right away, that I've just gotten a call from Lamartine, and he tells me that the tests show conclusively that Joan does not have leukemia."

"But darling, how absolutely *marvelous!* I couldn't be more pleased.

You are sweet to call me up right away, of course I'd want to know. But you all must be *so relieved.*"

"Well, it is a great weight off our shoulders, and Joan is naturally ecstatic. Personally, the only reason I'm not jumping up and down is that I never had the slightest doubt that she ever had any such thing. You see, I may not be a doctor, but I know enough to know that you couldn't possibly have leukemia and be as normal as Joan quite obviously is. So although I'm very pleased, especially for Alan, who was in fact practically frantic with worry—nothing I could say would do any good, I think he had himself convinced it was something fatal—all I can say is that the whole thing was very unpleasant, but I'm glad more than ever I didn't let them whisk her off into the hospital, as they kept badgering me to do."

"Darling, it's all too marvelous. Will she go back to college now?"

"Well, not for the time being. They still don't know just what this is. They'd like her to get more rest than she'd be able to at college, and they want her to put back some of the weight she seems to have lost. All in all they would be happier if she would stay down for a while. I think they're crazy if they think she'll get any rest in New York, but I'm delighted to have her here."

"They don't know what it is she's actually got, then?"

"I don't think they're going to be able to fit her into any of their categories, if that's what you mean. Which is fine with me. I couldn't care less what they call it. Whatever it turns out to be, something will still have to be done. That much is clear. Nobody's pretending Joan is the picture of health. Still—this latest is a great relief, I must say."

It suddenly struck Eleanor what a terrible strain her sister-in-law had been under, although hell would freeze over before she would ever admit it. Feeling somewhat remorseful, she said, "Peggy I hope you don't think I haven't been properly concerned—of course we have all been *sick* with worry—but I have to tell you, it never even occurred to me that it might have been . . . anything of that sort. I suppose that's very stupid of me. I would have been only too happy to have agonized with you if I had suspected anything like that. But it never even entered my head."

"Darling, the last thing I want is for anyone to worry unnecessarily. What's the point? It doesn't do Joan the slightest bit of good. I think the less fuss anyone makes, the better. Particularly in front of Mother, if you know what I mean."

"I know exactly what you mean. I won't say a word. You've spoken to her, I take it?"

"Yes, of course, I went right over to see her as soon as I heard from Lamartine."

"Well, please tell Joan we're all thrilled over the news, that we love her, and we'll of course see you all shortly. Seven o'clock, is it?"

"Dear, it's never been anything other than seven o'clock as long as I've been going to Mother's for dinner."

"Sometimes it's earlier, if Mother's going to the opera, or some such thing."

"There's no opera tonight, dear. Just us. Which is noisy enough, if you ask me," Peggy said with a laugh.

"It will be divine to see you all. Please give Joan our love."

The two women said good-bye.

Eleanor hung up the phone. Without taking her hand away from the receiver, she exclaimed aloud: "Leukemia! Ye gods!" And a moment later, shaking her head, she asked, "What next?"

She released the receiver, reached for John Gunther, and put her reading glasses back on. She read an entire page before she realized she hadn't registered a word, and had to read it all over again.

Nine

When you come into Frieda Altman's house on the north side of 71st Street, closer to Park than to Madison, the first thing you notice is the flowers. The house itself is not imposing—nothing along the order of the Frick mansion just a block to the west, or any of the other vulgarly ostentatious homes of the late-nineteenth-century tycoons. But it is a house with a great deal of elegance and lovely detail, and the paintings are magnificent, it goes without saying. Even people coming to look at the Altman collection, however, are struck first by the flowers; and if you're coming in from a raw, dismal November evening, you feel transported to an enchanted garden. Two large urns filled with jonquils flank the door, and there are vases of flowers on all the hall tables, as well as in the powder room and the men's cloakroom. After leaving your coat, or powdering your nose, as the case may be, you then climb a stairway past the medieval tapestries embroidered with exquisite millefleurs. Upon entering the living room on the second floor, you are met by an absolute onslaught of color and fragrance and soft sweetness that can only come from the most prodigious offering of fresh flowers. Everywhere you look you see another bowl of flowers. The pictures for the room all blend harmoniously: a plump, pink Renoir girl winks from her velvet cushion over the couch, and sensuous Fragonard lovers entwine each other beneath rosy bowers and arbors on the panel between the windows. Over the mantel, delicate, pastel Watteau ladies celebrating their fête champêtre seem to breathe the same rich scent that fills the room. Each painting overflows with flowers that appear to spill into the room, where numerous fresh bouquets add to the illusion that you have entered a floral paradise, heavy with the beauty of a warm summer's evening.

Mrs. Altman had already come down when the Gutheims arrived. She wore a deep blue dress with a gold and diamond pin, and sat, as always, in the corner of the sofa across from the fireplace. The only others there were Aunt Hilda and Cousin Sammy. Aunt Hilda was not, in fact, an aunt, or any relation at all of the Altmans; nor, so far as anyone knew, of anyone else's, except for a brother who had died some years before. She had been around forever. The family, that is to say, Mrs. Altman, looked after her as a matter of course, a condition she accepted as being in the natural order of things. Her recent increasing deafness, added to her lifelong dullness, guaranteed that she would not bother anyone too much with conversation. In fact, being seated next to her at a family dinner party had its compensations: You could count on a pleasant aural vacuum on at least one side, leaving you freer to cope with the cacophony of the rest of the gathering. For that matter, Cousin Sammy was no great wit. He had been a black sheep cousin for many years, until about the time of Nathan Altman's death, when he went over into a sort of emeritus status. By that time his lack of any useful occupation was no longer very conspicuous, and he also gave up gambling. He had always been considered amiable, he played a decent game of bridge, and he never embarrassed the family by appearing anywhere, public or private, with any of his mistresses. Much to the children's disappointment. They would have given anything to meet one of those mysterious scarlet women of the older generation. But it was not in his interest to exhibit them. For his discretion, he was tolerated as a frequent guest at the various Altman tables. Peggy described him as "perfectly harmless."

"Good evening, Sammy," Peggy said, letting herself be kissed lightly by her elderly cousin, who sprang up with the surprising agility of the chronic recipient of handouts. "Always nice to see you." She went over to the sofa to greet her mother, who was beaming. "Mother, dear," she said, kissing her.

"I like your hair that way," Mrs. Altman said. Peggy, who had never had the patience to maintain a carefully waved hairdo, had had a cut that morning that had left her hair nearly straight, slightly turned under at the neck.

"Do you, Mother? I had them do it this way for the simple reason that it was getting to be too damn much trouble. I told them, I couldn't care less what you do with it, just make sure I don't have to fuss with it all the time. Life's too short." Peggy had an almost ethical aversion to being complimented, even by her mother. If others found her attractive at all, she hoped it would be for her energy and willingness to help. It was true that when she came into a room, people were glad to see her, and were caught up in her liveliness.

"It suits you," Mrs. Altman said. Alan and Phil and Joan all came forward to kiss her, and they said good evening to Sammy and shouted something at Hilda. They also said good evening to Billingsly as he handed them their drinks, already prepared, on a silver tray: a martini for Peggy, Scotches for Alan and Phil, and a tomato juice for Joan. Joan had for several years taken a weak Manhattan, but Billingsly had kept his ears open, and knew that alcohol was forbidden for now.

"But where's Carl?" Mrs. Altman asked, anxious at not seeing her youngest grandchild.

Peggy looked around. "We had him with us when we came in. I know that."

"The call of nature, perhaps?" Phil asked slyly. He knew perfectly well that Carl had gone into the kitchen to say hello to the help, and was in fact in the hallway, about to enter the room.

At that time Carl was an awkward, plump boy of fifteen with a grave manner and a round face that took life too seriously. People had trouble keeping from smiling when they saw him. His clothes fitted poorly, a result of his fat boy's habit of buying a size too small out of embarrassment before the snobbish salesmen at Saks. He kept his jacket buttoned, which was a mistake: it rode up on his rear, and the button looked in danger of popping. He choked slightly in his shirt, and hadn't gotten his tie completely under the collar. A few flecks of dandruff speckled the shoulders of his navy blue jacket. Not the most dashing figure one might imagine.

"We were about to send out a search party for you," Phil said jovially.

"I was just saying hello to Helga," Carl replied humorlessly. He hated to have people think he was going to the bathroom. The last thing he wanted people to think about was his body. "Hello, Grandmother," he said, bending with an effort to kiss her. He was very sober, despite her unreserved affection for him.

Peggy, seeing that Carl was about to argue with Phil—always a losing battle for him—said, "Won't you say good evening to Aunt Hilda and Cousin Sammy?"

Carl thought he could really have done that without being reminded to, as though he were a small child. Sammy returned his handshake with mock solemnity and winked at the others. Carl considered him a buffoon, and resented being patronized by him, of all people. When Carl shouted hello to Cousin Hilda, he could see that she hadn't the foggiest notion who he was. She was fast losing the few wits she had ever possessed, poor soul, and had somehow gotten the notion recently that Peggy and Alan had only two children. She had been staying with Mrs. Altman in the country when Peggy had been rushed to the hospital with a miscarriage; she remembered that well enough. But by the time Carl came along, life was already beginning to fog in for her. Carl said nothing. He was used to going unrecognized. Peggy saw her bewilderment, too, and as a diversion told him, "Why don't you pull up a couple more chairs. We'll need them once your cousins get here." Now, Billingsly, who was in the room, had placed the exact number of chairs necessary in the circle around the couch; but neither he nor Carl said anything.

"Marian's not coming," Mrs. Altman said, trying not to sound disapproving of one of her grandchildren. Marian was a trial to even the most indulgent of grandmothers. Her latest escapade had been to join the Crusaders for Morality, a quasi-religious group noted for its charismatic right-wing leader, its shady methods, and its propensity for recruiting disaffected members of rich families, whom it then proceeded to suck dry. Eleanor had said nothing to Peggy about Marian not coming. Which was understandable, but unwise: Peggy liked to be kept informed.

Peggy gave up trying to count chairs for people who hadn't yet arrived. "That will do nicely for now," she said as Carl brought over a chair from the side of the room. Phil, Carl noticed, was never asked to draw up extra chairs, or in general to fetch and carry. "Don't drag it across the rug, dear, it leaves marks," Peggy explained.

"Glad to see you making yourself useful," Alan boomed cheerily. He was determined to compliment Carl whenever the opportunity arose, which was not nearly so often as with Phil. Also, he wanted to encourage Carl in any physical activity, no matter how minor. He still hoped that some day his heavy, unathletic son would slim down and learn to play at least one sport decently well.

Peggy was cross to hear his poorly disguised nagging. She would often tell him, "When he's ready to lose weight, he'll do it on his own." But there were some things she couldn't get through his head, for a smart man.

"And how is school?" Mrs. Altman asked. "I hear they've put you into this terribly advanced math course."

"Yes, they have." Carl was grateful for her tact, but he knew Phil would get him later for bragging.

"I'm dying to hear about it," she said.

"It's nothing special," Carl said self-deprecatingly. "I doubt you'd find it very interesting."

"You might let your grandmother be the judge of that," Peggy said. Joan and Phil snickered.

Carl rushed to explain, and started reciting the complicated topics he was studying, while Mrs. Altman smiled with uncomprehending pride. Joan and Phil looked at each other and rolled their eyes toward the ceiling.

"How do you manage it?" Mrs. Altman asked admiringly. Carl was only saved from further embarrassment by the arrival of the Altmans.

Eleanor Altman never entered a room without creating a stir. Even at her mother-in-law's, with just the family as audience, she swept in, looking stunning. In her blue sheath that Fiona had gotten the spot out of, smiling brilliantly, *her* hair elegantly piled on top of her head to leave bare her swan's neck, she still took one's breath away at forty-eight. Gerald accompanied her with a confident sense of his own importance. Dickie, a few steps to the rear, made a very doubtful contribution. He was decent enough looking, if never handsome, but he had started scowling so early in life that by now he gave the impression of perpetu-ally smelling something unpleasant. Probably himself. Dickie had never been considered to have many talents. He had confirmed this view of himself by flunking out of an impressive series of prep schools, culmi-nating in the military school he had been sent to after even Peddie, of all places, had given him the gate. Out of sheer perversity he had joined the Marines; a truly bizarre step for a member of the Altman family. But of course he hadn't been able to cut it there either. When the Corps let him go, he made a pathetic attempt to fend for himself. It wasn't long before he accepted the job at Altman & Sons. The fact that he hadn't been given a shred of responsibility made his position there pretty untenable, but no one could figure out what else to do with him. There was talk now and then of his moving to the West Coast, but so far nothing had come of that.

Only after Dickie had said his sullen hellos did Barbara come in. She had long since learned not to arrive in her mother's shadow. Not that she wasn't lovely herself, because she was; but she hadn't her mother's presence. Of course, no one did. Eleanor was in a class by herself. Dark and pale, with the only chest worth noticing in the family, Barbara was a very lovely girl, really. That was how people always described her: a very lovely girl, really. The "really" had various meanings to different people: It could indicate surprise; or insinuate that her looks were better than some of her other attributes; or allow that, in comparison with Marian—a girl of whom it could truly be said that her looks were not her fortune—Barbara was a knockout. Most often, though, you could hear a note of regret, or mild reproach: The girl was so lovely, why should she want so much more? Why would she never be satisfied? Everyone knew that Barbara, underneath that tense smile, was not happy. She was twenty-two, and already divorced. And why? George had been a perfectly decent boy. No ball of fire, to be sure, but then what would Barbara have done with a ball of fire, Peggy always asked. He was terribly attractive, there was that at least. But she had shed him almost as fast as she had bedded him. What on earth would make her happy?

If Barbara knew that people talked about her—no doubt she did— she kept her poise. She had the serene look of a girl who hasn't been asked to dance yet, but knows that she will be—or will she? She smiled radiantly as she came into the living room, pretty as ever. When she finished the lengthy business of saying hello and kissing everyone and shouting something at Hilda, she took her seat with an air of placid grandeur. Peggy had told Carl to pass around a tray of hors d'oeuvres. Barbara took one, saying, "Thank you, Carl," as though she were a visiting countess graciously accepting a tribute from the village half-wit.

Everyone settled down immediately to talk. Across the room a fire glowed, giving off not only warmth but a sense of comfort and pleasantness to the family group. Mrs. Altman smiled to see so many of her grandchildren together.

"Peggy, dear," Eleanor called over, "I love your hair that way. Who did it?"

"The same girl who's done it the past fifteen years," Peggy replied, amused.

Barbara had sat next to Joan, and whispered, "Don't change your expression. There's a new man. I can't wait to tell you about him. Mummy and Daddy don't know he exists." She giggled girlishly and looked around to see if her parents were wondering what secrets she was telling Joan.

"Are you going up to New Haven for the game?" Gerald asked Phil. "It should be a humdinger."

"I wish I were, Uncle Gerry, but I'm afraid I'm going to have to pass it up."

"Let me know if you change your mind. I can give you a lift up." Gerald was disappointed not to have Phil's company. Dickie pretended not to notice. His father hadn't taken him to the Harvard game since he was a small child. Not that he had the slightest interest in wasting a whole day. . . .

"The reason I particularly ask," Eleanor was saying to Peggy, "is that my girl is up and deserting me. Retiring, if you can imagine! And now I have to find a new one, at my age!" She smiled at her advancing years, knowing that people forever marveled at her youthful looks. "If she wants to go and sit on a bench in St. Petersburg and read magazines for the rest of her days . . ." She looked wistfully at Sammy, who knew how to take an interest in such matters.

"Maybe Carl would go up to the game with you, Gerry," Alan suggested. It was hard to know who was more alarmed by the suggestion, Gerald or Carl.

The conversations switched, in the same way a person sitting in a chair shifts himself to find a more comfortable position. Alan talked to his mother-in-law. Phil tried to find something in common with Dickie. Barbara was shouting at Hilda, but that was hopeless. Sammy asked Carl what he was up to these days, in the tone one adopts toward an eight-year-old in inquiring about his stamp collection.

Peggy found a moment alone with Eleanor. "Marian's in Westchester, I take it?" she asked discreetly but not entirely innocently. She knew there must have been a terrible row, for Marian to skip dinner at her grandmother's.

"She's with her 'group,'" Eleanor replied with distaste. "I told her

I didn't see why the group would mind if she stayed away one evening to come to her grandmother's, but that just shows how little I understand about the group, which does mind, terribly. To be honest, I don't understand much about it, and I don't care to."

Peggy made a sympathetic noise.

"I'll be a lot happier when she's over this particular one," Eleanor continued. "I actually think it's worse than that League." Before joining the Crusaders, Marian had for about a year been caught up in a paranoid political cell that had spent most of its time, and a great deal of Marian's money, planning outrageous schemes. Few of them came off, but they had aged Eleanor and Gerald considerably. The last straw had been an attempt to land several boatloads of mixed varieties of manure at the base of the Statue of Liberty. The Coast Guard, tipped off by a disaffected member, intercepted them before they were able to befoul Bedloe Island. Marian put up bail for everyone, and advanced loans for fines and legal costs. To no one's surprise, she never saw a penny of that money again.

The hors d'oeuvres were being handed around again, this time by Billingsly. "I adore these bacon things," Barbara said. "Why can't we have them at home?"

"There are certain things in life one can only get at one's grandmother's," Eleanor told her. Mrs. Altman looked pleased.

"How's your brother making out these days?" Phil asked Dickie. There had been some rumblings that Randy was having academic difficulties at Brown, and he guessed it would give Dickie some malicious pleasure to talk about it.

"He's getting ready to flunk out any day now," Dickie replied, grimacing with joy at his brother's imminent expulsion, an experience with which he had more than a nodding acquaintance, though never at Brown.

"I'm not sure it's quite as bad as all that," Gerald put in, overhearing his youngest being maligned. "They've put him on warning, I think they call it. I gather it's slightly less disgraceful than probation."

"It's the same thing as pro," Dickie assured Phil. "Except that he could still play on a team, if he played on one, which he doesn't."

"Not on a team?" Alan asked, disappointed. "He'll be on the tennis team, won't he?"

"I doubt it," Dickie said, smirking. "The Ivy League's a little tougher than Choate. He'd have to work his little derriere off to make the team, and knowing Randy I don't think that's very likely." Mrs. Altman closed her eyes in disapproval of Dickie's language.

"I should think Brown'd be lucky to get him on its team," Alan insisted loyally. "He's got one hell of a serve. Have you ever seen him play, Sammy?" Sammy shook his head, smiling regretfully. He didn't belong to the Silverlake Club, since no one had ever asked him to join, or offered to pay his dues; and if he did, he wouldn't have spent much time around the tennis courts. "You ought to some time. I've seen bullets that travel less fast than his first serve." Alan shook his head in recollected awe.

"When does he play next?" Sammy asked, whimsically drawing a small engagement book out of his inner coat pocket.

Billingsly was offering refills for the drinks. Everyone declined except for Gerald. Peggy looked at her watch. She was thinking it was time to go in, but said nothing.

"I must tell you," Mrs. Altman said to Eleanor, "that I had a call today from a Mr. Leonard." She looked amused.

"Oh, no!" Eleanor cried. "But that's *too awful*. I told him absolutely on no account was he to call you." The others were puzzled. She explained, "He's the curator of the Clark—in Williamstown . . ."

"I know where the Clark is, dear," Peggy said, smiling.

"At any rate," Eleanor continued, "they want Mother's Chardin for a show next fall. I told him I would discuss it with you, and he should not on any account pester you about it."

It was clear that Eleanor had wanted to push this through without the rest of the family around.

"It's perfectly all right," Mrs. Altman said graciously. "I assume they got to you via Walter?" Eleanor's brother had gone to Williams, Class of '28.

Eleanor shook her head. "That's a perfectly reasonable assumption, but in fact they got to me through Evie Justin, who is on their board."

"Who on earth is Evie Justin?" Peggy asked, mystified.

"She was Evelyn Harris," Eleanor explained.

"She's Vincent Harris's daughter," Alan added, to complete the identification.

"What are you going to do?" Peggy asked her mother.

"What do you think I ought to do?" Mrs. Altman asked in return.

"You should do exactly as you please," Eleanor rushed to say, lest anyone think she was trying to control her mother-in-law—the last thing in her mind! "Of course, they're dying to have it. But you should loan it only if it would give you pleasure."

"Didn't you just get the Chardin back from Chicago?" Peggy asked, as if only gathering information.

"It's been back for a time now. While it was away, I had gotten the Ingres, and when it came back I didn't want to move the Ingres. I finally put it where the Corot was, but if it goes out, I can put the Corot up there again."

"Doesn't Lattimore want the Ingres for next fall?" Lattimore was the director of the Metropolitan, a polished, unctuous man who often made a fourth for bridge with Mrs. Altman.

"I don't see why Lattimore thinks he can come to you the minute you buy a new painting," Eleanor said angrily.

"They have the Ingres in my will," Mrs. Altman pointed out apologetically.

"That should be enough, then. They can wait."

"I personally don't see why Mother has to do without anything at all, if it makes her even the slightest bit uncomfortable," Peggy said.

"It's just that I feel it's so selfish to have these things and not let as many people as possible see them," Mrs. Altman fretted.

"Oh, Mother!" the adults chorused.

"I never heard of such nonsense," Peggy scolded. "There isn't another collection in New York that's as much used as yours. What with loans and students and some professor or other in here day in and day out!"

Everyone agreed on that.

Alan, who had been looking troubled, said, "I would think the Clark would call on the locals first before coming down here. There must be some Chardins in Boston." He hated for Mrs. Altman's paintings to travel outside the city limits.

"There are Chardins and Chardins," Eleanor informed him. "And none of Mother's quality in Boston that I know of. Not very many in the country."

"The Avalons have a lovely Chardin," Mrs. Altman said generously.

Eleanor agreed. "The Avalons have one, and I wouldn't turn up my nose at the one those aluminum people have . . ." She groped for the name.

"The Douglases," Alan said, adding, "I still think if they can't support their museums up there themselves, they shouldn't come to us." In Alan's geography, there was New York, and there were the provinces.

"Look, darling," Eleanor said, sensing things were not going well. "This Leonard character should never have bothered you in the first place. Instead of your taking any more trouble over it, which is the one thing we want to avoid, why don't we simply tell him that you can't give him a definite yes just yet."

If she thought she could slip that one by Peggy, she was sadly mistaken. "That's all very well, dear," Peggy said, smiling to assure everyone that she had no personal stake in this, but only wanted to protect her overgenerous mother. "But is that what Mother wants, or is it what you want her to want?"

Eleanor's attempt to return her smile was quite hampered by her mixture of feelings: anger, embarrassment, but most of all the belligerency of a woman used to having her way up against another who was no slouch in that respect. Mrs. Altman, who knew perfectly well what was going on, stepped in: "Maybe Phil could take care of it. He manages these things so well. I wonder if you'd call him and say we'll let him know, but not to count on it one way or the other. You always know how to put it. That would be lovely if you would handle it for me, dear."

Everyone relaxed. "Wonderful," Eleanor said delightedly. She knew that Phillip would make sure all the options stayed open. He was very good at that.

"That makes a great deal of sense," Peggy commented, feeling vindicated, and proud of her son.

Everybody was pleased, except for Dickie, who had the wild idea he, as the eldest grandchild, should have been asked to do it. Which was one more example of how poor his judgment was.

Billingsly, who had stood poised at the door, saw his chance and announced, "Dinner is served, Mrs. Altman."

"Thank you, Billingsly," Mrs. Altman said, and got up.

Everyone stood at once, except for Hilda, who hadn't heard Billingsly and had to struggle out of her deep armchair when she saw the others going in to dinner. The men all stood near the door to let the women pass through first, and then Gerald and Alan each made a great show of Alphonse and Gaston after Sammy claimed his dubious precedence. The young men followed. Carl naturally came last.

They crossed the square hallway into the dining room, where they were met by the haughty Ingres noblewoman who glared elegantly at them as they came in. The humble Chardin she had ousted from the place of honor over the mantelpiece was now above the sideboard, where a lavish bowl of fruit and ornate crystal candlesticks contrasted with the pewter objects on the canvas. Peggy and Eleanor tried to seat the table together, never an easy task. Mrs. Altman sat down at the head of the table, and Gerald stood at the foot, so that was a start; but everyone else milled about while the two women agonized over the chaos of trying to seat a family. They finally agreed it couldn't be done. Peggy ceded it to Eleanor, and it went a bit better. Joan went next to Barbara; Dickie was sandwiched between Hilda and Sammy, not a very choice position, but not even his mother cared whether he liked it or not. Carl was put next to Mrs. Altman so he could talk to her about music, which was nice for both of them.

They served the first course immediately. It was a cream of chicken soup, laced with sherry. A special portion was served to Carl, of the same soup without the sherry, since children were thought not to like the taste of wine. Gerald did not take cream soups; he was brought a half a grapefruit. Mrs. Altman had her clear consommé. Joan allowed them to put the soup in front of her, but she took only a small spoonful of it. Peggy saw it—she paid close attention to such things—and with difficulty restrained herself from saying something. Not in front of everyone, she told herself; there would be plenty of time for a quiet word with Joan about it. Celery and olives were handed around in separate dishes, followed by toast, the crusts of which were, of course, trimmed. Eleanor was brought a glass of Evian, and milk was served to Dickie and Carl. Carl hoped no one knew his was skimmed. They might think he was on a diet, and comment endlessly on what he could or couldn't eat. If he could have dieted in peace, he might have conceivably have lost some weight; but in the face of the everyone's help, it was easier just to eat on.

Billingsly brought the bottle of wine over to Gerald to inspect, and handed him the cork, which he sniffed. Gerald nodded, waited for some wine to be poured into his glass, tasted it, and nodded again. His pretentiousness over wine was a standing joke in the family. The story of how he rhapsodized over an unknown vintage only to find it was Coca-Cola was a favorite of the Gutheims. They didn't serve wine at their dinner table, and Mrs. Altman wouldn't have either, except to please her son.

Billingsly asked Joan in a whisper if she wanted any wine. She shook her head almost imperceptibly. Peggy thought that Joan was abstaining from anything with a trace of alcohol in misplaced compliance to the doctors' orders and called across, "Would you like some of Carl's soup?" Joan shook her head. Peggy said nothing more, but she whispered to Billingsly to ask Joan if she wanted some fruit juice instead of the wine. Billingsly made the most discreet inquiry imaginable, and got a sharp no for his trouble.

Gerald liked to start off a meal with a toast. He had raised his glass and cleared his throat before Peggy cut him off. Not only were toasts horribly pompous, she thought, but she also feared he might say something maudlin about Joan, and she hissed to him to skip it. Gerald, who was as used to having his sister order him around as he was his wife, took another sip and put his glass down without a word.

With dinner launched, Alan opened the general conversation. "I don't like this situation in New Orleans at all," he said. He was referring to the violence that had erupted when they tried to put a little Negro girl into the public schools. "With all our difficulties, I'm glad to say you wouldn't find that sort of thing sanctioned by the leading members of this community. We have our problems, God knows, but fortunately this isn't one of them."

"That child!" Eleanor exclaimed. "Did you see her face in the paper this morning? So angelic! To have to go through something like that, at her age!"

"It's a terrible situation," Gerald said gravely. "I think this Reverend Whatever-his-name-is shows a lot of guts."

"Oh, I'll say this for the clergy," Alan said. "They've been in the vanguard of all of this. Whenever there's a march or whatever, you see a lot of turned collars right up there in front. No, I take my hat off to the clergy on this one."

"You have to," Sammy said. "It isn't polite to leave it on." He laughed heavily at his own joke.

Alan brightened. "That reminds me of the famous one: 'He didn't take off his hat.' You know that one, don't you, Sammy?"

Sammy didn't know it. As Alan geared up to tell it, Peggy complained, "Darling, that's as old as the hills."

"Besides which," Eleanor chimed in, "If you're going to tell the punch line first, do we really have to hear the whole joke?"

"It's just that Sammy was saying, you can't leave your hat on, so that reminded me of the famous joke. It seems this woman came into a church with her baby—I heard this from none other than Monsignor

Nugent, you know, the chancellor of the archdiocesan schools?—he has a delicious sense of humor, vows or no vows. It seems this woman came into a church . . ." He started to laugh, and had to start again: "This woman came into a church—"

"There's no stopping him, is there?" Eleanor appealed to Peggy.

"Darling, I've been trying to for twenty-six years."

" 'Sure'n I'd be glad to perform the blessed sacrament,' " Alan went on in his wretched brogue.

"It's like trying to stop the tide from coming in," Carl said. The others smiled. He was going to add something about King Canute, but decided to quit while he was still ahead.

"If only you could at least get him not to tell the punch line first," Eleanor said.

" 'And did the father have red hair too?' " Alan continued, oblivious to the heckling. He was wheezing with laughter. " 'I don't know,' she said, 'he didn't take off his hat!' " His last words were all but lost in his own roars of laughter, and Sammy never did get the point.

"Oh, God," Joan groaned.

"That's the famous 'He didn't take off his hat!' " Alan announced exultantly.

"At least he enjoys it," Eleanor observed.

"I'm glad someone does," Peggy replied.

Mrs. Altman looked down her table, glad to see so large a part of her family with her, enjoying her hospitality, looking happy. Nothing mattered more to her than that her children and grandchildren should be happy. Joan was, of course, her chief worry at the moment, but it seemed as though the worst was over now. At least she hoped so. The news Peggy had brought that afternoon was marvelous, but in its own way it was unsettling. Leukemia! Who would have dreamed such a thing! It couldn't be more wonderful that they had ruled it out, but what was next? It wasn't that she couldn't deal with adversity. She had buried her husband and gone on without a murmur. It wasn't even the unexpected that caused her difficulty. Nathan Altman, after all, had been struck down in the pink of health. But the unknown—who could deal with that? She looked over at Joan. The child was undeniably thin, and pale, and of course none of them sat up straight at the table. But all in all she didn't look bad. She was talking, listening intently, laughing gaily—she had that marvelous, infectious laugh. But what was inside?

Was there something that no one knew of yet but was there all the same, lurking unseen? Who could tell?

Her glance turned from Joan to Gerald, his face furrowed with worry. It upset her to see him like that. "How does it come along, this business?" she asked. She preferred not to have such matters discussed at dinner, but she felt she owed it to her son to show concern.

"*Ça va*, Mother. It's not in the bag, by any means. Don't quote me."

"It's an utter bore," Eleanor told Peggy. "And you can quote me."

"I'm glad you find it so boring," Gerald said testily. "It happens to butter your bread."

"It hasn't buttered a thing, so far," Eleanor retorted. "All it's done that I can see is to keep you on the phone constantly with Morty Pines." She turned back to Peggy. "I know when he's home by the fact that the phone rings, and it's that . . ." She shuddered with disgust at the thought of the unpleasant little man.

"Who is Morty Pines?" Joan asked.

"He's New York's next real estate tycoon," Barbara told her. "Nobody likes him."

"Whether or not anyone likes him is absolutely irrelevant," Gerald said angrily. "Morty Pines is a very smart man."

"Morty Pines is a horse's ass," Peggy put in.

"Peggy, that's not at all helpful," Gerald complained. He was quite flustered with the attack coming from every direction. "It's also not fair."

"It may not be fair, but it's true," Peggy said, turning away from her brother to laugh with the rest of the table at his discomfort.

Just then—virtually without precedent in modern memory—Hilda gave off a rumbling noise that indicated she was about to speak. Everyone turned toward her in amazement to hear what was going to shatter the years of silence. "Who is this they are talking about?" was her question.

The conversation stopped dead. Joan began to giggle. Alan leaned across the table to shout, "Mortimer Pines, Hilda. Mortimer Pines. I don't think you know him. He's in real estate."

"Of course I know him," Hilda said, flapping her hand at Alan in annoyance. "I know him very well. He used to be at Sid's all the time. Know him very well."

Everyone was stumped by that. "I don't think Morty Pines and Sid ever so much as laid eyes on one another," Alan said slowly, trying to reconstruct a hypothetical meeting between Hilda's brother, dead these fifteen years, and the brash upstart who had only come on the scene a few years back. Going as best as he could through Sid's circle, such as it was, and attempting some sort of psychic communication with Hilda's peculiar associations, he made a wild stab: "You're not thinking of Harry Elden, are you, by any chance?"

"That's the one! I know him very well!" Hilda cried insistently.

The kids were approaching the perilous brink of total collapse. Joan was already rocking in her chair, trying to suppress a scream of laughter.

"Isn't he the one you said?" Hilda asked nervously, sensing that she might not have gotten a completely accurate grasp of the conversation. It's possible that she might have reasoned that Harry Elden, who had also died some years since, was not likely to be doing business with Gerald.

"No, Hilda," Alan said as gently and gravely as he could. "We were talking about Mortimer Pines, as it happens."

"I thought you said he was in real estate." She looked down morosely at her soup.

"Yes, I did," Alan conceded. "They were both in real estate, you're right. That was what probably got you confused." He instantly regretted the unfortunate choice of the word, accurate though it was.

"I'm not confused," Hilda insisted, helping herself to more soup, which was being passed for seconds. Joan had begun to splutter like an outboard motor, and the others were having a bad time of it trying to control themselves. Carl alone managed to keep a straight face. He feared the poor woman's feelings would be hurt.

Alan quickly steered the conversation into safer waters. "I'm not at all happy about this transit situation." Mike Quill was making his usual biannual threats of a strike. Every New Year's Day when the contract ran out, the city faced the possibility of grinding to a halt.

"It's terrible!" Barbara cried. "What will people do if they can't take the subway?"

"Why do you care, Bobbie?" Dickie sneered. "The taxis will still be on the streets."

"Try getting one," Sammy said. Everyone else was appalled at Dickie's callous disregard for the general public.

"Speak for yourself, Dickie darling," Barbara shot back. "I happen to ride the subway a lot."

"Do you really?" Alan asked, astonished.

"Yes, I do. I used to take it all the time because my dancing teacher had her studio down in the Village, but I still use it if I'm going down to Lord & Taylor's, something way downtown."

"I'd be just as happy if she wouldn't use it," Eleanor said. "I don't think it's at all safe."

"You couldn't be more wrong!" Alan cried. "Not only is it perfectly safe, but a lot of our problems would be solved if more people would use it. I'm one of its most faithful riders. Many's the time, I can assure you, when I have to get downtown in a hurry, after a Mt. Sinai meeting, say, and Billy Landau or someone offers me a ride, and I always turn it down because I know I'll get there sooner than he will if I take the subway. Oh, no, I use it quite a lot."

"That's wonderful, dear," Peggy said, winking at the others.

"One of the biggest problems the city faces," Alan went on, ignoring his wife's needling, "is transportation. Great as it is, it needs a more efficient system. Do you know you could get from 42nd Street and the East River to 42nd and the Hudson quicker a hundred years ago than you can today? You know how?"

No one knew how.

"By horse!" Alan cried triumphantly.

" *'I sprang to the stirrup, and Joris, and he;*
"*I galloped, Dirck galloped, we galloped all three—'*

You know that famous poem, don't you?" He looked around the table until he caught the habitual blank expression on Dickie's face, which he took to mean Dickie didn't know the famous poem.

" ' *"Good speed!" cried the watch—*' "

"Darling," Peggy warned.

"Well!" Alan explained, "Dickie hadn't heard it."

"After this, just nod, please, Dickie," Phil advised.

"Oh!" Alan cried in horror. "How can you be such a philistine!" He raised his forefinger in the air, like Moses chastising the Israelites, and chanted:

" ' *"Good speed!" cried the watch, as the gatebolts undrew—*' "

"Dear, they're trying to serve you," Peggy informed him. Billingsly had arrived at Alan's elbow with a large platter, which he seemed prepared to hold there until the entire poem had been recited.

"Oh! Pardon me!" Alan apologized to the butler, adding as he served himself, "Although how anyone can be so barbaric as to prefer food to poetry . . ."

"If it's a choice between Mother's food and your poetry . . ." Peggy said.

"It's not mine! It's Browning's! The most famous example of anapestic tetrameter in the English language!"

Mrs. Altman put an end to it by announcing, "We're having roast beef in your honor, Joan dear, since it's your first meal here since you've been back. I asked your mother what you would like best, and she thought roast beef."

The large silver platter Billingsly was serving from was covered with thick slices of roast beef. Most of it was rare, although at one end were several well-done slices for Barbara and Phil, who didn't like their meat rare. Two maids followed. The first carried a bowl of roast potatoes, the second carried a divided dish with peas on one side and creamed spinach on the other. When Billingsly finished serving the meat, he came around again with a tray on which were placed a special little saucer of sharp English mustard, which he placed in front of Eleanor, and a larger glass dish of horseradish, which he passed. The maids made a second round to pass the toast and a large bowl of pink applesauce. The crescent glass salad plates were placed, and the salad passed, while the main course was being eaten. Gerald used to argue that the salad should not be served while wine was being drunk; but Mrs. Altman had always done it that way, and it never changed. An oozing Camembert was served with the salad.

The constant intrusion of one serving dish after another and the concentration required by the food caused a lull in the talk. Everyone fell to their plates, and spoke to the people next to them to fill in the gaps. Under the cover of the chatter and the noise of the serving dishes, Barbara was whispering excitedly to Joan about her boyfriend. "He's completely dreamy, to start with. He's over six feet, not *grotesque*, but tall and very dark. He's not you-know-what, which is fine with me." Barbara had never found Jewish men attractive; George's sole good point in her eyes had been his straight blond hair. "He has two smiles: one he uses in public, and the other is kind of dirty. You might not think much of his build if you saw him in a suit or something, but he is *incredibly* sexy, believe me. I haven't slept with him, I know you're thinking I have, not that I wouldn't like to."

Joan looked around, alarmed by the recklessness of Barbara's talk. But the others were absorbed in their own conversations, or their thoughts, or the roast beef. Only Hilda stared blankly ahead, and there was no danger of her overhearing anything, poor soul. The old woman put down her knife and fork, covered her mouth with her napkin, and erupted in a long, low burp. Everyone pretended not to hear.

"How old is he?" Joan asked, smiling in spite of herself at Hilda.

"He'll be twenty in July. You'd never know it to look at him. I always forget that he's younger than I am."

"What does he do?" Joan knew better than to ask where he went to college.

"Right now he's between things. He's trying to find himself. He wants to marry, settle down, get a job, maybe acting. He says he wasn't ready for it before, but he is now. If Daddy knew, he would have him locked up in a dungeon and have the key thrown into the deepest part of the ocean."

"Don't you think it'd be a good idea if they met him?" Joan asked, thinking to end the various deceptions.

"Good God, no. He would never survive that. I doubt that I would survive it. You have absolutely no idea how lucky you are that your parents let you lead your own life. They never interfere."

Joan looked over at her mother. It was strange that Barbara thought she was so free, when she felt so trapped. She on her part envied Barbara, who could fight her battles in the open, while she had to writhe and struggle against an invisible net. Peggy caught her eye and smiled fondly. Joan could hear her say, "I only want you to do whatever would make you happy," and then she would arrange every last detail down to the most minute. Eleanor at least never camouflaged her opinions, or her coercion.

Seconds were going around. Joan took a little more roast beef, since it had been ordered specially for her, but she had no appetite for it. It was easier, though, to take some on her plate than to have everyone carry on about it if she didn't. She couldn't take one more person asking her how she was feeling. She looked over at Carl. The little beachball, she always called him. He was next to Mrs. Altman, who urged him to take seconds. Joan had told Peggy not to let him sit there, that Mrs.

Altman indulged him horribly. It was perfectly true. He took everything except the toast. When the applesauce came around, there was no
more room on the plate, so he put it on top of the peas. Disgusting! No
wonder she felt nauseated at the thought of food. It revolted her, seeing
this orgy of eating covered over by the thinnest veneer of civilized behavior. She felt as though everyone was looking at her, watching every
bite she put in her mouth, checking to see what she ate, what she left,
what went in, what stayed out. It was as if she had no will of her own.

"I saw Edna Margolis at Percy's whatchamacallit on Sunday,"
Peggy called down to Mrs. Altman. "She sends you her best. I think it's
terrible they let her get off the board at Co-operating."

"She isn't getting any younger, you know," Mrs. Altman pointed
out. She was the only one present who could say such a thing.

Phil said to his father, "By the way, I forgot to tell you, I heard at
the commission that Fred Lowenthal is not getting the judgeship after
all. It was vetoed."

Alan looked perturbed. "Fifty-first Street?" he guessed.

Phil nodded. "So I understand."

"The gall of it!" Alan exploded. "They blackball a man whose great
crime is that his wife—not even him, but his wife!—is head of Planned
Parenthood. And then they expect us to vote for someone who takes his
orders from his confessor?" He eyed the doorway to the pantry, in case
one of the maids should suddenly come in. "This fellow Cushing, I
understand, is little better than Spellman. And on top of that there's the
old man! I have a hard time swallowing a president of the United States
of America who's the son of the biggest unjailed crook in the country."

"Would you rather swallow Nixon?" Peggy taunted him.

"Don't get me started on that snake!" Alan declared.

"Don't get him started on that snake," Eleanor begged her sister-in-
law.

"Who's getting the judgeship, then, did you hear, Phil?" Gerald
asked.

"I've heard it'll go to someone by the name of Finsterman," Phil
told his uncle. "He's been in Washington. At Justice. That's all I know
about him."

"I'll tell you exactly who he is," Alan said. "He married Nancy
Isaacson!" He grinned as he nailed the identification.

"Oh, I'd forgotten that," Eleanor said. "Nancy Isaacson was an old
flame of your uncle Walter's," she added for Barbara's benefit.

"Everyone seems to have been a flame of Uncle Walter's," Barbara observed.

"He had quite a few," Gerald agreed. "I always said, if there had been fewer flames, and more fires, you might have had another aunt. Hopefully not one of his chorus girls."

"Walter didn't take out chorus girls!" Eleanor protested.

"Not only did he take out chorus girls," Gerald insisted, "but that is giving some of them the benefit of the doubt. Sorry, Mother." Mrs. Altman had closed her eyes in silent protest against such talk at the dinner table.

It was dessert time. First came a molded ice-cream bombe, chocolate on the outside, then a layer of vanilla, and an inner nougat of orange ice. Next came a silver boat full of hot, thick chocolate sauce. The sauce, of course, didn't go at all with the orange ice, but neither one was felt to be dispensable. Then came a silver platter of small cylindrical yellow cakes that were glazed all over with chocolate icing, except for a few that were frosted with a butter cream, for Barbara, whose skin did not react well to chocolate. For Hilda there was a bowl of mixed stewed fruits, another reminder of the deprivations of old age. Gerald was brought a plate of wine-colored grapes, the same kind that were in the large fruit bowl in the center of the table, only his were cold. Coffee was served to everyone except Carl, and Hilda, who took tea. Mrs. Altman and Eleanor both took Sanka in the evening. Dickie asked for another glass of milk. A tray with cream, sugar, and saccharine was passed, and a saucer with lemon slices was placed next to Hilda's teacup. She didn't see it, and looked sadly on the serving tray for it—she didn't like to ask for anything special for herself—until the waitress whispered to her that the lemon was already at her place. Hilda couldn't hear what she was saying, and wouldn't have understood her Galway accent if she had, so the waitress had to point out the lemons. When Carl thought no one was looking, he took a chocolate-covered peppermint from the peacock-shaped dish at his end of the table and laid it carefully against his plate so it would be handy as soon as he finished his dessert.

Appreciative moans about the dessert were heard around the table. Mrs. Altman smiled in acknowledgment, as though she had personally baked or at least frosted the cakes. Surveying her family's contentment —she didn't notice that Joan ate nothing of the dessert—she said, "I was glad to see that your friend Felicia Reiner is engaged."

"Yes, it's very nice," Joan replied.

"Isn't it lovely," Eleanor agreed. "Although the picture wasn't very flattering."

"Considering what they had to work with, it wasn't bad at all," Peggy observed. "She's a perfectly sweet girl, but a photographer's dream she ain't."

"Still, I would have thought Florence could have gotten a picture that didn't make her look so washed out."

"She's pretty washed out in real life, Aunt Eleanor," Phil said.

"Well, I couldn't be more delighted," Mrs. Altman said. "I understand he's a lovely boy."

"He is, he's quite nice," Joan confirmed. "Quiet," she added.

"Quiet!" exclaimed Phil. "His personality matches Felicia's complexion."

"He doesn't talk a lot, which you wouldn't understand," Joan scolded. "But he's very nice."

"Isn't his mother Teddy Hiller's sister?" Eleanor asked.

"Cousin," Alan corrected her. "Her father was William Hiller, and Teddy is of course Edward Junior. They were brothers, William and Edward Senior—he was just called Edward, in fact—and I think there was one other boy. Wasn't there, Mother, besides the sister?"

Mrs. Altman nodded. "There was a younger brother, Frank, who died as a child. He had never been well. Something the matter with his heart. They had a house down at the shore, just next to your great-aunt Lucy's, and I remember he was never allowed to go in the water. The rest of them were all very hearty, and then there was this poor thin little boy who wasn't allowed to do anything. He used to have to sit on the beach, all bundled up, on the hottest days, while everyone else went bathing. It was such a shame, really: they could at least have let him enjoy himself in the little time he had. But of course in those days if you had the slightest thing the matter with you, you stopped everything and went to bed. Not like today." And then, worried she might have inadvertently offended Joan, or Peggy, she added hastily, "The sister, Norma, was the grandmother of your friends the Unger boys."

"Oh, really?" Joan asked.

You could see Alan gathering himself for the genealogy: "Norma Hiller was married twice." He always began as though reciting an epic. "The first time was to a man named Gordon Tollman, who was quite a distinguished surgeon in this town. If you ever God forbid broke your hip, you went to Dr. Tollman. He invented some kind of contraption, I think they named it after him, that they put in after everything you might have started out with gives out. They had a daughter, Ruth, who is now Ruth Weiler, she married Harold Weiler, and you know their children, I think, wasn't the girl in Barbara's class at Spence?"

"Marian's," Eleanor said.

"I stand corrected," Alan allowed. "Anyway, the Tollmans were divorced when Ruth was, I imagine, still a baby. There weren't that many divorces in those days, but I think he had a nurse in his operating room who was doing a bit more for him than handing him the scalpel. Am I right, Mother?" Mrs. Altman nodded her reluctant agreement, eyes shut tight. "Norma remarried, this time to Irving Unger, which is how she got to be the grandmother—or was, they're both dead now, she and Irving—to Dick and Larry Unger. She and Irving had three children. The oldest was Jeanne, who was the famous one who had to be carried off the *Normandie* on a stretcher. You remember, dear?" he asked Peggy.

"Do I remember! How could anyone forget?" Peggy took over the narrative. "It seems she had been in Europe, and evidently cut herself, and the cut got infected. In those days, of course, there were no such things as antibiotics, and it just so happened that at that very time the President's son—Calvin Coolidge's son—up and died of blood poisoning. You can imagine what a scare that provoked. It makes no sense but all I can tell you is that there was an *absolute hysteria.* People with the tiniest little scratches you could barely see would go to bed and not move a muscle for fear the poison would 'get into their system!' So when Jeanne Unger got this infection, and in Europe, no less, where the water isn't very reliable, she went completely to pieces. Or her mother did, no one was ever quite sure which. She came home immediately, or as immediately as she could be gotten suitable accommodations, because of course it would never do to cross to an unsuitable ship, never mind if you were dying. So evidently they managed to get her on the *Normandie*—"

"Than which there was nothing more suitable," Eleanor put in.

"It was considered one of the finest," Alan commented. "In those days there were four great liners: the *Normandie,* the *America,* and the two *Queens.*"

"I always liked the *Cristoforo Columbo,* I must say," Sammy ventured.

"Well, yes," Alan condescended, "but it wasn't one of the top four.

The *Normandie* was said to be the greatest restaurant in the world, land or sea. If you ordered a dish on the *Normandie* and the chef couldn't make it for you, it probably didn't exist."

"At any rate," Peggy continued, "there was a picture in all the papers of Jeanne Unger being carried off the *Normandie* on a stretcher, attended by God only knows how many doctors and nurses, because it turned out the line didn't want anything to happen to her until she was on American soil, and then the family had her met by an ambulance and several more doctors, so there was quite an entourage."

Alan took it up, chuckling: "Everyone saw the picture and assumed that Jeanne was as good as dead, so when she turned up about a week later at some social gathering or other, and none the worse for wear, there were quite a few raised eyebrows, you may be sure. But what was the poor girl supposed to do? She couldn't stay in bed for the rest of her life! Anyway, she made this miraculous recovery and went on to marry a man by the name of Niles. The perfect definition of a nobody. He was from somewhere down in Pennsylvania, Scranton, or Bethlehem, although he had nothing to do with coal at all. Everyone who knew the Vernon Nileses thought he must be related to the Lewis Nileses, and everybody who knew the Lewis Nileses thought he must be related to the Vernon Nileses, and it turned out he wasn't related to anyone! No one knew where Jeanne found him. She was back in town two years later, married Bob Hendricks on the second go-around, and that seems to have worked out all right."

"If you call having to drink a fifth of Scotch a day to put up with her working out all right," Peggy amended.

"In all fairness to Jeanne," Alan said, "I think Bob was hitting the bottle pretty heavily before she came into the picture."

"Why do I know the name Bob Hendricks?" Phil asked.

"I'll tell you why," Peggy answered. "When you used to go up to Martha's Vineyard to visit your friend, what's his name——?"

"Tony Holliger."

"Tony Holliger. You used to take that tiny little plane up, you know, the one that used to make your father so nervous?"

"I still say it was sheer madness to let him go up on that airline," Alan said, frowning with worry despite the safe return, some five years ago, of his son.

"I'm still here, Dad," Phil said cheerfully.

"It was still crazy. You know the song 'Comin' in on a Wing and a

Prayer?' That should have been the theme song for that airline." He
started to sing the song but was groaned down.

"Anyway," Peggy resumed, "the Ungers have, or used to have, I
lose track of such things, a place on the Vineyard, and Bob used to go up
for the weekend during July. You probably sat next to him one time on
the plane."

"Mother, if he was on the plane, I sat next to him. All the seats were
next to each other."

"It was madness," Alan insisted. "But anyhow, that's Jeanne." He
brightened as he returned to his history. "The next one in the family is
Alfred, who is of course Larry and Dick's father, and then there was
another daughter, named Lillian, who married Vic Gardner. He's, you
know, the man who really put Hamilton Industries on the map. Whit
Hamilton always gets the credit, but the real brains there if you ask me
was Vic Gardner. He's also, incidentally, an uncle of your friend Ellen
Frankel," he added to Joan, who was looking dazed. Everyone was more
or less stupefied. He had started out with Felicia Reiner, and now here
he was at Ellen Frankel. "His sister was Doris Gardner, now Doris
Frankel," Alan confirmed himself, nodding for further emphasis.
"That's right."

"Wait a minute . . ." Joan said, thoroughly confused. "What does
that make Ellen to the Ungers?"

"They must be cousins!" Barbara cried out.

"They aren't related at all!" Alan exclaimed in great excitement,
like a magician who, having put any number of objects into his hat,
whisks away a scarf and reveals the hat to be empty. "Ellen's mother's
brother married an Unger, don't you see? It's her uncle, their aunt.
They're no relation at all!"

"They're *mehuttin.*" Peggy corrected him.

"Distant," Alan conceded that much.

"But it does make cousins out of the Ungers and the Weilers," Phil
offered by way of consolation. "Stepcousins, at any rate."

"Half cousins, yes," Alan allowed. "Ruth Weiler is Alfred Unger's
half sister. So they're half cousins. But none of them is related to Ellen
Frankel at all."

"Well, I think it's lovely about Felicia," Mrs. Altman said, to end the
matter. She was the only one who could stop Alan. Unchecked, he
would have followed another branch of the family tree, along to the
farthest twig; or perhaps jump, squirrel-like, to yet another and start in

all over again. The Frankels were related, on the other side, to the Strassers, and if he got onto the Strassers they could have been there all night.

To forestall that, Mrs. Altman gave a nearly imperceptible push downward on the arms of her chair. She didn't change her position, but she galvanized everyone else into action. Billingsly materialized instantly from nowhere and put his hands on the back of her chair. All of the men sprang up together. The women reached for the handbags they had left in the living room. One of the maids stood at the doorway. Even Hilda could see that dinner was over, and she put her napkin to her mouth for one last eructation, hoping it would be lost in the general rising from the table. Carl saw that Phil had left a cake half-uneaten on his plate, and managed to wolf it down unobtrusively on his way out. Everyone said, "Thank you, Grandmother." She smiled and passed toward the door.

With everyone in transit, Dickie intruded himself in Alan's path and said, "I'd like a word with you, if I may, Uncle Alan." For no apparent reason his tone was quite provocative, and he looked, or tried to look, masterful.

Everyone stopped where they were. The room became very still. No one was used to hearing such belligerence in the presence of Mrs. Altman. Only Hilda, who hadn't heard Dickie, continued her dogged trudge toward the door. Seeing her hostess barring her way, she turned to see what had gone amiss.

Gerald was actually the one to reply. "This is hardly the time or the place," he muttered angrily. "You're behaving like a fool." Dickie blanched, but he continued to stare at his uncle. For a family that had a horror of any kind of public scene, it was quite sensational. Barbara started to titter, but she was scowled down by her father.

Alan looked uncertain. No one had told him about anything, but he always assumed the worst. He was ready to help anyone, everyone. Not this very moment, perhaps, but in principal. "I'd be only too happy to—" he began, but Gerald cut him off too.

"Thanks, Alan, but there's no need for that. If Dickie wants to talk to you, which incidentally would be a colossal waste of your time, he can make an appointment through your secretary. There's no need for him to disturb Mother."

Dickie was stung. "It's not Grandmother I want to talk to," he said valiantly, although it was clear his resolve was already crumbling. "I just want to speak to Uncle Alan for a few moments. It won't disturb anyone."

Gerald's face took on that peculiar tightness that was his sign of barely suppressed fury. "Who are you to decide whom it will or won't disturb? In point of fact you have already disturbed all of us. We've just had a perfectly delicious dinner and are about to enjoy hearing your cousin play the piano. No one has the slightest interest in sitting around and waiting while you pester your uncle about some nonsense that neither he nor anyone else ought to pay the slightest attention to. If you insist on pursuing this idiocy, at least kindly have the taste not to inflict it on the rest of us. Least of all your grandmother."

Everyone was mystified, but would have been patient had it not been for the provocation of the word *idiocy*, which drove Barbara to ask, "What's this all about?"

"None of your business, Bobbie," Dickie hissed.

"Since I've asked Dickie not to talk about it here, I'll ask the same of you, Bobbie," her father said, but in a much gentler tone that must have infuriated Dickie by its obvious favoritism.

"As a matter of fact," Dickie said, goaded into outright rebellion, "it's exactly because no one will listen to a thing I say that I want to talk to Uncle Alan. I want to invest some money, and Father of course won't hear of it. He doesn't know what the deal is, and he doesn't care. If I'm the one to find out about it, it must be worthless. Fine. I don't want to argue with him. All I want is to find out how to put my hands on my own money. No one else's, just what's rightfully mine. I don't think that's asking too much."

A fantastic episode! The idea of raising the sordid issue of money in front of Mrs. Altman, to say nothing of the rest of the family, was as outrageous as a shouted obscenity. Nothing Dickie had ever said or done had remotely approached this for sensation. It was completely without precedent. Everyone was too shocked to know what to say, except for Hilda, who asked plaintively, "What's this? What is it he wants?"

No one made any attempt to clear up her confusion—it would have been impossible at that point—but Gerald told Dickie, "It's a debatable point whether anything is rightfully yours, considering your past and present conduct. As I've told you, trusts are established for a purpose, and you are doing a good job of showing why, if nothing else. This whole thing is absolutely unacceptable talk for your grandmother's, and if you expect to be allowed to stay, you'll have to behave yourself accordingly."

With that, the group resumed its progress out of the room. Only Dickie stood his ground, defiantly, while the others more or less stepped around him. Mrs. Altman was quite distressed, but said nothing. She hoped that if everyone continued in their course, the scene that had just taken place would be caused never to have happened. It would simply be annulled. She passed on into the hallway, where the elevator was waiting, stepped in, waited for Hilda to join her, and nodded to Billingsly. He got in to take the two ladies down to the first floor, while the others walked down the staircase past the millefleurs tapestries. Everyone played it straight. Carl tried to catch Phil's or Joan's eye, but they wouldn't return his half smile. Dickie came last, shunned by his relatives. At the bottom he hesitated, thinking perhaps to walk out in protest, but on consideration followed the rest into the ballroom. No one looked at him.

Mrs. Altman came in, took her seat, and everyone sat down. As cheerfully as she was able, she said, "Now we can have the music. Carl, dear?" Carl feigned surprise, got up again, and went to the piano. Alan beamed in anticipation, and said to his mother-in-law, "He's got a Chopin Ballade he's been working on that he can really play the hell out of."

Carl hated performing. His bad nerves and his dislike of being looked at made it torturous, even among just the family. He was still feeling shell-shocked from the master class and would have been glad to be excused for once. But there was no escaping. At one time he used to protest, never to any effect. "Nonsense," Peggy would say, "you play beautifully, dear. It gives so much pleasure. Don't have to be coaxed." It was simpler to play and be done with it. Besides, it did make his grandmother inordinately happy. Carl would have been glad to do it for her. The others were a less gratifying audience.

He waited for the talking to stop. The mood was obviously jittery, after Dickie's pathetic eruption. Barbara was still whispering to Joan, but he decided to go ahead anyway. He was about to announce the piece when Peggy asked, "What are you going to play, dear?"

"This is an etude by Scriabin," he said glumly.

"An etude!" Sammy exclaimed. "That's very difficult!" He made it sound as though Carl were about to execute a backward somersault.

"Maybe he'll play the Chopin afterward," Alan said hopefully. Barbara continued her chatter, and Carl bowed his head in preparation for the hushed opening.

He chose the Scriabin because its sad beauty appealed to him that evening, and also because it was short; he didn't think the group was up to anything very taxing at that point, and he was certainly not up to the Chopin again. He loved playing this etude. He concentrated on making a rich, sonorous tone, and allowed himself to fall under its melancholy spell. He brought out the inner voices, and emphasized the tragic inevitability of the opening theme's return near the end. The harmonies became increasingly complex, and in their inexorable progression one could hear the note of fate. It really was a gorgeous piece. It would have been nice if Barbara could have shut up.

With the very first notes, a feeling of serenity and joy filled Mrs. Altman. She loved nothing better than to be surrounded by her family, and to hear such beautiful music as well gave her perfect contentment. She closed her eyes to give herself over completely to it.

Seated next to her on the sofa, Peggy was relieved that Carl had played without fuss. For a child who could give so much to others, and also have the attention she knew he craved, Carl could be extraordinarily temperamental. She was glad to see his face relax as he played. That tense, drawn look—if such a chubby face could be said to be tense and drawn—melted as he lost himself in the music. He was a different person when he was playing. She was uncertain about a musical career for him; it would be a difficult life. But he was fated to a difficult life. Her poor baby. She did worry about him. The others didn't find life half so perplexing. What a relief, she thought, to have this nuisance with Joan over with! Talk about a weight lifted from one's shoulders! Not that she had ever believed for a minute all the dire things they were saying before Lamartine came in and put a stop to all that nonsense. For some reason Joan was still restless, though; dissatisfied; troubled. No one else saw it, she was sure. Alan thought Joan didn't have a care in the world, now that she had been given a clean bill of health. The next event, in his view, was her wedding. Peggy doubted it. Sweet as he was, and getting handsomer by the day, Johnny would never keep pace with Joan. Joan wanted something different; not that she had the slightest idea what she did want. No, there were some storms ahead there too. It wasn't over. Not by a long shot.

Gerald, sitting across from his sister, sank into his armchair, exhausted. The proxy business would be plenty without the constant worries about his children. If one was temporarily quiet, another would be sure to create an uproar. Surely Job hadn't suffered more than he did. Where had they gone wrong with Dickie, he wondered. What should they have done? He had asked himself that question over and over, and never could come up with an answer. Let him have his way, he was tempted to say, and cut loose altogether. Good riddance. The only trouble was, he would be the laughingstock all over the city. Lord! It would be nice to enjoy the music, but with all he had on his mind . . . His eyes were heavy. He thought he would just close them for a minute . . .

Phil watched Gerald nod off. He understood his uncle thoroughly. Even though he was in a way the beneficiary of Dickie's failings, raising him in his uncle's estimation, this latest was really excessive. And it wasn't that helpful to him either. With the clerkship in the balance, the last thing he needed was a scandal in the family. He hoped Barbara wouldn't get pregnant again. They'd have to put an abortionist on retainer for her. And there was Marian, ranting and raving up in Westchester. No telling what mischief was being planned up there. Randy, at least, represented no greater threat than being booted out of college, but you could never be sure. If only they would all just stay put for another two months; then let them bust loose, if that's what they wanted. They would, he was sure. If you know you're never going to amount to anything, what else is there left in life but to create scenes?

Really, he thought, Carl had a knack for choosing the most tedious pieces. It was inconceivable that he would ever have any sort of career. Serkin notwithstanding.

Eleanor was struck by the contrast between the really quite lovely sounds coming from the piano, and the amazingly unprepossessing figure producing them. Her sister-in-law had her hands full with that boy. Maybe not as full as she had with Dickie. Barbara was by contrast child's play. They'd be rid of this current one of hers in no time, whoever he might be. How nice that she and Joan were rediscovering each other. They had been such great friends as girls. It might be good for Barbara, not that Joan was the model of stability. Whatever the tests might say, Eleanor knew Peggy was still worried. In truth, seeing Joan didn't totally reassure one. Felicia Reiner looked positively plethoric next to her. But one couldn't deny, she had a marvelous joie de vivre. Eleanor sighed. Whatever he might look like, the boy really did play beautifully.

Sammy looked at his watch and sighed inwardly. How long, he

wondered, before he could decently leave. It was sheer perversity in Frieda not to let him have a cigar after dinner. Nathan had never been without one in his mouth, morning, noon, or night. It was the old story: he who pays the piper . . . Sammy was, of course, not supposed to have a complaint in the world, they were so marvelous, these relatives of his. Really, he didn't know why he put up with all their little humiliations. A decent meal, yes, but was it worth it? To sit through yet another interminable rendition from this curious boy?

Well! Dickie thought, he had gone and done it. He had shot all his rockets, and had got nothing but duds. He had thought that by standing up, for once, to them all, they might take him seriously. Wrong again. They were all against him, that much was clear. He had no ally in the family, not one. Certainly not Phil, that prig. It was only a matter of time before he was pushed out altogether, and Phil put in his rightful place. That's what his father had wanted all along. He had never gotten one word of encouragement, one sign of trust from the bastard. He'd never get his hands on any real money, either. They'd all tied everything tighter than a drum: his father, Uncle Alan, the whole gang. Well, if he couldn't touch his own money, he'd just have to borrow. This was too good a deal to pass up. His father would be horrified, but screw him! He'd never know anyway. Not until the day Dickie had the pleasure of coming to him and informing him that his own son, who he thought didn't have a brain in his head, had just made a killing in the stock market! Beaten him at his own game! Dickie imagined the look on his father's face, and found it amusing.

Barbara saw her brother's mirthless smile, and wondered what the cause of it was. Probably some girl he was being horrible to. How awful, to have been stuck with him for a brother. Randy wasn't much better, just out of the way, thank God, for now. Even Carl, no bargain, would have been better. As for Phil! If he wasn't a cousin, she would definitely go to bed with him. She wondered if he and Betsy were sleeping together regularly. She bent toward Joan again, to tell her about the other night . . .

Joan wished Barbara would be quiet. She had heard all she wanted to, and then some, about this creep. He sounded dreadful. She was worried Barbara would mistake her silence for approval. Actually, she wanted to hear the music. She hadn't heard her brother play in a long time. She never admitted it, but she loved listening to him. If only the rest of him came anywhere near his musical ability, there might be a shred of hope for him. Bobbie's chatter was like static on the radio. What she could hear sounded quite pretty, really. But she didn't want to hurt her cousin's feelings by telling her to stop whispering. Underneath the giggles and the silliness Joan could hear the confusion, the anxiety, the unhappiness. If only she could help.

Alan was beside himself. It was sacrilege, to talk during the music! He watched his son's hands with great interest. Amazing, how such an awkward boy could move his fingers with that much dexterity. The piece was not entirely to his liking. He would have preferred a Chopin. But he didn't complain. To have a musician in the family! One day, Carnegie Hall. Nothing could make him prouder. One son on the Supreme Court bench, the other playing with the Philharmonic. As for Joan—she was the toast of the town. Thank God for her recovery. A bad scare, but now all was well again.

Whatever you might say, the boy could play the hell out of that keyboard.

Little more than a faint buzzing reached Aunt Hilda's ears. She felt an aching sadness to realize she would never really enjoy music again. She remembered the night she had been taken to hear the immortal Paderewski—that was heaven! Never to know it again! Tears filled her eyes. Life held so little for her anymore. She missed her brother terribly. Frieda was always so kind, but the others laughed at her, she knew that. What could she do? Where else could she go? Who would have ever dreamed, when she had been young, and—if she did say so herself— pretty, that it would all come to this. She had made a fool of herself at dinner. She knew perfectly well that Harry Elden was dead. He had died not long after Sid. They probably thought she was senile. Maybe she was. This boy, for example, playing the piano—she couldn't for the life of her think who he was. He couldn't be Peggy and Alan's: Peggy had lost that third child when she was carrying it. Hilda remembered it well. She had been staying with Frieda at the time, in the country. Sid was still alive then. The roses had been beautiful that summer. At least she could still enjoy the flowers. Frieda's heavenly flowers. But she would have given anything to be able to hear the music. It must be enchanting, she was sure.

Around the corner, out of sight, Billingsly stood in the hallway and listened. As soon as Carl had gone to the piano, he had opened the door to the back hall so the rest of the help could hear. They had come out of the kitchen and were crowded on the back stairs, straining to hear.

When Carl was a little boy, he would come on a summer morning to Rosefield, when the family was all out, and play the piano for the help. He'd play all their requests, all the old favorite songs, always winding up with " 'Tis the Last Rose of Summer." Kathleen would cry. They all stood on the stairs now, hardly breathing for fear of missing a note. When the piece was over, they stayed for a moment, until Billingsly came over to close the door, and they went down to finish the dishes and resume the nightly pinochle game. "When I die, I'd ask for nothing more than to have him play at my funeral," Kathleen said wistfully, knowing that no such sounds would accompany her soul's last journey. "He plays like an angel, that one."

In the ballroom, the end of the piece was greeted with gasps of "Ahhhh!" and everyone smiled. Carl came over to Mrs. Altman, who kissed him. "That was lovely, dear," she said gratefully.

Eleanor smiled brilliantly at Carl. "You play divinely, dear," she said.

Peggy commented approvingly: "You've been practicing, haven't you? It shows."

The others took up their conversations, except for Dickie, whom nobody paid the slightest attention to; and Alan, who looked a bit disappointed, and asked, of no one in particular: "No Chopin?"

Ten

The airless shroud that had enveloped Joan ever since she came home was gone the next morning. When she walked out of the door of 685 Park to go to work, a benign city greeted her. The air was mild again, the sky lighter. She was refreshed. The thick, cottony feeling in her head had dissolved. When the doorman asked her if she wanted a taxi, she told him she would be taking the subway to work now. He smiled fondly; he knew Alan's pride in riding those filthy trains. "Be careful, Miss Joan," he warned, touching his cap. Years before, he had always urged her to look both ways before crossing the street. Waving gaily at him, she turned to walk downtown.

She continued on Park to 68th Street, then turned east. The side street had a lovely, early morning feeling. Not many people were out yet. A few men were walking their dogs, standing primly and pretending not to notice the disgusting spectacle taking place next to their feet. The women she passed didn't look as though they lived in the neighborhood, but probably came from somewhere else to work there—shop clerks, or some of them might be cleaning ladies. In the middle of the block she recognized the girl who sold cosmetics and soap at Hancock's Pharmacy, and smiled at her; but the girl passed by with a stone face. She was quite young, and had no doubt been lectured not to so much as exchange glances with anyone in the street. The nuns would have told her that. She might not have recognized Joan. The usual crowd of girls one always saw hanging around Hunter College hadn't assembled yet. Classes wouldn't begin this early. Joan was pleased to be up with the working people.

It was election day. She had forgotten about it until she saw the bunting hanging in the window of the Democratic headquarters on Lexington Avenue. Now she noticed how many people were wearing campaign buttons. Up toward Third Avenue a group of men were drinking coffee, their picket signs resting upside down along the fence, policemen lounging nearby. There must be a school there, Joan thought. She hadn't registered. Her first year of being twenty-one, and she had failed her first test as a citizen. Feeling unpatriotic, she hurried down the stairs into the subway station.

A train was just pulling in. Joan allowed herself to be pushed into the crush of people who always stayed near the door so they could be sure of getting out at their stop. She made sure she clutched her purse to her side with her elbow as she reached with the other hand for the post, to steady herself. She hadn't quite grasped it when the train jolted off, and she lurched backward. She would have fallen if the car hadn't been packed. As it was, she was thrown against a nicely dressed Negro woman. She felt bad, but she was careful not to apologize too profusely. The woman said it was all right, and seemed not to mind. She was used to that sort of thing, and had long since learned not to complain; certainly not to a white woman. Everything would have been fine if it weren't that a man, seeing how unsteady Joan was, offered her his seat. Joan didn't know what to say. The offer was considerate, but there was the colored woman, older than she was, still standing up. She had probably been on her feet all the way down from Harlem, and would probably be on them most of the day. How did she like seeing a seat offered to a snip of a girl who had just boarded, wearing a coat from Bonwit's? Joan declined the seat politely, but she had still been party to an insult. Short of making a scene, though, there wasn't much she could have done. Maybe she should have made a scene, she thought. Her mother would have made a scene. Joan had a lot to learn yet.

The woman, thank God, got out at 59th. At Grand Central the car emptied considerably. Joan took a seat, knowing that she would also be on her feet most of the day, and then there was a fresh onslaught of passengers. They came in like a marauding army, crowding the car even more than it had been. Joan wondered if she should keep her seat in view of all the older women, some of them with large shopping bags or packages. But next to her were nothing but men, and she wasn't going to give her seat up for one of them. A young man in tight pegged pants stood directly in front of her. He wore the insolent air of someone who thought better of himself than he had any right to think, with his greased hair and bad complexion. Joan wondered if he would bump up against her, or in some way act rudely. He managed not to touch her at all. He just stood in front of her, swaying, thrusting his pelvis out toward her more than was necessary to keep his balance. In fact, it had nothing to do with balance, she saw. Of course she looked. It was revolting, but she couldn't take her eyes away. To her relief, he got off at Eighth. She was afraid he might have taken it into his head to follow her. The next stop was hers. Houston Street.

Houston is a broad street, really a boulevard, with benches on its wide sidewalks. The benches were empty at that hour, but the sidewalks were crowded. The autumnal smell of roasting chestnuts hung thick in the air. The brazier where they were being roasted was just next to the subway station. Down the street was a cart from which a man was selling pretzels, thick and doughy. He smeared mustard on them before handing them on to customers, and they looked delicious, although the idea of mustard at that hour of the morning was faintly revolting.

She crossed over Houston and turned downtown on Allen Street. It was exciting just to be there. The people seemed to her wonderful— simple, honest, friendly. Joan saw more goodness in them than in her rich neighbors uptown. She liked the tieless men and the women who looked old-world and earthy in their cloth coats, flat shoes, and babushkas. All the political signs, buttons, and placards here were for Kennedy and Johnson. No Republicans dared show their faces.

Allen Street was lined with stores on both sides, almost all of them already open. Racks of clothing were out on the sidewalks. The windows were crammed with more merchandise, not arranged in artful display but simply put there with their price tags. Sales, specials, clearances were all crudely crayoned on the windows themselves in white or colored soaps. There was no nonsense, no pretense: dresses, shoes, purses, appliances, secondhand books, lamps, bric-a-brac, used furniture, each store stuck to its own business. Occasionally there was an incongruous sideline: sheet music at the stationery, or the thicket of umbrellas in a TV store. Standing among the flickering screens, the uniformly black umbrellas had a guilty look, as if they had been swiped from elsewhere. But for the most part the commerce here seemed genuine, immediate, life-sustaining, not feeding the jaded appetites of an overindulged clientele.

She was glad to be there, and with a right, a purpose. She was no sightseer. Still, she didn't really belong. When people glanced at her, she thought they must know she was an outsider. How she would have loved to be taken for one of them. She wanted to live there. Maybe she could find an apartment with one or two other girls from the neighborhood, ones who had grown up there; or maybe one native, and Jenna. She saw her life simplifying, becoming closer to the people she was serving. Her father would of course have a fit. He would rant and rave and talk darkly of crime, which he otherwise hated to admit took place in New York. Her mother would take a different tack: She would seem to be pleased and helpful, but wind up just as impossible. Her list of perfectly realistic objections would never end. Joan knew she would never get out of the house.

Up ahead at the corner a man was panhandling. Joan found it hard to pass by someone in such sorry circumstances. Alan had always told the children not to give them anything. "They can go to the Salvation Army, which we in fact contribute to for that very reason," he would say. "Some of the Catholic churches, I'll say this much for them, have shelters for the poor. Anyone can go there. You might have to say a few Hail Marys, but you get a hot meal and a decent place to stay until you're on your feet again. This isn't Calcutta, you know. No one in this city has any real reason to have to beg on the streets."

She supposed he was right. But she would look at the faces of the people with their hands out, and they didn't look to her like drunks or drug addicts. They looked like miserable people who suffered. She saw hunger and loneliness and fear in those faces. Naked pain. How could she ignore that? How could she walk past a man shivering on the street and step on into 685 Park Avenue, where the door was held open for her by a man in a brown uniform? "They don't work for their keep," Alan argued. Well, neither did she. Neither did Alan, when you came down to it. He went to his office every day and did many good things, no doubt, but their way of life was not earned by the sweat of his brow. It was hypocritical, really, to turn around and deny a man a quarter, on moral grounds. And what if the pittance she might give them did go to booze? They would still know that someone cared whether they lived or died. They wouldn't be passed by as though they didn't exist. She would have gladly shared their plight if only she knew how she could do it. She

wanted to take some small portion of their burden and place it on her
own shoulders. If she couldn't do that, at least she could give them a
little money. If they wanted to throw it away on drink, let them. She
had her own policy: Whenever she saw a supplicant humiliating himself
on a street, she would furtively press a coin into his outstretched hand
and hurry on, ashamed to receive his gratitude, mixed as it always was
with scorn and detestation.

She got a quarter out of her purse and held it in her hand so she
could give it to the man quickly as she passed, and not have to stop and
fumble around. She was getting near Meyer House, and the last thing
she wanted was for anyone she might know to see her dispensing her
dubious charity. Her position at the settlement house was already ambiguous, what with relatives on the board and chauffeurs coming to call
for her. She didn't want people to see her tossing coins at the poor.
Clutching the quarter, she walked briskly down the street. The man was
turned partly away from her. Just before she reached him, she stopped
and looked over her shoulder to make sure she saw no one from Meyer
House. She took a step or two before turning back. By that time she was
almost upon him. She nearly collided with him. Seeing his face for the
first time clearly, she couldn't suppress a gasp of horror. She had never
seen such a horrible sight. The face seemed barely human, ravaged as it
was with some dreadful disease and distorted even further by an expression of wild fury. It was an incoherent face that seemed to have been
slapped onto its skull in a haphazard fashion. The nose was bulbous and
misshapen, the skin hideously pocked, and one eye smeared over with a
yellow, opaque discharge. When the man saw Joan about to give him
something, he drew his mouth back into a ghastly rictus and reached out
a hand partially gloved in a thin, cutoff sock. Only the palm was covered, and she could clearly see the gnarled stumps of three fingers.

Even though she had already reached out her hand, she recoiled and
drew it back sharply. She meant to give him the money, but she couldn't
bear to touch his flesh. The man only saw her withdraw the offering;
and whether in retaliation or perhaps in misjudged response to what he
took to be an attack, he raised his other hand as if to strike her. In that
split second she thought she saw a knife.

There are moments in everyone's life, even in the most familiar and
safe surroundings, when one loses his place. The sudden appearance of
an extra step on the staircase, or the unexpected drop of an elevator,
even the irregular leap of one's heart—in an instant, life itself becomes

uncertain; precarious. One is paralyzed, as in a nightmare at the moment between death and awakening, when the dreamer knows he is in mortal danger but cannot move to escape. Joan felt that terror when she saw the man raise his hand toward her. There were people around her on all sides, but they saw nothing, or in any event did nothing. They walked by as if everything was ordinary and safe. The instant froze—the hand remained raised. Joan couldn't breathe. Inside her chest a leaden mass ballooned, choking her as it expanded. Her legs turned to rubber. She was drugged, voiceless. With her last burst of strength, she lurched away from the beggar. Keeping her eyes fixed on his hand, which remained poised but didn't yet strike, she staggered backward. She didn't realize until she stumbled off the sidewalk that she had lunged blindly into the street. She could hear the screech of tires, and then everything went out.

By a stroke of sheerest luck, Peggy happened to have been home when they called from the hospital. She had been on her way to a meeting of the League, and in fact already had her coat on when the phone rang. She picked it up in the hallway. "This is Bellevue Hospital," a flat voice announced. "We have a patient here identified as Joan Gutheim." They pronounced the *u* short, as in *gut*.

Peggy was not given to losing her composure, but even she was shaken by the stark impersonality of the message. Feeling giddy, she sat down on the chair next to the telephone. She felt as though she had been assaulted in the street with a gun, so strong was the actual physical sensation. Still, curiously, the words sounded familiar, as though she had been expecting the call, or had heard it all before, somewhere.

"Will someone be coming to the hospital?" the voice wanted to know.

Peggy asked, as calmly as she was able, what was the matter.

"That information cannot be given out over the phone," they said. "The doctors are with her now."

"Why can't you give out that information over the phone?" Peggy demanded, as anger began to overtake her other emotions.

It was no use, though. She couldn't get anything out of them whatsoever. "Will someone be coming to the hospital?" was all they would say.

She hung up the phone. For a moment all she could do was to sit there. The important thing, she told herself, the important thing was to get to the hospital as quickly as possible. She would also have to get word to the League that she would be late. Noreen could do that, if she gave her the instructions simply and clearly enough. So much for the League. Lunch—? She drew a perfect blank on lunch. She tried to think, but for the life of her she couldn't come up with a name or visualize a place. It was written in her engagement book, but just at that moment she didn't think she could go back to her room to look it up. She told herself sternly that she was being very foolish, that she had better get ahold of herself if she was going to manage this at all. Then she got to her feet, took a deep breath, and went into the pantry. Very calmly, she told the maid she was going out. She wrote down the number of the League and told her exactly whom to speak to and what to say. Noreen was too nervous with the assignment to ask for a reason, which was just as well.

That done, she went back into the hall, picked up her purse, remembered to check to see that she had some gloves, and went out to ring for the elevator. It took much too long to come for the middle of the morning. The men always pretended they hadn't heard the buzzer, or that they were busy with a delivery man, when she knew perfectly well they were lounging around smoking and talking. But she made herself smile at Frank when the elevator finally did come, and said nothing about the delay. He said something about Joan going off earlier that morning, and she smiled again. She spoke to the doorman who got her a taxi, and asked after his wife, who was in the hospital again. From the frequency of her admissions she must surely either be an alcoholic or dying of cancer. Three children they had; not very nice for them, whichever the case. She would ask Alan if they couldn't do something extra for them at Christmastime this year.

It took until she was seated in the taxi and heard the driver ask her twice where they were going before she realized she wasn't in perfect control of herself. She wondered if she should have called Alan. He would be upset not to be notified. But it would have taken God knows how long to reach him, and then another eternity to explain to him that she didn't have the answers to all the questions he would ask, and then they would have had to arrange where to meet, and so on and so forth. No, she was glad she was handling this herself.

In truth, she never even considered phoning him. Quite frankly, she was glad she didn't have him to cope with on top of everything else. She was about to walk into a difficult situation and would have to deal with doctors and nurses and hospital functionaries of all sorts, and she could do it far better without Alan there. He would complicate matters enormously. He would start out by criticizing everything in sight, and would compare Bellevue unfavorably to Mt. Sinai. Which would be true enough as far as it went, but rather beside the point just now. He would tell everyone what they were doing wrong, and how it was done—correctly—uptown. That would help a lot. No, she would call him just as soon as she had anything to tell him. Anything definite. Alan didn't handle uncertainty too well.

What she would have liked would have been to have Phil with her just then. If she'd had her choice.

As the taxi U-turned around the island in the middle of Park and started downtown, she had a thought: What was in store for her? She'd already been through one phone call, when that idiot had called her from Bennington, although in fairness she had been quite civilized compared with this. Still, she saw it was becoming disturbingly familiar: sudden, jolting phone calls, life thrown off the tracks, trying to negotiate a rather complicated situation while inside the bottom is falling out. Was it to be that way now? Never knowing when the next thing would go wrong? Was the pattern, the expectability that she had always taken more or less for granted—namely, that life could be managed—in question? She felt suddenly fatigued and she thought, I'm not up to it. She had been foolish, to believe she could handle everything so smoothly. Everyone always said, Oh, Peggy manages everything so beautifully, so calmly. And she did. There was never the slightest outward show of perturbation. If she had any private anxiety, no one ever knew. But now she wasn't so sure. What lay in store for her? How many more chilling voices over the phone? What as yet unimagined turns of events? What might happen that she wouldn't be able, finally, to control?

For a frozen, terrible instant she couldn't avert the thought: How would it end?

The traffic slowed maddeningly. The avenue was choked with cabs. Huge packs of them crawled along, clogging the streets, blocking the intersections, making side streets completely impenetrable. If only they would let passengers double up, they would cut the traffic virtually in half. But the fleet owners would object, and of course some people were too snobbish ever to ride in a taxi with someone they hadn't been formally introduced to. They were the kind of people who never contribute. They never think of others, never consider the problems of the city. Peggy couldn't abide people like that.

She fretted that they ought to be farther east, on Lexington, or Second Avenue. She was about to speak to the driver, but decided not to. She had enough on her mind for once. Let him worry about the route.

"Identified as Joan Gutheim!" What on earth possessed them to use such an expression? It did nothing but frighten people. They were talking about her daughter, after all, not some vagabond. And it wasn't just that she was accustomed to being treated with deference that made her indignant. The ordinary people they called from that place day in and day out were entitled to the same respect, the same consideration she was. Nothing could be sillier than that they couldn't give out information over the phone. Why on earth not? As it happened, she had a pretty good idea what the trouble was: It was in all likelihood another . . . episode. But she might not have known. It could conceivably be something else. Joan could have had an accident. She could fall ill like anyone else. She could have been hit by a car. Or they could have been wrong all along, have missed something in the tests. Maybe the child had some dreadful illness after all. Lamartine could be wrong. It was always possible. If he was, what did it mean? What was going to happen to her Joan?

She really couldn't allow herself to think about it.

Well, what good did it do?

Now they weren't moving at all! Being stuck in traffic just then was excruciating, sheer torture. The light up ahead was green and they simply weren't budging. They had gone into a side street and gotten caught like a fly in a spider's sticky web. She should have told the driver to take a crosstown street. She twisted and craned her neck to see what was holding things up. She could see a passenger getting out of a cab half a block ahead. There was room for the taxi to have pulled over and let the traffic go by, but it had chosen to stop right smack in the middle of the street, whether out of disdain or sheer laziness. That sort of thing made Peggy so angry, that kind of thoughtlessness. She watched as the dismounting passenger turned to help someone else out. The second person was having great difficulty. Now he was out. Well, it certainly wasn't his fault. He looked elderly and unwell. Probably going to see his doctor. A lot of doctors still had offices on these streets, between Park and Lexington, or Madison and Park. Originally they had been the ground floor, or that floor just below street level, of their own homes. Now as often as not the offices were suites in apartment buildings.

Peggy wondered if Frank Lawler still had his office on this block. Where were they, 68th? 66th? She could see a subway stop up ahead, it must be 68th. Yes, there was Hunter, those girls must be students. One of them was Negro, which was good to see. The time was when you never saw a single colored girl at Hunter. Some things were getting better, at least.

They were going to miss the damn light again.

Suddenly she had the thought: If Joan was all right, why couldn't they say so over the phone? Or why hadn't Joan called herself? Did it mean something was really wrong?

Peggy tried to calm herself and consider the possibilities. They were probably examining Joan and the clerk was told to notify the family. They probably have instructions: Never tell anyone anything over the phone. Something like that. These people have limited capacities. You can't just tell them, Use your judgment. One procedure, no matter what the case, was probably all they were up to. That's the trouble with so many people, they can never make any distinctions. They have to be told to do the same thing every time. Which they then do, no matter what. Plodding, stupid, limited. Try telling them to try something different. Blank stares is all you get, if you're lucky.

Peggy felt horribly agitated. She could barely force herself to sit there in the taxi and not scream, at someone, anyone. What right had they to withhold information from her, even if it was to "spare" her? She didn't ask to be spared. She asked for one thing only: the truth. If they would just tell her the truth, she could handle the rest.

The taxi broke free and they got onto Lexington. Peggy's relief was enormous. The cars moved a little better, but there were still stops and starts, so the driver turned east again. They went past the construction site of the new skyscraper Abbott & Strawbridge was putting up. A huge cavity, nothing more. Soon the cavity would belong to Morty Pines. Not a reassuring thought. He was not the sort of man to build with any sort of vision, any feeling for how a building would fit into the city. He wouldn't go out and hire a Mies van der Rohe or a Philip Johnson to make a statement. He was only concerned with how cheaply he could build it and how much profit he could make. A loathsome man, really, the sort of person one could imagine running around, slipping envelopes stuffed with money into the hands of building inspectors, union bosses, the people you had to take care of if you wanted to leave girders on the street. How could Gerald be allying himself with such a man, she wondered. This had been a good block at one time, part of the old city of small businesses and family stores. Peggy couldn't remember just which ones had been there, but Alan would, on request, recite every one, north to south, in order. They were all gone now.

Turning south again, they crossed 42nd Street. The city south of Grand Central was quieter than midtown. There had been less change there in recent years. Murray Hill, Grammercy Park, the sections of town always referred to as "gracious." Meaning they had once been fashionable but were shabby now. Still, you saw some attractive buildings. Before she could really enjoy the charm of the neighborhood, the taxi turned once more and stopped abruptly at the hospital.

Bellevue! The name alone was enough to make one shudder. Hordes of infected immigrants, prostitutes with loathsome diseases, alcoholics, vagrants, tubercular indigents, madmen. What a dreadful place for her poor Joan. "I wouldn't be caught dead there," Alan always used to say. Phil would add, "You might not have much to say about it when it happens." It was funny at the time. Everything Phil said was funny when he said it. He had that knack. Timing, she supposed. In retrospect it wasn't funny at all. Her Joan!

But she did wish Phil was with her. He could cope wonderfully. He had his father's ability to analyze a situation and see what was called for, but he had the additional advantage that he always stayed calm. Alan started well, but sooner or later he would cross swords with the inevitable incompetent and get into a row. He would be right but he only made things worse, and where did that leave them? Peggy had never gotten him to see that, not in twenty-six years of trying. Phil, though, never got ruffled, no matter what. He could get people to do whatever he wanted them to. He was going to run things, there was no doubt about that in Peggy's mind. Being a lawyer would never be enough for him; people would turn to him to lead them. He would accomplish a great deal.

All that was some time in the future, unfortunately. Just now he was not available, and Peggy missed him. The taxi had stopped. They were there. Blocks and blocks of buildings in every size and shape, new and decrepit, a complete hodgepodge that had grown over the decades into a sprawling, undefined complex, blending at the edges into the decaying neighborhood. Peggy didn't know where in the world they were, and neither did the taxi driver. Everything around them revealed confusion, as one might expect. Peggy hadn't set foot in the hospital in years—how long had it been? Who had she gone to see? Rita, that's who it was. Her mother's laundress. She had been there a week until they got her transferred. Peggy had gone to see her. It had been shocking. Of course, Rita had never been quite "right," but it had made Peggy sick to her stomach to see the impassive, taciturn woman so wild and incoherent. Locked up in that dreadful place.

She paid the driver and got out. She went into the nearest building. People were milling about, looking as though they were there for no particular purpose at all. They didn't appear sick or seem to be waiting to see someone who was. They didn't look as though they had anything to do with the proper business of a hospital at all. It reminded Peggy of the crowd that used to assemble, in the old days, when an ocean liner was embarking or docking: some, to be sure, were there to meet relatives or friends, or to see them off; but most were there for curiosity's sake, or for some shadier purpose, such as picking pockets or shilling unsuspecting visitors. In some respects, of course, this crowd was very different. These people were predominantly Puerto Rican and Negro. Where did they all come from? Surely they didn't live near the hospital, not all of them. The respectable developments—Peter Cooper Village, Stuyvesant Town, the newer complexes—housed almost all white people. Didn't they use Bellevue for their medical care? And who were these people? Did they come down from Harlem? Across town from the West Side? Peggy was bewildered.

She managed to find some sort of information desk, although the people there weren't terribly helpful, to say the least. They kept sending her up the wrong corridor, through the wrong door, into the wrong building. There was a system of connecting subterranean passageways, but the place was laid out in such haphazard fashion that she kept finding herself emerging into strange basements, dank and foul and poorly lit. She didn't know which to fear more, muggers or rats.

When she finally located the emergency ward, no one there had so much as heard of Joan. They all treated Peggy with that special sort of rudeness and disdain limited people adopt when they don't know something it's their business to know. Did they think she had come to Bellevue, of all places, on a lark? Looking for a fictitious person? Whatever they thought, no one offered to actually find out where Joan was, and for a terrible moment Peggy thought they had taken her daughter to the morgue and were giving her another of their runarounds. She told herself not to panic, and started once more to tell her story to the imbecile woman they put at the front desk. But all she could elicit from the woman was a blank stare, followed by an abrupt shout of "What?"

Peggy turned away from her in exasperation and boldly walked toward a door marked NO ADMITTANCE—NON PASADA, deciding she would find Joan herself if need be.

"You can't go in there, lady!" the woman called, evidently better trained to prohibit than to facilitate. Peggy pushed on through, on the grounds that rules in a place like that don't deserve to be followed. A nurse at an inner desk who was writing in a chart glanced up at her, and took no further notice. They were clearly used to dealing with sheep. Peggy might be many things, but she was no sheep.

She continued past the nurse's desk into a corridor that ran between two rows of cubicles, partitioned only with curtains. Inside the cubicles, patients sat waiting to be examined, or lay on examining tables, or even on the stretchers that had wheeled them into the emergency ward. Gurneys with and without patients partially blocked the corridor, like carts in a supermarket. Equipment carts, intravenous poles, and machines for resuscitation further cluttered the cramped space. Nothing looked clean enough or functional enough for medical use. Sputum cups, bloody gauze, broken tongue depressors, discarded gloves, broken ampoules, and other medical detritus littered the floors, and the smell of carbolic permeated the air.

Peggy looked into the first cubicle—the curtain was only half drawn—and saw a man lying on the examining table. He was unshaven, and his face was caked with dried blood that had come from a deep gash along the top of his bald head. Something about him made Peggy think he wasn't simply a drunk. The curtain on the second cubicle was drawn, but Peggy could see enough to make out that Joan wasn't in there. The third cubicle was completely concealed by its curtain, but Peggy could hear someone calling out in rapid, anguished Spanish, punctuated by sharp cries of pain: "Aieee! Aieee! Aieee!"

Her search was interrupted when two policemen rushed in, half shoving, half dragging a man in total disarray. His clothes were torn and filthy, and as he passed, Peggy could see that they were spattered with something vile—vomit, at best. His graying hair was disheveled and he had a wild, unfocused look in his eyes. "Jesus will save!" he screamed. "Only the wicked will burn in hell!" In between shouts he spat on the floor. At first Peggy thought he was handcuffed, but when he was hustled past her, she saw that he had actually been straitjacketed. She had thought these medieval restraints weren't used any longer, and it alarmed her to see the long sleeves tied behind the man's back. His crazy eyes fixed on her for a moment, and she thought he might spit on her too. When he didn't, she feared that he had drawn her into his persecutory world and would attack her if he got the chance. She shrank back as the struggling trio passed, partly in order not to obstruct the police, and also in hopes of avoiding contact with his filth. In trying to get out of the way, she bumped into the gurney behind her. Looking around to find out if she had toppled anything over, she saw a pale young woman lying there. She almost turned back before she realized that it was Joan: nearly as white as the sheet that covered her, but alive.

Peggy hadn't fully understood how frantic she had been until she felt the tremendous surge of relief sweep over her. For a moment she couldn't speak, she was so shaken. When she did find her voice, she said, with a nonchalance that surprised even her: "Well, well, well! What have we here?"

"She's coming around."

Joan's eyes were closed. She supposed she must be asleep, that the words she heard were spoken in a dream. She couldn't see the speaker. Her head throbbed in back, so far back that the pain seemed not to belong to her. Jack fell down and broke his crown. There was something wet on her chin, but when she tried to reach up and wipe it off, she found her arm was somehow trapped. She was lying on it. She would have used the other hand, but she couldn't find it. Odd, not to find her own hand.

"Give her some air. Let her breathe."

She was lying in the street. The machine smells of tar and exhaust were strong. It struck her as peculiar that she should have fallen asleep on the street, where people could watch her, but she didn't dare wake up and face them. A stab of fear shot through her as she wondered if she had wet her pants. She couldn't tell: she felt no warmth or dampness there, but it seemed to her that she had let go. She thought she had better open her eyes after all, but the eyelids stayed shut as if they had been glued, or sewn together. Maybe she would go back to sleep, or just pretend to be asleep. If only they would all go away!

"Has someone checked for a heartbeat?" she heard a man ask. Her wrist was taken up gently, a finger pressed against her pulse. How odd, to have someone touch her in public like that.

"It's beating," said a voice close to her ear. "Is there a doctor here?"

"Someone should call an ambulance."

Joan remembered now what had happened. The man had stabbed her. She was bleeding to death. She didn't feel any pain, except for the back of her head, where it must have struck when she fell. She had the sensation of blood streaming from a wound. She was mortally wounded, and would die soon. She felt strangely peaceful, without sadness or fear. So this is what it's like. A moan escaped from her lips, to her surprise. It might have come from another person entirely, so little did she mean to utter it.

"Are you all right?" the man kneeling next to her asked.

She struggled to open her eyes. "She's opening her eyes," a woman above her reported.

Through a blur she saw people standing over her, looking down. They seemed far away, as if she were seeing them through the wrong end of a telescope. They looked worried, but their expressions were artificial, as if they were actors, or part of a general conspiracy, and their expressions of concern were a sham, a trick.

You're crazy, she told herself.

When she tried to turn her head, she found it was too heavy, weighted down with some dense material that had collected at the back of her skull. The man kneeling next to her was middle-aged. He had a sad face, worried eyes, a limp gray mustache. "I tried to stop, but you came out of nowhere. I didn't think I hit you. I tried to stop. Are you all right?" He spoke with a slight accent—Italian, maybe, or Greek. "She just come out of nowhere," he appealed to the crowd. "I didn't have no time to stop."

"She just ran out into the street," one of the women confirmed indignantly. What were they saying? That she had been hit by a car? This man's car? She had no memory of it whatsoever. The last thing she remembered was trying to get away from the man with the knife. The beggar. Where was he? she suddenly wondered, with a start of terror.

"I'm all right," she said, or tried to say. It came out garbled: "Iyawright."

"What's that?" the man asked her, bending closer to try and hear. His breath reeked of garlic and tobacco. "She's okay," he reported to the others. "Are you okay?" he asked her anxiously.

Joan nodded. She didn't feel okay, but she thought she ought to say she was, in consideration for the man. She still felt almost nothing, in fact, except for the ache at the back of her head, down toward the neck. She could move her left arm now, and she reached back to rub her neck.

"Don't let her move her head!" commanded the woman who had seen her run out into the street. "Her neck could be broken. She shouldn't be moved until the ambulance comes." She had a harsh voice and spoke with a thick German emphasis.

"Does your neck hurt?" the man asked her, his eyes pleading with her to deny it.

"No, it's all right. It's fine. I'm all right, really. Just a little . . ."

A little what? She didn't know what was happening to her. She was confused, embarrassed. If only everyone would just go away. It was horrible enough to lie in the street in the midst of Lord knows what sort of filth without having people stare at her. She tried to get up, but she couldn't pull her legs up under her, and the slightest motion of her head caused a sickening dizziness. The people, the street sign, the cars whirled above her, and she let her head drop back against the pavement. It made an audible thud.

"Don't move," the German woman warned. "You could snap the spinal cord. I know something about this," she added, nodding her head vigorously. She was a fat woman whose face, as best as Joan could make it out, was surprisingly soft for someone who spoke so stridently.

"My neck's all right," she whispered to the man. "I'm just a little dizzy, that's all." She wanted an ally against the woman.

"Don't get up too fast," he cautioned, helping her to sit up. "That's it. Take it easy. Sit there for a minute, before you do anything else." He gripped her around the shoulders in a fatherly embrace. He seemed like a kind man, an uncle to a flock of nieces and nephews he bought candy for and took to baseball games. Joan worried about the trouble she was making for him. She should make amends. She had delayed him, delayed all these people. They must have things to do, places to go, and instead they were here, attending to her. She felt awful.

"Where's the ambulance?" another woman asked. Joan felt better sitting up. They didn't all look so peculiar. "A person could die in this city waiting for an ambulance to come."

Another woman said, "My brother-in-law had a heart attack. It was forty-eight minutes before they came. They said another five minutes he would've died. And that was in Queens!"

The man with the mustache asked, "Did anyone call an ambulance?"

No one answered.

"I don't want an ambulance," Joan told him. "I don't need an ambulance."

He nodded in eager agreement, but the German woman insisted, "She has to go to the hospital." She was adamant about it.

"I don't need to go to the hospital," Joan pleaded. "Really, I'll be fine." But even as she spoke a wave of nausea swept over her, and she had to close her eyes to keep everything from spinning around her again. She didn't speak until the nausea had passed.

"She should go to the hospital and she should not be moved until the ambulance comes," the German woman said angrily. With that she turned and walked away, as if to wash her hands of the entire mismanaged affair.

"I can take you in my car," the man offered uncertainly. "It's quicker than waiting for the ambulance. You could wait all day for it to come."

Joan nodded. It seemed the easiest thing to do. She had no desire to go to a hospital. She was already late for Meyer House. But she couldn't lie there on the street with people staring at her, traffic being shunted around her, passersby pointing at her. She could agree to go to the hospital, and once everyone was gone she could get herself quietly to Meyer House. If necessary she could let him drive off a couple of blocks and then circle back. She wondered if she ought to give him something for his trouble. He was dressed in shabby clothing, his overcoat was threadbare. His teeth were bad, European teeth. On the other hand, he might be terribly offended . . .

With his assistance she struggled to her feet. People drew back deferentially. Joan wanted to thank them for stopping, for helping, for caring what happened to her. New Yorkers always come through in a pinch, Alan was fond of saying. She felt ashamed to have consumed so much help and kindness. Surely there were many people who needed it more than she did. She had so many advantages as it was. Remembering the beggar, she felt a rush of fear, and looked around to see if he was still there. She didn't see him. Thank God. It was childish to have been so frightened by him. If she was going to help people, she would have to be tougher. She couldn't panic like that.

When people saw she was going to leave in the same car that hit her, there was general disapproval. "He shouldn't be the one to drive her," said the man whose brother-in-law had had the heart attack. "He just wants to get her away before the ambulance comes. Where are the police, anyway? You can never find a policeman in this town when you need one. Double-park, and they're swarming all over you, but when something really happens . . ."

Joan had gotten into the car and didn't hear the rest. They were being unfair, she thought. The man was only trying to help her. It hadn't been his fault. She wished she had made that clear. But everything was so confused, she was so dizzy, it seemed hopeless to try to straighten it out. She didn't remember what street she was on, or where Meyer House was from there. She was still in a daze.

As they drove off she saw the last of the onlookers turn away and lose themselves among the crowd on the sidewalk. She had become an incident, a moment's curiosity. Something seen on the way to work, like a fire, or a public argument. If she had died, they might remember that. As it was, they would forget her before the day was over. It was all quite impersonal.

It suddenly hit her that she was riding in a car with a total stranger. He had driven into her, and now she had actually gotten into his car. She didn't know this man at all. She didn't even know his name. When he had closed the door for her, he had locked it. Maybe an automatic gesture, maybe not. Whichever it was, she was locked in. As they drove down the street, she glanced over at him. His face, which had seemed so gentle to her before, now had a tense, angry expression. Did he mean to kidnap her? Of course, he could hardly have planned it, but maybe he was taking advantage of the opportunity. She was insane to have gotten into his car. She thought of jumping out. The idea was absurd. She didn't even want to unlock the door for fear of arousing his suspicion, if he was planning something; or insulting him if he wasn't. She should have taken the opportunity when he was walking around to get in. Now she was trapped. She would have to be vigilant, and watch for her chance.

She had no idea where he was taking her. She didn't even know what direction they were going. It looked like the Bowery: deserted buildings, drunks on the streets, piles of filth. She and her mother had driven on this very street four days before. An ideal spot for a rapist. "Where are you taking me?" she asked, betraying her fear.

He hesitated a disturbing moment, and said, "Bellevue."

The very name of the hospital terrified her. She had never been there, but she had a vivid image of raving lunatics, violent drunks, the dregs of skid row. Timidly, she said, "I'd rather not go there." He didn't reply. "I don't really need to go to a hospital," she added.

"They'll take good care of you," he said. "I've gone there myself."

What could she say to that? That she was too good for Bellevue? That no one in her family would be caught dead there? And would he be so good as to take her up to Mt. Sinai, only a hundred blocks away? That he should understand she didn't receive her medical care among the hoi polloi?

Still, she couldn't stomach the thought of going into that place. "I'm feeling a lot better," she said. "If you could just let me off here, I could go on to my work."

"I don't think that'd be too good an idea," the man said. "You might of took a concussion. You oughtta go there, let them check you out." He kept looking over at her with nervous little sidelong glances. "I can pay, if that's what you're worried about. I work for the city. They'll pay the bill. It won't cost you nothin'."

Joan was terribly ashamed. "Oh . . . it isn't—I would never— Look, this was entirely my fault. I ran into the street like an idiot. I didn't know where I was going. There was this man—this beggar—I was trying to get away . . ."

The man nodded. "I thought you was running away or something. I said to myself when I saw you, She must be scared out of her mind, to run into the street like that. I hit the brakes, but it was too late. If I'd of swerved, I'd of gotten it from the traffic coming by on the left. You gotta stay in your lane in this town."

"I hope you didn't think I was going to ask you to pay for anything."

"You never know," the man said. "People get ahold of a lawyer, before you know it, they got the shirt off your back."

"I would never do a thing like that!" Joan said; but the man didn't look all that convinced.

He drove her up to the emergency ward entrance. As she got out he said he was going to park the car and would come back to make sure everything was all right. Joan protested, saying she could manage fine, he must have to get to work, et cetera, but she was glad when he said he would stay with her until she was given a clean bill. It was nice to know there were people in the city who would go out of their way for you. Here was this man, obviously neither rich nor particularly educated, ready to help. The common man, her family believed, was as capable of fine actions as any aristocrat.

The process of being registered and getting the usual information took an interminable length of time. Some of the clerks had gone off to vote, and the one remaining had to do everything: fill out forms, answer the phone, talk to the nurses. She had no time to waste on patients. Finally, Joan was told to wait in a little cubicle. She had to undress and get up on a gurney. An emergency case came in, and they had to take her out of the cubicle. They left her out in the passageway, and for a long time no one paid any attention to her at all. Everyone was talking about the election, no one had any interest in the patients. After a while she realized the man wasn't coming back.

It was so sad, really. That a decent, kind, basically good person should have to slink off like that. It was the money he was worried about. She probably couldn't ever have persuaded him that she wasn't out to sue him for every penny he was worth. Whatever that might be. It's far easier to act nobly when you don't have to worry about paying for it, she thought. Still, she was disappointed. He had seemed one step up from that.

A doctor finally came over and gave her a cursory examination— little more than a few halfhearted pokes in the stomach and waving a flashlight past her eyes—before sending her off to be X-rayed. There was a long wait at X ray, and another before anyone took her back to the emergency ward. They didn't put her back into the cubicle but left her out in the thoroughfare again. While she was lying there, strapped in and unable to move, they brought in a wild man straight out of every nightmare she had ever had about that hospital. Two burly policemen, aided by a straitjacket, couldn't control him. He was tall and wore a black coat that made him look weirdly like Abraham Lincoln. In his madness he seemed to have access to inhuman strength. He shouted disconnected phrases of piety and hate. The attendants circled him as if he were an escaped lion that no one wanted to come within striking distance of. The nurses were rushing about fetching syringes full of tranquilizers and calling in more and more doctors until the room was jammed with men in white. None of them, though, was willing or able to subdue the man. The other patients were all left to their quieter sufferings. Joan wasn't suffering, but watched, fascinated and horrified. She didn't notice the well-dressed woman who was shoved against the gurney until she heard that unmistakable voice saying, as if it would take a lot more than this to surprise her: "Well, well, well, what have we here?" and she realized that her mother had come to the hospital.

They had put one of those hospitals gowns on her that made her look like a cadaver. Her clothes were folded at the foot of the stretcher, with her purse on top where anyone could walk off with it. Peggy moved it up to where Joan could see it. It was a miracle no one had swiped it. It was a miracle Joan was alive. Peggy felt a sudden surge of gratitude. Joan's pallor, the fact that she was lying unattended among the dregs of the city were secondary for the moment. Only one thing counted: She was safe.

Joan's face came to life from the death-mask blankness it had fallen into when Peggy first saw her. "How did you know I was here?" she asked.

Peggy laughed. "They called, of course. Did you think they wouldn't?"

"But that's awful! If I had dreamed they were going to call you, I would have told them not to. Aren't you supposed to be at the League?"

"That's the silliest thing I ever heard. I can't say I'm exactly thrilled to have you here, but since you are, I can't imagine my not being with you. So much for that. Now, what I need to know is: What happened?"

"They didn't tell you that?"

"Darling, as far as they're concerned, you hardly exist, much less has anyone told me anything medical. They simply called me, said you were here, and that was that. I assumed you had a little . . . you know . . . one of your . . ."

Joan stared at her uncomprehendingly, then burst out laughing. "Mother! For God's sake! It has nothing to do with that! I was hit by a car!"

It was absurd, but the news was a great relief. Ordinarily, hearing that one's daughter had been hit by a car might not be the most welcome piece of information in the world. But there she was, in one piece; and at least it hadn't been the result of that other . . . whatever it was, or her own poor judgment in letting the child tear off to work and get exhausted when any sensible mother would have put her straight to bed. "Oh, it's only that!" she said; and realizing how stupid it sounded, added, "I had thought you had . . . Actually, I didn't know what to expect. They don't tell you a thing over the phone." Her voice trembled with uncharacteristic emotion.

Joan was sobered. "Oh, Mother! How dreadful for you!"

Peggy laughed to show how little it had bothered her. "Darling, I'm not the one we should be worrying about. You're the patient, after all. What about you? Are you really all right? Have you broken anything? Are you in pain?"

"None at all! Isn't that fantastic?" Joan exclaimed happily. "Here I've just been—I don't know what—and I feel absolutely perfect. Other than a rather splitting headache, which has nothing whatsoever to do with the accident."

Peggy frowned. "I'm not a hundred percent happy about a splitting headache, I must say. They've taken X rays?"

"Oh, they took about a thousand X rays. I told them not to bother, I had every one in the book last week, but they had to anyway since I was unconscious."

Peggy was alarmed by that, but didn't betray herself. "How long were you unconscious?" she asked. Joan shook her head in fatalistic resignation to a mystery never to be solved. "I think, dear, if you've been unconscious you don't know how long, plus you have a splitting headache, Lamartine should see you. We can go straight to his office from here."

Joan balked. "Why do I have to go there? This has nothing to do with any of that, after all."

"You really can't be sure," Peggy said. "You might have had a small episode."

"Mother, it wasn't anything like that! I was in the middle of the street, a car came out of nowhere and hit me. I don't know, some people said he ran a red light, I really didn't see."

"It still wouldn't do the slightest bit of harm to have Lamartine see you, just in case."

"Just in case what?" Joan flared up. "They checked me over here! Isn't that enough? Why do I have to go see Lamartine? I can't stand that man!" She was close to tears.

"Darling, I hardly think that this is the place to solve that particular problem." Peggy didn't know what to say, if Joan preferred the care of a hospital as notorious as Bellevue, with its madmen and criminals and carriers of contagion, to a clean, quiet office where she would be attended by a leading specialist. That woman in the cubicle was still moaning and crying. And this was where Joan wanted to cast her lot! "I really think the sooner we get you to Lamartine, the better. Just give me a few minutes to find out what we have to do to get you out of here and we'll be on our way. I'd also like to give his office a ring to let them know you're coming, so he can rearrange his schedule, if possible, and not keep you waiting." Peggy automatically looked at her watch, although she had already mentally canceled the rest of her day. It had come to her, when she wasn't trying to remember, who she was supposed to have had lunch with: Harriet Plaut. Hardly a tragedy, since Harriet was a deadly bore, except that she would have to make another date with her. If by some miracle she did get free, she could slip in late to the board meeting of the Home for the Aged. They always shilly-shallied around like a bunch of old women before getting down to anything of substance anyway. She made a note to try and call Harriet if she got a chance.

"You must have a million things to do today," Joan said, recognizing her mother's familiar abstracted look, which indicated she was organizing something in her head. "I'll be fine here, don't worry. The place isn't much to look at, but it is a hospital, after all, and besides which there isn't really anything wrong with me. Why don't you get back to the League, and whatever else you have on. I'll call you when they let me go. I'll call you from Meyer House."

It didn't work. "I have absolutely no intention of leaving," Peggy said. She had meant to be loyal, but what she said sounded stubborn. The thought of leaving her daughter on a stretcher in the Bellevue emergency ward was, of course, preposterous. As for Meyer House today . . .

A youngish Oriental man in whites—presumably an intern, judging by the filth of his uniform—ambled over, casual as a sightseer. He picked up the chart at the foot of Joan's stretcher and flipped through the few pages languidly. It might have been a magazine. Then he put it down and stared at Joan. He didn't say anything or ask any questions, he just stared. He had a faint, pubescent mustache that suggested he hadn't yet begun to shave. Peggy hoped he was under very close supervision. "Can you tell me what you've found out about this young lady's health?" she asked him, as if her cheerful, informal manner might somehow influence Joan's diagnosis favorably.

The intern didn't reply. He gave no indication of having heard Peggy at all, but continued to stare at Joan in an increasingly unnerving way. Suddenly he shouted, "Where is—area—of greatest—pain?"

Joan was so startled, she didn't reply at once. The intern, apparently uninterested in an answer, took a penlight from his pocket and clicked it on. Brushing past Peggy as if she were a low branch in his path, he seized Joan's head roughly and shone the light first in one eye, then the other. "Still the vision is—blurred?" he asked, or rather challenged, as if he were dealing with a tiresome and not very credible complaint of hers.

"I never had any blurred vision," Joan told him.

He picked up her chart again and scanned the illegible notes. "Yes. Good," he remarked with satisfaction and flipped the chart closed, as if his suspicion, whatever it was, had been confirmed. He pulled back the sheet covering Joan and poked her abruptly in the abdomen. "You experience pain when I press here?" he asked. Joan shook her head, discounting the effect of his jab. He looked dissatisfied, as if she was denying symptoms he perfectly well knew she had. With his exaggerated rigidity, he gave the impression that he had no idea what he was doing but was improvising on the spot. If a maniac had somehow gotten ahold of some soiled whites and was under the delusion he was a doctor, the performance could not have been better suited. He snapped out some instructions to a nurse who happened to be passing by. Neither Peggy nor Joan understood his staccato, eccentrically pronounced words. The nurse looked totally unfazed. "Sure, when I get a minute," she said, and disappeared. Peggy had been looking around for a phone to call Alan, but she decided she couldn't possibly leave Joan alone with this lunatic, who was liable to do something crazy any minute. It seemed entirely possible he could pull out a scalpel and make an incision on the spot. Peggy's response was to gather up Joan's things in anticipation of getting her dressed. The intern, who was already walking away, nevertheless saw her. He wheeled around and shouted, "Patient will stay twenty-four hours for observation!" and stalked off furiously.

"Just one moment," Peggy said, quietly but in her own calm way just as angrily. "My daughter is under the care of Dr. Arthur Lamartine, of Presbyterian Hospital. If there's no immediate danger, I would prefer to have her seen by him."

"We will put in for consult if you wish," the intern said without turning around.

"But I don't want him to consult," Peggy explained. "I want him to see my daughter today, and I intend to take her to see him now."

Turning on her, the intern yelled wildly, "You cannot remove the patient until I give the release."

Peggy did have a marvelous competence she could summon up when dealing with inadequate functionaries who resort to fascism. "I fully intend to remove her," she said. "Whether or not you 'give the release' is entirely up to you. It couldn't matter less to me."

The intern was in a full rage. "The patient has been unconscious. In addition, she is dangerously emaciated. Her condition does not permit release. Admission is mandatory."

Peggy pretended to ignore him. Turning to Joan, she said, "Let's get you dressed, sweetie, and get out of here as soon as possible."

The intern screamed at the nearest nurse, "Call hospital director!" and stomped off in a fury.

The nurse gave a sympathetic, don't-take-him-seriously smile to Peggy. She was a dark-haired, pleasant Puerto Rican woman in her forties who had obviously been through this all innumerable times before. She seemed to conceive her role as that of a tranquilizing influence, a soothing presence for disintegrating patients and decompensating doctors, as well as the occasional frazzled relative. Peggy was glad to see some sign of sanity in the place, but she couldn't rely on anyone. For all her goodwill, the nurse still hadn't intervened.

The intern returned with a sheaf of papers, which he thrust at Peggy. She gave them a brief glance and laid them aside. The infuriated intern, seeing he wasn't having his way, began to harangue the nurse. The tall man in the straitjacket had all the while continued his own stentorian warnings, and the woman in the cubicle resumed her cries of "Aiee! Aiee! Aiee!" The place had turned into a true bedlam.

Joan was content to remain passive and let them argue over her. She had come around to Peggy's point of view. Bellevue was a grim place, and the prospect of a night there scared her. Also, the intern had introduced the subject of her thinness, and she was terrified that others might spot it and make an issue of it. It had, of course, nothing to do with her being where she was. Strictly speaking, it was no business of theirs. It was no business of anyone's. She was glad, now, that Peggy was there to rescue her.

All the same, she thought it wrong to be whisked off by taxi to an expensive specialist's office, and possibly from there to a private room at Mt. Sinai that would be jammed with flowers and special nurses and doctors groveling over her. So many other sick people, most of them far worse off than she, had to accept the sordidness and the indignities or have nothing. Why should she be better treated than they?

Fortunately, there was nothing she could do. Peggy was in charge now, and when she had made up her mind, neither Joan nor anyone else could change it. Besides, Joan felt awful. Her headache had gotten worse, and successive waves of nausea swept her precariously close to vomiting. It took full health and vigor even to think of standing up to Peggy. Joan had all she could do to keep from throwing up in full view of everyone.

Another doctor, hearing the row, wandered over. Although he was also a foreigner—this one seemed to be Indian—he was an improvement in that his uniform was cleaner, his mustache fuller, and his demeanor less wild. His self-possession in fact didn't jibe with the turmoil. Peggy wondered if he was drugged, or had used some form of yoga to cope with the ordeal of Bellevue. He did relieve Peggy of most of the papers the intern had shoved at her, and asked her politely if she would sign the one entitled "Leaving the Hospital Against Medical Advice." Peggy knew that Alan would have a fit if she signed a document without reading it, but she had no intention of reading anything at this juncture. She signed it quickly. She had already decided she'd have to sign something to ransom Joan from that hellhole.

She did note that a parent's signature was required only if the patient was under eighteen, or for some reason unable to sign. Joan was of course perfectly able to sign, or not to sign if she wished. Peggy thought all in all it made sense for her to sign it, especially since Joan obviously wanted to leave. It's one thing, after all, to work in squalor, and quite another to entrust one's life to incompetent doctors. She almost pointed this out to Joan, but restrained herself. She knew Joan wouldn't want to hear it from her. And what was to be gained? Joan had all but admitted she was right.

It proved more difficult for Joan to dress than she expected. She was allowed to go into a cubicle, where she was glad to be alone and not have Peggy see her clumsiness and unsteadiness as she pulled on her clothes and fumbled with the buttons. She agreed to sit in the lobby while Peggy got a cab, but she still felt light-headed when she was riding uptown. Peggy assumed she was shaken and exhausted by the ordeal, and made no attempt to talk to her. When they got to the neurologist's office, the nurse took one look at Joan and went in to interrupt Dr. Lamartine.

Peggy waited outside while he examined Joan. After he finished, while Joan was dressing again, he called Peggy into his office. "Nothing serious," he said; but he looked troubled, as if he had something to say but didn't know how to put it.

"Something's bothering you," Peggy prompted.

"I suppose so," he admitted. "The pieces don't all fit together. Something about her reaction bothers me."

Peggy remained skeptical, although she had noted the same thing. "It would help me if you could be a little more specific," she said.

Lamartine sighed. He disliked saying unpleasant things, especially to someone like Peggy. "Frankly, I have some doubts as to whether Joan was in fact struck by this car. I don't find any bruises, or any other indication that she was actually hit."

Peggy didn't flinch. "You think she's not telling the truth?" she asked matter-of-factly.

Lamartine shifted uncomfortably in his chair. "I don't say that, no. She may not know just what happened. She may be confused. I'm sure she sincerely believes she was hit. All I'm saying is that I see no evidence she was. She may well have passed out and just assumed she was struck. Perhaps the people around thought she was. No witnesses came to the hospital? No one was with her?"

Peggy shook her head. "I gather someone called an ambulance, or the police, and when none came a passerby offered to drive her. I can't say I'm crazy about her having accepted the offer, but under the circumstances it was understandable. Whatever happened, she was obviously . . . upset."

"This isn't epilepsy," Lamartine said firmly.

"I never had the slightest doubt about that," Peggy agreed.

"Whatever it is, I think we'd be on more solid ground at this point if we could get her into a hospital where we could observe her for a few days, get a good look at what's really going on, once and for all."

Peggy frowned. "Is that absolutely necessary? What's to be gained by putting the child in the hospital, especially if you think it's nothing . . . physical? Putting her to bed would only make her feel worse. I should think it's the very opposite of what you want."

"I don't want her to feel worse, that's certainly true. However, it's still not clear, as I told you yesterday, what her diagnosis is. I do think a period of observation would help clarify things. Also"—he hesitated; he was stepping out now onto some very treacherous ice—"her weight does concern me. She really is quite thin, once you get the clothes off her. Her ribs are beginning to protrude, and there is some muscle wasting.

The dry skin, the general fatigue—these could all be simply the result of undernutrition."

"I don't see what her weight has to do with what happened today," Peggy said, a little color rising in her cheeks. "I don't like this business of finding out she's perfectly fine in one area, and then going to look for something wrong in another. If you see something the matter, fine. Let's fix it. But why on earth should she be 'observed' until someone comes up with a diagnosis? I personally have very little interest in what you call it."

Lamartine got out his handkerchief, realized he had no use for it, and replaced it in his pocket with much shifting around in his chair. "I just thought it would be the prudent thing to do. Just for a while," he added, seeing Peggy wasn't going for prudence.

"If you simply want someone to watch her, I can get a nurse in to do that," Peggy said.

Lamartine pondered the suggestion. It wasn't his first choice. Still, they'd ruled out the dread possibilities—cancer, the leukemias, the gruesome degenerative diseases. The girl was in no immediate danger. In all likelihood she was just going through a difficult phase. If it did turn out to be one of those mysterious eating disorders, there'd be plenty of time to call in the witch doctors. In the meantime, there wasn't much he could do anyway, that much was true. "I suppose, if you could get someone reliable . . ." he said, cutting his losses.

And so it was settled. He called Joan in and told her she could go home, but should stay put for a couple of days. Complete rest. They'd see. It wouldn't hurt if she ate a bit more either. "Put some flesh on those bones," he recommended. His manner was a bit hearty for Peggy's taste. She made a note to see if there was another specialist in the city who enjoyed as good a reputation as Lamartine. Not for now, but perhaps at some point. Lamartine might be an excellent diagnostician, but Peggy had her doubts about the long run.

When they got home, Joan fell into bed and Peggy got on the phone. The family had a Miss Trimble who had nursed various Altmans through heart attacks, strokes, and one terminal illness. Miss Trimble was insipid but reliable. Unfortunately she was on a case. She immediately offered to get someone to take her place where she was, so she could care for Joan, but Peggy wouldn't hear of it. She assured Miss Trimble of the family's gratitude for all her devotion in the past, and gave her to understand that she wasn't jeopardizing her future with the

Altmans; although she would have been delighted to have an excuse not to use Miss Trimble should her mother ever fall ill, God forbid. With that reassurance, Miss Trimble gave Peggy the names of several trusted colleagues so she wouldn't have to call a service and get a stranger. The second name proved to be free, and could come that evening.

That seen to, Peggy phoned Alan. It was the first he heard of the events of the day.

When the aptly named Miss Frost came, she turned out to be one of those people who is able to function only under the strictest of conditions. She had a clear conception of her duties, and had a long list of requirements. She would not, for example, consent to step into the kitchen even to return a tray for someone else to clean up. "She had so many conditions," Peggy told Eleanor over the phone that evening, "that as Alan put it, it's doubtful whether it would have been worth it for Florence Nightingale. And this gal ain't Florence Nightingale; not by a long shot, thank you very much."

Oddly enough, Joan liked her; or if not her personality, at least her presence. She created a great fuss over Joan, in contrast to the imposition she lay on everyone else. Joan put up not one iota of resistance to the invalidism that Miss Frost enforced rigidly. Normally she hated to be waited on, and always got things for herself. Now she suffered herself to be babied and bossed by the nurse until everyone worried if she wasn't sicker than had been thought. She gave herself over entirely to helplessness. It was soothing, lulling, calming; a dreamworld. When she awoke the day after the accident, her head still throbbed like a gong, but she felt happy. She thinned out her voice and looked so listless and weak that no one questioned Miss Frost's presence.

There was talk of having the nurse stay on indefinitely, and she might well have, had not the inevitable quarrel broken out between her and the rest of the staff. It was hard not to sympathize with the help. Miss Frost was impossible. She complained that her breakfast had not been properly prepared when her eggs were overcooked by a minute; that no one had given her fresh sheets for Joan's bed; that they wouldn't let her watch a particular television show in the maid's sitting room. The final straw came when one of the maids refused to take a letter of hers to the mailbox, and she left in a huff. No one was very worried except for Miss Trimble, who phoned in extreme consternation when she found out and offered to come straight over. By then the case for Joan's having a nurse was pretty thin.

With Miss Frost out the door, Joan all but sprang from her bed. She insisted on going back to Meyer House right away. She had missed almost a week of work, and she worried that her absence had created a hardship for the kids and the other workers. She was very anxious not to be seen as lazy, or frivolous. She fretted that the children, particularly Pearl, might feel she had deserted them. Everyone tried to persuade her to be sensible, but she was merciless in her self-reproaches and gave no one any peace. Not even Martin Perry, calling personally to reassure her that Meyer House was still functioning in her absence, could keep her away.

So she returned; too early, as anyone could have predicted. Sunday evening there was nearly a row. Mrs. Altman had offered her car, but the thought of Holberg appearing again at Meyer House horrified Joan. She came close to being rude to her grandmother, and insisted on going the next morning on the subway again. Peggy insisted that at least she take a taxi her first day back, on the ground that she would do no one any good if she arrived exhausted from the subway ride. Joan stewed about the ostentation of a cab, even though many of the clients of Meyer House arrived daily in a taxi paid by welfare. As a compromise, she agreed to go down by taxi, that one morning; after that it was the BMT.

Peggy phoned Martin Perry to find out if he knew of another worker who could discreetly make a slight detour on her way to work and pick Joan up on her way to Meyer House, and then come back with her in the evening. She could then stay on the subway to her own home, presumably north of 96th Street, although Peggy didn't say that. Martin Perry, of course, said he would have no trouble finding someone. Peggy mentioned a generous sum to be added to the worker's paycheck at the House. She suspected it might be hard for Martin to find someone; but the fact that he never mentioned any difficulty was one of the reasons she had always thought he was so splendid for the job.

In fact, he had no trouble at all. There were very few people who worked at Meyer House whose route brought them anywhere near 685 Park, but he had only to ask, and Jenna said right away she'd be glad to do it. The extra money was never mentioned.

Alan objected on principle to there being a washroom for the partners at Furrer, Gutheim. It went smack against his democratic instincts, and also it was a tremendous waste of space to have two men's rooms. The firm employed no male secretaries, God forbid, and personally it wouldn't have killed him to run into a client or an associate washing his hands. But there had always been one at the downtown office, and some of the stuffier partners—the firm had more than its share—had insisted on the prerogative when they moved. He hadn't liked anything about the move, and the partner's washroom was just one more irritation, but there it was.

The one thing it did have to recommend it was privacy. One could talk to one's partners there without fear of indiscretion. So when Alan ran into Murray Furrer there soon after his conversation with Gerald, he decided it was as good a time as any to broach the subject of the Abbott family. Murray's office was all of twenty feet from his, but he thought the discussion might benefit from a more informal setting. When a man's fly is unzipped, he tends to be a little less punctilious in other matters.

"I was just about to buzz you," Murray said as Alan came in. "You have anyone on for lunch?"

"I couldn't be sorrier, Murray," Alan replied. "I have a Federation finance committee meeting, which I have to leave early to get up to Mt. Sinai. Otherwise I'd love to have lunch with you."

"Everything okay?" Murray asked, alarmed by the mention of the hospital. Alan had said very little about Joan except that she had come down from college with some sort of worrisome something-or-other. She certainly hadn't looked well when Murray had spotted her at Percy Weinstein's funeral. Terribly thin. And then this mysterious accident, no one seemed very clear about that.

"Everything's fine," Alan said, seeing the misunderstanding. "No, Joan couldn't be better. This is for the new medical school. They want me to raise the dough."

"Don't they always," Murray observed. The firm had long since accepted the inevitability of Alan's outside commitments. They cut into his hours at the desk, but in the long run they brought in a good deal of business. What you lose on the peanuts you make up on the popcorn. He tented his fly to make sure everything was out of the way before pulling up the zipper.

"It was the last thing I wanted to do, believe me. But how can you say no to a great hospital? No, when it comes to saving lives, I don't think any of us can look the other way."

"It's good of you to do it, Alan," Murray said, wondering how much this was going to set him back. Alan never twisted his arm, but by the same token he could hardly be chintzy with his partner's favorite cause. Murray went to the sink and turned on the water.

"How's the latest grandchild, by the way?" Alan inquired, thinking a bit of small talk might ease the request he was about to make. Murray's youngest daughter had finally had a baby after several years of trying. Alan couldn't remember if it was a boy or a girl.

"Couldn't be better," Murray said happily. "Lucille's spoiling him worse than any of the others, which is going some, but I imagine he'll survive." He rinsed off his hands and turned off the tap. The time had come.

"I had something I wanted to mention to you," Alan said, furrowing his brow and pretending to grope. "Can't for the life of me . . . Oh, now I remember! Fred Wellman, that's it. Everything going all right over there?"

"Sure," Murray said, puzzled. He'd had nothing but the most routine dealings with Wellman ever since taking over the account. "Why do you ask?"

"Well, there's a situation developing with this Abbott & Strawbridge business that they may be drawn into. A bit ticklish, really." Alan glanced nervously toward the doorway of the washroom. "The fact is, the Abbott trust, as I understand it, is in pretty deep hock to Anspach & Wellman. They probably needed some cash to pay off the estate taxes, unless I miss my guess, and rather than sell off their stock at a loss they took out a loan and used the stock as collateral. My understanding is that Fred is sitting on a large pile of their paper."

Murray dried his hands carefully with one of the linen hand towels on the washstand. He might not have been the most brilliant lawyer in town, but he'd been around for a fair number of years and he knew what was what. "I can't think it would be in Fred's interest to call in the note, if that's the issue," he said, catching up rapidly to Alan's line of thinking. "I don't know the particulars of the situation, but if he tries to collect from the trust at this point they might well go under, and then I'd have the devil of a time trying to get Fred's money back for him."

"I don't think anyone wants that," Alan said hastily.

"Of course, the stock will go up with this tender offer," Murray said. "I suppose if they sold it, they could come up with the cash. If they don't sell it, and the takeover doesn't go through, the whole kaboodle might be worthless. So there is some rationale for their selling it now. Which they can't do without Fred's permission."

"Exactly," Alan said.

"Conceivably, Fred's permission might depend on who the buyer is. In theory, his only concern is whether the buyer can foot the bill. But he could call the shots on this if he wanted to."

"If he wanted to," Alan echoed.

"I guess the sixty-four-dollar question is, does he want to?" Alan nodded in agreement. "And I take it the other question is, who's going to find that out."

Alan didn't say anything.

Murray looked up at the ceiling for a moment before saying, "I've got to give this a bit of thought, you know, Alan, before I say yes or no. I'd like to be helpful to Gerry in any way I could. On the other hand, I have some responsibility to the clients here."

Alan was stung by the suggestion of impropriety. Hadn't he himself been the one to tell Gerald there couldn't be a conflict of interest? "I'd be the last person in the world to suggest that you do anything that in any way, shape, or form—" he protested, but Murray held up his hand.

"Now let's just hold on a minute, Alan! I didn't say I wouldn't do it. I just need some time to think about it. After all," he said, "finding compromises is our business." He dropped the soiled towel into a basket. "Let me get back to you on this," he said, and left the washroom.

Damn, thought Alan. First he let Gerald push him around, and now he had to listen to Murray Furrer, of all people, give him a lecture on ethics. And for what? He didn't stand to gain a thing by this whole business. It was what he got for trying to be helpful. From trying to please too many people. He didn't like it. He didn't like it one bit.

Damn.

In his preoccupation he had followed Murray out the door. He was trying to work out a better conclusion. It was tough to do. He rehearsed imaginary conversations between Murray and Fred Anspach, and then between Fred and whoever handled the Abbott trust, but no matter how he twisted and turned, it wound up looking fishy. Buried in his thoughts, he got halfway back to his office before he remembered why he had come out in the first place, and he had to retrace his way to the washroom.

Eleven

Johnny phoned constantly while Joan was recuperating. He would call at some ungodly hour in the morning before he went off to classes, and in the evening when he got home, and usually once or twice in between. He sent her flowers and fruit and books and if she had let him, he would have come over and relieved Miss Frost of her duties. He offered to come every evening, Miss Frost notwithstanding. He said he would come and talk to her, or read to her if she was too tired to read to herself, or watch TV with her, or just sit in her room and say nothing. He would have, too. If she let him, he would have watched her while she slept. He would have been thrilled just to sit there and watch her sleep. It was creepy.

Joan, taking advantage of the available truth, told him she was too exhausted to see him. She hinted that she was forbidden visitors, although that really defied belief. (Wendy had come the day after the accident, bringing a box of nonpareils from Flora Mir and six magazines, but Wendy didn't exactly count.) Joan did take most of his phone calls despite his becoming a nuisance with them. Who wanted to talk to Johnny, or anyone else, at a quarter before eight in the morning? If nothing else made the idea of marrying him impossible, the thought of having to talk to him every morning would have ruled it out. He'd be cheerful, energetic, solicitous, full of interesting tidbits from the newspaper, and in every way insufferable. Joan liked the evening calls, though. She was glad to hear his smooth, masculine voice after a day of

Miss Frost's harpy's rasp. As the afternoon wore on she would look forward to his call. Friday he didn't call until late—some meeting, he said—and she was actually upset. She said nothing about it, but she did tell him he could come over the next day, provided he didn't stay forever, and promised not to look at her.

He came indecently early, with a bunch of roses from Donatello's. Joan hadn't seen him since the night of the surprise party, and he looked terrific to her. He gave her his chastest brotherly kiss, ostensibly because Miss Frost was there. Of course, it wouldn't have made any difference if they had been marooned on a desert island. Miss Frost hung around like a duenna, bustling about and plumping up pillows and generally making herself obnoxious. She was obviously unable to tear herself away. Aside from his great looks, Johnny had a special way with servants, salesladies, waitresses, and other old maids who thought they could do very well without a man until he came along and broke their hearts with his anachronistic courteousness. He didn't even begin to talk to Joan, for example, until he had conversed with Miss Frost. He found out about her bachelor brother for whom she kept house except when she was on a case, her elderly aunt who was in a nursing home but whom she visited every week without fail and specialed whenever she went into the hospital, and her last two clients. He learned more about her in ten minutes than the rest of the family, Joan included, had in four days. When Miss Frost finally ran out of reasons to stay, she left the room with a backlong glance, blushing.

With her gone, Johnny settled in for a long visit. If he had counted on having any privacy, he would have been disappointed; but he knew the household. Alan came in as soon as Miss Frost left. He was on his way out for his Saturday walk. Every week, rain or shine, he set out on Saturday morning, coatless, to pay his calls. He stopped in on each of his sisters, on his Uncle Rudolf, and on a decrepit elderly cousin of his mother's who hardly knew who he was from week to week, but who it pleased him to believe lived for his visits. He went uptown as far as Mt. Sinai, where he would look in on any patient whose name was even vaguely familiar to him. On those rare occasions when he didn't know anyone who was sick, he visited the children's ward. He would buy a box of candy at the gift shop and distribute the sweets, Santa fashion, with benevolent comments and a little homily, to the totally bewildered children. Most of them never began to understand who he was. Before leaving he would "take the pulse" of the hospital, much to the bemusement of the assistant director on duty for the weekend. He would return home by a different route and would come back in bursting with information. He reported new buildings or demolitions under way, important street repairs, interesting or bizarre scenes he'd witnessed, what was showing at the Met, and the latest information on the astonishing numbers of people he'd seen on the street. His report took forever. Then he would get his own lunch, no one was to bother about him. (Gerta always said it would be a lot less bother for her to serve him on a tray than to have him getting it himself and leaving her kitchen in an uproar.) He would eat it while he listened to the opera broadcast, humming the familiar tunes of the overture between mouthfuls. It was a rare Saturday that he wasn't asleep on the library couch before the first intermission.

It being Saturday, Joan would have had to be much nearer death's doorstep than she was for him to forgo his walk. He stood in her doorway, rubbing his hands and inquiring of Johnny about all his professors at business school. He kept his thoughts about the propriety of the scene before him to himself. Whatever went on between his only daughter and her boyfriend was fine with him. He assumed Peggy had seen to whatever a modern girl required, and he would never in all his days have dreamed of mentioning it. But he didn't think it proper for an unmarried woman to entertain a male visitor in her bedroom. Especially when she was in bed. In her bathrobe. The innocence of the actual behavior had nothing to do with it. He knew he was old-fashioned, and that if he said anything Peggy would hoot him down, so he kept his mouth shut. He showed his true feelings only in an excessive cordiality toward Johnny, who in any case he hoped and expected would one day have a connubial right to sit at Joan's bedside. Alan's hands having been rubbed to a fine heat, he left, calling as he strode down the hallway, "Neither rain, nor snow, nor sleet, nor the winter's chill shall stay this messenger . . ." although it was in fact a lovely day.

Peggy came next, but didn't stay long either. She had no qualms whatsoever about Johnny's being in Joan's bedroom, but she doubted he would be there much in the future. "They're growing in different directions," she would tell Alan whenever he started rhapsodizing about their imminent engagement. Still, for the time being it was pleasant to see the young man. She had always been terribly fond of him, and used to refer to him as God's gift to women. He knew how to court mothers too. She wouldn't have minded lingering a bit. But Peggy Gutheim was not one to linger. She had a full schedule for the morning. She asked Joan if she wanted anything, and suggested any number of articles of clothing, toiletries, books, or food she imagined Joan might need. She mentioned several stores she could stop at, but Joan insisted she had everything she could possibly want. She had a stack of unread books on her bedside table that people had brought her. *To Kill a Mockingbird* was at the bottom of the pile. Peggy decided to get her something to eat. As much to keep Lamartine from threatening hospitalization at the drop of a hat as anything, Peggy had tried to encourage Joan in that department. She hadn't met with much success. Joan refused to talk about the subject, and on one occasion when Peggy had pressed her about it there was nearly a row. Clearly, nagging wasn't going to do the trick, as Peggy had had to tell Alan. There were moments—she said nothing about it to anyone—when she wondered if Joan, on top of everything, had this dreadful thing when girls stop eating, or whatever it is they do that makes them look like they just got out of Auschwitz. The Goldsteins' daughter, she understood, had all but died of it. Joan, of course, didn't look anywhere near that bad, but Peggy was uneasy all the same. She'd stop at Fraser-Morris; they were sure to have something Joan would like.

Before Peggy left, Phil came in, still in his pajamas. He brought his orange juice and coffee and the *Times* and sat on Joan's bed. Peggy said good-bye to the three of them. Phil settled himself in, spreading the paper out over her legs. Johnny didn't mind. It made him feel at home again, to be in on such a family scene. He knew that he needed to stay in Phil's good graces if he had any hopes of winning Joan. Any man in her life, he knew, would always play second fiddle to her older brother.

The paper provided Phil with a steady stream of material for his sardonic comments. There were two articles on the latest appointments to the administration. Everyone thought Kennedy was making surprisingly good choices. Phil knew more about the politics, and he took a more jaundiced view of some of the people named. Then he turned to the society columns, which he footnoted maliciously, and the other two were in stitches before he finished. Finally he reached the sports section, which was the one part of the paper that claimed his undivided attention, and that shut him up temporarily.

Carl didn't go in. He was practicing, and the sound of the monotonous exercises came in from the living room. Joan told Johnny crossly to close the door, but they could still hear the music. Joan hated to have to put up with hearing her brother practice. She occasionally asked him if there was any real reason to repeat the same passage over and over so many times. It was enough, she said, to drive anyone stark, raving mad. Over the years they had had several scenes over the subject.

Miss Frost came back and stunned them all by asking Johnny if he would like some coffee. It was the first time since she had come that she had offered to lift a finger for anyone except Joan. Even when Mrs. Altman had visited, the maid had had to be called to get her a glass of ice water. While Miss Frost was out getting the coffee, Phil made a lewd assessment of Johnny's opportunities with her. She played into it by blushing when she returned with the tray, and Joan came close to disgracing herself in a fit of hysterics.

They passed the morning lazily. The sun slanted through the window, casting a pale light on the lemon-colored walls hung with little Dufy gouaches, giving the illusion that the entire city basked in the same warmth that filled the bedroom. Joan found it delicious to lounge against the pillows piled up luxuriously on her sickbed, with her panda next to her for company, and her feet squished by her loutish brother. The two young men bantered about football and politics. Carl had temporarily abandoned the Chopin for the G-major Schubert sonata, the one with the heavenly melody above a rippling accompaniment, much more soothing to hear.

One could grow used to this, Joan thought, lying in bed. She felt more content than she had since coming back to the city. If only she wasn't plagued by the vaguest sense of guilt, a feeling that it wasn't right to be enjoying all this; that for every moment of pleasure she consumed, someone, somewhere, was suffering. She was taking more than her share. She had too much of everything: clothes, food, people to wait on her, material possessions. She felt too full, as though she had overeaten and fallen asleep in the afternoon, only to awake bloated, listless, gaseous. She ought to get up and do something strenuous. Do some physical work, ride a horse. Anything to purge herself. She ought to give some of what she had away. She should perform more good works, think better thoughts. Think about the poor and the deprived, instead of always herself. If only she could stop thinking of herself altogether!

But how was it possible, with everyone making such a fuss over her? With Alan wringing his hands and Peggy forever asking if there was something she could do for her or buy for her, Johnny continually throwing himself at her feet. Any moment now he was liable to ask if he could kiss the hem of her dress, or her feet, turn her into some sort of saint or religious shrine. Horrible! Only Phil treated her as she deserved to be treated, and of course he didn't give anyone the time of day. In truth, he treated everyone more or less badly, including Betsy. But his flip, irreverent manner suited Joan perfectly. If only everyone else would let up on her, she would do fine. When she was younger, she had the fantasy of becoming transparent, invisible, so that no one could see her. She would still be there, but she could come and go as she pleased and no one would know whether she was there or not. They might fret for a while, but then they would think she had gone away and would come back when she was ready. Eventually, she thought, they would forget about her. It was an ambiguous fantasy. At times she found it consoling, at others, scary. To think that she would become nothing more than an illusion, and dissolve away! She used to wonder what it would be like to be alone like that, torn away from the others, all ties cut. Would it be an escape from those omnipresent eyes of her mother, who always knew her every move? Or would she feel exiled, marooned? Buried alive, like Juliet. What if she wanted to return? How would she get back?

That afternoon Joan went out for the first time since the accident. Mrs. Altman was picking her up, and then they were going on to Rosenberg's. Joan loved nothing better than going to the galleries with her grandmother. Although in theory it should offend her, she took a secret delight in a bit of bowing and scraping now and then, provided it wasn't overdone. At Knoedler's, the fawning could get out of hand, but Rosenberg's had a lighter touch, not to mention some fabulous Impressionist paintings.

She was downstairs when the car arrived, fearful that she might keep her grandmother waiting. There had been several phone calls over who would call for whom. Ordinarily, Mrs. Altman let Peggy rule her, but she couldn't be persuaded that Joan could perfectly well sit in the car for the half minute it took Holberg to come in for her. She greeted her granddaughter warmly, skillfully concealing her mounting anxiety over Joan's health and well-being. "Grandmother!" Joan said, kissing Mrs. Altman. "You are *so wonderful* to take me with you. I hope I won't be in the way."

"Nonsense, dear. It only adds to the pleasure when you're with me. It's lovely to see you." She lifted her hands to allow Holberg to replace the gray lap robe he had pulled forward when Joan got in the car. "You're looking much better."

"I should hope so," Joan said airily. "I've been doing nothing but lie in bed and have everyone make a terrible fuss over me. Also, Miss Frost is leaving this afternoon, which is enough to make anyone feel better. Not that there was anything wrong with me to begin with."

Mrs. Altman smiled wryly. Joan was Peggy to the life, always denying that the slightest thing was amiss. Either one of them could be in extremis and not a peep out of them. She patted Joan's knee fondly and pointed out a fetching pair of little girls, just then crossing the street with their governess.

Holberg drove them up Fifth Avenue so they wouldn't have to cross the street at 79th to get to the gallery. It was pleasant looking into the park. The playground below the transverse was crowded, and judging by the number of boys in short coats carrying toy sailboats, there must have been a regatta on the 73rd Street pond. As they turned east, Joan could see people lounging on the steps of the museum up ahead, enjoying the unseasonable warmth of the day.

At Rosenberg's, by some marvel of unseen communication, the director was on the street when they drove up. Who knows, maybe he had been there all morning. He escorted Mrs. Altman and Joan into the gallery, where there was a show of pointillists. Joan barely took in the dotted landscapes as they were swept like royalty past the ordinary customers and shown into a back room. There they were seated on Louis Quinze chairs and handed cups of tea. Besides the manager and two assistants, a Mr. Poincaré was in attendance. It wasn't clear to Joan at the outset what his function was, but eventually she gathered he had something to do with the Met. When he was introduced to Joan, he spoke of her parents' Picasso and Matisse, which apparently established her identity for him.

As soon as Mrs. Altman and Joan were settled, the showing began. Pictures straight out of an art book were paraded in front of them. One of the assistants would bring out a painting and set it on a stand in front of a dark blue curtain while the director murmured a brief appreciation. Mr. Poincaré then dated the work, commented on its historical significance, and gave the provenance. Mrs. Altman would ask a question, or not, one assistant would remove the painting and the other would bring in the next. Mr. Poincaré would suggest ever so tactfully which paintings would especially complement the Altman collection, which he knew inside out. Joan understood, without anyone saying so, that he was indicating which ones the Metropolitan particularly had its eye on, it being clear that any purchase Mrs. Altman made at this juncture would wind up fairly soon on the museum's walls.

Mrs. Altman bought nothing that afternoon, but Joan guessed it wasn't done that way. No price had been mentioned the whole time. There had been one Pissarro that Mrs. Altman had wanted to look at for an extra moment before it was whisked away, but no one spoke of it again. Before they left, the director asked Joan if there was anything she would like to be shown. He spoke to her with almost the same deference he used toward Mrs. Altman, but she declined his offer, not wanting to arouse any expectations that she was in the market. Then he asked, did she have a particular favorite among the Impressionist painters? She mentioned Degas, thinking of the wonderful dancers in pink that hung in Mrs. Altman's third-floor sitting room. The director nodded to one of the assistants, who immediately brought out a small pastel of a young girl, sad and pensive. She struck Joan as having been abandoned, an orphan perhaps. It was marvelous how affecting a little sketch could be. "Charming," Mrs. Altman pronounced, looking to see her granddaughter's reaction. Joan was smitten with the drawing, but she only smiled, and thanked the director for letting her see it.

After they left the gallery, they drove to Schrafft's, at 88th Street. It was their tradition that after any afternoon outing—a movie, shopping, matinee, whatever—they would stop for a soda on the way home. Joan ordered her childhood favorite, a butterscotch sundae, while Mrs. Altman contented herself with the baked apple. Neither of them ate very much.

"You were so nice to bring me with you," Joan said, taking tiny sips of the sticky golden sauce.

"I hope it wasn't too tiresome for you, dear," Mrs. Altman replied anxiously. "There must be so many things you'd rather do on a Saturday afternoon."

"Grandmother! There's nothing I'd rather do! It was wonderful of you to let me come with you. It was terrific, really."

"I'm so glad," Mrs. Altman said. "I was so afraid you'd be bored."

"How could anyone possibly be bored? All those wonderful paintings!"

"They were charming," Mrs. Altman agreed. "I gathered you liked the little Degas drawing?"

"I have to admit, that was my favorite," Joan said.

"I would love to give it to you as a present," Mrs. Altman said, almost shyly. "Christmas is coming up."

"Grandmother!" Joan cried. "You can't give that to me as a Christmas present! I mean, it's too lovely for words, and you know I would love nothing better, but you really can't!" Mrs. Altman wrinkled her forehead in disappointment. "Grandmother." Joan reached across the table and took Mrs. Altman's hand in hers. "You just spoil me horribly, that's all there is to it. I can't think of anything more wonderful than to have it from you. But it's much too much for a Christmas present. Let's save it for an occasion." She gave her grandmother's hand an affectionate squeeze.

"Maybe graduation?" Mrs. Altman asked hopefully.

It was hopeless. The last thing in the world Joan wanted was to hurt her grandmother's feelings. How could she turn down a present, so generously offered? How could she explain that she didn't deserve it, didn't deserve all this solicitude and attention? How could she ever repay her debt?

"I would love it," she said warmly. She could cross that bridge when she came to it. She wasn't at all sure she was going to graduate, but she said nothing of that.

Mrs. Altman beamed happily, like a little girl who had just been promised a trip to the circus. Nothing gave her more pleasure than spoiling her grandchildren.

When they came out of the restaurant, the bright sunlight momentarily blinded Mrs. Altman. She became confused, and a look of panic swept over her face. Joan put her hand under the older woman's elbow to steady her, and guided her gently over to the car. When Mrs. Altman saw her chauffeur holding open the door, she became herself once more. As she got in the car she said to Joan, "Thank you, dear. I don't know what I'd do without you."

Joan couldn't do a thing about it. She was deceiving them all.

On Monday she went back to Meyer House. She had every intention of forgetting about herself, her accident, her illness, anything connected with her troublesome body. It was all very confusing to her anyway. One day she loathed her flesh, despised her appetites, wished she were incorporeal; the next, she was intoxicated with sensations and desires. She seemed to lack continuity. Today she wanted to clear her mind of everything physical so she could concentrate on the children. She wanted to devote herself purely to them.

She wondered what they would make of her, after her disappearing act. If they had any sense, she thought, they would wash their hands of someone so unreliable. But Mark, the first kid to come, gave her a big hello. Joan knew he was that way with everyone, from his grim-looking father, who left him off in the morning, to any perfect stranger who might wander into the room and stop for a moment beside the cute little kid in the wheelchair. Everyone got the same cheerful "Hiya!" and the same broad grin. There was no way you could tell if he really remembered you, although in fact he remembered everyone. Still, she was glad to see him again, and she gave him a big hug.

Claire had sunk deeper inside her shell over the week. There were now long, ominous silences when a question was put to her. It was as though she was making a decision whether to let anyone have the most fleeting glimpse into her world before she slammed the door shut again. Joan got the feeling that soon it would close for good, and Claire would be locked inside.

When Pearl was wheeled in and saw Joan was back, she went into paroxysms of joy. Leona said she had asked for Joan every day last week. As soon as Joan was able, they took up where they had left off. The work was slower, though. Joan could understand why people had thought she was retarded. At times her unintelligibility seemed willful. She had a habit of blurting out a phrase or a sentence almost perfectly, catching herself, and then repeating it in her usual garble. When she did that she would turn on her most lovable grin and drool fetchingly, but Joan didn't fall for that. She worked patiently until Pearl produced some words she could understand. It took the better part of the morning, but by lunchtime Pearl had made up what she had lost in Joan's absence. The two of them hugged each other happily, and Joan said, "That's *so* great, Pearl."

At lunchtime, Joan insisted again that Leona let her stay alone with the children. She hoped Jenna might come by for her. She had caught only a fleeting glimpse of her friend when Jenna came into the room with a note for Leona. She waved to Joan, who was struggling with Pearl at the time. Joan thought the greeting was cool. It could have been her imagination. She was probably reading too much into one wave. She wasn't the center of Jenna's life, she told herself. The girl had been nice to her, but that didn't make them blood sisters. She tried not to dwell on it.

But by the time Leona came back, Jenna still hadn't come. Joan thought of skipping lunch—she wasn't a bit hungry—but she decided to go down anyway. Entering the cafeteria alone was difficult. She was horribly self-conscious. The last time she had been there she had suffered the fiasco of Holberg coming for her. Now she felt like a child who is going back to a place where she has disgraced herself and had to be removed. She felt as though all the eyes in the room were on her.

Probably very few were, and those belonged mostly to the middle-aged ladies. Etta smiled and waved and carried on so that Joan had no choice but to go over and join her and the other mother hens. They were all relieved to see her back. They commented on how well she looked, and wanted to know all about the accident. They were horrified she had wound up at Bellevue. "What were you doing at such a place?" Etta wanted to know. "They should have taken you to Mt. Sinai. But you probably didn't let them know who you were."

Meanwhile, she wished she was across the aisle where all the younger people were sitting. No one there paid any attention to her at all. Jenna either didn't see her or pretended not to. She was sitting next to Kevin. Joan didn't know what was going on there. They didn't look like lovers, but they were more than friends. Once Kevin put his arm around Jenna's shoulder. It could have been a casual, kidding gesture, but Joan was bothered by it. She realized how ludicrously jealous she was being, considering that she had yet to speak to him. There were also about twenty good reasons why they couldn't and shouldn't have anything to do with one another, not then, not any time in the future.

"Is that all you're eating?" Etta was asking her. She had taken only a small salad and a cup of black coffee, and she hadn't touched the salad. She smiled wanly and mumbled something about not being that hungry. "You ought to have something substantial. Even if you don't feel like it. Cup of soup, at least. Food like home you won't get here, but a cup of soup will get you through the afternoon." Joan tried to explain that it had nothing to do with the food, which was fine, but clearly Etta thought it was not up to the Gutheim standard.

Across the way they were having a much better time. They were telling jokes and laughing uproariously, while the ladies at her table were groaning about tie-ups in the subway, the cold weather, the high prices of food. She felt like a child who isn't allowed to go out and play with her friends, but has to stay indoors and be good. She wondered if she would ever be accepted there, ever belong.

The ladies were still going nonstop when the crowd across the way started to break up. Joan wanted to join them, but she couldn't figure out how to get away from where she was. Kevin and Jenna went out together. He was laughing loudly. Joan thought probably nothing was very funny, but he just wanted to be seen laughing loudly. On his way past her table he saw her, and flashed a grin. He was wearing his white sweatpants. Jenna exulted in his attention. After they were gone, the ladies got up. Joan took her uneaten salad with her coffee cup to the pass-through window at the kitchen where the dirty dishes were collected. Everyone else had eaten what they had put on their trays. Joan felt wasteful and spoiled. No one mentioned the untouched food.

Jenna was outside the cafeteria, in the hallway near the stairs. She acted surprised to bump into Joan, but Joan knew she must have waited there. Kevin had gone, and so had the others. There was no other reason for her to have been there. She seemed ill at ease, as though the two of them had quarreled. She didn't refer to Joan's absence for the past week. She waited until they were alone in the stairwell, and then asked Joan if they'd be going home together that afternoon. Puzzled, Joan said that would be nice. It seemed a strange thing for Jenna to ask. Still, it was a gesture. Joan thought she understood now. Jenna wanted to see her, but away from Meyer House, where they could be on a more equal footing. She might even have worried that if they were seen together in the settlement house, people would think she was cultivating Joan. Nothing could be further from the truth, of course, but Joan could see how there was a chance of a misunderstanding. No, it made a great deal of sense. She herself should have realized how uncomfortable this all was for Jenna. She wanted to say something about it, but that would only make it worse. Of course they would go home together. Nothing would please her more. They arranged to meet when Joan was through for the afternoon. "Come up and get me," Jenna said, clearly more at ease. "I'll be in the gym." Joan was glad. They were back to normal again.

All afternoon, as the children limped and clumped and wheeled their way around the room, Joan kept hearing Jenna's casual "I'll be in the gym." As if she lived there. Joan was envious of Jenna's freedom. She could go where she pleased. To Joan, the gym was off-limits. Directly overhead, it intruded itself constantly. A steady crescendo of activity was taking place there. Toward the middle of the afternoon a basketball game started. Up and down the length of the ceiling it thundered. It was impossible not to follow the progress of the game. Between the increasing disorganization around her and the pounding feet overhead, she found herself distracted and disturbed.

She didn't know what she should be doing. During the morning, she had been useful, but she got lost in the shuffle in the larger group. The children she had worked with were still there, but they were absorbed into the general chaos. Claire's litter was pushed against a wall, and she watched the others with her usual listless stare. Mark darted in and out of various clusters of teenagers, listening in on their conversations. As soon as they realized he was eavesdropping, he would pivot his wheelchair and speed off to another group. He turned into a rascal, and got all the attention he wanted. Pearl was adopted by the older girls, who treated her as though she were a rag doll. They petted her and hugged her and passed her from one to another. Joan tried to get to know some of the other children, but it was too noisy. She couldn't do much more than wander from child to child and introduce herself. The only one who took any interest in her at all was Andrea, the little colored girl in a brace who had caught Peggy's attention that first day. She had a sad, waif's countenance, and was glad to let Joan sit and watch while she laboriously drew pictures of her mother, of the father she never had, and a home that could only have existed in her imagination.

Outside it began to grow dark. The children gradually departed. Some, like Andrea, went alone. Others were called for, by sisters and brothers, mothers and aunts, or family friends. Some of the older kids went downstairs to hang around the lobby until their normal counterparts came in. Leona and Joan went around the room picking up the debris of the day, putting some things away. Eventually everyone had left except for Mark. He offered to help, but there wasn't much he could do. He waited, intent, at the door. When he couldn't dash about, watching or listening or escaping, his face fell into the tense vigilant expression Joan had noticed when she first saw him. He looked out the door and stiffened every time the elevator stopped. After many false alarms, his father finally came. Mark burst into surprising tears. The father, a haggard, beaten-down man carrying a lunch pail, seemed inured to his son's outburst. He neither scolded nor comforted the boy, but wheeled him out the door without saying a word. Mark subsided into quiet sobs, and he wiped his wet cheeks with the palm of his hand. "I thought you weren't gonna come," Joan heard him say.

"He does that every night," Leona told her. "I tell him his father's coming, he might be a little late, and he always thinks something's happened. He worries he'll be left here, alone. I tell him that would never happen. I'd take him home with me first. But he always worries." She shook her head at the unsolvable riddle of a young child's fears.

The day was over. Joan relaxed into a pleasant fatigue. While she was putting on her coat, Leona asked her how she was getting home. Hearing that she planned to take the subway, Leona looked horrified. Leona had of course taken the E train out to Jamaica every evening of her working life, but it seemed to her that a Gutheim ought to be called for, or to take a taxi at the very least. Joan's assurance that she would be traveling with Jenna didn't satisfy Leona. She said nothing, but her lips tightened. It was obvious that she had deep feelings about having Negroes on the staff, but she didn't say anything. The two women parted at the end of the hallway and said a pleasant enough good night; but something of their goodwill had dissipated. Joan understood better why Jenna wanted to avoid her inside the settlement house. It had been indiscreet to mention her name to Leona.

Climbing up to the floor above, Joan thought of the last time she had been in that stairwell. No one came crashing down on her this time. When she reached the top landing, she stopped. She was reluctant to open the door. She thought she might walk in on something she shouldn't see. Her notion of a gym was a dirty, fetid dungeon where men in various stages of undress went about their sweaty business and told smutty jokes. It wasn't a fit place for a woman. She wished she had arranged to meet Jenna somewhere else, but it was too late. There was nothing for her to do but go in.

She was surprised to find herself on one side of a huge, brightly lit open space. The gym occupied the entire top floor of Meyer House, and its ceiling was twice as high as that of the rooms below. In the middle of its wooden floor a basketball court was marked off, and there were additional backboards against the outside walls. The game Joan had heard earlier in the afternoon was over, but some boys were still on the court shooting baskets. They were sharing a couple of balls among them, standing around between shots with blank, daydreaming expressions. A bunch of older boys and young men stood among an array of barbells and dumbbells and other metal apparatus. They were watching a young man who lay on a wooden bench, straining against a huge barbell on his chest. The others rubbed their bare arms and arched their shoulders as they waited their turn. Next to the weights were some dirty gray mats for tumbling or wrestling or exercising. Between the mats stood a couple of gym horses and a set of balance bars. Monkey bars ran up the walls between the high windows, and an overhead ladder was suspended from the ceiling next to them, although to get to the ladder required a daring leap, more than ten feet off the floor.

On the opposite side of the gym was a raised ring, with ropes, for boxing. Two men were sparring in it, one white, the other Negro. Near the ring, leaning against a pucnhing bag, Jenna held a towel. Joan looked back and saw that the white boxer was Kevin. The realization excited her. From the distance she could hardly recognize him. Except for the thuds of the basketballs and the clink of the weights, the only noise in the gym came from the scuffling feet and the dull thuds of the boxers' gloves. No shouts or profanity filled the air, but a grim seriousness was evident.

Jenna didn't see her, so Joan went over to where she stood, crossing carefully behind the basket. She had never seen a fight before, except in a movie, or maybe a brief glimpse on TV before someone switched the channel. She was both repelled and fascinated. The Negro boy was bigger than Kevin, and well enough built, but clearly overmatched. He was panting hard and looked tired, and although he wore only trunks and no shirt he was sweating heavily. Kevin wore his tight white sweatpants and a red undershirt and had not a trace of perspiration on him. He looked relaxed and assured as he bounced up and down between exchanges. Both of the boxers wore protectors with the word *Everlast* blazoned on them, grotesque black trusses with enormous pouches that Joan found embarrassingly explicit.

The boy was having a rough time. Kevin didn't attack him but was easily able to deflect all his punches. After knocking aside his thrusts, Kevin would land a short, hard blow to the midsection that would force a grunt of pain and a fine spray of spit from the confused boy. It was clear that he could do anything he pleased with his opponent, but the boy kept at him doggedly until almost by accident he slipped a glancing punch by Kevin's guard and clipped him in the ear. Kevin, stung, retaliated with a fast combination of hard body blows. The boy paled, dropped his gloves, and said in a trembling voice, "I think I'm gonna puke, Kevin." Kevin hit him again in the stomach and he staggered backward into the ropes. He hooked an arm over the top rope and sagged to one knee, hugging his waist with his free arm. His ashen face twisted, and he looked as though he was about to cry.

"Kevin!" Jenna called out sharply.

"Shut up!" he snapped at her. He was wearing a mouthpiece, and the words came out indistinct but angry. The boy coughed and some saliva dribbled down his chin. A few more coughs then turned into gags and he started to retch. He leaned into the corner of the ring, expelled his mouthpiece, and spat some mucus onto the canvas. "You okay?" Kevin called. He nodded, retched some more, and dislodged some sort of crud into the puddle. Kevin went over to him and put a glove on his shoulder. "You're all right," he said, a little uncertainly. The boy nodded his agreement and took several deep, gasping gulps of air. He retched once more and vomited up some greenish junk. Wiping his mouth with a glove, he straightened up and smiled sheepishly. He had tears in his eyes. Kevin pawed him on the shoulder. "Good man," he said, giving a light jab to the boy's arm. "You're all right," he said again, and pranced back across the ring, shadowboxing. When he got to the ropes, he tongued his mouthpiece out into his gloved hands, ducked between the ropes, and jumped lightly down onto the floor. He left his mouthpiece on the ring apron and came over to the two women. He put his arm around Jenna's shoulders, but she wriggled him off.

"You don't know when to stop!" she told him angrily.

"That's not what you said last night," he said, taking Joan into the joke with a grin and a wink. "Don't be a sissy," he said, taking the towel from her and wrapping it around his neck as best he could with his gloves on. "If you're gonna come into a gym, you can't be a woman about it."

He wasn't as fine-looking as Joan wanted him to be. His nose was crooked where it had probably been broken, and his cheekbones were high enough to give his eyes a pinched, almost beady appearance. His arm and chest muscles were blatantly overdeveloped and he kept flexing them. Joan wasn't used to being that close to a man who displayed his muscles so unabashedly, and she was disturbed by his acidic, gladiatorial smell. Her instinct was to move away, but since she couldn't she was forced to recognize an attraction she considered debasing. She was disquieted and ashamed. She could hardly keep herself from staring at his crotch. She was sure everyone could read her thoughts and know her desire.

Jenna carried on her pout and pretended to be mad at Kevin. "You know what you are? You're a bully. Was that supposed to be a lesson? You call that a lesson?"

"That was a lesson, all right," Kevin insisted. "Shit, if he's gonna come down here and mess around with wop hoods, he better learn to fight like a nigger at least, or he'll wake up with a shiv in his stomach. He's okay. You're okay, aren'tcha, Dennis?" Dennis had by then climbed shakily down from the ring. He didn't join the others, whether because of the humiliation he had suffered, or out of a greater sense of delicacy than Kevin's. Joan recognized him now as the boy who was being pursued on the stairway the other day. With his mouthpiece out he had the sweet, dumb look of a boy on his way toward bad trouble. One of the boys who had been lifting weights had come over and was unlacing his gloves. When he got a hand free, he picked up a towel from the floor where it had fallen and wiped his face and chest. When the other glove was off, he circled to the back of the ring and used his towel to sponge the mess he had made. "Don't worry about that," Kevin called. "That's woman's work. Jenna'll get that." He grinned again.

Jenna rose to the bait and shrieked, "You just see if I clean up this pigsty for you one more morning! You just wait and see!"

Kevin shrugged and laughed. "Come on, Jenna. Wanna go a few rounds?" He jabbed at her and danced a bit. "I'll teach you to fight dirty too. Only you already know about that, don'tcha? Huh? Maybe you could teach ol' Dennis a thing or two, couldn't you?"

"That's it. We're leaving," Jenna said to Joan, making a great show of outrage. She started marching huffily toward the door, but her heels were too high for dignity, and the effect was comical. The boys grinned, and Kevin burst into derisive laughter.

"You don't have to go," he called. "You can stay. It's fine with me."

Jenna stopped and wheeled around. "And as for woman's work, you can do your own cleaning up in the morning!"

"I never said that was woman's work!" Kevin protested, pitching his voice high so that it sounded whining and effeminate. "I said that was nigger's work!" He gave out a loud, raucous laugh, in which all the boys joined, including Dennis, who was in fact the only other colored person in the gym. Jenna made a fresh show of indignation, which was especially ineffective since she was a limited actress and was clearly enjoying the attention. "Aren't you gonna introduce me to your friend?" Kevin called. But they were at the door, and Joan had to leave before the introduction could be made.

They stood in the little hallway outside the gym, waiting for the elevator. "Ooh, that guy!" Jenna said. "He makes me so mad! He thinks he's God on earth and I don't know how he does it but somehow he gets me to do I don't know what-all for him, and then—ooh!" she ended in exasperation. The elevator arrived and the two young women got in. It picked up passengers at each floor, so they couldn't discuss the intriguing subject any further.

A swirling throng was gathered in the lobby. Workers coming in for the evening stopped to talk to those on their way home. Most of the elderly clients had vacated their chairs and sofas, but were reluctant to leave. They lingered about, taking in everything they could before going off to their solitary, probably hungry evenings. The teenagers were now pouring into the building in full force. They pushed their way rudely by the old people and headed for the recreation rooms or the gym. Each time the door to the stairwell opened, their shouts could be heard reverberating there. Martin Perry had come out of his office and stood smoking his pipe like a proud father, calling familiarly to the departing clients and staff. He boomed a hearty good night to Joan, and smiled at Jenna.

As the two young women had made their way across the crush, they were joined by several other workers. The group emerged into the dark evening in high spirits. Most of the shops in the neighborhood were still open. Progress to the subway was slowed by someone or other wanting to look through a rack of dresses or coats on the street. The pungent smell of Chinese food ambushed them, and an early supper together was proposed. They asked Joan to come with them. Johnny was coming over for dinner that evening. She envied the others their freedom. She wished she could decide on the spur of the moment when and where she was going to eat without having to worry about the table having to be reset back home, anxious questions to be answered, unspoken disapproval of anything left unexplained. She thought of just not showing up, leaving them all there to eat without her, her empty chair teasing them all during the meal. No one would say a word about her absence. They would all be churning about it, but no one would say a thing. Except perhaps Phil, who would make some grizzly speculation as to which hospital she had been taken to this time. With an inward sigh, she declined the invitation.

By the time they reached the subway station, Joan and Jenna were by themselves again. As they came down the stairs a train was pulling in, and they were caught up in the stampede to catch it. They reached the door in time, but there was a solid wall of bodies blocking their way. Joan would have waited for the next train, but Jenna charged in like a football player. Joan followed her even though there was no actual space, and the closing door bumped against them both. As it reopened they were somehow sucked in, and the door crawled closed again, this time only scraping their hips. Joan worried about being pitched out at the next stop and trampled to death.

They weren't trampled, but she and Jenna were both pushed out with the exiting horde, and they had to hold their ground near the door. This time they were able to squeeze themselves farther in. At each station, buffeted by succeeding surges of passengers pushing in and out, they worked their way farther into the car. As they approached Grand Central, Joan began to worry whether she stood any chance of getting off the train at 68th Street. When the car half emptied for the express, she was able to take up a position nearer to the door, which she defended desperately. It was a continual struggle, the entire ride, and there was no possibility of a conversation. At 68th Street she had barely enough time to wave good-bye to Jenna, who called that she'd see her the next morning, bright and early.

When she arrived home, she found that Phil and Alan were not in yet, and Peggy was having a bath. She was thankful for the respite before having to report on the day's activities to Peggy, with a shorter repetition of them to Alan. Phil wouldn't interrogate her, but he would expect to hear the juiciest details. She rarely held anything back from him, but she thought this time she might. The mere mention of a young man at Meyer House, no matter how casually she put it, would be enough to trigger off a merciless stream of jibes and innuendoes. If Phil ever got wind of the fact that he was a half-educated Irish punk, there would be no stopping the snide jokes. Phil saw everything in the most cynical light, and she would have no protection from his ridicule.

She went into her bedroom and undressed while her bath was running. By rights she ought to be exhausted, but to her surprise she wasn't. In fact she felt better than she had in some time. She was ravenously hungry, which contributed to her euphoria. She reveled in the anticipation of watching the others eat while strictly abstaining herself. The discipline allowed her to savor more fully her exquisite sexual excitement. She was too old for crushes, she told herself; besides, he was surely unavailable. If he wasn't sleeping with Jenna, there was bound to be someone else, or more likely several girls he slept with regularly. In any case, he wasn't for her. She could never bring him home, to start with. It wasn't so much that her parents would be horrified beyond belief, but it would be impossible for the boy himself. Everyone would be impeccably polite, but they would manage somehow to humiliate him all the same. No, if there were ever to be anything between them it would have to be in secret.

In secret! The very thought of it thrilled her, as if she wasn't already too aroused for her own good. She went into the bathroom and looked at her naked body in the full-length mirror. Ordinarily she avoided such a complete appraisal, daring to examine only parts of herself. She had never found pleasure in her appearance. Certainly Johnny had never indicated dissatisfaction; then again, he hadn't shown much interest in such matters. She wondered how she would look to a man who was so physical, so elemental. Staring into the mirror, she was uneasy. She had never before had any strong ambition to be more beautiful than she was, but now she wished for something to attract him with: sexiness, allure, mystery. Her breasts were tiny, her legs thin, her pelvis narrow. She had striven to be inconspicuous: straightforward and unadorned. That wouldn't do for him. He would want some curves, some complexity. She raised an arm, canted a hip, then quickly dropped the ludicrous pose. She swiveled to take a look at her rear, still round and lascivious. Suddenly repelled, she abandoned the inspection.

She tested the bath with a toe, found it too hot, and got in anyway. A first shock of pain gave way to a prickly feeling. She released her breath and allowed her muscles to relax. She was more tired than she had realized.

The water sloshed gently around her as she leaned her head back against the tub wall. She closed her eyes. The bathroom grew hot, the mirror misted over, she began to perspire lightly. She reached for the soap in the recess at the side and rubbed it over her shoulders and chest. She was too comfortable and lazy to push up and wash the rest of herself. She let her legs fall apart. Opening the gates of hell, Professor Grainger always said of girls who didn't cross their legs. Feeling wicked, she rubbed herself with the soap. She wondered what those hands were like outside of boxing gloves, what they would feel like on her. With her free palm she caressed her labia, then thrust back between her legs until she could grab hold of her buttocks, first one, then the other, then the forbidden crease between them. Would she allow him to do that? Would he want to? What would he require of her? How would it feel, all that bone and muscle, with that immensity poking out in the center? Would he make her take him in her mouth? She shuddered in a confusion of repugnance and desire. To what depths of depravity was she sinking?

"I just thought I'd find out when you wanted dinner." Peggy's voice penetrated the closed bathroom door like a bolt from an X-ray machine. Joan sat up sharply, splashing water over the side of the tub onto the floor. She might as well have been caught outright, she felt that guilty.

She forced herself to answer calmly. "I don't care, Mother."

"We can have it when it suits you, dear. It couldn't matter less to me."

Who gives a goddamn crap! she wanted to shout, but managed to restrain herself to a weary "What about seven o'clock? Johnny's coming then."

"That would be fine with me, but it might make things a bit tight for your father. He likes to take a nap if he has a chance, before eating. How would seven-thirty be? That way Johnny could have a drink."

Johnny didn't drink. "Whatever is good for you is fine."

"It couldn't matter less to me," Peggy insisted. "We'll make it seven-thirty then. I don't suppose the world would come to an end if you got a little rest in yourself, for that matter. I can entertain Johnny. How was your day, by the way?"

She didn't reply.

For a moment she thought her mother might have gone back to her room, but evidently she hadn't, because after a pause she said, "We're having veal. I seem to remember that Johnny likes Gerta's veal."

Was there no end to this? "That's lovely, Mother," she said. "He adores Gerta's veal."

Although the Knickerbocker Preparatory School had officially opened its doors to members of all faiths after World War I, it had not enrolled any significant numbers of Jewish boys until the Depression, when it was forced to liberalize its admissions policy in order to stay solvent. At that time it had also been found expedient to elect a Jew or two to the board, particularly as the endowment that had financed the school's first century didn't appear likely to see it through its second. Murray Furrer, one of the first outsiders in the student body, was the first Jew on the board. He was elected with the tacit understanding that he would offer advice on fund-raising but otherwise keep a low profile, so to speak. At first he came regularly to board meetings; but in recent years he attended sporadically. Truth be told, he was not sorely missed, since other, more effective fund-raisers now sat on the board. Chief among those was Fred Wellman, loyal alumnus, father of two more alumni, and donor of the new Wellman Gymnasium. Fred was chairman of the finance committee, and the hope of seeing him was the only incentive that could have brought Murray out on a foul evening to the November meeting of the Knickerbocker board.

It was so foul, in fact, that Murray had trouble getting a taxi, and arrived quite late. The meeting was well along by the time he got there. He came in as unobtrusively as he could to the faculty lounge on the second floor, where the board held its meetings. The members had all helped themselves to drinks from the makeshift bar laid out on the side table, and taken their places in chairs that had been drawn up into a circle. Murray came in on a heated discussion of the budget for FY '61. There was going to have to be a tuition hike, that much was clear. The question was, how much? One faction of the board was pushing for a substantial increase in order to bring faculty salaries up to a competitive level for private schools; which was anyway much lower than the going rate at public schools. The other group argued that these ruinous tuition raises could not be borne any longer. Already many families who had been sending their sons to Knickerbocker for generations were feeling the pinch. Sooner or later they would not be able to afford the school— an almost unthinkable situation. Naturally, everybody wanted to be generous, but the teachers had to understand the realities. If they couldn't, they were always free to go teach in Harlem and see how that suited them. Most of them lived outside Manhattan anyway, and their expenses were lower. One member of the board proposed that since most of the teachers had voted for Kennedy, they ought to accept the consequences of their folly, which, according to his logic, included a salary freeze until a Republican was back in the White House.

They were going at it hammer and tongs when Murray arrived. The chairman, Bradford St. Germaine, barely acknowledged his word of apology as he pulled a chair up to join the prominent men of affairs who made up the Knickerbocker board. There was no actual space for him, and the two men whose chairs he tried to squeeze between moved apart in only the most perfunctory fashion, leaving him still outside the circle. He didn't join in the discussion for fear of repeating something that might have been said already, and also because no one had paid attention to anything he said for years. Seeing him, however, must have triggered an association in St. Germaine's mind, since a moment later he turned to Fred Wellman to ask why in hell the endowment wasn't coughing up more income. Fred, placed on the spot, reiterated the school's long-established investment policy, which was as conservative as its educational methods. In its demand for safety over return, the board couldn't expect the yield to cover more than a fraction of the annual deficit. His explanation was not well received. A member inquired whether the time hadn't come—needless to say, one would be reluctant to do this except as a last resort—to trim some of these huge scholarship awards. It was all very well and good to give poor children the benefit of a Knickerbocker education, but it was becoming a frill the school could ill afford. There was evidently considerable support for such a step. Unfortunately, there weren't that many indigent students at the school, and it turned out that even if the whole program was gutted, the shortfall would persist.

Sensing a growing acrimony, and realizing that a consensus wasn't likely that evening, St. Germaine called for a motion to adjourn. He suggested that the executive committee could consider the various proposals and report back to the next meeting of the full board. Amid disgruntled mutterings, the motion was passed, and the trustees, without further ceremony, repaired to the bar. Fred lingered to talk to St. Germaine, and Murray placed himself so as to intercept Fred. It was awkward, appearing to eavesdrop like that. But he had come for the express purpose of talking to Fred; and in any case, no one had urged him to come over and have a drink.

At length the two men finished whatever they had to say to each other, and Fred came over to Murray. "I don't know how you did it, all those years," he began, shaking his head in disbelief. "I've told them I don't know how many times, they've got to have a drive to raise the endowment. Of course, they expect us to do all the work. I'll tell you, I would rather hang by my thumbs than raise money again from this crew. They all think it's a great idea until you suggest they dig into their pockets. This is the board we're talking about, not just your ordinary run-of-the-mill cheapskates. It's always the same story. Their great-grandfather already gave. I told them I've run my last drive for them. They can get one of their own for a change. Then that bastard has the gall to insinuate that they might switch the endowment account to another firm. He all but accused me of mismanaging it."

"What did you say?" Murray asked, aghast.

"I told him to go to hell," Fred replied, glancing over at St. Germaine, who by then had joined the others at the sideboard and was laughing too heartily at something or other. "In so many words," he added, responding to Murray's shocked look. "It's not as if I need the business. Besides, where are they going to take it? None of them has the slightest idea which end is up when it comes to handling investments, and of course hell could freeze over before they'd pay someone to do it. I'd call his bluff in a minute, except that I don't particularly like the idea of the school going out of business. Let's have a drink," he said, and started over toward where the others were gathered.

"Could I have one word before we do?" Murray asked. "This could easily wait until tomorrow, but I just thought, since I've got you now, we could save all that phoning back and forth. It's about a note I think you're holding."

"Let me guess, now," Fred said, pursing up his whole face in a caricature of thought. "This couldn't have anything to do with a certain proxy fight some of our mutual friends are engaged in, could it?"

Murray was taken aback by Fred's quickness. "Has someone spoken to you about this already?" he asked, wondering if Alan had jumped the gun.

Fred laughed. "No one had to. I wasn't born yesterday. The tender offer's public now. It's my job to keep tabs on these things, and I have a general idea which way it's going. Gerry doesn't need very much more stock on his side to get control. It was just a matter of time before he found out I was sitting on a rather sizable bloc. Then what was he going to do? He would never stoop to coming to me himself. So who was he going to send? I figured Alan." He shrugged his shoulders. "I wasn't too far off the mark there."

Murray flushed. He didn't like to be seen as Alan's lackey, though it was often enough the case. "I'm not here to do Gerry's bidding," he said, without a great deal of conviction.

Fred turned up his palms. "You're the lawyer, Murray. It's all the same to me. As far as I'm concerned, Gerry could have spoken to me himself. I have no problem with that. I would have told him the same thing I'd tell you."

"And what's that?" Murray asked, trying not to sound too eager.

Fred tantalized him with a pause. Then he leaned toward Murray and said, "I don't think I'm betraying any state secrets in telling you I have no great admiration for Gerry Altman. Which has nothing to do with anything that's happened between him and me. That's irrelevant. But you know as well as I do he's one of the bigger sons of bitches in this city. Which is saying a lot. As for Morty Pines, he doesn't even figure in. He's strictly a nonentity in my book, although why Gerry wants a jerk like that as a front man escapes me. But that's neither here nor there. The question is, what's the alternative? On the one hand you have Gerry Altman. On the other, you've got Will Strawbridge." He pivoted slightly and indicated with his hand the assembled trustees of the Knickerbocker School, who, after their brief and ineffective deliberations, were losing no time getting themselves collectively sloshed. "I give you Will Strawbridge," he said.

Brad St. Germaine, whose frustration over the financial difficulties of the school was dissolving in Scotch, saw Fred's outstretched hand. In his befuddled state he decided Fred was offering some sort of apology, and he waved back in grand forgiving gesture.

"If you see what I mean," Fred told Murray.

"It's them or us," Murray agreed.

Fred nodded. "It pretty much comes to that," he said, and added wearily, "When you look at it that way, there isn't much of a decision, is there? I mean, whatever you think of Gerry, we've got to stick together."

Murray looked at him anxiously, not wanting to misinterpret his response. "You mean . . . ?" he asked expectantly.

"That's what I mean," Fred confirmed. Before Murray could say anything more, he took the older man's arm and guided him over toward the sideboard. "And now I think we'd better get a drink while there's still some to be gotten. It's going fast."

The two of them went over to join the others.

Twelve

As Joan reached for the front door of Meyer House, she looked anxiously about her. Anybody watching her would surely have thought she was a burglar, she looked so guilty. The door was as always unlocked. Cautiously she pushed it open, half expecting to find Martin Perry himself standing inside, arms folded, prepared to give her a good scolding before packing her off home in a taxi.

Of course, Martin Perry wasn't there. He had better things to do with his Saturdays than to patrol the settlement house. And if he was there, he would hardly disapprove of her having come in on her day off to do some extra work. He might object, as Peggy had, that she was overtiring herself, she needed some rest, she would do nobody any good by collapsing with exhaustion. "I'm not exhausted, Mother," she had protested. Peggy didn't argue, but gave Joan a skeptical look as if to say, Who are you fooling? Joan knew that look well. Her mother never forbade anything outright, but that look had haunted all her disobediences, the tiny little rebellions of her childhood. But why? she asked herself. What was wrong about wanting to do something extra for her children? They needed so much and had so little. They deserved more than she could ever give them. A Saturday afternoon was a drop in the bucket. Why should she have such misgivings about it?

Why indeed? she thought. And who was she fooling?

The only people she saw when she came in were two old ladies who to all intents and purposes lived in the settlement house. Joan knew them well by now, they were such fixtures. Sitting guard over the lobby, they appeared to have taken root. They had shopping bags close at hand, like reassuring pets, but Joan knew they had come in well before any stores were open. They would rather spend the day dozing on a Meyer House couch, keeping an eye on who came in and went out, than brave the blustery streets or sit in a cold, meagerly furnished room and stare out the window. Who could blame them?

Joan's arrival jolted them out of their stupor. They whispered furiously to each other, but stopped abruptly as she came closer. Then they screwed their creased cheeks up into toothless smiles and nodded frantically, until she returned their greeting, at which point they nearly burst with gratification. As she opened the door to the stairway, she heard one of them say to the other, "The spitting image of her mother." Which was absolute nonsense, of course. Joan always denied that she bore a trace of the Altman family, or Gutheim either, for that matter. But the women probably weren't thinking about her looks. A moral resemblance was what they saw. Another Peggy Gutheim. Try as she might, she couldn't escape that. Not at Meyer House, at any rate.

The crippled kids' room seemed vaster in its emptiness than it did during the weekdays. She switched on the light and looked around. Curiously, she felt as though she shouldn't be there. She remembered a time she had gone up to Fieldston on a weekend. A janitor had let her in —what was it she'd gone there to do? Feed some lab animals? Mimeograph the newspaper? She had crept about like a sneak thief. She'd sat at the teacher's desk, itching to know what was in the drawers. But she hadn't opened them. She was always such a good girl. So *reliable*. Such good sense, her mother always said of her. Joan's never given me a moment's worry.

Of course she hadn't. Who would, when she could get everything she ever wanted without having to break the rules? She had not had to batter against the walls, test the limits. She had wanted what was good for her. She'd never had to struggle with her conscience. Her mother had been right not to worry.

She laid down the packages she had brought and looked around the room. She planned to clean it up. It was hard to know where to begin. The children's cubbyholes were chaotic. The books were thrown in the bookshelves in no particular order. The paint corner was a chronic mess. The toys needed sorting through to see which ones were still usable and which were beyond saving. None of the puzzles had all its pieces, and the games were all in hopeless disarray. A discouraging scene. Joan took off her coat.

She had gone that morning to Reiss Bros. to buy some games and puzzles and some toys for the younger kids. She took them out of their packages and laid them out on the play table. Their bright colors contrasted with the faded dreariness of everything that was already in the room. When she bought them, she had wanted the children to have something nice for once. Now she feared these new things would mock the poverty and harshness of the life the children led, and arouse longings that couldn't be fulfilled. She felt their disappointment keenly, and the idea that she might, in her blundering way, add to it brought tears to her eyes.

Work was the only way she could make it up to them, and there was plenty to do. She started in with the paint corner. She threw out the torn paper and caked, unusable paint cups, and cleaned the brushes, discarding the ones that remained stiff as boards even after a thorough soaking. She scrubbed the floors and the walls where paint had spattered, but much of it had become absorbed over the years and wouldn't come off. When she had done what she could, she turned to the bookcases. She had hoped simply to reshelve the books one by one, but soon realized she'd have to clear the shelves and start from scratch. She put the books in piles as she pulled them from the shelves, but it was slow going. Most of the books were unfamiliar to her, and she had to leaf through almost every one to decide which age-group it belonged in.

She had finished the picture books and was making some headway with the storybooks for young readers when she heard sounds coming from overhead. She tried to pay no attention, but they soon organized themselves into the pattern of a basketball game. It was no use pretending to herself that she wasn't interested. She had come that day for all the right reasons, but she couldn't quite hide from herself that there was one more: which was one floor above her, in the gymnasium.

She hadn't been looking for this. She was quite clear about that. The last thing she needed was another complication in her life. But she couldn't ignore what was happening. Every day this past week, Kevin had gone out of his way to speak to her. If she was late in coming down to the cafeteria, he would still be there. If she lingered on the way out, he would just happen to be in the stairway. Their conversations were inconsequential, with no ardent declarations. He'd been casual about it, very cool, and she had responded in the same vein. As yet, he hadn't made an actual play for her; but she was sure it was only a matter of time.

As for herself—she didn't know. She already had a boyfriend, and there were many other reasons to stay uninvolved. Even if she were free, Kevin wasn't someone she would have picked. He had his appeal, there was no getting around that, but his unmodified physicality was both an attraction and a liability. Beyond that, they had little in common. Until recently he'd been little more than a juvenile delinquent, and she wasn't sure how far beyond that he was yet. If he were to know her better, he'd see she was no bargain either. Education, tastes, values— all were incompatible. They came from different worlds, and they lived in different worlds.

So what was she doing there that afternoon? It was true she had come in to do some work; but it was also true she knew he'd be there. He had let her know that he came in on Saturdays to supervise the teenage boys and all but invited her to come. She had taken the invitation lightly, but he'd repeated it several times, and now here she was. Whatever her other reasons for being there, she couldn't deny that she wanted to see him. What more she wanted she wasn't sure, and she didn't really want to figure it out. By rights she should go home, then and there. By rights she shouldn't have come in the first place.

Suddenly the noise stopped. She listened intently. Maybe the game was over. Were they all leaving? How would he know she was there? Maybe he would go without her seeing him. She stood stock-still, straining to hear. She still heard people walking around above. There were some miscellaneous noises: someone running, heavy thudding sounds, a few uninterpretable thumps on the far end of the ceiling. Then the game started up again.

This was madness. She looked at the books still piled up on the floor, and knew she couldn't get anything more done until she saw him. She left the room and went back to the stairwell. As she climbed the top flight, she rehearsed her cover story, as though she was about to be interrogated. It was ridiculous, she knew. No one would ask or care. But then, this whole thing was ridiculous. She was ridiculous. With the word ringing in her mind's ear, she pushed open the door and walked in.

A mass of bodies was entangled on the court. Some of the boys were in shirts, the others stripped to their shorts and sneakers, and despite the presence of a basketball, they seemed to be more engaged in shoving and shouting than in a basketball game. On the sidelines, other boys were poised to rush in, and a group of girls shouted and jumped up and down. The place was about twenty degrees hotter than it had been the last time Joan had been there, and the heat had developed the latent aroma of leather and mats and dust and sweat. Some of the girls saw her come in and pointed her out to one another with nudges and hand-covered giggles. She felt a hot burst of shame, as if they knew why she was there and what she was after.

At first she didn't see him. He was refereeing the game. He wore his white sweatpants—she had never seen him wear anything else—and was bare above the waist—except for a chain with a crucifix, and also a cord for the whistle. He wasn't taller than most of the players, but against their skinniness his thick muscles gave him an appearance of maturity. Even though he wasn't playing, he threw himself into the action vigorously, racing down the court with the fast break or, when the play stayed in one end, bouncing up and down with his boxer's agility.

Despite her studied nonchalance, Joan worried that under the girls' scrutiny she couldn't loiter in the gymnasium. She estimated how long a staff member, presumably not there with ulterior motives, would remain; not more than a couple of minutes at most, she thought. Her time was quickly up, and he still hadn't seen her. She thought she would lose her chance, but she couldn't stay any longer. As she turned to go the whistle sounded shrilly and he called a time-out. She had to continue her exit, but saw that he had spotted her. He ran over and caught the door just as she was opening it.

"Hi," he said, taking the door from her and opening it as though he had run over for that purpose. It was a heavy door, with a pneumatic device at the top that pulled it closed. She stepped into the stairwell and turned around to face him. "Hello," she said. He wasn't smiling, so she didn't either.

Setting his foot against the door to keep it from closing, he put his bare arm up against the jamb. He looked at her intently. The muscles of his chest swelled with his hard breathing. His sweatpants were slung low, revealing the waistband of a jockstrap above them. No man Joan knew would ever have displayed such a thing in public. He was chewing gum, and the faint whiff of spearmint mingled with the stronger smell of sweat. She felt hot and flushed and giddy with arousal. "Kinda surprised to see you here on a Saturday," he said.

The remark flustered Joan. "I just came in to get some work done. In the room. It's been a mess, and you can never get it cleaned up while the kids are there. I was down there working when I heard something going on up here. It's right overhead." She was explaining too much, making it sound like the alibi it was. The teenagers were watching them, although they probably couldn't hear what she was saying, and she felt exposed, even half hidden in the stairwell. "I came to see what was going on."

"Oh," Kevin said, looking over his shoulder as if to remind himself what was going on in the gymnasium. "Some of the kids come in on weekends. I usually get a game goin', somethin' like that, keeps them outta trouble. Keeps them off the streets, like they say." He had used the same phrase the day before.

"I was just wondering what was going on," Joan repeated. Her voice trembled with nervousness, but she couldn't control it.

"So you come in on a Saturday to work?" he asked. She didn't know if he was being admiring or skeptical. When she didn't respond, he asked, "You gonna be around for a while?"

Despite everything, she wasn't sure what to reply. She didn't want him to think she had come in especially to see him. "I don't know. I've still got tons to do, I don't think I'll get it finished this afternoon." She looked at her watch, an automatic Gutheim reflex.

"You got someplace to go?" he asked.

"Eventually," Joan said. "Not right this minute."

" 'Eventually?' " He mocked the word.

Perhaps she was being too cautious. "I'll be here for a while," she admitted.

His grin was both triumphant and disarming. "Maybe I'll come down when I'm finished here, see if you're still around. This'll be over soon." He jerked his head toward the basketball court behind him.

Joan could see that the players were growing restive with the delay, and the girls were frankly gawking at them. "Don't let me keep you," she said.

He glanced over and confirmed that he was needed. "I gotta get back," he said, apologizing for his indispensability. "Maybe I'll see ya." He flashed his grin again, as though aware of its potency, and then turned and ran back onto the court, blasting the whistle and motioning for the ball to be thrown to him. The door wheezed closed, and the scene was cut off from Joan's view.

She waited in the semidarkness for a moment, confused and excited. She didn't know what to make of it all. It seemed stranger than before to think he was really interested in her, they were so different. If he wanted sex, surely he could do better than her, with her flat chest, sharp angles, bones, edges, spikes. Maybe he was after some money; maybe a conquest he could boast of. She would have to be cautious or she would find herself in over her head. He was not used to refusals, that was plain. If he thought she was leading him on, things could get ugly. She suspected he had a violent streak just under the surface. Heaven help her if she triggered it.

As she walked slowly down to the third floor, she realized she was getting ahead of herself. He hadn't asked her to go to bed with him. It was snobbish of her to think he was nothing more than a dumb brute, only interested in one thing. If anyone deserved that accusation, it was she: she had come all the way down here just in the hope of seeing him. She ought to be worrying about her control, not his. She was the one teetering on the brink.

Coming back into the room, she was filled with dismay. There was so much still to be done. She should have stuck to her work, instead of flirting like a bobby-soxer. She finished quickly with the books, and turned to the cubbyholes. They seemed a hopeless task. If she started in on them this late in the afternoon, she would only leave them in a worse mess than they were already. Still, she had to do something. She couldn't just hang around there, waiting for him to come. She was jittery enough as it was. She had to keep herself busy. Her mind was on the game overhead, and when it stopped again, this time for good, she found herself unable to continue working. She listened anxiously to every creak overhead, and when she satisfied herself that the gymnasium was empty, she strained to hear his footsteps in the hallway outside the crippled kids' room.

None came. She tried to imagine what he might be doing, but as the minutes dragged on, she had increasing difficulty accounting for the delay. It became possible, then likely, that he had left without keeping his promise. She felt horribly disappointed, then angry: he was making a fool of her. An eerie silence surrounded her, and she began to wonder if she was alone in the building. The vulnerability of her situation dawned on her, and she cursed her naive imprudence. She knew better than to isolate herself like that. Someone was coming down the hallway. She had been waiting for that, but now her excitement was contaminated with panic. She looked about frantically for something to defend herself with. This was New York City, she reminded herself: it could be Kevin, or it could just as easily be a maniac.

The person who appeared in the doorway was neither. It was Etta Sevitsky, of all people. Etta was even more surprised than Joan. "Miss Gutheim! Fancy seeing you here! You're the last person I ever expected to find. I thought it was some of them kids, having a smoke, or doing whatever it is they do in here. I don't know what that might be, but they're not supposed to. They're not supposed to be in here at all, comes to that."

Joan took Etta to mean that she wasn't supposed to be in there either. Flustered, she blurted out, "Oh, Etta! I just popped in. I'd been wanting to do some cleaning up for ages, but there never seems to be any time for it while the kids are here. So I decided now would be a good time. I'd have the room to myself, and no interruptions."

"Aren't you the angel!" Etta cried adoringly. "Still, you oughtn't to come in on Saturdays. You should be out enjoying yourself. You'll work yourself to death if you don't watch out."

"There's hardly a danger of that," Joan scoffed. "Anyway, what about you? Why aren't you out enjoying yourself on a Saturday?"

"Oh, Miss Gutheim, you're putting me to shame. I'm not here for any good reason at all. What it was, was that I was in shopping this afternoon—I like to come in and pick up the bargains on Saturdays—and I'm meeting some of the girls for supper. I just came in to drop off my packages, so I won't have to schlepp them all over the city, and probably wind up leaving them in the restaurant, knowing me. When I saw the light on in here, I thought to myself, those kids'll be in there, smoking or drinking or I don't know what-all. I've spoken to Mr. Perry about it I don't know how many times. Mr. Perry, I've told him, those kids'll burn the place down if we don't watch out. But he thinks they ought to have the run of the building, no matter what hour of the day or night. I suppose he knows best." She pursed her lips to show what she really supposed. "It did give me a turn to find you here. I just know Leona will die when she finds out you've been coming in Saturdays, to work! Imagine such a thing!"

Joan didn't know what to say to disavow her claims to a medal. A more immediate concern was what to do with Etta if Kevin showed up, although that seemed unlikely now. "It was just for a little while," she said. "I was just going, in fact, when you came in." She went over to the coatrack and took her coat off of it; but she didn't put it on, which Etta probably noticed.

In any case, Etta wouldn't be rushed. She was thrilled to be thrown in with Joan Gutheim, all to herself, and she settled in for a nice chat. "I shouldn't be surprised after all, seeing you're your mother's daughter. You do so much for these kids. Leona says she's never seen a volunteer work harder. Or been so popular with the kids. They really love you. I know you're doing wonders for Pearl. But you should be careful, if I may say so, Miss Gutheim. You don't want to overdo it. You've your health to think of. You shouldn't work on weekends." She was quite certain about it, adding, "Does your mother know you're coming in?"

Joan smiled at the irony of the question. "Yes, I got her permission," she said with a laugh.

Etta looked chastened. "Oh, I wasn't suggesting . . . Naturally, you're old enough to be doing . . . I just thought, your mother . . ."

She was interrupted by Kevin, who finally made his appearance. The situation threatened to become farcical: Etta was thrilled, Joan discomfited, Kevin completely unperturbed. "Hiya, Etta!" he cried exuberantly. "D'you buy out Delancey Street? Ready for a big night on the town? Which nightclubs are the ladies hitting tonight? I and my friends could join you, maybe take a little spin on the dance floor. A cha-cha-cha or two? You know that Etta's a really hot dancer, don't you?" he asked Joan. "What's it gonna be? The Stork Club? The Copacabana?"

Etta was clearly titillated. Her face radiated girlish delight, and she even managed a passable blush. "Oh! Kevin! I don't know where we'll go. I'm gettin' so tired of the Stork Club, you know? It's boring, seeing the same faces all the time. The Vanderbilts, the Astors, always the same crowd. We were thinking we might try one of those places you hang out in. They sound like such a lot of fun. Tell me, do any of them have names?"

Joan was amazed. She had never dreamed that Kevin so much as spoke to Etta, or any of the older women at the settlement house. She could see now that he basked in the admiration of women of all ages, and that he had the knack of turning any encounter into a sexual adventure. She and Etta were more alike, in his eyes, than different; although she doubted whether Etta would approve of her having anything to do with Kevin. Etta would certainly think he wasn't good enough for her. It was one thing to kid around with him, and quite another to be fooling around with him, especially if you were a Gutheim.

The worst of it was, she wasn't fooling around with him, not yet at least. They had no agreement as to what came next. They might well have very different expectations, and with Etta there they could hardly negotiate the next step. The most they could accomplish would be a vague understanding that they'd go somewhere together. It was all done with innuendo and looks, amid the bantering between Kevin and Etta. They hadn't put anything into words, and Joan hoped that Etta might not catch on to what was happening.

Etta, however, was no fool. She might be an old maid, but she knew what went on in the world. Kevin was no help, for that matter. He had no stake in being discreet. When it became clear that Etta was in no hurry to leave, he suggested that they could walk her to the subway. By implication, he and Joan would continue on from there. They all left the building together, which helped as far as the ladies in the lobby went but increased the awkwardness once they were out on the street. Kevin behaved in a proprietary, boyfriend fashion toward Joan as they walked, first taking her hand, then putting his arm around her. In a way, it was thrilling, but Joan had promised herself to keep it casual. She was constrained by Etta's presence, at the same time she was embarrassed by the open display of intimacy. When at last they left Etta at the subway stop, she felt hopelessly compromised.

Kevin lived not far from Meyer House, and he seemed to take it for granted she would come there with him. It was not what she had intended, but she could hardly play the innocent at that point. Although she had no idea what she would do once she got there, she agreed to come with him to his place. It was almost completely dark. Joan was afraid of dangers seen and unseen, muggers, rapists, criminals of one sort or another whom she imagined lurking in the alleyways. She was repelled by the filth on the sidewalks, the foul air, the thought that at any moment a rat might scurry out from the garbage that occluded the sidewalks. Kevin tightened his embrace around her shoulders, the way Johnny always did. It was strange to have this boy, whom she hardly knew, holding her so familiarly, so possessively. Leaning her head against his leather jacket, she felt at once safe and threatened. She wondered if he carried a knife.

They turned into a side street that she would never have ventured down alone, not even in broadest daylight. Now, in the evening, the narrow, lonely street was especially menacing. The building where Kevin lived had the sad look of a brownstone that had fallen on hard times. Its masonry was still solid, and a surprising garland of leaves and fruit decorated the frieze above the first story. It boasted a stoop that led up to a tiled vestibule, or rather a formerly tiled vestibule, now mostly gaping concrete. The mailboxes were all dented or smashed and piles of third- and fourth-class mail—ads, flyers, bills tossed aside, throwaways, junk mail—were strewn about. They had been discarded there over time by the tenants, or perhaps delivered only that far by the demoralized postman. Opposite, a board had once hooked up to a buzzer system, but it was evidently obsolete, since no names were displayed. There was no use for buzzers anyway, since the inner door had no latch and could easily be pushed open.

They walked up three dingy flights of stairs and down a long, almost pitch-black hallway. Joan saw a door open in the passageway. It was pulled only as far back as a safety chain would allow. Behind it there was darkness, with only the flicker of a television set. She had gone beyond fear by then. She felt unreal, detached, as though in a dream, or a foreign country. All the manners, customs, practices of her life had been left at the border.

An unlocked door opened directly onto a large room that was evidently the whole of the apartment. In the dim light Joan saw a refrigerator, a sink piled with dishes, a couch, a couple of chairs with wooden arms, a large round table with hi-fi equipment on it, and a frameless bed along one wall. The bedding, she saw, was already in disarray. The whole room was strewn with clothes, and a sense of clutter prevailed despite the sparse furnishings. A poster advertising boxing matches was on a wall, next to pictures of some fighters. In the middle of the room, amid underwear and sweatclothes, were weights and bars and a set of dumbbells. On the wall next to the bed was propped up a large, streaked mirror in a huge, ornately carved wooden frame. A radio was playing, and bits of music could faintly be heard in the static.

The shades were drawn on the two windows at the far end of the room, and the eerie twilight was further deepened by a pervasive haze. From the pungent sweetness that filled the room, Joan guessed that incense of some kind had recently been burned. Looking again in the mirror, she saw the murky reflection of a figure. She had to look around the room before locating the original of it. A man was sitting, Buddha-like, on the floor, partially hidden from Joan by the couch between them. In the obscurity she couldn't make out whether he was asleep or dead.

Joan hadn't counted on there being a roommate. In all her thoughts about going to a man's apartment, she had never imagined anyone else there. Maybe in college, but not in the real world. She had no plan for coping with it. She had used up all her courage just to get this far. A quick survey of the apartment indicated that there was no other room where they could have any privacy. Where could they go? She didn't believe even Kevin was exhibitionist enough to want an audience, but she didn't know. This man looked as though he was in a trance, but no trance was that deep. He could come out of it any time. It wouldn't do. She hadn't realized until then how much she was counting on having sex, despite her scruples. She felt exposed in her eagerness, and disappointed in the man's presence.

Kevin saw the consternation on her face and laughed. "He'll clear out of here," he promised. He went over to the apparently unconscious man and gave him a sharp kick in the ribs. The man's body listed to the side, but he showed no other reaction. "He's faking," Kevin said, and gave him another kick.

"I am not," the man said in a distant, toneless voice. "I am communicating with the soul of my ancestors. If you lay another foot on me, their spirits will descend upon you and tear you to shreds." Before he finished speaking, he had opened his eyes.

He was a slight, disheveled man with unkempt dirty blond hair and a flamboyantly scruffy beard. He wore jeans and a flannel shirt, both of which were torn and patched, and he was barefoot. He didn't get up when he opened his eyes. His legs were so thin that although they were crossed, both knees touched the floor.

"Fix the radio," he commanded Kevin, closing his eyes again.

"Listen, you fool, get out of here," Kevin said. "I got a guest here."

"That's cool," the man replied. "It won't disturb me."

"Out!" Kevin yelled, grabbing the collar of his shirt and yanking him roughly to his feet. The man hung limply, like a marionette on a string.

"Fuck, man, you don't have to get violent all the time!" His voice shook as Kevin jerked him about. "Just ask nicely. Don't you got no couth? Aren't you gonna introduce me to your . . . guest?" He said the word sarcastically.

"Shit, no. You're not fit to meet a lady. And stop turning this place into an opium den. I'm gonna get sick just breathing the air in here after you're through using it."

"What about me? I gotta inhale your sweatshit all day." Kevin gave him a last shake and pushed him away in disgust. He collected himself, walked over to Joan with mock dignity, and extended his hand. "I'm Lenny Bruce," he said. She accepted his hand uncertainly. His speech was not slurred as a drunk's would be, but it was slightly off in its rhythms, and something about him smacked of intoxication. Joan thought she recognized the name Lenny Bruce, but she couldn't place it. It didn't seem likely she would have heard of this man, whoever he was. She thought she was probably being made fun of.

"Asshole," Kevin snarled. "His name's Harlow," he told Joan. She didn't know if that was a first or last name.

"I like Lenny Bruce better," Harlow complained. "Lenny Bruce," he chanted. "Len—ny—Bruce. Lenny. Bruce. I like it. Harlow isn't right for me. It doesn't do me justice. I don't look like a Harlow, do I?"

"Get lost, willya?" Kevin said wearily.

"Nice talk! Is that any way to treat an old buddy? After all we been through together? After all I've done for you?" Kevin snorted and turned away from him. Harlow, rebuffed, paced around the room, looking for something. His steps were uncertain, heavy, like those of a man who has lost his sense of position and has to feel the ground come up under his feet before taking the next step. "Next time you need help, see if I come running. What's become of friendship these days? Loyalty? Gratitude? Where have all the old values fled?" In his mumblings and lurchings he stumbled over a barbell that was partially hidden among a tangle of towels and T-shirts. He fell sharply. "Fuck, why don't you put away your goddamn bodybuilding shit? While you're falling in love with yourself, the rest of us are breaking our fucking necks."

"You'll break your neck one way or another," Kevin told him. "It wouldn't matter if anything's there or not, you still couldn't stay on your feet. The shape you're in. And watch your mouth, by the way."

"Oh, *sorry*," Harlow said as he picked himself up. "I guess I'm just not used to you bringing home a *lady*." He grinned nastily.

Kevin glowered. "Get the fuck out of here," he said in a low, suddenly threatening voice. Harlow looked frightened. His face lost its bravado. He picked up a pair of sunglasses from the table next to the hi-fi and put them on. They made him look blind, but they masked his fear. "Pleasure to meet you, I'm sure," he said to Joan. "Hope we'll see you again. Y'all come back soon, heah?" He bowed in an exaggerated manner and glided eerily out the door. He was still barefoot. Joan wondered if he was going out onto the street without shoes.

"He's nobody," Kevin said in answer to her unasked question. He came over to her and with unexpected gallantry took off her coat. "I knew him back home. We came to the city around the same time. He stays here sometimes. He doesn't really live anywhere. He mooches off a lot of people. When one person gets fed up enough with him, which doesn't take long, he moves in on someone else. He's a total mess. Doesn't know where he is half the time. He never knows what he's saying. He'll wind up dead in some gutter one of these days. The way he's heading."

He had taken off his own jacket and laid it with Joan's on a chair. Now he came back over to her and stood in front of her, quite close. He looked serious and intent. "Forget him," he said huskily.

The time had come. So quickly. No preliminaries, no subtleties. Joan felt her heart beating painfully. She still hadn't really made a definite decision, but here she was, beyond the point of no return. It was already too late to stall, past the time of rituals, compromises, euphemisms. She had committed herself by coming there with him, and now there was no turning back.

There was still the intricate business of getting from where they were, fully clothed in the middle of the room, to being naked on the bed, but it had all gone much faster than she had expected. She felt exposed already, and she wasn't ready. The thought of undressing before his eyes shamed her. She wished the lights were out. She didn't want him to look at her body. It would disappoint him. She dreaded seeing his response: would he be cold, or condescending? If she failed to arouse him, would he be angry with her? She didn't know what she was supposed to do.

He seemed assured enough for both of them. He put out his hand and opened the top button of her blouse. She put her hand over his as he went down the row, opening each button. He took off her blouse and waited. She understood that she was supposed to take off her bra. He watched her while she unhooked it, like a connoisseur appraising a work of art. She wanted to cover her breasts. They were so meager. She could read no judgment on his face. Instead he came forward, dropped to his knee like a suitor, and kissed first one breast, then the other. He clasped her around her waist and laid his face sideways on her left breast, his mouth grazing the right one. She was confused and touched. Running her fingers through his hair, she wanted to thank him for his generosity.

He straightened up, reached back over his head and swept off his sweatshirt. The motion had the effect of a sculptor unveiling a torso, augmented by the release of his athlete's smell. At the sight of his chiseled abdomen, Joan was swept by a sharp excitement. She was surprised at the quickness of her desire, springing up acutely despite her nervousness.

When they had rid themselves of the rest of their clothes—he kept his crucifix on, which increased for Joan the sense she was sinning—he wrapped his arms around her and pulled her tightly against him. She found it disturbingly thrilling. She had never been like that before, naked in a brightly lit room, nothing hidden, beyond propriety and modesty. The tension that had grown within her burst and in the sudden discharge she became faint. She sagged in his arms. Holding the back of her head in his open palm he kissed her, almost devouring her. He plunged his tongue between her lips and cupped a hand over her breast. She responded by running her hand down the thick ridge of his back until it reached his buttock, which tightened at her touch to the same marble hardness as his flexed arm.

He lifted her up, bride fashion, and carried her over to the bed. "You don't weigh more'n a feather," he said, as though she was not a sufficient challenge to his strength. He knelt again and placed her gently on the bed. "God, you're thin!" he exclaimed, looking at her as she lay stretched on the bed.

She wanted desperately to pull something over her, to hide her gaunt body, but it was too late to hide. Perhaps thinking of her fragility, he asked her if she had any protection. Of course, she hadn't brought a diaphragm; she didn't carry one around with her. As for protection, she hadn't menstruated for months; but she didn't want to tell him that, so she just said she had nothing. He got up and walked over to where he had left his jacket. He got his wallet out and fished in it. Joan watched him walk across the room and back. He carried himself with the ease of someone who is accustomed to being looked at, who took admiration for granted. He came back to the bed, sat down, and unrolled the Trojan over his erection as unselfconsciously as if he were tying his shoe.

To her dismay, he hurt her when he tried to enter. She wasn't a virgin, and the other time she had felt no pain; she had felt nothing much at all. She didn't expect that now, of all times, she would be so taut. She tried to conceal it, but he was not so callow that he couldn't tell. "It's all right," she assured him when he withdrew. "Go ahead."

She hoped she would relax; or if she didn't, she was prepared to endure whatever was necessary. But he pushed himself off of her and moved down the bed. To her horror, he dipped his face down onto her pelvis and lapped at her with his tongue. The sensation was exquisitely tender, but too forbidden to be pleasurable for her. She felt a deep loathing of her organs, and was sure he must be revolted by his task. "You don't have to do that," she protested softly.

"I don't do anything because I have to," he told her defiantly, and continued.

She lay there passively, submitting to his ministrations. When he hoisted himself on top of her and entered her again, a miraculous flood of warmth replaced the pain. Her own orgasm was almost immediate, and she had to muffle her cry lest he think he was still hurting her.

After it was over, she wanted to show her gratitude, but she didn't know how. Words wouldn't be right, not for him. She wanted some reassurance as well, but she didn't dare ask for it. Uncertain and far from calm, she put her clothes back on. Kevin only pulled on his sweatpants, content to be gazed at whenever possible.

His hospitality surprised her. He asked her if she wanted a drink, and even offered to make her tea. When she said she thought she should go, he seemed disappointed; but he made no move to escort her out of the building, much less back to anything resembling civilization. She resigned herself to its being a one-night stand, another notch on his belt. She didn't even know if she wanted to see him again, so drained was she of feeling. She felt let down. She wondered if he expected her to give him something. Of course, he could use money and she would have been willing to give him some, but she didn't know how to do it without running the risk of insulting him.

As she was leaving, though, his face took on a queer, cold look that frightened her. She saw with sudden, terrible clarity that he wanted no money but submission. He was going to beat her before letting her go. She should have realized how violent he was. It had been insane to come like this to the apartment of a virtual stranger. As fear gripped her she estimated whether she could get out of the door before he attacked her. She saw that it wasn't possible. She supposed she could scream, but who would help? Resistance, she knew, only provoked such men to greater brutality.

In an instant the delusion was over. She understood that he wasn't going to attack her after all. Now she was exhausted. She had undergone too many contradictory emotions, and when he finally kissed her she felt numb. She clung to him more than she intended. She felt him grow hard against her body. "Just to let you know there's more where that came from," he boasted.

She said she wanted to see him again. She didn't know if that was true or not.

She hurried fearfully back to the subway and traveled home in a daze. The memory of their sex grew vague. What had she actually felt? Had there been passion, or only sensation? She couldn't re-create it for herself. She tried to call up his image, but it was difficult. He no longer seemed erotic, but instead menacing. The terror that had seized her just as she had been leaving returned. She longed to be home. She wanted to see Johnny. She almost cried out for him, so desperately did she want to be with him, to nestle in his safe embrace. She was shaking with fear, and wished he were there to protect her.

Johnny! It was the first time she had thought of him all afternoon. He was taking her out to dinner that night, and she was late. He would never reproach her. He was so good to her, and she had treated him so badly. She wanted to go directly to him, to lose no more time before throwing herself in his arms. But she had to go home first and take a bath. She had to clean herself, get one man's scent off before going on to the next. She shuddered with repugnance. Remorse swept over her.

By the time she got home, she felt cut off from the events of the afternoon. In the dark and familiar hallway, she leaned against the wall, and cried silently. When she got hold of herself, she resolved that she would never again return to that sordidness, that danger. It was over.

She had to go by her mother's bedroom before getting to her own. Peggy was sitting on her bed, propped up against the pillows, reading. As Joan went by she put down the book and smiled. She was always so glad to see her daughter.

"And how was Meyer House?" she asked.

The Gutheim family had an enormous refrigerator; some might have said monstrous. It was a brown, square, wood-paneled affair with two doors on top and two below, making it look like a huge armoire that had been put in the kitchen by mistake. Peggy had gotten it from a hotel supply chain. "It was the only way I could think of that we wouldn't be forever running out of something or other," she would explain to astonished visitors. By "running out," Peggy of course meant that someone might not find exactly what he wanted to eat at any given instant. Peggy couldn't bear the thought that a person might open her icebox door and come away disappointed. The actual chance of any real privation was slim. Fruit, soft drinks, salad ingredients, and miscellaneous oddments were kept in the pantry refrigerator, leaving the kitchen warehouse free for the basic needs of the household, plus leftovers. The Gutheim definition of a leftover included not only whatever was brought back untouched from the table but also dishes specially cooked to be "left" in the refrigerator. It was a rare midnight that a secret snacker couldn't find an entire roast beef or a fried chicken or a few lamb chops deep in the recesses. Dagwood Bumstead, introduced to the Gutheim refrigerator, would have thought he had died and gone to heaven.

Carl came into the kitchen dressed for the occasion in his pajamas, slippers, and a maroon bathrobe, which he tied above the protruberance of his stomach, making himself look five months pregnant. He was searching only out of habit. He'd had an ample supper and wasn't hungry. He would in fact have happily gone without any food at all, settling for a simple glass of milk, if he hadn't known that fully half a chocolate cake was going begging on a covered dish in the larder. Gerta had baked the cake the day before yesterday, and he knew from experience that tonight was the last night it would be soft. Its presence had haunted him all evening. He had been studying without a break, and he felt he deserved a reward.

He cut himself a modest slice and carried it reverently to the kitchen table. Then he poured a medium-size glass of skim milk and put it next to the plate. He had just sat down and taken the first luscious bite when a voice behind him broke the nocturnal silence:

"You absolute pig!"

He didn't turn around. There was no dealing with Joan when she was in one of her moods. He knew she would give him no peace but would hound him unmercifully about one lousy piece of cake until it tasted like ashes in his mouth. He gave up all thought of getting any pleasure from it, but he continued to eat it dutifully.

"I can't believe that even *you* can possibly want anything more after watching you stuff yourself at supper this evening." In the faded blue flannel pajamas that were much too big for her, she looked like a kid dressed up in grown-up clothes.

Carl didn't respond, but carefully scraped off the icing to be saved for the end, and washed down the already slightly stale cake—it was a good thing he hadn't waited another day—with swallows of cold milk.

"Aren't you afraid you're going to explode?" Joan asked with real curiosity, as if wondering how he was coping with the anxiety.

The milk gave out before he finished the cake. He was faced with the odious choice of eating the last part dry, or making another trip past Joan to the refrigerator. He knew he should have taken a full-size glass in the first place.

"Oh, great, he's getting something else," Joan announced as he got up and went to the refrigerator. "This I gotta see." He got out the bottle of skim milk and took it back to the table. "Why do you bother drinking skim milk?" she asked derisively. "Is that supposed to be a diet? Do you actually think you're going to lose weight drinking skim milk and gorging yourself on chocolate cake?"

"I happen to prefer skim milk," he answered. He was determined to avoid arguing with her. It was beneath him, and also he had never won an argument with her or Phil in his entire life. It had nothing to do with who was in the right: right or wrong, he always lost. He poured himself a judicious amount of milk, no more than he actually needed, but set the bottle on the table, just in case.

While he was finishing the last of his snack, Joan rummaged around in the larder and discovered the rest of the cake. She brought it over to the table. "Here. You left this behind. Why don't you have it all?"

"I don't want it all," he said with as much indifference as he could muster. What did she want now? She had already ruined whatever enjoyment he might have had. What more did she want?

Ignoring his answer, Joan took up the cake server from the platter and cut a huge slab, which she transferred crudely between the server and her hand onto his plate. She slapped it down like a lump of hash and said, "Here's another piece for you. Want some more milk?" She took up the bottle and poured it out into his glass. She kept on pouring until the glass overflowed and the milk ran across the table and down onto his lap.

"Are you crazy?" he cried, jumping up and trying to stanch the flow of milk with the napkin he had used. Some of the milk had also gotten onto the plate where the indecent hunk of cake lay, and the whole thing was turning into a soggy mess. "You've ruined it!" he cried. "That was perfectly good cake and you ruined it."

"Ohhhh!" Joan cooed. "How tragic. And it could have gone to the starving children of Armenia. Or you could have had it for breakfast."

"I don't see what you're trying to prove," he complained.

"I'm not trying to prove anything," Joan said. She sat down at the head of the table, at right angles to the chair he had been sitting in. She scraped some of the icing from the cake and tasted it. "Sit down," she commanded.

"Why? So you can go on insulting me?" he asked.

"Oh, stop whining," she told him. She had become absorbed in picking away the icing. She ate some of the fragments, but for the most part she mashed them together to form a glistening, dark ball in the pool of milk on the plate. She made a separate mound of the unfrosted cake, which she then crosshatched with the tines of the fork. Carl didn't sit down right away, but got a dishcloth from the sink to wipe up the milk that had gone onto his chair, as well as the trickle that was breaking through the disintegrating napkin. When he had tidied most of it up, he took his seat submissively.

"You've really done a job on that cake," he observed sadly.

"I'm just removing it from temptation. I'm doing you a service."

"Thanks," he muttered.

She picked at the cake some more. "What are you doing up so late anyway?" she asked.

"Studying."

"This late?" she exclaimed.

"They give us a lot to do."

"Jesus! I sure as hell never stayed up this late when I was a freshman."

"I'm a sophomore," he reminded her.

"God, that's right. I keep forgetting. Who do you have for history this year? Did you get Mr. Barlow?" He nodded. "That's *so* great. He's such a great teacher. He's the best teacher you'll ever have, anywhere. I'm glad you got him. Do you like him?"

"Yeah, I do. I mean, I'm not one of his favorites, like you and Phil were. He still has his clique, and I'm not in it. But I like him. We're doing the Reformation. He rants and raves about the Catholics. He's worse than Mom. I wonder what he'd do if there were a Catholic in his class."

"A Catholic? At Fieldston? That'd be the day!" She was still mauling the cake. "Does he still do the Diet of Worms, or whatever it was? Martin Luther's speech? 'Here I stand,' that bit? Does he still do it?"

"Oh, sure, he's just as big a ham as ever."

"God, this is so great, hearing about school. Tell me all about your other teachers. Tell Mr. Barlow hello from me, will you? Who else do you have? I ought to go up and see them. I miss them all. It's such a great school. I'm glad you didn't go to Music and Art. You'll have enough of that stuff when you go to Juilliard."

Carl wasn't used to such effusiveness from his sister. Usually she took no interest in him unless she was annoyed. This was a new experience. He wondered if it would last. Then he wondered if he could entrust her with a secret he had been harboring. At another time he might have hesitated, but he wanted badly to tell someone. In the flush of her unexpected sympathy, he succumbed to the impulse. "I'm not going to Juilliard," he told her. He sounded casual, considering the momentousness of the decision.

"You're not going to Juilliard?" Joan sounded surprised, but not that surprised.

He shook his head. "I don't know. It's a new idea for me. I mean, it was never should I be a doctor, or should I be a lawyer, or what? It was just, Carl's going to be a pianist. Period. I never thought about anything else. I never considered that there were other possibilities. I don't have anything else in mind, to tell the truth. But I really don't want to be a pianist."

Joan didn't answer right away. She was busy with the cake. She had made such a colossal mess of the piece dissolving on the plate that nothing more could be done with it, so she turned to the remainder on the platter. She poked at it with her fork, teasing out bits of icing that she licked off. She worked methodically, with concentration, until the entire expanse of icing was pockmarked, as if someone had gone after it with a shotgun. "Then don't be a pianist," she said.

He sighed. "It's not that easy. It's not entirely up to me."

"No one has to be anything they don't want to be."

"In this family?" he asked incredulously.

Joan looked over at him. "You know what your trouble is? You let everyone push you around all the time. You don't have to let them tell you what you can do or can't do." She tapped the top of the cake with her fork until it started to crumble apart. She extracted some of the exposed filling, eroding what was left of the cake's structure. As it started to list she added, "You could be anything you wanted, but you can't just lie down and let them walk all over you."

He gazed at the ruins of the chocolate cake, milk-soaked and demolished on its plate. "Oh, sure, I can do anything I want to do. I know, we lead our own lives. How often have I heard that! Of course, they don't actually tell you, do this, or don't do that. But you know how it is. You know how Mother works. Suppose I announced tomorrow that I wanted to be a fireman. Do you think anyone would forbid it? Would they say, That's ridiculous, no one becomes a fireman, you simply can't do that? Of course they wouldn't. They'd say, How *marvelous*! Carl wants to be a fireman! They'd let everyone know how terribly pleased they are. They'd run out and buy me a library of books about fire and water and pumps and ladder climbing and get me a little fire engine of my own to pedal around in and probably get me a Dalmatian. They'd find the absolutely best fireman teacher in New York and pay him a fortune to come to the house every Saturday morning to teach me how to slide down poles. They'd tell everyone in New York I was going to be the greatest fireman of all time, because God forbid I should just be a good fireman. That would never do. The painters would be in the next morning to redo my room in red. And so on and so forth. Oh, I'd lead my life, all right. I'd go stark, raving mad."

Joan nodded. While he was talking, she had gone back over to the refrigerator, and was moving everything inside it around until she found a bowl containing leftover custard. She brought it back to the table, picked up the fork she had used for the cake, sucked it clean, and started picking away at the custard with it. She meticulously peeled back bits of the skin, like a surgeon lifting a dermal flap, and scooped out some of the egg-white pudding beneath. "You let them push you around too much," she said absently. "You've got to ignore them. Let them buy you all the fire engines they want. It's no skin off your nose. Look at Phil. No one tells him what to do."

"Of course not," he replied bitterly. "He can do what he wants, because he wants to do what everyone expects him to do. Plus he's brilliant at it. You know how it is in this family. If you're a lawyer, you make the Supreme Court. If you're a tennis player, you win the Davis Cup. If you're a pianist, you play in Carnegie Hall. If not, forget it. There's no room for mediocrity."

Joan stared at him, a troubled expression playing on her face. "What about me?" she asked, troubled. "I'm mediocre."

He was taken aback. It had never occurred to him that Joan had any doubts about herself. He thought he was the only one with dark thoughts in the family. Surely not Joan. "No you're not," he asserted, but he wasn't convincing.

"What am I that's not mediocre?" she persisted.

He tried to think of an answer. "You're a saint" was all he could come up with. "Saint Joan."

She gave a wry look. "Ingrid Bergman, burning at the stake?" she asked. "No, thanks."

"That wasn't what I meant," he said, flustered. "It's just that everyone wants you. They come to you. You don't have to *be* anything or *do* anything. You don't have to prove anything. You have skillions of friends. You have a boyfriend who worships the ground you walk on. Everybody worships the ground you walk on. How could you want to be any different from what you are?"

She looked thoughtful. Putting down the fork, she pushed the bowl away from her on the table and sat back in her chair. "There's no reason I shouldn't be the happiest person on the face of the earth, I guess," she said, more to herself than to him. "Don't you think so?" she asked.

He did; or at any rate he always had. Her health could be better, but no one seemed to take that too seriously. Other than that, she seemed to him to have life pretty much on her own terms. Now, for the first time, he wondered. "I don't know what makes anyone happy," he confessed.

For a moment neither of them said anything. Then Joan spoke: "Did you know Johnny wants to marry me?"

Carl looked pleased. "I didn't know exactly. But I more or less figured that was the case. He doesn't exactly make a secret of it. Are you gonna?"

She shook her head. "I don't know. It's very complicated. What do you think I ought to do?"

He hesitated. No one in the family ever turned to him for advice, and now here was Joan, of all people, asking him what she should do about her love life. Him, the expert. "I think you should do what you want to do."

"Do you like Johnny?" she asked.

"Of course I like him. Everyone likes him. He's a great guy, and he's always been very nice to me. But I'm not the one who'd be marrying him."

Joan looked pensive for a moment, then asked, "Can you keep a secret?"

"Of course."

"No, really. Not tell anyone?"

"Joan," he pointed out. "Who would I tell?"

That much was true. Joan leaned toward him and said softly, "I'm seeing a guy at work."

That did get a reaction. "No kidding!" Carl said. Joan searched his face for disapproval, but could read no judgment. "When in hell do you see him?" he asked.

Joan laughed. "Incredible as it sounds, I have some time to myself. A few minutes a day. Anyway, it's not that big a deal. We're not going steady."

"Then why the secrecy?"

Joan shrugged. "It wouldn't work out at all. You know what it'd be like. They'd all want to meet him." She nodded her head toward her parents' room. "They'd have to know all about him. Who he is. Who his parents are. Believe me, he doesn't have any parents. He wouldn't fit in here. It'd be a disaster. Phil would make mincemeat of him. And Johnny would be terribly hurt."

"I think I get the picture," Carl said, smiling. "I guess you're better off keeping it to yourself."

"It's complicated," Joan observed. Carl nodded his understanding. "Do you think I'm being awful?" she asked urgently.

Carl found it hard to believe she really cared about his opinion; but evidently she did. He spoke carefully: "You just got through telling me to do what I wanted to do. I think there's too much guilt around this place. It's the family disease. Everybody's got it." He stopped himself, and added, "Everyone but Phil."

Joan smiled fondly at him. "You won't tell anyone?" she asked anxiously.

"I thought we'd settled that."

"And you won't think badly of me if I do something crazy?"

"I thought we'd settled that too," he said.

"I guess we have," Joan agreed. "You know what I want?" she asked, suddenly animated. "One piece, before you give up the piano for good."

He smiled. "I'm not sure even Dad would like to be woken up at two A.M. by my dulcet tones."

"You could play something really soft. That piece I always loved? You could play it pianissimo."

He knew which one she meant. The *Träumerei* from the "Scenes of Childhood." "I'll have to play it pianissimo, or I'll wake up the house," he warned. They went together into the living room. A half-moon threw in just enough light to see by. He sat at the keyboard in the darkness. Joan went to the window next to the piano and stood looking out. "No talking, now," he insisted.

The *Träumerei* is a night piece anyway, and lent itself to a pianissimo performance. It didn't wake anyone up. Toward the end, Carl thought he heard Joan sigh; but he didn't know if it was for the music, or some regret it had called up. Maybe she was thinking of a scene from her childhood; he wouldn't know. He imagined she might be remembering Rosefield, the summers during the war. He had missed out on that part of her life.

When he finished, Joan didn't say anything. She stayed where she was, looking out over the city. It lay, silent and immense, under the clear, cold sky. After a moment she came over to him and leaned over. He had remained at the piano, listening to the final dying sound of the last chord. "Thanks, Carl," she murmured, and she kissed him.

The Harvard Club of New York contains a dining room, several function rooms, a reading room, guest rooms for out-of-town members, and the best squash courts in the city. For Roger Montgomery, however, the heart and soul of the club was in none of those places, but in its bar. There, daily, he could stop off on his way home after work and find refuge from the helter-skelter of city life. Elsewhere he was obliged to deal with people he would much prefer to avoid. They accosted him everywhere, thrust themselves on him, buffeted him, and challenged him, as well as his way of life, at every turn. He—a Montgomery, with Howard blood in his veins, whose wife just happened to be an Islington —was brought day in and day out into distasteful contact with the great unwashed. The Harvard Club was his castle. The college, it was true, had let the standards slide disastrously in recent years, and the club was unfortunately open to any alumnus who wanted to join. There were many members, sad to say, he did not care to know. But by some miraculous operation of an underlying order in the universe, these people seldom if ever came to the bar. There, in the quiet of the late afternoon, Roger Montgomery could sink into the deepest crimson chair and sip that blessed first drink, secure in the knowledge that he was among his own.

One of his own—one of his very own—was Chip Holliwell, whom he was expecting momentarily. Chip and he went back a long way. Their families were close. They themselves had gone to the same prep school, and of course they were in the Porcellian together at college. Not only that, but their sons had followed along in their footsteps—St. Paul's, Harvard, the Porcellian Club—until young Chas Holliwell had the misfortune to have a bit of cheating during an exam be observed by the proctor. In Roger's day, if a Holliwell had gotten caught with his pants down, the dean would have called him in for a stern chat. Nowadays, other, more malevolent forces were in operation, and the boy had been unceremoniously dismissed from the college seven generations of his family had attended. Roger, who was godfather to young Chas, had had the devil of a time finding a decent job for the boy after that. Sometimes he didn't understand what the world had come to.

That had happened a few years back, but the world hadn't become any saner in the interim. A Catholic in the White House! The machine running City Hall; not for the first time, to be sure, but this outfit was damn hard to deal with. Negroes, not content with all that'd been done for them, raising all sorts of ruckuses down South. Alan Gutheim, of all people, suggesting with a straight face that they put one on the board of the executive committee. Alan Gutheim, come to think of it, being seriously considered for presidency of the Bar Association of the City of New York. Alan Gutheim! Over his dead body.

And now Chas Holliwell again. Chas was evidently in some sort of trouble for a change, though it wasn't yet clear to Roger just what it was. When Chip had called him earlier that day, he'd been nearly incoherent. He'd mumbled something about a trust, some stocks, a loan, Roger could hardly make head nor tail out of the whole thing. Chip was getting harder and harder to follow these days. Rather than try and disentangle the mess over the phone, Roger had told Chip to meet him at the club. Whenever possible, Roger liked to talk things over at the Harvard Club. Even the thorniest problems appeared more solvable in those hushed and protected environs. Often the very people who could be most helpful were at hand, or at least they were fellow members. The world, which elsewhere seemed out of control, was more manageable there.

And now here was Chip, looking even more distraught than Roger had expected. Years of hitting the bottle had taken their toll on a face that in its day had caused many hearts to flutter. Chip's fine features had long since sagged into boozy shapelessness, and as he sat down next to Roger they were positively quivering. He could hardly speak, and Roger didn't press him for details until he had a stiff double under his belt. Only when the waiter had brought over a second drink was he able to talk at all.

"He's a good kid, Roger," Chip pleaded. "He may have made a couple of mistakes along the way, but he's basically a good kid. I hope you'll bear me out on that." The poor man was close to tears.

"Maybe you'd better tell me the story," Roger said, trying to retain his impartiality. As a lawyer, he knew he ought to hear the facts before reaching a judgment. But then again, this was not his first encounter with Chas Holliwell.

The story took Chip some time to tell. Chas, as Roger well knew, had been salted away at Colonial Fiduciary, a backwater little firm that managed estates and trusts. Over the years, Colonial had tended the affairs of some of the city's oldest and best families. Although it had acquired no new business for decades, it still gave satisfaction to most of its special clientele. By virtue of investment policies that were cautious almost to the point of paralysis, it rarely lost any large sums of money for its accounts, and the erosion of capital was not obvious to widows whose bills were paid regularly. In recent years a few hawk-eyed clients had switched to banks that were more aggressive in their tactics, but enough remained to keep the firm afloat. Among those who stayed were the Abbott family. In accordance with the firm's long-standing practice, all contact with Mrs. Abbott was handled by a partner—in this case the senior partner, Francis Tremayne—but the actual management of the estate was left to an assistant trust officer, who for the Abbott family was Chas Holliwell.

After a rocky start, Chas had worked out quite nicely at Colonial. At first it had been a near disaster. Naturally, Chas hadn't been pleased to have his carefree college days so precipitously interrupted. To find himself instead stuck behind a desk from nine to five every day, doing stultifying clerical work alongside men old enough to be his grandfather, was not what he had bargained for. His father hadn't perhaps helped him understand how much trouble it had been for Mr. Montgomery to find anything at all for him, and he despised the job. He performed his few tasks poorly, and was almost let go. Before giving him the sack, Frank Tremayne had the courtesy to notify Roger Montgomery, who came and read Chas the riot act.

Things went better after that. Chas, to his credit, shaped up. He realized that his options weren't particularly attractive, and he decided it was in his interest to do well at Colonial. It wasn't that hard. He had the Holliwell name and looks. He knew how to comport himself. Despite his early departure from Harvard, he had picked up the air of superiority that generally goes far in the absence of actual accomplishment. He did creditably enough to move up a notch, and was in time given responsibility for several accounts. He made no decisions regarding portfolios—very few were in any case made at Colonial—but he kept track of dividend receipts, maturation of bonds, tax payments, dispersals, and so on. The Abbott estate was one of his assignments.

The estate itself was in a shambles. Most of it was tied up in Abbott & Strawbridge stock which in recent years had kicked in precious little income. In part because the trust had not been properly updated, the death of J. Harrison Abbott had triggered off a ruinous tax bill, with nothing much to pay it with. With the company on the skids, the stock was practically worthless on the market. The only out that Tremayne could see was to borrow against it, and the only lender he could find was Colonial's broker. In view of the poor risk, the brokers could have charged astronomical interest, which they were only persuaded to forgo by an arrangement of payment on demand. This meant that on a moment's notice they could require full repayment of the principle, and failing that they were entitled to foreclose on thirty percent of Abbott & Strawbridge. Will Strawbridge yelled bloody murder, but what could Tremayne do? These were hard times for old families and old companies alike. The wolf was at the door.

The loan itself was arranged by Tremayne, and it fell to Chas Holliwell to monitor the cash flow. This consisted mainly of depositing the borrowed money as it came in and immediately paying it out in taxes. If there was any surplus, it was to be invested in short-term tax-exempts. Up until then it all seemed pretty straightforward to Roger; but at that point, Chip's account grew vague. "The figures just didn't add up," he kept mumbling.

"What's that supposed to mean?" Roger asked sharply. He didn't really want to hear the answer.

"I don't know, exactly. They couldn't find all the money. The figures just didn't add up," he repeated, as if it was too mysterious to comprehend.

"When figures don't add up, there's usually a reason," Roger said. "And in nine cases out of ten, the reason is misappropriation."

"The boy's no thief!" Chip cried desperately. Roger glanced around nervously. Even in the bar of the Harvard Club, there was such a thing as indiscretion. "He's a good boy, Roger. You know that," Chip said, still too loudly. He was overwrought, and the alcohol—he'd had another drink by then—didn't help him modulate his volume.

"Whether he's a good boy or not has absolutely no bearing on the situation. The only question is, did he or did he not take some money?"

Chip's face was already about as flushed as it could get, but he swallowed hard, and tears sprang to his eyes. For a moment he couldn't get the words out. "If he took any, it was only temporarily. He always meant to put it back," he explained.

Roger sighed. "I think it would be a very good idea if he put it back right now," Roger advised. "Then we can pick it up from there."

Chip nearly broke down entirely. "I don't know if he can put it back! He doesn't have it, and I'm not sure that I do myself."

"How much are we talking about here?" Roger asked, mentally reaching for his checkbook. He was prepared to do what he could for the sake of an old friend and honor of the Porcellian Club, but he didn't propose to cut off his arm.

"I don't know exactly," Chip said morosely. "It isn't so easy to figure out. He didn't keep exact track of it all. He always meant to put it back—"

"Just a rough estimate will do," Roger interrupted him impatiently.

"Thirty, forty thousand, something like that. It might go higher, even," Chip replied, as if the figure were some voracious organism that could grow on its own.

It was going to be damn inconvenient, Roger thought. He didn't have thirty or forty thousand dollars lying around, as it happened. His own daughters were costing him a pretty penny these days, and he sure as hell didn't need Chas Holliwell to suck him dry. He wondered, was there another way out of this mess without his having to actually shell out hard cash?

"What does Tremayne know about this?" he asked, seeing the glimmer of a possibility there. "Does he suspect any hanky-panky?"

Chip looked resentful at the use of the term, but was in no position to protest. "He doesn't yet, but it's bound to come out."

"Why is it bound to come out?" Roger wanted to know.

"The brokers are calling in the loan!" Chip moaned. "The estate doesn't have the cash, and they may have to declare bankruptcy. The auditors are sure to turn up something," he added with a groan.

"Why in hell are they calling in the loan?" Roger asked. "Why do they want to push the estate over the brink? They'll never get their money that way. Why are they calling it in now?" He paused, struck with his last thought. "Why are they calling it in now?" he mused. It didn't make sense. Something was missing. "Who's the broker, anyway?"

"I don't remember," Chip replied dully. He was not used to retaining large quantities of information these days. "Does it matter?"

Roger looked at him incredulously. "Yes, it matters," he said, barely concealing his contempt.

"If it's important, I could find that out," Chip offered, happy to have found a way to be helpful.

"Why don't you do that, Chip," Roger replied, staring off into the dimly lit room. "Why don't you find that out."

Chip hesitated, waiting for some further instruction. When none came, he asked, "You mean, now?"

Roger still didn't look at him. "Now, Chip," was all he said.

Sending Chip off to the telephone gave Roger a chance to think. It was all terribly sad, really. The Holliwells had been one of the really important families in New York, at one time boasting a governor and a senator serving simultaneously. That was well over a century back, true, but up until recently there was a Holliwell on every important board you could name. And now here was Chip Holliwell—the same man who once stroked the Harvard crew to victory at Henley—turned into a sniveling lush, while his only son was proving to be somewhat worse than that.

Still, something had to be done. Roger was never one to throw up his hands in despair. In his experience, there was always room to maneuver; it was mainly a matter of knowing whom one was dealing with. Frank Tremayne, for instance, would be a pushover. The man didn't know his ass from his elbow. He hadn't yet discovered a rather sizable embezzlement taking place under his nose, and if he ever did he could be manipulated without much difficulty. Roger had a fair amount of influence with several of Colonial's most important clients, and if worse came to worst, the firm could be persuaded to see that it was not in its best interest to make a fuss over a few thousand dollars.

The broker was another matter, however. He was less likely to be a pushover. If he was an old-line man, from a good family, it might not be too bad. Roger personally might not know him; but if he didn't, he was bound to know someone who did. Something could be done. He could talk to the man. They would speak the same language. Reason would prevail.

But there were the others—the many others—who would be more difficult, and Roger suspected the broker in question was one of them. Probably one of Them. As soon as he had heard mention of high interest rates, naturally his thoughts had turned to the Jews. It came to him, now that he thought about it, that Abbott & Strawbridge, which one might have thought would have died in peace by now, was involved in an ugly takeover fight. He tried to remember who was bidding for it, but he couldn't for the life of him think who it was just then. Some front man, that was it, a strict nonentity. But whom was he fronting for? Roger couldn't remember. The more he thought about it, the more he was convinced that the proxy fight was behind this inopportune foreclosure. If that was so, they might not be as interested in the money as in control of the stock. Which might also give Chas Holliwell time to slip back the thirty or forty thousand dollars, or whatever the figures finally added up to. If only Roger could remember who was trying to get control of Abbott & Strawbridge. He struggled to think, but only drew a blank.

His efforts were interrupted by Chip, returning from the telephone. "I got the name you wanted," he told Roger. For the first time since he had come into the club, he was smiling, obviously pleased to have carried out his assignment without a hitch. He was still good for something, old Chip. "The brokerage house is Anspach & Wellman. That mean anything to you?"

Roger kept a poker face. "In a general way, yes," he said. And then, suddenly, his lips drew back in a grim, satisfied smile. "Gerald Altman," he said.

"What's that?" Chip asked, puzzled.

"I think Gerald Altman's behind this," Roger answered. "And I have a pretty good idea who's behind him. I'll want my name kept out of it, but I may be able to help."

He didn't elaborate, but he did call the waiter over and ordered another round of drinks.

Thirteen

No one was surprised when Joan and Johnny got engaged. After all the expectation, the event was something of an anticlimax. Not that anyone thought it would be sentimental: no moonlight for Joan, or lapping water, soft music, passionate embraces, tears. Still, there was something awfully no-nonsense about it. They had been out shopping—it was a Saturday afternoon—or rather Joan had been shopping and Johnny had made approving noises and carried her parcels. They had just come from Tru-Form, where Joan still bought her shoes instead of going to a grown-up shoe store. As they strolled down Madison they looked in the windows of the art galleries. It was a sunny day, but cold, and one didn't linger long even at a masterwork. Rosenberg's had put the Degas pastel in a window, and Joan asked Johnny if he liked it. He said he adored it; Joan's notice was recommendation enough for him. As they turned away from it Joan said casually, "We could ask Grandmother to give it to us as a wedding present."

Johnny didn't take it in all at once. "I don't see why—you're not saying—?" He got tongue-tied. "Does this mean— Oh, God!"

Joan looked put out, as if she didn't like his stopping and holding them up for no reason at all. "That's what it means," she said, and started to walk downtown again. Johnny didn't move.

"Let me get this straight," he said. "Are you saying we're going to get married?"

Joan sighed, already regretting it. "I suppose so."

"Really?" Johnny asked in sheer disbelief.

"Yes, really," Joan said crossly. "Now please don't make a big fuss about it, will you? You know I can't stand a big fuss."

"How about a little fuss?" Johnny pleaded. "You've got to allow me that much. It doesn't happen every day. Not to me. You are serious, aren't you? You're not just kidding around."

"Oh, Jesus!" Joan cried. "I'm not kidding, but if you're going to go on and on about it . . . I've said we can, now let it go. I'm cold." She walked on in earnest. Johnny caught up with her and tried to get her to soften her stance, but she remained adamant. No carrying-on. No scenes. Absolutely no mush.

"Can we at least tell people?" he asked, "Or is it a secret?"

"Oh, tell whoever you want," she said irritably. "But no announcement in the paper." He started to protest. "And no ring," she added, like a judge tacking a few extra years on a sentence.

"No ring!" Johnny cried. "Joanie, let's be reasonable about this."

But if reasonableness was what he wanted, he was barking up the wrong tree. Joan wasn't in a reasonable mood. She probably wouldn't have agreed to get married if she had been. Ever since she had gone to Kevin's apartment, she had felt unreasonable, touchy, on edge. The memory of that afternoon was disturbing. It was bad enough that she had sunk to such depths; but she hadn't even gotten it out of her system. She wanted to see Kevin again, be with him, make love to him; if anything, more than before. Her attraction to him only became sharper, while he, she was sure, could take her or leave her. In the intervening days, when she had seen him at Meyer House, he hadn't revealed a thing to her. He behaved toward her the same as he had before she came to his apartment: no more and no less. It appalled her, and frightened her, too, to be so enthralled by him, so desirous of seeing him again. He had her entirely at his mercy. She needed a shelter from him. Johnny was her refuge.

She wasn't toying with him, though. Joan didn't treat people like that. She would go through with the marriage all right. She had no second thoughts. But she wasn't ecstatic and she wouldn't pretend she was for anyone. She hadn't so much accepted him as given in. Everyone wanted her to marry him and she was almost too tired to care. It might as well be Johnny as anyone, and it might as well be now as later. It would make him happy, and God knows she wanted him to be happy.

Joan wanted everyone to be happy. If she had it within her capacity to bestow happiness on one person, and that person happened to be Johnny Krieger, fine. She would marry him. She owed him that much. Whether being married to her would turn out to be a bed of roses, she herself seriously doubted, but she had given up trying to convince him of that. If he wanted it so badly, let him have it. The thought went through her mind: It's his funeral.

But she wouldn't put up with any hoopla. No party, no announcement, no ring. She was stubborn as could be about that. Johnny, as it happened, didn't care a bit whether he had a party, and no announcement was necessary: everyone in town knew about it practically by nightfall. But he was desperate to give Joan a ring. Johnny hadn't an ostentatious or pretentious bone in his body, and he wasn't exactly rolling in dough. When his old man had taken a dive from the seventeenth floor of 35 Wall Street, not much was found left in the till. But Johnny would have spent his last buck and gone into hock up to his ears just to be able to walk into Tiffany's holding hands with Joan and emerge an hour later with a ring on her finger. It didn't have to be a diamond. Of course, Joan wouldn't want a diamond. Diamonds were far too glittery and conventional for Joan. Fine. Let it be a sapphire, then. A star sapphire, sky-blue, all its brilliance concentrated into one intense point of light. That would be just as good. Or if she didn't want a sapphire, she could have whatever she chose: an emerald, a ruby, whatever; no jewel at all, if she insisted on being austere. But it hurt him that she wouldn't accept any ring at all, wouldn't wear one. Whenever he looked at her empty left hand, he felt a small pang of sadness. He said nothing about it, though. On the whole, he was delirious with joy.

The whole city seemed to smile on the couple. Joan had her work cut out to keep her friends from throwing a party. They didn't buy her argument that the surprise party at Betsy's was all the celebrating she could take. "What about Johnny?" Wendy wanted to know. "He deserves a party, even if you don't. We'll have one for him, and you can feel free to stay away." Of course she went. It was a blast. The whole gang was there. Ellen threatened to come down from Bennington, and would have if she hadn't had to finish her last project before leaving for San Francisco. But everyone else came, even the Danzigers this time. Johnny was practically in tears with happiness and pride, and everyone said it was the best time they'd had in ages.

Alan and Peggy were of course tremendously pleased. In Alan's eyes, the thing had been decided long since, and even Peggy, not one to be proven wrong by events, told everyone she wasn't a bit surprised. She convinced herself that she had predicted it all along, which was a comfort to her, and amused Eleanor, who knew better but said nothing. When Joan called on her grandmother to give her the news, Mrs. Altman was so moved that she couldn't speak for a moment. She held Joan in a tender embrace and when she recovered the use of her voice she immediately called Rosenberg's and told them to take the Degas pastel out of the window. Eleanor was also, to her surprise, a little teary when she heard the news. "I couldn't be more thrilled, darling," she told Joan. "Give Johnny my dearest love, and let me know what you want for a wedding present once you've made up your mind. But something *really* nice. I want that understood." When all was said and done, Eleanor could really be a dream.

The only people to complain, not surprisingly, were Alan's sisters, Cecile and Marjorie.

"No ring?" shrieked Cecile. "Whoever heard of such a thing. It's impossible. It's not done."

"I don't care what she says," Marjorie asserted flatly. "If there's no ring, there's no engagement."

The two of them carried on like maniacs. "What is it you said the father did?" Majorie asked.

"The father's dead, Marjorie," Alan explained wearily. They'd been through this before. Marjorie and Cecile both had a habit, when they weren't satisfied with an explanation, of demanding that it be repeated, in the hope that it would improve the second time around.

"Yes, I know that! But presumably he did something before he died."

It was terribly awkward. Bob Krieger had never amounted to much. He had flitted uneasily on the outskirts of the financial world. He was an entrepreneur with so little self-confidence that he could rarely persuade anyone to go in on his schemes. He typically lost his nerve at the eleventh hour and pulled out with tremendous losses just before the success of the enterprise he had deserted. He limped along for a number of years until, in his first really decisive act, he pitched himself out the window of the offices of the Chase, where he had just been refused further credit. Alan had done his best to make some order out of the chaos he left behind, but the family had been in pretty dire straits. A number of people, including Alan and Gerald Altman, had helped out on the q.t., but there wasn't a hell of a lot for the widow and children to fall back on. The suicide itself had been hushed up, but everyone knew, and Johnny always looked in agony whenever his father's name came up. "He was in investments," Alan told Marjorie.

She wrinkled her nose. "I'm surprised you allow this, Alan," she scolded.

"The boy's done marvelously," Alan declared. "He's worked very hard and he's really made something of himself. And he couldn't be nicer."

"I'll have to take your word for it," Marjorie huffed, "since evidently we're not to have the great honor of meeting him."

"Of course you'll meet him," Alan said imprudently.

"How?" she pounced. "They refuse to have a party. Of course Joan never comes to see us. None of your children do. I'm not complaining, merely stating a fact. Where am I going to meet him? On the street? Am I supposed to go up to him and say, 'I'm your future aunt?' That'll be the day!"

Alan was trapped. He had to promise that Joan would call on her aunts and bring Johnny. "I won't hold my breath," Marjorie said.

She had a point. Joan was reluctant to drag Johnny around to meet her dreadful Gutheim relatives, and Peggy backed her up. "I don't give a damn what they think," she told Alan. "They've never approved of a thing this family has done anyway. They're not going to start now, whether or not Joan calls on them. You know perfectly well they'll still find something to criticize. I had a party and a ring and an announcement and I called on all of them, not to mention every one of your aunts, all of whom were alive at that point, and they still wanted you to call it off. They thought you could do a lot better." She laughed at the memory. "I don't know that they weren't right about that!"

"Oh! You're wrong there!" Alan protested. His recollection had long since prettied up the ugliness of his own engagement. "They had no objections whatsoever. They couldn't have been more delighted, in fact."

"Delighted, my ass," Peggy said. Alan looked crestfallen. He hated his wife to use such language, especially when the servants were around, as was just then the case. But he couldn't do anything about her tongue. He'd tried for twenty-six years without the slightest success.

Joan did not call on her aunts. As a compromise, she and Johnny were to drop in for drinks before the next family dinner. "They'll probably stay for the evening," Alan promised his sisters.

"Half an hour will do it," Peggy assured Joan.

Cecile Hirsch's living room was overstuffed. You could never be in that room for any length of time without feeling dyspeptic. It was a hodgepodge of sofas, antique chairs, fussy butler's tables, teetering lamps, knicknacks, curios, objets d'art, bric-a-brac of every description, all thrown together in an impossible jumble. There was no sense of harmony in the room, no ease, no breathing space. The mustard drapes were always drawn, night and day, blocking out all light, air, view, or possibility of escape. An odd group of paintings filled the walls: a dull Dutch landscape; a disagreeable lady in the style of Van Dyck; a still life of astonishing ugliness; and a remarkable huge biblical scene by an obscure French painter of the Barbizon school that depicted Susannah being stoned by the Elders. "No Rembrandt has gone up in value like that painting has, since we bought it," Edgar Hirsch would point out proudly, perhaps in answer to the tacit question: How could anyone tolerate it in his home? But Edgar, to give him his due, put up with a lot.

So did Peggy. When she was first married, she and Alan were supposed to spend every Friday night with his family for Shabbat. Not until Alan's mother died was she able to get out of the weekly ordeal. There continued to be intense pressure for family togetherness. Cecile conceived the idea that her daughter, Audrey, and Joan, who were the same age, should be the best of friends. Peggy scotched the idea from the beginning. Audrey was as vacuous as her mother, without the nastiness, in fairness, but with not much else to offer in its place. Cissy had always resented—among her many, many resentments—that Audrey was not included in all of Joan's parties, outings, summer plans, any activity she got wind of. She complained bitterly to Alan. To Peggy's face she was cloyingly sweet, but behind her back she accused her of putting on airs. Her great dream was to be able to high-hat an Altman. There were never many opportunities, and she was particularly delighted to announce that when Joan brought Johnny to meet the family, Audrey would not be there. "She's much too busy to drop everything and come running at the snap of Peggy's fingers," she told Alan.

"You're supposed to be crushed," Peggy warned Joan. "It's meant to be a terrible snub."

"I'll be mortified," Joan promised.

These family gatherings, even though they were no longer weekly affairs, were still pretty dreadful. "Your aunts are impossible. How your father managed to turn out the way he did will always be a mystery to me," Peggy told her children. "Leonard is an idiot, and Edgar isn't good for anything much except opening doors at funerals. Their friends are all deadly bores. Which is hardly surprising. Why would someone who had anything at all to contribute want to throw away an evening on them? If I had my way, I'd spare you ever having to waste any time on them."

But family was, after all, family, and they did have to meet Johnny at some point. Joan and he were to drop in Friday night, for drinks, at Cecile's. Only Cecile and Edgar—Audrey being otherwise engaged—Marjorie and Leonard and Kenneth; poor Etta, Alan's youngest sister; and, inescapably, Uncle Rudolf were to be there. And Monica. Monica came with Uncle Rudolf. She was not, to be sure, family. It was hard to say just what she was. To all appearances she was Rudolf's mistress; but that, at his age, defied belief. Rudolf, who had never married, was reputed to have had in his younger days voracious and rather despicable sexual appetites. The women who satisfied them must have been more or less sluts; even he never dared bring them into any family gathering. With the passage of time and the ravages of some well-deserved venereal disease, one would have thought his capacity had abated, presumably his desire following suit. If that was so, it was hard to know what function Monica served him. Monica was no slut. You couldn't say much more for her, but you had to give her that. She was a sour, dried-up woman, old before her time, and so unappealing, it was impossible to think that she adorned even Rudolf's idiosyncratic fantasy life. She had no physical or intellectual charm at all. She exuded an air of put-upon gentility, although Marjorie swore up and down that she came from no family whatsoever: her people were strictly Long Island with a hard *g*, by way of Seventh Avenue. What Marjorie called the "Oy vey! set." No evidence of any money. Rudolf kept her fed and clothed and gave her a pittance. He might have led her to believe he had mentioned her in his will, she should live so long. Alan had drawn it up, and although he was usually the soul of discretion, he did let slip that Monica stood to gain little by Rudolf's death. They didn't live together—Rudolf was too stiff-necked and hypocritical for that, and not even someone as craven as Monica could have survived it—but she was at his beck and call day and presumably night, if such a thing could be borne. Altogether a pretty horrible existence, one would think.

Peggy and Alan arrived before Joan and Johnny. The rest of the family was there, except for Rudolf and Monica. Peggy braced herself as she came into the living room. Marjorie saw her first. "Oh, I love your hair!" she screamed. "I just love your hair!"

"Do you?" Peggy asked dubiously. "I had them do it this way simply because it was too damn much trouble before."

"Well I just love it," Marjorie said defiantly. "Cissy, don't you just love Peggy's hair this way?"

Cecile loved it.

"I just love it," Marjorie insisted.

Etta's opinion was not asked. That earth-shattering subject having been settled, Peggy went to sit next to Kenneth, who was the only person there she could stomach. But Leonard came and plunked himself heavily on her other side and asked gravely, "How's the little girl doing, Peg?"

Peggy feigned complete puzzlement. "What little girl?" she asked. She knew perfectly well whom he meant, but he goaded her with his oozing solicitude.

"Didn't they tell me . . . ?" He looked at Kenneth in a panic. "Didn't Joanie . . . wasn't there some sort of accident . . . ?" Now he thought he had the wrong person. He never paid much attention to anything that was told to him. Maybe it was someone else. He looked to his son for help, but Kenneth gave him a contemptuous look and said nothing.

"Oh, Joan!" Peggy exclaimed, as if suddenly enlightened. "When you asked about the 'little girl,' of course I hadn't the foggiest idea who you were talking about, Joan being twenty-one, and the accident having taken place so long ago."

"Yes, but I thought . . . it didn't have any effect on the . . . on her . . ." He groped for words, not wanting to say something indelicate.

"You see, it doesn't work that way," Peggy said, as if explaining something to a backward child. "The one had absolutely nothing to do with the other. But people never understand that, no matter how many times it's explained to them."

"Oh!" Leonard nodded without in fact understanding. How could he? Here was this girl, said to have something rather ghastly the matter with her, although no one would say just what; and instead of putting her into the hospital, as any normal mother would have done, Peggy had insisted on running the child all over creation at the same insane pace the entire family for some reason insisted on maintaining. Before you could say Jack Robinson she was hit by a car and damn near killed. Next thing you knew she was engaged. Without a ring. It boggled the mind; Leonard's mind, at least.

Cecile saw her brother-in-law being made a fool of. "How about some drinks!" she shouted at her husband. Edgar dutifully got up and plodded around taking orders. Marjorie shouted over to Peggy, "What do you think of Boca Raton?"

"I don't think much of it," Peggy answered, too quickly. Smelling a rat, she said, "Why do you ask?"

"Etta was thinking of going there," Marjorie answered with distaste.

Two tiny spots of red invaded Etta's cheek, her version of a blush. "Some of the girls were thinking of going," she explained apologetically. "Ordinarily I wouldn't be able to get away, but by a fortuitous chain of circumstances it might be feasible. The January lecture at the museum has been postponed because the curator who gives the course is going to be in Florence. Lucky he! Therefore, when Pam asked if I would go to Boca Raton with some of the girls, I said I might possibly be able to get away in January. But you say it's not very attractive?"

Peggy was furious. She had been drawn into that favorite Gutheim pastime, vetoing Etta's plans. "I've actually never been there, Etta, but people do go there, year after year, so I would gather they must like it." In fact, Peggy couldn't think of a duller place to go; but what was dull for any normal person might be the last word in excitement for Etta. She could play bridge in Boca Raton as easily as in Majorca.

Cecile frowned. "I've heard it's terribly cold in Boca in January. Who was down there, and it was so unbelievably cold, hon? Wasn't it the Neumanns?"

"The Neumanns go to Palm Beach," Edgar answered, staring dully into space.

"Palm Beach, Boca Raton, what's the difference? It's the same weather. They were there in January and they said they might as well have gone to Antarctica. They were simply miserable. Simply miserable! You may have to wait until later. February, possibly, or better, March."

"I don't think some of the girls can go later," Etta said nervously.

"Where were you going to stay?" Marjorie demanded.

"I don't know," Etta admitted abjectly. "I think Pam's travel agent has some place in mind. I didn't inquire as to just where."

Marjorie shook her head and put up her hands. "Travel agents! They just sent you wherever they get the biggest rake-off."

"I'll call Dolly Neumann and ask her where you should stay," Cecile said.

"The Neumanns go to Palm Beach," Edgar chanted, still staring blankly.

"Etta can go to Palm Beach, then," Cecile decided. "In March."

"In March they're giving us Michelangelo!" Etta wailed, tears of disappointment gathering in her eyes.

They badgered her for some time more. It was the same old story, except that the issue was rarely as vital as the weather in Boca Raton in January as opposed to the weather in Boca Raton in February. More typically it was a question of whether Etta's cook should order her meat from Gristede's or from Bristol Market, or if she should return a pair of shoes that pinched her feet. By now, on those rare occasions when Etta was allowed a small say in the running of her own life, the poor woman suffered such agonies of indecision that it seemed a kindness to let others do her thinking for her.

Poor Etta! At one time she was supposed to have been a vivacious young woman. It was hard to believe, looking at her ghastly pale face, watching her fluttering hands plucking at her shawl. Family legend had it that a young man had been so smitten with her that he had proposed. Old Mr. Gutheim had died by then, and even though his wife was still alive, Uncle Rudolf had assumed the role of arbiter in important family matters. He determined that the man in question was unsuitable; in just what way was never explained. The engagement was called off, and whatever juice flowed in Etta thereupon dried up. By the time Peggy knew her, she was a pathetic, utterly empty woman who was browbeaten by her sisters every time she opened her mouth.

Peggy, to avoid listening to the harangue, turned to Kenneth. "And how does the writing go?" she asked. Kenneth had declared himself to be a writer. The ambition was mild, but it was an ambition nevertheless, which was something, considering his parents. In the absence of any visible occupation, he might as well call himself a writer as anything, Peggy supposed. It suited his languid, affected manner and provided an excuse for his irregular hours and even more irregular friends. Except for some charming letters written from the Adriatic coast of Greece and circulated among the family, no one had yet to see much evidence of any feverish literary activity. Kenneth made it clear, however, that his vocation and his acquaintance with some famous writer or other entitled him to the prerogatives of an artist. Peggy was happy to let him have them, although she doubted that he had a shred of talent, let alone the perseverance to finish a book. It wasn't inconceivable that he might end up someday in a small publishing house or a little magazine where, in return for a hefty chunk of capital, he could be given a decent title. It would be a more rewarding life than joining his father and spending the remainder of his days shuffling aimlessly around the floor of the Exchange.

Kenneth beamed at Peggy's interest. "It's rather hard just now, thank you, Aunt Peggy. I'm blocked. It happens to everyone. I'm thinking of going to Corfu."

"I suppose Corfu isn't a bad place to have writer's block," Peggy observed.

Kenneth smiled good-naturedly. "I think my trouble is that I don't drink. Faulkner, Hemingway, Fitzgerald, O'Neill—all great drunks. Alcohol loosens the pen, you know."

His mother was monitoring the conversation, though, and not finding it to her liking, called over to Peggy, "What's this about Dickie Altman?"

"What's what about Dickie Altman?" Peggy asked, playing dumb.

"Peggy, darling, it's all over town. You needn't protect your brother. Although I'm sure he must be fit to be tied. Simply fit to be tied."

Peggy remained unperturbed. "I really haven't discussed it with him at any great length, so I can't tell you what he intends to do about it, which I gather is what you're dying to know?"

Marjorie was caught off guard. "I'm not *dying* to know anything, Peggy dear. I have no wish to pry whatsoever. The only reason I inquire at all is that we naturally take an interest in anything affecting you and Alan."

"Thank you, dear. I hate to disappoint you, but this will not affect me. Or Alan."

That shocked Marjorie. "I assume it will affect your seeing Dickie in the future!" she said, scandalized.

Peggy shrugged. "I see very little of Dickie in the present. I hadn't planned on seeing much more of him, but if I did, this wouldn't affect it one way or the other."

Cecile tried another tack. "I for one haven't the slightest interest in the whole affair. I haven't seen Eleanor and Gerald in ages. They travel in different circles nowadays." Cecile had often complained to Alan of being excluded from what she imagined to be the Altmans' glittering social life.

"Dear, they travel in exactly the same circles they've always traveled in," Peggy assured her. "I wasn't aware that you ever saw that much of them."

"Ellie Weil?" Cecile cried.

"Darling, she hasn't been Ellie Weil in well over twenty-five years."

"Well, when she was Ellie Weil, we were practically inseparable." The others were dumbfounded. Even from Cecile this was astonishing information. No one in the room had the slightest recollection of any friendship between the two women. "Don't you remember our last summer in Lake George? They were there. Not the old man, he had taken off by then, and of course the mother drank like a fish. Poor little Ellie practically *lived* at our place that summer."

"I'm not sure I remember . . ." Alan said, trying to recall his future sister-in-law among the images of sailboats, band concerts, sarsaparilla, swimming parties, buzzing flies.

"She would be on our doorstep while we were still at breakfast," Cecile said, shutting her eyes to more perfectly recall the details. "I remember Mam'selle had to literally send her home at night. Of course, it was terribly lively *chez nous* in those days, while she, poor thing—I can still hear Mam'selle saying, 'Mam'selle Elainor, you must *faire la retour journée* now, ze muzzer, she will be fretting about hair leetle gairl.' As if ze muzzer gave two hoots about hair leetle gairl, she was too soused to care. Poor Ellie would go off to that wretched little cottage they rented. You remember it? It was back in the woods, not even on the lake. I went over there once, that was enough. You couldn't believe the mosquitoes. And hot? The Black Hole of Calcutta was a refrigerator compared to it."

The others nodded mechanically. "Oh, she had time for us then!" Cecile cried. "Not that we've ever so much as been invited up to them in Westchester." Another famous grudge. "Audrey was there, though. Once. One of those huge, perfectly vulgar parties they used to throw for Barbara. Of course, *they* didn't invite Audrey, but they had invited a certain young man, and it so happened that he was simply crazy about Audrey. Simply crazy! Don't ask me which one it was, I can't keep them all straight." She laughed shrilly. "But whoever it was, he said he wouldn't go to the party unless he could bring her. Oh, he was head over heels about her, that one!" Her face took on the shining, wide-eyed look she adopted when spinning her fantasies. "Audrey told him: Go ahead, you'd be a fool to pass up a chance like that, just because I'm not invited. She had scads of invitations, she didn't exactly sit home pining for an invitation from the high and mighty Altmans. But he said, no, if she wasn't going, he wouldn't either, and that was that." Cecile put on her best pout.

"What could they do?" she shouted gleefully. "They said, bring whomever you please. And that's how it was that a member of the Hirsch family finally set foot in your own brother's home."

The conversation had given out. Everyone was done in by Cecile's harangue, which bore only a tangential relationship to what anyone else remembered. The buzzer rang, and they listened to hear whether it was the young people or Uncle Rudolf.

Peggy was glad to hear that it was Joan and Johnny, but when they appeared in the doorway, she was upset to see how pale her daughter looked. Pale, and so terribly thin. She was wearing the dark blue dress they had bought at Bonwit's that first day they went shopping, and it hung like a sack on her. It had probably never been properly fitted; there was such a thing as being in too much of a rush. But it wasn't just the dress. Although Peggy had seen her only that morning, looking at her now, seeing her as the aunts' penetrating eyes would, she realized how gaunt Joan had become. It was as though a blindfold had been taken away, and she saw her daughter in a harsher, truer light; and it troubled her.

She realized she should have postponed this entire dreadful evening. Joan wasn't ready for it. Peggy could have kicked herself for allowing her to be paraded in front of those harpies when she was looking so rundown. Not that Peggy gave a damn what they thought, but they would carry on to Alan, and nothing she could say would persuade him, after all these years, to ignore his sisters.

Cecile, for reasons best known to herself, decided to play the loving aunt. She greeted Joan with nauseating effusiveness. Marjorie, taking the other tack, cried, "Ahh! Their *majesties* have arrived." Johnny looked very handsome, of course, which didn't hurt. Although he had probably met everyone in the room, with the possible exception of Etta, he didn't really know them. Joan introduced him around. Cecile took him under her protection, treating him with cozy intimacy, asking after his mother as though Mrs. Krieger was as close a friend as Eleanor was supposed to have been. They probably wouldn't have recognized each other if they passed on the street. Marjorie remained icy, no doubt on the theory no ring, no congratulations. Poor Etta gave Joan an affectionate peck on the cheek and told both of them, "My heartiest, my dears;" which would have been easier to take if Phil hadn't predicted those exact words the evening before. Joan had her usual trouble keeping from breaking down in hysterics.

There was some desultory small talk, but now everyone was waiting for Uncle Rudolf. The tension built until finally his strident voice was heard in the hall. There was a short delay while he finished hectoring Monica, or the maid, or both, and then he marched into the room.

Uncle Rudolf was always said to have mellowed over the years. God knows what he had been like before the mellowing. Considering that he had been treated far more generously by the world than he deserved, he was a remarkably disagreeable old man. He complained constantly of being slighted, insulted, deserted by his friends. Even allowing for the fact that most of them must have died by now, it wasn't hard to understand why the rest would keep their distance. He was forever scolding Alan because Peggy didn't bring the children over regularly to call on him. From time to time Alan would appeal to her to mollify the old man, but her reply was invariably "Over my dead body." In fairness, if she thought it would give Rudolf an ounce of real pleasure, she would have brought them. But she knew he only insisted on it in order to be unpleasant. Cecile and Marjorie, who had produced their children regularly for inspection, complained to Alan as well; but Peggy stuck to her guns.

"I would apologize for being late," Rudolf said as he came in, "but it wasn't my fault." This was entirely gratuitous, since no one expected him ever to accept the blame for anything. "That idiot of a doorman didn't keep the taxi when Monica came for me. When I came down it was gone, and they took forever getting another." The hope that Rudolf might take a car and chauffeur had been the subject of many a long and futile family discussion. He hadn't the slightest intention of doing it, Peggy pointed out, since he had long since discovered that, for a lot less money and very little inconvenience to himself, he could have the pleasure of keeping everyone else waiting for him.

He settled himself down now in the deepest chair in the room and permitted Edgar to provide him with a drink. Ignoring Joan and Johnny, he scowled over at Alan and said, "Nice ratfight your brother-in-law's got himself mixed up in now. I suppose he likes that sort of thing?"

"I don't think he likes it," Alan answered. "He feels someone has to take a stand if we're to keep businesses vital in this city."

"Take a stand, is that what he calls it? He's not interested in making a buck, I suppose? Morty Pines is going to keep business vital, eh? That's his stand? But then, you're calling the shots, aren't you?"

Alan looked uneasily around the room. "I'm not handling this particular matter."

"Oh?" Rudolf pounced. "You're not his lawyer any longer?"

"I still advise Altman's, of course. But they have someone outside for this. Man by the name of Bernstein. Younger fellow, quite a hotshot, by all accounts. You have to be up on the latest law for this sort of thing. I told Gerald right away he'd better have a specialist handle it."

"A specialist!" Rudolf cried with glee. "First the doctors, now the lawyers. I suppose if someone sues me and I call you, you'll tell me to call a specialist?"

"In the unlikely event you get sued, Uncle Rudolf, I think I could handle that."

"And Phillip? Is he going to be a specialist? They tell me he is going to Washington."

"That's still very up in the air," Alan said, discomfited; he had already told his sisters it was in the bag.

"What will he do there? Lobby?" Rudolf took the view that the only reason anyone would ever go to Washington would be to offer someone a bribe. "He must be busy. He certainly hasn't enough time to come and see his oldest living relative. Not that any of them do. You wouldn't be here unless you were dragged in kicking and screaming, would you?" he snarled at Joan.

There wasn't much Joan could say to that. It was perfectly true, of course. She tried to be amiable, but there was no placating Rudolf when he wanted to be belligerent.

"Let's have a look at this young man, then. I'm not to call him a fiancé, they tell me. It isn't modern, or some such." Johnny had already been placed near him, a lamb prepared for the slaughtering. "They tell me you're at the business school, then? Columbia? Is that a decent place these days? It's not Harvard, but I suppose they can teach you how to get blood from a stone just as well, eh?"

Not an easy question to field. Johnny mumbled something about management techniques, financial analysis, economic planning. It didn't satisfy Rudolf.

"You learn all that fancy stuff and then go out and take over the family business and everyone counts themselves lucky if you don't run it into the ground. Isn't that so? Do you go into your father's business?"

Johnny still smiled valiantly. "My father died some years ago. There's no business for me to go into."

But Rudolf persisted like a bulldog: "And what did he die of?"

The light chatter in the rest of the room stopped. Everyone listened to hear what Johnny would say. Peggy was sickened. She had seen this coming, but there wasn't a thing she could do. It was like trying to stop a Mack truck from rolling down a hill.

Johnny turned ashen, and the smile vanished from his face. "My father committed suicide," he answered quietly.

Peggy had never admired Johnny so much as she did at that moment. His fine face tautened as he answered Rudolf's questions, but he bore up bravely. Peggy wondered whether the shame might not have worn off by now. Why on earth should a son be made to feel ashamed for something his father had done? Besides which, she always said, what was so shameful about suicide? It wasn't her particular cup of tea, to be sure, but if a person found it impossible to go on, and chose that way out, she was not one to condemn it.

She still would have liked to strangle Rudolf, but then no one expected him to be anything short of detestable.

His ordeal over, Johnny was taken away by Joan. Dinner was announced, and after a considerable delay while Rudolf visited the powder room—Peggy said the trouble must go beyond the prostate—they went in. Peggy, as the 'outside' daughter, was invariably seated next to Rudolf, where she was subject to his complaining conversation and disgusting table manners without respite. By the time he left, she was exhausted. Rudolf always departed abruptly while they were still at the table, in order, Peggy was sure, to deprive Monica of her one great pleasure in life, the consumption of rich desserts. Peggy would have been glad to forgo the Bavarian cream herself, if it meant she could leave, but unfortunately she didn't have that choice.

As soon as the front door was closed behind Rudolf and Monica, Marjorie announced, "I'm not at all happy with the way he looks. He didn't look at all well."

"I couldn't agree with you more," Cecile said. "He looks dreadful."

"There's nothing wrong with his appetite," Alan observed. "If he ever loses it, I hope a poor man doesn't find it."

"I'm not talking about his appetite," Marjorie said crossly. "I'm talking about the entire way he looks. His face is as red as a beet, and he has that vein or whatever it is that bulges out on his neck. Honestly, it scares me to death to see it bulge out like that. I'm sure he's going to have a stroke any minute. I swear."

"That vein's been there ever since I've known him," Leonard offered.

"He looks terrible," Marjorie snapped at her husband. "His color is poor and anyone with eyes in his head can see that the man is not well. I don't know about the rest of you, but I, for one, do not intend to stand around and do nothing."

"What do you intend to do?" Alan asked nervously. He had a foreboding about this.

"I intend to put him in a hospital," Marjorie replied emphatically. "He needs a decent checkup."

"Darling," Peggy said, "I wonder how you're going to get a man with the constitution of an ox into a hospital when he's not sick. Besides which, the last time I heard, he had a perfectly competent doctor, who might be expected to tell him if he needs a checkup or not."

"Finsterwald may be competent, I don't say he's not, but he's very busy, and he rushes you through as fast as he can. I'm getting him on the phone first thing in the morning and *insisting* he put Rudolf in for a complete checkup. The works. Alan, you can arrange for a room."

"Now, just a minute," Alan said in alarm. "It's not quite that simple. You just don't call up and say I'd like a room with a nice view of the park. There's quite a waiting list just for elective surgery, you know. Of course, emergencies get handled as always, but this isn't an emergency. I don't like it, but what else can we do? It's the price we pay for being one of the leading hospitals in the world."

"You . . . know . . . perfectly . . . well"—Cecile shook her finger at her brother—"that you have only to flick your little finger and he would be in the hospital tomorrow. What are they going to say? Sorry, Mr. Gutheim, we don't have room for your own uncle? In the pavilion you raised the money for? I'd like to be there when they say that. *That* I'd like to hear!" she screeched in delighted anticipation.

"First of all, Cissy"—Alan raised his hand to try to stem the tide that was roaring in—"before you have me getting him in with a flick of my little finger, which I wish were as easy as you seem to think it is, I'd like equally for you to be there when they ask what's wrong with my uncle, that they should kick some really sick patient out onto the street, and I say, 'Oh, my sister thinks his face is too red.' I hope you'll stay for that. It'd be the last time anyone paid the slightest attention to anything I said over there. And what's more, they'd be dead right."

"Would you rather wait until he keels over dead on the street?" Marjorie demanded. "When you want to, you do it. When you don't, nothing on earth can get you to. Don't give me this no-beds routine. There were beds when you wanted to get Wilma Klein in, after they told her doctor it was impossible. Or do you claim you had nothing to do with that?"

"Of course I had something to do with it. I was glad to do what little I could, a lot of good it did poor Wilma, rest her soul."

"You can do it for her, but not for your own father's brother?"

"Marjorie, for God's sake, Wilma was dying!" Alan said in exasperation.

"She . . . wasn't . . . family!" Cecile shrieked. "Everyone knows you will never lift a finger for a member of your own family."

"Now, Cissy—" Alan put in.

"Don't 'Now, Cissy' me!" she shot back. "Just tell me one time you have ever lifted a finger for anyone in your immediate family. One single instance. I don't speak of the other side. Peggy's relatives. Everyone knows you're at their beck and call, Gerald has only to snap his fingers and you come running. But as for your own flesh and blood, that's another story. I can't think of a single, solitary occasion when you have done a thing for any of us. Can you, Marjorie?" Marjorie shook her head grimly. Clearly it was an oft-rehearsed grievance. Etta sat, petrified, to hear such things said of her brother, who eased her life in countless ways. She wanted to speak in his defense, but she didn't dare oppose her sisters; and she could do nothing more than sit in misery, twisting her pearls until they were in danger of breaking apart and spilling all over the Sarouk carpet. "I can't think of a single, solitary occasion," Cecile reaffirmed, bolstered by Marjorie's corroboration.

"I'm the last one to blow my own horn," Alan stammered, "but I think I had a little to do with Audrey's getting a job at Saks." Which was an understatement, since without a call from him to Bernie Gimbel himself, Audrey would never have been considered for anything beyond a salesgirl; certainly not an assistant buyer, which was the job she got.

"That was only after you refused to get her into Vassar, as you could so easily have done!" Cecile cried.

"Cissy, how often have we been over this?" Alan said wearily. "I don't know where you ever got the idea that I had Vassar College, of all places, in my back pocket. I got in touch, against my better judgment, with Miriam Ackerman, who was good enough to look into it, and was told that even if the college waived their admission requirements, which Audrey didn't meet, the feeling was that Audrey would have been miserable there. I thought it had all been settled long since."

"Oh, it was settled all right. Only you weren't the one who had to tell Audrey. Your own children, of course, have but to *conceive* of a wish, and no sooner said than done. Whatever the cost, the sky's the limit. You spoil them within an inch of their lives, and then have the chutzpah to tell me that my daughter shouldn't go to the one college she had her heart set on?"

"Cissy," Alan said, "I don't think any of our children exactly qualify as hardship cases, but I don't agree that mine are spoiled."

"Not spoiled!" she exclaimed. "Are you going to sit there and tell me to my face that you aren't moving heaven and earth to get Phillip this precious clerkship? And do you mean to tell me that you don't let Carl eat whatever he pleases even though any sensible parent would have long since put a stop to that kind of gluttony? And as for Joan—"

"What about Joan?" Alan flared, goaded beyond patience by the aspersion cast on his daughter, about whom he was already sick with worry.

"Alan, dear," Peggy warned. She had vowed to herself to stay out of the whole thing, knowing that nothing she or anyone else could possibly say would stem the venomous outpouring from her sisters-in-law. It was an old story. Not that it made the slightest difference to her what they said, but she knew it hurt Alan terribly. If she could just get him to ignore them, they would lose interest; but he never learned.

Peggy's mild caution seemed to have freed Cecile from whatever

fragile restraint she had felt until then: "Here's your own daughter—
your own daughter!—wasting away before your very eyes. Anyone with
half a brain knows perfectly well she ought to be in a hospital. She
ought to be put there and kept there until someone finds out what is the
matter with that poor child and does something about it. I would have
thought that any parent who had an ounce of concern for their daughter
would have done that long ago. But of course you don't work that way.
God forbid she should do anything she doesn't want to. She's too used to
having her own way. Nothing will do except for her to traipse around
town, going down every day to that horrible neighborhood, exposing
herself to filth and disease and God only knows what else. Well! Is it any
wonder she looks the way she does? We have all begged you, literally
begged you, to do something about it, just use a little common sense, but
of course she had to have her way. No one's in the least bit surprised
she's having these terrible accidents. The only surprise is that nothing
worse has happened yet. And now to hear that she's thinking of getting
married to that terribly nice young boy. She's no more well enough to
get married right now than she is to swim the English Channel. It's
impossible for her to even be thinking about it, I can't imagine how
anyone can encourage her to be planning a wedding, in her condition.
You mark my words: If she goes on like this, I can't answer for the
consequences. I cannot answer for the consequences." She looked over
at her sister, and Marjorie nodded to indicate that she, also, would refuse
to accept responsibility for the imminent catastrophe.

"Cissy!" Alan groaned, wondering how to get her to stop saying
such terrible things about his beloved child.

"Don't say you haven't been warned," Cissy steamed on. "If something terrible should happen, which God forbid, don't say I didn't warn
you. Many, many times."

"Cissy!" Alan pleaded in anguish.

"Alan, dear," Peggy said wearily, "save your breath."

But that only goaded them further, and they returned to the attack
with renewed vigor.

"How utterly ghastly for you," Eleanor said when Peggy recounted
the scene for her the next morning. They were having their midmorn-
ing phone call, and Eleanor naturally had wanted to know how it had
gone with the sisters the night before.

"It doesn't bother me in the slightest," Peggy assured her. "They couldn't be sillier if they tried. The whole bunch of 'em. No, I wouldn't mind a bit, if only Alan didn't take the whole absurd business to heart. It's just that it makes him perfectly miserable. He was a wreck afterward. Not so miserable, I'm sorry to say, as to keep us from having to go there; but miserable enough, thank you very much."

"I feel badly for Alan, and I feel awful for you, my darling," Eleanor said with sympathy.

"Me?" Peggy asked, reluctant that anyone should concern themselves about her for one minute. Whatever Alan's sisters might choose to think, she was in fact sick with worry about her daughter; but the world would never know.

"It must be so dreadful for you to sit there and listen to them say such spiteful things," Eleanor pointed out.

"They can say what they want," replied Peggy. "It couldn't matter less to me." She laughed pleasantly to her sister-in-law, adding, "I pay no attention whatsoever."

Fourteen

The soft ending of the concerto's slow movement was just dying out when the door to Mrs. Altman's box opened and Gerald slipped into the anteroom. He had intended just to take off his overcoat and sit down without disturbing anyone, but inevitably there was a little commotion on his arrival. Onstage Francescatti closed his eyes as he drew out the exquisite final notes, and when he lifted his bow the audience exhaled a collective sigh. The finale began without pause, and Gerald had to edge his way into the little gold seat in the box while the music continued. Social imperatives clashed with art. Mrs. Altman felt obliged to turn and greet her son graciously, much as she regretted the disruption. Eleanor gave him an icy smile and muttered, "Glad you could make it," between her teeth. Alan nodded, taking note of Gerald's troubled look— *very* troubled look. Peggy saw no reason whatsoever why she should acknowledge her brother's entrance. He was no busier than anyone else, and there was no earthly reason why he couldn't get places on time. The Heymanns predictably made a great fuss over him, and Mrs. Heymann even started up a conversation as though they were at a dinner party and not Carnegie Hall. Peggy, who always thought Mrs. Heymann was a horse's ass, had no qualms about shushing her. Mrs. Heymann turned red, caught between playing up to one Altman and offending another. Mr. Heymann was sleeping too soundly to pay any attention even to Gerald.

Carl was seated next to his grandmother in the front row of the box. He leaned forward in a desperate attempt to blot out his uncle's entrance and the attendant flurry. It caused him real pain to hear a masterpiece desecrated. He loved nothing more than coming to concerts with his grandmother, but it wasn't worth it if boors and philistines ruined the music. A man in the next box, if it could be believed, actually leaned across the velvet-covered partition in order to shake Gerald's hand. He must have wanted something awfully badly. Meanwhile, Mendelssohn was rolling in his grave.

The concerto reached its glorious conclusion without further opposition from box 45, although it had to be said that the audience as a whole was having a particularly bronchial night of it. Nevertheless, Francescatti received warm applause, and Lenny went into raptures on the podium. Mrs. Altman beamed and said to Carl, "That was charming, don't you think?" He thought it was a good deal more than that, but he didn't correct his grandmother. He didn't even need the warning frown from Peggy.

Everyone got up for the intermission except for Mrs. Altman. She made the slightest of adjustments in the position of her chair so that she could receive visitors without having to move. Maurice Heymann, of course, bolted for the bar; no great loss. Peggy shooed Fanny Heymann out of the box as well, knowing that Mrs. Altman would want to be rid of her but would never say so in a million years. Peggy could not for the life of her understand why her mother felt she had to be kind to every soul in New York, including the deadliest bores. The Heymanns had nothing whatsoever to contribute; but Peggy said nothing on that score.

Carl thought his grandmother might like it if he discussed the performance with her, and he offered to stay. She told him he couldn't be sweeter, but he should go along and enjoy himself. She thought he might like a Coke. Peggy thought it would be nice to keep Carl company and introduce him to all the people he would run into and wouldn't have the slightest idea who they were; generally second cousins. Eleanor stayed with Mrs. Altman, and Gerald asked Alan for a word.

Poor Alan! He had been so looking forward to intermission. He liked to hurry around to all the lobbies and talk to as many of the people he had spotted during the first half as was humanly possible for one man without roller skates. He would have liked Carl to go with him so he could introduce him to everyone. "You know our youngest, of course; quite a musician himself, you know. Oh, yes, he's studied at Juilliard for years!" But Gerald upset all that. And it wasn't even his case! He'd been fired. Let Gerald interrupt Jack Bernstein's evenings.

But he said nothing, and went along docilely. The two men found an out-of-the-way staircase behind a fire door where they could talk in relative privacy. Except for the occasional musician in tuxedo who came by on his way to the men's room, they had no interruptions. Gerald came right to the point. "They're printing an article in the *Journal* tomorrow morning about calling in the notes of the Abbott estate," he said gravely, "and they're laying the whole thing at our doorstep."

"I don't suppose they're too wide of the mark there," Alan observed.

"That's neither here nor there." Gerald brushed him aside. "The point is they're saying some extremely derogatory things about me. In the *Journal!*"

"What are they saying?" Alan wanted to know.

Gerald glanced around nervously to see if anyone was lurking about within earshot. "They've seized on this business of the surcharge on the interest rates. They're acting as if we're the first ones in history ever to impose it. They're using the word *gouging.*" He paused, and said in hushed, outraged tones, "They're using the word *usury!*"

Alan waited, thinking there was something really grievous coming. Seeing there was not, he said, "It's not very pleasant, Gerry, but if that's all—"

"Pleasant!" Gerald exploded. "It's libelous, that's what it is!"

"Well, I hardly think—"

"Alan, God damn it, it's libelous, that's all there is to it. It's scurrilous, it's unfair, it's false, and it's sure as hell defamatory. If that isn't libel, I'd damn well like to know what is!"

"I suppose in the strictest construction of the term—"

"Strictest construction, my ass!" Gerald shouted. "It's actionable, and I'm going to sue."

Alan groaned inwardly. Aside from the language, which wasn't fit even for a deserted stairwell, he deplored his brother-in-law's hotheadedness. "Gerry, I'd advise you to go slow on this. I haven't read this thing, of course, nor have you, I suspect. Even if it says what you say it says, libel isn't the easiest thing in the world to prove. It's very difficult to impeach a statement like that, even if it's in some ways untrue. The word itself is a very loose term. What you're objecting to, I take it, is that it has a certain, I'll grant you, objectionable connotation. That might absolutely be the case, but you can't collect damages for insinuations."

"This isn't an insinuation, dammit, Alan! This is anti-Semitism!"

"I don't say it isn't. What I would say is it would be difficult to prove in open court. And if you could, the damage to your reputation would be far worse than one article could ever inflict. The smart thing for you to do at this point is to let it go. If you start yelling and screaming and giving out counterstatements and threatening action, they'll all smell blood and the sharks will really circle then."

"What do you suggest I do, then?"

"Nothing. Ignore it."

"Ignore it! Alan, they're turning this into an alley fight."

"You can hardly be surprised about that, Gerry. If I remember correctly, you said you were ready for one."

"I wasn't ready to be slandered in *The Wall Street Journal*."

"Maybe you ought to have been ready."

That gave Gerald pause. But after only brief reflection, he said, "There must be some way of getting at them. Why should we come out the bad guys all the time? They've been calling Jews dirty names for centuries now and getting away with it. Why should they get off scot-free?"

"If you win the proxy fight, the names won't bother you so much. You can cry all the way to the bank."

"It won't do, Alan," Gerald insisted. "Here's *The Wall Street Journal*, which I would have thought would above all stay neutral in a thing like this, allowing itself to be used for a smear. I can't stand by and allow that."

A thought struck Alan. "Have you wondered why they're doing this?" he asked.

Gerald looked puzzled. "I don't know. Does it make any difference?"

"I think it may," Alan replied. "Look at it this way: Why would they bother with this sort of stuff? What are they trying to accomplish? They can't seriously think it would affect the proxy situation. No one holding stock gives a damn about this sort of thing. It's all very fishy. I think it's a smoke screen. I think they did this to get your attention, which they did. Which leads me to ask, what are they trying to hide?"

Gerald asked, "You think they're trying to hide something?"

"I don't know, but it's worth looking into. If I were in your shoes,

I'd do a little digging of my own. You never know what you might turn up. Who knows?" Alan added with a little smile, "you might be able to feed the *Journal* some material for a follow-up article."

"I still would like to sue the bastards," Gerald said.

"I wouldn't advise that. Not now, at least. You never know, you may need them yet. They owe you one." The bell rang for the second half. "We'd better get back. I'm not sure how much Mother appreciates having us walk in late."

Gerald frowned. "I don't know that I feel much like listening to music just now."

"It might be just the thing," Alan suggested. "Shall we?"

They went down into the main corridor and came up the public staircase. Alan managed to salvage something of the intermission by lingering at the top of the stairs, where he could at least say hello to people who were returning to their seats. They were only a fraction of his acquaintances in the hall, but he consoled himself that one could accomplish only so much in a finite period of time. He waited until they were actually blinking the lights before scurrying back to the box, and he took his seat just as Bernstein was returning to the stage. As the conductor acknowledged the applause, Mrs. Heymann asked giddily, "What are they giving us now?" She had a program on her lap.

Mrs. Altman leaned back and whispered, "Shostakovich. Carl tells me it's lovely." That wasn't quite the word he had used to describe the severe piece they were about to hear, but Mrs. Heymann wrinkled her nose anyway. She didn't care for modern music. She shuffled her chair, trying to settle herself more comfortably for the ordeal. Gerald rubbed his face with both hands, and Eleanor looked anxiously at him. She knew she should have insisted that he go home at intermission. This thing was killing him.

No one at Meyer House knew about the engagement. Joan made no particular attempt to conceal it; on the other hand, there was no reason to mention it to anyone there. She in general avoided talking about herself or her family at work. It was another world, after all, and she thought it would be in poor taste to bring it up at the settlement house. She might possibly have mentioned it to Jenna, who after all traveled with her every day, but she didn't. Her relationship with Jenna was friendly enough, but it had never deepened. Neither of them confided in the other. The differences in their backgrounds, their experiences, and particularly their financial situations prevented the kind of total sympathy that is necessary for intimacy. Jenna knew of Johnny's existence in the same vague way Joan knew the names of boys Jenna dated. It seemed easiest to leave it at that, rather than trying to explain the peculiarities of a betrothal even Joan didn't completely comprehend.

Kevin: now there was a problem. There wasn't enough history to their relationship that Joan felt any obligation; still, she wondered if in fairness she oughtn't to tell him. She didn't fear his jealousy. She knew he would pass the information off as irrelevant, unimportant. He would have no compunctions about sleeping with another man's fiancée. In itself the knowledge would gratify him. Still, there was danger in his knowing. He might not have the slightest wish for an emotional involvement, but he wouldn't tolerate being second fiddle. He wouldn't put up with it, not for a minute. Joan kept her silence.

Even in her silence she had to face the harsh and inescapable fact that she was engaged to one man and sleeping with another. The engagement might be unconventional and the sleeping not as yet an established institution. Still, they didn't go together well. She went from Kevin's apartment to her own with the smell of him still lingering, the taste of him sharp, the surprising roughness of his chin scraped into the hollow above her collarbone. While she was with him she thought of no one else. Yet she walked out the door to responsibilities, expectations, a life he played no part in. She couldn't shrug them off, and she couldn't avoid the awareness of her duplicity. She hadn't had to lie to Johnny yet, but truth was becoming shallow, irrelevant; the whole thing was a lie. In her guilt she began to see Johnny as impossibly constrained and deferential to the point of weakness. Being with him was becoming more and more claustrophobic.

Keeping this all to herself was ultimately too difficult for her to bear. Joan was not a solitary, inward person. She lived among others, her life was reflected in their regard for her, she only really existed in the company of her friends. The only person who knew anything of her secret was Carl. She hadn't spoken to him about it since that night in the kitchen. Needing someone to confide in, she turned to the least probable person she knew: Harlow.

Harlow was an odd choice for any number of reasons, but he was also inevitable, given his unique position. He was often at the apartment when Kevin was out, and he was easy for her to talk to. Perhaps because of his very instability, he appealed to her as a confidant. She could pour out her heart to him with the comforting illusion that his soggy brain retained only a fraction of what passed through it. He had the makings of an ideal listener.

Moreover, they had plenty of opportunity to talk, since Joan and Kevin came to the apartment separately now. After that first Saturday, Joan had decided they couldn't be seen leaving Meyer House together. Both of them, in different ways, were objects of curiosity and gossip around the settlement house, and if they were linked together they would be envied and resented. Even that would have been manageable; but not rumors flying uptown. She wasn't prepared to let that happen. They could be explained: there are few stains that can't be removed somehow; but anyone looking closely can see where the spot had once been, and to all intents and purposes, the fabric is as good as ruined.

So she resorted to stealth. Her medical condition provided an excuse for leaving in the middle of the day (if you have to lie, use the available truth). She would slip away at lunchtime and find Kevin still in bed. He would make love to her before he was fully awake. She liked the musty odor of his somnolent body, the crush of his dead weight, the sudden urgency of his dream-kindled lust. But it wasn't always easy to get away, and she did feel guilty abandoning the children for an afternoon shack-up. More often she went after work. She would give Jenna some excuse for staying late, and then slip through the evening throng like a fugitive to his place. She was no longer afraid to walk those miserable streets. She wondered if she was degenerating, shedding her sense of danger along with that of propriety. Maybe she hadn't yet become a fallen woman, but she was on the way down.

She would let herself into the apartment. Harlow was almost always there, listening to his weird music, puffing away at a joint, flowing through various stages of euphoria. As far as she could tell, Joan had never seen him cold sober. He could always talk, though. He was never so far gone that he couldn't talk. He had a mordant view of the world and an endless collection of stories about himself, and once he started in there was no stopping him. It was impossible to distinguish the true tales from those he invented. For all she knew, his entire life could have been fictional. She never saw him outside that room. Once he passed out the door, he ceased to exist for her. He might as well have been a figment of her imagination.

They would sit together, the two of them, in the gathering dusk. Harlow would smoke away, supplementing his pot with liquor, pills, junk he crammed up his nose, and on one occasion he used a hookah, an apparatus that went well with his oriental proclivities. Joan never saw him eat. Drugs were, to her knowledge, his sole nutrition. Despite his apparent poverty, he always offered to share whatever he had with her. She had made up her mind from the start that she would never take anything from him. She feared she would get hooked if she started. She had the idea that once under the influence of his drugs, her mind would snap and she might never come out of it.

But she did talk to him. She told him more than she had ever told anyone. He never commented, never judged, only listened. If he said anything in return, it was only stories of his own life, or imagination. He would play her records of strange, monotonous Indian music, and they would sit there in the near dark, spellbound by the hypnotic plucking of sitars. Gradually, Joan would fall into a trance virtually as profound as Harlow's. She felt so peaceful that when Kevin came in she almost resented his intrusion.

He was not to be denied, however. He would barge in, flushed and sweaty, sweep the needle off the record with a sickening scrape, and kick Harlow out without the slightest civility. He treated Harlow like dirt. He would start his sexual preparations before Harlow even got out the door, slamming around the apartment, cursing that he couldn't find his rubbers, which turned up among his socks or in some discarded pair of pants, never anywhere sensible or sanitary. If Harlow was too slow to leave, he would start stripping down right in front of him. He would probably have gone right at it with Harlow looking on, and loved it too. He made no pretense of being in the throes of unbridled passion, only of impatience and a refusal to be deterred from what he wanted immediately. Joan might have liked to believe she was the cause of all this ardor, but she didn't fool herself. It had nothing to do with her, specifically. Any female would have done. She didn't protest. Kevin was not a man to protest to. He conducted himself strictly as he pleased, take it or leave it. He would have considered politeness to be soft, unmanly. She was there, he implied, under his conditions, and she could go if she didn't like them. He called all the shots. He didn't want anything from her. He needed nothing from any woman; from any person, if it came to that. Despite his vanity, he never looked for approval. He had supreme confidence in his virility and his power to excite, and no sign Joan could give or withhold would affect him one way or the other.

She had no recourse. She knew it was one-sided and untenable, but there was nothing to do about it. She couldn't risk being cut off by him. She had succumbed to an addiction far more dangerous than anything Harlow could draw her into. Her fix could not be bought or stolen, and its availability lay completely beyond her control.

Strangely, the nature of their lovemaking changed. As their encounters grew more frequent, they also became shorter and blunter. That wasn't Kevin's doing, though. He was surprisingly correct in his observance of postcoital etiquette, and in fact he usually wanted to prolong their intercourse. Joan was the one who cut it short. She didn't realize at first what was the matter. She thought it had to do with the sordid circumstances, the undisguised carnality, the knowledge of exploitation on both sides. Then the bleakness of the apartment depressed her, she thought it might be that. Only gradually, reluctantly, did she recognize that immediately after they coupled her desire was transformed into disgust. Kevin's body, which had only moments before sent her into a frenzy of arousal, underwent a metamorphosis. The very attributes that had attracted her—his thick shoulders, his sleek haunches, his aggressiveness—repelled her. His face struck her as that of a thug. His muscular odor, once compelling, now offended her. She couldn't bear to look at his naked genitals. As soon as she decently could, she would dress and leave. Once away, her repugnance would fade, and when she saw him the next day at Meyer House she felt only intense desire. A word, a glance, or a gesture would ignite her afresh and she would burn until they were locked together again.

Her reaction seemed to her inexplicable, possibly pathological. She tried to encapsulate her trysts with him, isolate them as much as possible from the rest of her life. At Meyer House she could avoid him much of the time. Their paths didn't need to cross. She stopped going to the cafeteria at times he was likely to be there. She changed the subject if his name came up. At home, no one knew of his existence, and she could more easily put him out of her mind. When she did think of him, he was blurred and insubstantial, as if he had appeared to her in a half-forgotten dream.

One afternoon, when she was at his apartment waiting for him to return, she idly took the reefer Harlow was smoking and inhaled several times. She did it without thinking, and was surprised at herself. Despite her fears, she didn't go crazy. In fact she felt no different at all. All that she noticed was a heightened sense of unreality about where she was and what she was doing. When Kevin came in, she became agitated as always; but the intercourse was more pleasurable, and afterward she felt no reaction, only a pleasant indifference. She stayed longer than usual. During the subway ride uptown her mind was completely blank. She emerged into the familiar surroundings of Park Avenue like an amnesiac who has just woken up and doesn't recall how he got there. What memory she had of Kevin was mild and innocent.

The next time she repeated the experiment, and got the same result. After that, she asked Harlow to leave her a joint if he wasn't going to be there when she came. It was only to help her through, she was firm about that. The fact that she felt no direct effect from the marijuana reassured her that she wasn't susceptible to it, and she never took anything stronger. She knew she could easily do without it. She only took it at all because she knew she didn't need it. On weekends, when she didn't see Kevin, she did fine without it, proving—if proof were needed—that she had no addiction whatsoever. If the weekends were bad, that was because she couldn't see Kevin. It was he she craved, not any drug.

At the end of the Gutheim apartment down toward Lexington Avenue was a room that when the children were young had served as a playroom. All the major toys were kept there—forts, castles, electric trains, blocks—and there was a table where they were served breakfast and sometimes supper. When the children got older, it was done over into a room where everyone could lounge around, and where all but the most formal company was entertained. It was comfortably arranged, with squishy armchairs and a chaise longue, and ottomans all over the place since no one in the family could read so much as a letter without putting their feet up. The walls were cheerful with Kandinsky and Delaunay, the upholstery all bright yellows and oranges. Underneath the bookshelves were cabinets for games, stationery, pads, pencils, photo albums from many years back—no one took pictures since the last governess had left—and a candy drawer. On top of the cabinets were piled the latest books, read and unread, and recent issues of the magazines the family took: *Life, Time, The New Yorker, Sports Illustrated, Saturday Review, Art News, The New Republic, National Geographic,* and *Cue.* Nobody read the *National Geographic,* but Alan thought it important to support. The room would have been called a sitting room except that Peggy couldn't stand the name. "It always sounds as though the only thing you're allowed to do there is sit. If people want to sit, that's fine with me, but if they want to do something else, why on earth shouldn't they? I don't like the feeling that someone else has already decided what you should do." Peggy was a great libertarian. Gutheims could hardly have a "den," or a "rec room," so it continued to be called the playroom.

Peggy and Joan were sitting there the day following Cecile's dinner party. They were by themselves. Phil was at Betsy's, ostensibly studying; Carl was in his room, really studying; and Alan was late getting back from his Saturday walk. The two of them were reading: Joan had the latest *New Yorker*, and Peggy was looking through the evening paper, which the maid had just brought in. On the radio, a Wagnerian soprano was making a terrific fuss.

Peggy looked up and wrinkled her face at the horrendous sound; but she didn't turn down the radio, which would have meant getting up from the chaise she was sitting in. "Your father's missing his opera," she said.

Joan didn't reply right away. She was absorbed in the magazine, and hadn't really heard what Peggy said. "Mmm?" she asked.

"I said, I was worried your father's going to miss his opera. Aren't you uncomfortable like that?" Joan had her legs tucked up under her instead of stretched out, which Peggy would have thought would be much more comfortable. They were sure to go to sleep. "Wouldn't you rather have an ottoman?"

"I'm fine," Joan said. She looked up and asked, "Do we have to have that on, if Daddy's not here?" she asked.

"Of course not, dear," Peggy said, getting up to turn off the radio. "The only reason it's on is for our enjoyment. If we don't like it, what earthly reason is there for keeping it on?"

Joan thought she had been selfish. "If you want it on, I can live."

"It couldn't matter less to me," Peggy assured her. "I couldn't be happier with it off." That was true. She was delighted to have her daughter's company, that was all she cared about.

"Where is Daddy, anyway?" Joan asked, noticing the time.

"He said he might be late because he was going to pay a call on Sophie Edelman."

"Jesus!" Joan exclaimed. "Why on earth?"

"I asked him the same thing. Your aunts have been carrying on like maniacs about Sophie, and won't give him any peace until he calls on her. Of course, they won't give him any peace then, either, so what's the point?"

"What's the matter with Sophie Edelman?" Joan asked.

"She hasn't been at all well. Aunt Marjorie says she doesn't always know where she is these days. Of course, if you ask me, she's never known where she is."

Joan rolled her eyes to the ceiling and then looked back at the magazine. She smiled at a cartoon.

"I'll be a lot happier when this Bar Association thing is decided," Peggy commented. "Your father, you know, is being considered for the presidency."

Joan made a noise that indicated she knew. How could she not know? It was discussed endlessly.

"I'd love him to get it. He's dying to have it, and he's worked terribly hard for them."

Joan made the same noise, this time to indicate agreement.

"If anyone deserves it, he certainly does," Peggy observed, and she bent to the paper once again. "Oh, for heaven's sake!" she cried. "Richard Hudnut died. Remind me to tell your father when he comes in."

Joan looked up absently, and after a minute registered what Peggy had just told her. "Who on earth is Richard Hudnut?" she asked.

"He was a partner of your Grandfather Gutheim's. He retired from the firm ages ago. In all honesty, if you had asked me I would have said he died years ago. His wife was one of the first woman judges on the family court in this city. A really capable woman. Something of a battle-ax, I always thought, and a perfect *horror* to look at. She had one of those pinched-up faces that always look as if she had the sun coming in her eyes"—Peggy screwed up her face to show Joan—"but she really accomplished a great deal. He himself was no great ball of fire. He was a little wisp of a man"—she thinned her voice to approximate a vocal wisp—"who looked as though a strong wind would blow him away. But perfectly harmless. I hope your father won't feel he has to go to the funeral. If I let him go to every funeral he thinks he ought to, he wouldn't have time for anything else."

Joan had stopped listening. She was reading a review in the magazine and only heard enough to know when to murmur and nod. Peggy saw that she wasn't being listened to, and went back to the paper.

After a minute Joan looked up and said, *"The New Yorker* gives *A Raisin in the Sun* a good write-up. I'm dying to see it."

"Just let me know when you want to go, dear. I'll be only too happy to get you the tickets. Daddy and I are seeing it at some benefit or other, I think the Urban League, if you want to go then."

"Oh, that's nice, but I'll probably go with Johnny."

"Just let me know which night you want tickets," Peggy said.

"Mmm," Joan replied, slightly less eager to go than before. She had stopped at an ad for a dazzling Steuben piece done in the shape of a gothic arch with choirboys singing at the bottom and angels hovering over. Two thousand eight hundred dollars. Who would spend that kind of money on a piece of glass? she wondered.

The phone rang. Peggy picked it up on the first ring. She asked who was calling, covered the mouthpiece, and said to Joan, "It's for you. Donna Something-or-other." Joan looked puzzled. She got up and went to the door. "You can talk right here. It won't bother me in the slightest," Peggy offered, but Joan either didn't hear her or chose not to hear her.

As soon as she heard voices talking on the extension, Peggy hung up the receiver. She turned back to the paper, but she was preoccupied and didn't take in anything she read. She continued to turn the pages, and was surprised to find herself already in the editorials before she had read the gossip columns. She told herself she was better off skipping them. Still, there was always the outside chance one might miss something written about a friend. Although, of course, the columnists confined themselves pretty much to café society, people who did nothing, contributed nothing, and, on those rare occasions when Peggy encountered them, had absolutely nothing to say.

She reluctantly turned back, and was halfway through Earl Wilson when Joan came back into the room. A storm cloud had gathered. When she had left the room she had been reasonably cheerful, if exhausted; now she looked angry and upset. It must have been bad news, Peggy thought. But what? Lamartine surely wouldn't call on a Saturday afternoon, or if he did he would certainly speak first to Peggy. Then she remembered it hadn't been Lamartine, or anyone medical. It had been a girl. Peggy couldn't remember the name, except that she knew she hadn't recognized it, or the voice either. Hannah? Something of that sort.

Joan didn't return to her chair, but stood at the doorway looking shaken. "That was Donna Something-or-other on the phone," she said. It was obvious she was angry, although Peggy couldn't for the life of her figure out why.

"I don't think I—" she began.

"Her name happens to be Jenna Rollins. She also happens to be the person you hired—I certainly don't expect you to keep track of all the people you *hire*, certainly not get their names straight, especially if they're *Negro*, for God's sake—but she just happens to be the person you hired to take me to work every day."

"Darling, I can see you're upset, but I really haven't the slightest idea why."

"You haven't?" Joan challenged. "You couldn't guess?"

"Don't you think it would be easier if you simply told me?" Peggy asked. She had never known Joan to be this openly rude before, and it worried her. Not the rudeness, of course—that couldn't matter less; but the fact that Joan was losing control.

"I'll tell you why I'm upset. Jenna just called me up to tell me that she wouldn't be able to come and pick me up on Monday. I said it was nice of her to let me know, but she certainly shouldn't feel she had to do it every day. She said, oh, but she did. 'After all,' she said, 'your mother's paying me to do it.' I nearly died! I've never been so ashamed in my life!"

"But darling, what on earth is there to be ashamed about? Besides which, I'm very puzzled why you should be so upset about this just now. It's been going on for weeks. It's nothing new."

"I never had any idea you were *paying* her to come to work with me!"

"I'm sorry if you didn't know. I always assumed you did."

"How would I know?" Joan was on the verge of tears. "You never told me. You never tell me anything. You just sneak around my back and do what you please."

Peggy was stung. "I'm sorry, but this was not done behind your back. In fact, I distinctly remember discussing with you that I was going to speak to Martin about it."

"What you call discussing is always you telling me what you're going to do, so where is there any discussion? Besides which, you *never* said anything about money, so don't tell me you did!"

"I'm sorry you're so upset about it, darling, but I must say it never even entered into my head that you wouldn't know she was being paid. Naturally, Martin asked someone he thought you would find congenial, but it never occurred to me that you thought she was doing it for nothing, or else I would have mentioned it to you. I had not interest in hiding it. I just never gave it a thought."

"You should have. You should have given it a thought, and you should have asked me if I wanted someone hired to walk me to work, like a dog. Or doesn't what I want matter?"

"Of course it does. Although I think you're being a little dramatic about it. I don't see that it would have made the slightest bit of difference if you'd known she was being paid, she still would have had to come with you."

"No, she wouldn't. I wouldn't have allowed it. I would have quit the job first."

"I can't think of anything that would have been more foolish," Peggy said.

"Why is everything I do foolish?" Joan cried indignantly.

"Now just a minute, sweetie. I've never said everything you do is foolish. I don't think it, so how could I have said it?"

"You don't think it?" Joan asked. "Only that it's foolish for me to want to stay in college when I'm 'so sick,' and it's foolish for me to get tired when I'm 'so sick,' and it's foolish of me even to care that you're hiring some flunky—naturally she has no name, how could she?—to walk me to work in the morning, as though I was an imbecile who can't be trusted to cross the street alone. Every time I've tried to do something on my own, you've wheeled and dealed until I either have to give it up, or else it gets watered down to where you want it to be."

"Darling, that simply isn't the case." Peggy's own composure was beginning to unravel. "I don't want to get you more upset than you already are, but I do have to say it isn't the case and it never has been."

"Don't worry about making me upset, please. It's what you do that makes me upset, not what you say. And it is so the case, it always has been. You never wanted me to go to Bennington, and when I finally got there you couldn't wait until you could get me away from it. I'm sure you were overjoyed when I got sick and you had your excuse to get me down here where you could have me under your thumb again."

"That's a terrible thing to say! It's very hard for me to deal with you when you make that sort of accusation."

"Then don't deal with me. Maybe I don't want to be dealt with. Maybe I'd just like to be left alone to run my own life my own way."

Peggy didn't like to leave such distortions unanswered, but Joan simply had to be calmed down. "There's no point in arguing the matter when you're overwrought. You know perfectly well you run your life to an extent most girls your age wouldn't even dream of doing. In fact, I've been criticized quite a bit for letting you have things your way too much

of the time, not that that's either here nor there, because I pay no attention whatsoever to what people think about how I raise my children.
There never was any question in my mind that you should run your
own life, and you always have. You've done what you wanted to. I never
had any objections to Bennington, as a matter of fact. It wasn't the
college I would have picked for you, but I didn't pick it. You did, and I
didn't offer the slightest objection when you did. Not the slightest."

"No, you didn't. You never do. You don't object. You just go behind
the scenes and make good and sure everything comes out the way you
intend it to. Of course, you're not so stupid as to order me to do this or
that. But you know you never leave me or anyone else alone until I do
what you want, in the end."

"That's just not true," Peggy said. "You do as you please, and you
always have."

"Oh, I've heard that a thousand times. The party line. In fact I do
what everyone else wants me to, and especially what you want me to.
You've always let the boys have their way—Carl could eat his way into
the grave and you wouldn't say a word—but with me you always have
to have the final say. If I object, you take what I say and twist it around
until it sounds completely idiotic, and then you can tell everyone how
foolish I'm being. When Daddy comes home, he'll want to know what's
wrong with me, and you'll say, 'Oh, who ever knows what that *child* gets
upset about. She made no sense whatsoever.' That's what you always
say, I make no sense, you haven't the slightest idea what I'm talking
about. 'If you'll just tell me calmly what it is you want, dear,' that's what
you always say, and it sounds oh so *reasonable*. I mean, no one can blame
you if your daughter is so *incoherent*, you can't even tell what she wants.
Of course, you have to decide on whatever it is I would decide if I
weren't so incoherent. You figure out what I really want, and then go
ahead and do it, get me a paid companion, or whatever it was I wanted
in the first place. You always know better than I do what I want. You
know better what I think, what I feel, everything. You know better!"
She was sobbing with bitterness and rage.

"Darling, I do think it would help if you would calm down a bit,
and we could talk about these things a little more reasonably. For one
thing, I can't think that you're this upset simply because I arranged to
have this young lady—I forget her name—"

"Jenna, Mother! Jenna. Is that such a difficult name?"

"Jenna, then. I may not have specifically told you she was being paid, but if you're old enough to run your life, as you seem to want to do, then you're old enough to realize certain facts of life, one of which is, if you expect people to go out of their way for you, you have to make it worth their while. It doesn't always have to be a matter of money, you don't necessarily buy everything you want; but there has to be some sense of reciprocation. You can't expect a perfect stranger to do a rather big favor for you purely out of her goodwill. It would be unrealistic to expect her to, and frankly I think it was unrealistic of you to assume she wasn't being paid."

"I knew it! I knew sooner or later it would work out to being my fault, something wrong with me. Unrealistic. I was fascinated to know what it would be, because you always find something, I'll say that for you. Something about the other person. You're never the one at fault. You've never made a mistake in your life. Oh, no. It's just that I'm . . . unrealistic. Either unrealistic, or foolish, or immature, or thought-less . . ."

"Darling, I've never said you were thoughtless, I've never—"

"You have!" Joan yelled in anguish. "Or if you haven't, you've thought it! No one can ever pin anything on you. You've got an answer for everything. You're always right! You're never wrong! If only every-one would just do what you want, and save themselves so much trouble! Just turn their lives over to you. You'd do such a much better job of it than we could ever hope to do!" Tears streaming down her face, she ran out of the room, leaving Peggy shaken, bewildered, terribly hurt by the unfairness and ingratitude and the inevitable grain of truth blown up into an essentially unjust indictment.

A few moments after Joan's door slammed, Alan's voice was heard in the hallway, singing in his unmelodious rasp:

> *"East Side, West Side,*
> *All around the town . . ."*

He appeared in the same doorway his daughter had just vacated, and, rubbing his hands, sucked his breath in sharply and said, *"Nu?"*

Peggy made a face. She hated him to use that kind of expression, but she said nothing about it. Summoning up all her reserve, she said, in the calmest imaginable voice: "Richard Hudnut died."

On Monday, Joan set out grimly for work. She left the apartment house by herself and didn't return the doorman's good-bye. The sky was a dismal gray. It was the first of the unrelenting days of winter, without snow or wind, but with a damp cold that penetrates and grips and eventually wears one down. Fewer people than usual were out on the streets, and they were too intent on shielding themselves from the cold to smile at one another. The subway platform was deserted, which meant that a train had just pulled out. The next one was a long time in coming. The transit workers were staging a slowdown to try to get their contract concessions, but a strike seemed inevitable. Two express trains charged toward each other on the center tracks. The local still didn't come. The small band of people waiting grew until at length the platform became choked with a restive crowd. People were talking about being late to work. Several leaned out over the tracks, peering anxiously for signs of the oncoming downtown train. Rumors of tie-ups, accidents, a fire on the tracks began to circulate. Joan waited without interest. It made no difference to her whether she was early or late or didn't get there at all. They would carry on as well without her as with her. She was superfluous. Work held no interest for her. All she looked forward to was the end of the day, when she could go home and lie down. She no longer took any pleasure in her job. She would go to Kevin's after, or not, it didn't matter. She went out of habit now. It did nothing for her. Pretty soon she would stop. Johnny would be waiting for her like a faithful old dog. She supposed they would get married soon. She didn't care about that either. She was sleepwalking through her days. Nothing held any meaning for her. The holidays were coming up. She wished they were already over.

There was still no train. The crowd was becoming agitated. The platform wasn't wide enough for the growing accumulation of passengers. Joan, who had paid no attention to what was going on, was near to the tracks. She pulled herself out of a daze and saw that she was being pushed slowly but relentlessly toward the edge. She thought it wasn't possible that she could be shoved off the platform, but she found herself slipping closer to them. She couldn't identify the force that was moving her. No one else seemed to be alarmed. A tinge of fear gripped her and she saw that she would be thrown onto the tracks. She wanted to cry out for help, but her voice stuck in her throat and she couldn't squeeze the sound out. Fear progressed to terror, and she became aware, in addition to everything else, that her heart was pounding violently. The familiar dreadful dizziness filled her head. She took refuge in the thought, This isn't happening to me; I am dreaming this; any moment I will wake up.

But the dream—if it was a dream—wouldn't end. She remained poised precariously at the edge of the platform. In the distance the rumble of the approaching train was finally heard. The crowd's excitement grew as the train neared, and they surged toward the track. Joan felt herself teetering, and saw a man running wildly at her. He means to throw me over, she thought to herself. He sees me in danger and intends to finish the job. She tried to scream but still couldn't summon any sound. The man was shouting. The noise of the crowd was so loud, with the train bearing down on them, that she couldn't hear what he was saying until he was almost upon her. He was yelling, "Stop her! She's going to jump! Someone stop her!" It was a ruse, of course, since he meant to throw her off himself. She swayed, trying to find a place to escape him, but the crowd wouldn't yield. The train screamed by, grazing her arm, and she lost consciousness.

When she came to, the crowd had gone and the train was no longer there. They had stretched her out on a bench at the wall, underneath an ad for Ringling Bros.–Barnum & Bailey Circus. A few people were staring at her. She recognized among them the man who had rushed at her.

"He saved your life," an elderly woman told her. "You was going to jump, and he pulled you back. You owe your life to him." She nodded in agreement with herself.

Joan stared at her, then at the others. "I wasn't going to jump," she said. She was surprised at the flatness of her voice. She sounded drugged.

"You looked like you were going to jump," the man explained apologetically. "I couldn't tell for sure. I was trying to get to you, but I would have been too late. I think the train saved you. It brushed by before you fell. You weren't trying to jump?"

She shook her head. She didn't want to talk. Her face hurt. Maybe she had hit it when she fell, she didn't know. She didn't imagine she was dreaming anymore. The man looked vaguely familiar, as people look in dreams, appearing as they do from some other part of one's life; but she couldn't place him.

"I'll be all right," she said, wanting them all to go away and leave her alone. "I'm fine."

They didn't believe her, she could see that. They thought she had been about to jump and had been rescued from the abyss temporarily. It is well known that a would-be suicide, having been rescued from death, will want to live again and is in no immediate danger of another attempt; but that unless something is done, eventually she will make a second attempt, and if that fails, a third, and so on until finally she succeeds.

As Joan gradually revived the onlookers all walked away slowly, shaking their heads sadly. The last to go was the man who had run toward her. He departed reluctantly. He was clearly not reassured by her robot-like repetition of the words *I'll be all right*. Which was all she would say, except that once or twice she added, "I'm fine."

In front of Low Library on the Columbia campus sits Alma Mater, an irresistible figure for generations of graduation photographs, collegiate pranks, and pigeons. Phil had chosen the statue for a meeting place because he doubted that Dickie Altman could find any other place in the university. But it was already five minutes past two, and he wondered if the task of getting himself anywhere on time was too much for Dickie. The day was warm, for December, but not that warm, and Phil had too much to do to wait for his cousin. He wouldn't have agreed to the meeting at all had it not been for the urgency in Dickie's voice when he'd called the night before; that, plus his own curiosity. It's not every day one is told, "I've got to see you. I can't talk about it over the phone." Whatever Dickie's shortcomings, and they were many, he certainly had a flair for the melodramatic. Wild horses wouldn't have kept Phil from meeting him; but he'd had the presence of mind to name a time and place at his convenience. It should always be clear, Phil thought, who is doing whom a favor. Keeps accounts straight in the long run.

Dickie used to be an interesting figure, his continual scrapes a constant source of wonder and amusement. You never knew what he'd do next. The other Altmans were by comparison predictable in their troubles: Marian and her causes, Barbara and her men, Randy and any rule that got in his way. Dickie, by contrast, was versatile, one might almost say inventive. It was impossible to tell what he'd do next. But he was no longer a boy. More was at stake now than whether he got kicked out of another school, or made a fool of himself at a party. One of these days he would cause a full-fledged scandal. Phil only prayed he would wait until after Mr. Justice Klingor made his decision. Until then, it would be best to keep an eye on him.

Phil looked at the time and swore to himself. He had too much to do to waste the afternoon waiting for his cousin. He was on the verge of going back to the law library when Dickie came sauntering along, the picture of a man of leisure who hadn't a care in the world. As he approached he called, " 'Lo, Phil. They can't be serious about this, can they?" he asked, indicating the statue. "It is a joke, *n'est-ce pas?*"

"What's on your mind, Dickie?" Phil asked, unsmiling.

"Where can we talk?" Dickie replied. "I'd like a drink."

Phil looked at his watch. "I haven't got all the time in the world. Maybe we should talk, and you can have your drink at home." He nodded at a second-year law student he knew who came by on the path.

Dickie shrugged. "Whatever you say, Phil. Just if you don't mind finding a place where we're not likely to run into anyone. I'd be just as happy if it didn't get back to Father that we're talking. It could lead to all sorts of boring questions."

"How many people do you know up here, Dickie?" Phil asked skeptically.

It was too cold to stay outside for a talk of any length, so Phil took Dickie over to a coffeeshop on Amsterdam Avenue. It was a hangout of the beatnicks and motorcycle freaks, and not a place he frequented ordinarily. But they were unlikely to run into anyone either of them knew, and they could have a table to themselves for the afternoon, if they liked. Once they were seated and their coffee brought, Phil asked brusquely, "What can I do for you, Dickie?"

Dickie eyed him uneasily. It wasn't easy for him, coming like this to his younger cousin, and he wondered if there wasn't some less painful way out. Finding none, at least for the moment, he said, "I'm in a bit of trouble, as a matter of fact." Hoping that would suffice, he stopped.

When he didn't continue, Phil said, "If I'm going to be of any help to you at all, Dickie, I really think you're going to have to tell me what the trouble is, and it would save both of us a lot of time if you wouldn't beat around the bush."

Dickie flushed with anger. In the old days, when Phil corrected him, he would have overturned the game they were playing, or created some sort of mess. Now, his options were more limited. He could stalk out of the coffeeshop, or he could stay and humiliate himself. "It involves money," he said.

"It usually does," Phil commented, wondering, has Dickie gotten a girl into trouble? Is that why he wasn't going to Gerald?

"Actually, it has more to do with time than money. You know that investment I called you about a few weeks ago? Well, it was supposed to have paid off by now, but things have gotten stalled." Phil looked dubious. "It isn't what you think, Phil. This is no platinum mine, believe me. It's practically a sure thing. But I had to borrow the money to stake myself, and they're calling it in."

"Dickie, I get very nervous when I hear someone talk about a sure thing. Especially when they don't have the money to pay for it. If it was such a sure thing, why did you have to borrow the money? Your father would have put it up if it was a halfway decent investment."

"He wouldn't even listen to me!" Dickie cried. "He didn't have the decency to even ask me what it was for, he just went ahead and refused me, as he always does. When I tried to pry loose some of my money—my *own* money—all I got was the runaround. I tried to talk to Uncle Alan, and he wouldn't see me. You yourself wouldn't put in a dime, if you'll remember. You don't like risks, of course," he added bitterly.

"I don't like throwing my money away, no."

"Phil, believe me, this was a good deal. I'm just running out of time. If I can hang on a little longer, I'll be raking it in. If not, I'm off to the cleaners."

"How much are we talking about here?" Phil asked.

Dickie looked around to see if any of the nearby patrons were listening before replying. "Fifty thou," he said with a bravado Phil recognized from countless Monopoly games.

"And what is this investment, if it's not platinum mines?" Phil asked dubiously.

Dickie looked insulted. "I'd just as soon not say, if it's all the same to you," he huffed.

"Dickie, this isn't a game," Phil said wearily. "What's your money in?"

Dickie leaned closer and said, in a near whisper, "Abbott & Strawbridge."

"Jesus Christ, Dickie!" Phil exclaimed.

Dickie, thinking Phil was impressed, went on: "I got in on it in October, when it was going for a song. I could get out today with a nice profit if they hadn't suspended trading. As soon as this takeover goes through, I'll be sitting pretty. All I need is a little time."

"All you need is a few brains," Phil said contemptuously.

"This wasn't my fault! Everyone thought it'd be settled by now. No one thought it'd drag on like this. Father thought it'd be settled by Thanksgiving."

Phil brushed aside his excuses. "You bought this stock in October on, what, a hunch? You were shopping around for a good buy and just happened to choose an outfit on its last legs that by sheer coincidence was the target a month later of a takeover bid? With, more coincidence, your father's bank behind the acquiring corporation?"

Dickie still didn't catch on. "Of course I knew something was up. I keep my ears open," he said with pride.

Phil smiled grimly. "You can't do that," he informed his cousin. "That's inside information. You can't use it. It's against the law."

Dickie was unconcerned. "Who's to know?" he asked.

Phil assumed his sternest expression. "Dickie, it's a federal crime. You can go to jail for it."

Dickie's face, never a tower of strength at its best, sagged horribly. "That's just a theoretical possibility, I suppose. I mean, they don't really put people in jail for something like that, do they?"

"You're damn right they do. And they'd be delighted to do it for you, believe me. From what you've told me, they wouldn't have much trouble proving their case."

"Phil, honestly, I never thought I was breaking any law."

"Ignorance of the law is not a viable defense," Phil said coldly.

"Jesus, Phil, what should I do? You've got to help me."

Phil bristled at the suggestion of any such obligation; but all he said was "You'll have to tell your father."

"I'm not going to do that!" Dickie cried. "I'll do anything else, but I'm not telling him."

"There is no 'anything else.' You've put him in a very bad position by doing this, and he could be implicated. He has to know. If you won't tell him, I'll have to. But it would be a lot better if he heard it from you."

"I can't, Phil!" Dickie pleaded. "You don't know what it's like, having to listen to his eternal lectures. Also, this is hardly the time for me to be appealing to his so-called good side."

"You can't do anything about that now. You got yourself into this."

For a minute, Phil thought Dickie would break down, right there in the coffeeshop. But he managed to control himself, and only said, "If I do that, you're sure everything will be all right, though?"

It was exasperating. "No, I'm not sure everything will be all right. Not everything always comes out right, Dickie. You better learn that. Jesus, what were you trying to do, fooling around with that kind of deal anyway? You don't need the money."

Dickie stared at him with fury. "You don't have the slightest idea what I need, Phil. My father treats me like a child. I'm nothing more than a lackey down there. No office boy is treated like that. He thinks nothing of barging into my office whenever he pleases and shouting at me, never mind the whole world can hear him. He's moving heaven and earth to get you this precious clerkship. As for me, he wouldn't give me the time of day. I'm twenty-seven years old and he's got me on an allowance! An allowance! So don't tell me what I need. What I need right now is fifty thousand dollars, and no more sermons. I came crawling up here today to get it. If you want me down on my hands and knees, I'll get down on my hands and knees."

"I don't want you down on your hands and knees, Dickie," Phil said.

"Can you get me the money then?" Dickie asked cravenly.

Phil considered his response. "If it was money you needed, of course I'd get it for you, Dickie. You know I'd do that for you."

Dickie replied with sudden harshness, "Let's cut the crap, okay? Do I get the money, yes or no?"

"If you want to frame it that way, then no, I guess not."

"Fine." Dickie stood up. "Thanks for your valuable time. I know how busy you are." He turned to walk out.

"I'd still like to help if I could," Phil said to his back.

Without turning around, Dickie called, "Go fuck yourself, Phil," and continued on out the door.

Phil sat where he was, trying to avoid the stares of his fellow customers. When they had turned back to their own business, he put some money on the table and walked out.

Well, Dickie had really hit the jackpot this time. He'd made the big time. The first criminal in the family. Well, probably not the first, but certainly the stupidest. Ignorance of the law didn't quite cover it: ignorance of *anything* would be more like it. It was a sobering lesson, if one were needed, that if a person is determined to ruin himself, no one can stop him.

The problem was, Dickie could bring down a few other people with him. If this business got out, the whole takeover bid would be in jeopardy. The fact that Dickie was acting on his own, without Gerald's knowledge or permission, wouldn't hold water in court. The SEC would have a field day, and so would Will Strawbridge. Altman & Sons would be in a terrible position, and the family could well lose its shirt.

Not to mention that he could kiss the clerkship good-bye.

Much as jail seemed too good for Dickie just then, obviously something had to be done. But what? The idea of keeping the whole thing a secret was tempting, but terribly risky. These things always come out. The proxy fight had become fierce and both sides had their bloodhounds out, sniffing around for something that could be turned to their advantage. They were bound to stumble on Dickie sooner or later.

The only hope, it seemed to Phil, was that the other side's hands weren't one hundred percent clean. His father had intimated that their financing might not be completely on the up-and-up. If they could be discovered having dipped into some comparable cookie jar, they might be persuaded to reach an accommodation over Dickie: a sort of prisoner exchange. The legalities would have to be seen to, of course, that went without saying. But Phil had already been around long enough to know that there is always a wide latitude for interpretation on that front. His work for the commission had taught him that, if nothing else. The art of compromise, as they say. Not a bad definition.

As soon as he got back to the library, he put in a call to his father. Alan was at a board meeting, and Phil left word for him to call back and told the librarian where he could be found. He went back to the carrel where he had left his books. He had an exam in constitutional law the next day, and he thought it might be a good idea if he passed it. He was able to put Dickie completely out of his mind for the next two hours, until they came to tell him that his father wanted to speak to him.

Every year, on the first day of Christmas vacation, Carl wandered around New York City. If he could have had just one Christmas present out of the surfeit that was the family's custom, it would have been that one day on the town. When he was younger, he used to go on excursions. He wasn't above the landmarks. He went to the top of the Empire State Building, visited the Statue of Liberty, took the Circle Line tour around Manhattan. One year he walked across the George Washington Bridge, so he could feel like the Colossus, with one foot in New York, the other in New Jersey.

In later years he took the subway out to Queens to visit Trude and her sister. Trude was the Gutheims' former cook, retired and pensioned for some years now. She would fix him lunch—she knew his tastes—and they would play gin rummy for old times' sake. When he got back from Trude's, he would take the double-decker Fifth Avenue bus all the way up to Fort Tryon Park and go into the Cloisters to gaze at the Unicorn

Tapestries. He had a passion for those tapestries. He especially loved the
Unicorn in Captivity, that pure white magic beast who lived forever,
imprisoned, suffering from a mortal wound.

By the time he was in high school, the sights were familiar and the
Cloisters no longer an adventure. He still went out to visit Trude, but
that could no longer constitute a special treat. His roaming became less
adventuresome: he shopped, went to a movie with a stage show, and
ducked furtively into Hicks's or Schrafft's for a banana split, which he
couldn't enjoy for the guilt. Last year he had taken an actual girl, Hilary
Klein, out for lunch. They met at Longchamps, had an awkward meal
together, and he walked her home. He was in seventh heaven. It was his
best first-day-of-vacation ever, until his euphoria came to an abrupt end:
under the awning of her apartment house she told him she couldn't ask
him up because Jeff Marks was coming over. He considered himself so
hopelessly outclassed that he didn't even consider a protest. The walk
home was among the more dismal of the many demoralizing episodes
that characterized his life at the time.

This year he decided to skip the outing altogether. He had another
reason beside the painful memory of Hilary Klein. The Juilliard recital
was coming up in a week, and the prospect of that ordeal ruined any
thought of pleasure until it was over. He supposed he was prepared for
it. He had learned the damn Chopin Ballade as well as he was ever going
to learn it, and if it wasn't note perfect—which it wasn't by a long shot
—he could get through it without completely falling on his face. Madame pronounced it ready. It may have been. He was not. Whenever he
thought about the concert, he felt nauseated, and he began having bad
dreams. They had nothing to do with music or recitals, but he knew
they were caused by the upcoming ordeal. For the first time in his life he
had trouble concentrating on his homework. If he could have lost his
appetite and shed a few pounds, he might have gotten some good out of
it, but like most fat people, he ate more rather than less under stress.
There were no fringe benefits for him.

Under the circumstances, he decided that an outing would be useless. He couldn't see any point to it, and he had to practice. He had
reached that stage of anxiety where the only respite came from being at
the keyboard, going over and over the piece in a desperate attempt to
master it. On that first morning he woke up early, and forced himself to
stay in bed so as not to squander the luxury. Then he got up, ate a very
light breakfast, and went straight to the keyboard. He did his scales and

exercises, as congenial to him as sit-ups and push-ups would have been, and started in on the hateful Ballade.

After twenty minutes or so of this warfare, he smashed his hands onto the keys and bolted away from the piano. He looked back at it and saw an unremitting slavemaster, a cold, unyielding black box that held imprisoned the music he despaired of ever reaching. Somewhere there existed a beautiful piece by Chopin—although he couldn't conceive of it anymore—which bore no resemblance whatever to the lifeless succession of notes he was producing. He hated the work he was to perform in a few days' time, and he began to hate all music. The thought of a lifetime spent hacking away at that instrument filled him with disgust and terror. He was not given much to temperament, but he had to get out of the apartment, get away from the piano. If he could have found a way, he would have killed it, then and there.

With no thought but escape, he went out. The day was cold but bright. The first snow of the winter had come and turned to slush, leaving only a few gray mounds of ice in the gutters. Even so, the city had a festive aspect. The Christmas trees had been set out up and down Park Avenue and wreaths hung on the front doors of brownstones. The shop windows on Madison were in full holiday dress. Green and red ribbons, sprays of holly and mistletoe, evergreen branches, glittering balls, icicles, silver streamers, ersatz snow, and blinking colored lights decorated the merchandise, which itself was spiffed up and polished and sparkling. Santas, rotating trees, gaily wrapped presents, figurines of shepherds, Magi, barnyard animals, carolers, choirboys, reindeer, lambs were placed among the wares. Windows were bordered with stars, crusted snow, lettered greetings. The shopkeepers had selected their most attractive goods for display: jewelry, toys, bright sweaters, picture books. The bakeries offered elaborate decorated cakes, and when their doors swung open the fragrance of warm dough and spices was intoxicating. The Salvation Army bell ringers were on several corners, and at 57th and Fifth, right outside Tiffany's, four soldiers were playing carols on their gleaming brass instruments. The city was decked out for Christmas. It was his to enjoy.

Or was it? His family did observe Chanukah, after a fashion. Phil and Joan had a few friends in, everyone got presents, a menorah made a fleeting appearance on the piano. The Bible teacher was brought in to have supper, say something in Hebrew, sing a song or two, and spin the *dreidel*. The older children thought it was hilarious. Carl never understood a thing. His parents would come in while this nonsense was going on and smile happily before going in to take their baths. They had dinner later in those days, but they would come back and sit with the children at dessert, to mark the special occasion. No one considered for a minute that it was a substitute for Christmas. "It's the original holiday," his father would argue. "Christmas is just a later version." No one cared about that. Chanukah was never anything more than a minor holiday, elevated in importance to soothe the feelings of the Jewish kids who had to miss out on the real fun.

Of course, the Gutheims didn't miss out on it, not by a long shot. "Why should we?" his mother would ask. "Christmas isn't a religious holiday. It's an American holiday. It would be a shame to deprive the children of it. And for what?" Not to celebrate Christmas was the equivalent of allowing oneself to be pushed into the gutter. In America, everyone shared the sidewalks.

And so he enjoyed Christmas, with all the relish of the outsider who had crashed the party. He walked through the festive city alone, a tourist in his hometown. Walking down 58th Street to Fifth he came to F.A.O. Schwarz. The toy store had been one of the sacred shrines of his childhood. The arrival of the Schwarz catalogue in the mail was the true harbinger of the profane Christmas they celebrated. He no longer played with toys, but nothing else had taken their place in his life, and he missed the immoderate pleasure they used to give him. The sight of the F.A.O. Schwarz windows stirred the childlike feelings he was trying to suppress. He inspected the newest versions of chemistry labs and erector sets and Schuco cars and regretted that he would not be unwrapping a new game on Christmas morning, or staying up late Christmas night tinkering with a new gadget. He was tempted to step inside for a moment to see what else new they had, but there was always the danger of running into someone he knew and having to explain his anachronistic presence among the stuffed animals and lead soldiers.

Tearing himself away from the windows, he continued down Fifth Avenue. On the next block, Tiffany's looked disapprovingly down on the Salvation Army band, while inside its thick show windows necklaces and pendants were tossed carelessly on fantastic landscapes. Guiltily, he dropped a quarter into the kettle and received too warm thanks from the trombonist. He hurried on downtown. Although wreaths and red ribbon adorned the doors and decorated the facades of the great stores, the windows were less seasonal, and the haughty mannequins seemed to resent any suggestion of festivity. On the west side of the street stood the Fifth Avenue Presbyterian Church, where he had been taken once to play the organ. He couldn't reconstruct how a nine-year-old boy, clearly not a parishioner, came to be given the unrestricted run of that gigantic four-keyboard, ninety-six-stop machine. He guessed he had expressed a passing fancy for the instrument, and his parents, fore-seeing the emergence of another J. S. Bach, pulled the necessary strings. He did remember the uncanny sensation of producing such a magnifi-cent noise, the enormity of which overwhelmed whatever slight ambi-tion he might have had to study the organ, even if his feet could have reached the pedals.

The Protestant churches, on Fifth Avenue and elsewhere, always seemed to invite the curious or the footsore to come in, and he had explored several of them over the years. St. Patrick's was another mat-ter. He somehow formed the impression that he was forbidden entrance to Catholic churches, no matter what the sign on the door might say. He was probably influenced by the unspoken prejudices of his mother. Whatever the reason, he still, in his midteens, could not bring himself to enter the cathedral, even at Christmastime. Instead, he crossed the street to pay his respects to the Rockefeller Center tree.

The skaters were for the moment off the rink while they smoothed the ice. It would have been more picturesque to have seen couples glide around the perimeter while in the center a girl in a red costume dazzled the onlookers with jumps and turns and breathtaking spins. He had never seen such a sight, in all his years of passing the rink. Children stumbling around in snowsuits, teenage girls clinging precariously to unflinching instructors, elderly men with their hands clasped behind their backs were the more usual fare. Once in a great while an over-weight girl spilling out of a ludicrous outfit would do her Sonja Henie routine, but the effect was more comical than graceful. He studied the geometric pathway traced by the motorized roller and moved on before the rink reopened.

He headed toward Broadway. He told himself he might take in a movie, but he was well aware of baser motives. Sandwiched in between the shabby but respectable revival houses on 42nd Street were several theaters showing skin flicks. Timidity, not morality, prevented him from going in, but he was at that stage of life when just looking at the stills flanking the entrance could make him sweat. His real destination was the back-date magazine store next to the penny arcade, where, on the pretext of searching for an old *Life* or *Popular Science*, he could sneak a surreptitious glance at some truly astonishing periodicals. It was a shameful business at any time of year, but during the Christmas season it had the special thrill of blasphemy. As he walked over he glanced around nervously to see if anyone he knew was witnessing his criminal journey. He was safe as far as the Paramount, where *The Apartment* was playing. Beyond that he would be in no-man's land, without an alibi.

His route took him past Hanfmann's, a music and record store he frequented. He went in to it out of habit, and also to insert a bit of decent human contact into what was turning into a sordid outing. They knew him there, and greeted him with the usual condescension. It was a store where, despite his being a fairly good customer, he would imagine, he always felt like a pest. There was almost always a general conversation among the clerks about the latest musical events in town, but whenever he tried to put in a comment it was received with scorn. The clerks themselves were not active musicians; in fact, they despised everyone who performed in public. They knew he studied with Tamarovna, and dismissed him as a dilettante.

They were talking about the Philharmonic concert he had been to. Edwin, the pockmarked opera buff, had seen him during the intermission, and made a snide reference to his being in a box. Then they tore down Shostakovich. There was very little holiday spirit at Hanfmann's. In protest to the ubiquity of Christmas carols, which they abhorred, they were playing a record of some Chopin. The Ballade was not on the program, but it was enough to remind him of the practicing he should have been doing, and he was driven back out onto the street.

On 49th Street, passing by cheap hotels, he wondered what sex would be like in one of them, amid the filth and danger. At the end of the block, just east of Seventh Avenue, he paused outside the World Theater, where the best foreign films were shown. They were respectable enough to go to, and there was always the possibility of a bit of nudity. Unfortunately, *The Bicycle Thief* was playing. Nothing erotic, and anyway he had seen it. The memory of the poverty and desperation of postwar Rome reproached him for the overindulgence of his life. He should have felt chastised and warned, and headed for home before he sinned anymore. But he was too far gone to turn back now. He continued on, determined to have his sordid little eyeful.

Times Square was crowded. With all the schools out for vacation, hordes of kids jammed the entrances of all the movie theaters. The Capitol, the Palace, the Criterion, and the Astor all had their ropes out on the sidewalk, and the ushers were patrolling the unruly lines. He walked down to the Paramount. Even if he had wanted to see *The Apartment,* he would have had a long, cold wait. That would be his excuse, he thought, if someone asked why he hadn't gone to the movie. He was forever inventing elaborate cover stories for his self-condemned activities, not that anyone knew or cared what he was up to that afternoon, or any other afternoon. Thumbing through dirty magazines was pathetically tame stuff, in fact, but he imagined it a perversion he alone had discovered.

Still fearful of being seen slinking over to 42nd Street, he took an elaborate route, planning to go west on one of the side streets and approach the forbidden area from Eighth Avenue, where there was virtually no chance of running into anyone he knew. He walked over on 43rd, which by an unfortunate coincidence took him straight past the *New York Times* building. The *Times,* of course, didn't publish tidbits on the scandalous doings of younger sons of semiprominent New York families, but he went over one more block to Ninth Avenue, where he finally felt safe from exposure.

Ninth Avenue, to tell the truth, was not a street he spent a lot of time on. He may have been there two, maybe three times before. It lay outside the boundary of his New York City. His family would have considered it unsafe to begin with, and admittedly he would not set foot there after dark. In broad daylight, however, particularly during the Christmas season, he had no reason to feel afraid. There was, in fact, a pleasant, neighborhood atmosphere. The shops, perhaps a bit down-at-the-heel, resembled those on Lexington, or at least Third, near home. He tried to think if he knew anyone who actually lived in the area. He imagined it might be convenient for actors and other theater people, but he didn't know any of those. The only person he could think of who used to live around there was his old piano teacher, Seymour Bloom. That was several years back, and he thought—he hoped—Seymour might have moved up in the world by now. Out of curiosity, he went over to a phone booth to see if he was still in town. The Manhattan phone book was pretty beaten up, with a lot of pages torn out, but the *B*'s were intact, and he found the name: Seymour Bloom. On an inexplicable whim, he put a dime in and dialed the number. To his dismay, it was answered.

He was so surprised to hear a voice on the other end that he hardly knew what to say. He really had no idea why he had phoned. He had seldom thought of Seymour Bloom over the years. He had no desire to see him, certainly not when he was hot in the pursuit of pornography. If he had had his wits about him, he would have said it was a wrong number. But his morbid fear of detection made him fear Seymour might recognize his voice—probability never helped when he was feeling guilty—so he identified himself. He said he was nearby and asked if he could drop in. Seymour, for his part, couldn't very well ask the obvious question of why Carl would want to do such a thing, so he said, "Sure, fine, come on ahead." He sounded neither pleased nor annoyed, but Carl was certain he would resent the intrusion. Artists, Carl always thought, devoted their lives entirely to creativity and sex in strict alternation. Inevitably he would be interrupting either practicing or coitus.

When he arrived, there was no evidence of either pursuit. Seymour was disheveled, but Seymour had always been disheveled, and he didn't look like someone torn from intense activity of any kind. Carl had never been in the place before. That degree of barrenness was novel to him. There was a broken-down couch, a card table, a couple of chairs, a phonograph on the floor, a board-and-brick set of shelves with books and a few records. That was about it. In the corner, a music stand with some scores on the floor beside it. The walls were bare, a torn shade was drawn on one of the three grimy windows. He didn't know if Seymour was forced to live this way because of poverty, or whether he chose asceticism in order to further his art. There wasn't even a piano. Carl wondered how he practiced. When he had come to the Gutheims to give lessons, he hadn't seemed particularly down-and-out, but that had been some time ago, and Carl thought maybe he had been too young or too insensitive to notice.

They had a short, uncomfortable visit. Carl didn't want to say anything that might reflect on Seymour's destitution, and Seymour had the manners not to ask what on earth had impelled Carl to look him up. That narrowed the range of conversation considerably. Seymour asked if Carl was still studying with Tamarovna. Carl told him about the upcoming recital. He would have asked him to come, but he wasn't sure how it would be for him to go up to Juilliard and have to see old colleagues who must be doing better than he was. Carl in turn asked Seymour what he was working on. He regretted the question immediately. Seymour was playing in the pit for *The Fantasticks*. It must be terrible, Carl thought, for someone who had dreamed of performing at Carnegie

Hall to languish in the pit eight times a week in an off-Broadway show.
At least it wasn't burlesque, but that was about all that could be said for
it.

They had little else to say to each other. Seymour asked if Carl
would like to hear a record. It seemed the simplest thing to do. He
looked through his meager collection, as if searching for something glorious enough to overcome the joint depression. He looked through it
twice—it didn't take very long—before pulling out an old ten-inch al-
bum dating back to the days of the first LP's; Carl recognized the old
blue Columbia cover with the white scroll on it. Seymour put it on
without saying what it was, but the opening chord identified it as the
Meistersinger overture. One of Carl's favorites. He wondered if Seymour
remembered, and was playing it as a generous, sentimental gesture to
their brief musical acquaintance. Played on his tinny phonograph, in
that bleak setting, it lacked its grandeur. When it was over, Seymour
said nothing, but took the record off and put it back in its sleeve. Carl
tried to find something to say, about the performance, or Wagner, or
music, but he could find nothing. He thanked Seymour, and got up to
leave. Seymour didn't seem to care whether Carl went or stayed. The
last time Carl had seen him, he had still maintained a dream of success.
Now he seemed to have given up on himself. New York, like a cancer,
had devoured him. Only his shell remained. As Carl left, Seymour
wished him good luck at the recital. It was a heroic effort for him. There
was no way Carl could reciprocate. He would have wished Seymour a
merry Christmas, but it would have been a mockery.

Reaching the street, Carl found himself strangely confused. He
must have thought he was on the downtown side of the street, and he
turned to his right. He was puzzled by the blankness of the horizon up
ahead, but it took a minute for him to realize he was walking toward the
Hudson. He was in the middle of the immensely long block between
Ninth and Tenth Avenues, or between Tenth and Eleventh, he couldn't
remember which. The street was deserted. He should have been afraid,
alone in an unfamiliar place, but when he turned around he saw the
spire of the Empire State Building. He was in New York after all. This
was his home.

Brushing up against the sad life of Seymour Bloom had taken the
edge off his sexual appetite. The idea of sidling to the back of a store and
standing next to some stubble-faced degenerate in the comradeship of
depravity disgusted him. It had all the appeal of a public urinal. He was

ashamed of himself. In a few days he would have to walk out on a stage
and perform. He had to get home, as quickly as possible, and practice.
There wasn't enough time. Panic seized him. He knew he wouldn't be
prepared. He tried for the thousandth time to think how he could get
out of it. For a crazy moment he entertained the notion of disappearing.
The impossibility of doing it only heightened his feeling of desperation.
He hurried up the street.

Something cold and hard hit him in the neck. He hoped it had been
something falling from above, but when he looked down he saw it was
an iceball. His assailants were across the street. Two boys, young but
tough-looking, had appeared out of nowhere. Puerto Rican. They yelled
out something unintelligible but probably obscene. They were tearing
away some chunks from a pile of frozen slush at the curb. Carl didn't
know if they were challenging him to a snowball fight, or harassing him,
or preparing to come after him. He had no doubt they could beat him up
if they wanted to. He was a coward under any circumstances, and he
would certainly not put up any resistance here. He considered whether
he could get away, but he was sure they could catch him, and his attempted escape would only goad them into treating him more harshly.
He looked up the street to see if there was anyone to intervene in case he
got hurt. The only person he saw was a young man coming toward him.
An unlikely protector. He could have been in league with the others.
Two more iceballs were thrown. One of them hit him in the head. It
was as hard as a rock, but he was too scared to cry out. They were out to
hurt him, he thought. The boy walking toward him broke into a trot.
"Hey!" he yelled. It was all over now. Carl wondered if he'd pull a knife.

But he was yelling at the two boys. "Cut it out, you shitheads." He
was running now. "What the fuck you trying to do?" They let fly with
two more missiles, one at Carl, the other toward the young man, and
took off in the other direction. The young man outran the iceball aimed
at him, dodging it like a broken-field running back. The other one hit
Carl in the chest, since he was too surprised and still too frightened to
move out of its way. "Don't worry about them," the young man said as
he ran up to Carl. "They're just a couple of punks."

Grateful though Carl was, he was dubious about his rescuer. He
was bigger, faster, and more athletic—you would have had to go some
not to be more athletic than Carl was—and he looked Puerto Rican also,
although Carl hadn't heard any accent. He wore a thick short jacket and
a woolen cap, the kind worn by outdoor laborers in cold weather. He

reached over to an ice pile next to where Carl was standing and scooped up a chunk. Without bothering to sculpt it into a ball, he heaved it at the two boys who were running off. It was an astonishing throw, overshooting them by some distance. One of them turned around and gave him the finger: He grinned with satisfaction. He had a front tooth missing. "They won't give you no more trouble," he said.

"Thanks," Carl said.

"That's okay," the young man replied. "I don't like to see people getting picked on. You don't live around here, do you?"

"No I don't. I was visiting a friend."

"Oh, yeah? Who's that?" the man asked.

"His name is Seymour Bloom."

"Oh, I know him. I know Seymour. He's a nice guy. He's your friend?" Carl nodded. He didn't think for a minute the man knew Seymour, but he wasn't about to call him on that. "You going to see him now?"

"No, I just saw him. I was going home." Carl knew he was saying too much, but he didn't want to appear suspicious and ungrateful.

"You going this way?" the young man asked, jerking his thumb eastward. "I'll come with you to the corner. Make sure no one else gives you any trouble." He started walking back along the block he had just come down.

Carl didn't know what to do. He was already in the young man's debt, but he didn't trust him. His appearance and manner made Carl uneasy. If he had been smart, he would have made up an excuse to return to Seymour's place. But there wasn't time to form a plan, and above all he didn't want to be rude. There was still the outside chance the man was on the up-and-up, and Carl thought it best not to provoke him.

All the same, he wasn't really surprised when he was suddenly pushed into a narrow alley and thrust up against a wall. His stomach contracted automatically with fear, but despite that he felt quite calm. His predicament was ridiculously inevitable, and his only thought was that he had been a damn fool. The young man grabbed his coat in one hand, and curled the other into a fist, which he cocked menacingly. "Hand over all your money if you know what's good for you," he said. He had dropped the pretense of friendliness, and spoke with a sudden harshness.

Afterward, Carl couldn't figure out why he didn't simply hand over the money. He wasn't carrying a great deal—probably ten or fifteen dollars, if that—and he knew perfectly well that the loss of even a much larger amount would be inconsequential. It would have been nice to believe that some latent but essential instinct of courage, or even masculine pride, wouldn't allow him to submit to such a humiliation; but it wasn't a creditable explanation. His emotions at that moment were complicated. Fear, certainly, predominated. Oddly, he had decided his life was in no danger, which was not necessarily the case. What bothered him most was the possibility of being hit in the face, not because of the pain so much as the danger to his eyes, which was probably very slight. He also knew that he had been up to no good that afternoon. He had sin in his heart, and he was paying for it now. The loss of money, a noticeable injury, even torn clothing, would reveal his guilt. His only hope was to get away unscathed and avoid having to explain anything. The fear of exposure gave him the burst of bravado he wouldn't otherwise have found. He struck out clumsily with both arms, more shoving than punching his attacker. The young man was unprepared. He hadn't expected the slightest resistance from a fat, soft rich kid who wouldn't miss his pocket money, and he stumbled backward, almost falling in his surprise.

Having made the first move, Carl was committed to following through. He didn't fool himself that he had any chance in an actual fight. His only hope was to get away. He bolted out of the alley and ran up the street. He didn't know whether the young man actually pursued him. He must have made such a sight, with his overcoat flapping and his arms extended to keep his balance over the icy sidewalk, that his attacker may have been immobilized by mirth. Or he may not have thought it worth his while to take any more trouble with someone who had seemed an easy mark but now looked a little nuts. Carl didn't look back, and didn't know if he was out of danger. He continued at what was for him full speed up the block, driven by fear mixed with shame. Since there were no cars coming, he crossed the street diagonally, heading for a store not quite at the end of the block as the nearest place of refuge. The street was his undoing. It was even more treacherous than the sidewalk, with a patch of ice hidden beneath the slush. Carl skidded ludicrously on one foot, arms flailing desperately, and toppled backward, a perfect banana-peel maneuver. He put out a hand to break the fall, and landed his entire considerable bulk on it. He had no time to luxuriate in his pain, but even as he picked himself up and limped along the opposite sidewalk, he could tell that his wrist was not in working order.

He got himself home without further incident, slinging his left arm through his overcoat, Napoleon fashion. He didn't take a taxi, partly because he didn't travel in taxis in those days, and also because he needed some time to think. He was no doctor, but he knew he wasn't going to be able to get up in public and perform in a week's time. He had no idea how he was going to face Madame, or what he would tell his family. The truth was one possibility, but it needed to be heavily edited, and he didn't know if he could bring it off. He concocted and threw out a series of implausible stories. He wasn't very creative, and he was constrained by the idea of being cross-examined by the lawyers in the family. Although his actions had been innocent, his intentions hadn't been. He rehearsed and changed and put back what parts of the day he thought would pass inspection, but by the time he got home he still hadn't come up with a solid version he could count on. He crept into the apartment, holding his throbbing arm and wondering what they would say.

But as it turned out, no one took much notice of his injury. Only after a couple of days, and no improvement, did his mother think enough of it to send him to a doctor. The orthopedist poked at the wrist and ordered an X ray, which revealed a greenstick fracture of the bone. It wasn't in the least serious, but it turned out he would have to be in a cast for six weeks.

Ellen called Joan the minute she got down from Bennington. "I haven't even taken my coat off," she said, as if still catching her breath. "I couldn't wait to find out how you *are*. I can't *believe* everything that's happened since I saw you. I knew I should never have let you out of my sight. I knew I should never have let Johnny out of my sight. The minute I turn my back he ups and gets engaged to the first girl who comes along. I'll never trust a man again. How's Meyer House? How are *you*, for God's sake? When are we having lunch? You know I'm going to San Francisco the day after New Year's, if we don't get together *this minute* I'll be gone and we'll never see each other again!"

Ellen was quite capable of going on like that for quite some time. Joan had missed her terribly, but now that she was back in town it wasn't so easy to fix a date. Not that Joan wasn't eager to see her. She was. But her life was busy, and lunch with Ellen meant the better part of the afternoon would be shot too. "I'm a working woman these days," she told Ellen. "I'm not on vacation, you know. Won't I see you at Debbie's?" Debbie was having an informal party, the first one of the Christmas holidays. Joan had thought of not going. She was exhausted as it was, before the parties even began. But if she did go, they could see each other then.

Ellen, though, wasn't so easily fobbed off. She knew Joan too well, and was quite familiar with all her evasive tactics. She offered to do all the schlepping, if it came to that, but she wouldn't get off the phone until they agreed on a date. Bowing to the inevitable, Joan suggested the next day. Trying to think of a place they could go near Meyer House, Ellen suggested Mehlman's, on Allen Street. Joan had never heard of it. "Of course you've never heard of it," Ellen said. "It's kosher."

The next day, Joan worked it out with Leona so she could get away to meet her friend. When she got to the restaurant, Ellen was naturally nowhere to be seen. It was conceivable that Ellen was caught in traffic, but more likely she was simply late. As ten, fifteen, twenty minutes went by, Joan wondered if she had forgotten altogether; not beyond the realm of possibility. With anyone else, Joan would have been furious, but Ellen was Ellen. She'd never been on time the last sixteen years, and there wasn't much reason to think she'd change now.

She sailed in with her usual breathless spiel and hugs and spilling packages, generally creating enough of a commotion that no one could call her to account. It was wonderful to see her. Joan didn't know how she had survived the fall without her. It didn't seem possible she'd be going off in a couple of weeks to San Francisco. So far away!

There had been a long line when Joan arrived, but by the time Ellen came, they were near the front. When their turn came, no one showed them to a table, but a waiter clearing one told them they could sit there as soon as he sponged it off. After they had seated themselves, he came back with doilies and menus and he also slapped some silverware down. Paper napkins were already on the table, along with the salt, pepper, and what looked like a honey dispenser. "That's *schmaltz*," Ellen told Joan. "You put it on bread, like butter."

"That's the most revolting thing I've ever heard," Joan said. "What's all this about *schmaltz*, anyway? And kosher restaurants? What's come over you, Frankel? Is there something going on I don't know about?"

Ellen giggled and shook her head.

"There *is* something going on," Joan cried. Ellen shook her head insistently, until Joan gasped, "My God! You've got a new boyfriend!"

The two of them burst out into shrieks of laughter that even in the din of the place attracted attention. "Ellen Frankel!" Joan wailed. "I'm never speaking to you again. The most important event of the year, and I don't hear a word about it!"

"Joanie!" Ellen protested. "We've been here what, three minutes? You wanted to hear this over the phone? By letter?"

"You should have sent a telegram!"

The waiter came back, looking stern, and asked them if they wanted to eat. Joan didn't, really, but when she tried to order a tossed salad, Ellen wouldn't hear of it. "I know very well this is the first time you've ever eaten kosher food, you're not having a salad." To placate her, Joan ordered the stuffed cabbage. She disliked cabbage, the few times in her life she had eaten it—it wasn't served too often in the Gutheim home—but she didn't intend to eat anything, and it was immaterial to her what sat on her plate.

"So tell me about this guy," Joan said when the waiter had gone off. "I still can't believe I haven't heard about this."

"You've heard about it," Ellen said breezily.

"Liar! You've never so much as breathed a word. Not to me, at least. I don't know what you told Wendy."

"You've met him."

"No! Who is he?"

"Trepanoff. You remember him?"

"The painter?" Joan asked. "With the beard? With the motorcycle?"

"That's the one." Ellen nodded happily.

"I don't believe it!"

"That's the one!"

"With the sexy eyes? Omigod! This is *so* great! Tell me everything! When did this all happen? The last thing I knew, he was just this man who buzzed through campus all the time, making a lot of noise and getting everyone all hot and bothered."

Ellen laughed at the description. "Actually, he got rid of his motorcycle. He has a jalopy."

"God, this *is* serious!" Joan searched Ellen's face. "Is it serious?"

Ellen raised her eyebrows in question. "I don't know. We're not engaged. He's going out to San Francisco."

"He's following you! That's the most romantic thing I've ever heard in my life!"

Ellen smiled. "I'm following him, it's more like. Anyway, he was going out there before—this all happened."

"It's just a wild coincidence," Joan said skeptically.

"It's just a wild coincidence," Ellen repeated. They both started giggling again.

"Are you going to live together?" Joan asked, lowering her voice and glancing around the room.

"Do you think my mother would ever let me go out there if she thought I was going to cohabitate? With a man?" Ellen asked.

"You didn't answer my question," Joan pointed out.

Ellen shrugged. "Let's not rush things. We haven't even slept together." Joan looked dubious. "Well, don't give me that look. You haven't slept with Johnny. You think I'm some kind of fallen woman?"

"How do you know I haven't slept with Johnny?" Joan asked. This was getting a little deep, even for Ellen. They'd talked about sex endlessly, of course, but mostly in the abstract. Ellen knew about the Williams boy, but only indirectly. She knew nothing of Kevin.

"What do you mean, how do I know you haven't slept with Johnny? This is Ellen you're talking to. Your old roommate. Remember me?"

It's been a long fall, Joan thought. So much has happened. She was engaged to one man, having a clandestine affair with another. Ellen was going to San Francisco to paint, and maybe move in with this man Joan barely knew. Both their lives had speeded up, but they were going off in different directions. They were no longer in on each other's day-to-day existence. Ellen was her closest friend in the world; and yet, seeing her across the table, she might almost have been a complete stranger, there was so much distance between them.

The waiter brought their food, but they continued talking nonstop. Joan wanted to hear everything about Trepanoff. She remembered him only vaguely. He wasn't attractive in the usual sense. She herself had been repelled by his beard. Still, all the girls had noticed him. He was an intriguing figure, at least in Vermont. Joan wouldn't have put him and Ellen together in a million years. She thought they were an interesting but unlikely match. Not because he was an artist—that was to be expected—but the kosher business was hard to take in. "Who would have thought any of us would ever be involved with a real Jew?" she said.

"It's not so bad as you think," Ellen said. "He doesn't sit around all day rocking and mumbling prayers. He actually believes in the religion, if you can believe it, but he's not orthodox. He doesn't wear a yarmulka. The beard isn't Jewish, it's beatnik."

"It must be strange. What if you wound up having to convert!"

"Or emigrate to Israel," Ellen suggested. "He's always talking about that."

"Oh, God, Ellen," Joan begged. "Promise me you won't go off the deep end!"

"I haven't gone yet," Ellen said. "And Israel isn't off the deep end, no matter what your mother thinks. How is your mother, by the way. Was she delighted you were having lunch with me?"

"You're always saying that," Joan scolded her. "Mother really likes you. She always has. Really. She sent you her love, as a matter of fact. I just forgot. She did." She grinned at Ellen, who had her eyes shut as if to deny what Joan was saying. "No, really. It was always Bennington she didn't like. Her only complaint against you was that you got me to go there. And that's all over with now, I'm not going back, so she's happy. She got what she wanted."

But Ellen was suddenly serious. "What do you mean, you're not going back? What's all over with?" She sounded quite upset.

"Oh, we all know I'm never going back there," Joan said lightly.

"I didn't know that, Joanie," Ellen said. She was truly concerned, all the more so because Joan was so nonchalant, or pretending nonchalance. "When was this decided?"

"Oh, you know how it is. Nothing gets decided in our family. It just sort of . . . happens. You know? You might think you're going to do one thing, and without realizing it, you wind up doing something else entirely. It's all very painless. You never know what hit you until it's all over. Anyway," she added, "it really couldn't matter less."

Ellen had put down her fork and stopped eating altogether. "Joanie," she said softly. "What's happened to you?"

Joan was taken aback by the change in Ellen's mood. She didn't know what had caused it. One moment they had been laughing and joking, and the next thing she knew, Ellen was treating her as though she had a terminal illness. "I'm *fine*, Ellen. Don't worry about me."

"Joanie, I worry about you all the time, and never more than when you tell me not to worry about you."

"Well, please don't," Joan said, with the beginning of a temper.

"Everyone's always worrying about me. I really can take care of myself."

Ellen looked at her seriously. "Joanie, something is going on. I don't know what it is, but I'm scared, I really am. You're not telling me something. What did they find out? Are you holding something back on me?"

"Nothing's going on!" Joan insisted. "They didn't find anything!"

"They must have," Ellen said. "You can't sit there and tell me you're fine, and expect me to swallow it."

Joan's eyes filled with tears. "I never wanted to come down to New York. Everyone ganged up against me, so I had no choice. They got every doctor they could lay their hands on and did every test known to man, and they all said nothing was wrong. Nothing! I'm fine! I've got a clean bill of health! So don't you start in on me now."

"I can't help it, Joanie. I don't care if they gave you a clean bill of health. It isn't true. You look awful."

"Thanks a lot."

"I'm not saying it to insult you. But I've got eyes. I don't care what the doctors say, you're not at all well. You're exhausted, you're white as a sheet, and you're wasting away in front of me. Is everyone else blind? Doesn't anyone else see it? I thought you were too thin when you left college, but it was nothing next to what I'm looking at now. Believe me, I don't like telling you this, but if no one else will, I guess I'll have to be the one. *Someone's* got to."

"Don't you think they do? Don't you think I hear the same thing night and day, from everyone in the city?"

Ellen stared at her for a moment. "I don't know if you do or not," she said finally. "Or if you do, maybe it's not getting through. Maybe you're not really listening."

"I *do* listen," Joan said bitterly. "I have my mother. Remember her? She offers a bit of advice now and then. So does everyone else. Everybody's trying to run my life for me. Why can't people leave me alone?"

Ellen reached across the table and grasped her friend's hand. "I care about you too much to leave you alone," she said. "I'm sorry if it makes you mad, but I can't just sit by and let something terrible happen."

Joan wanted to pull her hand away, to free herself from the urgent grip; but seeing Ellen's earnestness, and remembering all the years of their friendship, she left it there. "I'm not mad," she said sorrowfully. "And nothing terrible is going to happen."

Ellen looked at her doubtfully. Joan looked so frail, so utterly for-

lorn. It seemed heartless to continue. "Make sure it doesn't," she begged.
"I can't afford to lose you." She tried to soften her urgency with a laugh,
but nothing would come out.

Joan, too, wanted to assuage her friend's anxiety; but her voice was
tight with her own fear. "Just don't *worry* about me," she said. "I'm *fine.*"

Nothing more was said on the subject. Both of them steered the
conversation into the more neutral waters of friends and family, and
when they parted they hugged each other as warmly as always. Despite
her best intentions, Ellen couldn't bring herself to point out that Joan
hadn't touched her lunch.

Arriving home that evening, Joan was intercepted by the maid
while she was taking her coat off in the hallway. Noreen had a characteristic panic-stricken look whenever she had a message to deliver, and
for a moment Joan thought someone had died. But all that Noreen said
was, "Trude is here," and she vanished as suddenly as she had appeared.

Trude never gave any notice of her visits. Since leaving the
Gutheims, she materialized twice a year, no more, no less. She always
came in the late afternoon in hopes of catching the family as they came
in. Joan had no desire to see her, or anyone, just then, but it was out of
the question that she would snub the old servant. She passed through
the dining room and pantry into the kitchen, where Gerta's grim expression confirmed the presence of Trude. Although Gerta could cook
circles around Trude, she had never held a comparable place in the
family's affections. She probably knew this, and she didn't disguise her
resentment of her predecessor. She suffered Trude's visits under choked
protest, and remained stonily silent when Joan bade her good evening.
Joan went quickly into the servants' sitting room, where Trude sat bolt
upright on the couch, looking as though she had come to interview for a
position on the household staff.

"Trude!" Joan exclaimed, going over to kiss the old woman. "It's so
great to see you. You look wonderful. I'm so glad you waited. I would
have been furious with myself if I had missed you."

"Hallo, Joan," Trude said, so subdued that one wouldn't guess that
the visit was the highlight, if not the only light, of her existence over the
past six months. She sat stiff and unsmiling in her black dress, fingering
the brooch the family had given her when she retired.

"And how is everything in Astoria?" Joan asked. Astoria was
thought of in the family as a kind of Valhalla for retired servants—

Queens being a place you went only to catch airplanes—and Joan still had difficulty pronouncing the name without smiling.

"Shust fine," Trude replied, adding, in an effort to recapture old customs, "Hunky-dory und fine und dandy."

"And Irmgard? How is she?" Trude's sister had been with the Hellers—Wendy's parents—during most of the years Trude had been with the Gutheims, both women having originally entered into service with Mrs. Altman when they first came over to America before the war. When Trude retired, they had bought the apartment in Astoria, or rented it, no one knew which, and Irmgard had followed a couple of years later, even though Trude always looked the younger of the two. But then, nobody believed Trude to be only sixty-five when she retired. The progression of her years had meandered like a gently undulating stream running alongside the straighter path of conventional time.

"She's all right," Trude said. "She don't get around too gut t'ese days. She had de problem mit her breat', it gets short, und I haff my eyes, so betveen us ve got about enough for vun old person. But vot you going to expect, when you get old, you fall apart. But vot about you? Dey tell me you got sick now, ach? Vot a shame! Und dot you got to come down from de college?"

"What have they been telling you?" Joan asked lightly. "I'm fine! It's all a lot of fuss of Mother's and Father's!"

"Und you vere alvays de healt'y vun," Trude said with a slight reproach, as though Joan had betrayed her trust. "Und now to have diss happen, ach!"

"Trude, just look at me! Do I look sick? Do I really now?"

"I don't know, I don't bring mein glasses mit me. Venever I take dem, I leave dem on de subvay. I tink you kind of t'in."

"You just say that because you're used to stuffing all of us. I'm fine! I'll be going back to college soon. After Christmas. Anyway, you haven't said anything about my big news! Did you hear I'm getting married?"

"Ja, dey told me. Dot's nice." Trude sounded less than ecstatic.

Joan persevered against the old woman's indifference. "You remember Johnny, don't you?" Johnny had been a favorite of Trude's, as he was of all servants, whom he always treated with great courtesy and attention. But Trude's face clouded in an effort to pluck a face out from the throng of young people who were always in and out of the house—dinner parties and unexpected visits in the wintertime, and during the summer, in the country, an endless picnic, swimming all day, baseball on the lawn, houseguests for breakfast, constant traffic through the kitchen for snacks and ice cream and icebox raids. She couldn't recall a specific face. "He's the nice-looking tall boy. One of Phil's friends? He's the one I'm marrying."

"Is dot so?" Trude commented vaguely.

Joan understood. She had frozen for Trude as a permanent teenager, and she would never grow older, never marry, never change. She saw that, but all the same she was hurt not to have a smile of approval from the woman into whose ample breasts she had so often buried her face in misery, always to find comfort, followed by something good to eat. "Did you see Carl?" she asked, resigned.

Trude's face lit up. "Oh, ja, ve had a nice long visit."

"And your gin rummy? Did you have your game? Did you let him beat you again?"

"Ach, I couldn't beat Carl anymore. Not since he vass a little boy. Ach, he is so shmart, dot vun. He was alvays de shmart boy. I tell him dot."

"Not smarter than Phil?" Joan protested. She had her loyalties too.

"I don't see Phillip anymore." Trude no longer had any need to disguise her bitterness. Phil was no longer even informed when she came nowadays. He had never been close to her.

"He's going to be a brilliant lawyer, you know. He graduates this year. He may go to work for the Supreme Court of the United States!"

"Phillip make a gut lawyer," Trude said ambiguously; and added, stubbornly, "But Carl, he iss de shmart vun."

"You know, it's Carl's health you should worry about, not mine," Joan chided.

"Ach, he iss too fat. I told him so." She had in her day indulged the boy shamelessly whenever he had set foot in her kitchen. "I told him he got to look handsome for de girls." Her face darkened with worry for Carl's prospects. "He got to haff de girlfriends. But how is *deine* grandmama? Und Mr. und Mrs. Altman?" Trude inquired only to change the subject, and out of politeness. She would already have been filled in on all the family news by Noreen; possibly even Gerta might have unbent for the sake of gossip.

"They're all fine. Grandmother is as great as ever. The Altmans are okay. Marian is crazier than ever. She goes to this strange group up in Katonah, they pray or something. Dickie's in trouble as usual."

"Ach!" Trude gasped in disgust. She had never liked any of the

Altman children except for Barbara. "Diss Dickie. He iss lucky if he don't go to jail diss time. But den he vas alvays such a spoiled boy, diss Dickie."

"Poor Dickie!" Joan said. "You remember when he wanted that treehouse? And how he carried on when he couldn't have it?"

It was a good try, but Trude wasn't up to it. She was getting too old for such feats of nostalgia. Joan could see the hard struggle as the elderly woman tried to keep the flame of the past burning. No, now she looked truly aged. Before long she would be dead. This visit, any visit, might be her last. Joan peered closely at her face. It was so lined, so tired. Her eyes had always been a little red, as if she had just finished crying, or was about to cry. She seemed to live perpetually on the verge of tears.

"I got to be going," Trude said, looking about her and gathering up her purse, her gloves, her sad little fox stole.

"Must you? Already?" Joan asked. She was relieved, though.

"Oh, *ja*. I haff nach a long trip. I don't like to be out after dark too long. Irmgard vorries, und she don't like to be alone. I shust say goodbye to *deine* mama." She would go to the door of the bedroom, never crossing the threshold, and bid Peggy good-bye; or if Peggy was in her bath, she would slip out without a farewell at all. Except that she would stop for one more word with Carl. "I hope dot you be better," she said with a sigh.

"I'm fine now, Trude," Joan insisted. "Don't worry about me."

Trude's failing eyes looked sadly at Joan. "You looking too tired. Too t'in. You got to eat more. You vear you'self out. Iss no gut. Not gut for you."

"Oh, Trude!" Joan kissed her. "How you carry on!"

But it was a relief to say good-bye to her, even granted that the visit might be her last; or if not this one, perhaps the next.

Fifteen

Christmas began on Christmas Eve in the Altman family. The gathering at Mrs. Altman's, with the tree and the presents, supper and carols, had been the occasion of frantic excitement when the children were young. Over the years, though, a sense of the routine had crept in. As the children got older, they became blasé about family customs, and the dinner at Mrs. Altman's was just one more event of the Christmas season. No one except for Marian would have dreamed of missing it, but no one was very enthusiastic about it either.

This year the holiday found the family under more than its usual tension. Gerald's proxy fight overshadowed everything else, but there were other problems, rarely spoken of, worrisome all the same: Carl's arm, broken under mysterious conditions virtually on the eve of his Juilliard recital; Marian, showing no signs of coming to her senses regarding this cult she was being sucked into; and most of all Joan, who seemed to be fading away under people's eyes. No one ever spoke about her health, but it was apparent to anyone with eyes that she was not well. The family hadn't found out about the episode in the subway; but later that day, Leona had gone to Martin Perry in alarm over her assistant's pallor, and a protesting Joan had been sent home in a taxi. That had been only a few days before Christmas, and although she'd returned to work the next day, it was clear she couldn't go on as she was for much longer.

For these reasons a strange combination of expectancy and foreboding modified the more traditional feelings on the day before Christmas. There had also been some question as to who would be included. Dates were never brought to Christmas Eve, but fiancés were considered family. Johnny wanted nothing more than to be with Joan, but he finally decided that he had to stay with his mother on Christmas Eve. Everyone understood. Mrs. Altman had very graciously asked Joan if Mrs. Krieger would like to be invited as well, but that prospect had been really too grim for words, especially for Johnny. As for Betsy, if Phil had said the word, she would have been warmly welcomed at Mrs. Altman's. She was dying to come, too, but Phil didn't want her there. There was no discussion. Peggy had asked Phil if Betsy would like to come this year, and he had simply replied, "She's not coming." That was that.

So it was just the five Gutheims, after all, going over together. They were standing in the little foyer outside the door waiting for the elevator, and Carl was being inspected. Phil was brushing the dandruff off the shoulders of his blue serge suit. Usually Carl carried most of the presents, but this year, with his left arm in a sling, he could carry only a few small ones that could rest on his cast. The others were on the foyer table. Alan would wait until they arrived at Mrs. Altman's to insert the envelopes with the crisp ten-dollar bills for the help under the ribbons of the packages. (Irene, Mrs. Altman's maid, who had been with the family forever, got a check for twenty-five dollars.) The elevator came and Peggy stepped in. "Can we all fit?" she wondered.

Phil felt he had to respond, "That all depends on how many cheese bits Carl has already eaten."

Alan took the bait. "I must say, I don't see how you can fill up with those things when you're going to have supper at your grandmother's, which isn't exactly to be sneezed at," he said.

"I didn't fill up on them," Carl answered crossly.

"That would be impossible," Joan chimed in.

"For God's sake," Carl cried, "it's Christmas Eve. I would think once a year you could lay off the nagging."

"I could care less if you explode on them," Joan retorted.

Peggy said, "Now shush!" spreading the blame equally as usual. Carl felt it was very unfair, but said nothing more.

Everyone had to squish into the elevator with the packages, and the crush did raise their spirits by the time they reached the lobby. They wished the elevator man and the doorman both Merry Christmas, and

their replies confirmed Alan's fears that he had been too generous with
their bonuses. Stepping out onto the sidewalk, Alan waved aside the
doorman's suggestion of a taxi. "We'll walk," he said with the hearty air
of an Arctic explorer forgoing a dogsled.

It was a brilliant, clear, cold New York evening. The air was perfectly still, with enough snap of winter in it to give a tinge of exhilara-
tion when you breathed it in. The well-shoveled sidewalk crunched under people's galoshes, but the footing was firm. All up and down Park
Avenue the trees, with clusters of yellow and white lights, looked as
though they had been placed there and decorated for the family's espe-
cial enjoyment this one night. Every apartment building had a Christmas wreath with a cluster of holly and a shiny red ribbon, and the early
stars sparkled down from a moonless sky.

The Gutheims passed many other happy-looking families, also carrying presents, and everyone smiled and wished one another a merry
Christmas, even though they might be perfect strangers. It made one
feel as though everyone was a single big family in the city that night. At
70th Street they stopped at the corner while Alan and Phil, with Carl
tagging along, went down the block to Donatello's to pick up carnations
for their buttonholes. Mr. Donatello would never let them pay for these
Christmas Eve traditions, even though every year he and Alan had a
strenuous and friendly argument over it. "You have to make a living at
Christmastime, just like any other time," Alan would protest, and Mr.
Donatello would always say, "Once a year, let me say thank you for
bein' the nice folks you are." It pleased Alan to think he was referring
not only to the business the family gave him throughout the year, which
was considerable, but to their being true friends as well. "You have to let
people do things for you too," Peggy always advised the children. In the
end the flowers were accepted with thanks. They called out Merry
Christmas to Mrs. Donatello, sitting in the back, making up last-minute
arrangements of poinsettias, and sent more wishes home to the daughter, who had lain for years and years, a hopeless cripple following that
tragic car accident.

The men rejoined the ladies and continued up the avenue. They
had to stop three times on their short journey: once to greet the Friedlanders, who were on their way to Mrs. Friedlander's sister's; and the
next time to say hello to old Mr. Levine, out for his usual evening stroll,
he told them, as though this was just another evening, which it was for
him; and a third time to wish the merriest of Christmases to Mr. and

Mrs. McLaren and seemingly innumerable little McLarens, one cuter than the next. They were all in a fever pitch of excitement because they were going to *their* Grandma's too, think of that! And for the very same reason! In addition the Gutheims nodded to several other familiar faces, and exchanged Christmas greetings with all the other passersby. For Alan it was the highlight of the evening.

On Mrs. Altman's door there was, of course, a beautiful wreath, all browns and golds, with pine cones and gilt-sprayed leaves, shining in the doorlight. Carl had gotten Kathleen's present ready so he could thrust it at her when she opened the door. She laughed with surprise and pleasure. The others wished her a merry Christmas and came in, stamping the snow off their boots.

"I'm going to be watching the midnight mass at St. Paddy's tonight on television," Alan told Kathleen, "and I expect to see you right up there on the screen."

"Oh, Mr. Gutheim!" Kathleen always blushed when spoken to by an adult member of the family, or a guest. "I wouldn't be going there. Even if I did go to midnight service, it wouldn't be there."

"Oh?" Alan was disappointed. "I never miss it. I think it's one of the most moving things I've ever seen. Those little choirboys out there in the front of the procession, looking like cherubs, singing their hearts out? They probably all have their slingshots under their robes, but they sing like little angels. No, I find it terribly moving."

"Well, it's a bit grand for me," Kathleen said, laughing shyly.

"Too grand? For you? How could it be too grand for you? You have as much right as anyone to be there. More so, if you ask me." Alan was indignant to think that democracy should be flouted, and on Christmas Eve, of all times.

"I wouldn't get there in time, what with the cleaning up," Kathleen said. She didn't want to explain to him that she hadn't taken communion in years, not since she left her parents' home in Galway and came over to work for Mrs. Altman, and that if she went to confession the priest would tell her her soul was in danger of eternal damnation.

"Oh! Well, anyway, a very merry Christmas to ye'." Alan always slipped into his pseudobrogue when he was trying to be chummy with any of the servants, even the Scandinavians or the Scots. It pained him that someone should be kept from a religious observance in order to wait on table, and he felt guilty to be a contributor to her deprivation; but as it was outside his jurisdiction, he said nothing more.

The ladies went into the large anteroom, where Kathleen took their coats, while the men took theirs off in the cloakroom, unassisted. Carl took the presents for the rest of the servants and went off to the door to the back stairs. When the others met in the hallway, Carl wasn't yet back. "I think we ought not to keep Grandmother waiting," Peggy said. "Carl will get to talking down there, and I see no reason to wait. Shall we go in?" She turned, not to the staircase but to the large ballroom straight ahead, where the huge tree was framed by the open doors, and led the others in.

The tree, an enormous Scotch pine, was thickly clustered with lights of every color, surrounded by ornaments of gold and silver and red satin, shining rather than glittering, every branch draped with silver icicles that reflected the light in a diffuse glow. To the left, on two couches facing each other were piled the colorfully wrapped presents, overflowing onto the armchairs there. To the right was a group of chairs and another sofa. These were arranged in front of a large fire. Mrs. Altman sat on the edge of the sofa, facing the door. She wore a full-length dark green gown for the occasion, with a large brooch of diamonds and emeralds, and she was nearly laughing with pleasure and excitement. "I'm so relieved you made it here all right, with all that snow on the ground," she said in greeting. "I had the most awful worry that someone might slip on the ice. I should have sent the car for you."

"Nonsense, Mother, there wasn't a bit of ice anywhere on the streets," Peggy told her. "We had a perfectly lovely walk over. The Friedlanders send you their love, Holly and Ed McLaren send you their love, it couldn't have been nicer. Merry Christmas, by the way." She laughed and leaned down to kiss her mother.

"Merry Christmas, dear," Mrs. Altman replied, repeating the greeting in turn to each of the others as they came up to kiss her.

As Joan bent down to give her a kiss, Mrs. Altman's smile was clouded for a fleeting moment by a troubled look. She seemed about to say something, but perhaps on reflection—it was Christmas, after all—she smiled again and said nothing. Joan had seen the look, and knew what it meant, but said nothing either.

"The others will be late," Mrs. Altman explained. "It seems that Randy isn't down yet. Eleanor just phoned. They're going to give him a few more minutes and then come on without him." Randy had gone straight from college to visit a young lady somewhere in the wilds of northern Connecticut, and was supposedly arriving back in the city in plenty of time for Christmas Eve.

"I was sure he was cutting it too close," Peggy said crossly.

"The roads are not at all good," Mrs. Altman said, always ready to excuse one of her grandchildren, even a reprobate like Randy.

"People have been known to allow for that," Peggy said. It made her angry that her mother should be inconvenienced—that they should all be inconvenienced—by her inconsiderate nephew. "The only thing that worries me in the slightest is that it wouldn't be beyond the realm of possibility for him to have a drink or two before he started off."

"I know, I've spoken to Gerald about that, because I don't see why the boy should be allowed to drive if he's going to drink. Usually I say nothing."

"Of course you don't," Peggy reassured her. "Ah, here's Carl now." Carl had appeared opportunely, to show up by contrast his truant cousin.

"Hello, dear." Mrs. Altman smiled at him. "Merry Christmas. How is your arm?"

"Merry Christmas, Grandmother," Carl intoned gravely. "It's fine." Carl had decided on pure stoicism, not only because people didn't complain of illness in that family, but also in order not to fuel the unspoken suspicion that he had in any way brought this on himself.

"Did you deliver all the packages?" Alan asked, adding to Mrs. Altman, "What do you think of our own private United Parcel Service?" Carl knew Alan liked to encourage any physical activity, no matter how slight, but wished he wouldn't refer to him as if he were about four years old.

"I delivered them all except for Stella's. She'll be back the day after tomorrow. We should have brought hers earlier, so she would have had it for Christmas."

"She always spends Christmas with an aunt, apparently, in Garden City," Mrs. Altman explained. "It causes a bit of trouble out back"—she checked to see that Billingsly was out of the room—"because some of the others don't think it's fair she should have it off every year."

"But the others don't have any place to go!" Peggy remonstrated.

"Which is why I let her go. But they of course feel it's not fair."

"I don't think they should complain to you about that, Mother."

"Oh, they don't say a word to me. But I find out about it, somehow. And I don't like to have them feel at Christmas—" She broke off abruptly because the butler had come back into the room. He had gone downstairs to accept his Christmas package with the rest of the help. He carried a silver tray with a glass of tomato juice for Carl.

"I put a little Worcestershire in it," he whispered. "Merry Christmas," he added, deadpan.

"Merry Christmas, Billers," Carl said. "It's perfect. Thanks."

Aunt Hilda came at that point. When she wasn't there at the Gutheims' arrival, everyone had hoped that something this side of death might have happened to deny the family her company for Christmas. Everyone would have been willing for her to have a three-days flu in return for just one family holiday without her. But there she was, fit and deaf as ever, looking a shade too happy in response to Christmas greetings and the prospect of some presents. Sammy came soon after, and still no Altmans.

Instead, Cousin Alma appeared, her arms filled with presents, crying out "Merry Christmas, everyone" in her appealing husky voice. "Let me just set these down here and I'm all yours." She spilled her packages on one of the couches and watched, laughing, as several tumbled onto the floor. She picked them up and balanced them precariously on the pile, then came over to greet the family, beaming and breathless.

Alma Schuler always came on Christmas Eve. She was the daughter of a cousin of Mrs. Altman's who had died some years back, and although she had plenty of closer relatives, she preferred the Altmans for the holiday. They were all glad she did. She and Peggy had been close since childhood, and she was one of the few relatives Peggy genuinely admired. She was regarded as a great oddity in the family, in that not only was she a professor of biology at NYU, but she took her work very seriously. She had a lab and wrote papers and no one in the family had the foggiest notion what she was up to except for Carl. He had been fascinated to have a scholar for a cousin, and he used to quiz her at length about her work. He was thrilled the year she first invited him down to see her lab, and she in turn took a great interest in his scientific education. She always urged him to become a doctor, despite the fact that no member of the Altman family on either side was in medicine. To the others it seemed an exotic idea, except for Alan, who was irritated that someone should suggest anything to Carl other than a musical career.

Alma had never married. Presumably she hadn't wanted to, because she didn't lack for opportunity. She had never been a beauty, but her intellect and energy had given her distinction, and then, too, she was no pauper. For years she had been escorted by one of two men: Freddy Irvine and Bunny Gelber. Bunny was by coincidence a distant relative of Alan's. Both men were apparently content with being shuffled to and fro, although how Alma decided which one would appear with her where remained a mystery. The two men never showed up on the same evening, but for all anyone knew they might have played cards together regularly for years. Some people said that Freddy was the serious boyfriend and that Alma only kept Bunny on tap to stave Freddy off. Others said it was platonic all around, and of course it was inevitably whispered that both men were queer. In the end, no one had a better explanation than that the arrangement apparently satisfied the people involved, which was, after all, the only thing that mattered.

"Isn't Freddy here yet?" Alma asked. "I could murder him."

"No, dear. Why, should he be?" was Peggy's amused reply. Both men were chronically late, which everyone except Alma expected after all these years.

Before he could be murdered, Freddy bustled in the door. " 'The first to a feast, and the last to battle,' as my great and good friend Sir John Falstaff would say," he called out, clapping his hands and rubbing them together as if they were still cold. "You know your Shakespeare, I hope," he said to Carl as he strode by on his way to Mrs. Altman. "Frieda, Merry Christmas. Peggy, Alan, assorted young Gutheims, Merry Christmas, one and all! Sammy! Hilda!" he shouted at the old woman, who looked confused to be addressed so familiarly by what she must have thought to be a total stranger. "Hello, Alma, my dear," he closed rather formally. They never kissed in public.

"Hello there, Freddy," Alan said cordially. He really liked Freddy, and he was also glad not to have his Christmas spoiled by Bunny, whom he disliked on account of some sharp dealings down on the Street, family ties or no family ties.

"Alan, m'boy," Freddy returned warmly. "I was in Chicago last week, saw Milt Glickman, he asked after you, complained he doesn't see you anymore, wanted to know if you were still alive and breathing. I told him that, barring some catastrophe in the previous twenty-four hours, I knew of nothing seriously amiss with your respiration."

"It's true," Alan admitted. "I haven't seen Milt in I don't know how long. How is he? I heard *he* hadn't been all that well."

"He's completely recovered. It was very mild, I understand.

They've cut down on his cigars, but otherwise life goes on pretty much as before."

"It's like your uncle Otto," Peggy told Alan.

"My grandfather had a brother Otto," Alan explained, "—this was my Fleischman grandfather—he was so addicted to cigars that he had one in his mouth and lit before he got out of bed in the morning. You never knew anyone more attached to his cigars than Uncle Otto. Anyway, he had a mild attack, a little like Milt's, as a matter of fact, except that Otto was deep into his seventies at the time. The doctor came to him and said, 'Mr. Fleischman, I'm sorry to have to tell you this, but either you give up those cigars or you'll have another attack before we know it, and the next one, God forbid, could finish you off.' And my uncle Otto looked him in the eye and said, 'If I gave up my cigars, *that* would finish me off.' So the doctor, seeing he was getting nowhere fast, told him, at the very least he'd have to cut down. He told him, if he would smoke half as many cigars as had been his habit, there was the outside chance he might survive. So you know what Otto did? He had his cigars custom-made, twice as big!" Alan burst into appreciative laughter at the memory of his great-uncle's resourcefulness. "He had them make up special cigars! The doctor never knew a thing, and Uncle Otto died in his sleep at the age of ninety-two! That's what he did! He had them custom-made!"

While Alan recovered from his story, Mrs. Altman said, "I feel very badly to keep you all waiting for your presents, but I suppose we should wait for your cousins."

"Why don't I call them?" Peggy offered. "We could at least get some idea as to their timing. How did Eleanor leave it with you?"

"No way in particular," Mrs. Altman said unhappily.

"She didn't say when they'd come?" Peggy asked incredulously.

"I gather it all depended on when Randy got there."

"Well, it's up to her," Peggy said. "Personally, I see no reason whatsoever why they should wait for him. He's perfectly capable of walking over on his own."

"I think they wanted to be there in case he called. They've let the help off for Christmas Eve, and if they're not there he would get no answer if he was trying to reach them."

"Mother dear, if he called and there was no answer, I think even Randy might figure out that he could reach them here."

"I'm a little worried about the roads, I must say," Mrs. Altman confessed.

"Oh, Mother! The roads are just fine." Peggy was angry that her mother should be made anxious by this thoughtless boy who didn't deserve anyone's concern. "Why don't I call Eleanor so you'll at least know when to expect her."

"If you think you ought to . . ." Mrs. Altman consented doubtfully.

"It couldn't matter less to me," Peggy insisted. "I just hate your having to worry. You might want to tell Helga if they're going to be late." Peggy, of course, didn't care when the Altmans got there. She just wanted them to worry less about Randy and more about her mother. If there had been an accident, sitting around and stewing about it wouldn't do him the slightest bit of good. Everyone shared the view of Randy, to be brutally honest, that if he were at that very moment splattered over the Hutchinson Parkway, the loss to mankind wouldn't be tragic. It was a terrible thing to think about a member of one's family. Still, there it was.

"Well, I don't know about anybody else, but I'm not sure how much longer I can wait to open my presents, and I'm sure Carl feels the same way," Sammy cried with forced cheeriness. Like many childless people, he had little grasp of the nuances of maturation, and imagined Carl was beside himself with impatience.

Sounds of a flurry came from the hall. "That must be them," Peggy said, her agitation only increased by the Altmans' arrival. "Carl, why don't you go ahead and start opening your presents."

Carl knew what she was after: She wanted the festivities to be in progress, to impress on Randy how inconsiderate he had been. But he had his own dignity, after all, to worry about. "I can wait for the others," Carl said.

"That's so silly, why should you wait?" Peggy asked. "I see no reason why everyone has to be unwrapping their presents at exactly the same minute. Come on, now, you know you're dying to get started."

"I really can wait," Carl pleaded.

"Just go on ahead," Peggy told him with annoyance.

The joy of Christmas! Carl walked over to the other side of the room and began to rummage around in the piles of presents for one with his name on it. He was saved from having to open it in complete isolation by the entrance of Eleanor, accompanied by Marian and Barbara. Barbara was flushed and radiant, Marian scowling fiercely.

"I couldn't be more dreadfully sorry, Mother dear," Eleanor said. "But here we are. Randy will follow. Merry Christmas everybody. I see that Carl couldn't wait, I don't blame you in the slightest, darling. We were abominable to keep you waiting so long. Alma, dear, how heavenly to see you. Freddy, my angel. Sammy. Hilda." A long and exhausting round of kisses.

"I could have waited," Carl said plaintively, but no one was listening.

Eleanor went on: "Randy just this minute called from somewhere in Connecticut and asked to speak to his father. As soon as I heard his voice and knew he was all right I told him we were all terribly cross with him, wished him a merry Christmas, and handed the phone over to Gerald. I scooped everybody else up and came over. Gerald will come as soon as he's off the phone. Thanks so much, Billingsly. Merry Christmas," she murmured fervently as the butler handed her a drink.

"Merry Christmas, Mrs. Altman," Billingsly replied warmly.

Dickie came in and made the rounds without causing any further break in the conversation. No one paid him the slightest attention.

Eleanor got herself up close to Peggy. "Darling," she said in a low voice, "if it's any consolation to you, I could wring his neck too. I may yet, but I don't propose to let it spoil my Christmas Eve, and particularly not Mother's. We'll deal with him later. Thank God at least he's in one piece."

"I'm sorry you had to go through all that worry," Peggy said, disarmed by Eleanor's obvious distress. "You needn't have rushed, actually. We were all perfectly happy."

"I hated to keep the children waiting. I knew Carl would be chomping at the bit." She smiled indulgently over at Carl, who was still standing alone among the presents, feeling forlorn. He wondered if anyone was planning to come over or if he was to open his presents in solitary. "I'm so relieved, darling, that you've gone ahead, which is so sensible," Eleanor called over. "What have you got there? Oh! You haven't opened it yet."

"Why don't you just open it, dear," Peggy said, irritated at what she took to be his sulking.

Barbara edged up to Joan and whispered, "Johnny's not coming?"

Her conspiratorial sotto voce suggested there was some hidden sexual meaning in Johnny's absence.

"He's with his mother," Joan told her. "I didn't see any reason to subject him to this before he absolutely has to."

"George always loved Christmas Eve. Both of them," Barbara recollected. "But then that was George. He was always put next to Aunt Hilda, and wouldn't you know, he *loved* it. And people wonder why I gave him the gate! You're so lucky. Johnny is a dream."

Joan smiled uncomfortably, and said nothing.

Gradually the family drifted over to the other side of the room, where Carl still hadn't opened his first present. "I'm not sure I can stand the suspense any longer," Freddy joked.

Everyone was now gathered to watch the first present being opened. Carl looked at the card and announced, "It's from Aunt Eleanor and Uncle Gerald."

He had difficulty opening the package with one arm in a cast. Eleanor provided a running commentary. "It comes from Mark Cross," she said, "so you can take it right straight back if it isn't exactly what you want, or if there's something else you're dying to have instead."

Carl opened the box cautiously, steeling himself for something too grotesque to act delirious over. "It smells like leather," he said, slowly removing the tissue paper.

"A brilliant observation, seeing as it comes from Mark Cross," Phil observed.

Carl lifted from the box a handsome brown leather briefcase. "It's a briefcase," he declared, adding with what he hoped would pass for enthusiasm, "It's lovely. Thank you very much."

"I thought you might be able to use one," Eleanor explained. "I had your music in mind, but of course you can use it to carry anything you like. I thought you should have a really nice one, because you're doing *so marvelously* with your piano, dear."

Carl felt he was accepting it under false pretenses, but all he said was, "It's lovely. I'll use it for my music."

Eleanor had more instructions: "If you want to keep it, take it back to Mark Cross, because they'll engrave your initials on the outside. I didn't have them do it because then you wouldn't have been able to return it. Or else you can take it back and exchange it for something you'd really enjoy."

"I'm not going to exchange it. I'm going to keep it and use it. Thank you. Thank you very much, Aunt Eleanor."

"You're so welcome, my pet. Merry Christmas." Eleanor smiled, relieved that her first offering was appreciated.

Alan was inspecting the briefcase. "That's real leather," he said reproachfully, thinking it was much too extravagant, which was certainly true.

"From Mark Cross?" Peggy exclaimed. "You won't find a single thing in that store that isn't real leather."

"Oh, really? I thought they had some things in that synthetic whatever it is."

"There isn't a synthetic thing in the whole store."

"You'd better save the box," Alan cautioned Carl. The credit on that would go a long way for a suitcase, he thought, and meanwhile he had a perfectly usable briefcase somewhere that Carl could have, if he needed one.

"Darling, he said . . . he wanted . . . to keep it," Peggy told him. She could see through her husband any day of the week. As who couldn't.

"I just mean . . . so it won't get wet on the way home . . ." Alan always stammered when he got caught. "I vouldn't vant it should get vet."

"We know what you want, dear," Peggy said sarcastically. She disliked Alan's mock-Yiddish accent. "Why shouldn't he have something nice? He works hard enough for it. I think it was a marvelous choice, Eleanor dear."

"I do my best. I'll get Alan something nice in Naugahyde next year."

"It's terribly nice," said Alan, abashed.

The ice having been broken, the others set about their tasks of opening presents. The two sisters-in-law presided, finding packages and handing them out. Every single gift was opened to the accompaniment of disclaimers and apologies and elaborate instructions on how it could be returned. Mrs. Altman was moved to an armchair near the presents so she could have the pleasure of seeing her grandchildren's surprise and delight. "It's just something to tide you over for tonight," she would tell each one. "You'll get your real present tomorrow, under your own tree."

Hilda sat next to her, smiling uncomprehendingly. Occasionally a gift would be brought over to her and unwrapped on her behalf, the donor's name being shouted in her ear so she would know she hadn't been forgotten at Christmastime. It was anybody's guess whether she got the idea.

In the midst of the chaos, Gerald arrived. Peggy saw him first and knew immediately something was wrong. Eleanor asked him when Randy was going to get there, and he replied tensely, "I'm not sure." She started to ask him a follow-up question, but he cut her off, saying only: "Later."

Someone handed him a present. He half opened it, glanced at the card, registered nothing, and put it aside. Even Mrs. Altman couldn't ignore his worried look. "Shall I have them save something for Randy?" she asked.

"Don't have them go to the trouble, please, Mother," he replied. "I doubt he'll get here before we're through. He's going to call us when he gets home, if we're still here. He can get himself something out of the icebox."

"There's no one there to give him supper," Mrs. Altman observed sorrowfully. "It seems so dreary, on Christmas Eve."

They were interrupted by a scream of delight from Barbara, who rushed over as if she had just been stung by a bee and threw her arms around Mrs. Altman. "They're absolutely divine!" she cried, holding up a pair of purple slacks. "How on earth did you ever know this is the one color I'm absolutely *mad* about?"

"I hoped you'd like them. If not, they're from the shop on the sixth floor in Saks. A Miss Sally. She'll be happy to exchange them for you."

Carl had opened all his presents, and was free to watch the others. No one was more interesting to him than Marian. She was there under protest, as she made unmistakably clear. She had asked that in lieu of presents this year, people would take whatever money they were planning to spend on her and donate it to her group. The request had, of course, been ignored. Now she sat to one side, glowering. She looked uncannily like the Altmans' onetime governess, Miss Georgina, who had clearly had a strong, baleful influence on her personality. Christmas must have been a trial to Marian. Her presents reflected everyone's view of her: a sweater from the Gutheims, in a gloomy brown; a sensible purse from Mrs. Altman; a book from Alma, obviously chosen with the assistance of a clerk who specialized in the hard-to-please. She opened them all joylessly, picking off the tape so as not to tear the wrapping paper, slowly pulling out boxes that held the drabbest gifts imaginable, thanking her relatives in her funereal and faintly disapproving manner. No one could remember the last time she had had fun.

When all the presents, except for Randy's, had been opened, Barbara went to a side table and took up a large package that had been left conspicuously for the last. "Now, Grandmother," she declared dramatically, "it's your turn."

Mrs. Altman never opened her present until everyone had finished. She didn't think it was right to keep the children from their excitement while she unwrapped a gift for herself. She would have preferred not to receive any present at all. She was a giver, through and through. But everyone insisted that she should have one. She relented, on the condition there was to be one, only, from everyone. It shouldn't be extravagant. The grandchildren were not to use their allowance on her. And so on and so forth. In the end, her present became an object of great anxiety to everyone. Peggy and Eleanor alternated picking it out from year to year. This year was Eleanor's turn, and she watched with uncharacteristic nervousness as her mother-in-law struggled with the package.

"I can't imagine what it can be," Mrs. Altman said, postponing as long as possible the dreadful moment when the object would be revealed, demanding from her an instantaneous public response. "It's terribly heavy, for such a small box."

"Let me help you, Mother," Gerald said, fretful that the present was proving a burden.

"Well, not *that* heavy." Mrs. Altman laughed. She was trying to tear off some tape that held together a swathing of corrugated wrapping, and there was more laughter as people tried to help. The only thing that would do was a sharp fingernail, something not to be found in a family of biters. Finally, by joint effort, it was opened, and Mrs. Altman lifted out the object itself and removed a final layer of tissue paper. It was a sparkling pony of solid Venetian glass, amber and ruby and deep green, smooth all over except for its pointed ears. A mane swirled over its neck like a glass wind. It had lain in a bed of excelsior like a newborn colt, and when Mrs. Altman held it up everyone gasped in admiration.

"It's perfectly charming," she said. "I couldn't be more delighted with it. Thank you all, it's darling."

"I thought it would look lovely on your entrance hall table," Eleanor said, to remove any possible doubt as to whose taste was being admired.

"I know just where I'm going to put it," Mrs. Altman said. "I'm going to put it on the mantelpiece upstairs, where it will catch the morning sunlight." She saw the flicker of disagreement in her daughter-in-law's face. "Do you think it would be all right there? Should I put it downstairs?"

"You should put it wherever it gives you the most pleasure, Mother dear," Eleanor said, gallantly concealing her chagrin that so few guests would see it, and ask who had found it.

"It's a marvelous choice," Peggy told Eleanor, seeing she needed consolation.

The giving and receiving of presents had its intended effect of kindling the flickering embers of family warmth and affection. By the time the prancing horse was displayed, glittering, on the table next to Mrs. Altman, the Christmas spirit had indeed taken hold. Whatever their feelings toward one another, they were a family, come together to celebrate the holiday. This gathering, under Mrs. Altman's benediction, was the center of their lives. Whatever their ambitions or disappointments, resentments or hopes, they were a close and loving family. If peace and joy were to be found anywhere, they would be found there.

But Joan felt neither peaceful nor joyful. She had gone through the motions with a good face, smiling and laughing and opening her presents with the required show of delight and gratitude. Inwardly, she was in a turmoil. Her life seemed to consist more and more of elements that couldn't be held together but were pulling farther and farther apart. Here she was in the midst of an opulent Altman Christmas, whose leavings were strewn around the room. The children of Meyer House were enduring, for the most part, a meager, cold holiday. She was being admired and envied for her engagement to a paragon, but she wanted to be with someone who couldn't even set foot in that room. Physically, she was falling to pieces. The sensations of sexuality, modulated increasingly by marijuana, dominated her. She barely touched food, but felt no hunger. She saw herself as voracious in every other respect; the one way she could deny herself was by not eating. She had too much as it was.

She couldn't bear to look at the surfeit of presents and wrapping paper and boxes. She had suffered over the bleak Christmas her children would have. She had wanted to provide them with everything they wanted, if only for one year. It seemed almost cruel not to, when she could so easily afford it. She had flirted with the idea of buying gifts to be delivered anonymously. That would have been the selfless thing to do. She had even gone so far as to raise it with her father, who hadn't much liked the plan. He thought it would come to a pretty hefty tab, as he put it, and said the money could be better spent on something more enduring—a special room bearing her name, where they could come and play games, for example, something solid that would outlast this one Christmas. He offered to donate it if she particularly wanted to do something for Meyer House, although, he pointed out, the Altmans and the Gutheims practically kept the place afloat single-handedly as it was. He calculated the cash equivalent of the time she was donating to the settlement house, and pointed out that it represented in itself a very generous contribution. Joan appealed to Peggy, who of course had no objections. Although she did wonder if it was right to raise unrealistic expectations in the children. What would they think, suddenly to be inundated far beyond their previous experience? Was it fair in terms of the rest of their lives? But—if Joan really wanted to do it, she suggested talking it over with Martin.

The matter died there; but the memory of it came back now to Joan, and she grieved inwardly for the children. Barbara came over so the two of them could see each other's presents. Joan managed a semblance of gaiety—"That's *so* great, Bobbie!" she cried, laughing and hugging her cousin.

Peggy saw the troubled look before the laughter—she didn't miss much—and was sure she knew the reason. Joan still resented her having arranged for that girl to help her get to work and back every day. But what should she have done? Sat by idly until the next disaster struck? It was terribly unfair. Everybody told her she was too lenient with Joan, letting her get thinner and thinner without doing anything about it, and then Joan turned around and accused her of interfering. Of course, it wasn't true. Joan led her own life. All the children did. Peggy would never have complained, but she had not been allowed to do what she wanted when she was Joan's age. She wanted nothing more than to give her own children perfect freedom, to do with their lives as they wished.

But it was hard. To look at Joan was to feel that something terrible was about to happen. Peggy had felt that for some time now. True, no calamity had yet taken place. Still, everyone said that she wasn't taking proper care of her own daughter. Could it be true, she asked herself. If only the child wouldn't look so deathly pale!

She would speak to Lamartine, she decided. Right after Christmas. Before it was too late.

Meanwhile, Carl had been asked to go to the piano. When the children were young, he had played carols at this point, but with the passing of years no one wanted to sing. The custom couldn't be entirely abandoned, and Mrs. Altman didn't want to give up the music altogether, so a compromise had been reached: one carol only. This year, with his left arm in a sling, the accompaniment was rudimentary. He felt like one of those cripples who, failing to elicit a miracle, throws away his crutches only to fall flat on his face. But with a little faking and a lot of pedal he managed to make it through "Adeste Fideles." With no one singing it sounded austere and grave, and people fell silently to their thoughts.

The music was the last event before dinner, which Billingsly now announced. The family went up to the dining room and were seated according to the plan Eleanor had worked out with great care; except that, of course, Randy wasn't there. His place had to be removed and the remainder closed in over the gap. Everyone sat down, somewhat subdued by the absence of a grandchild and the somber influence of the music. An unaccustomed hush descended over them all.

Peggy found herself next to her brother. They rarely talked intimately anymore, but Christmas Eve had stirred dormant feelings in both of them. "Difficulty with your youngest, I take it?" she whispered. Her tone was sympathetic rather than critical, and Gerald turned gratefully toward her.

"This time I'm afraid he's in pretty hot water," was Gerald's answer.

"I hadn't the slightest doubt the moment you walked into the room."

"You were right. I didn't want to say anything for fear of spoiling the evening for Mother. But the truth of the matter is he's been involved in an accident. I didn't get all the details completely straight, as you might understand, but I gather one person in the other car was hurt. It may be serious, they don't know yet. Randy's completely unharmed, thank God, but there seems to be some question as to whether he wasn't responsible. It isn't clear if they'll let him go. There wasn't much I could do. I spoke to the officer in charge at the police station where he's apparently been taken. He seemed rather decent for someone in upstate Connecticut, I must say, but he couldn't tell me if there would be any charges. I couldn't stay on the phone all evening without alarming Mother, so I told Randy to do as he was told, for once, and to say nothing beyond the barest essentials until we can get a lawyer in there."

Peggy took a deep breath. Even for Randy, it sounded bad. "Is this something Alan should be in on?"

"I'll speak to him after dinner. I think we'd do better to have a local man, someone who knows these people."

"You probably didn't have a chance to find out if he'd been drinking," Peggy suggested.

"I as a matter of fact asked him point-blank and he swore he hadn't touched a drop. I'm inclined to believe him." Peggy raised her eyebrows almost imperceptibly. Gerald saw it. "Or at least to give him the benefit of the doubt for the time being. There'll be time enough to go into all that. The important thing now is to get him down here and then we can assess the situation and see what needs to be done. If he can't drive down, or they won't let him, I can slip away quietly after supper and be up there in an hour and a half." He looked out the window. "Say, two at the most."

Peggy would have liked to know something about the person who had been injured, but she didn't want to press that just then.

"I must say, I'm pleased at how well Randy's handling himself," Gerald said, brightening a bit. "When all is said and done, he didn't fall to pieces, as one might reasonably expect of a boy of nineteen. No, I really think something from all those years on the tennis court may finally be paying off. Standing up under pressure, that sort of thing. He's taking it awfully well."

Peggy couldn't refrain from asking, "You don't think possibly too well?"

But Gerald didn't get her point. After a moment, he said, "And then there's Dickie, of course. After this little escapade of his, I'm ready to pack him off to military school all over again."

Peggy shook her head. "Not that that was any howling success when you tried it."

"I suppose not," Gerald mused. "What do you think—I'm serious—what do you think we ought to do with him?"

"Do you really want my opinion?" she asked. "I don't think you ought to *do* anything with him. His whole problem is that you're trying to lead his life for him. He'd be much better off if he had to stand on his own two feet. Outside the firm, I'd say. Outside New York, if possible. I don't say you should send him away, but if he could succeed or fail on his own, and not lean on you all the time, he'd be a damn sight better off, if you ask me."

Gerald looked interested. "I wish you'd tell Eleanor that."

"Sweetie," Peggy said with a smile, "if I've learned one thing in life it's not to give advice when it's not asked for. Nor wanted, I may add."

"Oh, but that doesn't apply to you and Eleanor!" Gerald said.

"*Especially* to me and Eleanor."

Gerald would have argued the point, but just then Mrs. Altman called over, "I must tell you, I had the loveliest Christmas card from Jeanne Grant."

"Isn't that nice," Peggy said.

"Who in God's name is Jeanne Grant?" Gerald asked.

"She was Jeanne Latour" was Alan's explanation.

"Jeanne Latour!" Alma exclaimed. "How many years is it since I heard that name! What's ever become of her?"

"She married a man by the name of Phillip Grant," Alan told her. "He's a big cheese at the Cleveland Trust, and she moved out there to marry him. They have two children who must be almost school age, I imagine."

"I can tell you exactly," Mrs. Altman said, "because she always sends along a charming picture of the children. The girl is seven, and the little boy is five, and they're both simply adorable."

"Hardly surprising," Alan said, adding to Phil and Freddy, "she was what you might call a looker in her younger days."

"She still is," Peggy said. "And if anyone deserves all the happiness in the world, she does. I always wonder, how does a woman like that manage to pick herself up, with an alcoholic mother and no father in the picture, and make something of herself. I'm always amazed at that sort of thing." She snuck a glance at her sister-in-law, whose parents also fit that description, but Eleanor didn't bat an eyelash. But then, Eleanor had made something of herself against the odds too; and deserved perhaps more happiness than her children were at the moment allowing her.

"Wasn't the sister a little odd?" Gerald groped with his memory of the Latour family.

"Darling, she spent eight years in Bloomingdale's, so I think she has a right to be odd," Eleanor replied, using the familiar name of the asylum.

"She was in Hartford, actually," Peggy corrected her. "I still see her from time to time. She copes, although barely. They have her on some kind of medication, and she calls me occasionally to see if I'll help with whatever little charity she collects for, she always has something like Muscular Dystrophy, or Save the Children, some such thing, perfectly harmless. I give her tea, and a check, which seems to keep her happy. So there she is, and there's Jeanne, who somehow managed to pull through it all. Albeit in Cleveland," she added, everyone smiling at the notion of trying to find happiness in such a backwater.

"She wrote me the nicest note," Mrs. Altman said. "I don't know why she goes to the trouble every year, but I must say it's lovely to hear from her."

Peggy differed: "I think it's very nice, but you're the only person I can imagine who would be surprised. The woman lived in your house for a month. When you take a perfect stranger in off the street, you might at least expect to hear from her at Christmastime."

"She wasn't a perfect stranger at all, she was a close friend of yours," Mrs. Altman protested.

"She was a perfect stranger to you," Peggy insisted.

"It was a terrible sacrifice for me," Mrs. Altman said. She allowed herself the mildest possible sarcasm, only when deprecating herself.

For a moment everyone fell silent. They were thinking of Jeanne Latour Grant, perhaps, and how she had managed when she had no place to go; and how marvelously life had turned out for her, albeit in Cleveland; and of her sister, wandering harmlessly around New York in a haze of medication, accepting tea and a check from Jeanne's old college friends; of the many who had come through it all; and the many more who hadn't; and of the occasional Frieda Altmans, who took strangers into her home and was astonished to receive annual Christmas cards in thanks.

The time seemed right to Barbara, who pushed back her chair and stood up, smiling in slight embarrassment and peering at a sheet of paper she had brought in with her. "Ah!" Eleanor cried, and Alan tinkled on his wine glass with a spoon to signal attention for the toast.

"What's this?" Hilda cried out in confusion. Freddy bent over to try and explain it to her, but it was a hopeless task. Alma told him to shush so Barbara could begin. The servants had come noiselessly out of the pantry and stood behind the screen that hid the door, so they could hear.

Lowering her paper, Barbara looked toward Mrs. Altman and began:

> *"Another year's gone by now*
> *And here we are once more.*
> *Let's raise a glass on high now*
> *As in the days of yore."*

An appreciative murmur greeted the successful completion of an entire stanza, whose unexpected extra rhyme gave promise of a special treat this year.

> *"As in the days when—"*

She stopped, suppressed a mischievous grin, and looked around the table until she spotted her oldest cousin. She spoke his name with a little cry of surprise, as if she had just selected him to be "it" in a game of hide-and-go-seek:

> *"—Phillip,*
> *Made rules for every game;*
> *Soon he'll be in Washington,*
> *Then on to greater fame."*

Phil gave a modest little smile while all the others applauded his next success. Barbara continued:

> *"When Dickie, now at Altman's,*
> *Could for his start well thank*
> *That famous game of Monop'ly*
> *The day he broke the bank."*

The recollection was perhaps not the most fortunate one Barbara could have chosen. Dickie, who never came off too well in these ditties, looked no more peevish than usual.

> *"When Marian played the violin—*
> *That famous 'Air in G';*
> *She no longer plays the fiddle*
> *But sings 'Nearer My God to Thee.'"*

Marian didn't join the nervous laughter. Barbara smiled at her to indicate that the whole thing was meant in pure fun, but she evidently didn't agree.

> *"When Bobbie only cared for*
> *Her trading cards and gum;*
> *Does anyone remember when*
> *She thought that boys were dumb?"*

A little polite laughter for her sense of humor about herself.

> *"When Joanie feared our attic*
> *Where Dickie saw that mouse;"*

Joan gave a little scream of remembrance, and Barbara cried, "Do you remember that, Joanie?" To which Joan replied, "How could I ever forget?"

> *"To think that now she travels*
> *By subway to Meyer House!"*

People turned to smile at the subject of each stanza. They all nodded at Joan in approval of her good works, and also because they were all still worried about her. Barbara lowered her paper and said, "The next one's about Randy, so I don't know whether to read it." The others thought she should, so she continued:

> *"When Randy left for camp*
> *In a tidal wave of tears;*
> *They say he's now in college*
> *Tho' we haven't seen him in years."*

The unplanned aptness of the verse left everyone in embarrassed silence, and Barbara pressed on to the next:

> *"When Carl—"*

She stopped and looked around for her cousin before going on. Carl braced himself for some reference to his weight, which he always dreaded at these occasions. Finding him, Barbara continued:

> *"When Carl would play at Rosefield*
> *To the great delight of all,*

Everyone knew that someday
He'd be at Carnegie Hall."

"On the stage!" Alan stipulated, lest anyone think that spectator status would suffice for his talented son. Carl blushed guiltily, knowing as he did that he would never fulfill the prediction.

"Oh! for our carefree childhood—
The good old days gone by—
But the future holds much promise
And so we must not cry."

Barbara stopped there because the next two sheets of paper were out of order. During the pause, people reflected on the good old days gone by, and thought, perhaps, of Rosefield: Rosefield, during the summers of the war, when the family spent its happiest times. No one quite believed that the future, whatever its promise, would bring such happiness again.

Finding her place, Barbara continued:

"A little birdie told me
In strictest confidence
That the New York Bar will soon have
One of its greatest presidents."

Alan frowned amid the congratulatory sounds. "Now that really *is* in strictest confidence," he said, but everyone could tell how pleased he was. Freddy added, "You could say 'its greatest,' without qualification, and the line would scan better as well." Barbara smiled, not knowing what he was talking about, and went on:

"For Daddy, all we wish for
Is no more proxy fights
For Mummy, no more phone calls
Through endless sleepless nights."

"I'll drink to that one," Eleanor called out.

"All day Aunt Peggy's meetings
Take her uptown and down
Her tireless work for others
Is the toast of all the town."

"Thank you, dear," Peggy responded to her niece's gracious compliment. She reflected that, when all was said and done, Barbara was a very sweet girl.

> *"Our learned cousin Alma*
> *Whom all of us adore;*
> *And since you bring us Freddy*
> *We love you even more."*

"It's luck for you," Freddy put in, "that 'Freddy' and 'Bunny' have the same number of syllables." Everyone laughed in appreciation of his savoir faire.

> *"Cousin Sammy, we're so happy*
> *You're with us on this day;*
> *And Aunt Hilda whom we love to see—*
> *As all who're here will say."*

People smiled at Hilda to indicate that she was being honored, but the poor old woman had long since given up the struggle to follow what was going on.

> *"And now I ask you all*
> *To join in happy toast—"*

Barbara raised her glass, and the others reached for theirs.

> *"To the one we all most cherish*
> *To the one we love the most."*

Looking at her grandmother, Barbara put down her paper and recited the last of the ode from memory:

> *"A Merry, Merry Christmas*
> *A Happy New Year too;*
> *Our dearest, dearest Grandma*
> *From all of us to you."*

Freddy cried, "Hear! Hear!" as everyone rose and lifted their glasses toward Mrs. Altman, who was beaming in happy appreciation. Her eyes glistened as Barbara came around the table to give her a special hug and to receive the compliments for her prodigious effort. Gerald smiled proudly at his daughter. He was quite moved. In fact, everyone was amazed, year after year, that Barbara could produce such a poem. While

Barbara kissed Mrs. Altman, Alan began to sing, conducting the others with his glass: "For she's a jolly good fellow." The others joined in, but only Alan wanted to continue through the second verse: "Which nobody can deny." He ended with his invariable cadence: "And she lives . . . in . . . our alley!"

The maids, brushing away tears from their cheeks, were led in by Billingsly to serve the main course.

On the morning after Christmas day, Peggy went to the phone and dialed Lamartine.

Having forced herself to the unpleasant task, she was not pleased to be stalled by the office nurse, who insisted on knowing what she was calling about. Then there was a long wait before the nurse came on the phone once more to say, "Doctor will speak to you now, Mrs. Gutheim." It particularly grated on her to hear a grown woman refer to her employer as "Doctor." She disliked the affectation, and she didn't have to be reminded that Lamartine was busy. Who wasn't?

Still, the man had proved himself useful; and besides, you don't get rid of a perfectly competent doctor simply because his nurse puts you on hold.

"Mrs. Gutheim!" he said when he came on the phone. "I'm so sorry they kept you waiting. I've left instructions you are to be put through immediately whenever you call, but this is a new girl. What can I do for you?"

Peggy was not one to dwell on unimportant details. She came straight to the point: "I'm not a hundred percent happy with the way Joan is looking recently," she told him.

"Neither am I, Mrs. Gutheim."

"She's looking terribly drawn, and she's tense all the time. Her weight hasn't improved one iota so far as I can see. I've tried to leave her eating alone, she's after all an adult, and these endless discussions don't seem to help in any case. All they do is get her terribly upset, and she's as thin as ever. She's more exhausted than she was when she first came down. Of course, she insists on burning the candle at both ends. There's nothing we can do about that, she leads her own life. But leaving that aside, I would think there was some way we could help."

Lamartine proceeded cautiously. "Do you have any ideas, Mrs. Gutheim?"

"I would have thought that was your department."

He paused. He didn't want to overreach himself. Still, maybe the time had come to pull out the stops. "I had thought it might be useful to put her to bed for a short time, in the hospital, where we can keep an eye on her, run some more tests, chart her input and output, monitor various parameters. Really get an accurate picture. I know you've always been dead set against it," he added.

"I've never been wild about the idea, I'll admit that, but I wouldn't say I was dead set one way or the other."

"If you'd permit it, I think it might help. I don't guarantee anything."

"I'm not asking you to. All I'm asking is that there be a purpose to it. I still see no reason to put her to bed simply for the sake of making an invalid out of her."

"Believe me, Mrs. Gutheim, the last thing in the world I want to do is to make an invalid out of Joan. Even if such a thing were possible, which I seriously doubt."

That was the right thing to say. "Not as long as I have anything to say about it," Peggy said.

"There's no question about that, Mrs. Gutheim. Nothing—as you know—nothing has been done, nor will be, without your express approval. Or Mr. Gutheim's, it goes without saying."

He was too smooth for her taste; but a damn good doctor. "It's Joan's approval that concerns us," she reminded him.

"Have you discussed her coming into the hospital?" he asked.

"How could I, when I didn't know a thing about it until this minute?" Peggy said sharply. "But of course I will. Shall we leave it, the day after New Year's? Can you get her a bed then?"

Lamartine, invisible at the other end of the phone, allowed himself the luxury of a smile. "I daresay it can be arranged," he assured her.

Etta Sevitsky, also, had a matter to attend to before she could see the year out with equanimity. Her task was hard, and not made easier for her by the fact that she had to carry it out in Martin Perry's office. Etta hadn't been in the director's office more than a handful of times since first coming to Meyer House. On those few occasions when she needed to ask something of her boss, she preferred to collar him in the lobby, where conversations tended to be brief and requests more readily granted. But for what she had to say, she needed privacy. The door was even closed.

"I didn't know if I should say anything to you about it, Mr. Perry," she said. She was perched nervously on a chair set close to his. Martin Perry never allowed a desk to come between him and someone who had come to him.

"Of course you did the right thing," he reassured her gently. "I need to know what's going on in the House. After all, it's not as though this is a crime. There's no rule against it here. These things happen."

"If I thought it was just the one time, I would have let it go without another thought," Etta explained. "After all, who could blame her? If I were her age, you'd have a hard time keeping me away from him. Of course, I'm not speaking as a member of her family," she added with reverence.

"As I say, it's no crime," Martin Perry repeated. "He's a handsome boy."

"He's that, Mr. Perry," Etta said, her eyes moist with a spinster's longing for Kevin's barrel arms. "I'm very fond of him. But he's not for her."

"I wouldn't think so, no."

"She's—she's like a daughter to me. I couldn't stand by and see her hurt."

"Of course not."

"Not that I like to report on people," Etta added. She had in her time traveled in leftist circles, and she hated informants.

"I don't consider that's what you're doing," Martin Perry said. "We're all close to one another at Meyer House. I naturally take an interest in the welfare of everyone here—clients, staff, whoever. Everyone's family, as far as I'm concerned."

"It's why I've stayed here all these years, Mr. Perry."

"We wouldn't want it any other way, Etta," Martin Perry said warmly. He got up, to indicate that whatever needed to be said had now been said.

"I feel better, now I've talked to you," Etta said.

"Etta, I'm grateful to you for letting me know about this. It's always good to have a chat with you. Come by more often, will you?"

"Happy New Year, Mr. Perry," she said as he opened the door for her.

"Happy New Year, Etta," he returned. "Behave yourself New Year's Eve, now."

"Oh, Mr. Perry!" she cried, tears springing up again as she left, so that this time she had to take out her handkerchief and wipe her eyes.

After she left, Martin Perry sat down behind his desk and allowed a sigh to escape. A pity. The boy was doing a fine job with the hoodlums, and he had himself come such a long way. Martin Perry hated to let him go. But there was no choice, really. The only question was, how to break it to him without his suspecting the real reason. Without anyone suspecting.

It might be easier after the first of the year. But then again if he told the boy now, it could be passed off as a budgetary matter. They could give him a warm and affectionate farewell at the end-of-the-year party, and then the young people could send him off in style at their New Year's Eve dance in the gymnasium. Maybe he ought to come this year, Martin Perry thought, but vetoed the idea. The dance was strictly for the kids. They'd be uncomfortable if he came.

Now to decide what to tell the boy. Nothing sprang immediately to mind. He'd think of something, though. That was what they paid him for.

Although Lamartine was the one to tell Joan he wanted her to go into the hospital, she knew very well who had made the decision. She knew perfectly well that he would never do it on his own hook. That night there was another row. Alan was at a meeting, Phil was off somewhere, and Carl was holed up in his room pretending to be oblivious to what was going on around him. The two women were free to battle on uninterrupted. They wound up exhausted, and accomplished nothing. The air was no clearer than before. Joan went off the next morning without speaking either to Peggy, or to Alan, who was completely mystified. He never quite caught up on what went on when he was out.

Joan wasn't good for much of anything at work. She knew she would be away for some period of time after the New Year. It was possible she wouldn't be back, ever. But she couldn't bring herself to say a real good-bye. There was talk of a school placement for Pearl. If that was so, she wouldn't be coming to Meyer House anymore. The uncertainty was difficult for her; it was difficult for them all. Pearl lost some of the ground she had gained. Her speech became worse, and she became clinging with Joan. Mark was having his problems with the holidays too. All morning he did nothing except career around the room and drive everyone nuts. He couldn't be contained. Claire was retreating farther and farther, looking more irretrievable than ever. Leona, who was usually so unflappable, seemed to have a bad case of nerves. Losing Pearl would be hard on her. Losing Joan would be devastating.

Kevin wasn't in the cafeteria when Joan went down at lunchtime. He wasn't in the settlement house at all that day. No one seemed to know where he was, or if he was coming in. Rumors were flying: that he had been fired; that he had left town; that he was in some kind of trouble with the law. People were saying that he had been arrested by the police and taken into custody. No one knew the facts, but feeling ran high against Martin Perry. Perhaps because of her special status with the director, Joan found the others cold. When she came over to sit with the younger staff, the conversation changed in that ostentatious way that indicates ostracism without coming out into the open with it. There was talk of a New Year's Eve dance, but when Joan tried to find out about it she got cryptic responses. No one put it into words, but she understood she wouldn't be welcome. Feeling unjustly treated, she spoke to Jenna about it afterward. She found no sympathy in that quarter. "It's not what you're used to," Jenna said coldly, and added, "If you have some other party to go to, you'd probably have a better time there. With your friends."

By the end of the day Joan was bewildered and hurt and agitated. The gymnasium had remained ominously silent throughout the afternoon. Joan knew she shouldn't go up there, but when she was through with work she went up anyway. Kevin wasn't there. A few tough teenagers stood about. They stared insolently at her and didn't speak to her. Jenna, who no longer escorted her to and from work, was in the lobby when Joan left for the day. She was still out of sorts. Joan considered confronting her, but shrank back.

She forced herself to stay in the building until Jenna left. When she did go, she was so anxious to get to Kevin's apartment that she almost overtook Jenna and gave herself away. She had to duck into a doorway to avoid being seen, and she felt like a spy, or a thief, sneaking through the streets. There were few people out. The holiday cheer was fading fast, and the neighborhood had returned to its everyday bleakness. Joan hardly noticed. Too many other thoughts troubled her.

Arriving at Kevin's building, she mounted the stairs with increasing dread. What if he were angry with her too? What if he believed she was in some way responsible for whatever had happened to him? How could she explain it, when she didn't know what she was accused of? Or he might turn on her for no reason at all. He was perfectly capable of doing that. She was prepared—she thought she was prepared—to say good-bye, but she didn't think she could bear to be kicked out. What if he got rough with her? Violence was never far from the surface, it could erupt any time. She had no plan of how she would deal with him. When she got to his door, she realized she wasn't ready to face him.

As it turned out, she didn't have to. He wasn't there. She found only Harlow, disconnected as always from the real world. He didn't know where Kevin was. He had no interest in the subject, but talked of Kevin as of some distant acquaintance he saw infrequently. "Did you check out that . . . you know, like, *settlement* house, man? What's its name? He works there?" He offered Joan marijuana, pills, tequila. Joan didn't believe he was that drugged. He seemed to know more than he let on, but there was no way of getting anything much out of him. He crossed his legs and went into a seeming trance. He refused to respond to her. She left in greater turmoil than when she had come.

She was reaching the end of her rope. She didn't know where to go, whom to rely on. Her relationship with Kevin—whatever in the world that had been—was disintegrating. Probably it was gone already. The forces against it were too overwhelming for such a tenuous thing to survive. She felt she could accept its being over if only she could see him and talk to him. One more time, that was all she asked, just one more time with him. She wanted to see his face, hear his voice, feel his body. Was that too much to ask?

But when? She couldn't find him, and she had her own obligations to think of: her friends, Johnny, the family. The affair with Kevin had taken place within a small gap in her life, between Meyer House and home; that gap was fast closing. Any day now it wouldn't exist. If she was going to see him, even to say good-bye, it had to be soon. But first she had to find him, and he was nowhere to be found. Time was running out. Soon the new year would be upon them.

Sixteen

Alan Gutheim's days lengthened with the coming of the winter solstice, as befitted a true man of the city. Holiday festivities competed with the year-end press of business, and he put in longer and longer hours as December wore on. During the last week of the year he was never home before seven, sometimes eight. Every year it got worse, but this year he seriously wondered for his sanity. So much was happening at once. The commission officially ceased to exist at midnight, December 31, and all business had to be wound up. The fund drive for the new medical school, which he had been wheedled into chairing, was being launched immediately in the new year, and a thousand things needed his personal attention. Aside from his own regular cases there was this takeover mess of Gerry's, which was coming to a head. Considering he'd been summarily dismissed by his brother-in-law two months before, it had taken far too much of his time, none of which was being paid for, incidentally. On top of everything else he had Phil's clerkship as well as the Bar Association to worry about. Both those decisions were due any day now. There was no denying he was on tenterhooks. Not for himself: these things were of little consequence to him. But Phil had, after all, worked hard, and he deserved this as much as anyone possibly could. As for the presidency, if Alan sought it at all it was not for any personal ambition, but for everyone of the Jewish faith who cared about New York City.

Also, he had to admit, Peggy would be pleased.

Still, despite the terrific press of business, he was not unhappy. If anyone thrived on a hectic schedule, it was Alan Gutheim. He could take some provisional satisfaction on several fronts. The commission's report was ready for final approval. Phil had practically written it single-handed, not that he had received proper recognition. The report would be submitted to the mayor with appropriate hoopla early in January. Excerpts would be reprinted in the *Times* and copies given to all the appropriate agencies and organizations, where they would gather impressive amounts of dust. The Problems of Youth would continue pretty much as before; but then, whoever thought they wouldn't? Certainly not Alan.

As for the fund drive, he had less reason for cynicism. That achievement would be real, and lasting. There was a lot of hard work still to be done, but he had no doubt they would do what they set out to accomplish. He himself was setting an example with a pledge that would put to shame any four-flushers who hoped to get a free ride out of this. Alan envisioned Mt. Sinai Medical School as a tribute to the generosity and pride and public spirit of a community prepared to live up to its responsibilities. By the same token it would stand as a permanent rebuke to any who failed in theirs. Alan Gutheim would know who was who, make no mistake about that. He already had a pretty good idea.

What else? There was Gerry's Folly, as he called it (only to Peggy). It did look, he had to say, as though Gerry might pull it off. Abbott & Strawbridge was about to wave the white flag. With the Abbott estate no longer in their camp, they had pretty much caved in. Word was they would make a formal announcement the next day. Gerry was delirious, Alan less so. It had proven ugly, far uglier than he had anticipated. All the mudslinging, acrimony, sharp tactics, shaving it close—it was not Alan's cup of tea. Keeping Dickie Altman out of jail had been no picnic, and by the same token there had been no pleasure in finding out that there had been hanky-panky on the other side. Initially he'd resented being pushed aside for Bernstein (who hadn't, incidentally, panned out as such a hotshot after all; Gerry had come running to Alan whenever the going got rough). But now he was glad to have stayed behind the scenes. His hands were clean. Well, his conscience was clean, at any rate. "To thy own self be true, and it must follow, as the night the day, thou canst not then be false to any man." Polonius knew what he was talking about. Of course, he only had Laertes to deal with, not Dickie Altman.

Signing the last of the letters on his desk, Alan pushed back his

chair and looked at his watch. It was past seven. He'd outstayed everyone at the office. It had been a busy day, a full day, back-to-back appointments, conferences, board meetings, dashing from one end of the city to
the other, no letup, the kind of day he loved the best. Now for a brisk
walk home, and the best part of all: his children. They were truly his
jewels. The mother of the Gracchi had nothing on him. He couldn't
wait to see them. Not that it would be for long: they'd all be off before
the evening was over. The holiday social whirl was in full swing, and his
children were in the thick of it all, needless to say. Dinners, dances,
parties, one on top of the other, they weren't getting in until two, three
in the morning, it was madness, but then they were young, and hadn't
he done the same thing at their age? Joan, it was true, looked as though
she might drop with exhaustion any moment now, but the doctors had
given her a clean bill of health, no matter what one's eyes told one.
Anyone could see Joan was still much too thin. Even now he thought
they ought to talk to her, urge her to get more rest, insist that she at least
eat more sensibly. He'd tried his damnedest with Peggy about that, but
Peggy had told him, in no uncertain terms, that he was to keep . . . his
mouth . . . shut. Which ended the matter as far as anything he was
ever able to do.

Enough! He roused himself from his reverie, gathered his things,
and left the office. He had hoped to run into the cleaning lady on the
way out, but didn't see her. It was too bad. He enjoyed their chummy
exchanges, and he also wanted someone to witness how late he was
working. In the hallway, he had a moment's uncharacteristic anxiety,
wondering if the elevator might arrive harboring some unsavory character. But when it came, the car was empty and he chided himself for his
foolish fears.

Stepping out onto Park Avenue, he braced himself against the evening's chill, but the air was surprisingly mild, with virtually no wind.
That was a bonus. He could endure any amount of cold without much
trouble, but a stiff wind severely tested his no-coat policy. He looked
with pleasure at the line of lighted Christmas trees visible as far as
Lenox Hill, and exulted in being out in his beloved New York, the most
exciting city in the world.

In honor of the season he decided to walk straight up Park. That
way he would run into the maximum number of people he knew, and
also the route would take him by the Waldorf. Not that he had any use
for the hotel itself, which was vastly overrated in his book. The Empire

Room was the last word in phony chichi. As for the Starlight Roof, it didn't hold a candle to the St. Regis. Nevertheless—he liked to walk by, particularly at this time of year, and see what was going on. The Grand Ballroom was in constant demand, particularly for the most fashionable parties of the upper crust. With any luck, he might see some of the young people, resplendent in their evening clothes: the boys in tuxedos more often than tails nowadays, but the girls looking as fetching in their gowns as their mothers had some thirty years before—a topic on which, if he did say so himself, he was something of an authority.

It was too early for a dance, but sometimes there were preliminary dinner parties, and Alan hoped to catch people arriving for one of those. He saw a cab pull up to the entrance when he was still some way off, and he quickened his pace. But it was only an out-of-town family, midwestern most likely, judging from the dumbfounded expressions of the wife and evidently two daughters as they got out and waited for their husband/father to pay off the cabbie. The bellboy was carrying in their bags, and they seemed overawed by it all. Alan had an impulse to say a few words of welcome, thinking someone should extend the hospitality of the town to these bewildered people. In another life he wouldn't have minded being the city's official greeter. Jimmy Walker, for all his failings —and he had more than his share—had a gift for that sort of thing. But while he was searching for something to say that wouldn't give the impression he was a crackpot, they disappeared into the hotel itself, where they would get a strictly routine reception at the desk. Pity.

The idea of playing the host took on a sudden irresistibility, and Alan thought he might give it at least one more shot. Just a friendly word or two, then quickly disappear before they even had a chance to thank him. Call it one New Yorker's eccentric gesture. He didn't want to hang around the entrance, though. He looked respectable enough, but there was no telling what the doorman might think, and there was always the outside chance he'd be told to move along. He retraced his way down to the corner of 49th, where he could linger without anyone noticing. Just to be safe, he pretended to look around on the sidewalk as though he had dropped his keys. It occurred to him he might really have lost them, but a quick check of his pocket reassured him they were there. Then he wondered what explanation he'd give if someone called him on it; but that was, after all, unlikely.

He must have hit a slow period. For several minutes no guests arrived at the hotel. He began to have misgivings about the whole enterprise. Even if he were looking for a needle, he would have found it long since. Also he really ought to get home. Feeling a bit foolish, he decided to give it up. He pantomimed his resignation to the supposed loss of his keys, and started decisively up the block. As these things happen, a taxi pulled up, and he stopped courteously to allow the passengers to alight.

He was rewarded for his patience by the appearance of a young woman dressed for a ball, accompanied by presumably her parents, also in evening clothes. From her white gown and long white gloves, Alan guessed the girl to be a debutante. It seemed to him there must be one of those ultra-exclusive cotillions tonight, hadn't he read, the kind you need a blood test to attend? This young woman would pass with flying colors, with her perfect nose and vacant expression and not a strand of blond hair out of place. The mother stood even straighter than the daughter, her skin stretched tautly over the high cheekbones, her thin lips pressed together in permanent disapproval of the world. Her looks were so familiar that Alan put it down to type, until he realized he really did know her. She was Harriet Montgomery, née Islington; and sure enough, who should follow her out of the taxi but Roger himself.

Alan was amazed by his luck. Who would have ever dreamed that his odd little project would yield up Roger Montgomery? Not that he was so delighted to see Montgomery per se, but with the executive committee about to come to a decision, such a chance encounter could be very helpful. Without saying anything about the presidency, or even the Bar Association, Alan could get in a little subliminal lobbying. A friendly hello, a compliment to the daughter, perhaps a remark or two on some neutral topic—that would be plenty. He'd have to be careful not to let his gregariousness get out of hand. Harriet Montgomery didn't look as though she tolerated curbside pleasantries too well. Already, seeing Alan about to speak and not recognizing him, she was trying to glare him off. Undaunted, he called out, "I'm not sure if I'm well enough dressed even to say good evening, Roger."

The words were barely out before he regretted his little joke. From Montgomery's disdainful look, it was clear he disliked Alan's greeting him, whether on sartorial or other grounds. He did manage to respond correctly, if coldly, and he introduced Alan to his wife and his daughter, Gina. Regina, probably; old man Islington's name was Reginald, if memory served, for years commodore of the New York Yacht Club. Alan, who had met Harriet Montgomery twice before, was going to say something about their being old friends, but thought better of it. "You're here for the . . . ?" he asked.

"The Assembly," was Montgomery's terse answer, as if no civilized person would require further identification of the event.

"What a pleasant coincidence for me. I'm just on my way from the office, and then to run into this happy band of revelers," Alan said. That seemed about right, with its suggestion of his industry while others were amusing themselves. Fearful of any implied criticism, he hastened to add, "It's a wonderful time of year. My own young ones will be at some similar event, I've no doubt."

Harriet Montgomery's eyebrows arched at the suggestion of any similarity. Alan was about to modify his claim when Montgomery interrupted impatiently. "Yes, yes. Well, terribly sorry to have to hurry on, Alan. Happy New Year." The debutante switched on a fleeting icy smile as she glided past Alan. Her mother, having expended her entire stock of goodwill in saying good evening, rustled into the hotel, and Montgomery was about to follow them when he stopped and turned around. "Actually, if you have a moment, Alan, I'd have a word with you," he said.

This was too exciting. What could Montgomery possibly have to tell him, other than some expression of support for the presidency, possibly even his premature but knowledgeable congratulations? He looked grim as death, it was true, but then, that was his fashion. Alan had never seen him otherwise. Trying to rein in the excitement was difficult. Who would have ever expected to hear the news so unexpectedly? And in this unlikely setting? The Waldorf would take on a whole new dimension in his estimation. Montgomery had stopped at the revolving door to let Alan go in first, but Alan's courtesy wouldn't permit that. Putting his hand on Montgomery's back to indicate his deference, he didn't notice, through the thick overcoat, the responsive shudder. His heart pounding, he followed his colleague into the hotel.

Christmas still proclaimed itself at the Waldorf. The outer lobby was full of poinsettias, wreaths, and red velvet ribbons festooned the walls, and two large Christmas trees, gay with red and silver balls, marked the passage to the elevators. Gina Montgomery had already merged into the crowd of white-gowned debutantes milling about with their escorts, tall, thin-faced young men in white ties and tails, affecting an air of boredom. Harriet Montgomery turned a withering glance on Alan as he came in the door and hissed, "Don't be long. We have a daughter coming out tonight, in case you've forgotten." Alan blinked before the onslaught and was trying to stammer out some sort of apology until he realized she was scolding her husband, not him. Without waiting for a reply, she went off to join a group of older women clustered about an especially terrifying-looking dowager who was holding court on the elaborate mosaic that decorated the lobby floor.

"Let's find a place where we can talk," Montgomery said, slicing his way uncompromisingly through the crowd. The press of people forced Alan to tag along behind. Montgomery pushed through to the inner lobby and made straight for Peacock Alley. Without waiting for Alan he sat down at a table. He kept his black Chesterfield coat and long white scarf on but fairly tossed an ashtray and bowl of nuts onto the adjacent table to make room for his top hat. "What will you have?" he asked Alan, the waiter having come over instantly in response to some imperceptible signal he was trained to pick up.

"Nothing for me," Alan protested with an air of grand renunciation. He assumed he'd be urged to have something, if only for the occasion's sake, but Montgomery didn't care, and ordered himself a Canadian, which was brought immediately.

"Well . . . !" Alan said, rubbing his hands together in anticipation, as well as nervousness. It was certainly not a situation he'd ever have envisioned in his wildest dreams, hearing this news from Roger Montgomery, of all people, over drinks in Peacock Alley. What a family story it would make.

"Let me get right to the point," Montgomery offered. "There's no sense beating around the bush." So much the better, thought Alan. "You know as well as I do that this whole takeover deal smells to high heaven. It was bad from the beginning, and has, if possible, gone downhill from there."

Alan's head swam. He was so completely unprepared for what he heard that at first he thought Montgomery was somehow alluding to the upcoming election in the Bar Association. Thank God he wasn't, although this other didn't bode too well. Clearly it was premature to celebrate. "I'm not sure I quite—" he temporized, but Montgomery cut him off curtly.

"Don't play the innocent with me, Alan. I know you've stayed pretty much out of sight, as have I, but that doesn't mean we don't both know the score. Which is that this whole episode has been marked by some rough fighting and some very low blows. I won't go so far as to say they've all been on one side: there's been enough dirty business to go around, and we've all got skeletons in our closets, as you and I are well aware."

Alan started to speak, but he was too flabbergasted to know what to say. Who would have ever guessed that Roger Montgomery was involved with this whole business? Now that he knew, it seemed logical enough, but it came as a shock nevertheless. He tried frantically to think what he, personally, had done that could have given offense, but everything blurred together into one great avaricious swamp. And none of it was his fault! Hadn't he warned against the whole enterprise from the beginning? Hadn't he pleaded with Gerry to keep things on the up-and-up, if for no other reason than to avoid just such a confrontation as this? He'd been a voice crying in the wilderness, and now to have to sit there and take this from the likes of Roger Montgomery! He all but choked on the unfairness of it.

In any event, Montgomery didn't seem to require a response. "Let's not waste time here, Alan. We're both busy men, and we've got better things to do—I know I have—than to rehash this whole sordid business. That's not what I asked you to come in here for, anyway. I just wanted to let you know—you'll find out tomorrow in any case, and I thought you may as well hear it from me—that Will Strawbridge is through. It's all over. Gerald will get the company, or Pines, or whoever is supposedly bidding for it. I can tell you frankly, I was against giving up, and I said so, but as is so often the case, my advice was ignored. I tell you this so you won't be under any false apprehensions as to my position. I thought that the idea of a perfectly respectable firm being swallowed up by a parvenu is outrageous, and I still think so. But there were other considerations, as I'm sure you know."

Alan didn't know what to think. Montgomery was only telling him what had undoubtedly been said in certain circles all along. In and of itself it was hardly surprising to hear. He didn't like to let the half-truths and aspersions stand, but they weren't his main concern just then. His main concern was that the man sitting across from him, misinformed and prejudiced as he might be, was in a position to do him enormous harm. All his hopes, his accomplishments, his efforts over the years, stood to go down the drain because of this one man's malice toward him. And all because of a completely unrelated affair in which he had played the smallest possible role. In addition to which he, Alan Gutheim, was personally innocent of the slightest wrongdoing. Innocent! But what good did his innocence do if Roger Montgomery had already convicted him? It wasn't enough, he saw now, to have clean hands, a clean conscience, to be true to oneself: the rest of the world had to agree. Roger Montgomery had to agree. And he didn't.

"There's a lot here that needs clarification, Roger," Alan said cautiously. "I hope that, whatever else may have happened, there's no misunderstanding between the two of us as regards my own part in this whole thing."

"I don't think there's been any misunderstanding, Alan," Montgomery replied, allowing himself the first faint smile Alan had seen so far. It was not reassuring.

"There's one thing I do want to say, and that is, that I was not in favor of this takeover, and said so from the beginning. Maybe not for the same reasons as you, but I did argue against it, and I think Gerry would bear me out on that. As you probably know, he got outside advice on this, in large part because we didn't see eye to eye about it. I won't say that I didn't try to be of some help to him once it was under way. I think you can understand the reasons for that, and I hope that whatever your opinion of this whole business you realize that my part in it was quite minor."

"I think I have a good idea of your part in it, Alan," Montgomery said, with the same sardonic smile.

"It wasn't what you think, Roger," Alan said, beginning to feel desperate. "It wasn't what you think." He realized he was sounding desperate, too, which could hardly be helping his case.

Montgomery looked at him, the smile having vanished. "As I said at the outset, I have no wish to rehash this. It could hardly serve to clarify anything at this late date. We've all done what we've done, and we've all formed our own conclusions. Mine may be different from yours, perhaps, but I really don't see any point in debating it. It's late, you no doubt want to get home, and I have a daughter to introduce to Society." He extended his glass toward Alan in a mock toast, drank down the last of his whiskey, and stood up.

Alan had little choice but to follow him. Montgomery had called the meeting, and he was ending it. Any idea of setting the record straight now seemed hopelessly beside the point. Only one question mattered to Alan now: how Montgomery stood with regard to the presidency of the Bar Association. He tried to avoid realizing that he already knew the answer.

No! It wasn't possible that the prize should elude him at this late date! Only fifteen minutes earlier it had seemed in the bag. He had prepared himself to receive the congratulations of the very man who was now brushing him off. Such a precipitous change in fortune was hard to grasp. Alan wasn't ready to accept it. In fact, nothing had been said about the presidency whatsoever. If there was any justice in the world, the one situation would have nothing to do with the other. Surely Roger Montgomery was a big enough man to put his feelings about a purely private transaction to one side when considering matters of great public import.

That consideration, improbable as it was, represented the only glimmer of hope for Alan as he glumly traipsed along after Mongtomery back to the lobby. He'd just have to trust to the man's professionalism, his decency, his concern for the larger interests of the people of New York. A long shot, to say the least, but it was all he had. He burned to ask Montgomery point-blank where he stood, but he knew better. Now was not the time to press for an answer. Even if Montgomery was angry, given a little time, and distance from the heat of battle, the man might well do the right thing.

As they emerged from Peacock Alley an ocean of debutantes closed in over them. In their absence a signal had reached the lobby that dinner was to be served shortly. The escorts fanned out through the crowd to find their young ladies, and with a thrill of anticipation everyone prepared to go on up. As they streamed by the two men everyone said good evening to Montgomery. No one, of course, recognized Alan. Harriet Montgomery, on the arm of a distinguished-looking man with an impressive head of white hair and a magnificent walrus mustache, passed them with her face set in a mask of haughtiness, never deigning to acknowledge the return of her husband.

"My father-in-law hasn't missed one of these things in fifty-six years," Montgomery observed. Alan now recognized Reginald Islington, who in his slightly younger days was frequently photographed at the helm of his yacht, *Victoria*.

He was buoyed by the faint hint of bonhomie in Montgomery's remark. Maybe he'd misjudged the man. Here, after all, was a prominent lawyer, a fellow member of the executive committee, a pillar of society. As a lawyer, he knew that Alan was obliged to do his damnedest for a client, as he undoubtedly had for his own. If the two of them happened to have found themselves on opposite sides of a dispute, well, that was par for the course. You fought your hardest, and after the verdict was in you went out and had a drink together. Hadn't they just done that, in fact? Wasn't Montgomery honoring the custom—the ethics, really—of the profession?

Encouraged by his reanalysis of the situation, Alan was reconciled to leaving. He turned cheerfully back to Montgomery and said, "I think I'd better let you rejoin the festivities. It was good of you to let me know how things stand. This whole business has been unfortunate in many ways, and I'm glad that we've put it behind us."

"I'm not sure I know what you mean by putting it behind us," Montgomery said, frowning.

"Well . . . I only meant . . . it shouldn't stand in our way with regard to . . . other matters . . ." Now Alan was confused. Montgomery seemed to have turned sour on him again. All these sudden shifts in mood were impossible to follow. His confidence was slipping away. "This won't affect . . ." He knew he shouldn't say it, but he couldn't stop himself: "The presidency . . . ?" He was plunging again into despair.

Montgomery's mirthless smile reappeared. "You know what I like about you people, Alan?" he said, and actually waited for Alan to shake his head in abject response. "I like the fact that you always think you can get anything you want. If you just push hard enough and squeeze tight enough and wait long enough, it'll all come to you. That's your philosophy, isn't it? Anything you want?" He leaned nearer to Alan and said, in a voice almost too low to be heard in the general hubbub, "Unfortunately, though, sometimes you little shits can't have everything."

And with no further word, Roger Montgomery turned his back on Alan and was lost in the crowd. As the cream of New York society swept by, Alan stood there dumbfounded, crushed by the enormity of his disappointment, still not really believing what he had just heard with his own ears.

The journey home was a weary one. In his misery, Alan thought of taking a taxi. He dreaded meeting someone he knew. He decided to walk, but he went all the way over to Third, and still ran smack into Harvey Silverstone before he'd gone a block uptown. They exchanged the usual greetings, Harvey couldn't have guessed what had just taken place, but Alan still didn't want to talk to anyone. He was too defeated. He could take no pleasure or interest in anything he saw. He felt useless, cast aside, without a future. It was as if New York itself had turned on him. For the first time in his life he felt like an outsider in his own city.

Behind him rose Gotham Tower. In a few days it would be Gerry's; or Morty Pines's, it amounted to the same thing. The parvenu. Montgomery had a point there. But then, they were all parvenus in Montgomery's eyes. Maybe it was so. Alan had always considered himself as rooted in New York as anyone could possibly be, but tonight, among the Montgomerys and Islingtons and the rest of them, he felt as shabby and unwashed as any immigrant off the boat. Perhaps it was true that these people were no better than he was, that in truth society counted for nothing anymore. He'd told himself that all his life. But now he wasn't so sure. He'd just been pushed into the gutter, like that, and there was nothing he could do except to pick his way onward through the garbage.

In the middle of a darkening city stood the latest—the last—project of Abbott and Strawbridge. By the eve of its corporate transfer, Gotham Tower had already become a massive structure rising twenty-five stories above the street. A rough shell of plywood forms had been slapped onto the frame of the building to provide a temporary skin until the concrete was poured. Inside, one could see the jungle of pillars and girders that constituted a huge steel skeleton. Looking at them through the peep-holes provided on the street level, sidewalk viewers were impressed by their solidity, their strength, their seeming impregnability. It would have taken the experienced eye of an engineer to detect the early signs of danger: the faulty welds, the deviations from true vertical, the minute cracks in some of the beams. A thorough inspection of the building would have proved disquieting.

But inspectors were infrequent visitors at Gotham Tower. Their sporadic tours were brief and amiable, and no inspector at all had come for the past three weeks. Bertino Bros. might not be the most experienced outfit in the city, as Irv Friedman had suggested to Alan; but no company enjoyed more pleasant relationships with the people it had to deal with: the unions; the suppliers; the subcontractors; the traffic department; and especially Mr. John Walsh of the Inspection Section, Building Authority of the City of New York. All of which had contributed to the gratifyingly smooth progress of Gotham Tower to date.

Many buildings in New York were put up under fairly similar conditions. The building codes of the city might have been appropriate for Utopia, perhaps, but for no real-world metropolis. Everyone knew that if they were enforced to the last letter, nothing would get built. No offices, no hotels, no apartment houses; not even public institutions. Construction would come to a halt. The city would stagnate. No one wanted that. No one ever intended that, not even the enacters of the code. It was a set of ideals, really, an incentive for everyone to do their best. No one expected anything more.

And indeed, Bertino Bros. did its best. It set out to build the finest building possible, given the constraints of time, materials, weather, and finances imposed on it by the real world. If the product happened to turn out shoddy, that was unfortunate. No one wanted it that way. No one had any stake in shoddiness per se. There were flimsier buildings in the city than Gotham Towers; it was really only a matter of good fortune that some of them were still standing.

By the same token, it was only a matter of ill fortune that, in the early hours of the next morning, a girder on the eighth story of Gotham Tower began to buckle. It didn't give way, or collapse, it just buckled. Not much else happened right away. The only immediate consequence was that the girder no longer supported the entire weight it was supposed to bear. An imperceptible shift was made, and the weight was redistributed. Some of the other girders and beams could accept the added stress. Others couldn't. A beam cracked, another girder buckled, then several more gave way in rapid succession. For a while the rest of the structure held, but only briefly. During the course of the night the process repeated itself in various parts of the supporting structure until shortly before dawn, when an uneasy equilibrium was reached.

By some miracle the entire building didn't collapse, although some boards slid off one of the high scaffolds and crashed onto the street below. If it had happened in the middle of the day, several people would have been killed. As it was, no one was around to get hit, and the sparse traffic on Third Avenue was able to dodge around the debris. When the crews arrived later that morning, they wondered what had happened but did nothing except to shove the splintered wood back to the curb. In fact, if the makeshift elevator, a platform attached to a pulley device, hadn't jammed on its way up, construction might have continued as usual. But the men who had to scramble off the stuck lift down to ground level swore they weren't going up again until the building was checked out. The supervisors were still having coffee. The foremen couldn't do anything. It took a couple of hours to determine that something was seriously wrong, and the better part of the morning passed before anyone got an idea what had happened. By the time the damage had been assessed, the work day was pretty much shot. The Bertinos had been notified by phone calls to a warehouse in Queens, and after lunch Vinnie Bertino drove over in a black Eldorado. He took one look at the building, shrugged his shoulders, and told everybody to go home. Then he got into the Eldorado and drove back to Queens, where he told his brother Sal what had happened. Sal was winning big in a poker game, and couldn't do anything until the game was over. Then he told Vinnie to call Abbott & Strawbridge and speak to no one but Will Strawbridge. The secretary told Vinnie that Mr. Strawbridge was in conference and couldn't be disturbed. Vinnie reported that information to Sal, who told him to forget it.

"Let the fuckers find out for themselves" was Sal's final comment on the subject.

Seventeen

Mrs. Nathan Altman
At Home
December 31, 1960
From ten o'clock in the evening
The favor of a reply is requested   Black Tie

The days between Christmas and New Year's were always hectic with the anticipation of Frieda Altman's New Year's Eve. What had started as a modest family custom had grown over the years into an elaborate dance for grandchildren, cousins, friends, friends of friends, and the many hangers-on to the Altman family. Half the city fought like maniacs to get an invitation to it. Members of the family were besieged throughout December by near-strangers who hoped to get onto the list. Once asked, no one would think of staying away, and every year saw more and more people gathered at 71st Street to celebrate. For many, it was the only place in New York where the old year could be properly bade farewell.

It was hastily decided to go ahead with the party despite the crumbling of Gotham Tower, even though to some it seemed as if the rest of the world might well follow in its wake. Everything was in complete disarray: the ownership of the company, the condition of the building, the reasons for its collapse, the consequences, all was utter confusion.

Nothing was clear. The proxy fight had ended, but the victory looked ominously Pyrrhic. Gerald was, of course, in a state. He'd been closeted all day with lawyers trying to sort the thing out and had made little progress. Will Strawbridge was having a last laugh, washing his hands of the entire affair and insisting he'd been bought out. No one could reach any of the Bertino brothers. They might as well have vanished off the face of the earth, although their warehouse in Queens continued in full operation. Morty Pines was going to pieces. As for Gerald himself, Eleanor wasn't a hundred percent sure he was going to make it through.

For some reason, she decided not to change her own plans, despite every incentive to do so. The Altmans always gave a formal dinner before Mrs. Altman's party, and Eleanor didn't like to disappoint her guests. This year it had promised to be tense even before the debacle on Third Avenue. Dickie, whose financial escapade had been dwarfed by subsequent events, had already forgotten the closeness of his call, and he was feeling aggrieved. Marian, never a great asset to her mother, had been forbidden to spend New Year's Eve with the Crusaders. In retaliation she refused to go to her grandmother's, where admittedly she wouldn't be missed, but her absence would be noticed. Randy was also not going to Mrs. Altman's. Although no charges had been lodged against him, the girl he had injured was still in the hospital, and it was felt he shouldn't be seen ostentatiously celebrating a week after the accident. He had objected to the banishment, and instead of telling him to shut up and count his blessings, Eleanor was allowing him to invite some of his friends over so he wouldn't have to spend New Year's Eve brooding. It wouldn't make that girl any better if he became crushed with remorse, was how she put it to Peggy; although Peggy doubted if Randy would recognize remorse if it came and hit him over the head.

At the Gutheims, although everyone was affected by the tense situation over at Altman & Sons, the mood was somewhat more optimistic. Alan, always resilient, had discounted his own setback and put all his hopes into Phil's appointment. He wanted to offer a toast at supper, but no one was drinking wine. Peggy never gave a dinner party on New Year's Eve, but instead gave the help the night off, and the family got their own supper in the kitchen. Everyone fixed what they wanted, and they always had a wonderful time. Dates, houseguests, friends, whoever happened to be around, all were welcome. This year, Ellen and Wendy came over to help "raid the icebox." Betsy and Johnny were there, of course; but then, they were family.

When they finished eating and had stacked the dishes in the sink, Joan took Ellen and Wendy and Betsy off to her room so they could dress together, and the men went to change into their dinner jackets. Peggy stayed to talk to Johnny, who had come already dressed. She needed only five minutes, if that, to throw something on. She never made a fuss over clothes, although for New Year's Eve she always wore the lovely jade brooch she'd been given by her grandmother Totenberg on her eighteenth birthday.

She liked Johnny, there was no question about that. She hadn't really had him to herself since the engagement, and she liked what she saw. She found him more interesting than she remembered now that he was at business school. More important, he had good values. That mattered more than anything to Peggy. He had ideas, ambition, energy. Everyone assumed he would go into some banking house or other, but after their talk Peggy wasn't so sure. He might well surprise people; he could well end up contributing. No, Joan could have done worse, she decided; a lot worse. And he did look like God's gift to women.

None of which stopped the time. It was getting on. Peggy went off to throw on her ancient green brocade gown to go with the brooch, and everyone gathered in the front hall. Phil untied Carl's bow tie and retied it stylishly. *"Très distingué,"* Alan pronounced, and they were off. They stopped again at Donatello's for the men's boutonnieres, and Peggy saw that Joan was shivering. Her coat wasn't nearly warm enough for such a cold night. Peggy begged Joan to take her own fur coat in exchange, but of course Joan wouldn't hear of it.

When they arrived, the band was playing, but the dancing hadn't started. The men left their coats in the ladies' powder room, tonight filled with coatracks. The women were escorted upstairs in the elevator by Kathleen, who was liberated from the pantry for the occasion, to leave their wraps in the third-floor sitting room. While the girls attended to their last-minute necessities, Peggy admired the lovely Degas, and noted that the glass pony had not yet made it onto the mantelpiece. The ladies then descended by the staircase to the second floor, where the men joined them, and the family went in together to wish Mrs. Altman a happy New Year.

On this one night of the year, Mrs. Altman received her guests in the library rather than the living room. The library was the smaller room off the second-floor hallway, and had a second doorway that gave onto a balcony overlooking the ballroom below. The balcony had been designed originally for musicians, in the fashion of a rococo palace, the idea being that bewigged musicians would supply minuets for the dancers below. When Nathan Altman, who had rather grand notions regarding entertainment, had been alive, a band had played on the balcony, without wigs. But it made conversation in the library all but impossible, and after his death the band had been sent down to the dance floor. Mrs. Altman used to make an appearance on the balcony once or twice during the evening to watch the dancing; but it was awkward, with its aura of a papal audience, and she had long since given up the custom. The unused balcony was now banked with flowers, which made an overwhelming impression, brilliant in the dead of winter, the strong fragrance descending on the dancers like a mist.

When the family came into the library, Mrs. Altman was as excited as a bride. Several guests were there, and Aunt Hilda had already taken up her position for the evening. Aunt Hilda had unfortunately gotten the notion, some years back, that duty required her to spend the entire evening seated next to Mrs. Altman. No one could dissuade her. It couldn't have been pleasant for her, when no one really wanted to talk to her, but she stuck it out. At one time she had served a slight function, chatting with people, talking to Mrs. Altman if there was ever a break in the stream of guests coming or going, occasionally running some small errand—carrying a message, or summoning someone. But now that she was all but stone deaf, poor soul, she couldn't carry on even her vacuous conversations of bygone years. She gamely asked from time to time if she could "make herself useful"; but how could anyone ask her to struggle out of a comfortable chair onto her arthritic legs to go fetch someone? "What would be useful," Eleanor observed, "would be if she would go home, and let someone sit there who might conceivably help Mother entertain her guests." But Hilda came on the stroke of ten, year after year, and refused to abandon her post until Mrs. Altman finally went upstairs herself, earlier and earlier with the passage of the years.

After saying good evening, the young people went downstairs. The rest of their gang would be arriving soon, and they wanted to get in some serious dancing. Alan went off to Mrs. Altman's bedroom, where the day's agonizing was continuing. Jack Bernstein had been summoned to join Gerald and the two or three Altman & Sons partners who would be coming to the party anyway; and Morty Pines was expected. Peggy hated these New Year's Eve conclaves—this wasn't the first, by a long shot—but this year she offered only a mild objection, mostly to Morty

Pines's presence. Even she conceded it was an extraordinary situation, although what would happen if they waited until the next day wasn't entirely clear.

She herself remained at the head of the staircase, where she could say hello to people coming up or down. She found it saved her the trouble of tracking down people she might want to see, or feel obliged to see, and from there she could act as an auxilliary hostess. Also, she liked to see who had come, find out who they were with, and generally keep an eye on what was going on. Her highest priority was to avoid being backed into a corner. In a corner one is always in danger of getting stuck with a bore who has nothing to say but who lacks the sense to move on. Hell on earth for Peggy.

Carl stayed at her side. No one his age had come as yet. Some of his second cousins would come later and he could dance with their dates. He always had a secret hope that he would meet the girl of his dreams on New Year's Eve. He had it all worked out: She would cut her date, and they would slip out together just after midnight to make the rounds of the wild parties he had heard so much about but never been to. He would arrive home after the sun was up, his tux in disarray, wearing a sheepish grin. Phil would rib him for weeks about it.

A woman came up to Peggy and wished her a happy New Year. "How are you, Edith, dear," Peggy said. "You know Carl, don't you?" The woman and Carl exchanged blank looks. "This is your cousin Edith Farnham, dear."

"This isn't the one in law school, I take it?" Edith asked.

"No, dear, please don't rush things any more than they are already," Peggy replied. "You're thinking of Phil. My oldest. This is my baby." She patted Carl's hand.

"What did you manage to do to your arm, dear?" Edith inquired.

Carl told her he had broken it.

"When his arm isn't in a sling, he plays the piano beautifully," Peggy said.

"Oh, of course. You're the musician. I remember hearing you play at your grandmother's. It was darling. Your feet didn't reach the pedals. That's why I didn't recognize you. You still keep it up, do you? I'd love to hear you play again sometime. And what about Joan? Is she still loving Bennington? Or am I behind the times on that too?"

"Well, you are, but it's understandable. Joan has been at Bennington, and she loves it, but she's had some medical something-or-other, they still haven't decided just what's wrong. Dear," she said to Carl, "why don't you move over a little that way so people can get by you more easily. You see, you're blocking where people want to come around. That's better," she approved after Carl moved over a foot.

"I do hope Joan's all right," Edith said, not knowing how alarmed she should be in the face of Peggy's breezy account of Joan's illness.

"She couldn't be better! She's here tonight, you'll see her downstairs. It's too silly for words that she should have to miss any college on account of it, but there it is. In the meantime she's working at Meyer House and loving every minute of it. How is Charlie?" Edith's father-in-law, Charles Farnham, had had a stroke several years before and had been no use to himself or anybody else since.

"About the same, I would say."

Peggy wrinkled her face into a sympathetic wince. "Give him my best, will you?"

"Dear, I would, but he doesn't know what's being said to him anymore."

"I had no idea!" Peggy cried. "What a shame! He was such a lovely person."

"He was that. But what can you do? He's not going to get any better, he gets nothing out of life, but one can't go around injecting air into the veins, you know. We haven't come to that yet. It's terribly hard on Joe; that's what I mind the most."

"What a shame," Peggy said again; and sensing that nothing more could usefully be said on the subject, added, "It's lovely to see you, dear. Have you seen Mother yet?"

"I was just on my way in. Well, Happy New Year. Good luck with your music, Carl. I hope your arm is better soon." She went into the library.

They stayed there for nearly an hour, saying hello to everyone; or rather, Peggy said hello to everyone and Carl was introduced. Occasionally someone would stop for a chat, but the stream was too steady for much conversation. People mostly just kissed Peggy, asked what Carl had done to his arm, and wished them both a happy New Year. Carl wished his cousins would come. When he was younger, he used to go and sit next to the band, sipping ginger ale out of a champagne glass and accepting the obsequious attention of the bandleader. But he was too old for that. Supper wouldn't be laid out until after midnight, and if he wandered off he ran the risk of being ambushed by an elderly relative and trapped in an inane conversation. So he stayed with his mother. She did like having him there.

As midnight approached the meeting broke up temporarily, and Alan came to take Peggy down to the ballroom. He liked to be dancing when the hour struck. Carl had no one to dance the New Year in with, but he went down too. He would have preferred to go back to the kitchen and see the old year out with the help; or else be with his grandmother at midnight. But he was too old to duck out with the servants now, and the density of old fuddy-duddies in the library was by then truly stupefying. So he trailed along after his parents to the ballroom, where at least he wouldn't be by himself at the crucial hour.

The floor was jammed. Everybody wanted to be dancing when the lights went out. People were checking their watches and swaying perfunctorily, intent only on the time. Eleanor appeared at the doorway and tried urgently to get through the mass of bodies to the bandleader. She had her tautest expression, since by her watch it was already past midnight, and they hadn't dimmed the lights. She also wanted to rush upstairs and kiss her mother-in-law before the music stopped, so she had no time to spare. Her brother Walter just then danced by jauntily, tapping his watch. "It's two past twelve, but at my age who's counting?" he asked, winking devilishly. He danced off in a cartoon two-step, pumping his partner's arm up and down vigorously. The lights dimmed finally. People shouted "Happy New Year" as the band played "Auld Lang Syne." Eleanor shouldered her way back, smiling grimly and saying Happy New Year to everybody as if it was her special, onerous obligation. "Happy New Year, dear," Peggy told her as she rushed by. Peggy knew that Mrs. Altman would greet the new year calmly with or without Eleanor; as she had for the many, many years before Eleanor came into the family. Peggy would wait until later to wish her mother a more private and genuine happy New Year. Eleanor managed to force a smile and Peggy looked around to find her own children. Joan and Johnny were near, so it was easy enough to kiss them, and then Phil and Betsy glided over in a smooth dance step, accepting their kisses without skipping a beat. Only Carl was missing. "Where's Carl?" Peggy asked Joan.

"He's right over there, waiting for everyone to come over to him."

"Carl, dear," Peggy called. "Over here!" Carl was—Joan was right —staring off in the opposite direction with a woeful expression, as if to provide some explanation, perhaps temporary blindness, for not seeing the others fifteen feet away. He hadn't focused his eyes on anyone, so that he appeared to be hallucinating rather than searching. He turned sharply at the sound of Peggy's voice, feigned surprise, and came over to get his New Year's kisses.

"What, no partner?" Alan asked heartily. "Didn't I see the lovely Miss Heldman here?" Carl had been assigned to escort Molly Heldman to one of the huge dances earlier in the vacation, and Alan had gotten it into his mind that they were going steady, or very near it.

"She came with Art Totenberg," Carl said. He despaired of convincing his father he was not another Phil with women.

With the New Year properly welcomed, the band broke out into a Charleston. There was cheering from Joan and Phil's gang, now assembled in force, and some of the older guests ceded the floor to them. It was still too crowded for their usual wildness, but they all kicked out jubilantly while the onlookers snapped their fingers. Joan, who had looked gaunt and tired up until then, sprang to life, grinning happily at Johnny. Everyone's eyes were on the two of them. Peggy thought Joan looked wonderful in the blue chiffon dress, and silently congratulated herself on its purchase.

After the Charleston, the band reverted to a fox-trot, which brought more couples onto the floor. "Happy New Year, Gutheims et al.," called Willard Stolmeyer as he danced by with his wife, May. Try as she might to look happy for the occasion, she was as forlorn as always. She forced a wan smile as her husband whirled her away. All those years, from one doctor to another, not one of whom had been able to do a thing for her, so far as anyone could tell.

"They say she had shock treatments this fall," Alan said in a hushed voice.

"Dear, you're behind the times," Peggy informed him. "That was last year. She's been in and out again at least once since then. They have her on some new drug, I understand, and I gather it's been about as successful as all the others."

"Poor Willard." Alan sighed.

"Poor Willard indeed," Peggy snorted. Willard Stolmeyer was a notorious fanny-pincher. How much further anatomical progress he had made was in some dispute, but he was not one of Peggy's favorite characters.

"Well, God knows, if any man was driven to it, he was," Alan sympathized.

"Here are the Fleischmans," Peggy announced as some cousins of Alan's danced by. "Dorothy? Alf? Happy New Year."

"What a stroke of luck," Dorothy Fleischman said. "All the Gutheims together so I can wish you a happy New Year and not have to find you one by one." She kissed Peggy and beamed at the others. "Betsy, darling," she added.

"You know Johnny Krieger, don't you?" Peggy asked, assuming Mrs. Fleischman had forgotten Johnny's name.

"Know Johnny Krieger? I'll have you know, Johnny Krieger and I used to meet in train stations. Every July first we schlepped down to Grand Central Station with Jeff to hand him over to 'Uncle George' or 'Uncle Hank' or Uncle Whoever-it-was-that-year, there would be Johnny Krieger, and when we went, two months later, to Harmon, at the crack of dawn—camp trains never come in during the civilized day —to catch him as they threw him off the train with his arrows and snakes and what little clothing he had left, he and Johnny Krieger would stand there with tears streaming down their little faces and bid each other the most heartrending farewells, until the next summer, when the whole thing repeated itself. And you ask me if I know Johnny Krieger? How are you, dear? I haven't seen you in an age. What are you up to these days?"

"I'm at business school. Here at Columbia." Mrs. Fleischman gasped at the transformation. "And how is Jeff liking med school?"

"How does anyone like med school? He hates it! He's up at Stowe, which is why he isn't here tonight, but he took so many books up there with him, I can't imagine he'll get out on the slopes. Poor dear! He's perfectly miserable! I'll tell him you asked after him. He'll be delighted."

"Please do," Johnny said. He and Joan excused themselves to go back onto the dance floor, Phil and Betsy already having whirled away. Only Carl hung around, having nowhere better to go.

Mrs. Fleischman turned to Peggy and Alan and said, "He's a lovely boy. You must be so pleased." Peggy smiled in graceful acknowledgment, and Alan glowed with pride. Lowering her voice, Mrs. Fleischman continued: "How is your mother taking this thing with Gerald? They've told her, I assume?"

"Of course they've told her," Peggy said indignantly. It grated on her that anyone should think her mother needed to be protected, that she was too fragile to bear the burdens of the world.

"She's a wonderful woman," Mrs. Fleischman added quickly, sensing she had taken a wrong turn. "I don't know how she keeps on having these, year after year. It must be a strain for her, although you would never suspect it, to look at her."

"I think it's a lot for her," Peggy agreed. "But it gives so many people so much pleasure, and of course she likes nothing more in the world than to give other people pleasure."

"I hope she never stops," Mrs. Fleischman said.

"These things have to end sooner or later," Peggy observed unsentimentally.

"Oh, dear! Don't say so! Not tonight, anyway. Happy New Year!" she called as Mr. Fleischman, who obviously feared another faux pas, abruptly danced her away.

They were replaced immediately by Barbara, who had draped herself over a young man who looked like a baby-faced gangster. He was far too pretty and, if his eyes were any indication, not to be trusted with the silverware. "Happy New Year!" Barbara cried in a delirium of excitement. "This is Terry Kincaid. Terry, this is my aunt and uncle, Mr. and Mrs. Gutheim, and my littlest cousin of all, Carl." She kissed them all, giving Carl one of her sickliest-sweet smooches.

Peggy, to her credit, almost laughed out loud at the preposterous young man. "Hello, dear," she said to Barbara.

"Did you have a nice supper? The Gutheims always have supper in the kitchen before coming over," she explained to Kincaid. "It must be divine. Ours was worse than ever. If you can imagine. Terry couldn't get free in time to come to dinner, so I was even more bored than usual. I had to sit next to Hy Conover, who lectured me the whole time about taxes. Of course I don't know a thing about them, but he acted as though *I* was responsible for their being so high. It was too tiresome. Randy was banished to his room, and Marian of course wouldn't come to the dinner table. Someone has to help out Mummy and Daddy, but really, next year I'm coming to you, Aunt Peggy. Anyway, I'm already starving to death, and Terry hasn't even had dinner, so we're going up to get something to eat. Would you like to join us?"

"Not just yet," Peggy replied. She knew that Barbara wanted a buffer between her date and her parents, but figured, she got herself into this, she can get herself out of it.

Barbara looked disappointed. "We'll go on up, then. Will we see you upstairs?" she asked eagerly.

"Very likely," Peggy said affably, on the grounds that it cost her nothing to say so.

Phil danced Betsy over just in time to see the two of them disappear into the crowd of people by the door. "Damn! Just missed," Phil said. Betsy was laughing, breathless. "We wanted to get over so Betsy could meet Barbara's gigolo."

"Phil, really!" Alan protested. No one had heard, but still . . .

"You were the one who was dying to meet him!" Betsy exclaimed. "You couldn't wait to get all the dirt on him, and make Bobbie miserable at the same time. You really are the worst person in the world!"

"The minute that guy walked into the room, you couldn't wait to get your hands on him," Phil insisted. "I had to forcibly restrain her."

"Phil!" Betsy cried, laughing.

"You didn't miss anything much, dear," Peggy confided to Betsy, "unless your taste runs to fairies."

"Now, just a minute, dear," Alan put in, horrified that his wife should talk so bluntly, let alone on such a subject. "I don't see how you can quite say that."

"Darling, you have only to take one look at that face. There's not the slightest question about it. It's a weak face."

Joan and Johnny had come around the floor, and they stopped. "Did you see Barbara's latest?" Joan asked.

"Relax," Phil advised her. "He's a fairy. Mother's already determined that."

"Mother!" Joan wailed. "What, did you give him some sort of test?"

"His face is weak," Phil explained.

"There's something about him that makes me nervous," Peggy said.

"How do you think Aunt Eleanor feels?" Phil asked.

"Poor Aunt Eleanor," Joan said. "I think she's going to have a nervous breakdown before the evening's over."

Carl drifted over toward his cousins and their dates. Being a grandson of the house gave him a limited droit du seigneur, which had few prerogatives but did make him confident enough to ask Molly to dance. He saw Art roll his eyes upward in sympathy as he cut in, but she had the decency to look pleased. Unfortunately, the band was playing a Latin piece, some kind of samba, which made it difficult to talk. The dance had one section in which you were supposed to swing yourselves apart and then pull back together in a rather tight embrace. Phil had always advised him to avoid dances in which he might have to "bounce," but there wasn't much he could do. Out of the corner of his eye he could see his brother and sister nearly breaking down, watching him. The dance ended, mercifully, and he brought Molly over to say good evening to his parents. He was sweating already, and had to mop his face while everybody wished Molly a happy New Year.

"You look just lovely, dear," Peggy said kindly. "Are you enjoying the party?"

"It's terrific, Mrs. Gutheim, thanks. I've never been in this house before. I can't get over these pictures. They're fabulous!"

"Aren't they? I must say, I never get over seeing them, as often as I have. Every time I come into this room I get a thrill. Have you seen the ones upstairs?"

"No, I haven't. Are there more?"

"Oh, some very fine ones. Why don't you take Molly upstairs, she can see the pictures there," Peggy suggested to Carl. "And that would also give her a chance to say good evening to your grandmother," she added.

"I do want to thank her for having me." Molly took the hint well. She darted a glance toward the people she had come with, but Art was dancing with one of the other girls.

"You could have supper," Peggy said, seeing Molly's dilemma, and trying to galvanize Carl into action.

"The food here is not exactly to be sniffed at," Alan said. "In fact— why don't we go up with them?" he asked Peggy.

"Now look," Peggy scolded him; Alan was often slow on the up-take. "First you drag me down here ostensibly to dance, then you decide you want to eat. If you want to dance, better do it now, or not at all. I'm not planning to traipse up and down that staircase. You kids go on up, we'll see you later." She led Alan onto the dance floor, saying, in response to his bewildered look, "You just have to learn to keep out of the way, dear."

"I just thought—" he began piteously.

"Relax, and dance," she cut him off. "Happy New Year," she replied to a couple who had wished it to them. She hadn't the foggiest idea who they were. The party was getting so big.

Joan was putting on a good front, but she didn't know how long it would last. Phil, Betsy, and the others had gone on to Wendy's, where the gang traditionally wound up on New Year's Eve. She and Johnny were to join them later, after putting in at least an appearance at supper upstairs. Carl had said good night to his grandmother and left with Molly for parts unknown. Peggy and Alan were in the dining room, expecting her there. Joan was exhausted. The noise, the crush, the hordes of people, half of whom she didn't so much as recognize, were closing in on her. Everyone who spoke to her had some garbled notion of what was wrong with her and she'd had to explain over and over again that she was fine. If she had to go through it one more time, she was sure she would scream. She was acutely aware of how artificial it was, the politeness, the smiles plastered on people's faces no matter what they thought; the emptiness. The total hypocrisy of it. She saw that the life they were leading, and she was leading, too, had absolutely no meaning. Everyone was a phony. She was the worst phony of all, her whole life lies piled on lies. She lied to everyone, and especially to Johnny. She felt remorseful about Johnny. He was a good person; too good for her. He deserved better than to be sucked down by her. She had all but decided that before the evening was out she would break off their engagement. She almost did it at the stroke of midnight, but she couldn't bring herself to what would seem to him an act of cruelty, no matter how much it would benefit him in the long run. But if she couldn't do that, she couldn't stay with him either. She couldn't bear his goodness any longer. She had to get away.

She would have given anything to have been at Meyer House that night. She felt banished, and trapped at the wrong place in a gaudy costume. She felt miserable not to be there, seeing in the New Year with warmth and love, people hugging one another genuinely, a happier family than the one she was stuck in. She hadn't had a chance to say good-bye to anyone. She longed to be with them this one last time.

Most of all she wanted to see Kevin. She knew that whatever it was they had had together was over with. She wasn't going to make a scene. She wouldn't plead with him. But she had a terrible sense of incompleteness, of a chapter in her life that hadn't ended but had simply been interrupted. She wanted to see him once more so he could tell her what she had meant to him. That was all she asked: no gratitude, no flattery, no false sentiment. All she needed was to hear his voice once more, to have him tell her those things, and she would close it out.

She had to get away. She had to be by herself for even a few minutes, or she thought she would go crazy. She told Johnny she was going to the powder room. She told him to go up to supper and she would meet him there. Before he could say anything, she rushed out into the hall and pushed the button for the elevator. While she was waiting for it, old Cousin Hattie Totenberg descended on her with a quivering smile. Cousin Hattie was a sweet, dotty old lady, and she didn't have the slightest idea what was going on around her. She had Joan confused with Barbara. She had heard something about an engagement, she said, but it had been such a short time since the divorce—wasn't Joan rushing things a bit? When the elevator came, Joan told her she wasn't coming, and sent the old woman up in it alone.

She took refuge instead in the narrow part of the hall that led to the front door. She could be alone there. A few latecomers straggled in from other parties, and one couple left, but the traffic had thinned out. The Pinkerton man was there to answer the door and keep an eye on who came into the party, but he was paid, among other things, not to fraternize with the guests. He wore a tux, which lent an air of refinement to his otherwise bruiser-like appearance, and smiled politely at Joan. He knew who she was, and he didn't expect her to speak to him. She was glad to be left to herself.

In the quiet hallway she calmed down. Maybe she could stick it out after all. She said something friendly to the Pinkerton man, and prepared to rejoin the party. As she started to go back in, a man in his sixties, wearing an old-fashioned vested white-tie-and-tails strode briskly out toward the door. He had a cloak over his arm, which he intended to throw over his shoulders as soon as the cold hit him. He stopped, looked at Joan, and appeared thunderstruck. "Joan!" he cried out. "Joan Gutheim!" as though she was the last person in the world he expected to find at her grandmother's New Year's Eve party.

Joan didn't have the vaguest idea who he was. He didn't even look familiar. She was sure she'd never seen him before. He could have been a total stranger but for the fact that he knew who she was; or her name, at any rate. She saw, to her horror, that he had a glass eye. She wanted to look away, for fear he would see her staring at his dead orb, but despite herself her gaze was drawn back to it. "Good evening," she said, trying to sound as though she knew him. She was used to pretending to know people she didn't recognize, but this man insinuated something more intimate; some not altogether savory experience or secret that they shared. She couldn't think what it was if her life depended on it.

"You don't know who I am!" he said teasingly, as if he had asked her a riddle that had stumped her. "I'm James Lipmann!" he cried. She was no better off. The name meant nothing to her. It was not a family name, and she couldn't recall any friend of her parents' by that name. "How are Peggy and Alan?" he asked. Surely he could have found that out himself if he cared. "How are *you?*" he asked, alluding perhaps to her illness, perhaps to something else entirely.

She felt a chill. Who was this strange, unknown man who appeared out of nowhere at her grandmother's party, seeming to know her so well. She would have gone back in, but he blocked her way. The Pinkerton man stood facing the door with his back to them. Nothing in the tone of their conversation would have alerted him to any danger. This man—this . . . Mr. Lipmann, if that was who he really was—could take it into his head to do something crazy before anyone could stop him. He could pull out a gun and shoot her. "Do you like my eye?" he asked gleefully, having caught her staring at the forbidden spot. "I'll show you something you'll like even better." He reached into the pocket of his vest and pulled out a gold watch that hung at the end of a chain. "Look at this beauty, will you? Isn't she something? I've had it all these years. You can't find a watch like this anymore these days. She keeps perfect time, and you don't have to wind her. In fact, you can't. You know why?" His mouth hung open, waiting for her answer. She shook her head. The man must be unhinged. "Because there's no stem!" he shouted maniacally, as if he'd just given the punch line of some profound joke. Joan wanted desperately to get away from him.

He put the watch back into its pocket. "Of course, one of these days it'll run down. Bound to. Nothing lasts forever. When d'you think that'll happen? Eh?" He edged closer to her. She took a step backward. "Take a guess."

"I couldn't possibly." She glanced back over her shoulder, but the Pinkerton man was still facing away from her.

The man answered by singing in a cracked, tuneless mezza voce:

> *"And it stopped—short—never to run again—*
> *When the old—man—*

Died!" he whispered harshly. He stepped past her and the Pinkerton man to the door, opened it, and looked back at her. "I'll let you know when that happens," he said as he opened the door. "Happy New Year to all," and he disappeared into the night.

Joan shuddered.

Unsettled, she went back to the party. She looked into the ballroom to see if Johnny was still there, but she didn't find him. She headed for the staircase, feeling limp. It took her forever to get up the stairs to the second floor, so heavy was the crush. Everyone had to stop her to wish her a happy New Year. The word had spread during the evening that she and Johnny were engaged, and people who had seen her already didn't know quite what to say. She, for her part, didn't want to hear their congratulations, and it was generally uncomfortable. By the time she reached the second floor, her face was clenched in a forced smile, and her cheeks ached with the strain of it.

Johnny was waiting patiently for her outside the dining room. Round tables crowded with people eating filled the room and spilled out into the hallway. Mrs. Altman had just left. Her visit was these days largely ceremonial. She took nothing to eat at her own party. She was forbidden most of the food she served, and she no longer had the digestive flexibility for a postmidnight supper. She only went in for a change of scene during the long evening, and to encourage others to enjoy themselves. When she left, people fell all the more earnestly to the food. Claude, gotten in every year to cater the party, was prowling back and forth between buffet tables making sure the platters were continuously replenished. A smoked salmon had been placed on each, and there were cold turkeys, hams, salads, rolls, chafing dishes with hot food, several aspics. The desserts were laid out separately on the sideboard, cut fresh fruit and ice cream and sauce and a magnificent *dobosch* torte, under the Corot. "Shall we go in?" Johnny asked.

Peggy and Alan were sitting at a large table with a crowd of their own friends. Peggy was just stifling a yawn when she spotted Joan. She cried out, "There's Joan!" as if a celebrity had arrived. Her tablemates continued eating nevertheless. Joan waved and looked for somewhere else to eat, but all the tables were full. Peggy somehow managed to commandeer two chairs and directed the men sitting on either side of her to manufacture space for Joan and Johnny to sit. When they were finally shoehorned in, Peggy suggested they go to the buffet to get themselves something. "You must be starved," she said anxiously. Johnny was, and Joan went along on the theory that it was always easier to do what Peggy wanted than to debate the matter.

When she returned with her food, Peggy smiled fondly at her. "I like that dress," she said, inspecting her daughter for signs of fatigue.

"Who is this Mr. Lipmann?" Joan asked by way of reply.

"I don't know any Mr. Lipmann," Peggy said. "Who on earth are you talking about?"

Joan described her encounter.

"Well, I don't know any James Lipmann, and I don't know anyone with a glass eye."

"You don't mean Lipkin, do you?" Alan asked. "There was a James Lipkin, he's dead now, but he'd be in his sixties. Or wait a minute: he'd be more like about seventy-five, I guess. About your grandfather's age."

"Daddy, I just saw this man with my own eyes. He wasn't a ghost."

"What on earth would James Lipkin be doing at Mother's New Year's Eve party anyway?" Peggy asked Alan. "He never set foot in this house so far as I know in his whole life. He barely knew the family."

"Now, hold on a sec," Alan countered. "Didn't he used to play golf with your father? I thought they played golf now and then."

"My father never played golf with James Lipkin in his whole life," Peggy stated flatly.

"What are you talking about!" Joan burst out. "This man was here! Tonight!"

Alan looked stumped. "There are some Lipmanns in Cincinnati," he offered. "One of them married one of the Rosenthals. I think Billy. Wasn't she a Lipmann? I'm sure she was." He looked relieved, as if he had solved the puzzle. "Yes, she was a Lipmann. From Cincinnati."

Joan closed her eyes. Her parents were capable of continuing indefinitely, and meanwhile she was left trying to make some sense of a weird encounter. It was scary.

"Good God," Peggy suddenly exclaimed. "There's Marian." The others looked at the door. Marian had indeed appeared and was glaring around the room in a fury.

"She looks like a hornet just stung her," Alan observed. Everyone immediately turned toward Eleanor, who was presiding over a table near the window. She, too, had seen her daughter and was eyeing her nervously, still trying to smile and converse with the person next to her. There was a general lowering of voices in anticipation of some sort of scene. Marian must have known that all eyes were upon her, because instead of going over to her mother, she stayed right where she was, looking like one of the Furies. Eleanor rose at her place, evidently hoping to come over to Marian and hear whatever she had to say in private. But the room was too crowded, and before she could make her way over, Marian shouted out to her, "Do you know what Randy is up to now?"

The few people in the room who were still talking now stopped. "And those friends of his? Do you know?"

"Darling," Eleanor breathed as she struggled through the under-brush of legs and chairs. "It's divine to see you." She was smiling brilliantly, but the effort it must have cost her was painful to watch. "I can't imagine what Randy is up to, but now that you're here, why don't you join us and enjoy yourself. Have you seen Grandmother? She'll be thrilled that you came." She had almost reached her daughter. Edging past the last table, she reached out to kiss Marian, or perhaps to guide her toward the library where she could be defused. But Marian brushed her arm aside and drew back. The action itself was slight, but she might as well have slapped her mother in the face, so harsh was the effect.

"Those boys are getting drunk!" she declared. "They're behaving like pigs, and exactly one week ago he drove his car smack into a sixteen-year-old girl and almost killed her!" She was near to tears with indignation and rage. Her indictment of her brother, particularly as many of the people there knew nothing of the incident, was extraordinarily shocking. Except for the sound of voices in the hallway and the faint strains of "I Could Have Danced All Night" drifting up from the ball-room, the room had become deadly silent.

"Darling," Eleanor pleaded, "Come in and see Grandmother." She spoke quietly, obviously hoping that everyone would go back to their own conversations, but of course nothing else remotely as interesting was being said, and only Donald Lindeman, who was quite deaf, continued to talk, much to the annoyance of the other people at his table. Eleanor put her arm around Marian's waist and moved her toward the library. Marian allowed herself to be taken away from her moment of sensation, but as she went she continued:

"Are you going to let him carry on like that? He's *drunk!* Eddie Saperstein has passed out. They've broken the lamp in the hallway." Her list of grievances faded away as they made their way across the hall, and people reluctantly resumed their conversations, which were hope-lessly flat by contrast.

"Not one of your aunt's better evenings, I'd say," Peggy observed to Joan.

"I feel terrible for Mrs. Altman, I really do," Johnny said generously.

"I do too," Peggy agreed. "Although to some extent she brings this on herself."

"How does she bring this on herself?" Joan demanded hotly.

Peggy stuck to her guns. "By trying to run those kids' lives all the time."

"Aunt Eleanor runs Marian's life?" Joan asked incredulously.

"Well, not now, of course, although she would if she could. But when she was younger that child wasn't allowed to breathe in and breathe out without being told when. That's all very well as far as it goes, but this is what it leads to. Still," she added, "she doesn't deserve this."

Joan didn't reply. Peggy saw she was disturbed, but couldn't think why. Marian's scene had probably upset her in some way. This was not the time to go into it.

Some of the ebullience had drained from the party. People got up from the supper tables and there was talk of going on to other parties. The crowd in the dining room thinned out. Word came in that Mrs. Altman would go up soon, which didn't mean the end of the evening but did cause an exodus of guests to the library to wish her a final happy New Year.

Joan abruptly stood up. "We're leaving," she told Peggy. "I'll say good night to Grandmother. Don't wait up for me. I'll see you in the morning. Happy New Year. Happy New Year all," she called out to the rest of the table. Johnny obediently got up and said good night. The other guests waved back at the young couple, and they were gone.

Peggy sat for a moment after they left, brooding. Joan was clearly much too exhausted to be making the rounds. There was no law she had to go to every party being given tonight. Wendy lived way up in the Nineties, what if they couldn't get a taxi? The subways were on strike, not that anybody in their right mind would take a subway. It was much too cold an evening to walk. The whole thing made Peggy nervous.

The more she thought about it, the less she liked the whole thing. It was no easy trick to get herself out from her chair, but she managed it. Leaving Frank Eckstein, who at his best was a deadly bore, she made her way in pursuit of Joan. To her great relief, Johnny was still in the hallway. There was still time to head them off. "I'm glad you're still here," she said. "I wanted to see if I couldn't persuade Joan to skip Wendy's party and go on home." She did wonder why he wasn't downstairs, waiting for her.

"Joan's gone, Mrs. Gutheim," he told her. He looked upset.

Even so, Peggy didn't catch on. Joan couldn't have left, she reasoned, if Johnny was still there. "You mean she's upstairs, getting her coat?"

"No, she's left the party. She said she had promised some friends she'd stop in tonight."

"What friends was she talking about?" Peggy asked. She was thinking, what friends could Joan have that she wouldn't take Johnny to see?

"I don't know," Johnny said miserably. "I said I'd take her, but she wanted to go by herself. She said I wouldn't like it. As if that made any difference!" he added vehemently. "I told her I'd a hell of a lot rather go and not like it than let her be out on her own. Tonight of all nights! But that didn't cut any ice with her. You know Joan. She insisted there was nothing to worry about. We went back and forth about it until finally she told me she'd call me first thing in the morning and she wished me a happy New Year and that was about it."

"You let her go?" Peggy asked in astonishment. Seeing the abject look on his face, she quickly said, "I'm sorry, dear, of course there wasn't anything you could have done. I'm just a bit worried about her. I don't like her going off by herself tonight. I have no idea where she's going, but wherever it is, I doubt it's one hundred percent safe."

"Neither do I, Mrs. Gutheim. But I didn't see what else I could do."

"Of course you couldn't have," Peggy said gently. Johnny was wretched. She could have kicked herself for making him feel responsible. "I'm sure she'll be fine. She does have a head on her shoulders."

He seemed grateful. "She can take care of herself," he agreed hopefully.

"Of course she can. Now—would you like to come back and join us? Or maybe it would be more fun for you to go on to Wendy's."

"It's very kind of you, Mrs. Gutheim. I think I'll call it an evening, if you don't mind." He did look beat. "We'll start it right tomorrow. I'll just go in and thank Mrs. Altman. Happy New Year." He leaned over and kissed her. It was the first time. Peggy thought of how hard it must have been for him, getting through all these years with no father, and a mother who was more of a burden to him than a help. How did he do it? She reached up and gave him a little hug. They don't come any sweeter than that, she thought.

"Happy New Year, dear," she said.

Or more handsome.

But she was worried about Joan. Looking back on it, it was clear the child had been agitated all evening. She hadn't had a good time. Something was bothering her. Peggy had seen it, but had put it down to fatigue. Maybe she was upset about going into the hospital. Peggy wondered if they should cancel it, or at least postpone it. She tried to convince herself that Joan was getting better. It wasn't an easy task.

Where in the world had Joan gone? Peggy tried to think if she had spoken of any other party, but she couldn't remember hearing of one. Most likely it was connected with Meyer House. Some of the younger workers were probably having a New Year's Eve party of their own. They had probably begged Joan to come, and she was too generous to refuse. It was like her to extend herself that way. A bit unwise, perhaps, and it would have made more sense to let Johnny come with her, but then that was Joan.

Peggy only hoped that it wasn't the colored girl giving the party. Harlem was not a place she'd feel easy about for Joan, at night, alone, New Year's Eve or no New Year's Eve.

Instead of going back into the dining room to join Alan and the others, Peggy went upstairs to see Mrs. Altman, who had by then taken her leave of the party. She wanted to have a moment by herself with her mother, to say good night and wish her a happy New Year. As she climbed the stairs, a feeling of sadness stole over her. There wouldn't be that many more of these parties, she reflected. This one might not be the last; but then again, one never knew.

The gymnasium at Meyer House was crowded and dark and in confusion. It wasn't at all what Joan had expected. The place was filled with people she didn't know. The ones she recognized paid no attention to her. She couldn't find Kevin anywhere.

Even without any real decorations, the gymnasium had been transformed for the evening. The whole basketball court served as a dance floor. Chairs had been brought up from the cafeteria and were scattered in disarray throughout the room. Young men without partners lounged on them, drinking from liquor bottles in paper bags, which they passed back and forth. On the far side, where it was darker, couples were pawing one another laboriously. The drunk stags yelled lewd comments about the dancers and the gropers and any unattached woman who strayed into their view. A band had been placed inside the boxing ring, with only the piano outside the ropes, and with the help of a crude but powerful amplification system it was blasting out an unholy amount of noise. The place was complete pandemonium.

She shouldn't have come. She was out of place and conspicuous in her blue evening gown, with her coat draped over her shoulders. People stared at her inhospitably, as if she had crashed, or wandered in off the street and found a party going on quite by chance. None of the social workers were there, nor was Martin, or any of the older staff. She recognized a couple of the younger secretaries and clients, but no one spoke to her. She tried to remain on the periphery and avoid attention, but the drunks made loud, rude remarks about her which she couldn't avoid hearing. Some of them insulted her directly, laughing raucously at their own boorish humor. No one defended her. She was on her own.

She couldn't see Kevin. She hoped she might just have missed him in her first look around the room, but as hard as she searched she couldn't locate him. She didn't see Jenna either. It occurred to her that they might be together. They might have left already, or maybe they hadn't come at all. She might have come all this way for nothing. It was crazy, to have come so late in the evening, hoping to find someone who wasn't expecting her and had no particular interest in seeing her even if he had been. She lost track of her reasons for coming. Even if Kevin were there, what good would it do? What could she accomplish, with all these people around?

A worker she recognized smiled and wished her a happy New Year, the first person to speak to her in friendliness since she had walked into the building. But the girl was with a young man, and Joan didn't know her well enough to join them.

She doubled back, still hoping she would see Kevin. She felt the terrible awkwardness of having to inspect the intertwined bodies coupled under the windows, but it had become urgent for her to know if he was there or not. People looked up from their obscene clinches and saw her staring at them. It was no good. She had to abandon her search.

She decided she ought to leave. She shouldn't have come. There was nothing to stay for. She passed by the basketball court and took one last look at the gyrating dancers, but she couldn't see Kevin among them. Not watching where she was going, she tripped over a pair of outstretched legs and nearly fell to the floor. She excused herself automatically, even though the fault wasn't hers. "Tha's all right, *Miss* Gutheim. I walk on them myself. Feel free." She saw that it was the Negro boy who had been sparring with Kevin the first time she had come up to the gymnasium. The same one who had fled by her on the stairway. He was sitting with a group of his colored friends, all of them drunk. Whether it was the liquor, or the need to settle a score on someone who had seen him humiliated twice, he spoke insolently to her. She understood that he meant to insult her, and was going to move on when he called out again: "If you're lookin' for your stud service, you might as well forget it, 'cause Kevin ain't here. He's ballin' someone else tonight." He laughed derisively, and the others joined in.

Dennis. His name was Dennis. She had felt sorry for him when he puked in the corner of the ring.

She stood there, defenseless to their hoots and catcalls. She had abandoned all caution in coming here tonight, as she had abandoned it by throwing herself at Kevin in the first place. She had been reckless from the start. If she had imagined there was any privacy, that was only more evidence of her delusion. Of course he had reported every detail of his exploits back to his admiring fans. What had she expected? That he would be discreet? That he would pass up a chance to boast of his sexual prowess? Of his conquest of the rich Jewish girl who was slumming it? Whatever made her think he would give a damn about her reputation. She herself had never given it more than a passing thought. If she stood there now, exposed and debased, she had only herself to thank. She could tell herself that these were nothing but a gang of unjailed delinquents, that their opinion didn't count for a thing; but if they knew, everyone knew.

She understood now why Kevin had been fired. She might as well have been fired too. She could never come back to the place again.

She stood where she was, frozen with shame. Dennis, seeing her predicament, asked, "Did anyone wish you a happy New Year?" He turned to the others. "Didn't anyone wish the *lady* a happy New Year?" It was ugly. Joan knew she ought to get out of there, but she was paralyzed. "Shit, *I'll* wish you a happy New Year." He staggered onto his feet and put his arm around her waist. She didn't resist. Pulling her in to a tight embrace, he inserted his knee between her thighs and kissed her hard on the mouth. His breath stank of bourbon and half-digested food. Joan felt no disgust, though, nor outrage. She felt almost nothing. She thought it was strange that this should be happening, but it didn't bother her. She wasn't there. People weren't seeing this. It was a dream. She would wake up any minute.

He pushed her roughly away from him and said, "There. Happy New Year." He leered at her. "Whatsamatter, ain't I as good as he is. Or is it just that you don't like niggers? Maybe you never tried one before. Ever tried dark meat?"

She wanted to undo the brutality, but there was nothing she could do. She reached back to pull her coat more closely around her shoulders, shivering as if she had felt a draft. She moved slowly toward the door. Stupidly, she said, "Good night," to him. People were staring. She knew she must look drunk herself, or possibly deranged. She didn't know, maybe she was. She might as well have been.

She made her dazed way as best she could through the crowd until she reached the stairwell. The heavy door was nearly too much for her. She pulled it open finally, and when it wheezed shut again the noise of the party was cut into the distance. Her throat ached as though she had been crying, but her cheeks were dry. She became aware of where she was. The stairwell was almost pitch-black, and forbidding. The terrifying thought struck her that someone was lurking in the shadows, waiting to attack her. She crept down a flight with her back to the wall, partly to keep herself out of the dim light, but also so she wouldn't be near the central well. She imagined herself being pushed over the railing, and fear gripped her.

By the time she got to the third floor, her heart was beating so hard that it hurt, and she was panting audibly. She couldn't go on, and she couldn't stay in the stairwell. She would go into the crippled children's room, where at least she could catch her breath. It deserved a last farewell, anyway. She probably would never come back after tonight. She felt for the door into the third-floor hallway. There was no light on. Clinging to the wall, she felt her way down the corridor, running her hand along until she came to the door. She fumbled for the knob, opened the door, and groped inside until she found the light switch. Even before she clicked it on, she knew someone was in the room; but the realization came to late to stop her hand.

In the first instant of recognition, when you see something you don't want to see, a powerful distortion comes to your aid and alters the unwelcome scene. When the light went on, Joan believed she had surprised two perfect strangers, people she had never seen before, in the act of making love. The shock, the fright, the forbidden sight of nakedness and copulation, all conspired to persuade her that she didn't know them. During the few seconds it took her to locate the switch again and plunge the room back into darkness, she shut her eyes tight in an effort to eradicate the scene she had just witnessed. Not until she opened them onto the void of the blackness did her vision clear, and she knew who they were. The sight of a white man and a black woman locked together should itself have made a split second's glance sufficient. She couldn't have avoided the revelation even if Kevin's voice had not shattered the silence: "What the fuck!"

If she had had her wits about her, Joan would have fled like a thief discovered in a crime, and hoped that she herself had not been recognized. But the last shred of her instinct for self-preservation had left her, and all she was able to do was to stand there in the darkness and say, "I'm sorry. I'm so sorry," over and over again, idiotically. There could be no question as to her identity, or that she had seen everything. She left no room for doubt.

The apology was futile. She was looking in the wrong place for forgiveness. If she had lit out of there, she would have had only her own chagrin to deal with, but she stayed and drew their attack. Jenna was actually the one to speak: "Don't you have enough parties of your own to go to?" she called out angrily. "You have to come all the way down here where you don't belong? Aren't wanted? Come barging in on people who just want to be left alone? You got everything a person could possibly want, but you just gotta have more. Well, let me tell you one thing: You may be used to having everything on a silver platter, but this one's not for you. You can forget about him. He ain't interested."

Joan stood there, dumb. She didn't know what to say. None of it was true, or all of it was true, she didn't know which. She knew she hadn't intended to come upon them any more than they intended for her to discover them. But who would believe her? Her case was hopeless.

She waited a moment more, hoping Kevin might say something to her, might make it a little better. But after his one outburst he said nothing. She finally left the room. She had never been more wretched. There seemed to be no respite from it, no pocket of hope. A black despair possessed her and held her completely in its thrall. She had neither the energy nor the will to resist it. Fate now ruled her life entirely. She could do nothing except to submit meekly to it. She stumbled down the corridor like a drunk and pushed her way back into the stairwell. She saw a man there, but she dismissed it as one more phantasm of the nightmare she was having. She had gone beyond fear. With the boldness of a sleepwalker, she brushed past, and only when a hand reached out and gripped her forearm did she acknowledge the reality of a presence.

Her scream was genuine enough, even though no one could hear it through the thick doors and over the music. If they had, they would probably have dismissed it as part of the revels. No one could save her now. She yelled with the desperation of an animal caught in a trap, but only alarmed the person who had grabbed her. It was Harlow.

The discovery didn't help much. Joan had been buffeted by too many emotions to be reassured now. She cried hysterically, alternating her sobs with short, piercing cries that frightened even the implacable Harlow. Unaccustomed as he was to helping someone else, he nevertheless did his best. He guided her down the stairs into the lobby, where she collapsed on one of the couches. She was still not in control of herself. He dug deep into the pockets of the long black coat he wore and came up with a handful of pills. He urged them on Joan. She was too far gone to offer any resistance, and obediently swallowed them all. Having no water, she gagged on one of the large capsules.

Too soon for the pills to take effect—probably owing to whatever calming effect Harlow himself had, or more probably out of sheer exhaustion—Joan quieted down. Harlow offered to take her back to Kevin's place, and even said she could spend the night there. Oblivious to partygoers passing through the lobby, he rolled a joint for her. She smoked it quickly and he rolled another, chain-lighting it from the first. He repeated his offer to take her back to the apartment, but she persisted in her violent refusal. He possibly understood. He asked her if she wanted to come upstairs with him—he had been on his way to the party —but she wouldn't go there either. Having exhausted his scant supply of charity, he wished her a happy New Year and went upstairs by himself, leaving her alone in the lobby.

As she sat there quietly, a gradual feeling of numbness took over. She had been too overwrought to experience any true comfort, but she gave herself over to a kind of lulling apathy. Her only remaining wish was to be alone; to be protected from any fresh emotional assault. It alone was strong enough to overcome her profound fatigue. She gathered what remained of her strength and got up from where she sat. She crossed the lobby to the far side. Pulling open the heavy front door, she had no sense of finality, of leaving the settlement house for good. All she knew was that she was getting away.

She welcomed the cold air. After the claustrophobic oppression of two parties, it was good to be outside. The night was clear. Although the streets were deserted, she wasn't afraid. The city was friendly, benign, safe. It would protect her. She could find refuge in it. She walked by dark alleys and obscure entryways without fear. Even the occasional body of a sleeping drunk offered no threat. As she walked the familiar route to the subway, she felt strangely refreshed. The events of the evening faded back into a hazy oblivion. If it hadn't been a dream, it was at any rate a part of her life she could now turn her back on. What was Meyer House to her? And who were these people, that she should tear herself up over their opinion of her? She had others to go back to, after all. She had a net to fall into before she hit the bottom.

The subway station entrance was barred by a locked gate. A crude, hand-lettered sign read ON STRIKE, and underneath it someone had already scrawled the word *Motherfucker*. She had forgotten about the strike. It didn't matter. She would take a taxi. She looked around. Several were speeding up and down Houston Street, bringing celebrants away from their parties, shuttling people back to their homes. None were empty. The few with lights on the top were off-duty, or in any event they didn't stop. Joan didn't care. She was perfectly happy to walk until she got one. Or she could get a ride from someone going uptown. It was New Year's Eve. Surely she'd be safe. If necessary, she would walk home. The air would do her good. "I learn more from a brisk walk of a mile or two through any part of this burg than I do from a week's worth of the *Times*," she heard her father say. She would look at the faces of the passersby. "You can always find something interesting in a person's face," her mother always said. "Everyone has at least one story to tell." She had learned how to get around New York, at least.

Perhaps it was a bit cold. What of it? It couldn't matter less.

She paid no attention whatsoever.

A cab pulled up to Meyer House, and Johnny Krieger got out. He told the driver he would be ten minutes. It wouldn't take longer. If Joan didn't want to come with him, he wouldn't argue with her. He hadn't come to drag her away. He just wanted to make sure she was all right. If he could just lay his eyes on her, that would be enough. Then he could go home.

He didn't know what he would say if he did find her. He hadn't come out of suspicion or jealousy—Johnny didn't have a jealous bone in his body—but he was worried. Joan had said good night to him with great tenderness, and apologized for going off like that and asked him to understand. If she had asked him to forgive her, he would have done it

in a moment; but understanding her was another matter entirely. Joan
had been an enigma to him from the first day he had known her up until
she'd kissed him good night less than an hour before; never more so than
now. He was very worried.

He had started to walk home after leaving Mrs. Altman's. He lived
fifteen blocks uptown, but he didn't notice the distance, or the cold. He
had too much on his mind; too many questions, too many fears. Letting
Joan go had been a mistake. She hadn't looked right when they said
good-bye. He should have trusted his instincts. He should have insisted
on going with her. There was no telling what might happen. In his
alarm, he barged past a waiting couple into a vacating taxi and ordered
the driver to take him to Meyer House.

He walked up to the massive front door, and wondered how to get
in. Trying the handle, he found it unlocked. The vast lobby was deserted. An elevator lay open at its far end, but he didn't want to get into
it. He looked for a stairway, and found the door. The stairway was dark,
and threatening, even to him. Joanie! he cried to himself. How could he
have ever let her do this?

He'd come to Meyer House on a hunch, that was all. She'd given
him no clue. She hadn't said anything about it, but all evening he could
tell she'd been distracted. When she had laughed, it had been brittle,
strained. Her heart wasn't there. She'd said nothing to him about wanting to be somewhere else, but he knew she did. It could only be Meyer
House.

He walked into the gymnasium and took stock. It was too large and
crowded to see if Joan was there or not. He spoke to no one, but circled
the room, searching for Joan. When he had gone completely around, he
walked back the other way, hoping he might have missed her. After his
second search, he asked several people if they had seen Joan Gutheim;
but everyone he asked shook their heads, or said they'd never heard of
her, or just shrugged their shoulders. One drunk colored boy, on hearing Joan's name, laughed nastily and said, "Yeah, I know her." But if he
had seen her that night, he wasn't admitting it.

Quitting the gymnasium, Johnny wondered if he should look
through the rest of the building; but he realized it was over. He left the
settlement house and found the taxi had waited for him after all. He got
back in and asked the driver to go slowly. He wanted to look out the
window, in the futile hope he'd see her walking along. But once they
had passed Houston Street, he told the cabbie to resume his normal

speed. The only people on the street he saw were drunks and bums. He knew that Joan would never have come there alone. He returned uptown, discouraged by his failure and more scared than ever for Joan. But there was nothing more he could do. There was really nothing more he could do.

She walked up the Bowery, but there were no cabs, no cars. The wind had come up and was whipping her face. A profound weariness overcame her. She had lost track of the time. It must be very late. They would all be in bed by now. She longed to be home, stretched out in her own bed. She walked by the street she would have taken to get to Kevin's, and automatically turned. She stopped. She could go there, gather her strength, and walk the rest of the way home if she had to then. The thought of a rest tempted her. But then she thought he might come back and find her there. He might bring Jenna with him, and they would both find her there. It would be unbearable. Bowing her head against the wind, she made her way uptown.

It was no use. She was utterly spent. Her legs wouldn't carry her. She couldn't go farther. Lifting her head, she searched the avenue as far as she could see, but she saw no taxis. She saw no cars at all. The street was deserted. An occasional drunk slept in a doorway, but she was the only one up and about. She was alone.

Alone, but safe. She was out on the streets of New York, her city, her family's city. New York would take care of her. The greatest city in the world. It had opened its arms to generation after generation of immigrants, refugees, lost souls, those fleeing oppression, the needy of the entire world. It would open its arms to her, too. Give me your tired, your poor . . . How good it was to accept its hospitality. A narrow alley, snug between two tenements, beckoned to her. She would just rest awhile, and then be on her way. No harm would come to her, she was sure. She was in New York. How good it was to slump down, to rest. Her legs had gone numb. As soon as they were stronger, she would resume her journey. She wouldn't stay long.

She closed her eyes. She wouldn't go to sleep. She would only stay a moment, she thought, only a moment. No sleep.

The city cradled her in its arms.

Peggy Gutheim lay in her bed, fully awake, staring at the faint shadows thrown onto the ceiling by the streetlight outside. Alan had finally gotten back from his last meeting with her brother, and she'd heard Carl come in after that. Phil she hadn't heard, but he was probably at Betsy's. It was unlikely he'd come back until morning.

Johnny had come by to tell her of his unsuccessful search for Joan, and to find out if she had returned home. He hadn't wanted to call, for fear of waking Peggy up, or alarming her needlessly. But she had never gone to sleep, and as for the other—it was, after all, her daughter. She'd been terribly grateful to him, and had asked if he wanted to stay for the rest of the night. He said he'd better go home, but asked if she would call him the minute she heard anything. Hopefully, it would be to tell him that Joan had just walked in the door.

Lying in her bed, Peggy strained to hear anything—the elevator's whirr, a footfall in the hall outside, the scratch of a key in the lock—that would signal Joan's return. She gave over the whole of her consciousness to the vigil. It was almost as though through the intensity of her wish she might control another person's actions. But even as she tried to will her daughter home, she prepared herself, as she always prepared herself, for whatever was to happen. Supine, motionless, ready, she waited for the phone to ring.

Eighteen

Not even the charm of Eleanor Altman's dining room could dispel the gloom of the January day. At the table, Eleanor and Mrs. Altman toyed with their lunch. Only a week had passed since the funeral, and neither woman had any appetite whatsoever. "I had them set a place for Peggy," Eleanor explained. "But of course if she allowed herself to have a nice, quiet lunch, she'd think she was indulging herself, which she won't do. Or let anyone else do it for her," she added, shaking her head. "Even now, of all times . . ."

Mrs. Altman stared dully at the pink and white miniature carnations arranged prettily in the center of the table. "Those flowers are nice, dear," she brought herself to say.

"I do think Fiona does a nice job with them. Mr. Sullivan sends such exquisite things." Mr. Sullivan always personally selected the flowers sent in each week from the greenhouses at Rosefield.

"Peggy says she's still completely overrun with flowers, so I didn't have them send her any this week."

Eleanor said, "I don't know why, I've never understood it, why people insist on sending flowers after the family has put in the request not to."

"I suppose some people don't see the announcement," Mrs. Altman suggested. "They hear the news and send the flowers right away without thinking to look in the paper."

"Well, they ought to look," Eleanor said angrily. "At a time like this they ought to. It may be a small thing, I suppose, but at times like these small things can be a terrible nuisance."

"I suppose they all mean well in doing it."

"I know they mean well." Eleanor sighed. "I suppose the hospitals can always use them."

The two women fell silent again, listening to hear if Peggy had come yet. Mrs. Altman looked wistfully out the window. She could see a woman sitting on the park bench opposite, feeding crumbs to the sparrows from a bag she carried. It seems such a pity the birds hadn't reached a warmer place for the winter, Mrs. Altman thought. The woman didn't seem so very well protected, either. She wore what looked like a terribly thin cloth coat. Worried about the woman—who would look after her?—Mrs. Altman withdrew her gaze back into the room again, where it fell on one of the filmy white curtains. The cord tied around it was slightly awry. For some reason it bothered Mrs. Altman. She hadn't noticed it before. It would be easy enough for one of the maids to fix, but she didn't want to say anything about it to Eleanor. She hated to interfere.

"Well, at least this whole dreary takeover business is over with," Eleanor said. "Of course, it ended in a complete mess, as I always thought it would, and Gerry is still making himself sick over it. At least I'm getting him off on a vacation. Now if we could only get Peggy to go away, I'd be satisfied about that."

"She absolutely refused to," Mrs. Altman said, drawing her breath in sharply.

"You can't be surprised."

"Of course not, but it would make so much sense for her."

Eleanor agreed. "It would make sense for her, and it would be good for Alan. I'm particularly worried about Alan."

"I'm worried about both of them, if you want to know the God's honest truth," Mrs. Altman said with a rush of anxiety. She would have continued, but stopped on hearing voices in the hallway.

The two women suspended their conversation to wait for Peggy to come in. She lingered a little, apparently whoever answered the door was offering condolences, it all took a little time. Finally she was there. They both smiled brightly at her as she walked into the room, but they also scrutinized her face to see how things were going. Their inspection left them no wiser; she looked tired, but otherwise there was little evidence of the devastation wreaked by the loss of her only daughter ten days before.

"Darling," Eleanor murmured with warm affection.

"Hello, dear," Peggy answered briskly. "Hello, Mother," she added more soberly. She in her turn was anxious to see how her mother was bearing up, and was as little informed as the others had been about her. Mrs. Altman looked grave and sad, but Peggy couldn't tell whether she was coming out of the worst period, or if the grief still lingered on stubbornly. "How are you?"

"Hello, dear," Mrs. Altman said. "I'm all right. How are you all?"

"We're as well as could be expected, I would say, considering everything. Nothing for me, thanks, Fiona," she said to the waitress, who had come in and was standing patiently. "If you had some tomato juice, I'd take some tomato juice."

"Nothing to drink, dear?" Eleanor asked solicitously.

"No, I've found the one thing this has done is that I can't take a drink. I can't for the life of me tell you why, because otherwise I don't feel any different, but if I have even a little I feel perfectly dreadful."

"How awful," Eleanor sympathized.

"It's the least of my problems, I can assure you."

"I still wish I could give you something to eat, though."

"Thanks, dear, I'm not in the least hungry, as you can imagine. I'll have a bite at home if I feel like it. I can't stay long."

"You can't?" Eleanor asked, disappointed.

"Oh, sweetie, not with everything I have to get done this afternoon."

"Does it all have to be done this afternoon?"

"It has to be done sometime. Do you know how many letters and telegrams we've received so far? Well over seven hundred." Mrs. Altman gasped in appreciation.

"You have someone, I trust?" Eleanor asked, alarmed at the prospect of Peggy sitting down and writing out well over seven hundred acknowledgments.

"Of course I have someone, but all the same there's a great deal to do. For one thing, I do have to read them all. Then, someone has to decide who gets what kind of response—who, for example, I will put a personal note on for, who Alan, occasionally Phil, and so on. No, we have a marvelous girl, but it's still a tremendous amount of work."

"Do you really have to read them all?" Eleanor wondered.

"Oh, yes, I'm afraid so. For one thing, some of them are quite touching. You know, one never quite realizes just how much of an impression Joan had made on people I wouldn't have thought even knew her. I was just reading a letter from Gertrude Silverman. I was on my way out the door, and it happened to have been at the top of the pile, so I looked at it. Now, I wouldn't have guessed, if you had asked me, that Gertrude would have known Joan if she passed her on the street. Do you know what she said? She said it was such a tragic thing to lose someone 'with so much sensitivity to the feelings of others,' was how she put it." She paused for a moment, to let the slight constriction in her throat release itself. "Now, who would have dreamed that Gertrude knew Joan well enough to have gathered that about her?" The other two women shook their heads in appreciation. "Then, too, I like to know what people have said, on the off chance I might run into them, it's nice to know what they've just written to you in a letter. Some of them mention some bit of news, even if it is a condolence letter, and I'd hate to draw a blank if it should come up. No, I'm afraid there's no getting around it. They really have to be read."

"Yes, but do you have to be the one to do it all?" Eleanor persisted.

"Who else is going to do it? Alan is frantically busy, trying to make up for the time he lost. I can hardly ask the boys to do it."

"I wish you'd let me help," Eleanor said kindly.

"You couldn't be sweeter, dear, but really, I have to do it myself. You're doing enough as it is, what with helping Mother, and then you have your own." It wasn't the time to go into Gerald's troubles.

"I could really spare Eleanor, I should think," Mrs. Altman offered. "Not that she hasn't been a great help."

"There's no earthly reason to, Mother, really. Now I'm not going to have you go into a stew over this, you two. Of all the things to worry about, my having to read condolence letters isn't very high on anybody's list."

"Do you have to do them so quickly? People surely don't expect replies instantly."

"I suppose not, but then it would just drag on and on, and frankly the sooner I get them out of the way, the better. I don't propose to spend the rest of my life reading condolence letters. Martin is coming over this afternoon, by the way."

"Oh, is he?" Mrs. Altman said.

"Yes. I offered to go down to Meyer House, but he insisted, and frankly I didn't object very strenuously. It's a lot easier for me, and it gave me an excuse to have Alan skip it. He would have joined us, if it had been at Meyer House, but he can't come all the way up town, he's at City Hall nearly all day today. I'm just as glad. He agrees that we should do something for the House in Joan's memory, but just now anything to do with the place upsets him no end. It makes no sense, but of course if it upsets him, it upsets him. We don't have to decide anything right this minute. I wanted to get an idea from Martin of what they might really need, what might be useful, as opposed to giving them something they don't really want. What I had in mind was that they might want to start a new program that they wouldn't otherwise be able to. Something innovative, that hasn't been done before, if possible."

"What did you decide about Bennington, dear?" Mrs. Altman asked.

Peggy's face tightened slightly. "Nothing as yet. Alan still wants to do something there. I personally see no reason to. Bennington never meant that much to Joan. I would rather do something for Fieldston, which was terribly important to her. Alan feels that Bennington could use it better, which may or may not be true, but somehow that's not one of my highest considerations at just this moment, if you see what I mean."

"Maybe I could do something for Bennington," Mrs. Altman offered.

"Mother, dear, that's very sweet of you, but you're doing enough as it is. Actually, in Joan's will, something is left to charity. I think it's twenty percent, at the discretion of the executors, so it may be that Bennington could be taken care of there. It doesn't have to be decided today. Alan really shouldn't have to be making these decisions just now. It only sets him off again, which is the last thing I want just now."

"There's no chance of your getting away?" Mrs. Altman asked cautiously.

Peggy made a face. "I suppose we'll have to, sooner or later. If it were up to me there would be no reason on earth, I'm fine right where I am. But I have Alan to think of. He's working himself to the bone, and I can't get him to be sensible about it. He uses the excuse that the work has piled up. I know perfectly well he's trying to keep himself so busy, he has no time to think about it, but of course it's no use. How could it be? We all think about it all the time." She stopped, struck with her own thought, and for a moment she paused. In that moment her face was swept by a sudden bleakness; but it recovered quickly, and she went on. "Meanwhile he's exhausting himself, which is terribly hard on him. No, I really have to get him off somewhere. Even if it means pretending it's for me."

Eleanor glanced at her mother-in-law. "Where might you go?" she asked.

"Well, people have been very kind. Tommy Simon has asked us down. Alan could get some rest, and sun, and have his golf and bridge and plenty of company. The only drawback is that I would have to put up with Marjorie. I can assure you, a week with Marjorie Simon would not be any great help to me just now."

"But there must be somewhere you could go where you wouldn't have to put up with Marjorie, although I must say they have a beautiful place down there. Have you ever been there?"

"No, and I haven't the slightest desire to go, either. Not that it isn't terribly nice of them to offer it."

"You couldn't go somewhere else?"

"I suppose we'll go somewhere. One complication is that I don't want to up and leave Carl at this particular juncture. I could take him, but I think he's much better off being in school right now. It means a great deal to him, and it takes his mind off the whole thing much better than if he were to go down to some beach where there isn't a soul his age, he'd be bored to tears and have nothing to do but sit around brooding, which as you know he is quite capable of doing. And Phil couldn't leave law school in any case. He would of course manage perfectly well on his own, but I'm not mad to leave him by himself just now either."

"Couldn't the boys come and stay with me?" Mrs. Altman suggested.

"Well, of course, that would be lovely, Mother, it's very thoughtful of you, but I think it would be best if I just stay put for the time being. I'd really rather."

"How is Carl?" Mrs. Altman asked with concern.

"I think he's beginning to come out of it. The funeral was terribly hard on him, poor lamb. I could really kick myself, because if I had had any idea how upset he would be by it, I would have urged him not to go. But who would have ever known?"

"I thought he handled himself marvelously," Eleanor said.

"Oh, he handled himself just fine. I was very proud of him, I must say, but it was terribly hard on him. On the way out to the cemetery he all but broke down."

"I suppose he had a right to, at his sister's funeral," Eleanor observed.

"He had every right," Peggy agreed. "In a way I was much happier than if he had held it in. But it was quite hard on him. He was nearly distraught. Of course, there were difficulties between them, as we all know. He idolized her. She was in fact devoted to him, but I don't think he knew it. At times she didn't make it very clear. She could be quite critical of him, as sisters can be. He's left feeling he was the one person she had no use for. It's all terribly difficult for him. He said something the other day—I know he doesn't mean it, but he did say it—he said he felt responsible for her dying," Peggy shook her head in bewilderment and sympathy.

"The poor child!" Eleanor cried.

"What I'd like is to get him some professional help. I'm sure it would make it easier for him to accept this. He's talking about giving up his music, which of course wouldn't solve anything, but it's hard for him to see that. It's clear it doesn't make any sense in the long run, but needless to say I'm not pushing the issue just now."

"Is there something I could do?" Mrs. Altman asked. "I was wondering if he'd like to go somewhere some Saturday or Sunday, on a little trip. I didn't have anything particular in mind. If he liked, we could go out to Rosefield for the day."

"I think he'd like it a great deal. It would be just lovely, Mother, if it isn't a lot for you. I'm afraid he's not very good company just now."

"I don't expect him to be, dear," Mrs. Altman said gently.

"Well, it would be lovely. Why don't you ask him yourself, he'd have all the more pleasure out of it if the invitation came from you rather than from me."

"What about Phil? Shouldn't I do something for him? Separately?"

"You couldn't be nicer, but I wouldn't worry about Phil. He's doing fine. He has Betsy, which is a great help to him, but he really is such a steady person. He's been a wonderful help to me during all this. I don't know what I would have done without him."

"Betsy is such a lovely girl," Eleanor said.

"I couldn't be more fond of her," Peggy said. "My only worry is that this whole thing might throw them together too quickly. Not that I have the slightest doubt they'll wind up together, but I only hope this doesn't precipitate anything prematurely. I don't think it's a great way to make that particular decision. Alan, of course, would like them to get married as soon as possible. He feels it would be a great comfort to Phil. I keep on telling him Phil doesn't need any great comfort. He's getting what he needs, he always has. It's all I can do to hold Alan off from proposing to her himself. Fortunately, neither he nor I has anything to say— Oh, I almost forgot to tell you: Phil's decided to accept the clerkship after all."

"Thank God!" Eleanor exclaimed.

"I was never in any real doubt that he would. Although he was quite sincere about giving it up. He would have thrown over the whole thing if he thought it would help his father. And then I had all I could do to prevent Alan from taking him up on it. He couldn't see that Phil was only trying to be thoughtful to him. He had himself convinced that Phil really didn't want to go to Washington."

"He will go, then?" Eleanor asked, anxious over the possible waste of her husband's influence.

"Yes, he's written his letter. I think it's the sensible thing to do. Nothing would be more foolish than to give up an opportunity like that. I always think it's a great pity when people suddenly change the whole course of their lives because of something like this. This business of stopping everything! It's sheer nonsense. Who's it for anyway? Who's any the better off for it?"

No one could say. After a moment Eleanor said quietly, "I suppose it will be hard on you, when he goes."

"It will be very hard. I'll miss him terribly. But can you imagine his not going, just because we'll miss him? I certainly wouldn't think of suggesting that Carl not go away to college. Although I may say, thank God it's not next year. It would be terrible to have them both leave at once. I feel selfish to say so, but I'm glad I have Carl for a while yet."

"It's nice that both of the boys are with you now," Eleanor said.

"It certainly is," Peggy agreed. "I make no bones about it." She took a sip of her tomato juice. "I'll tell you who I *am* worried about, and that's poor Johnny. I understand he is inconsolable. Completely. He hasn't gone back to school yet. I've tried to get him to come and see me, but he evidently can't bring himself to do that. I can't think of a thing I can do. He blames himself entirely for what happened. I've talked to him. Alan's talked to him. Phil went over there the night after the funeral, they were up until God knows when, and he still won't believe that no one holds him in the slightest degree responsible for what happened. Even if he were, of course no one would dream of so much as saying a word, but in fact there wasn't a thing he or anyone else on earth could have done."

"I suppose he feels he should have gone down there with Joan," Eleanor said.

"Yes, but how could he have? She refused to let him."

"I know that, dear, but a person quite understandably thinks of anything he might have done that would have led to a different outcome."

"He really did everything he could."

"Everyone knows he did, but I'm sure he's gone over it again and again, accusing himself, and by now he probably has himself convinced he could have prevented it."

"Which is exactly why I tried to get him to come and see me, so I could persuade him to stop blaming himself."

"If you'll pardon my saying so, darling," Eleanor said, "you may not be the ideal person to do that."

"No?" Peggy was genuinely astonished. She thought for a moment, and said, "You may be right, I suppose. Still, something has to be done. He can't go on tearing himself to pieces over something he couldn't do anything about. It's such a shame, really, because he is a wonderful human being. I told him—the first thing I said to him was how grateful we all were that he had brought Joan so much happiness. And I really meant it. I hope he won't feel he has to cut himself off completely from us, because it would be a shame. And for no reason whatsoever." She paused, and added, "But maybe you're right. I don't suppose I am exactly the person to tell him these things."

"I'm sure he'll come out of it," Eleanor assured her.

"I hope he does. He's such a lovely young man." The corners of her mouth fell almost imperceptibly, a tiny quiver playing over her lips as she thought of Johnny, suffering the second unendurable tragedy of his young life. She worried about how he would come out of it, how they all would come out of it: Alan, Carl, her mother; even Phil, her Rock of Gibraltar.

Peggy didn't ask how she herself would come out of it. It was not a question she knew how to frame.

The three women fell silent again. Mrs. Altman noticed that the woman feeding the birds had gone away. The park bench was empty now. The day was darkening. They might have snow before it was over. She hoped she would get home before it started. A few sparrows still hopped near the bench, looking for a stray crumb that might be left, unlikely though it was.

"I'm still trying to figure out some way for you to get away," Eleanor said.

"Well, Alan was at one time planning to go to London for the Bar Association meetings. That was before this happened, and at the time he was as you know hoping to go in an official capacity. But if everything is on an even keel here, we might possibly go there for a few days."

"That would be nice," Mrs. Altman said.

"Why do they have these conferences in London?" Eleanor asked. "The food is so dreadful there, and it is dreary in February. Why don't they have them in Paris, as long as one is going over there anyway?"

"I don't suppose they're that interested in what the French have to say about law," Peggy said, amused. "Anyway, London's fine with me."

"I'm hardly an authority," Mrs. Altman said, "since I can eat so few things anyway, but I must say the last time we were in London I thought the food was much improved. We stopped at the Connaught and took several meals there, and I have to say everything was perfectly delicious. Tony Hirsch came to see me, and I gave him lunch, and he simply raved about it. He knows what he's talking about, I should think."

"I didn't know you had seen Tony Hirsch," Peggy said. "How was he?"

"He was very well," Mrs. Altman answered. "And just as good-looking as always."

"He was one of the most divine-looking young men I knew," Eleanor said. "I never could understand why he never got married."

"How could you have any question about that?" Peggy scoffed. "Wasn't it perfectly obvious?"

"You think he's that way?" Eleanor asked.

"Darling, there never was the slightest doubt in my mind. You had only to take one look at his face."

"Well, he's a lovely person," Mrs. Altman reaffirmed. "And very amusing."

"I remember," Eleanor reminisced, "one time when he was over here, during the war. Gerald brought him up from Washington, he spent the weekend at Rosefield. Arthur Reinstein came to lunch—"

"I must say, I don't have any recollection . . ." Mrs. Altman strained to remember.

"Arthur had just bought his Corot, and you were considering getting one after the war, so you asked him to lunch so you could discuss Corot, and instead he spent the entire time pontificating on the conduct of the war, which he didn't think Roosevelt and Churchill were running as well as he would have done. Tony, of course, was quite high up in their government at the time, but naturally couldn't say anything because everything was so hush-hush in those days. He was terribly patient with Arthur, who was making a fool of himself. As usual."

"Darling, how do you ever remember such things, after all these years?" Peggy asked.

"Well, I never should have brought it up in the first place, but I remember that particular weekend because right after lunch you started to have your miscarriage."

"Oh, was that the weekend?"

"That was the weekend. I particularly remember because Tony was so very helpful and Arthur was such an imbecile. He didn't have any idea what to do or where to go or anything. And then—do you remember?—when we finally had you in Mother's car—Gerald had gone down to the garage to get ours, to follow—you and Mother and I were in the car, after all the confusion and the calling back and forth to whatever that portly man's name was you used to deliver your babies, and the hospital, and so forth, and when we were just about to pull out of the driveway, down the steps came running Miss Georgina! Do you remember Miss Georgina?"

"How could I forget Miss Georgina?" Peggy asked, smiling at the memory of the eccentric governess.

"I can still see her running down the steps," Eleanor said. "She did not cut a very graceful figure, as you may remember—shouting, 'Mrs. Gutheim! Mrs. Gutheim! Joan will not take her nap!' The fact that the child's mother was being rushed to the hospital, and the whole place was in an utter uproar, made not the slightest difference. Joan had to have her nap, come hell or high water. Do you remember?" The three women were all laughing at Eleanor's description of the scene. "All I could think, when I saw her running down the steps so frantically, was that something had happened to one of the children—what else could one think, after all?—and I remember thinking to myself, Well, we're on the way to the hospital anyway. And then it turned out that it was only that

Joan wouldn't take her nap. I must say, through no fault of her own Miss Georgina did make what would have otherwise been a pretty grim trip into something a bit more tolerable."

"She certainly did," Peggy agreed. "How we howled! I remember the look on poor Gerry's face when he came up in the car from the garage, because of course he hadn't the vaguest notion what was going on, there were the three of us, ostensibly worried to death over this terrible thing that was happening, except that we were laughing until the tears rolled down our cheeks."

Eleanor said, "I told Tony to tell him on the way, but I don't know to this day whether Gerry ever did understand what was so funny. Certainly Miss Georgina didn't."

"She was an idiot," Peggy said with surprising sharpness. "Here was Joan, who was all of, what, five or six at the time, her father was off in a war, and her mother going to the hospital, I'm sure she thought I was going to die. I remember trying to reassure her that I was fine, but I don't think I convinced her. And then this virago, who wasn't even her governess, expects her to have a nap in the middle of everything. I ask you, how stupid can you be?" On reflection, she added, more softly, "But Joan recovered and I recovered and I daresay Miss Georgina recovered. No one was very much the worse for it."

The other two pondered that idea for a moment. Peggy looked at her watch. "Well—I'd love to stay, but I think I'd better run."

"Would you like the car, dear?" Mrs. Altman asked.

"Thanks, Mother, I'm going straight home. The walk will be fine. You know, it's funny you should have mentioned that weekend, because Alan brought it up, right out of the clear blue, a couple of nights ago. I don't suppose we'd mentioned the miscarriage more than two or three times since it happened. There never seemed any reason to talk about it, especially as Carl came along not that long after, so why dwell on it? But Alan asked me if I knew whether it had been a girl or a boy. Poor man! What difference could it possibly make, particularly after all these years? But he wanted to know."

"Do you know?" Eleanor asked.

"Darling, how would I know? No one told me, and I certainly had no interest in knowing at the time. Alan was away, so he never had a chance to ask. Frankly I'm just as glad not to know. I don't see what possible good it would do to know. Except if it gave poor Alan something to grasp at. Just now he could use it. . . ." She was thoughtful for a moment, then added briskly, "But at any rate, I didn't know." She got up to go.

"Give Alan my love, will you?" Mrs. Altman asked.

"I will, dear," Peggy promised.

"And the boys, of course."

"Of course. I'll see you—when? Thursday?"

"I thought I might stop in, if I wouldn't be disturbing anybody, and see the children tomorrow afternoon, around five. Would that interfere with anything?"

"How could your stopping in possibly be anything but a pleasure, Mother? But why don't I have them come over to you, and save you the trouble."

"It's no trouble," Mrs. Altman said.

"I can never tell what Phillip's schedule will be."

"If Phillip is there I'll see him. I'll see Carl, at any rate."

"And you'll see me. I'm there, these days."

"Darling," Eleanor said as Peggy bent to kiss her good-bye. "It was lovely of you to stop by. I wish you would have let me give you something to eat."

"I wouldn't lose any sleep over it. I'm not exactly ravenous these days."

"Let me know if there's anything we can possibly do," Eleanor said.

"Thank you, dear. At the moment everything is under control. But I'll let you know, it's very sweet of you. Mother, dear." As she bent over for the kiss Peggy reached around to embrace her mother, and for a brief moment the two women clung together. A casual observer would have made nothing of it, but Mrs. Altman knew just what it meant. She reached up and patted her daughter's forearm tenderly. Peggy straightened up and said, "I'll see you tomorrow, then. I'll probably call you this evening."

"Please do, dear."

"Or maybe I'll catch you when you speak to Carl. If not, I'll call you. Eleanor."

"Peggy, darling. My dearest love to Alan and the boys."

"Thank you, dear. Good-bye, both of you. Thank you, Fiona, I can see myself out. Please don't bother."

"It's no bother, Mrs. Gutheim," Fiona said. She had been given firm instructions to see Peggy out, and she went with her.

The two women, left in silence, listened to hear Peggy make her departure. They heard the door close. Finally Eleanor spoke:

"I'll say one thing for that daughter of yours. She's indomitable."

"She is that," Mrs. Altman replied, but with somewhat less conviction. She had known Peggy longer, after all, and knew her better than even a perceptive and loving sister-in-law ever could. After a moment, she said, "Let's hope so."

The two women said nothing more until Fiona returned. Eleanor told her she could clear. She took away the dishes and laid the dessert plates. But when she passed the dessert, neither woman took any, and it went back into the kitchen completely untouched.

Epilogue

Not too long after Joan died, Carl went to Rosefield with Mrs. Altman. The outing had a slightly unreal air, like the embarkation to some never-never land in Mrs. Altman's exquisite Watteau. Although the house was kept open year-round, Mrs. Altman seldom went there after Thanksgiving, until the spring, when the first crocuses pushed their way through the snow. Carl himself had never been there in the wintertime. The stated purpose of the trip—a new garden was being planned, and the superintendent wanted Mrs. Altman's approval of the site—was only a pretext. The real reason was Carl. He was thought to be making a poor recovery from Joan's death, and it was hoped that a day in the country with Mrs. Altman would help his convalescence. None of this was said, of course—in the Gutheim family, how could it have been? It wasn't necessary to put it into words. Carl knew perfectly well, from the gingerly way everyone talked to him, that they thought he was doing poorly; that he hadn't "gotten over it" yet. Essentially they were right, although he felt patronized by their concern. He nevertheless fed it in various ways, most notably by avoiding playing the piano, although the cast was off and his forearm not much the worse for wear. His reasons for staying away from the keyboard were too complicated for anybody, himself included, to understand at the time, and only partially connected to his sister, who admittedly took a mixed view of his music. At any rate, although he thought the family was overconcerned with his

emotional health, he was touched by Mrs. Altman's characteristic generosity. The trip would have been a treat under any circumstances, and
although he hated to cause his grandmother any trouble, he accepted the
invitation gratefully. He held out the hope it might be pleasant for her
as well; after all, she had her own considerable grief to contend with.

They drove up Saturday morning, to return by supper. Kathleen
came with them, ostensibly to serve lunch, but also to get her out in the
country too. She, of all Mrs. Altman's household, had been the most
affected by Joan's death. The day was cold but clear, with a cloudless,
intensely blue winter sky. To get out of the city, they took the same
route as the funeral procession only a few weeks earlier. It was a little
eerie. Carl and Mrs. Altman spoke very little during the trip. In front,
where Kathleen was sitting across from Holberg, there was no conversation at all. If they'd wanted to talk, the glass partition could have been
raised; but Holberg had a Scandinavian's taciturnity, and Kathleen was
wrapped up in her own thoughts.

As they came down Rosefield's long driveway, Carl thought how
strange it looked. It wasn't just because of the time of year, although he
wasn't used to seeing snow on the grounds and the trees bereft of leaves.
It was more the thought that Joan would never come there again. She
had been passionately attached to the place, and it seemed to him wrong
that he, of all people, should be taken there when she could no longer
come.

They were met at the door by Bess. Bess and the elderly house-
keeper, Gwendolyn, lived permanently at Rosefield. During the summers, when the full staff came up from the city, they had no detectable
duties except to participate in the running pinochle game that went on
in the back sitting room. On the fall and spring weekends, Gwendolyn
did the beds and the general tidying up, and if Helga didn't come up,
she cooked. Carl had never known what Bess did. Obviously, if the
house were to be occupied in the winter, you could hardly expect one
octogenarian woman to stay there by herself, even with the superintendent and the head gardener on the grounds. Whatever function she
served, Bess was a dependable font of sympathy when the injustices of
family life became insupportable, and although she was something of a
fright to look at, the children often sought refuge in her ample bosom.
She greeted Carl that day with a silent, comforting hug. He was struck,
as he hadn't been before, by how old she was getting; but he might have
been overly preoccupied with mortality that day.

On arriving, Mrs. Altman went up to her room, attended by Bess. Carl went out to the kitchen to say hello to Gwendolyn, and find out what was for lunch. He hadn't seen Gwendolyn since Joan's death, except for a distant glimpse at the funeral, and she told him how sorry she was. He felt he was accepting the condolence on false grounds. The help knew as well as anyone—better than anyone—Joan's opinion of him. Kathleen, who had been driven around back, came in through the back door. While she was taking off her coat and hat, Bess came down the back stairs. As she entered the kitchen she said, "I can't believe she's gone." She took out her handkerchief and wiped her eyes. (They were more or less permanently watery, an occupational hazard, the children always assumed, of long winter evenings with but two possibilities of entertainment: gin, or Gwendolyn. "And what choice is that?" Phil would ask.) But these tears were certainly for Joan.

"It's hard to believe," Carl agreed.

As he spoke he was looking at Kathleen. She didn't return his look but said, "I'll see to the table," and moved toward the pantry.

"I set the table already, darlin'," Bess said. "Aren't you going to have a cup of tea, after your trip?"

"I'll have it later," Kathleen replied, hastily pushing her way through the swinging door.

Bess and Gwendolyn exchanged glances, and Gwendolyn looked disapproving. "I think she's still very upset over this whole thing," Carl explained.

"Aren't we all?" Gwendolyn said. "I remember when your mother carried her home from the hospital."

"Well, it's very sad for everyone," he observed, hoping to avoid any competitive bereavement.

"I still can't believe she's gone," Bess said. "She always had so much fun."

Gwendolyn said crossly, "What has that got to do with anything?"

"But she did!" Beth insisted. "She was always on the go! Morning, noon, and night. I don't know where that girl got all her energy! She was never still for a minute, she wasn't, from the time she got up till after she should have been asleep. And she wouldn't take her nap! Not her. She hated to take her nap. She didn't want to miss out on anything. Not that she ever did, she was always in the middle of everything. And mischief! Could that child get into mischief! You remember Miss Georgina's wig?"

Carl had to remind her that he wasn't born yet when that notorious theft took place. "But I was there for the pillow fight, Bess," he pleaded, hoping to insinuate himself into at least one legendary scene. There was a tradition of huge pillow fights at Rosefield, one of the few, it seemed, that lasted into his day. They were riotous affairs that could only take place well out of earshot of grown-ups, which meant they were confined to the third floor, where the boys slept. By the time Carl came along, it was relatively rare that enough children were staying at Rosefield to get a good melee going. But one autumn weekend when he was four or five, they were for some reason all there together, Gutheims, Altmans, Astrid Holberg, an overnight guest or two: the whole gang. The weather obliged with a terrific thunderstorm on Saturday afternoon. The Monopoly game degenerated more quickly than usual, and a pillow fight soon broke out. It happened that Bess came upstairs to get something out of the attic, and for some unimaginable reason she joined in on the mayhem. Floored as the children were to have her in the thick of the battle, it nevertheless continued. On that day she revealed a side of herself no one dreamed existed. When Carl thought of that gentle, arthritic woman, then well into her seventies, laying wildly about her, a half-crazed expression on her face, he almost doubted whether it really happened; or if it was another apocryphal story that had been repeated so often that everybody came to believe it had actually taken place.

"Oh! Don't bring that up!" Bess cried. "If your mum ever found out about that, I'd have my notice. Or your aunt!"

Carl smiled at her worry, after all these years, not to mention her belief that anything could have happened at Rosefield that those two women didn't know about. "I think they'd give you a medal for bravery," he told her.

"For lunacy, maybe," Gwendolyn snapped. Turning back to Carl, she asked in a gentler voice, "How is your mother, though?"

"Oh, she's doing fine," he said breezily. "You know how she is—she's terribly busy. She has to keep everything going."

Gwendolyn looked skeptical. "She was never one to show her feelings," she said, pursing her lips.

"I still can't believe she's gone," Bess said again.

Kathleen, who had composed herself by then, reentered the kitchen and announced, "Mrs. Altman is ready now."

Carl excused himself from the company of the ladies to join Mrs.

Altman. Mr. Sullivan was there, and the three of them went out to see about the new garden.

There were already many gardens at Rosefield. The main flower garden, a gorgeous expanse of color in the summer, was down the hill from the house. Next to it were the greenhouses, with the vegetable garden beyond. At the side of the house was a formal garden of hedges and boxwoods, laid out in rather severe geometric arrangements. Near the swimming pool, in constant jeopardy from stray baseballs and hide-and-go-seek players, was Mrs. Altman's adored rose garden, containing roses whose variety and delicacy of hue were renowned throughout Westchester County. Farthest off lay the rock garden, an out-of-the-way, gently hilly ramble of moss and flowers and ferns at the edge of the woods. In recent years when Joan and Phil had been off at college, Carl had spent many weekends at Rosefield with just Mrs. Altman and his parents, or perhaps one guest, but no other children. To break up the tedium of homework and practicing, he would walk down to the rock garden to see the lilies of the valley and velvet carpets of pansies in the spring, or the shroud of gold and brown fallen leaves in the autumn. It was his favorite spot at Rosefield.

Privately, Carl was against the idea of another garden, or indeed any change whatsoever. Rosefield had not been altered in any way within his memory, and he thought of it as one of the immutable constants of life. If it had been left up to him, he would have vetoed the whole scheme. But his only role was to keep Mrs. Altman company, and to take her arm when the footing was uncertain. He said nothing.

They tramped over the entire estate that morning. Mr. Sullivan described what kind of garden would do well in the various locations. They looked at the lower terrace, the meadow, the apple orchard, the field on the far side of the vegetable garden. Nothing seemed right. They even walked into the woods where they considered, briefly, some sort of planting by the brook. That was dropped too. Poor Mr. Sullivan made suggestion after suggestion; but Mrs. Altman, who was ordinarily so receptive, found nothing to her liking. It gradually became evident that the project was fraught with difficulties, few of which were horticultural.

At first Carl was puzzled as to what the problem was. It would have seemed the simplest thing in the world to put in another garden at Rosefield, if one wanted to do it. Not until they came out of the woods onto the back road did he begin to understand what was the matter.

Mrs. Altman thanked Mr. Sullivan for his time and said he needn't
trouble returning with her, that she had Carl to make sure she got home
all right. Mr. Sullivan looked a little dubious as to whether Carl was up
to the responsibility, but he only tipped his hat and turned toward his
own cottage, which was at the farther end of the road. As they began the
walk back, Mrs. Altman said to Carl, "I had my doubts about this from
the beginning."

Carl still didn't quite get what she meant, but said nothing. A minute or two later, as though continuing the same thought, she said, "Your
sister wasn't much of a one for gardens." They had come to the pond,
which was half frozen over. The ducks had flown south long since, and
the pond was uncharacteristically still. Mrs. Altman looked over to the
far side, where willows bent over the water and the pond was darkest.
"The water lilies will do, I think," she said. "She did love Monet."

Lunch was served when they got back. A fire had been lit in the
dining room fireplace, making the large room cozy on the winter's day.
They ate off plates painted with scenes of scarlet-clad huntsmen on
horseback. "These were given to your grandfather and me as a wedding
present," Mrs. Altman said. "They were his favorites." Carl hadn't
known his grandfather, and he was surprised to be brought in on the
intimacy.

During the meal there were long stretches of silence, punctuated
only by murmurs of thanks to Kathleen as she served. The silences
weren't uncomfortable, but they seemed charged with thoughts not spoken. Except for the one reference to Joan by the pond, her name hadn't
been mentioned all day. There was no need to. Her memory was inescapable. All the same, the enigma of her death lay between them, as
palpable as an unopened telegram containing dire news that no one
wants to hear.

When they finished eating, they went into the sun parlor. This was
a large room furnished informally with cushioned wicker settees and
armchairs, filled with plants and potted trees and, in one corner, a small
pool in which water cascaded from a fountain statue of a young maiden
carrying a jar. The side of the room opening onto the terrace was
screened in during the summer, but now windows and glass doors kept
out the cold. The February sun streamed in, and the day was clear
enough that they could see all the way across to the Long Island Sound
in the distance. The radio had been turned on to WQXR, which was
broadcasting from the Met. Mrs. Altman asked Carl if he knew which

opera it was. He could only identify it as Mozart, until the familiar aria of Papageno came on and he realized it was *The Magic Flute*.

Mrs. Altman had a book, and he had brought some homework, but neither of them read. Instead they gave themselves over entirely to the opera; conspirators in shirking their respective duties. When the applause sounded for the end of the first act, Mrs. Altman gave a rapturous sigh. "That was charming," she said, turning down the radio so they wouldn't have to endure Milton Cross's doleful commentary.

"Grandmother," Carl said, pretending to scold her, "that was the last opera Mozart ever composed. A few weeks after he finished it, he died in abject poverty. The plot is about good and evil, freedom and slavery, the brotherhood of man. I *won't* let you call it charming."

She smiled indulgently, and said, "I loved listening to it with you. I always enjoy music more when I have you with me. We missed you at the Philharmonic last week. It's not the same without you."

Carl felt abashed. "I was sorry I couldn't come. It sounded like a wonderful concert."

"Maybe next week?" she asked, looking around for her book, purse, glasses. It was time for her rest. Afterward, they would drive down to the city.

"I'd love that," he said, and stood up with her. "It's an all-Wagner program." As they walked to the door of the room, he asked, "Would you like me to do the themes for you?" He would often come early before a concert, and play for her some of the music they were to hear. It was easy for him to do, and she enjoyed those little previews immensely.

"That would be wonderful!" she said, adding, "I'm so glad."

From her reaction, he could see that she had resigned herself to never hearing him play again. He didn't think it would be a great loss; still, he was sorry to cause her any pain. "I haven't given up the piano, you know," he told her.

She did look surprised. "I'm so glad," she said warmly.

Carl accompanied her out through the hall. She was preparing to climb the wide, curved staircase when she stopped and said to him:

"You know, your sister adored your music. Sometimes she didn't let you know, but she loved nothing better than to hear you play. She spoke of it quite often to me. She would have been very sorry if you'd have given it up . . ."

She didn't finish the sentence, but bent toward him so he could kiss her, and then she continued on up the stairs. He waited until she got to the second floor, and then turned around. A large grandfather clock stood in the entrance hallway opposite the staircase. On its face the sun, the moon, and the stars were painted on a dark blue sky. He had never seen it wound, and at one time thought it must run by perpetual motion. He stood for a moment, watching its deliberate pendulum through the glass front.

It was probably true, he thought. Whatever else she thought about him, Joan had liked him to play for her. He remembered the night not long before she died, when she asked for the *Träumerei*. That turned out to have been the last time he played for her. He wished he had known it then. He wished it hadn't been the last time.

Suddenly, his eyes stung with regret.

He went back into the sun parlor to get his books, but rebelled at the thought of studying just then. He left the books where they were and went instead back through the pantry and the kitchen to the help's sitting room. In his younger days he used to spend a lot of time in there, but in recent years he didn't go in there so much. He found Kathleen alone, sitting at the dining table, reading a pocket book. She was wearing glasses, which he supposed he had seen before, but which were a shock nevertheless. She got up as he came in, and said, "Can I get you anything, Mr. Carl?"

He had protested when she started addressing him as "Mr. Carl" the previous summer, reminding her that she had known him ever since he was a little boy. "You're not a little boy anymore," she had replied. He'd had no answer to that.

"Oh, please, no," he said quickly. "What are you reading?"

"It's just a book," she said with a slight blush. She had put it down on the crocheted tablecloth, and he looked at the title. *Peyton Place.*

"Shocking!" he teased her. "Isn't that on the Index?"

"I don't pay much attention to the Index these days," she replied, with a little more heat than he would have expected; but then, he knew nothing of her religious life. It wouldn't have surprised him one bit to find that Kathleen was secretly a Freemason.

"Are you going to play your piano now?" she asked. He usually waited to practice until Mrs. Altman went for her rest, so he wouldn't bother her; although she always insisted it was a pleasure to hear him.

"I'm not going to practice today," he told her. "My wrist is still stiff." The wrist was a handy available truth.

"It's not too stiff to play for us, is it?" she asked. "Just a little? Or will it hurt too much."

"No, it won't hurt," he said. "But it will sound terrible. I haven't touched the piano in weeks."

"Oh, go on," she chided him. "You know we'd never know the difference. You could play with one hand, and it'd still sound like the angels to us. Bess and Gwendolyn made me promise to get them when you started playing."

"I don't like to disturb their rest," he stalled. "Why don't we wait until they get up."

"If you waited for that, it'd be time to go, and we wouldn't have a chance to hear you. They'd never forgive me for that. Just let me get them." She ran off to the back staircase before he could make any further objection, and returned in a moment. "They'll be right down," she told him. "They're just fixing themselves up."

"They don't have to do that," he protested.

"I think Gwen'd better put in her teeth," Kathleen said, deadpan.

The piano at Rosefield, a very fine old Bechstein, was kept in the formal living room. It was draped when not in use with an elaborate oriental cloth on which rested framed photographs going back to the last century. Carl spent vast amounts of time, when he should have been practicing, studying these sepia ancestors, despite not having the slightest idea who any of them were. Many of the faces had a vaguely Altman look to them, but a number of them could not possibly have been related to the family; at least he hoped not. The whole room, darkened, solemnly furnished, seldom used, often struck him as a tomb in which he had been buried alive, interred there to practice for eternity.

The four of them—Kathleen, Gwendolyn, Bess, and Carl—trooped in for his little recital. Bess was terribly concerned about his arm, but in truth he could have played for them even had it still been in a cast. They didn't expect any novelties, just a few old favorites: the Beethoven minuet he had played as a very little boy; some Chopin; a waltz by Schubert; and some songs. The songs were what they liked the best. No one sang. If the full staff had been there, they might have gotten up the collective nerve, and Billingsly sometimes shook off his butler's decorum to croon a verse or two of "Loch Lomond." But with just the three ladies, two of them well past the possibility of carrying a tune, the only participation was barely audible humming.

Still, they were happy just to hear him play. He supposed that they, too, had wondered if he had given up his music for good. They thought that the past had died with Joan; that nothing would be the same again. Listening to him play, they could imagine that it wasn't true; that the old times would return.

Of course, nothing would ever be the same; but the hope that the past can be lived again persists. For those who were there—Bess, Gwendolyn, Kathleen—the happiest times ever were the summers of World War II, at Rosefield. Carl had missed out on those days, but he shared the special sad wish that they would come again. They never did and they never could have: not for him, not for anyone else. Even if Joan hadn't died, they would still have been irretrievably in the past.

That afternoon he played the old favorites. He played "A Tavern in the Town"; "The White Cliffs of Dover"; "Bye, Bye, Blackbird"; "If I Loved You"; "Jeannie with the Light Brown Hair"; and Bess's favorite, "Annie Laurie." "Annie Laurie" was his own favorite, too, with its painful yearning for a lost loved one. But he always ended with " 'Tis the Last Rose of Summer," notwithstanding the fact that Kathleen always cried. When he asked if he should play it, the three ladies looked wistful; but they knew the time had come. He gave the melody a slightly different accompaniment than usual, but they didn't seem to mind. They may not have noticed. It was his final song for the day, and Kathleen cried.